SUPERMAN
BATMAN
alternate
HISTORIES

Brian Augustyn
and Mark Waid
Jon Bogdanove
and Judy Kurzer
Bogdanove
John Byrne
Chuck Dixon

Writers

Alcatena
John Byrne
Humberto Ramos
Joe Staton

Pencillers

Alcatena
John Byrne
Horacio Ottolini
Ron Boyd
Dan Davis
Wayne Faucher
Dennis Janke
Andy Lanning
Rob Leigh
Ande Parks

Inkers

David Hornung
Glenn Whitmore

Colorists

Clem Robins
Starkings/Comicraft
John Byrne

Letterers

DAVE DOWKINS '96

Batman created by Bob Kane
Superman created by Jerry Siegel and Joe Shuster

SUPERMAN/BATMAN: ALTERNATE HISTORIES

Published by DC Comics. Cover, introduction and compilation
copyright © 1996 DC Comics. All Rights Reserved.

Originally published in single magazine form as
ACTION COMICS ANNUAL 6,
BATMAN: LEGENDS OF THE DARK KNIGHT ANNUAL 4,
DETECTIVE COMICS ANNUAL 7, and STEEL ANNUAL 1.
Copyright © 1994 DC Comics. All Rights Reserved.
Elseworlds, all characters, their distinctive likenesses and related
indicia featured in this publication are trademarks of DC Comics.
The stories, characters, and incidents featured in this publication
are entirely fictional.

DC Comics, 1700 Broadway, New York, NY 10019
A division of Warner Bros. - A Time Warner
Entertainment Company
Printed in Canada. First Printing.
ISBN: 1-56389-263-4
Cover painting by Dave DeVries.

table of
CONTENTS

So (I hear you ask), what is
an alternate history and why should we care –
and furthermore, who are you and why are you
writing this introduction anyway?

Good questions, all.

To answer them out of order,

let me start by introducing myself:

I'm Mike Resnick, I'm a science-fiction

writer, I've won some Hugos and

Nebulas, and — more important for the

purposes of this book — I'm the editor

of the popular series of alternate

histories published by Tor Books:

Alternate Presidents, Alternate

Kennedys, Alternate Warriors,

Alternate Outlaws, and

Alternate Tyrants.

BY MIKE RESNICK

Science fiction — *good* science fiction — has always questioned reality, and looked at alternatives.

The best super-hero comic books have always been good science fiction. What would happen if a child from Krypton were raised in a small town in middle America? Or if an Amazon princess secretly walked among us? Suppose there were a weapon the shape and size of a ring that could do just about anything its owner willed?

But "Suppose aliens lived among us?" or "Imagine that plutonium were as common as lead?" are questions that require a specialized audience, one attuned to science-fictional concepts. That audience is getting larger every day, but there's still a huge mass of people out there who couldn't care less about aliens or science or any of the other trappings of the field. So what kind of supposition can reach them?

The answer to that is the alternate history. After all, you don't have to be a science-fiction or comic-book fan to wonder what life might have been like if Abraham Lincoln and John F. Kennedy had lived, or Richard Nixon hadn't resigned from the presidency, or the Nazis had won World War II.

"Science fiction - good science fiction -has always questioned reality, and looked at alternatives."

It's fascinating stuff. Even British Prime Minister Winston Churchill wrote a book of alternate history. In fact, perhaps the most famous alternate history was written not by a science-fiction writer, but by historian MacKinlay Kantor: *If the South Had Won the Civil War.*

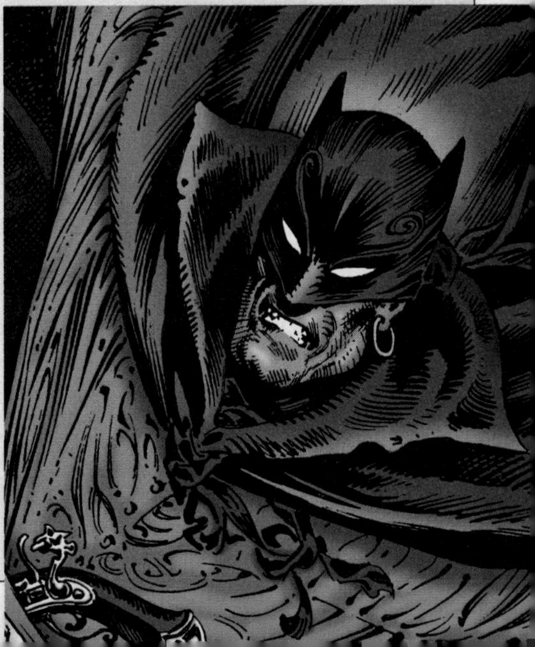

What you hold in your hand is actually a double twist on the typical alternate history. First, you are asked to accept the concept that the DC Universe — populated by such exotic heroes and villains as Superman, Batman, Green Lantern, Flash, Luthor, the Joker, Wonder Woman, and that whole crowd — is real. (Easy enough. We've been doing it for close to 60 years.)

Now comes the second twist: the DC writers and artists have taken that universe and written a number of alternatives to it. In other words, they have created the now-famous Elseworlds concept: they have not only changed things about the

"What you hold in your hand is actually a double twist on the typical alternate history."

character's life and past, but they have changed the entire world in which he exists and must function.

For example, they've created a wonderful pirate who just happens to bear a striking resemblance to a Caped Crusader we all know and love. Of course, simply making him look like Batman isn't enough, not for an artful alternate history. If they play fair — and believe me, the DC creative team always plays fair — they have to imbue this pirate with most or all of Bruce Wayne's/Batman's skills, and, even more, with his morality and world view, and then turn him loose and see what happens, what effect he has on his friends, his foes, his environment.

In a very altered Colonial America, a visitor from Krypton would set everything right and be elected President by accla-mation, right? Well, nothing

is ever as simple as it seems, and what we have in *Legacy* is a story of what absolute power does to its possessor, and in the sure hands of Team DC it becomes a tale of idealism and sacrifice rather than Redcoat-bashing.

Citizen Wayne skews history in a different way. Gotham City, crime-ridden home of Bruce Wayne, has a mysterious vigilante — and it's not Wayne. Honestly handled, that is simply the premise, not the story, which concerns Wayne's interaction with the vigilante and his ultimate effect on the millionaire.

The Steel story is perhaps the best of the lot, mainly because it accomplishes so many things: it uses the concept of the super-hero to reexamine the story of American slavery, to create a brand-new myth, and to eventually join an existing piece of folklore.

You know, there's nothing new about DC's creating alternate histories. I can remember the "imaginary" Superman stories, and the creation of Earth-Two to explain away the existence of two Flashes, Green Lanterns, Atoms, and so forth. Under the leadership of Julie Schwartz, Mort Weisinger, and their successors over the years, DC has been writing alternate histories for close to half a century. They've done their home-work, and learned from their many successes and small handful of failures.

I think when you finish reading this book, you'll agree that it can't be done much better.

Mike Resnick

ELSEWORLDS

In Elseworlds,
heroes are taken
from their usual
settings
and put into
strange
times and places —
some that have
existed
or might have existed,
and others
that can't,
couldn't or
shouldn't exist.
These are some of them.

leatherwing

herwing

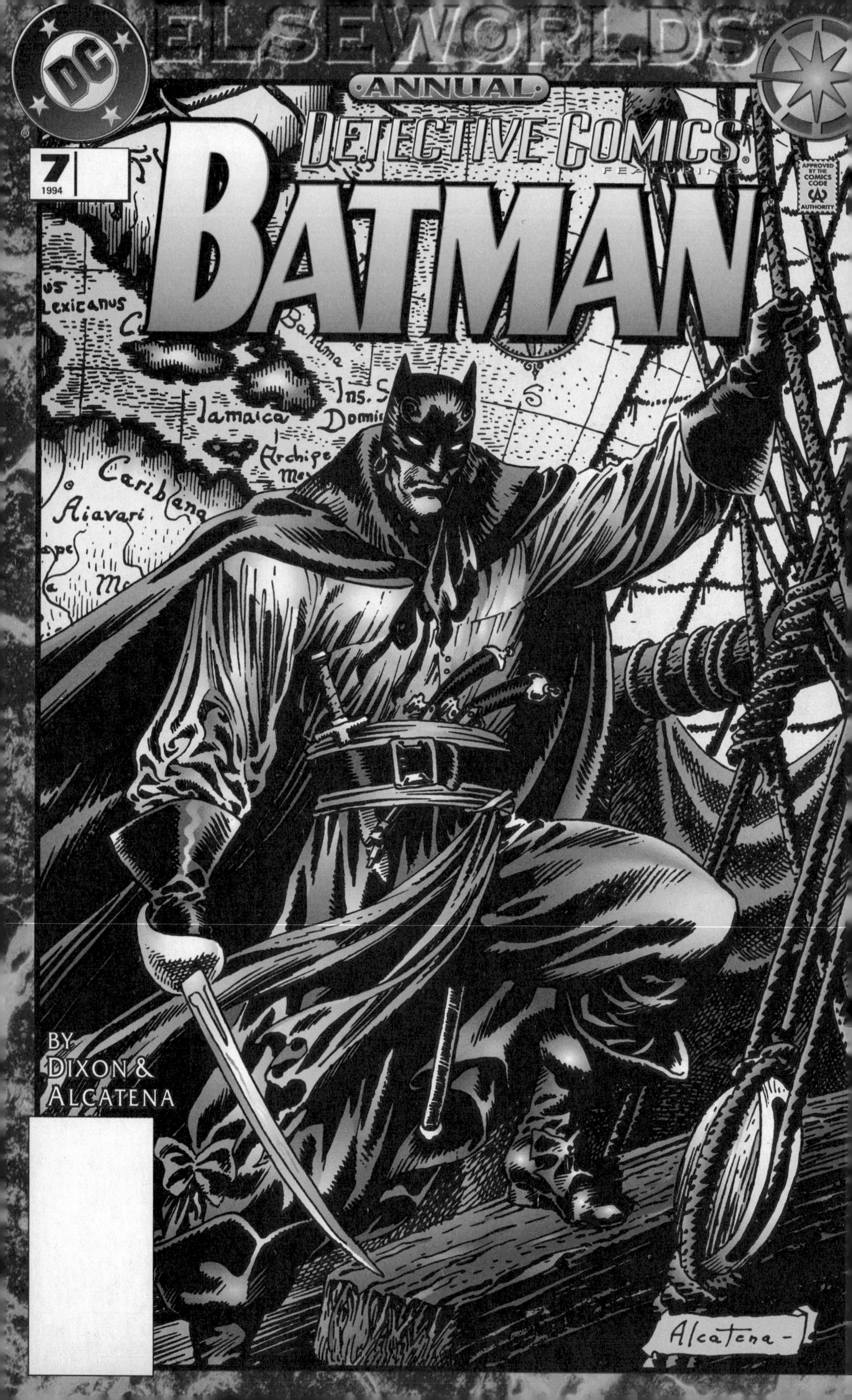

ELSEWORLDS
DC
ANNUAL
DETECTIVE COMICS
FEATURING
BATMAN
7
1994
APPROVED BY THE COMICS CODE AUTHORITY
Bahama
lamaica
Caribana
Aiavari
BY
DIXON &
ALCATENA
Alcatena-

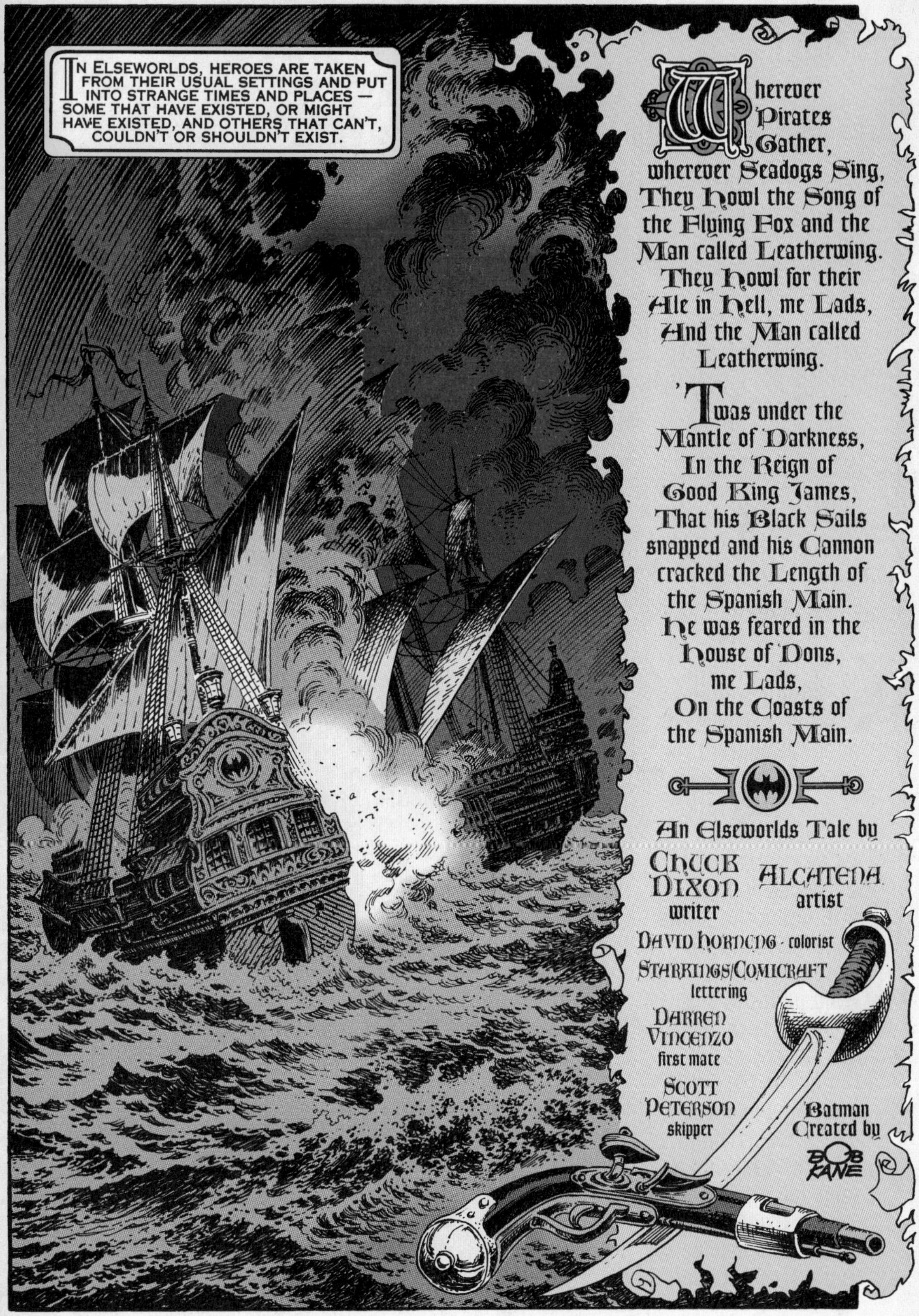
In Elseworlds, heroes are taken from their usual settings and put into strange times and places — some that have existed, or might have existed, and others that can't, couldn't or shouldn't exist.
Wherever Pirates Gather, wherever Seadogs Sing, They Howl the Song of the Flying Fox and the Man called Leatherwing. They Howl for their Ale in Hell, me Lads, And the Man called Leatherwing.
'Twas under the Mantle of Darkness, In the Reign of Good King James, That his Black Sails snapped and his Cannon cracked the Length of the Spanish Main. He was feared in the House of Dons, me Lads, On the Coasts of the Spanish Main.
An Elseworlds Tale by
Chuck Dixon writer
Alcatena artist
David Hornung - colorist
Starkings/Comicraft lettering
Darren Vincenzo first mate
Scott Peterson skipper
Batman Created by Bob Kane

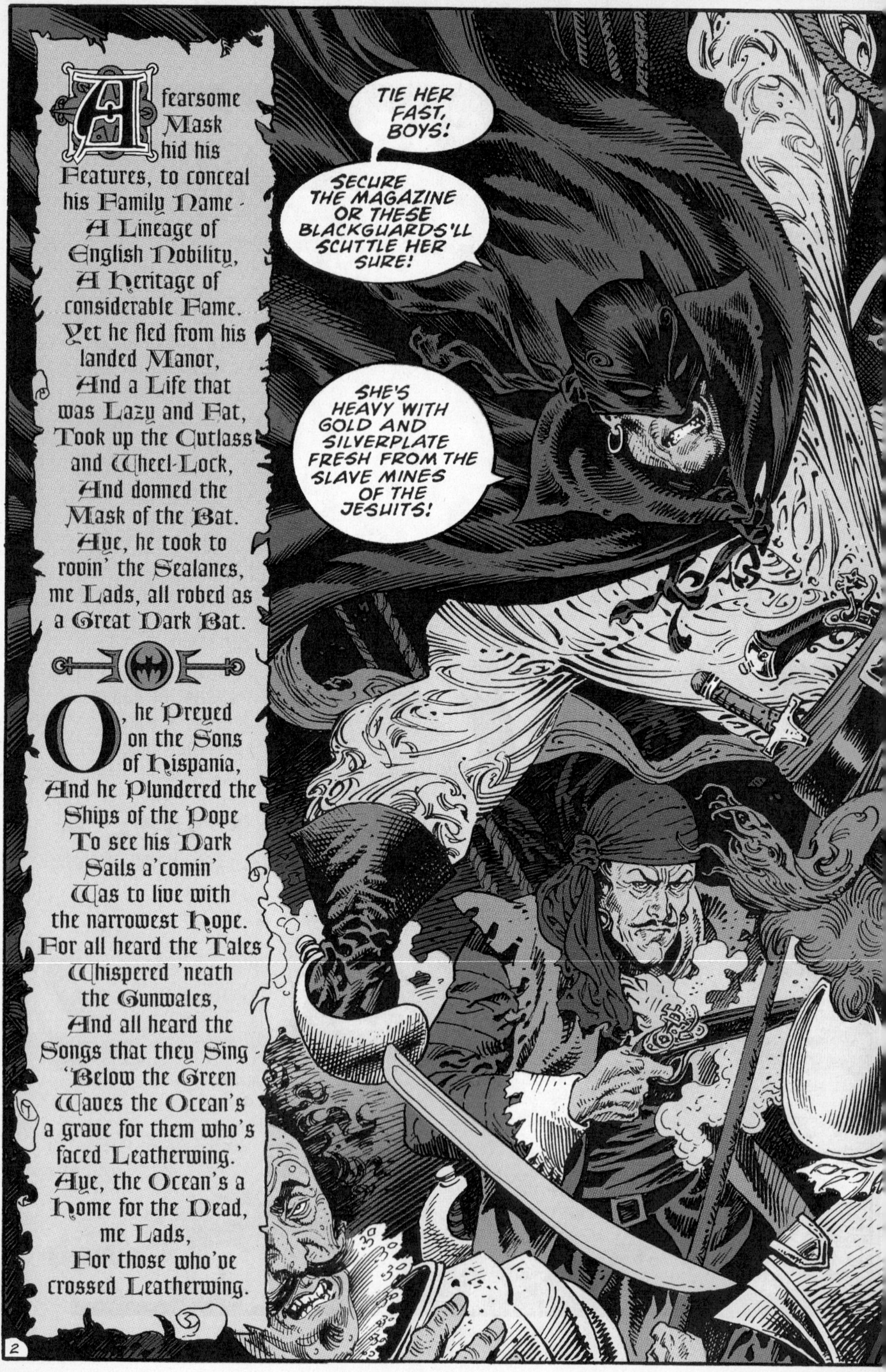
A fearsome Mask hid his Features, to conceal his Family Name - A Lineage of English Nobility, A Heritage of considerable Fame. Yet he fled from his landed Manor, And a Life that was Lazy and Fat, Took up the Cutlass and Wheel-Lock, And donned the Mask of the Bat. Aye, he took to rovin' the Sealanes, me Lads, all robed as a Great Dark Bat.
TIE HER FAST, BOYS!
SECURE THE MAGAZINE OR THESE BLACKGUARDS'LL SCUTTLE HER SURE!
SHE'S HEAVY WITH GOLD AND SILVERPLATE FRESH FROM THE SLAVE MINES OF THE JESUITS!
O, he Preyed on the Sons of Hispania, And he Plundered the Ships of the Pope To see his Dark Sails a'comin' Was to live with the narrowest Hope. For all heard the Tales Whispered 'neath the Gunwales, And all heard the Songs that they Sing - 'Below the Green Waves the Ocean's a grave for them who's faced Leatherwing.' Aye, the Ocean's a Home for the Dead, me Lads, For those who've crossed Leatherwing.
2

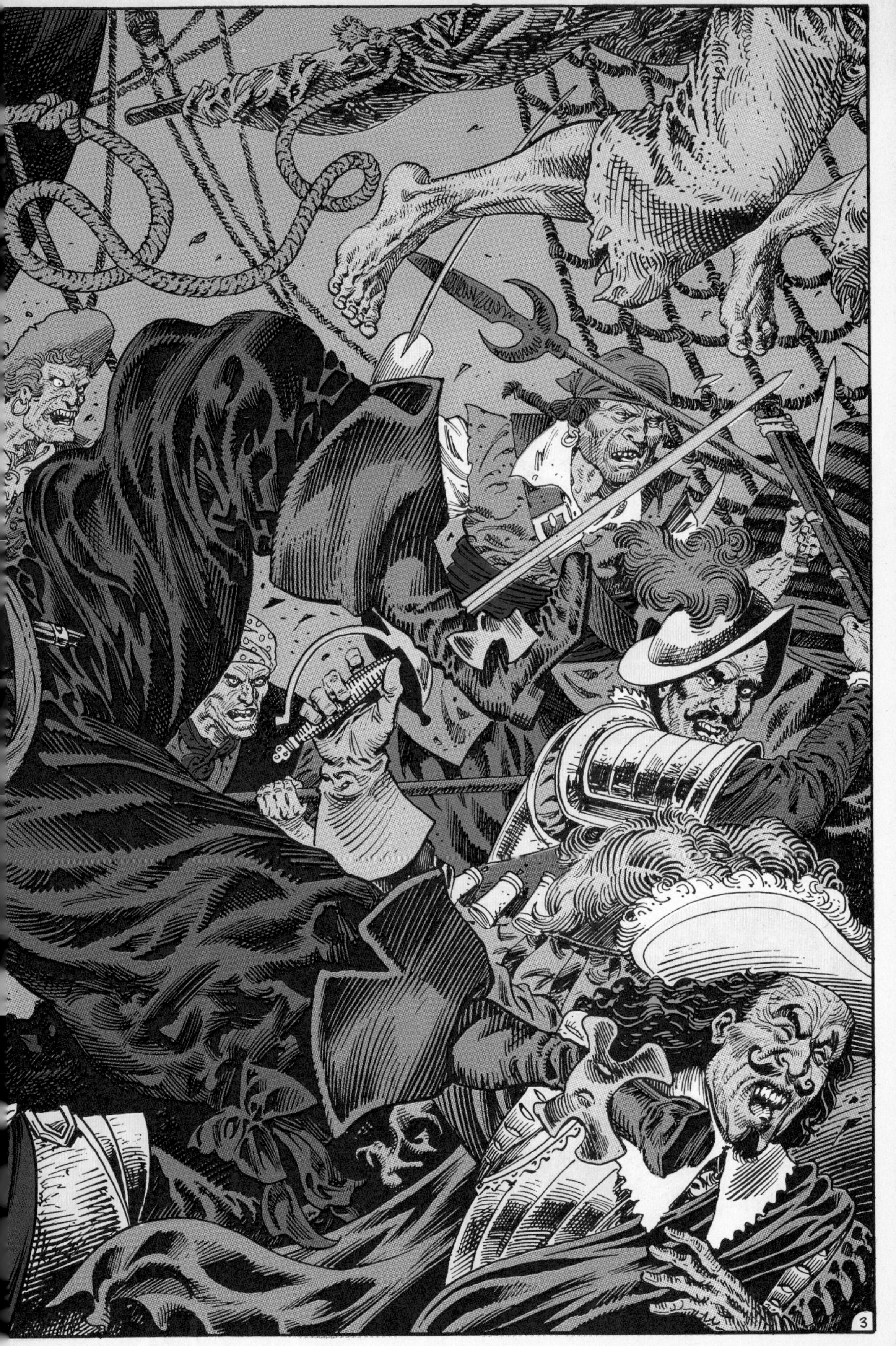
3

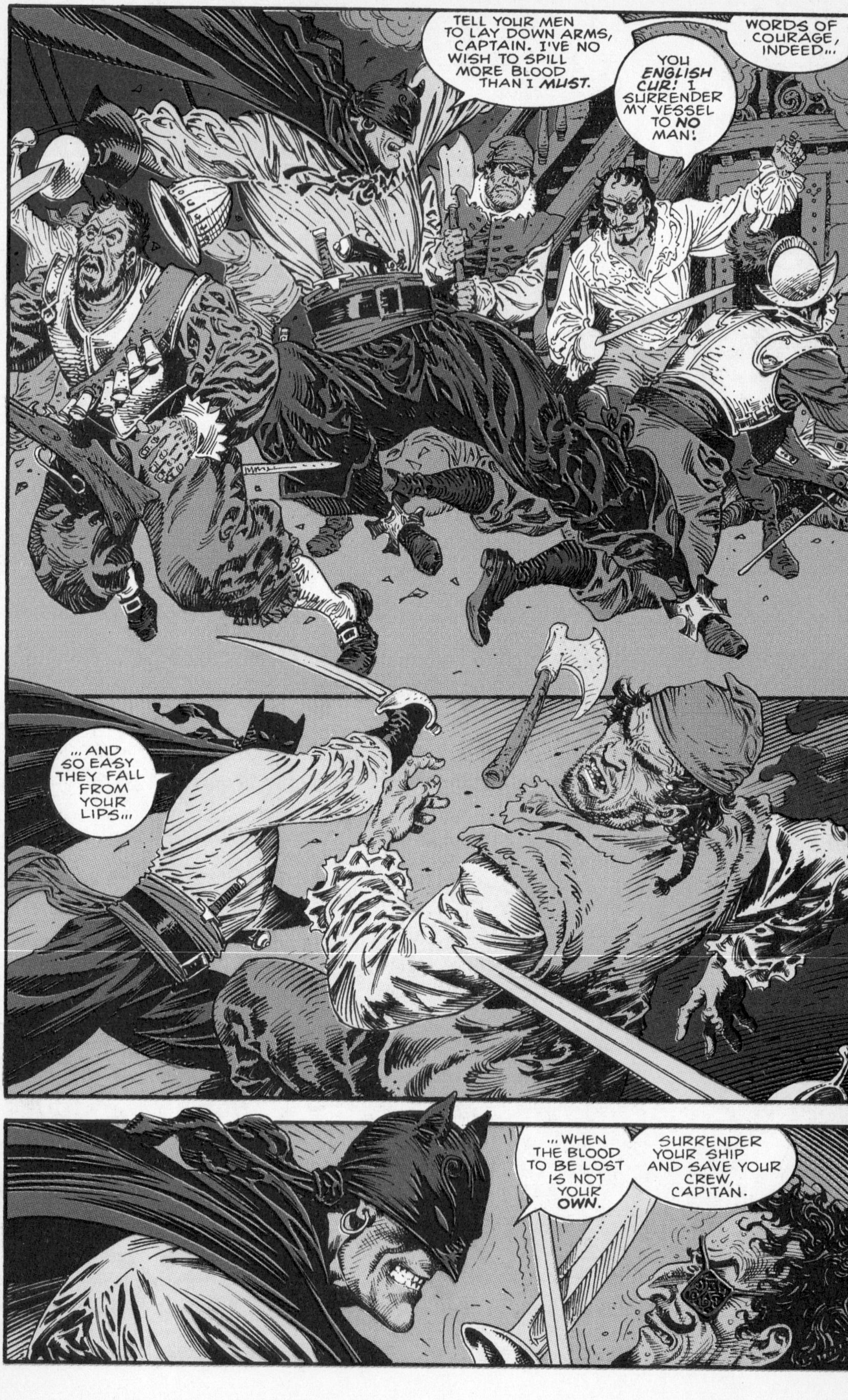

TELL YOUR MEN TO LAY DOWN ARMS, CAPTAIN. I'VE NO WISH TO SPILL MORE BLOOD THAN I MUST.
YOU ENGLISH CUR! I SURRENDER MY VESSEL TO NO MAN!
WORDS OF COURAGE, INDEED...
...AND SO EASY THEY FALL FROM YOUR LIPS...
...WHEN THE BLOOD TO BE LOST IS NOT YOUR OWN.
SURRENDER YOUR SHIP AND SAVE YOUR CREW, CAPITAN.
4

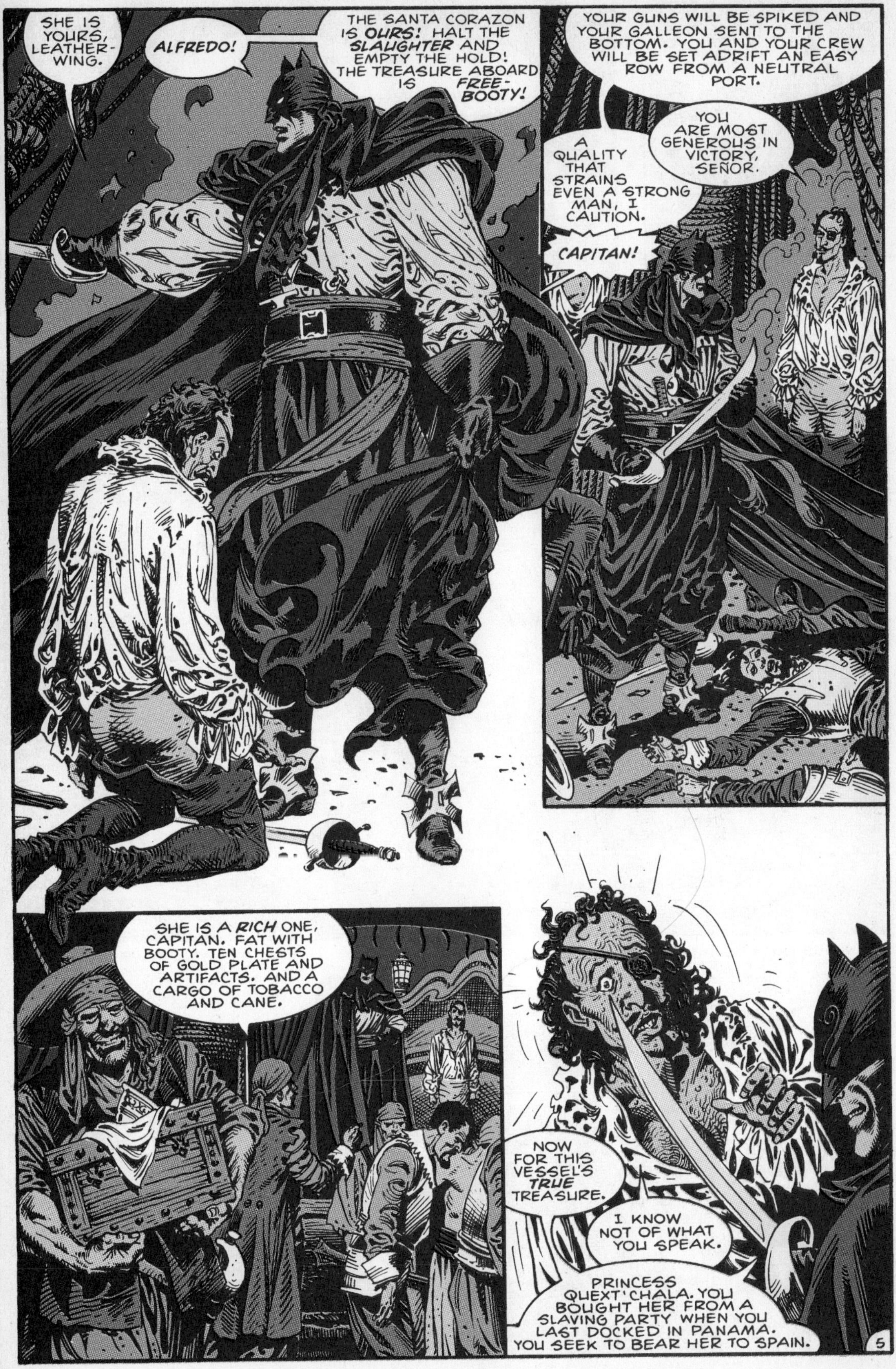
SHE IS YOURS, LEATHER-WING.
ALFREDO!
THE SANTA CORAZON IS OURS! HALT THE SLAUGHTER AND EMPTY THE HOLD! THE TREASURE ABOARD IS FREE-BOOTY!
YOUR GUNS WILL BE SPIKED AND YOUR GALLEON SENT TO THE BOTTOM. YOU AND YOUR CREW WILL BE SET ADRIFT AN EASY ROW FROM A NEUTRAL PORT.
YOU ARE MOST GENEROUS IN VICTORY, SEÑOR.
A QUALITY THAT STRAINS EVEN A STRONG MAN, I CAUTION.
CAPITAN!
SHE IS A RICH ONE, CAPITAN. FAT WITH BOOTY. TEN CHESTS OF GOLD PLATE AND ARTIFACTS. AND A CARGO OF TOBACCO AND CANE.
NOW FOR THIS VESSEL'S TRUE TREASURE.
I KNOW NOT OF WHAT YOU SPEAK.
PRINCESS QUEXT'CHALA. YOU BOUGHT HER FROM A SLAVING PARTY WHEN YOU LAST DOCKED IN PANAMA. YOU SEEK TO BEAR HER TO SPAIN.
5

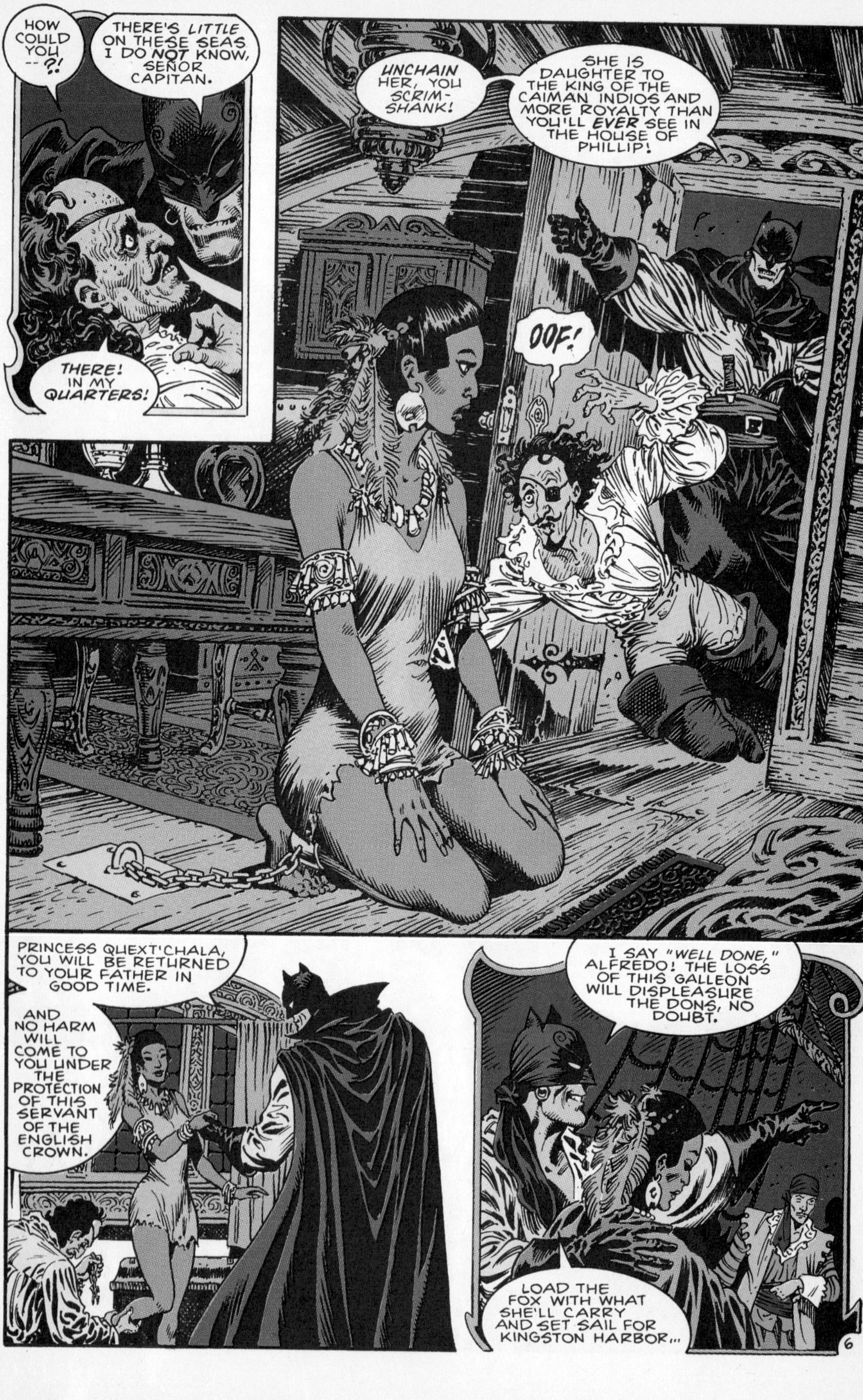

HOW COULD YOU --?!
THERE'S LITTLE ON THESE SEAS I DO NOT KNOW, SEÑOR CAPITAN.
THERE! IN MY QUARTERS!
UNCHAIN HER, YOU SCRIM-SHANK!
SHE IS DAUGHTER TO THE KING OF THE CAIMAN INDIOS AND MORE ROYALTY THAN YOU'LL EVER SEE IN THE HOUSE OF PHILLIP!
OOF!
PRINCESS QUEXT'CHALA, YOU WILL BE RETURNED TO YOUR FATHER IN GOOD TIME.
AND NO HARM WILL COME TO YOU UNDER THE PROTECTION OF THIS SERVANT OF THE ENGLISH CROWN.
I SAY "WELL DONE," ALFREDO! THE LOSS OF THIS GALLEON WILL DISPLEASURE THE DONS, NO DOUBT.
LOAD THE FOX WITH WHAT SHE'LL CARRY AND SET SAIL FOR KINGSTON HARBOR...
6

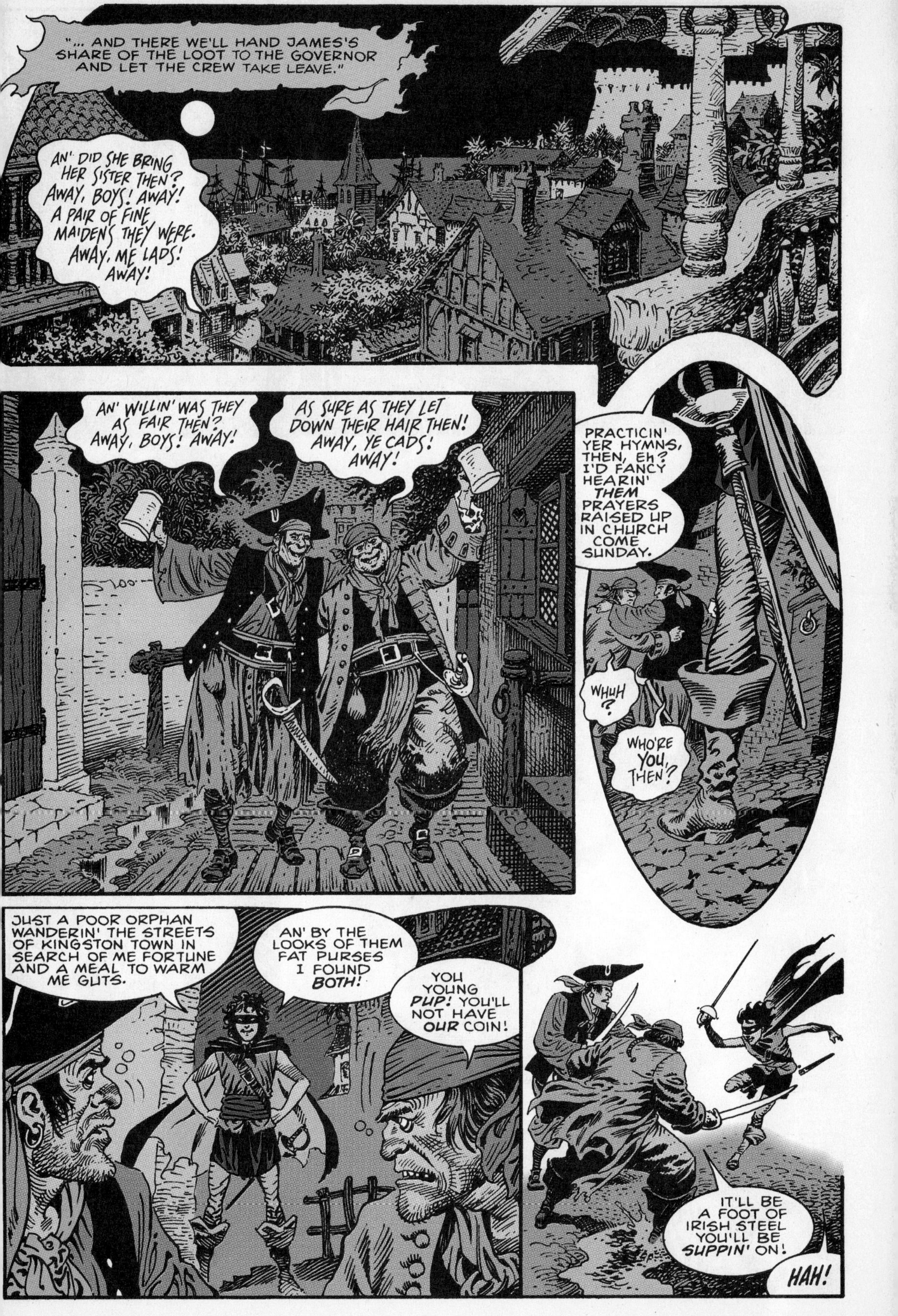
"... AND THERE WE'LL HAND JAMES'S SHARE OF THE LOOT TO THE GOVERNOR AND LET THE CREW TAKE LEAVE."
AN' DID SHE BRING HER SISTER THEN? AWAY, BOYS! AWAY! A PAIR OF FINE MAIDENS THEY WERE. AWAY, ME LADS! AWAY!
AN' WILLIN' WAS THEY AS FAIR THEN? AWAY, BOYS! AWAY!
AS SURE AS THEY LET DOWN THEIR HAIR THEN! AWAY, YE CADS! AWAY!
PRACTICIN' YER HYMNS, THEN, EH? I'D FANCY HEARIN' THEM PRAYERS RAISED UP IN CHURCH COME SUNDAY.
WHUH?
WHO'RE YOU, THEN?
JUST A POOR ORPHAN WANDERIN' THE STREETS OF KINGSTON TOWN IN SEARCH OF ME FORTUNE AND A MEAL TO WARM ME GUTS.
AN' BY THE LOOKS OF THEM FAT PURSES I FOUND BOTH!
YOU YOUNG PUP! YOU'LL NOT HAVE OUR COIN!
IT'LL BE A FOOT OF IRISH STEEL YOU'LL BE SUPPIN' ON!
HAH!

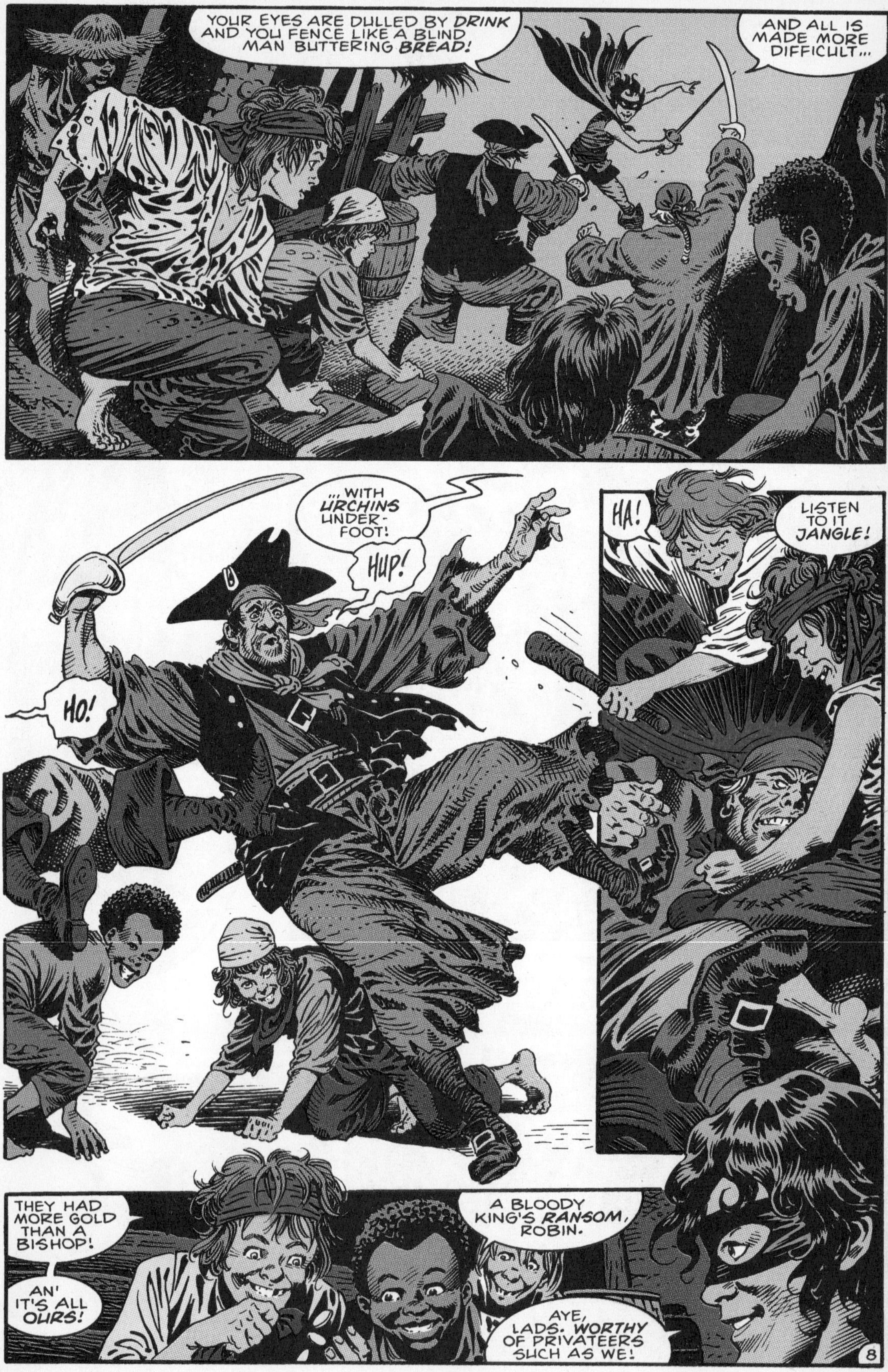
YOUR EYES ARE DULLED BY DRINK AND YOU FENCE LIKE A BLIND MAN BUTTERING BREAD!
AND ALL IS MADE MORE DIFFICULT...
...WITH URCHINS UNDER-FOOT!
HUP!
HO!
HA!
LISTEN TO IT JANGLE!
THEY HAD MORE GOLD THAN A BISHOP!
AN' IT'S ALL OURS!
A BLOODY KING'S RANSOM, ROBIN.
AYE, LADS. WORTHY OF PRIVATEERS SUCH AS WE!
8

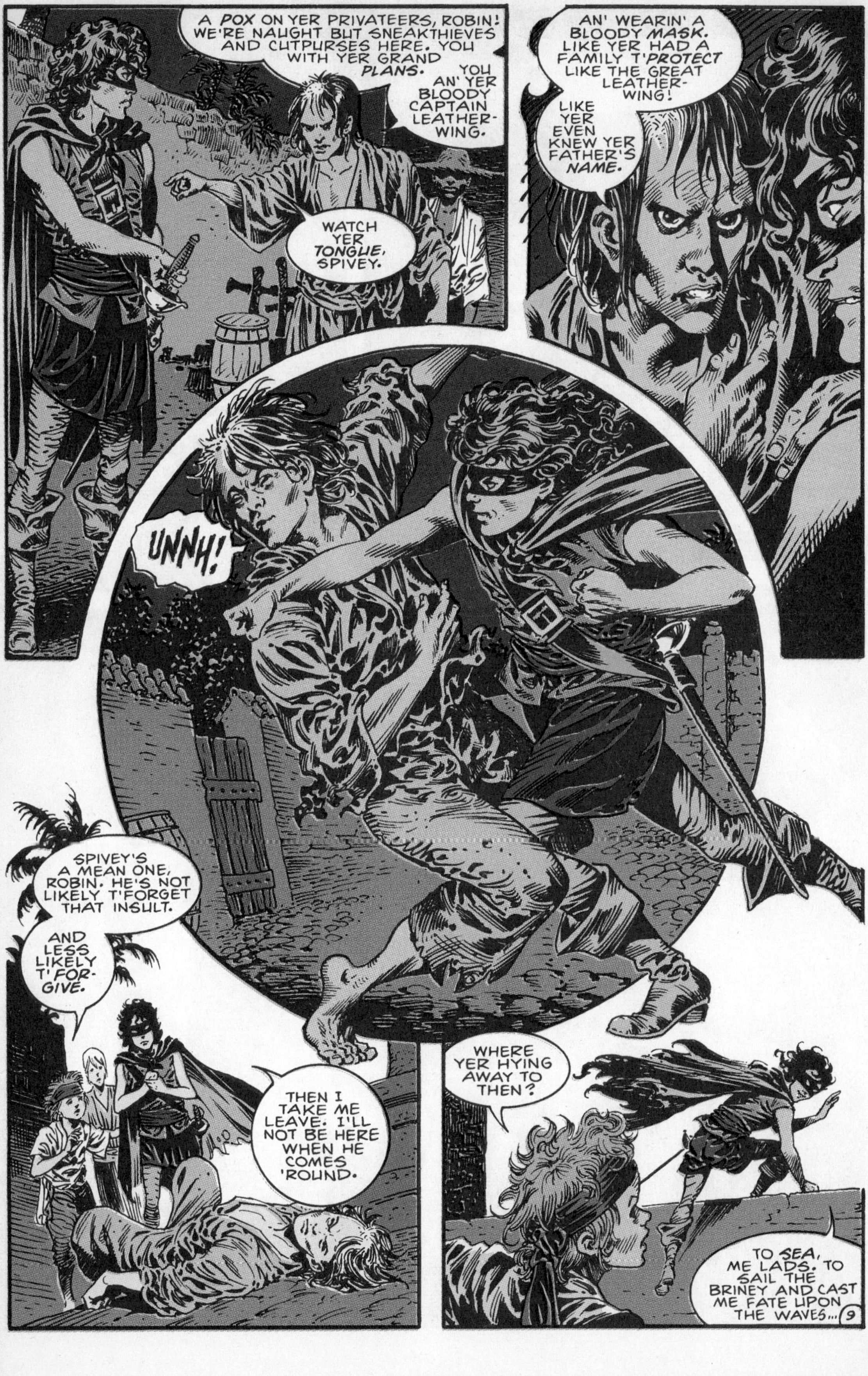
A POX ON YER PRIVATEERS, ROBIN! WE'RE NAUGHT BUT SNEAKTHIEVES AND CUTPURSES HERE. YOU WITH YER GRAND PLANS.
YOU AN' YER BLOODY CAPTAIN LEATHER-WING.
WATCH YER TONGUE, SPIVEY.
AN' WEARIN' A BLOODY MASK. LIKE YER HAD A FAMILY T'PROTECT LIKE THE GREAT LEATHER-WING!
LIKE YER EVEN KNEW YER FATHER'S NAME.
UNNH!
SPIVEY'S A MEAN ONE, ROBIN. HE'S NOT LIKELY T'FORGET THAT INSULT.
AND LESS LIKELY T'FOR-GIVE.
THEN I TAKE ME LEAVE. I'LL NOT BE HERE WHEN HE COMES 'ROUND.
WHERE YER HYING AWAY TO THEN?
TO SEA, ME LADS. TO SAIL THE BRINEY AND CAST ME FATE UPON THE WAVES...
9

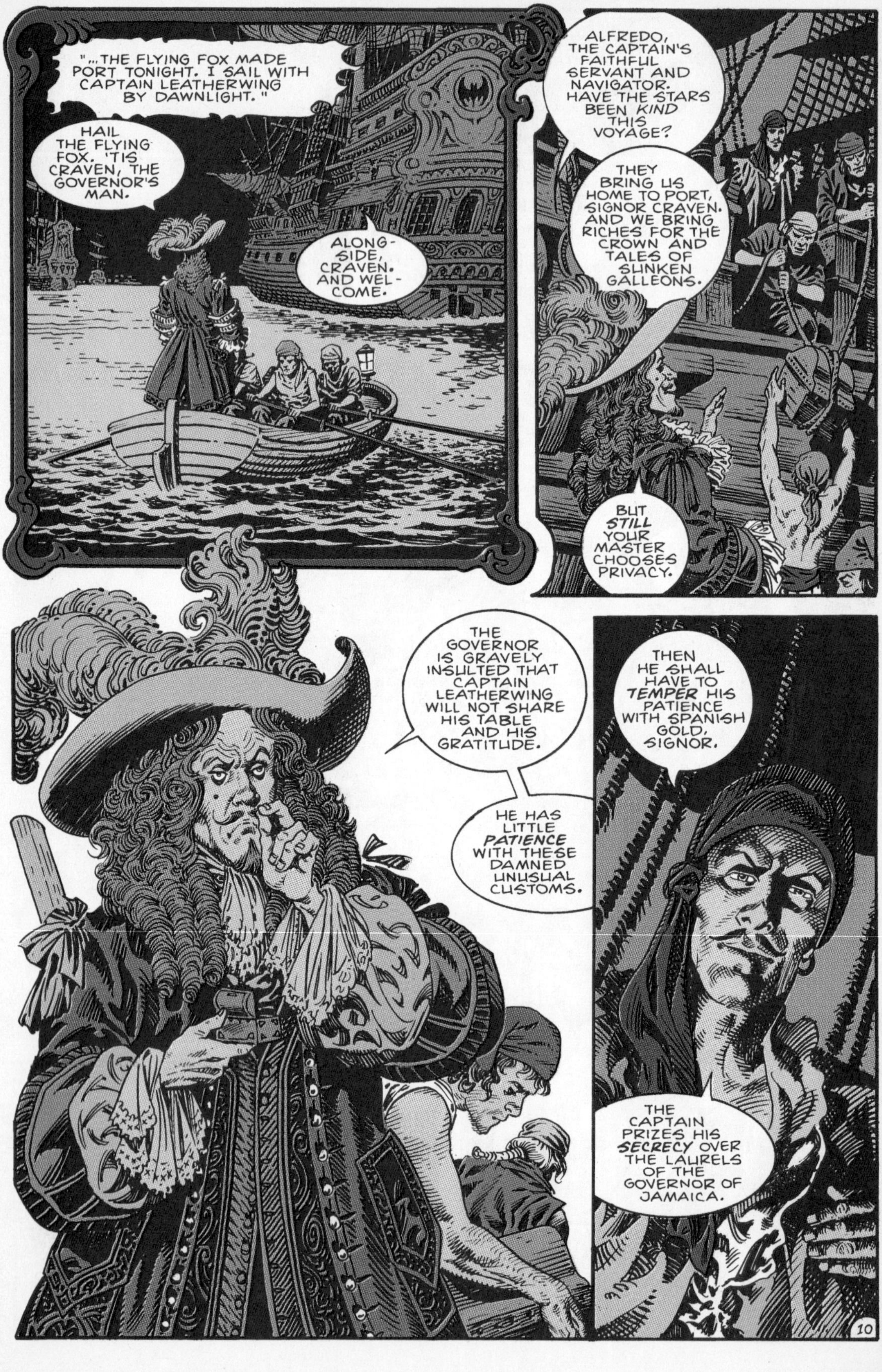
"...THE FLYING FOX MADE PORT TONIGHT. I SAIL WITH CAPTAIN LEATHERWING BY DAWNLIGHT."
HAIL THE FLYING FOX. 'TIS CRAVEN, THE GOVERNOR'S MAN.
ALONG-SIDE, CRAVEN. AND WEL-COME.
ALFREDO, THE CAPTAIN'S FAITHFUL SERVANT AND NAVIGATOR. HAVE THE STARS BEEN KIND THIS VOYAGE?
THEY BRING US HOME TO PORT, SIGNOR CRAVEN. AND WE BRING RICHES FOR THE CROWN AND TALES OF SUNKEN GALLEONS.
BUT STILL YOUR MASTER CHOOSES PRIVACY.
THE GOVERNOR IS GRAVELY INSULTED THAT CAPTAIN LEATHERWING WILL NOT SHARE HIS TABLE AND HIS GRATITUDE.
HE HAS LITTLE PATIENCE WITH THESE DAMNED UNUSUAL CUSTOMS.
THEN HE SHALL HAVE TO TEMPER HIS PATIENCE WITH SPANISH GOLD, SIGNOR.
THE CAPTAIN PRIZES HIS SECRECY OVER THE LAURELS OF THE GOVERNOR OF JAMAICA.
10

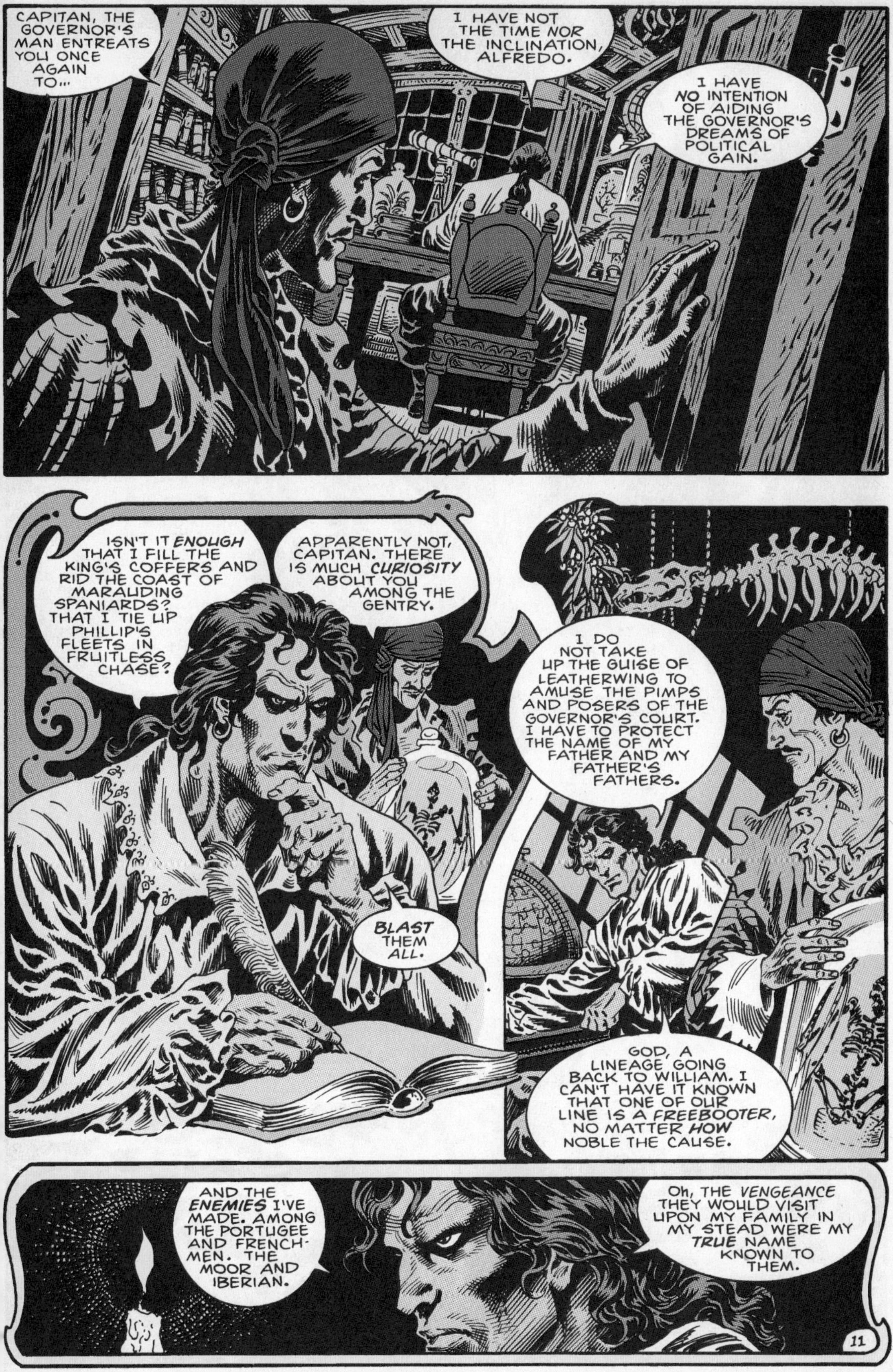
CAPITAN, THE GOVERNOR'S MAN ENTREATS YOU ONCE AGAIN TO...
I HAVE NOT THE TIME NOR THE INCLINATION, ALFREDO.
I HAVE NO INTENTION OF AIDING THE GOVERNOR'S DREAMS OF POLITICAL GAIN.
ISN'T IT ENOUGH THAT I FILL THE KING'S COFFERS AND RID THE COAST OF MARAUDING SPANIARDS? THAT I TIE UP PHILLIP'S FLEETS IN FRUITLESS CHASE?
APPARENTLY NOT, CAPITAN. THERE IS MUCH CURIOSITY ABOUT YOU AMONG THE GENTRY.
BLAST THEM ALL.
I DO NOT TAKE UP THE GUISE OF LEATHERWING TO AMUSE THE PIMPS AND POSERS OF THE GOVERNOR'S COURT. I HAVE TO PROTECT THE NAME OF MY FATHER AND MY FATHER'S FATHERS.
GOD, A LINEAGE GOING BACK TO WILLIAM. I CAN'T HAVE IT KNOWN THAT ONE OF OUR LINE IS A FREEBOOTER, NO MATTER HOW NOBLE THE CAUSE.
AND THE ENEMIES I'VE MADE. AMONG THE PORTUGEE AND FRENCHMEN. THE MOOR AND IBERIAN.
Oh, THE VENGEANCE THEY WOULD VISIT UPON MY FAMILY IN MY STEAD WERE MY TRUE NAME KNOWN TO THEM.
11

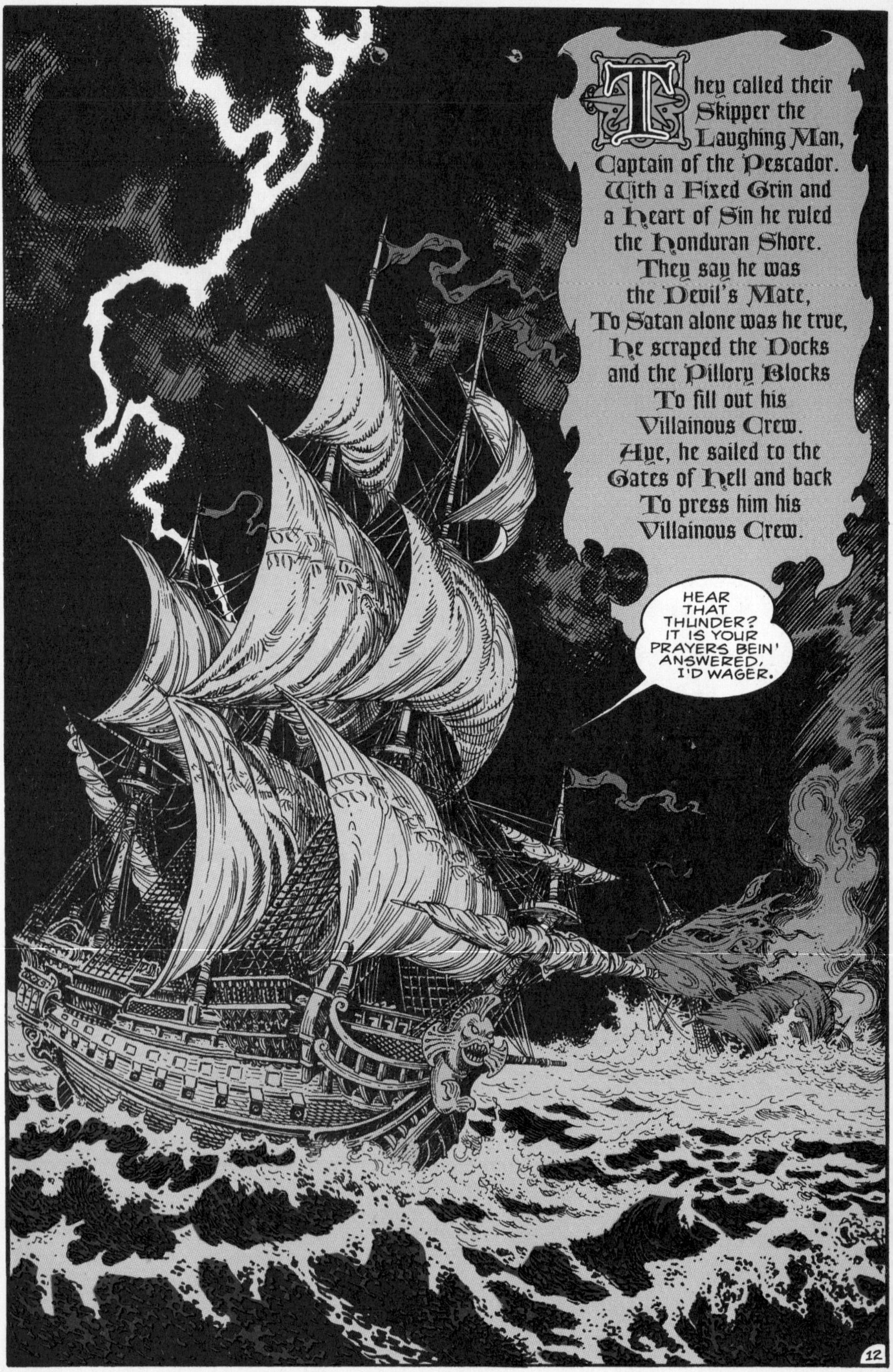
They called their Skipper the Laughing Man, Captain of the Pescador. With a Fixed Grin and a Heart of Sin he ruled the Honduran Shore. They say he was the Devil's Mate, To Satan alone was he true, He scraped the Docks and the Pillory Blocks To fill out his Villainous Crew. Aye, he sailed to the Gates of Hell and back To press him his Villainous Crew.
HEAR THAT THUNDER? IT IS YOUR PRAYERS BEIN' ANSWERED, I'D WAGER.
12

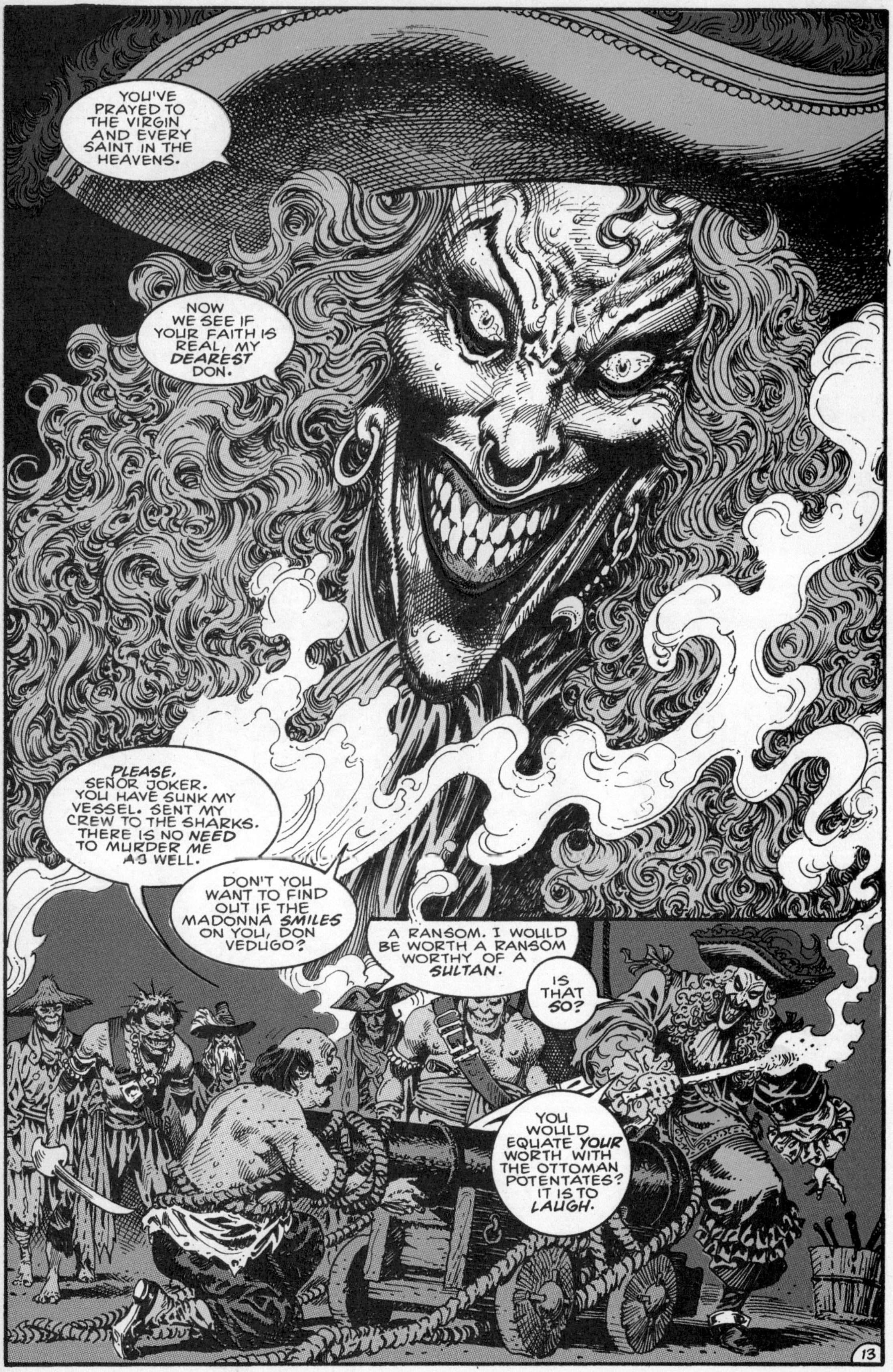
YOU'VE PRAYED TO THE VIRGIN AND EVERY SAINT IN THE HEAVENS.
NOW WE SEE IF YOUR FAITH IS REAL, MY DEAREST DON.
PLEASE, SEÑOR JOKER. YOU HAVE SUNK MY VESSEL. SENT MY CREW TO THE SHARKS. THERE IS NO NEED TO MURDER ME AS WELL.
DON'T YOU WANT TO FIND OUT IF THE MADONNA SMILES ON YOU, DON VEDUGO?
A RANSOM. I WOULD BE WORTH A RANSOM WORTHY OF A SULTAN.
IS THAT SO?
YOU WOULD EQUATE YOUR WORTH WITH THE OTTOMAN POTENTATES? IT IS TO LAUGH.
13

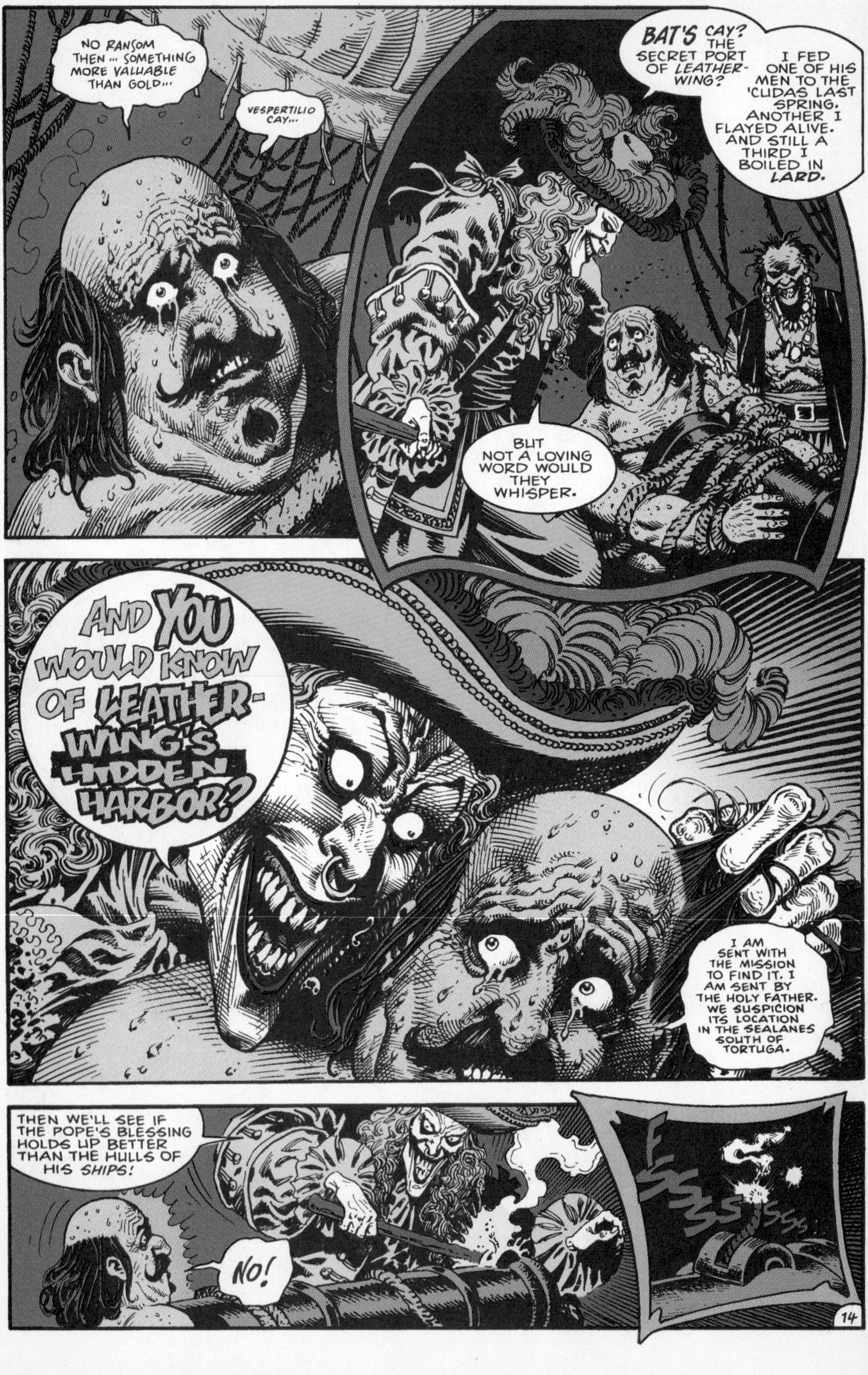
NO RANSOM THEN... SOMETHING MORE VALUABLE THAN GOLD...
VESPERTILIO CAY...
BAT'S CAY? THE SECRET PORT OF LEATHER-WING?
I FED ONE OF HIS MEN TO THE 'CUDAS LAST SPRING. ANOTHER I FLAYED ALIVE. AND STILL A THIRD I BOILED IN LARD.
BUT NOT A LOVING WORD WOULD THEY WHISPER.
AND YOU WOULD KNOW OF LEATHER-WING'S HIDDEN HARBOR?
I AM SENT WITH THE MISSION TO FIND IT. I AM SENT BY THE HOLY FATHER. WE SUSPICION ITS LOCATION IN THE SEALANES SOUTH OF TORTUGA.
THEN WE'LL SEE IF THE POPE'S BLESSING HOLDS UP BETTER THAN THE HULLS OF HIS SHIPS!
NO!
FSSSSSSSSS
14

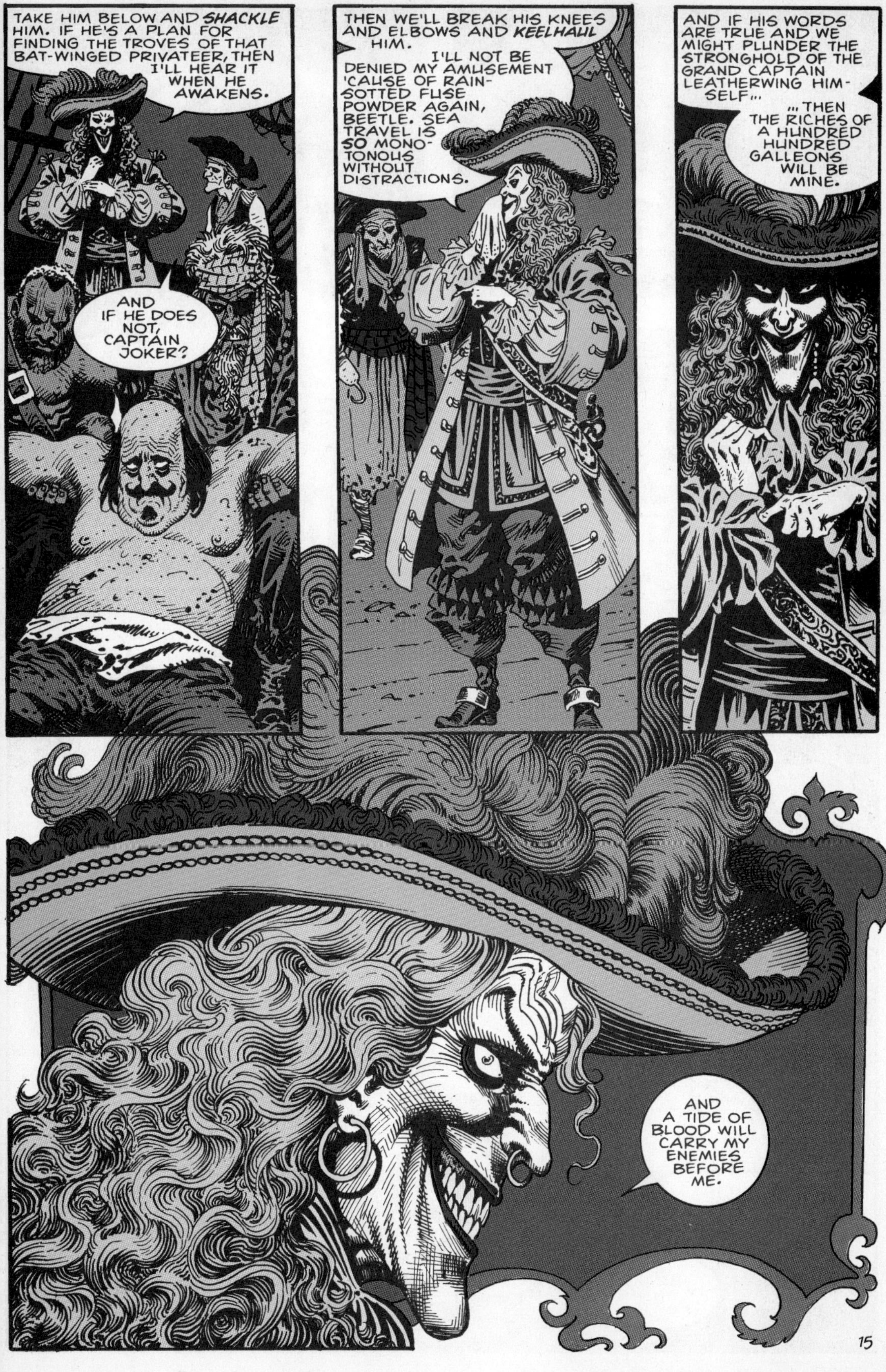
TAKE HIM BELOW AND SHACKLE HIM. IF HE'S A PLAN FOR FINDING THE TROVES OF THAT BAT-WINGED PRIVATEER, THEN I'LL HEAR IT WHEN HE AWAKENS.
AND IF HE DOES NOT, CAPTAIN JOKER?
THEN WE'LL BREAK HIS KNEES AND ELBOWS AND KEELHAUL HIM.
I'LL NOT BE DENIED MY AMUSEMENT 'CAUSE OF RAIN-SOTTED FUSE POWDER AGAIN, BEETLE. SEA TRAVEL IS SO MONOTONOUS WITHOUT DISTRACTIONS.
AND IF HIS WORDS ARE TRUE AND WE MIGHT PLUNDER THE STRONGHOLD OF THE GRAND CAPTAIN LEATHERWING HIMSELF...
...THEN THE RICHES OF A HUNDRED HUNDRED GALLEONS WILL BE MINE.
AND A TIDE OF BLOOD WILL CARRY MY ENEMIES BEFORE ME.
15

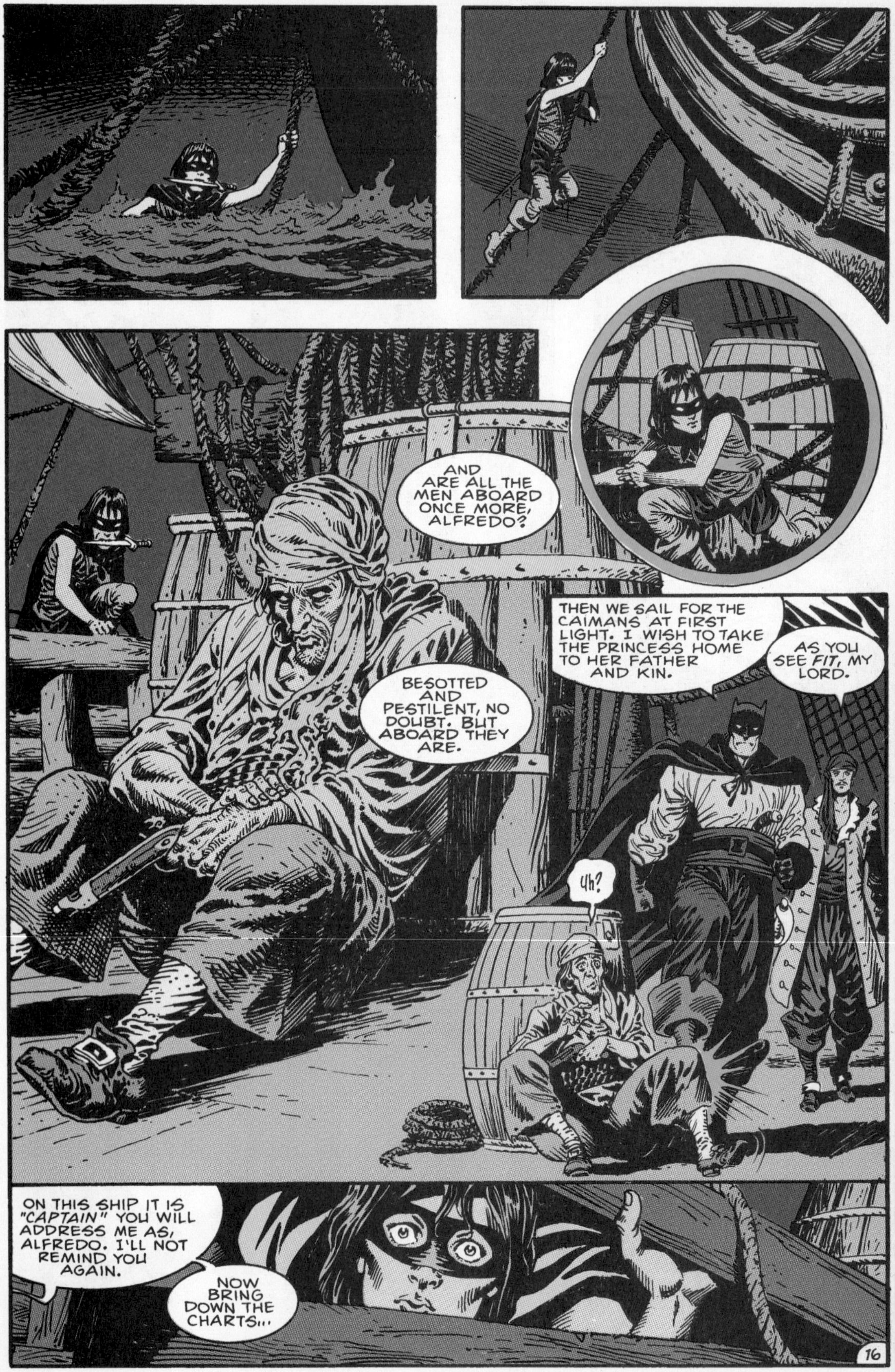
AND ARE ALL THE MEN ABOARD ONCE MORE, ALFREDO?
BESOTTED AND PESTILENT, NO DOUBT. BUT ABOARD THEY ARE.
THEN WE SAIL FOR THE CAIMANS AT FIRST LIGHT. I WISH TO TAKE THE PRINCESS HOME TO HER FATHER AND KIN.
AS YOU SEE *FIT*, MY LORD.
UH?
ON THIS SHIP IT IS "*CAPTAIN*" YOU WILL ADDRESS ME AS, ALFREDO. I'LL NOT REMIND YOU AGAIN.
NOW BRING DOWN THE CHARTS...
16

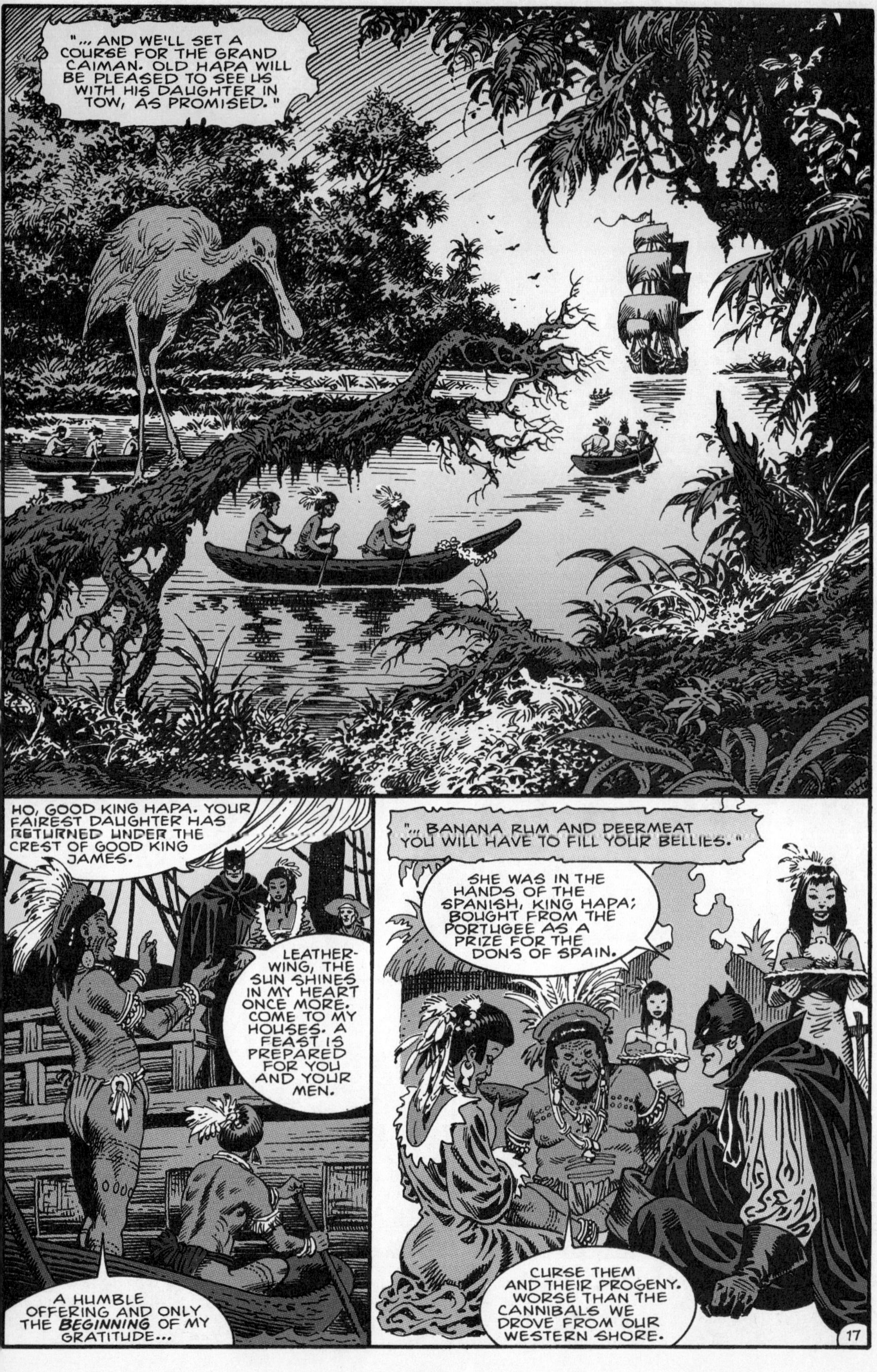
"... AND WE'LL SET A COURSE FOR THE GRAND CAIMAN. OLD HAPA WILL BE PLEASED TO SEE US WITH HIS DAUGHTER IN TOW, AS PROMISED."
HO, GOOD KING HAPA. YOUR FAIREST DAUGHTER HAS RETURNED UNDER THE CREST OF GOOD KING JAMES.
LEATHERWING, THE SUN SHINES IN MY HEART ONCE MORE. COME TO MY HOUSES. A FEAST IS PREPARED FOR YOU AND YOUR MEN.
A HUMBLE OFFERING AND ONLY THE *BEGINNING* OF MY GRATITUDE...
"... BANANA RUM AND DEERMEAT YOU WILL HAVE TO FILL YOUR BELLIES."
SHE WAS IN THE HANDS OF THE SPANISH, KING HAPA; BOUGHT FROM THE PORTUGEE AS A PRIZE FOR THE DONS OF SPAIN.
CURSE THEM AND THEIR PROGENY. WORSE THAN THE CANNIBALS WE DROVE FROM OUR WESTERN SHORE.
17

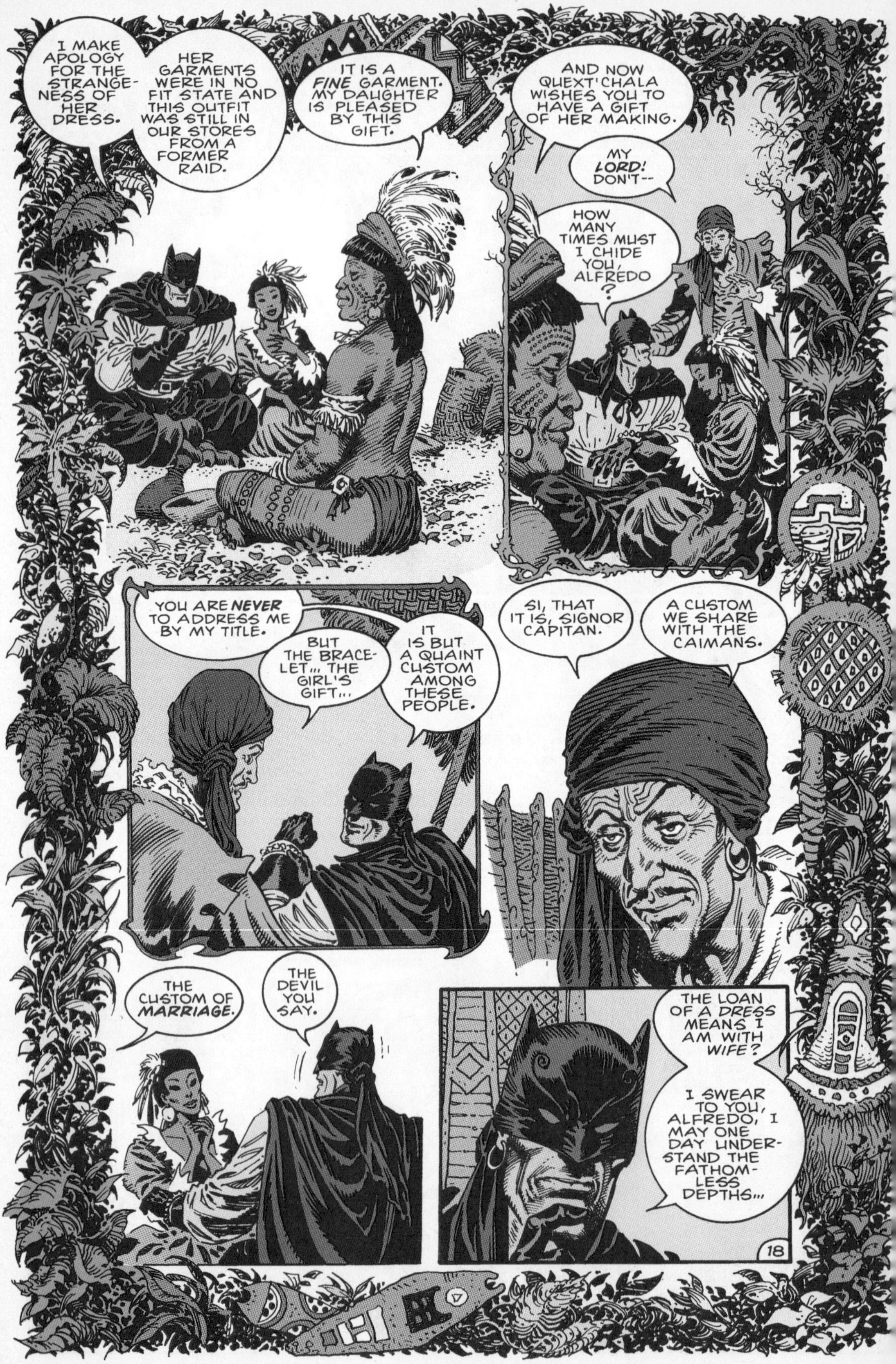
I MAKE APOLOGY FOR THE STRANGENESS OF HER DRESS.
HER GARMENTS WERE IN NO FIT STATE AND THIS OUTFIT WAS STILL IN OUR STORES FROM A FORMER RAID.
IT IS A FINE GARMENT. MY DAUGHTER IS PLEASED BY THIS GIFT.
AND NOW QUEXT'CHALA WISHES YOU TO HAVE A GIFT OF HER MAKING.
MY LORD! DON'T--
HOW MANY TIMES MUST I CHIDE YOU, ALFREDO?
YOU ARE NEVER TO ADDRESS ME BY MY TITLE.
BUT THE BRACELET... THE GIRL'S GIFT...
IT IS BUT A QUAINT CUSTOM AMONG THESE PEOPLE.
SI, THAT IT IS, SIGNOR CAPITAN.
A CUSTOM WE SHARE WITH THE CAIMANS.
THE CUSTOM OF MARRIAGE.
THE DEVIL YOU SAY.
THE LOAN OF A DRESS MEANS I AM WITH WIFE?
I SWEAR TO YOU, ALFREDO, I MAY ONE DAY UNDERSTAND THE FATHOMLESS DEPTHS...
18

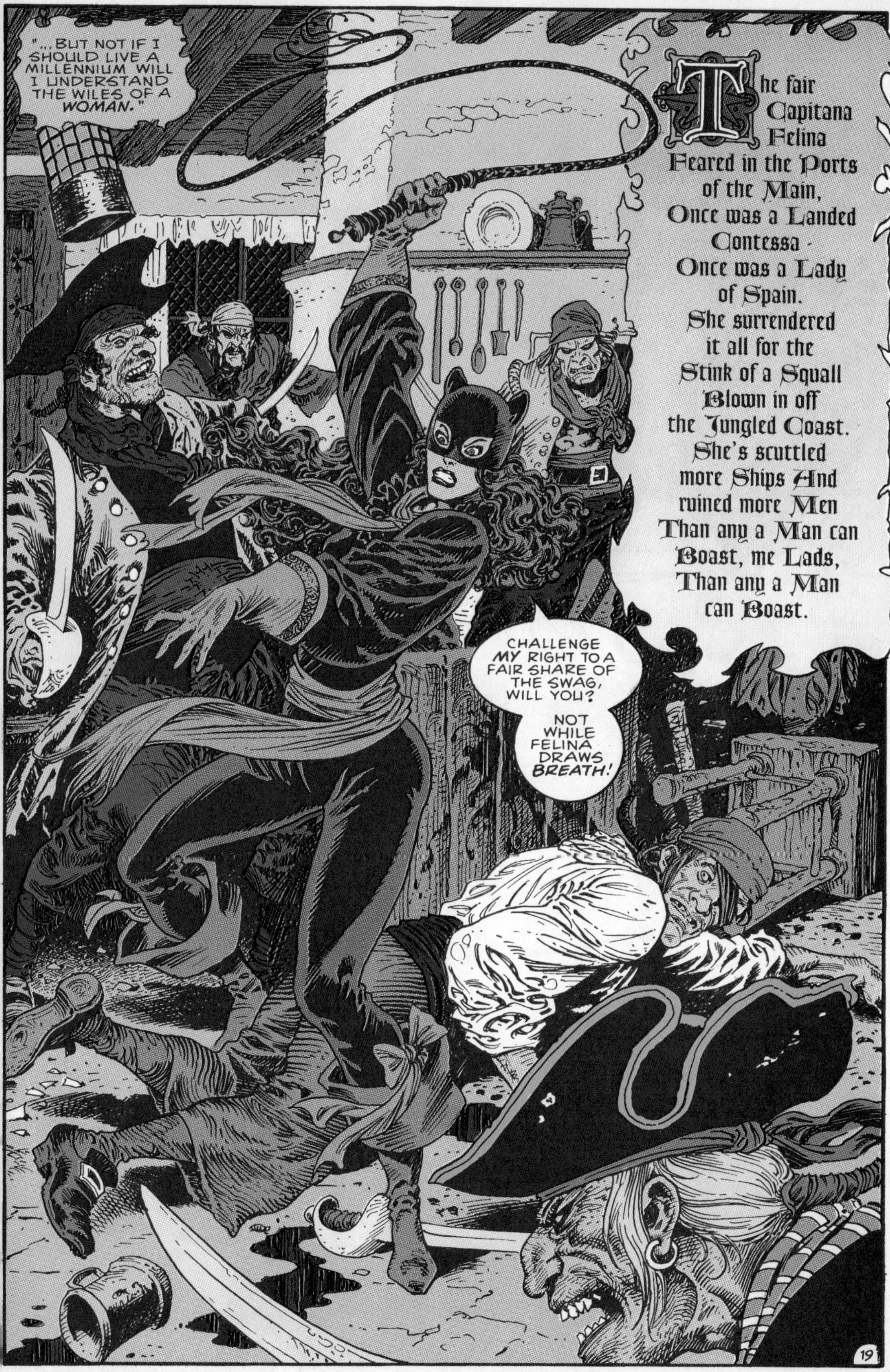
"...BUT NOT IF I SHOULD LIVE A MILLENNIUM WILL I UNDERSTAND THE WILES OF A WOMAN."
The fair Capitana Felina Feared in the Ports of the Main, Once was a Landed Contessa - Once was a Lady of Spain. She surrendered it all for the Stink of a Squall Blown in off the Jungled Coast. She's scuttled more Ships And ruined more Men Than any a Man can Boast, me Lads, Than any a Man can Boast.
CHALLENGE MY RIGHT TO A FAIR SHARE OF THE SWAG, WILL YOU?
NOT WHILE FELINA DRAWS BREATH!
19

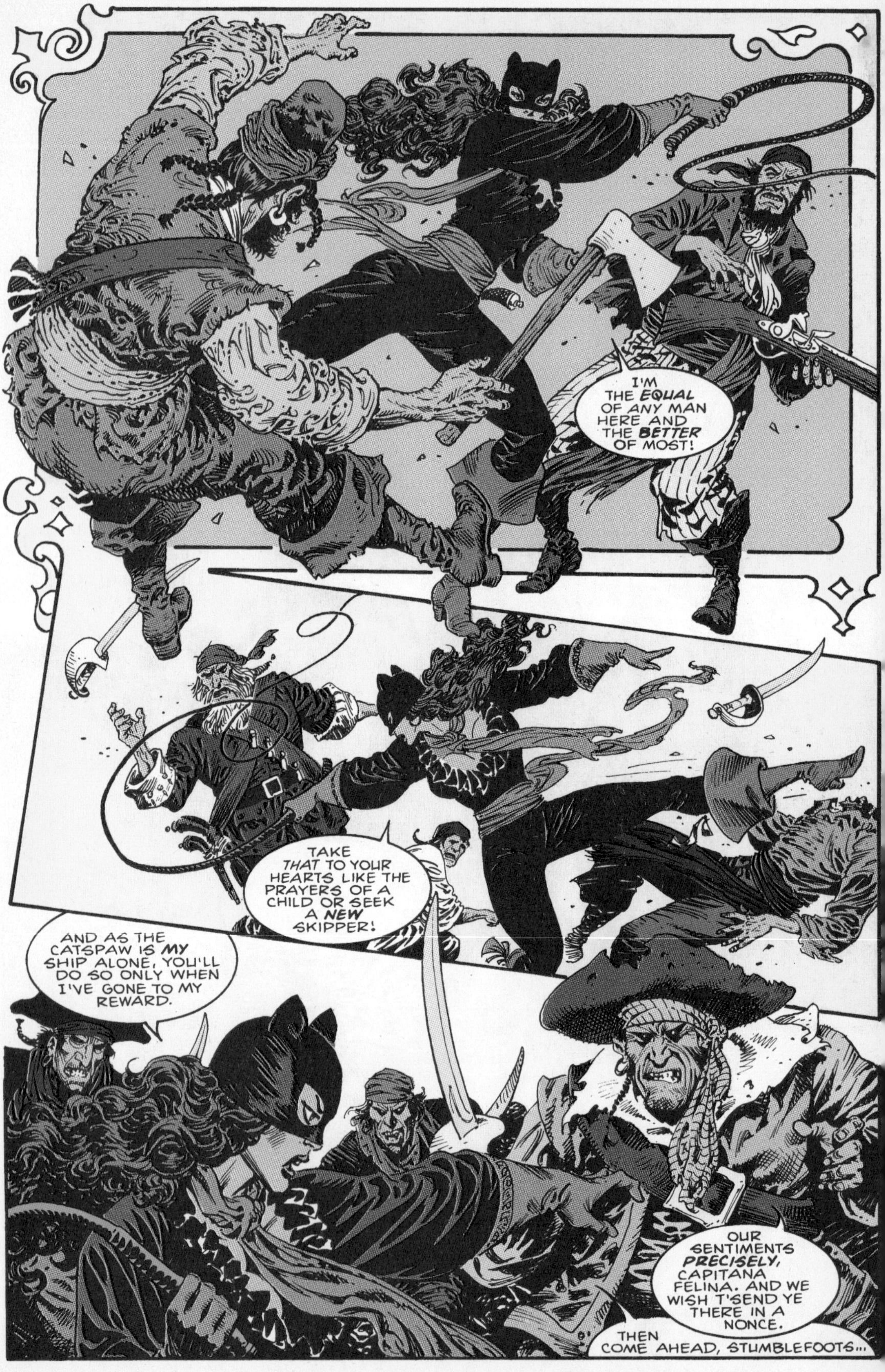
I'M THE EQUAL OF ANY MAN HERE AND THE BETTER OF MOST!
TAKE THAT TO YOUR HEARTS LIKE THE PRAYERS OF A CHILD OR SEEK A NEW SKIPPER!
AND AS THE CATSPAW IS MY SHIP ALONE, YOU'LL DO SO ONLY WHEN I'VE GONE TO MY REWARD.
OUR SENTIMENTS PRECISELY, CAPITANA FELINA. AND WE WISH T'SEND YE THERE IN A NONCE.
THEN COME AHEAD, STUMBLEFOOTS...

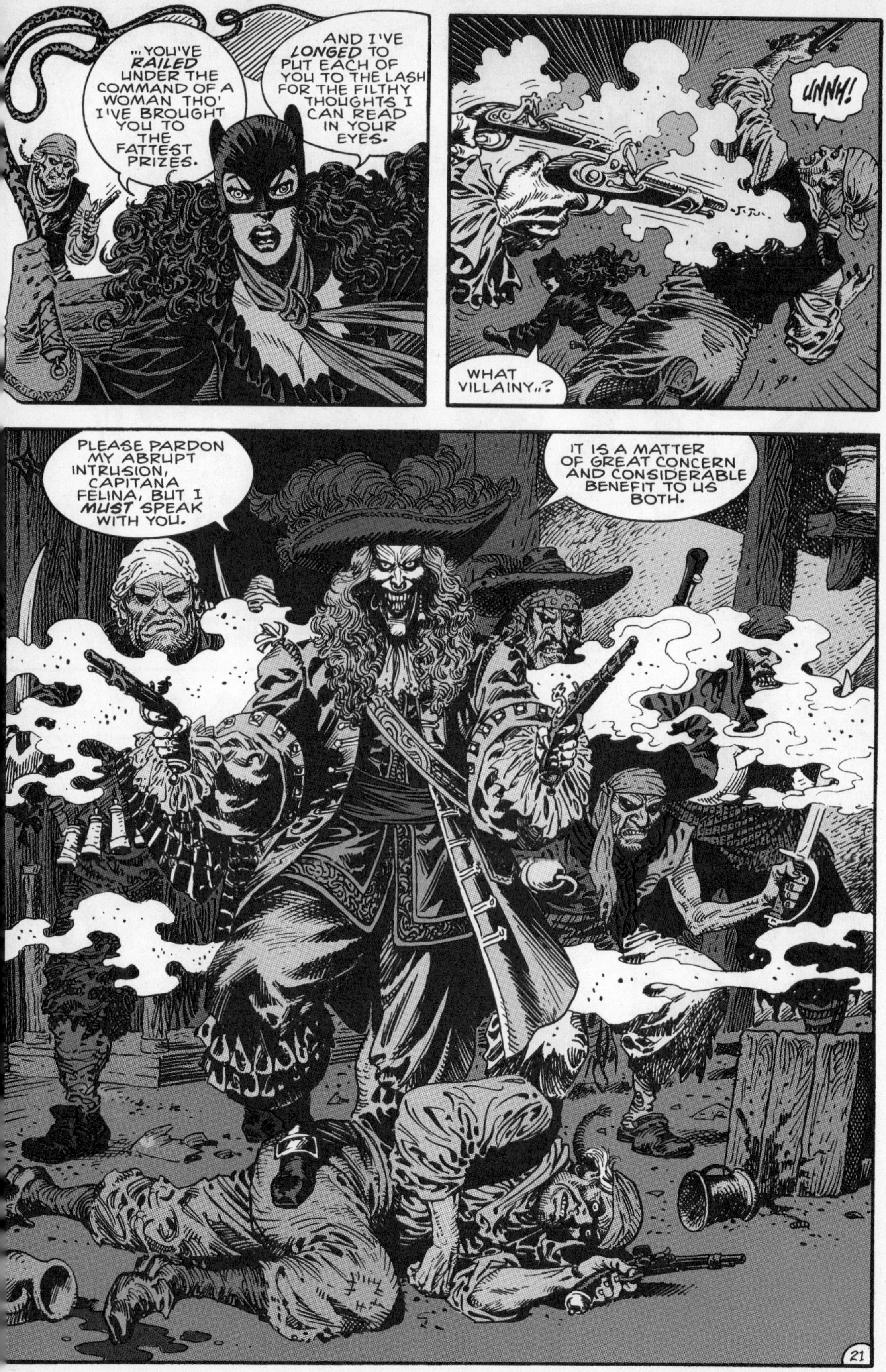
...YOU'VE RAILED UNDER THE COMMAND OF A WOMAN THO' I'VE BROUGHT YOU TO THE FATTEST PRIZES.
AND I'VE LONGED TO PUT EACH OF YOU TO THE LASH FOR THE FILTHY THOUGHTS I CAN READ IN YOUR EYES.
UNNH!
WHAT VILLAINY..?
PLEASE PARDON MY ABRUPT INTRUSION, CAPITANA FELINA, BUT I MUST SPEAK WITH YOU.
IT IS A MATTER OF GREAT CONCERN AND CONSIDERABLE BENEFIT TO US BOTH.
21

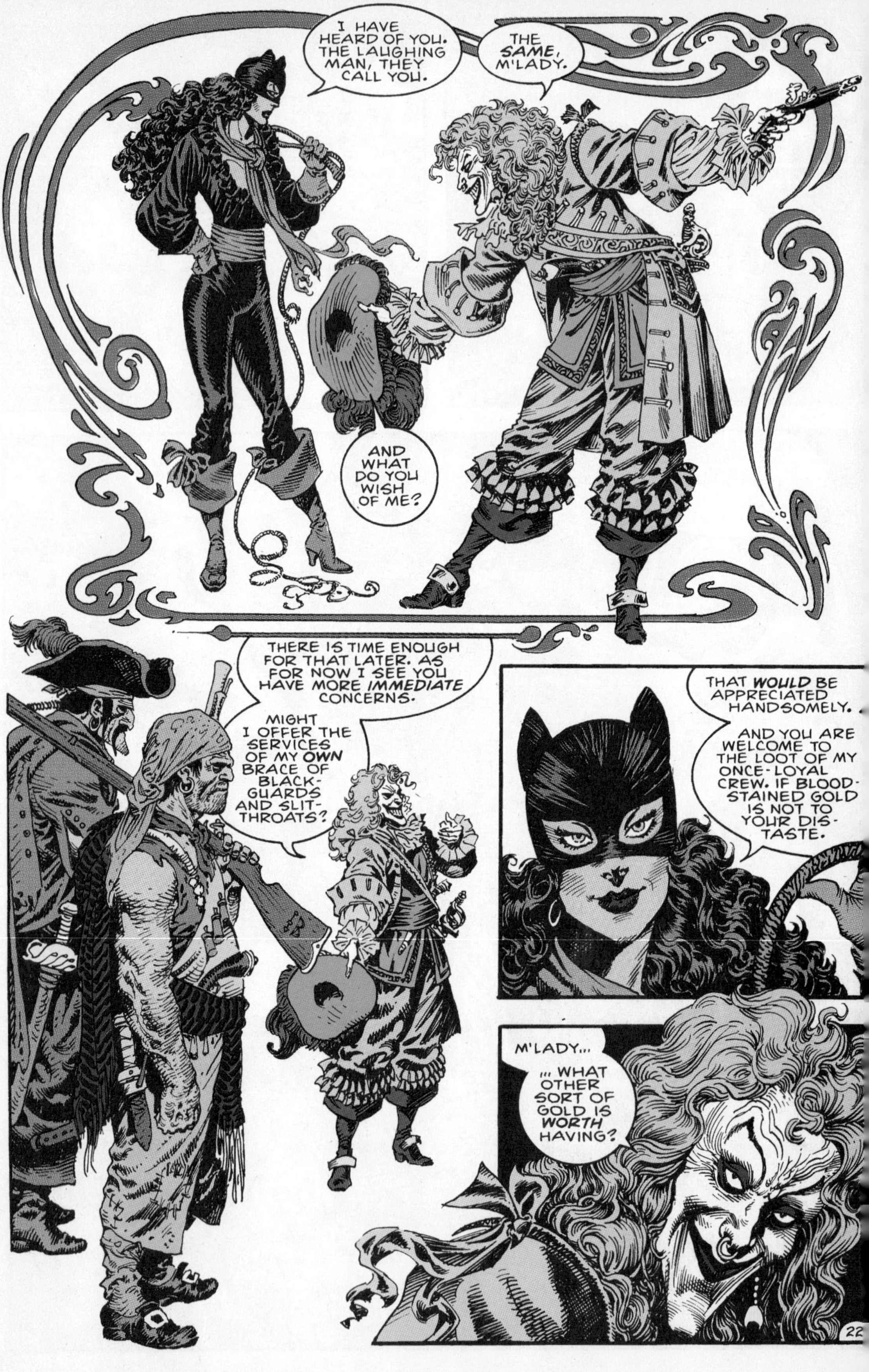
I HAVE HEARD OF YOU. THE LAUGHING MAN, THEY CALL YOU.
THE SAME, M'LADY.
AND WHAT DO YOU WISH OF ME?
THERE IS TIME ENOUGH FOR THAT LATER. AS FOR NOW I SEE YOU HAVE MORE IMMEDIATE CONCERNS.
MIGHT I OFFER THE SERVICES OF MY OWN BRACE OF BLACK-GUARDS AND SLIT-THROATS?
THAT WOULD BE APPRECIATED HANDSOMELY.
AND YOU ARE WELCOME TO THE LOOT OF MY ONCE-LOYAL CREW. IF BLOOD-STAINED GOLD IS NOT TO YOUR DIS-TASTE.
M'LADY...
... WHAT OTHER SORT OF GOLD IS WORTH HAVING?
22

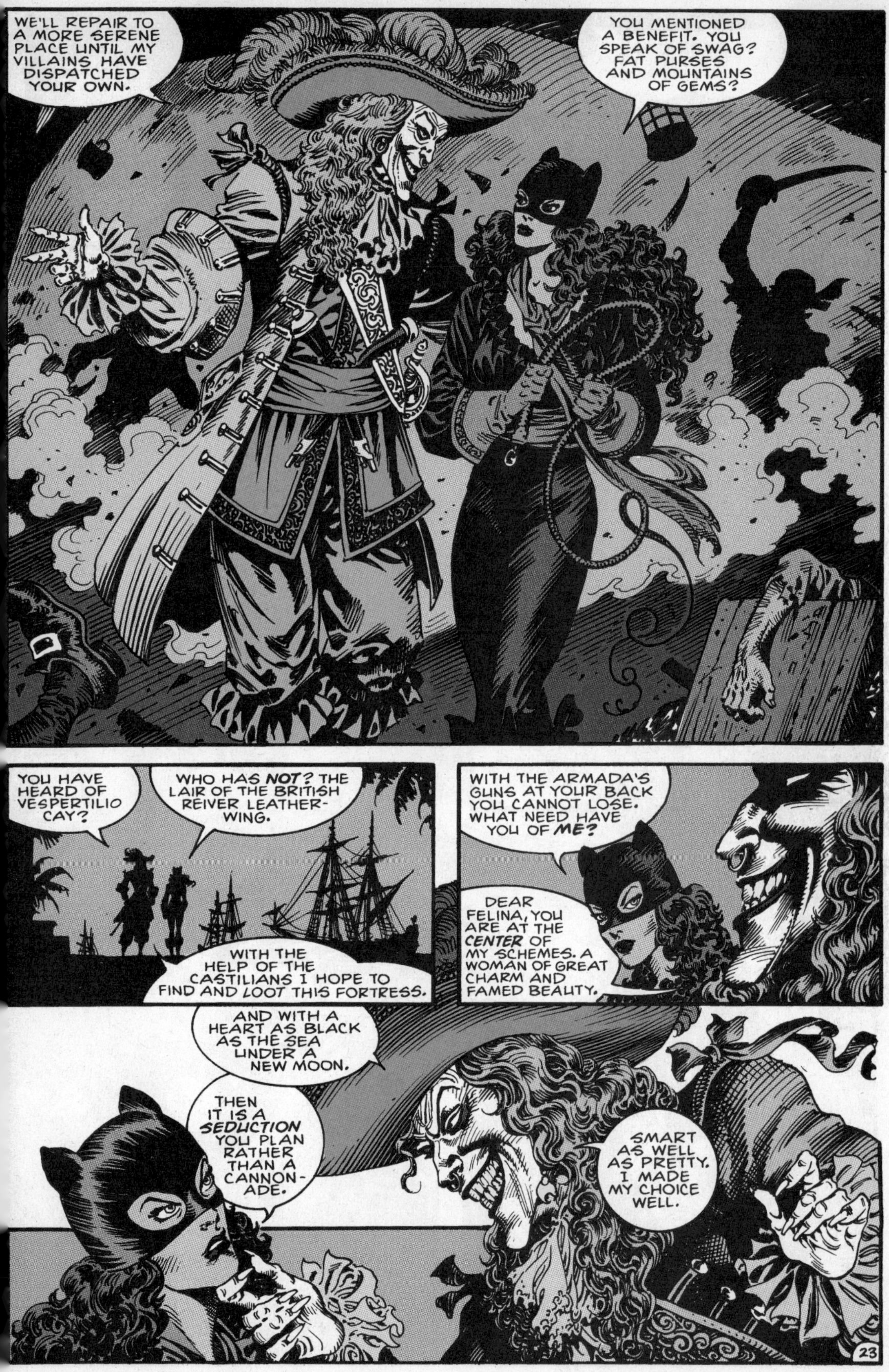
WE'LL REPAIR TO A MORE SERENE PLACE UNTIL MY VILLAINS HAVE DISPATCHED YOUR OWN.
YOU MENTIONED A BENEFIT. YOU SPEAK OF SWAG? FAT PURSES AND MOUNTAINS OF GEMS?
YOU HAVE HEARD OF VESPERTILIO CAY?
WHO HAS NOT? THE LAIR OF THE BRITISH REIVER LEATHER-WING.
WITH THE HELP OF THE CASTILIANS I HOPE TO FIND AND LOOT THIS FORTRESS.
WITH THE ARMADA'S GUNS AT YOUR BACK YOU CANNOT LOSE. WHAT NEED HAVE YOU OF ME?
DEAR FELINA, YOU ARE AT THE CENTER OF MY SCHEMES. A WOMAN OF GREAT CHARM AND FAMED BEAUTY.
AND WITH A HEART AS BLACK AS THE SEA UNDER A NEW MOON.
THEN IT IS A SEDUCTION YOU PLAN RATHER THAN A CANNON-ADE.
SMART AS WELL AS PRETTY. I MADE MY CHOICE WELL.
23

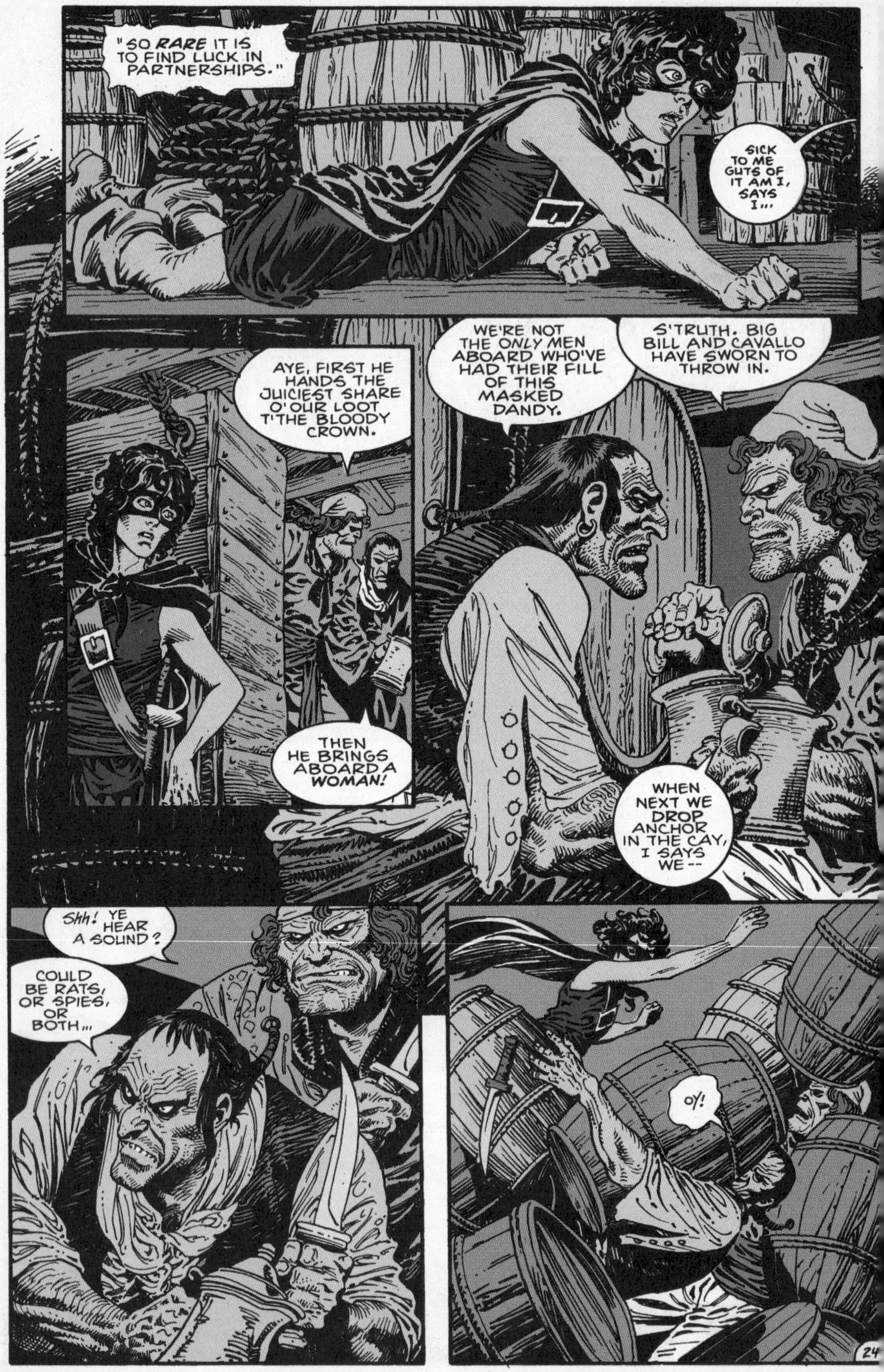

"SO RARE IT IS TO FIND LUCK IN PARTNERSHIPS."
SICK TO ME GUTS OF IT AM I, SAYS I...
AYE, FIRST HE HANDS THE JUICIEST SHARE O'OUR LOOT T'THE BLOODY CROWN.
THEN HE BRINGS ABOARD A WOMAN!
WE'RE NOT THE ONLY MEN ABOARD WHO'VE HAD THEIR FILL OF THIS MASKED DANDY.
S'TRUTH. BIG BILL AND CAVALLO HAVE SWORN TO THROW IN.
WHEN NEXT WE DROP ANCHOR IN THE CAY, I SAYS WE --
Shh! YE HEAR A SOUND?
COULD BE RATS, OR SPIES, OR BOTH...
OY!
24

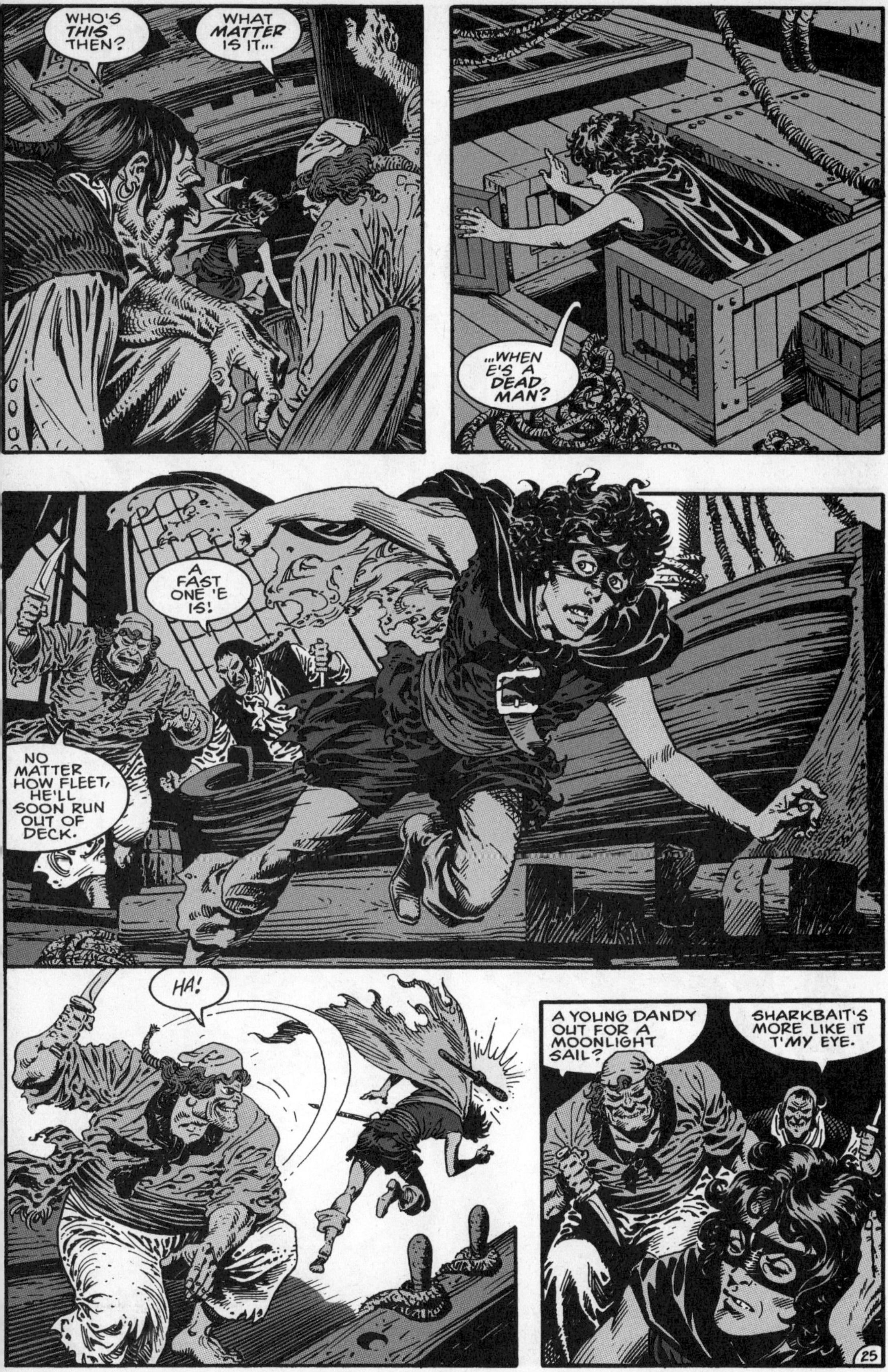
WHO'S THIS THEN?
WHAT MATTER IS IT...
...WHEN E'S A DEAD MAN?
A FAST ONE 'E IS!
NO MATTER HOW FLEET, HE'LL SOON RUN OUT OF DECK.
HA!
A YOUNG DANDY OUT FOR A MOONLIGHT SAIL?
SHARKBAIT'S MORE LIKE IT T'MY EYE.
25

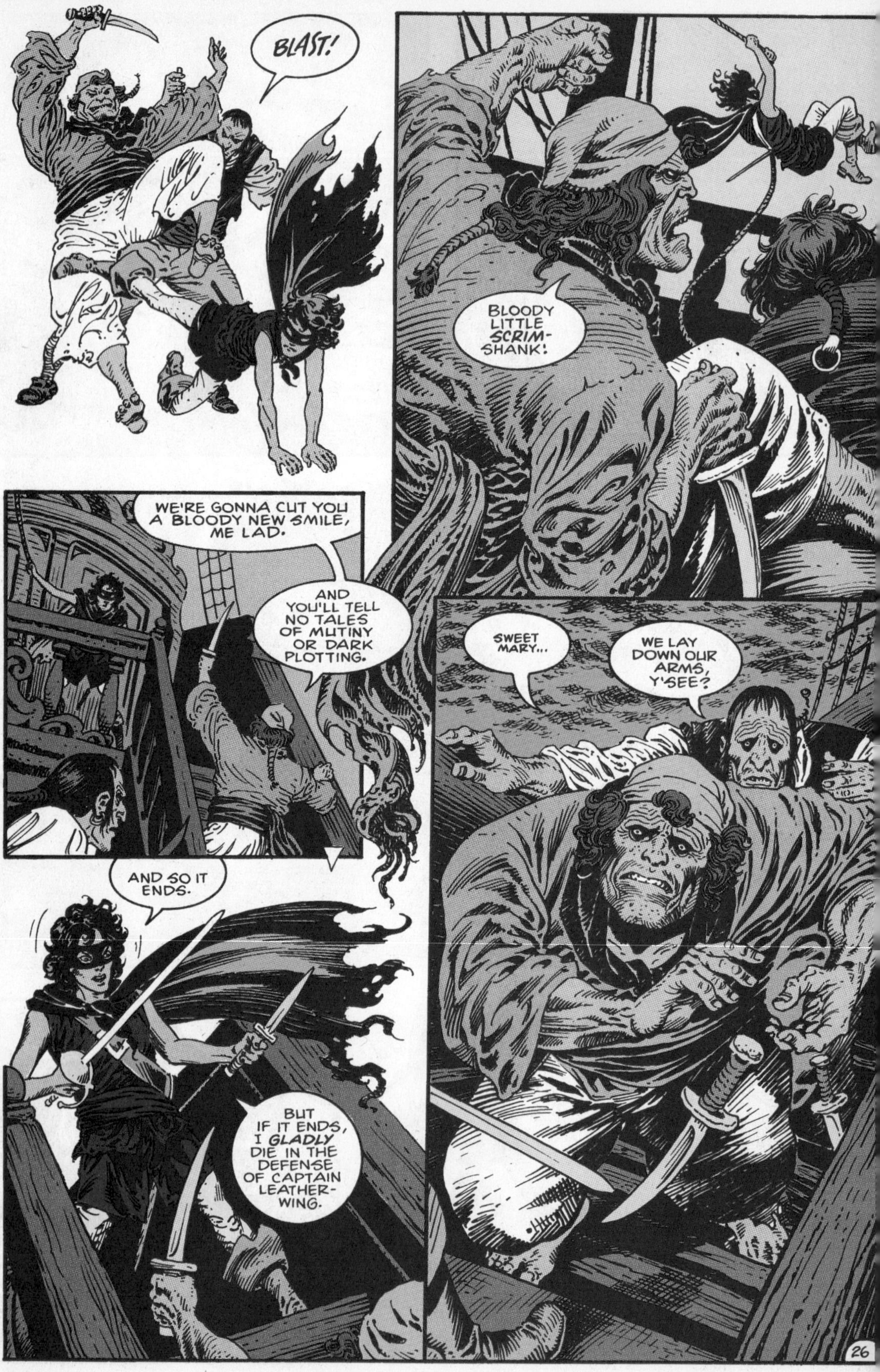

BLAST!
BLOODY LITTLE SCRIM-SHANK!
WE'RE GONNA CUT YOU A BLOODY NEW SMILE, ME LAD.
AND YOU'LL TELL NO TALES OF MUTINY OR DARK PLOTTING.
AND SO IT ENDS.
BUT IF IT ENDS, I GLADLY DIE IN THE DEFENSE OF CAPTAIN LEATHER-WING.
SWEET MARY...
WE LAY DOWN OUR ARMS, Y'SEE?
26

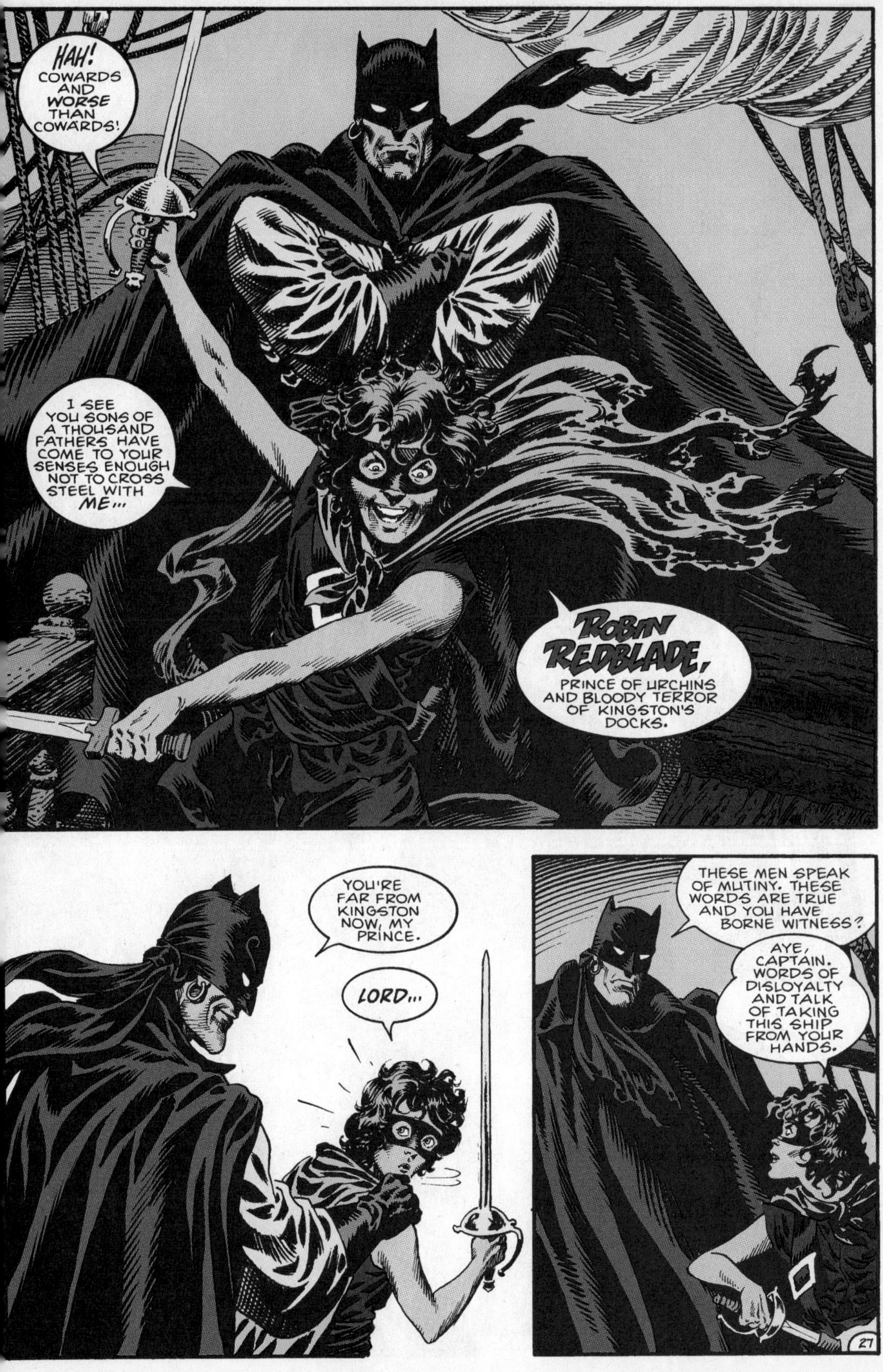

HAH! COWARDS AND WORSE THAN COWARDS!
I SEE YOU SONS OF A THOUSAND FATHERS HAVE COME TO YOUR SENSES ENOUGH NOT TO CROSS STEEL WITH ME...
ROBIN REDBLADE, PRINCE OF URCHINS AND BLOODY TERROR OF KINGSTON'S DOCKS.
YOU'RE FAR FROM KINGSTON NOW, MY PRINCE.
LORD...
THESE MEN SPEAK OF MUTINY. THESE WORDS ARE TRUE AND YOU HAVE BORNE WITNESS?
AYE, CAPTAIN. WORDS OF DISLOYALTY AND TALK OF TAKING THIS SHIP FROM YOUR HANDS.
27

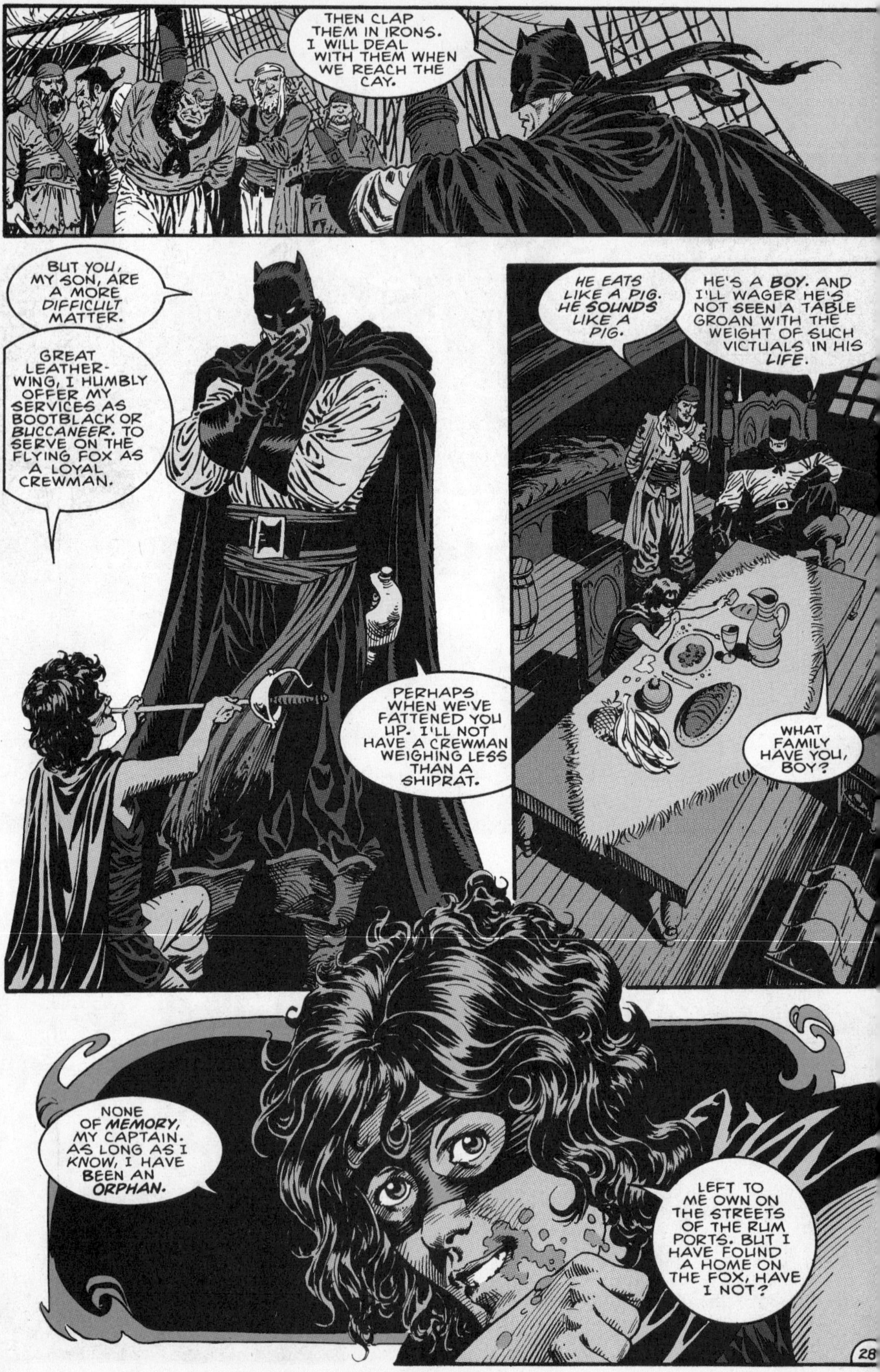
THEN CLAP THEM IN IRONS. I WILL DEAL WITH THEM WHEN WE REACH THE CAY.
BUT YOU, MY SON, ARE A MORE *DIFFICULT* MATTER.
GREAT LEATHER-WING, I HUMBLY OFFER MY SERVICES AS BOOTBLACK OR *BUCCANEER*. TO SERVE ON THE FLYING FOX AS A LOYAL CREWMAN.
PERHAPS WHEN WE'VE FATTENED YOU UP. I'LL NOT HAVE A CREWMAN WEIGHING LESS THAN A SHIPRAT.
HE EATS LIKE A PIG. HE ***SOUNDS*** *LIKE A PIG.*
HE'S A **BOY**. AND I'LL WAGER HE'S NOT SEEN A TABLE GROAN WITH THE WEIGHT OF SUCH VICTUALS IN HIS **LIFE**.
WHAT FAMILY HAVE YOU, BOY?
NONE OF ***MEMORY***, MY CAPTAIN. AS LONG AS I KNOW, I HAVE BEEN AN ***ORPHAN***.
LEFT TO ME OWN ON THE STREETS OF THE RUM PORTS. BUT I HAVE FOUND A HOME ON THE FOX, HAVE I NOT?
28

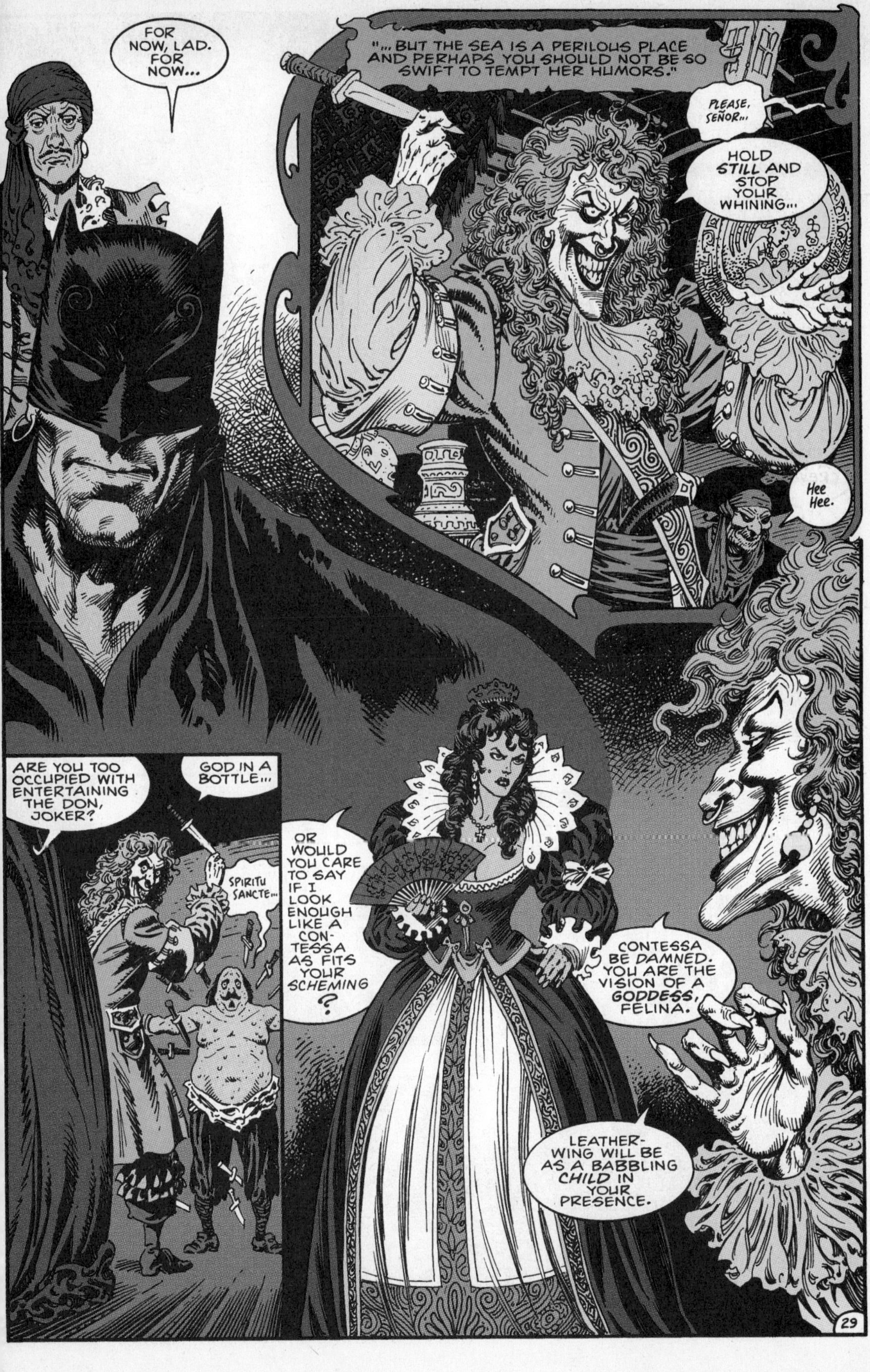

FOR NOW, LAD. FOR NOW...
"...BUT THE SEA IS A PERILOUS PLACE AND PERHAPS YOU SHOULD NOT BE SO SWIFT TO TEMPT HER HUMORS."
PLEASE, SEÑOR...
HOLD STILL AND STOP YOUR WHINING...
Hee Hee.
ARE YOU TOO OCCUPIED WITH ENTERTAINING THE DON, JOKER?
GOD IN A BOTTLE...
SPIRITU SANCTE...
OR WOULD YOU CARE TO SAY IF I LOOK ENOUGH LIKE A CONTESSA AS FITS YOUR SCHEMING?
CONTESSA BE DAMNED. YOU ARE THE VISION OF A GODDESS, FELINA.
LEATHER-WING WILL BE AS A BABBLING CHILD IN YOUR PRESENCE.
29

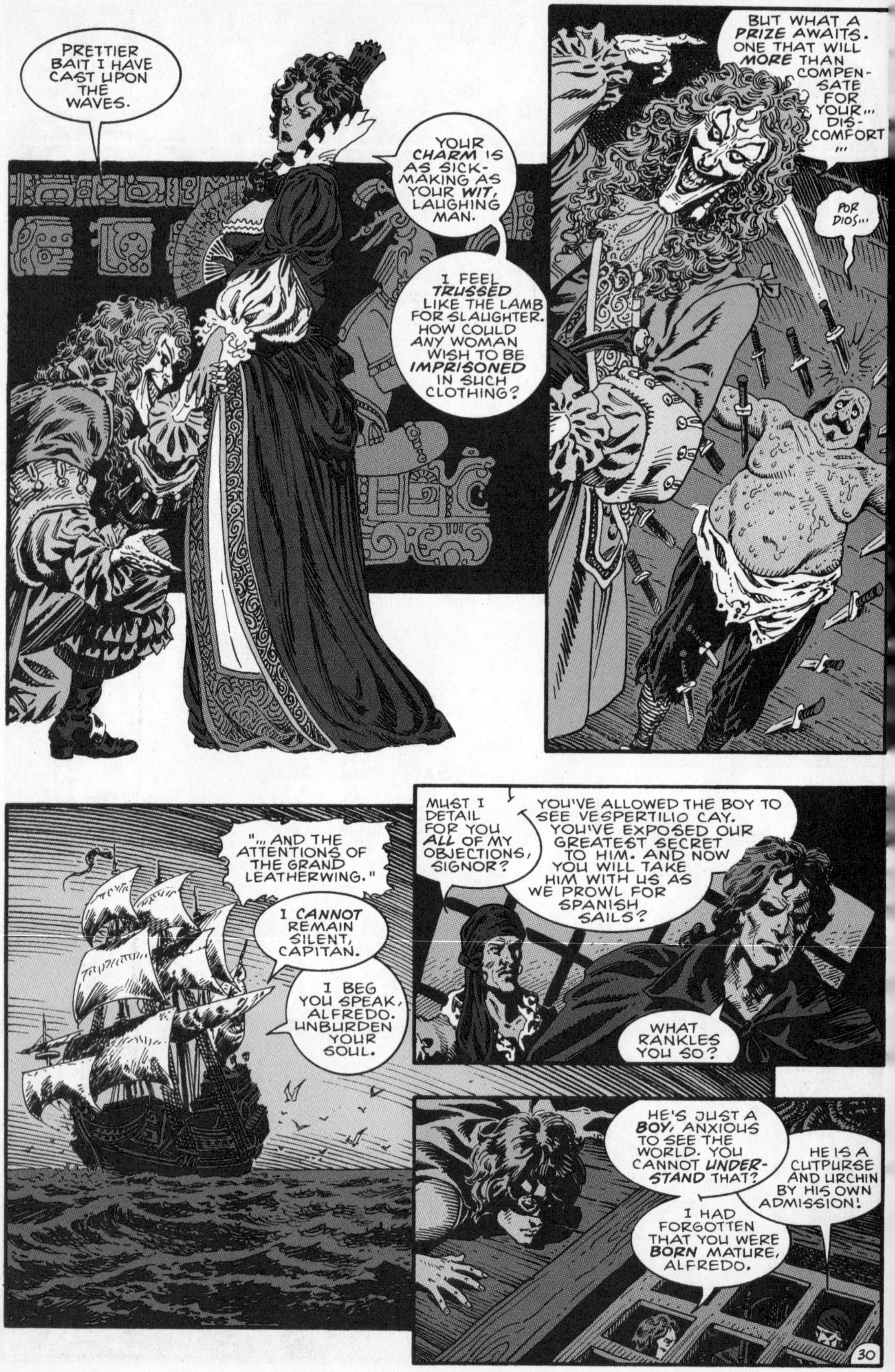
PRETTIER BAIT I HAVE CAST UPON THE WAVES.
YOUR CHARM IS AS SICK-MAKING AS YOUR WIT, LAUGHING MAN.
I FEEL TRUSSED LIKE THE LAMB FOR SLAUGHTER. HOW COULD ANY WOMAN WISH TO BE IMPRISONED IN SUCH CLOTHING?
BUT WHAT A PRIZE AWAITS. ONE THAT WILL MORE THAN COMPENSATE FOR YOUR... DISCOMFORT...
POR DIOS...
"... AND THE ATTENTIONS OF THE GRAND LEATHERWING."
I CANNOT REMAIN SILENT, CAPITAN.
I BEG YOU SPEAK, ALFREDO. UNBURDEN YOUR SOUL.
MUST I DETAIL FOR YOU ALL OF MY OBJECTIONS, SIGNOR?
YOU'VE ALLOWED THE BOY TO SEE VESPERTILIO CAY. YOU'VE EXPOSED OUR GREATEST SECRET TO HIM. AND NOW YOU WILL TAKE HIM WITH US AS WE PROWL FOR SPANISH SAILS?
WHAT RANKLES YOU SO?
HE'S JUST A BOY, ANXIOUS TO SEE THE WORLD. YOU CANNOT UNDERSTAND THAT?
HE IS A CUTPURSE AND URCHIN BY HIS OWN ADMISSION!
I HAD FORGOTTEN THAT YOU WERE BORN MATURE, ALFREDO.
30

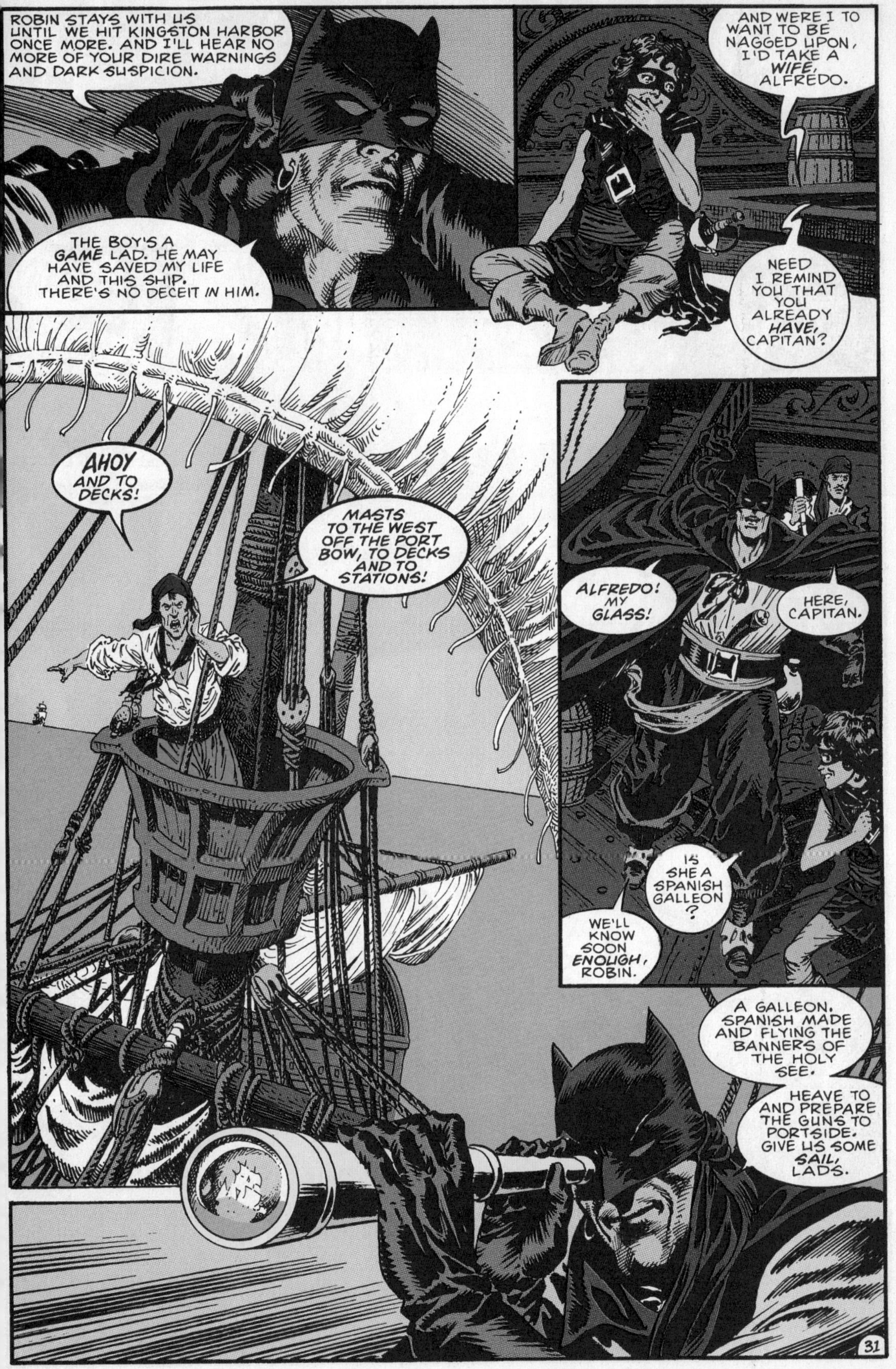

ROBIN STAYS WITH US UNTIL WE HIT KINGSTON HARBOR ONCE MORE. AND I'LL HEAR NO MORE OF YOUR DIRE WARNINGS AND DARK SUSPICION.
THE BOY'S A GAME LAD. HE MAY HAVE SAVED MY LIFE AND THIS SHIP. THERE'S NO DECEIT IN HIM.
AND WERE I TO WANT TO BE NAGGED UPON, I'D TAKE A WIFE, ALFREDO.
NEED I REMIND YOU THAT YOU ALREADY HAVE, CAPITAN?
AHOY AND TO DECKS!
MASTS TO THE WEST OFF THE PORT BOW, TO DECKS AND TO STATIONS!
ALFREDO! MY GLASS!
HERE, CAPITAN.
IS SHE A SPANISH GALLEON?
WE'LL KNOW SOON ENOUGH, ROBIN.
A GALLEON. SPANISH MADE AND FLYING THE BANNERS OF THE HOLY SEE.
HEAVE TO AND PREPARE THE GUNS TO PORTSIDE. GIVE US SOME SAIL, LADS.
31

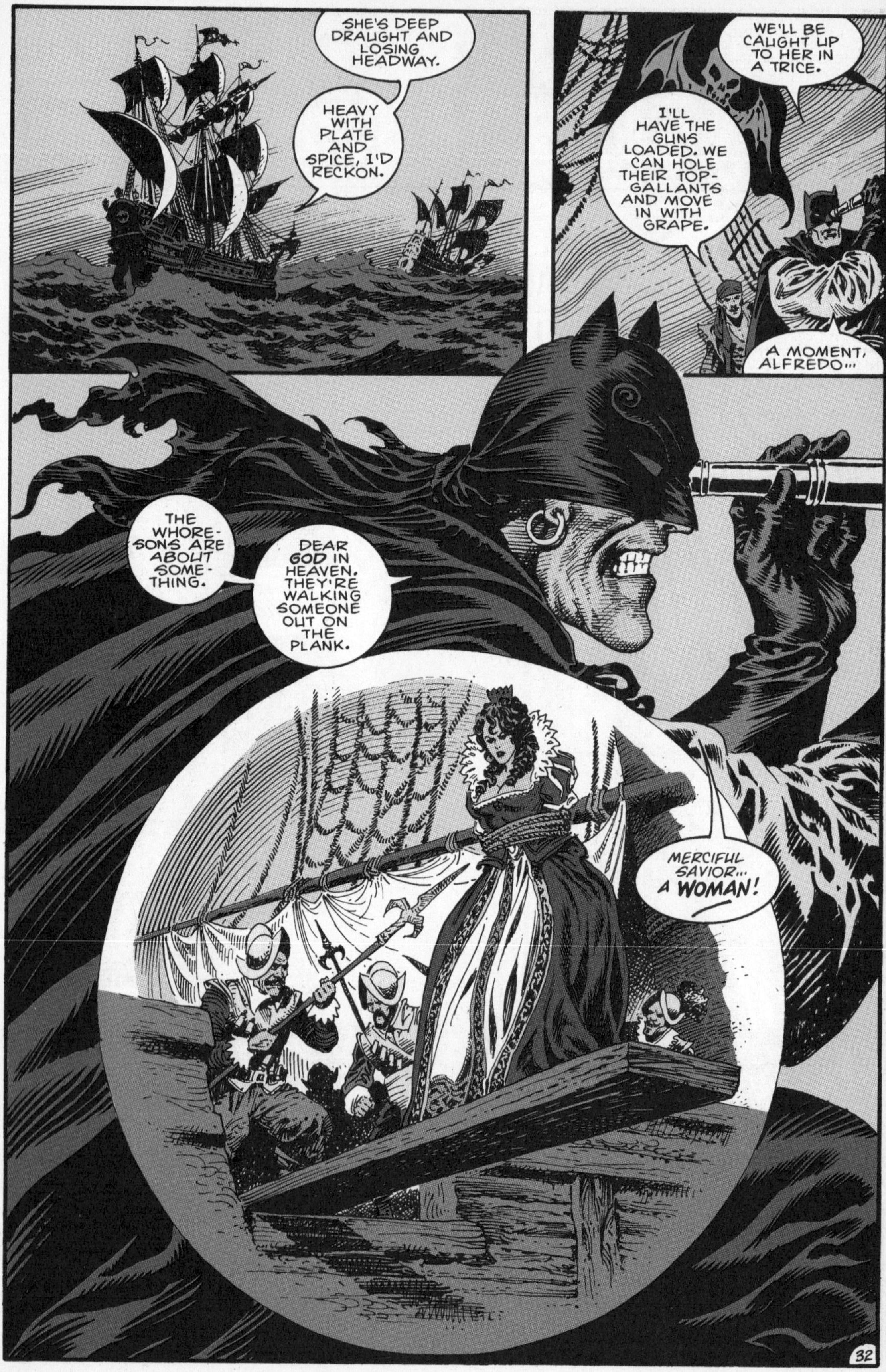
SHE'S DEEP DRAUGHT AND LOSING HEADWAY.
HEAVY WITH PLATE AND SPICE, I'D RECKON.
WE'LL BE CAUGHT UP TO HER IN A TRICE.
I'LL HAVE THE GUNS LOADED. WE CAN HOLE THEIR TOP-GALLANTS AND MOVE IN WITH GRAPE.
A MOMENT, ALFREDO...
THE WHORE-SONS ARE ABOUT SOME-THING.
DEAR GOD IN HEAVEN. THEY'RE WALKING SOMEONE OUT ON THE PLANK.
MERCIFUL SAVIOR... A WOMAN!
32

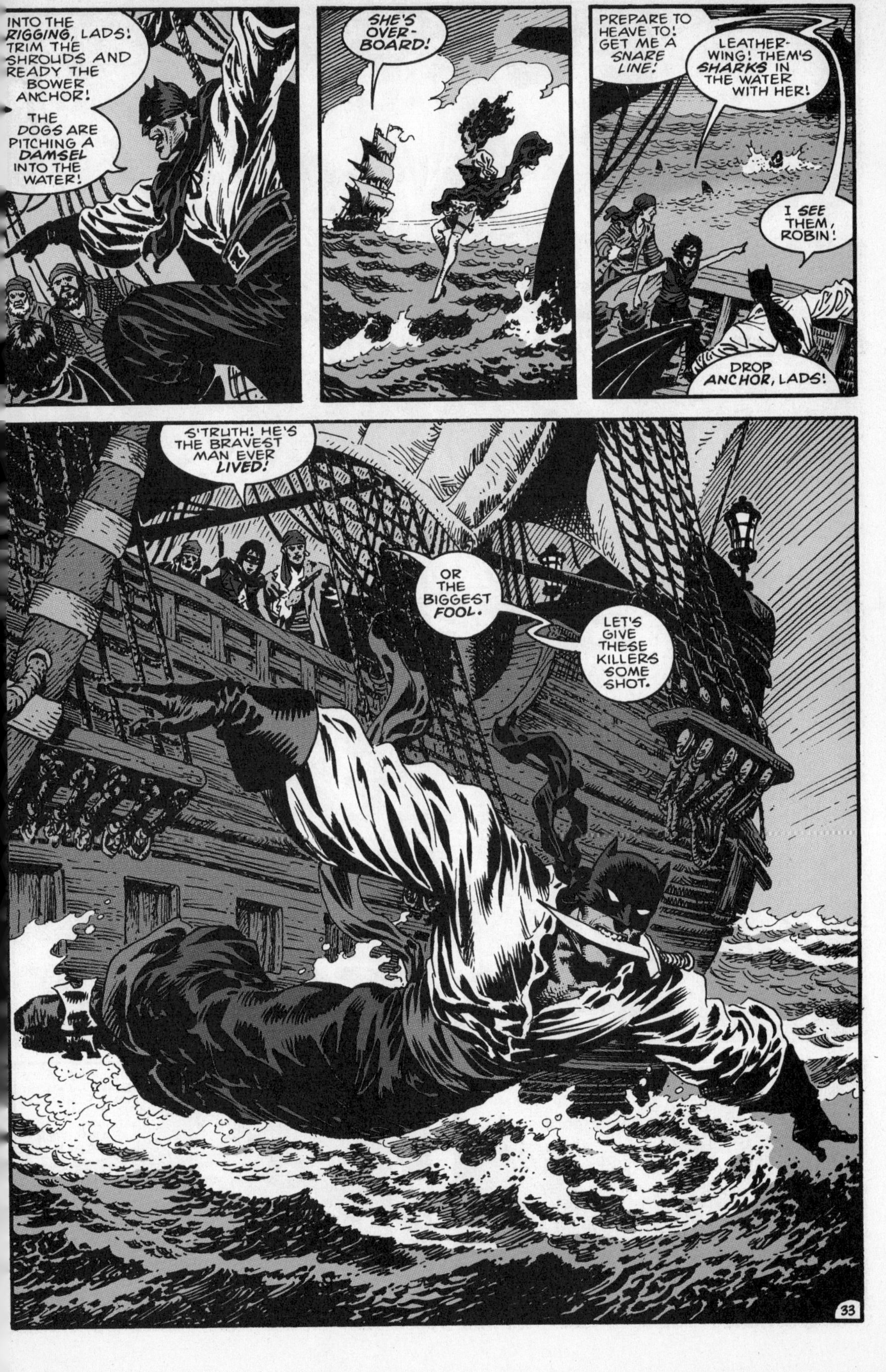
INTO THE RIGGING, LADS! TRIM THE SHROUDS AND READY THE BOWER ANCHOR!
THE DOGS ARE PITCHING A DAMSEL INTO THE WATER!
SHE'S OVER-BOARD!
PREPARE TO HEAVE TO! GET ME A SNARE LINE!
LEATHER-WING! THEM'S SHARKS IN THE WATER WITH HER!
I SEE THEM, ROBIN!
DROP ANCHOR, LADS!
S'TRUTH! HE'S THE BRAVEST MAN EVER LIVED!
OR THE BIGGEST FOOL.
LET'S GIVE THESE KILLERS SOME SHOT.
33

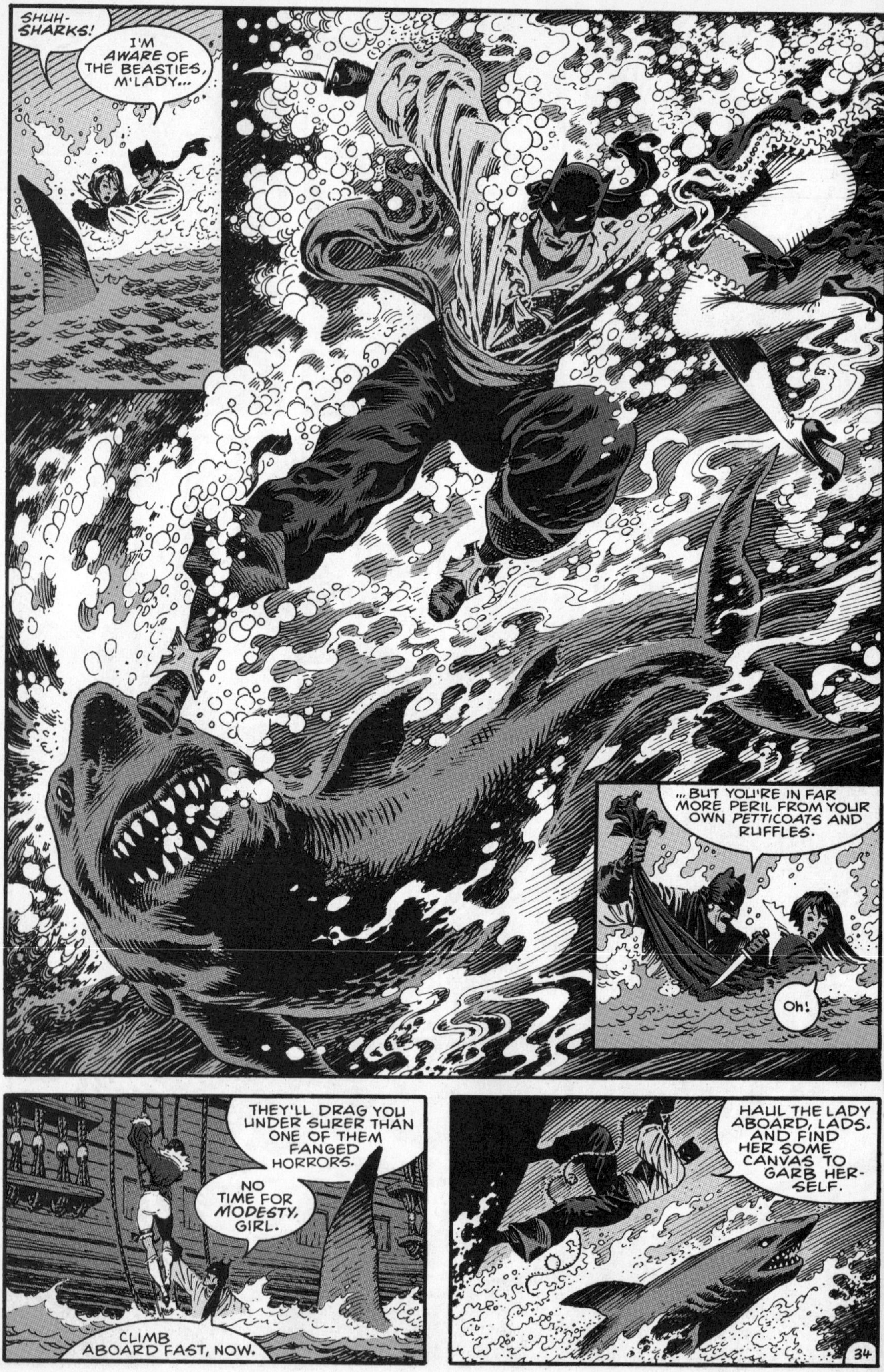

SHUH-SHARKS!
I'M AWARE OF THE BEASTIES, M'LADY...
...BUT YOU'RE IN FAR MORE PERIL FROM YOUR OWN PETTICOATS AND RUFFLES.
Oh!
THEY'LL DRAG YOU UNDER SURER THAN ONE OF THEM FANGED HORRORS.
NO TIME FOR MODESTY, GIRL.
CLIMB ABOARD FAST, NOW.
HAUL THE LADY ABOARD, LADS. AND FIND HER SOME CANVAS TO GARB HER-SELF.
34

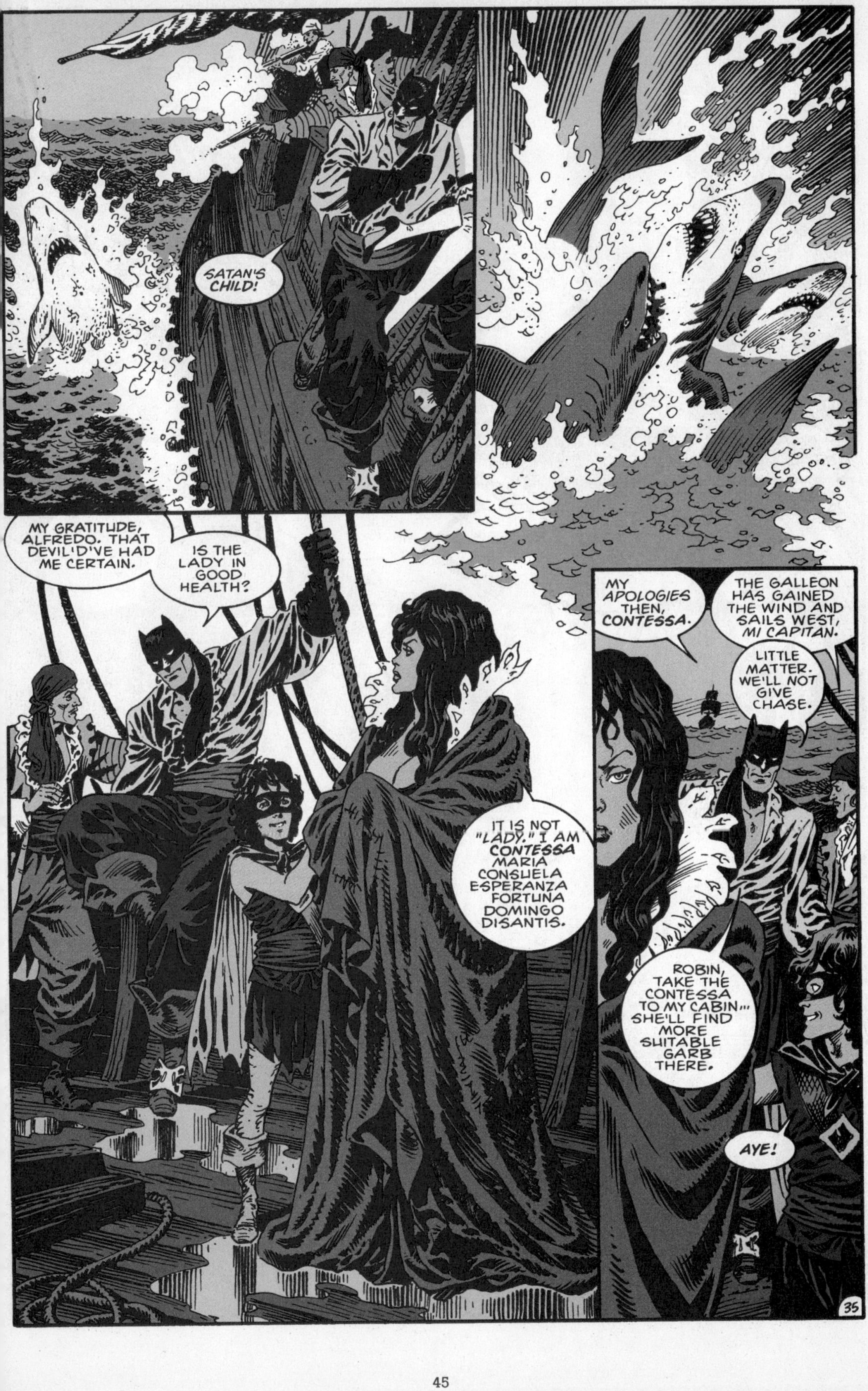
SATAN'S CHILD!
MY GRATITUDE, ALFREDO. THAT DEVIL'D'VE HAD ME CERTAIN.
IS THE LADY IN GOOD HEALTH?
IT IS NOT "LADY." I AM CONTESSA MARIA CONSUELA ESPERANZA FORTUNA DOMINGO DISANTIS.
MY APOLOGIES THEN, CONTESSA.
THE GALLEON HAS GAINED THE WIND AND SAILS WEST, MI CAPITAN.
LITTLE MATTER. WE'LL NOT GIVE CHASE.
ROBIN, TAKE THE CONTESSA TO MY CABIN... SHE'LL FIND MORE SUITABLE GARB THERE.
AYE!
35

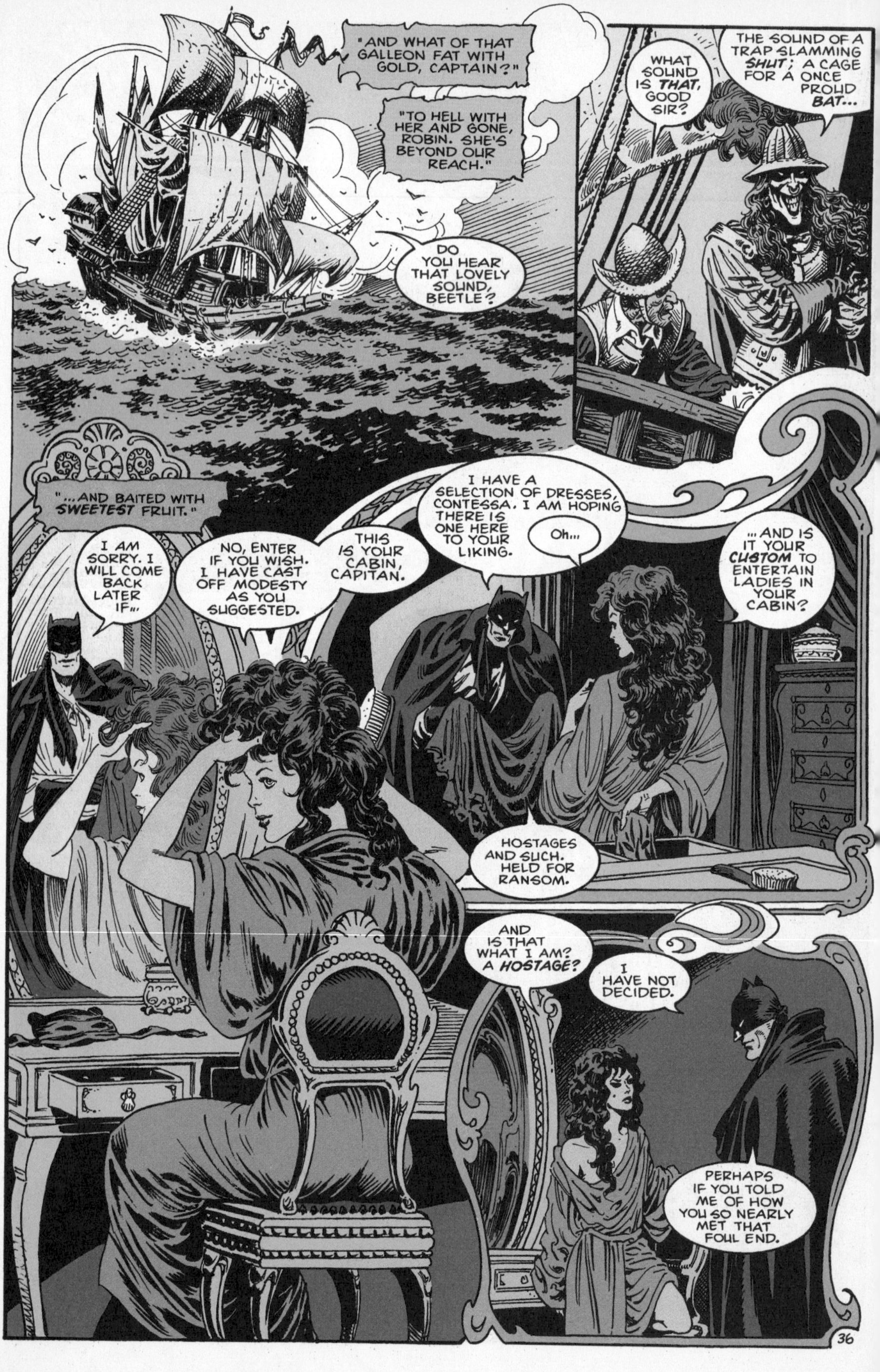
"AND WHAT OF THAT GALLEON FAT WITH GOLD, CAPTAIN?"
"TO HELL WITH HER AND GONE, ROBIN. SHE'S BEYOND OUR REACH."
DO YOU HEAR THAT LOVELY SOUND, BEETLE?
WHAT SOUND IS THAT, GOOD SIR?
THE SOUND OF A TRAP SLAMMING SHUT; A CAGE FOR A ONCE PROUD BAT...
"...AND BAITED WITH SWEETEST FRUIT."
I AM SORRY. I WILL COME BACK LATER IF...
NO, ENTER IF YOU WISH. I HAVE CAST OFF MODESTY AS YOU SUGGESTED.
THIS IS YOUR CABIN, CAPITAN.
I HAVE A SELECTION OF DRESSES, CONTESSA. I AM HOPING THERE IS ONE HERE TO YOUR LIKING.
Oh...
...AND IS IT YOUR CUSTOM TO ENTERTAIN LADIES IN YOUR CABIN?
HOSTAGES AND SUCH. HELD FOR RANSOM.
AND IS THAT WHAT I AM? A HOSTAGE?
I HAVE NOT DECIDED.
PERHAPS IF YOU TOLD ME OF HOW YOU SO NEARLY MET THAT FOUL END.
36

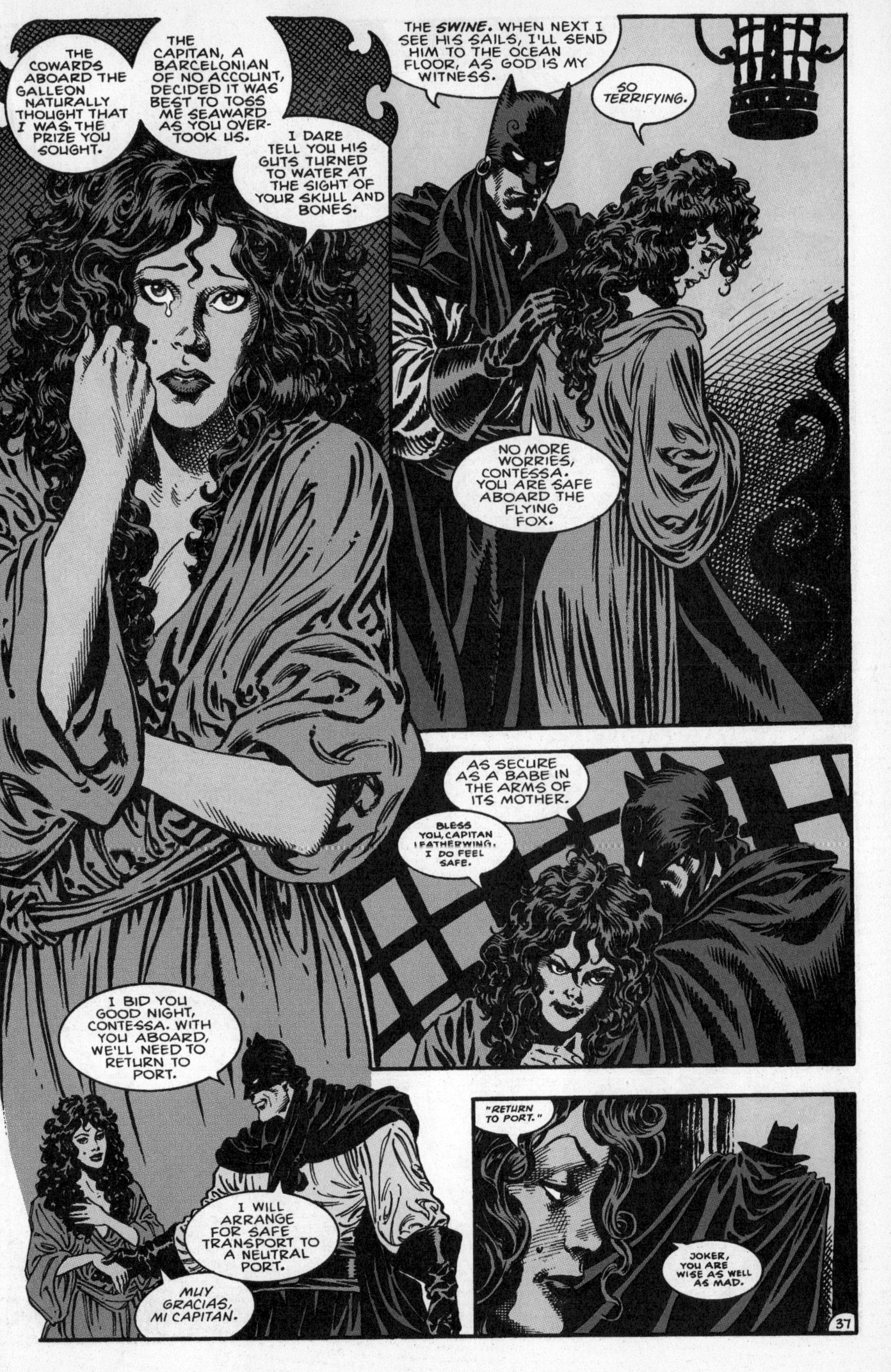
THE COWARDS ABOARD THE GALLEON NATURALLY THOUGHT THAT *I* WAS THE PRIZE YOU SOUGHT.
THE CAPITAN, A BARCELONIAN OF NO ACCOUNT, DECIDED IT WAS BEST TO TOSS ME SEAWARD AS YOU OVERTOOK US.
I DARE TELL YOU HIS GUTS TURNED TO WATER AT THE SIGHT OF YOUR SKULL AND BONES.
THE ***SWINE***. WHEN NEXT I SEE HIS SAILS, I'LL SEND HIM TO THE OCEAN FLOOR, AS GOD IS MY WITNESS.
SO TERRIFYING.
NO MORE WORRIES, CONTESSA. YOU ARE SAFE ABOARD THE FLYING FOX.
AS SECURE AS A BABE IN THE ARMS OF ITS MOTHER.
BLESS YOU, CAPITAN LEATHERWING. I DO FEEL SAFE.
I BID YOU GOOD NIGHT, CONTESSA. WITH YOU ABOARD, WE'LL NEED TO RETURN TO PORT.
I WILL ARRANGE FOR SAFE TRANSPORT TO A NEUTRAL PORT.
MUY GRACIAS, MI CAPITAN.
"RETURN TO PORT."
JOKER, YOU ARE WISE AS WELL AS MAD.
37

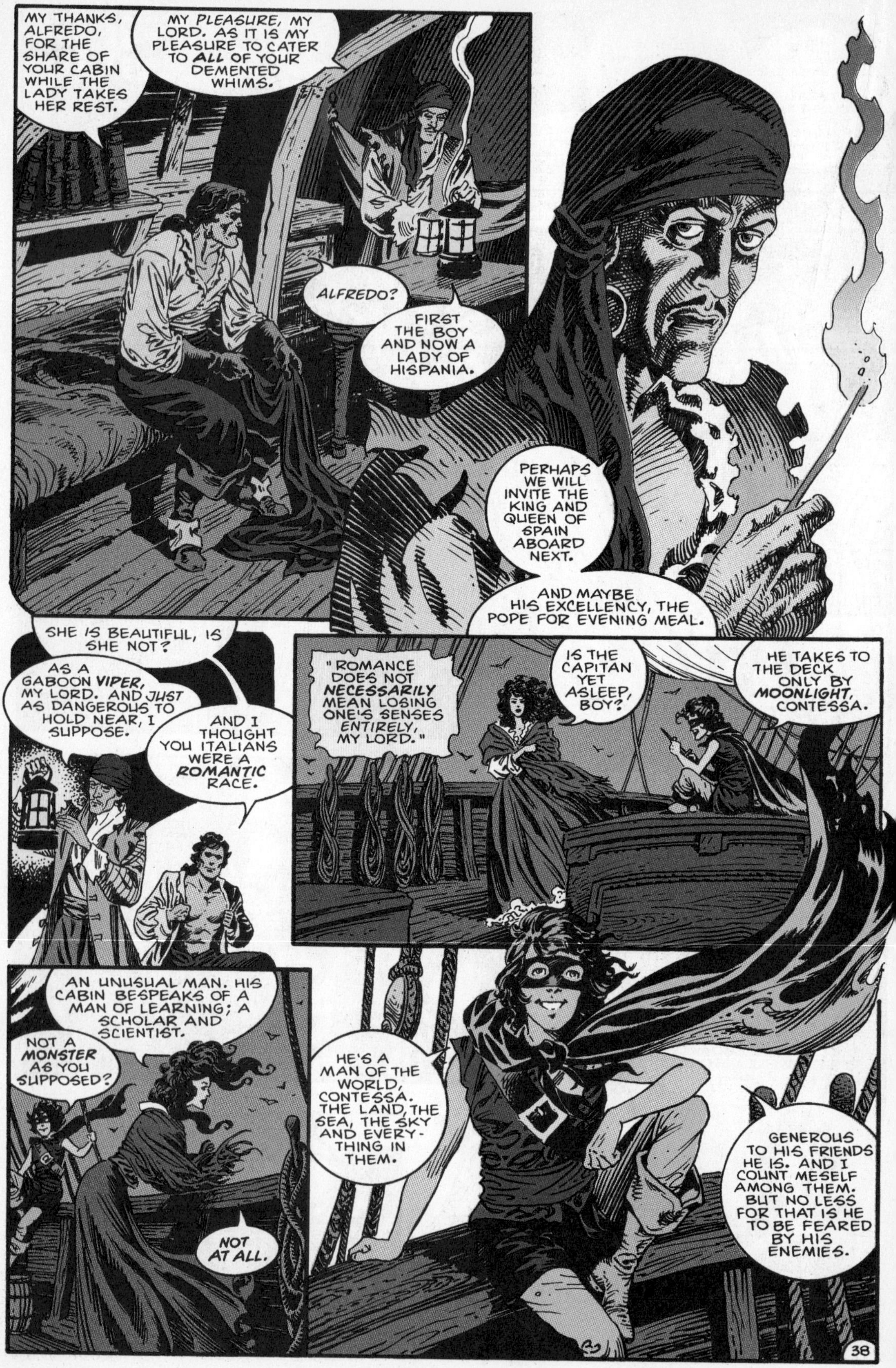
MY THANKS, ALFREDO, FOR THE SHARE OF YOUR CABIN WHILE THE LADY TAKES HER REST.
MY PLEASURE, MY LORD. AS IT IS MY PLEASURE TO CATER TO ALL OF YOUR DEMENTED WHIMS.
ALFREDO?
FIRST THE BOY AND NOW A LADY OF HISPANIA.
PERHAPS WE WILL INVITE THE KING AND QUEEN OF SPAIN ABOARD NEXT.
AND MAYBE HIS EXCELLENCY, THE POPE FOR EVENING MEAL.
SHE IS BEAUTIFUL, IS SHE NOT?
AS A GABOON VIPER, MY LORD. AND JUST AS DANGEROUS TO HOLD NEAR, I SUPPOSE.
AND I THOUGHT YOU ITALIANS WERE A ROMANTIC RACE.
"ROMANCE DOES NOT NECESSARILY MEAN LOSING ONE'S SENSES ENTIRELY, MY LORD."
IS THE CAPITAN YET ASLEEP, BOY?
HE TAKES TO THE DECK ONLY BY MOONLIGHT, CONTESSA.
AN UNUSUAL MAN. HIS CABIN BESPEAKS OF A MAN OF LEARNING; A SCHOLAR AND SCIENTIST.
NOT A MONSTER AS YOU SUPPOSED?
NOT AT ALL.
HE'S A MAN OF THE WORLD, CONTESSA. THE LAND, THE SEA, THE SKY AND EVERY-THING IN THEM.
GENEROUS TO HIS FRIENDS HE IS. AND I COUNT MESELF AMONG THEM. BUT NO LESS FOR THAT IS HE TO BE FEARED BY HIS ENEMIES.
38

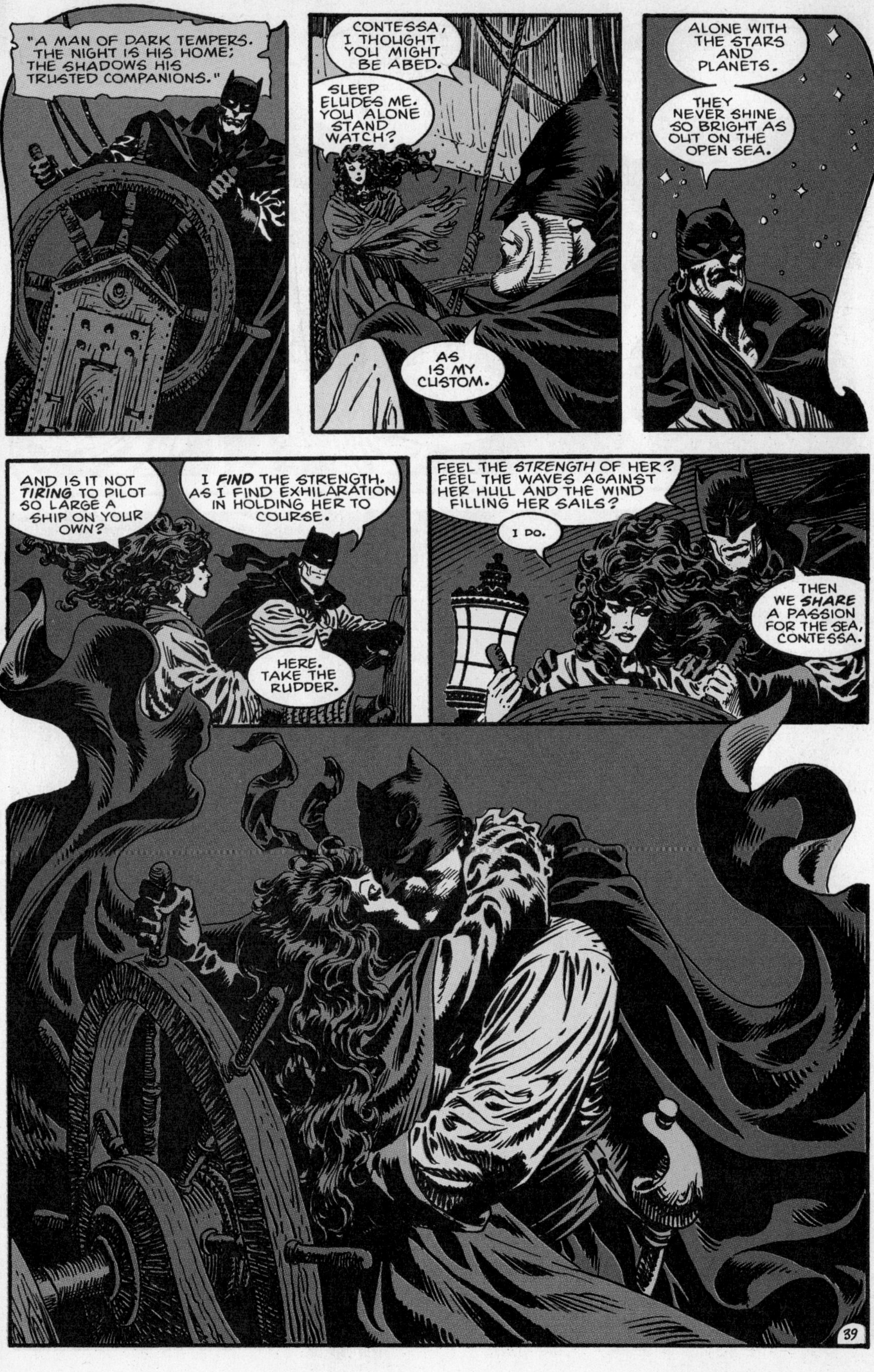
"A MAN OF DARK TEMPERS. THE NIGHT IS HIS HOME; THE SHADOWS HIS TRUSTED COMPANIONS."
CONTESSA, I THOUGHT YOU MIGHT BE ABED.
SLEEP ELUDES ME. YOU ALONE STAND WATCH?
AS IS MY CUSTOM.
ALONE WITH THE STARS AND PLANETS.
THEY NEVER SHINE SO BRIGHT AS OUT ON THE OPEN SEA.
AND IS IT NOT TIRING TO PILOT SO LARGE A SHIP ON YOUR OWN?
I FIND THE STRENGTH. AS I FIND EXHILARATION IN HOLDING HER TO COURSE.
HERE. TAKE THE RUDDER.
FEEL THE STRENGTH OF HER? FEEL THE WAVES AGAINST HER HULL AND THE WIND FILLING HER SAILS?
I DO.
THEN WE SHARE A PASSION FOR THE SEA, CONTESSA.
39

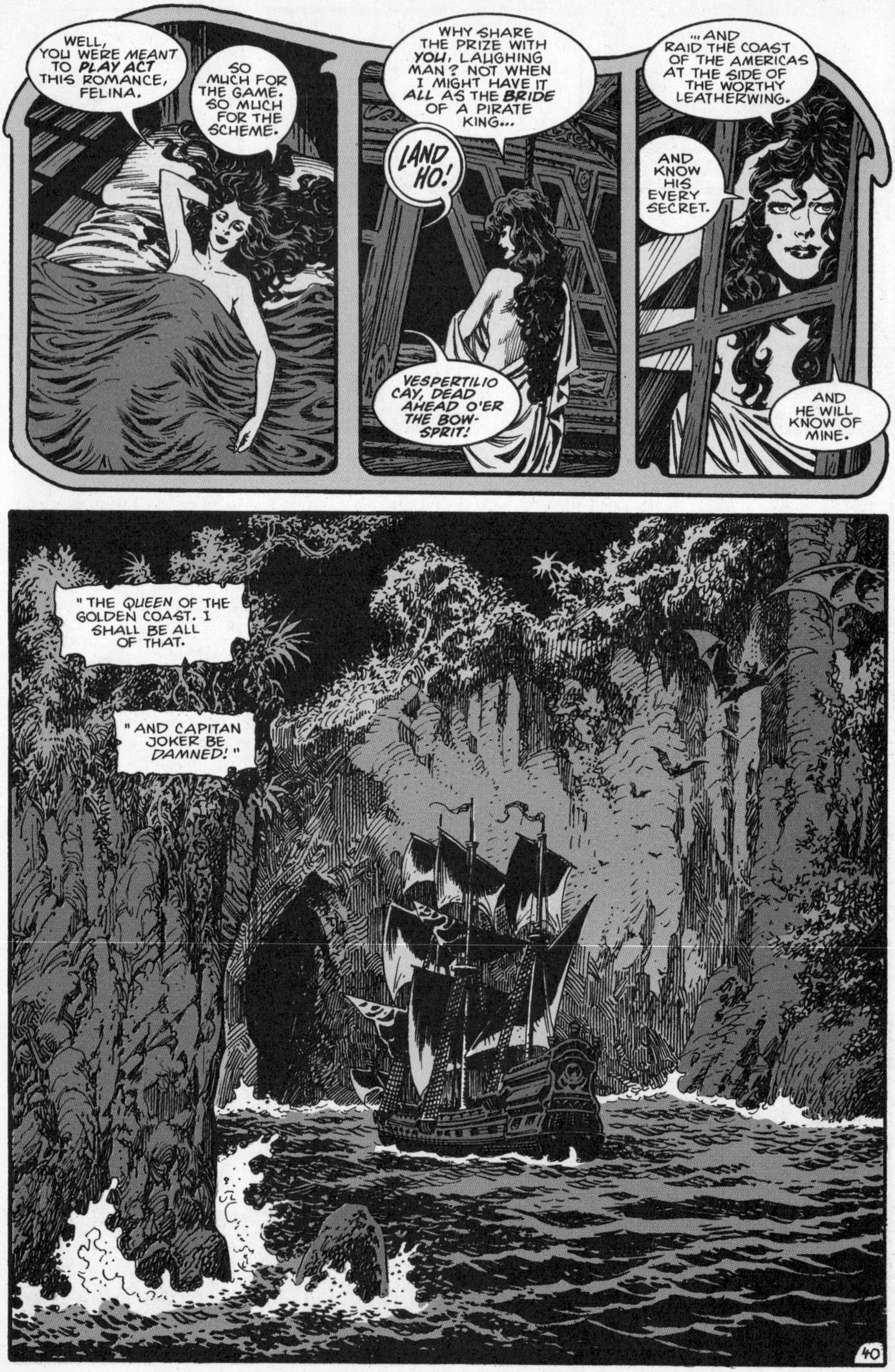
WELL, YOU WERE MEANT TO PLAY ACT THIS ROMANCE, FELINA.
SO MUCH FOR THE GAME. SO MUCH FOR THE SCHEME.
WHY SHARE THE PRIZE WITH YOU, LAUGHING MAN? NOT WHEN I MIGHT HAVE IT ALL AS THE BRIDE OF A PIRATE KING...
LAND HO!
VESPERTILIO CAY, DEAD AHEAD O'ER THE BOW-SPRIT!
...AND RAID THE COAST OF THE AMERICAS AT THE SIDE OF THE WORTHY LEATHERWING.
AND KNOW HIS EVERY SECRET.
AND HE WILL KNOW OF MINE.
"THE QUEEN OF THE GOLDEN COAST. I SHALL BE ALL OF THAT.
"AND CAPITAN JOKER BE DAMNED!"
40

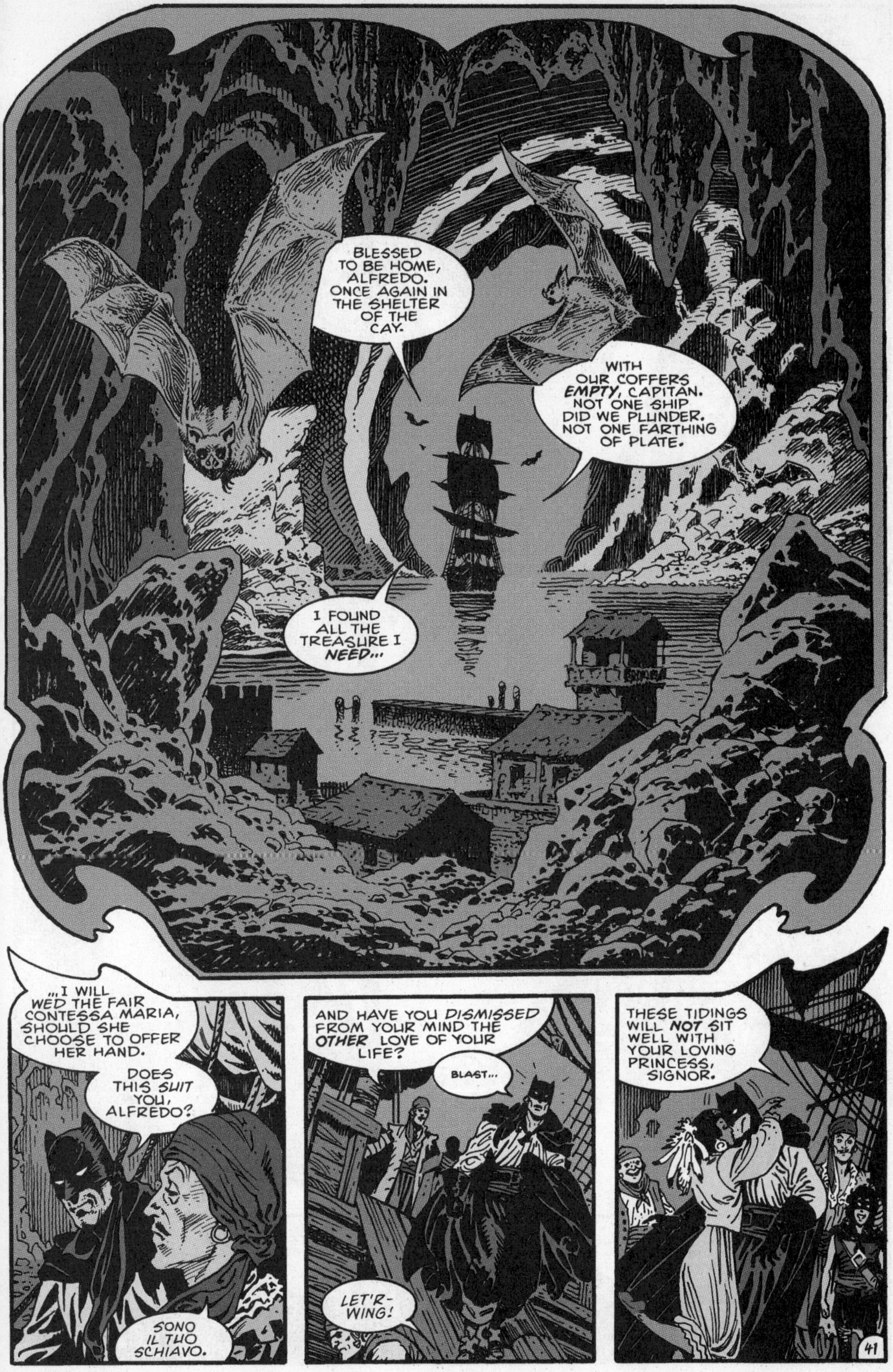
BLESSED TO BE HOME, ALFREDO. ONCE AGAIN IN THE SHELTER OF THE CAY.
WITH OUR COFFERS *EMPTY*, CAPITAN. NOT ONE SHIP DID WE PLUNDER. NOT ONE FARTHING OF PLATE.
I FOUND ALL THE TREASURE I *NEED*...
...I WILL WED THE FAIR CONTESSA MARIA, SHOULD SHE CHOOSE TO OFFER HER HAND.
DOES THIS *SUIT* YOU, ALFREDO?
SONO IL TUO SCHIAVO.
AND HAVE YOU *DISMISSED* FROM YOUR MIND THE *OTHER* LOVE OF YOUR LIFE?
BLAST...
LET'R-WING!
THESE TIDINGS WILL *NOT* SIT WELL WITH YOUR LOVING PRINCESS, SIGNOR.
41

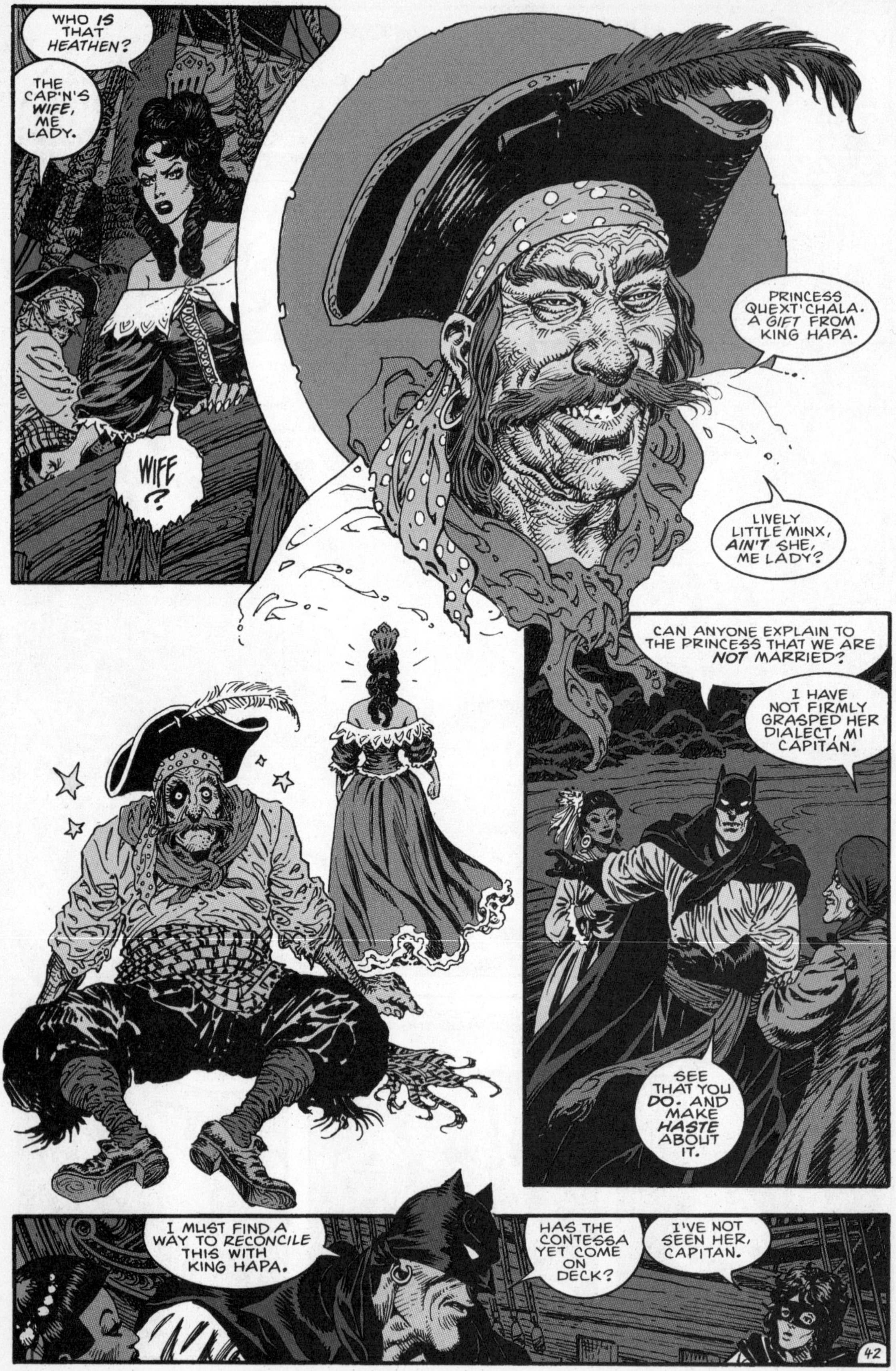
WHO IS THAT HEATHEN?
THE CAP'N'S WIFE, ME LADY.
WIFE?
PRINCESS QUEXT'CHALA. A GIFT FROM KING HAPA.
LIVELY LITTLE MINX, AIN'T SHE, ME LADY?
CAN ANYONE EXPLAIN TO THE PRINCESS THAT WE ARE NOT MARRIED?
I HAVE NOT FIRMLY GRASPED HER DIALECT, MI CAPITAN.
SEE THAT YOU DO. AND MAKE HASTE ABOUT IT.
I MUST FIND A WAY TO RECONCILE THIS WITH KING HAPA.
HAS THE CONTESSA YET COME ON DECK?
I'VE NOT SEEN HER, CAPITAN.
42

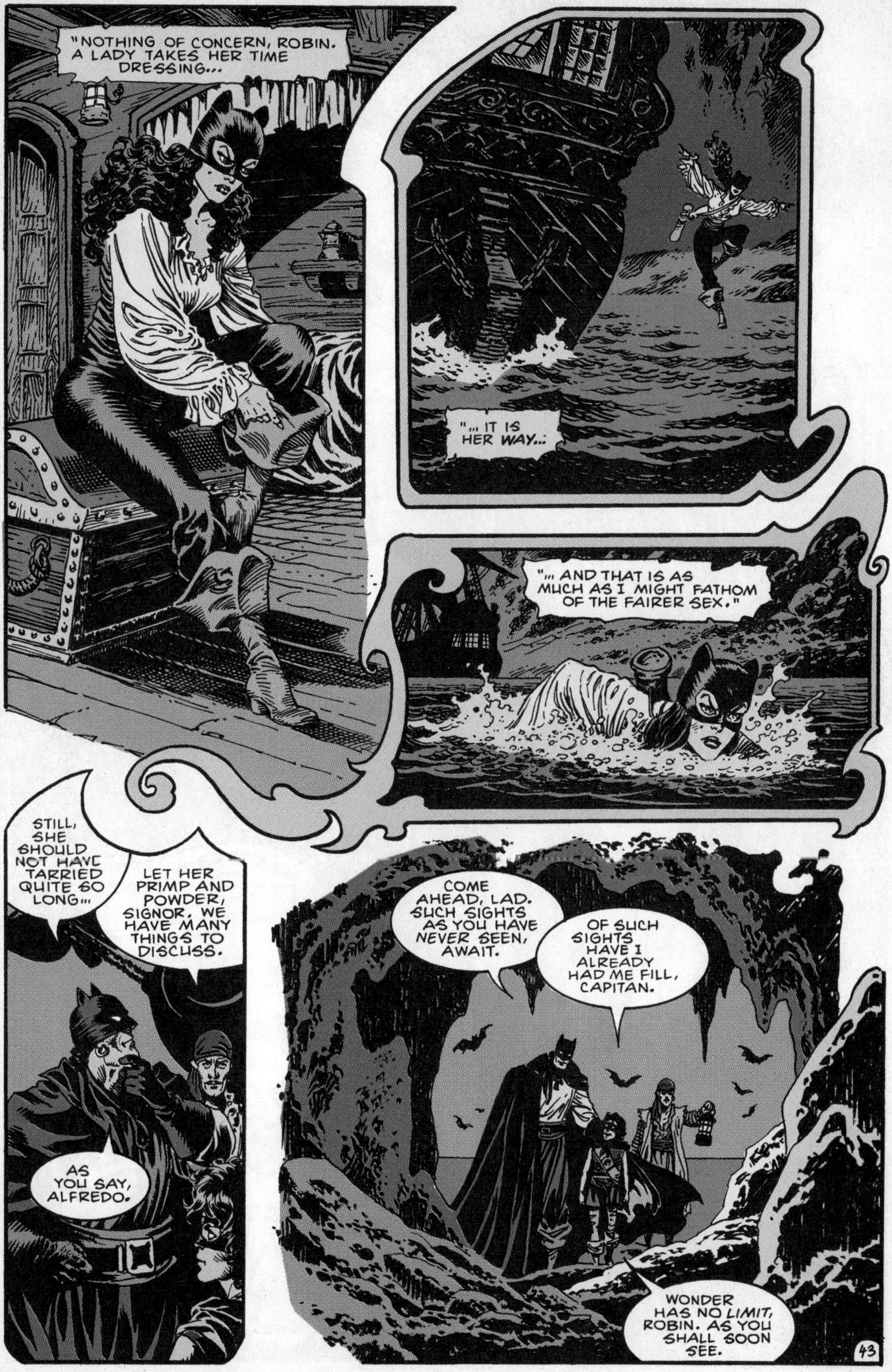
"NOTHING OF CONCERN, ROBIN. A LADY TAKES HER TIME DRESSING...
"... IT IS HER WAY...
"... AND THAT IS AS MUCH AS I MIGHT FATHOM OF THE FAIRER SEX."
STILL, SHE SHOULD NOT HAVE TARRIED QUITE SO LONG...
LET HER PRIMP AND POWDER, SIGNOR. WE HAVE MANY THINGS TO DISCUSS.
AS YOU SAY, ALFREDO.
COME AHEAD, LAD. SUCH SIGHTS AS YOU HAVE NEVER SEEN, AWAIT.
OF SUCH SIGHTS HAVE I ALREADY HAD ME FILL, CAPITAN.
WONDER HAS NO LIMIT, ROBIN. AS YOU SHALL SOON SEE.
43

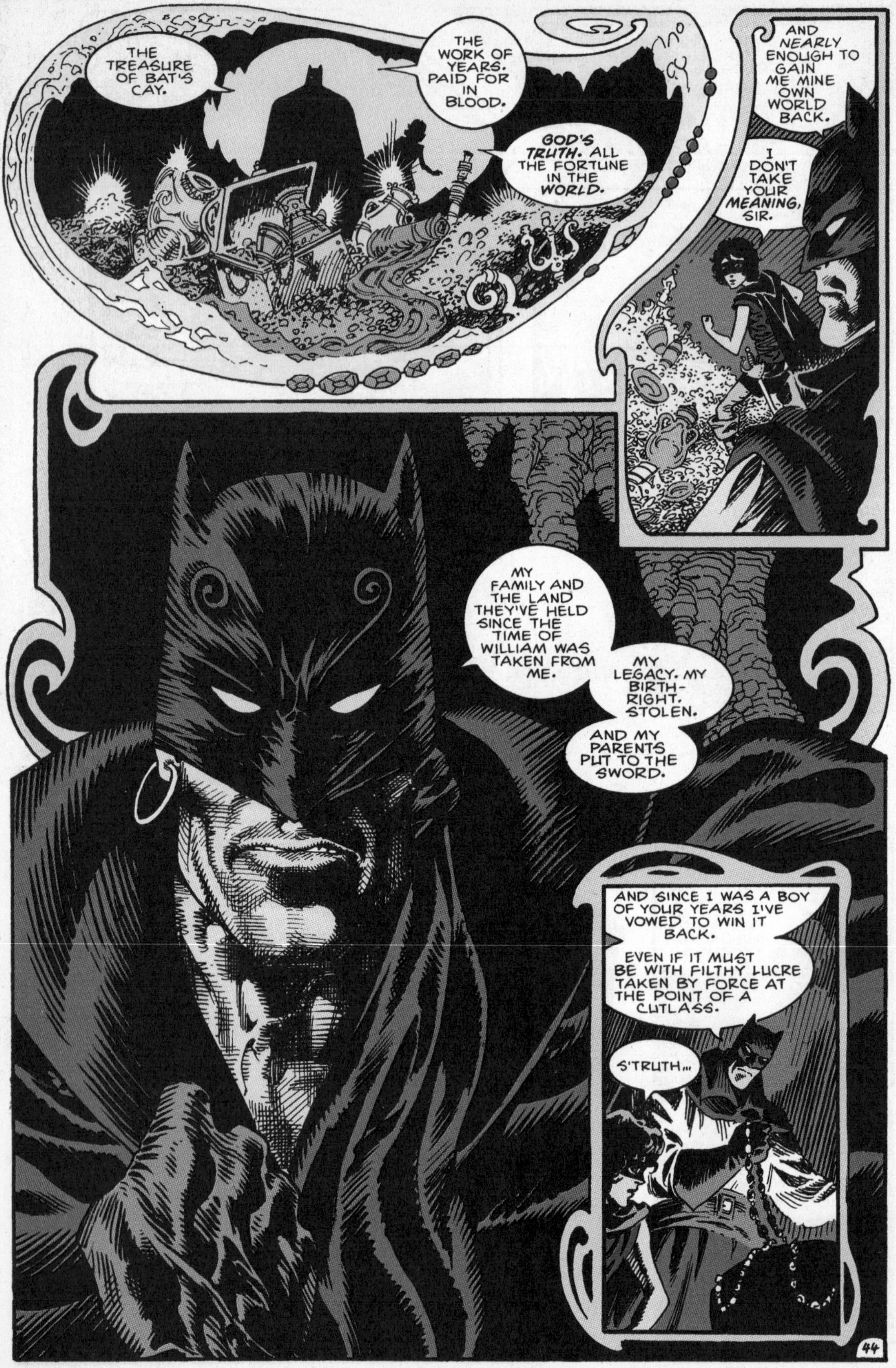
THE TREASURE OF BAT'S CAY.
THE WORK OF YEARS. PAID FOR IN BLOOD.
GOD'S TRUTH. ALL THE FORTUNE IN THE WORLD.
AND NEARLY ENOUGH TO GAIN ME MINE OWN WORLD BACK.
I DON'T TAKE YOUR MEANING, SIR.
MY FAMILY AND THE LAND THEY'VE HELD SINCE THE TIME OF WILLIAM WAS TAKEN FROM ME.
MY LEGACY. MY BIRTH-RIGHT. STOLEN.
AND MY PARENTS PUT TO THE SWORD.
AND SINCE I WAS A BOY OF YOUR YEARS I'VE VOWED TO WIN IT BACK.
EVEN IF IT MUST BE WITH FILTHY LUCRE TAKEN BY FORCE AT THE POINT OF A CUTLASS.
S'TRUTH...
44

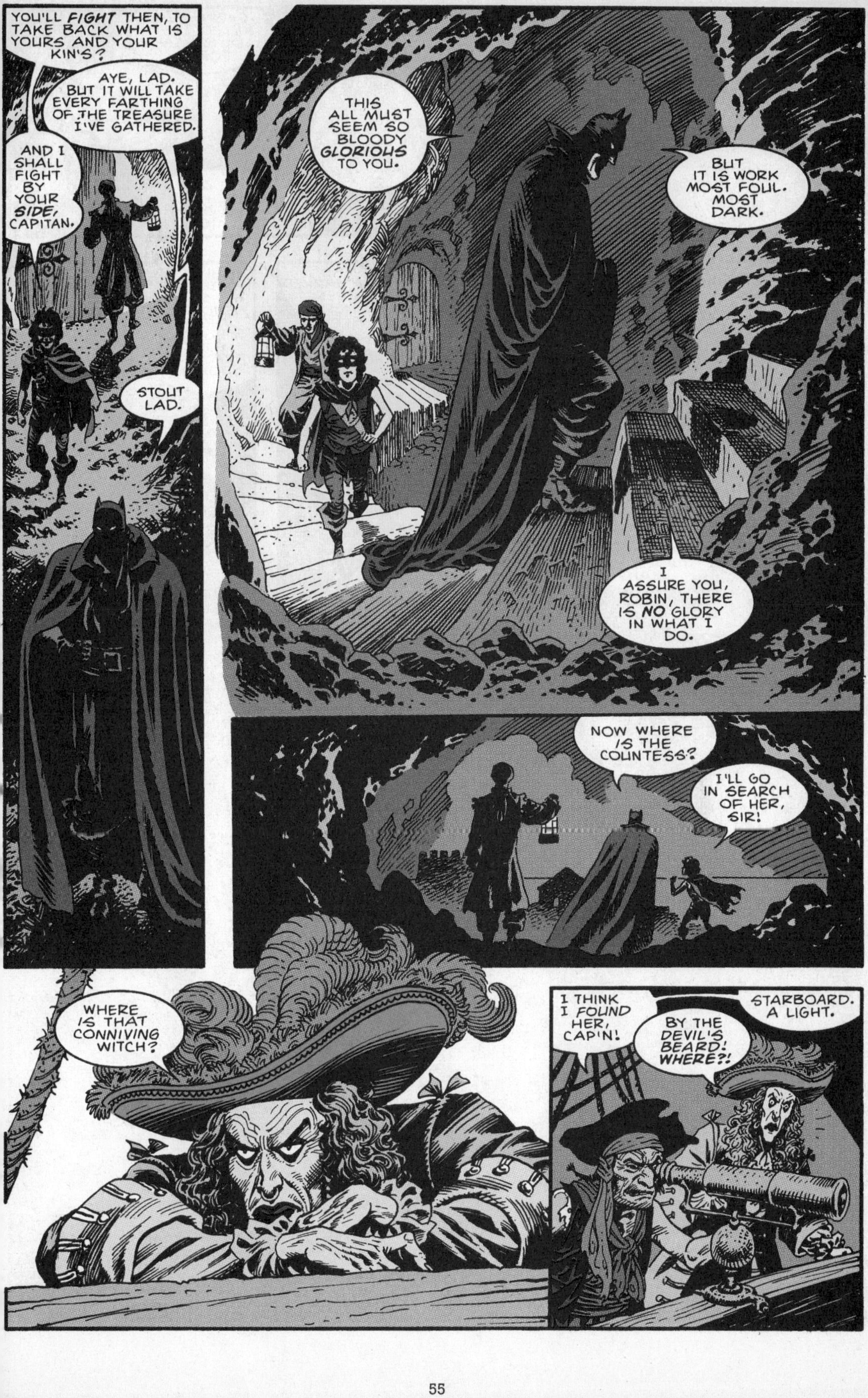

YOU'LL FIGHT THEN, TO TAKE BACK WHAT IS YOURS AND YOUR KIN'S?
AYE, LAD. BUT IT WILL TAKE EVERY FARTHING OF THE TREASURE I'VE GATHERED.
AND I SHALL FIGHT BY YOUR SIDE, CAPITAN.
STOUT LAD.
THIS ALL MUST SEEM SO BLOODY GLORIOUS TO YOU.
BUT IT IS WORK MOST FOUL. MOST DARK.
I ASSURE YOU, ROBIN, THERE IS NO GLORY IN WHAT I DO.
NOW WHERE IS THE COUNTESS?
I'LL GO IN SEARCH OF HER, SIR!
WHERE IS THAT CONNIVING WITCH?
I THINK I FOUND HER, CAP'N!
STARBOARD. A LIGHT.
BY THE DEVIL'S BEARD! WHERE?!

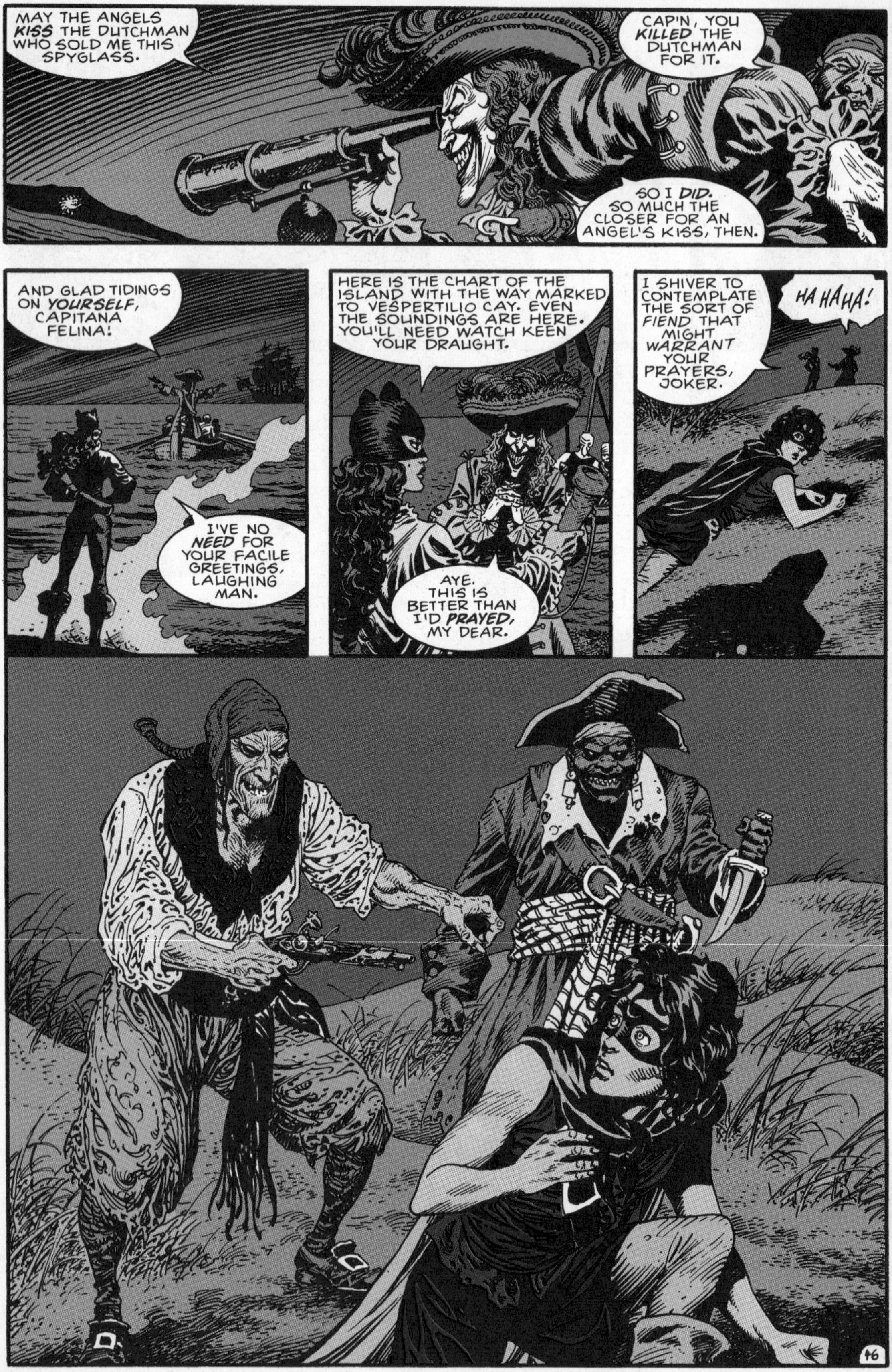
MAY THE ANGELS KISS THE DUTCHMAN WHO SOLD ME THIS SPYGLASS.
CAP'N, YOU KILLED THE DUTCHMAN FOR IT.
SO I DID. SO MUCH THE CLOSER FOR AN ANGEL'S KISS, THEN.
AND GLAD TIDINGS ON YOURSELF, CAPITANA FELINA!
I'VE NO NEED FOR YOUR FACILE GREETINGS, LAUGHING MAN.
HERE IS THE CHART OF THE ISLAND WITH THE WAY MARKED TO VESPERTILIO CAY. EVEN THE SOUNDINGS ARE HERE. YOU'LL NEED WATCH KEEN YOUR DRAUGHT.
AYE. THIS IS BETTER THAN I'D PRAYED, MY DEAR.
I SHIVER TO CONTEMPLATE THE SORT OF FIEND THAT MIGHT WARRANT YOUR PRAYERS, JOKER.
HA HAHA!
46

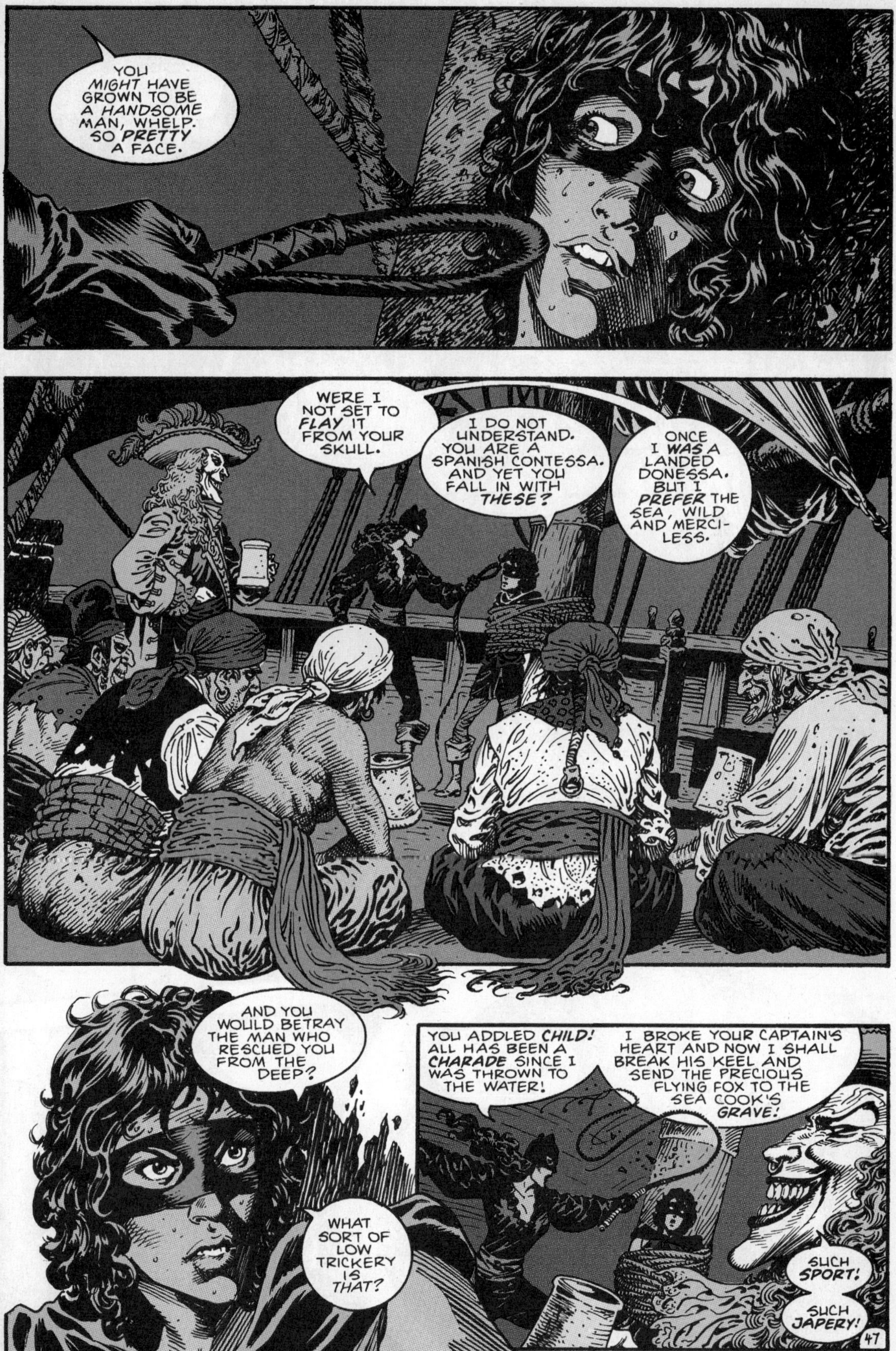
YOU MIGHT HAVE GROWN TO BE A HANDSOME MAN, WHELP. SO PRETTY A FACE.
WERE I NOT SET TO FLAY IT FROM YOUR SKULL.
I DO NOT UNDERSTAND. YOU ARE A SPANISH CONTESSA. AND YET YOU FALL IN WITH THESE?
ONCE I WAS A LANDED DONESSA. BUT I PREFER THE SEA, WILD AND MERCI-LESS.
AND YOU WOULD BETRAY THE MAN WHO RESCUED YOU FROM THE DEEP?
WHAT SORT OF LOW TRICKERY IS THAT?
YOU ADDLED CHILD! ALL HAS BEEN A CHARADE SINCE I WAS THROWN TO THE WATER!
I BROKE YOUR CAPTAIN'S HEART AND NOW I SHALL BREAK HIS KEEL AND SEND THE PRECIOUS FLYING FOX TO THE SEA COOK'S GRAVE!
SUCH SPORT!
SUCH JAPERY!
47

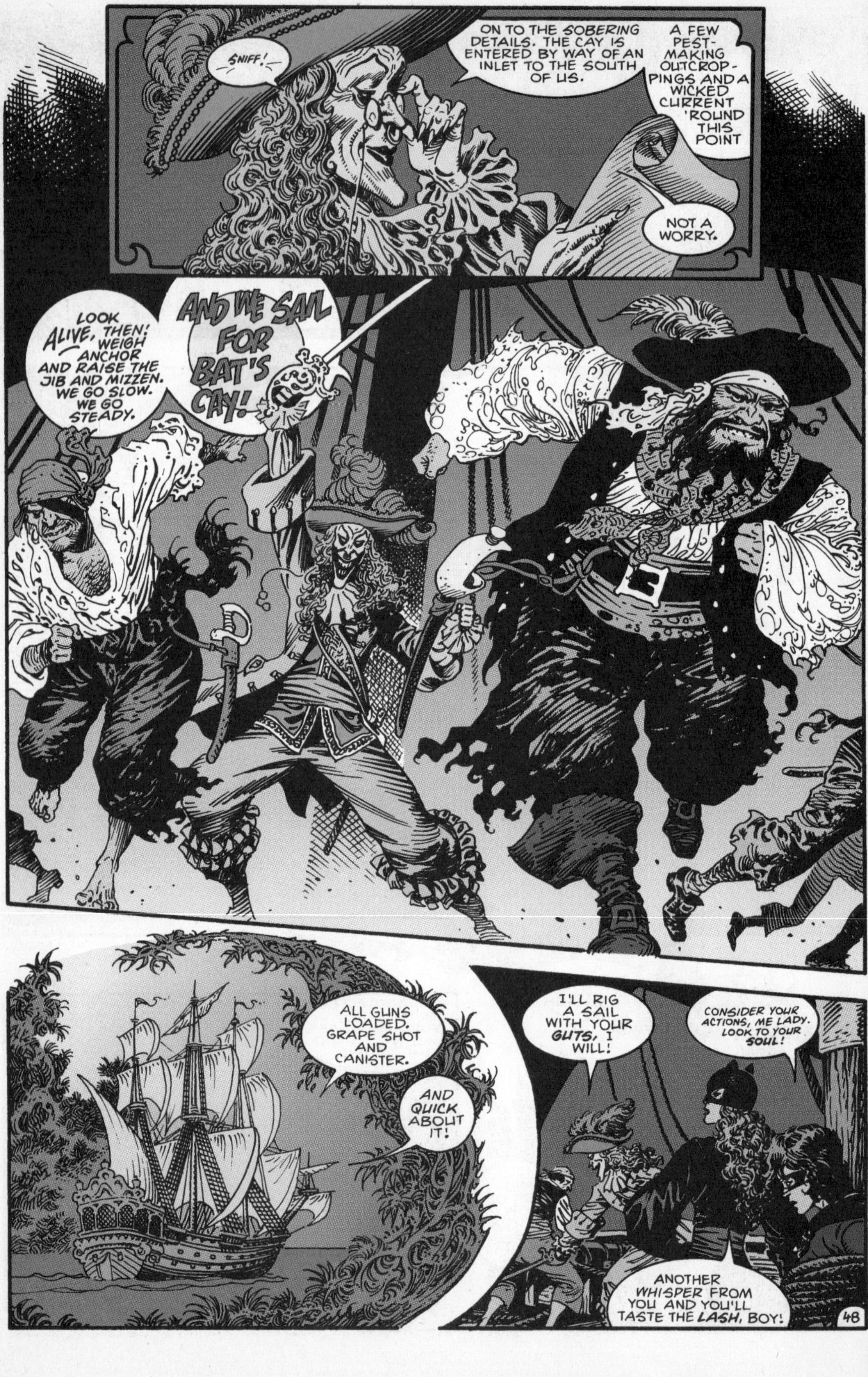
SNIFF!
ON TO THE SOBERING DETAILS. THE CAY IS ENTERED BY WAY OF AN INLET TO THE SOUTH OF US.
A FEW PEST-MAKING OUTCROP-PINGS AND A WICKED CURRENT 'ROUND THIS POINT
NOT A WORRY.
LOOK ALIVE, THEN! WEIGH ANCHOR AND RAISE THE JIB AND MIZZEN. WE GO SLOW. WE GO STEADY.
AND WE SAIL FOR BAT'S CAY!
ALL GUNS LOADED. GRAPE SHOT AND CANISTER.
AND QUICK ABOUT IT!
I'LL RIG A SAIL WITH YOUR GUTS, I WILL!
CONSIDER YOUR ACTIONS, ME LADY. LOOK TO YOUR SOUL!
ANOTHER WHISPER FROM YOU AND YOU'LL TASTE THE LASH, BOY!
48

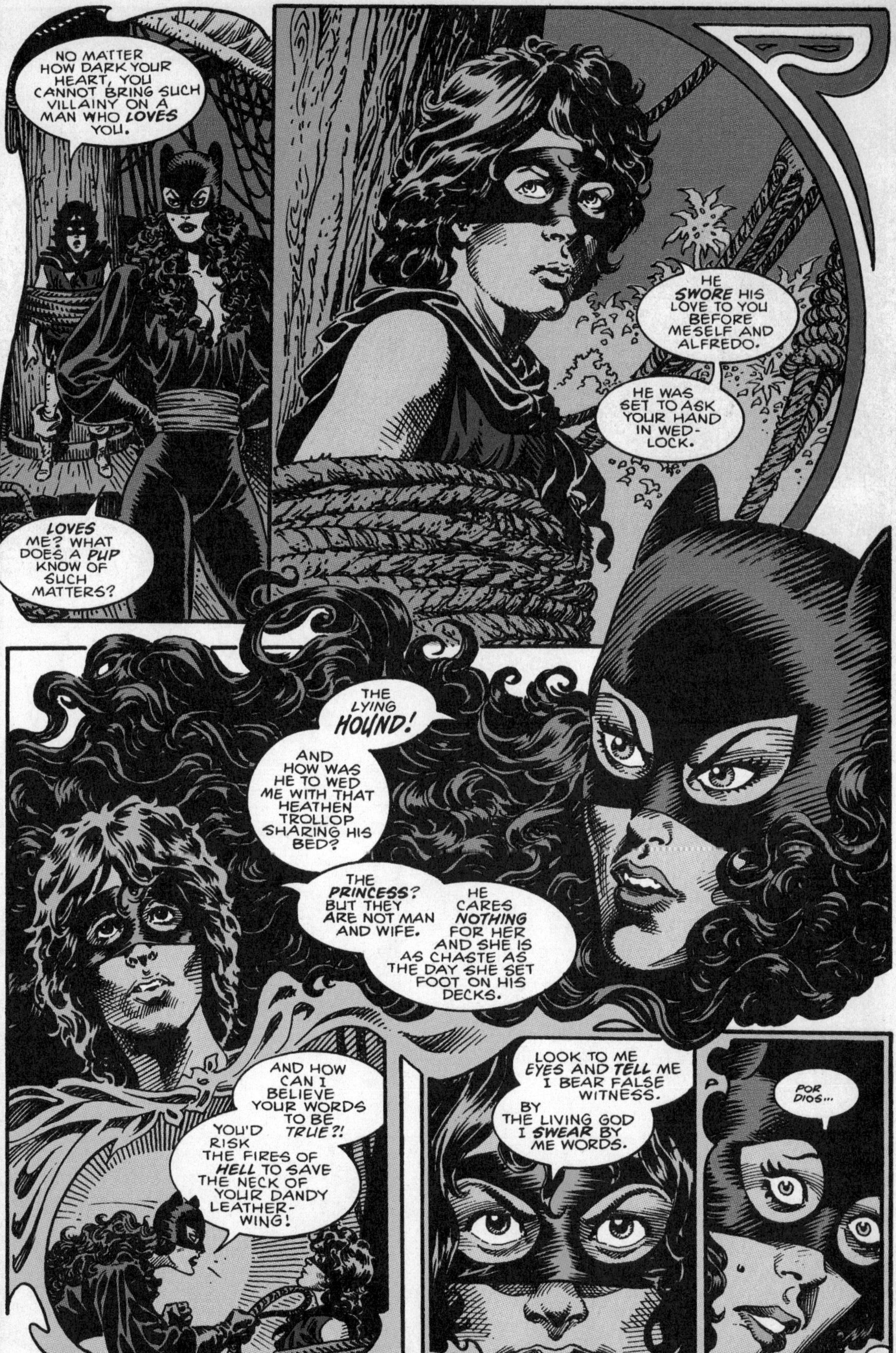
NO MATTER HOW DARK YOUR HEART, YOU CANNOT BRING SUCH VILLAINY ON A MAN WHO LOVES YOU.
LOVES ME? WHAT DOES A PUP KNOW OF SUCH MATTERS?
HE SWORE HIS LOVE TO YOU BEFORE MESELF AND ALFREDO.
HE WAS SET TO ASK YOUR HAND IN WED-LOCK.
THE LYING HOUND!
AND HOW WAS HE TO WED ME WITH THAT HEATHEN TROLLOP SHARING HIS BED?
THE PRINCESS? BUT THEY ARE NOT MAN AND WIFE.
HE CARES NOTHING FOR HER AND SHE IS AS CHASTE AS THE DAY SHE SET FOOT ON HIS DECKS.
AND HOW CAN I BELIEVE YOUR WORDS TO BE TRUE?!
YOU'D RISK THE FIRES OF HELL TO SAVE THE NECK OF YOUR DANDY LEATHER-WING!
LOOK TO ME EYES AND TELL ME I BEAR FALSE WITNESS.
BY THE LIVING GOD I SWEAR BY ME WORDS.
POR DIOS...
49

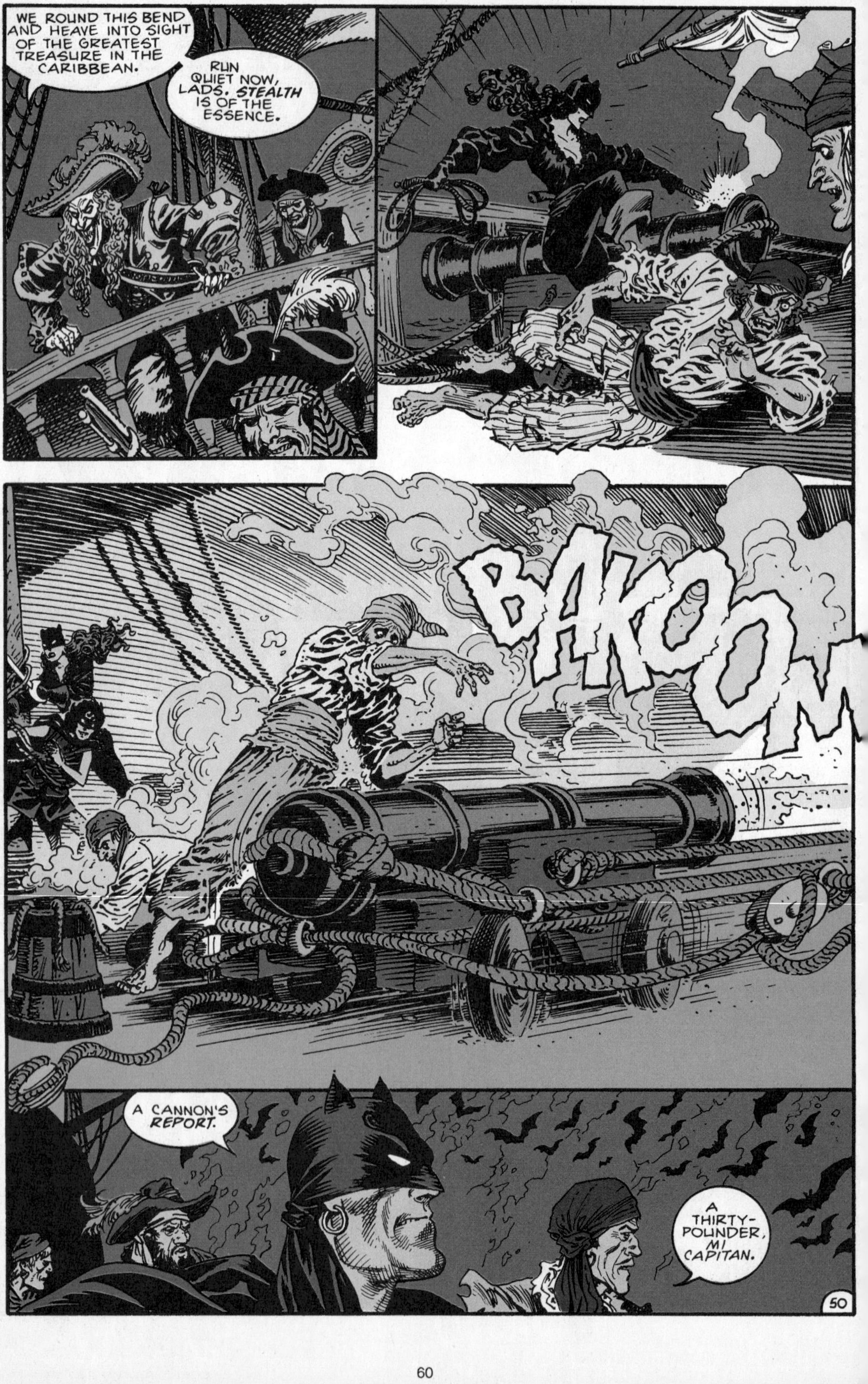
WE ROUND THIS BEND AND HEAVE INTO SIGHT OF THE GREATEST TREASURE IN THE CARIBBEAN.
RUN QUIET NOW, LADS. STEALTH IS OF THE ESSENCE.
BAKOOM
A CANNON'S REPORT.
A THIRTY-POUNDER, MI CAPITAN.
50

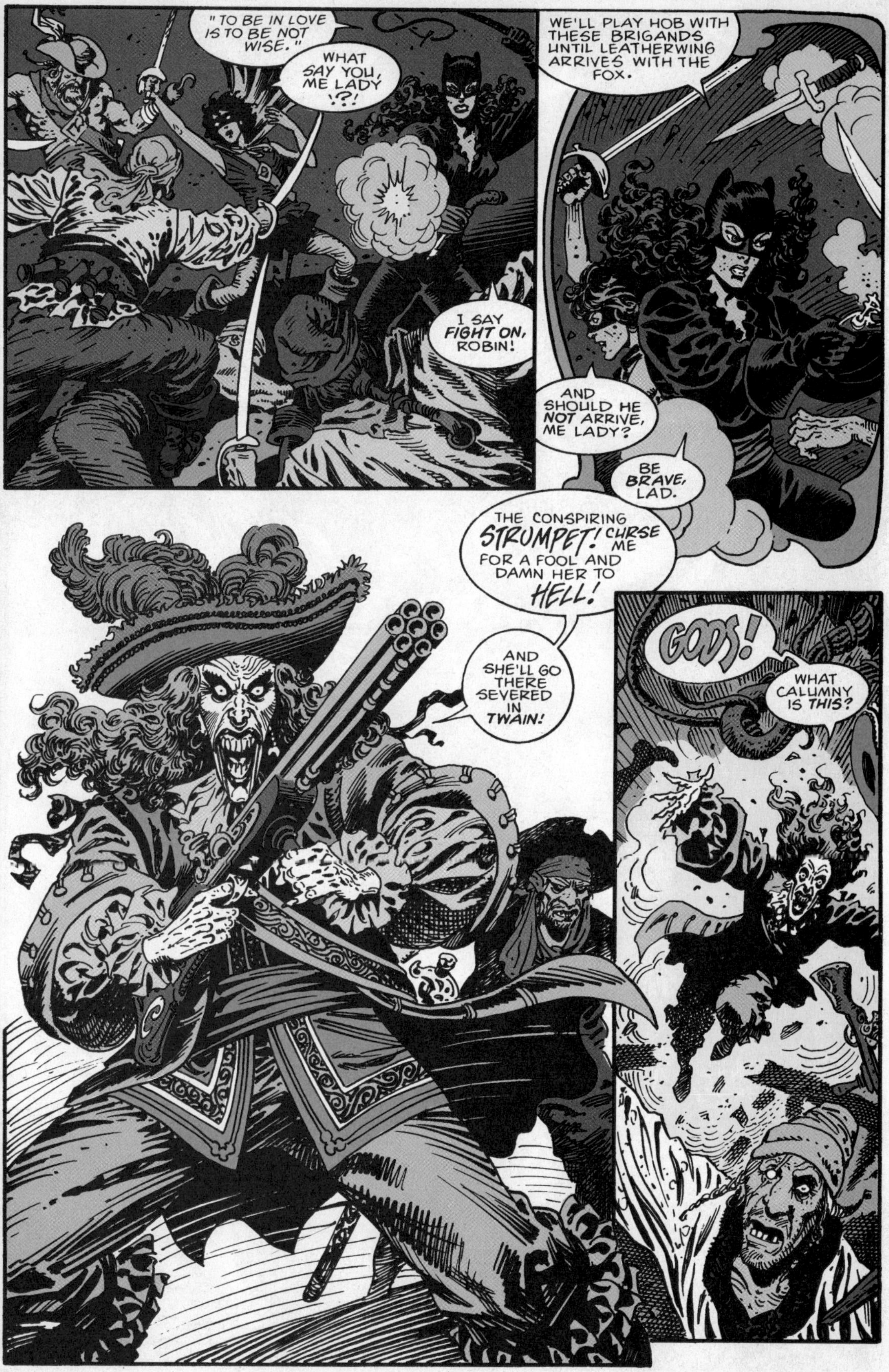
"TO BE IN LOVE IS TO BE NOT WISE."
WHAT SAY YOU, ME LADY !?!
I SAY FIGHT ON, ROBIN!
WE'LL PLAY HOB WITH THESE BRIGANDS UNTIL LEATHERWING ARRIVES WITH THE FOX.
AND SHOULD HE NOT ARRIVE, ME LADY?
BE BRAVE, LAD.
THE CONSPIRING STRUMPET! CURSE ME FOR A FOOL AND DAMN HER TO HELL!
AND SHE'LL GO THERE SEVERED IN TWAIN!
GODS!
WHAT CALUMNY IS THIS?

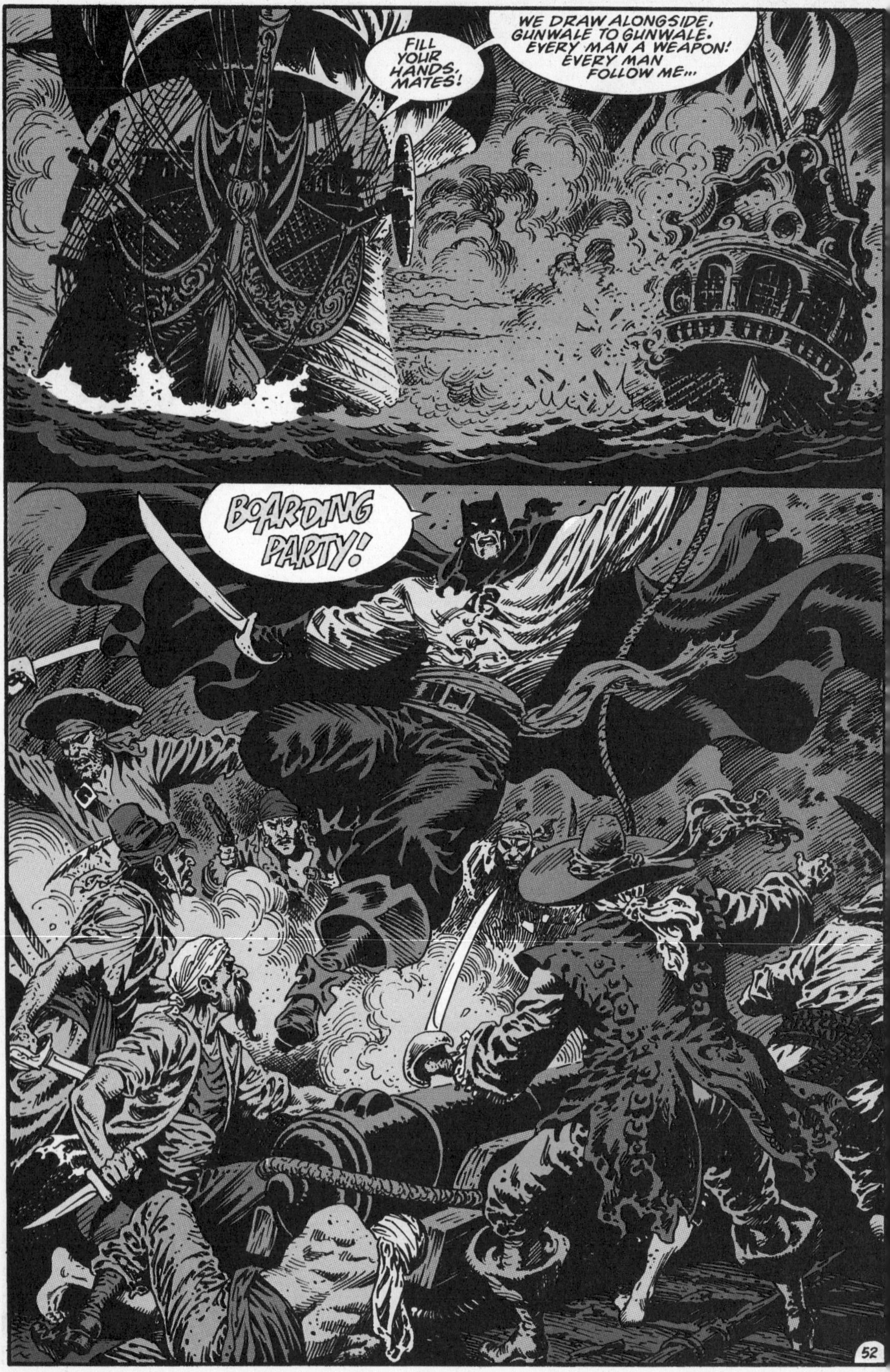
FILL YOUR HANDS, MATES!
WE DRAW ALONGSIDE, GUNWALE TO GUNWALE. EVERY MAN A WEAPON! EVERY MAN FOLLOW ME...
BOARDING PARTY!
52

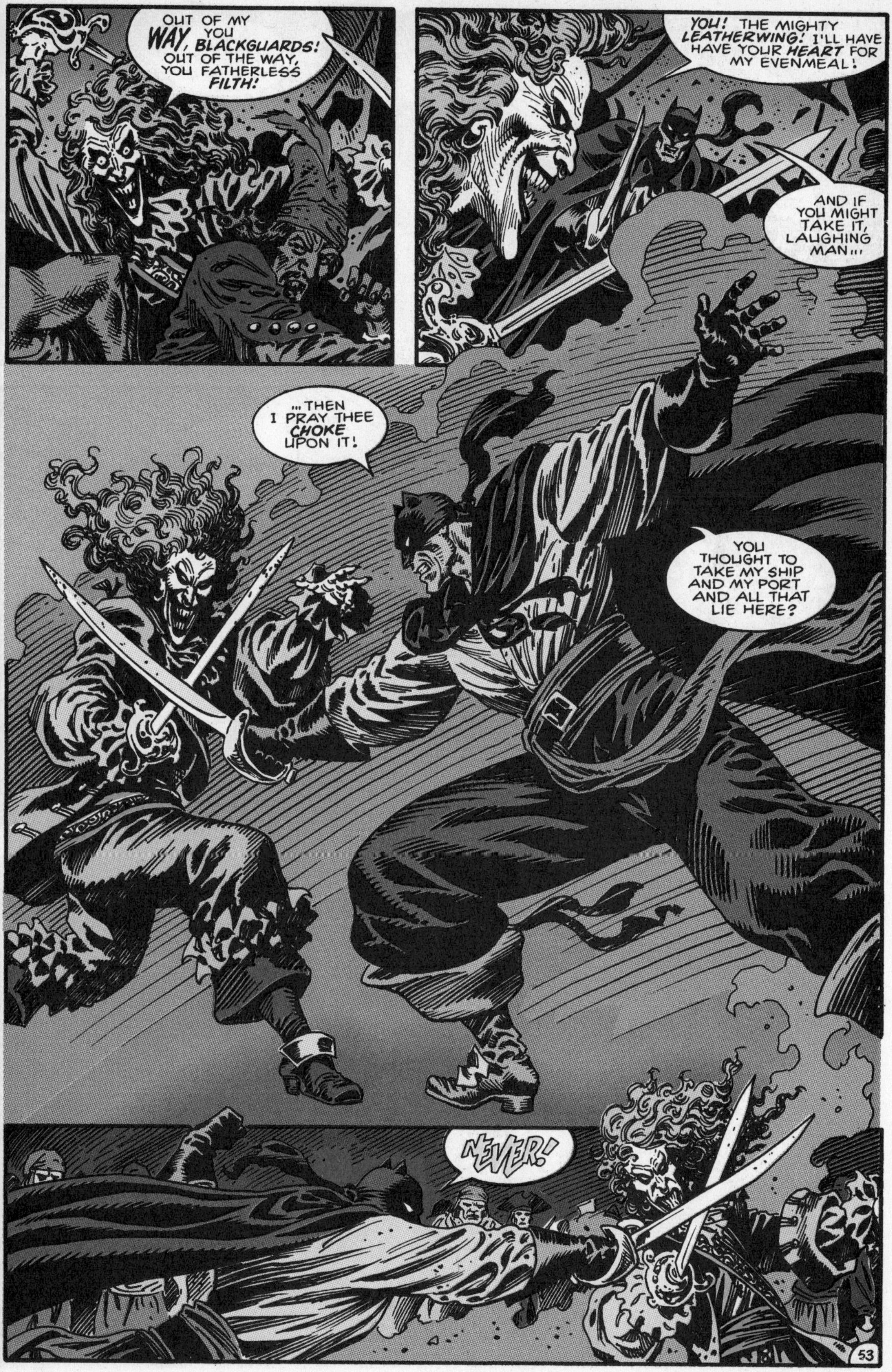
OUT OF MY WAY, YOU BLACKGUARDS! OUT OF THE WAY, YOU FATHERLESS FILTH!
YOU! THE MIGHTY LEATHERWING! I'LL HAVE HAVE YOUR HEART FOR MY EVENMEAL!
AND IF YOU MIGHT TAKE IT, LAUGHING MAN...
...THEN I PRAY THEE CHOKE UPON IT!
YOU THOUGHT TO TAKE MY SHIP AND MY PORT AND ALL THAT LIE HERE?
NEVER!
53

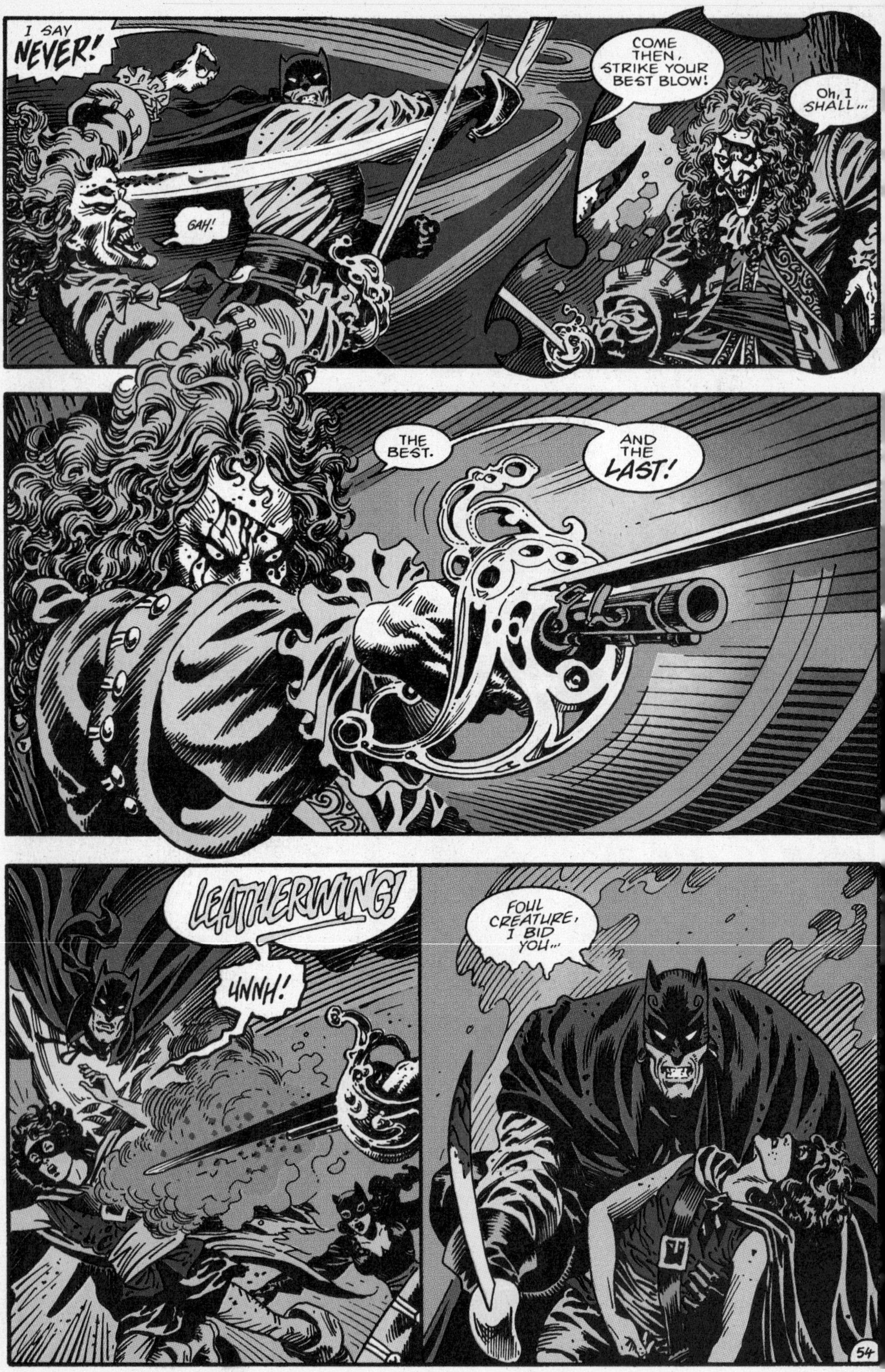

I SAY NEVER!
GAH!
COME THEN, STRIKE YOUR BEST BLOW!
Oh, I SHALL...
THE BEST.
AND THE LAST!
LEATHERWING!
UNNH!
FOUL CREATURE, I BID YOU...
54

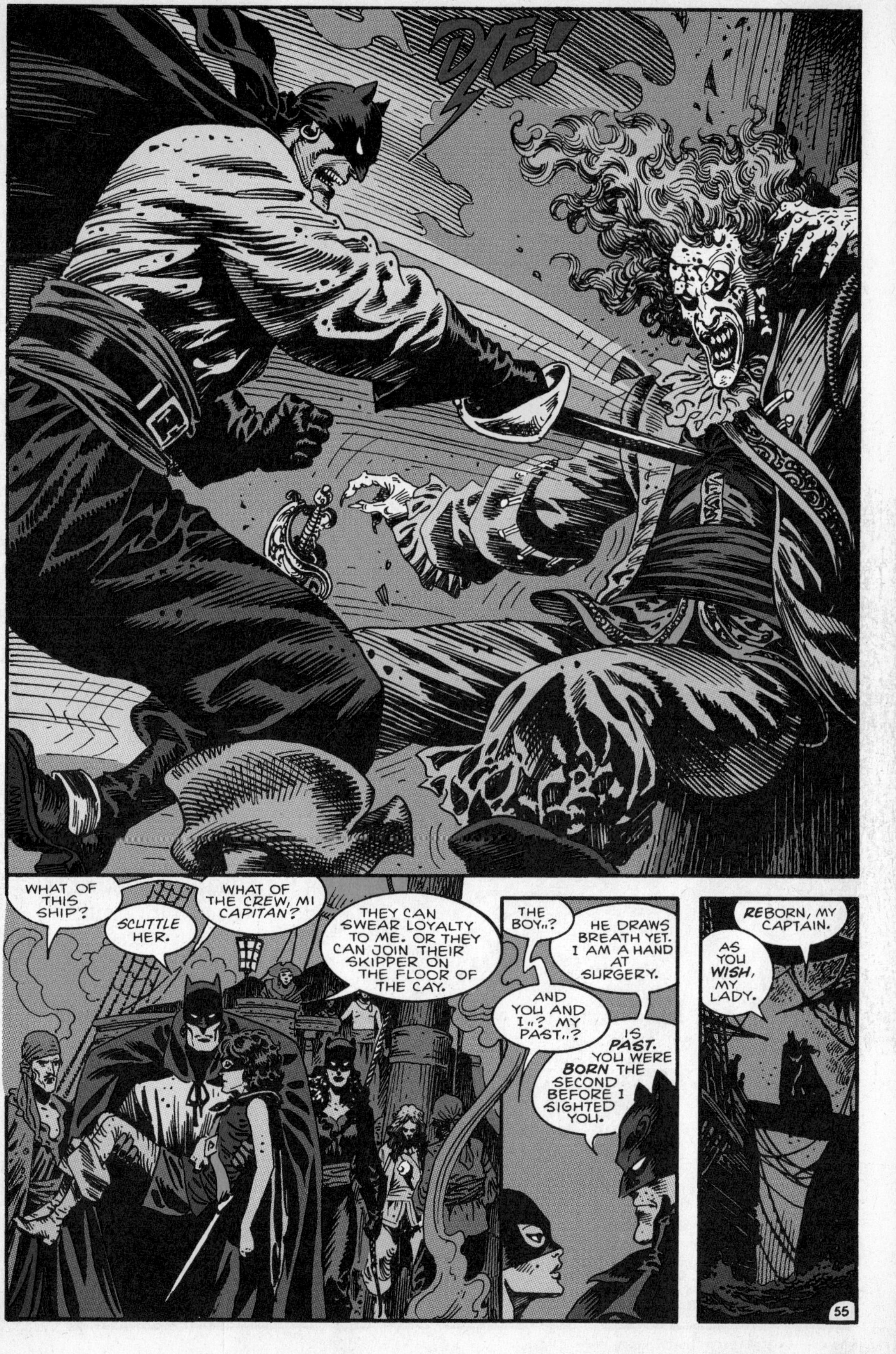
DIE!
WHAT OF THIS SHIP?
SCUTTLE HER.
WHAT OF THE CREW, MI CAPITAN?
THEY CAN SWEAR LOYALTY TO ME. OR THEY CAN JOIN THEIR SKIPPER ON THE FLOOR OF THE CAY.
THE BOY..?
HE DRAWS BREATH YET. I AM A HAND AT SURGERY.
AND YOU AND I..? MY PAST..?
IS PAST. YOU WERE BORN THE SECOND BEFORE I SIGHTED YOU.
REBORN, MY CAPTAIN.
AS YOU WISH, MY LADY.
55

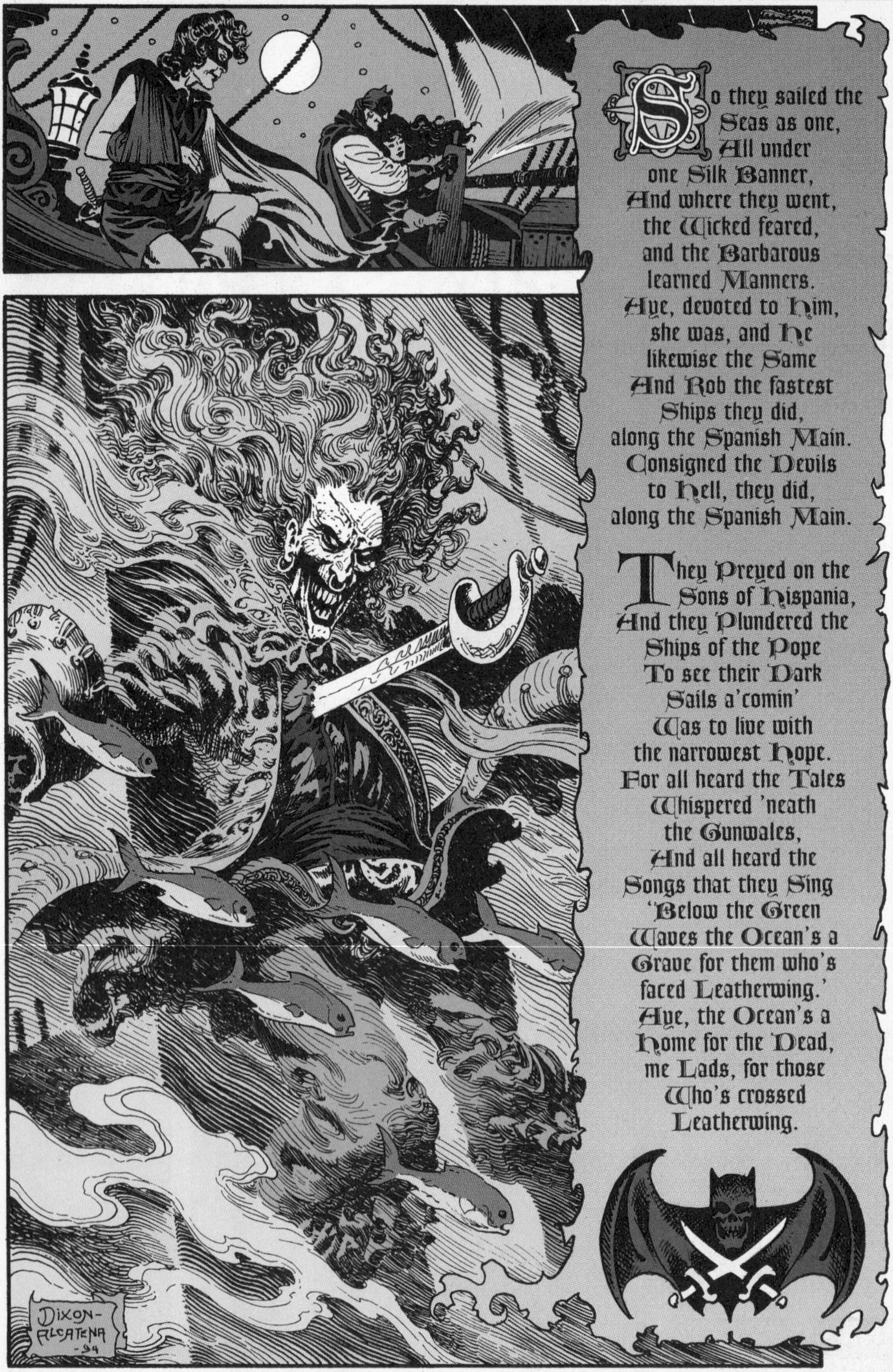
So they sailed the Seas as one,
All under one Silk Banner,
And where they went, the Wicked feared,
and the Barbarous learned Manners.
Aye, devoted to Him, she was, and He likewise the Same
And Rob the fastest Ships they did, along the Spanish Main.
Consigned the Devils to Hell, they did, along the Spanish Main.
They Preyed on the Sons of Hispania,
And they Plundered the Ships of the Pope
To see their Dark Sails a'comin'
Was to live with the narrowest Hope.
For all heard the Tales Whispered 'neath the Gunwales,
And all heard the Songs that they Sing
'Below the Green Waves the Ocean's a Grave for them who's faced Leatherwing.'
Aye, the Ocean's a Home for the Dead, me Lads, for those Who's crossed Leatherwing.
DIXON-ALCATENA -94

legacy

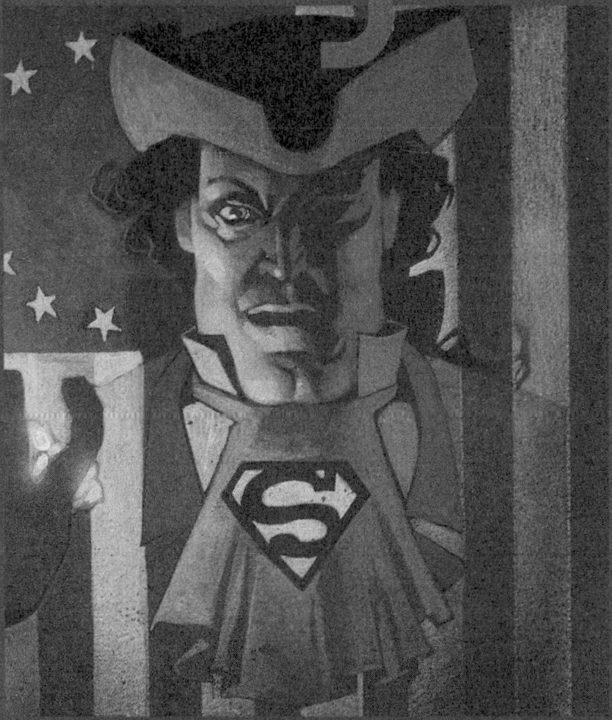

legacy

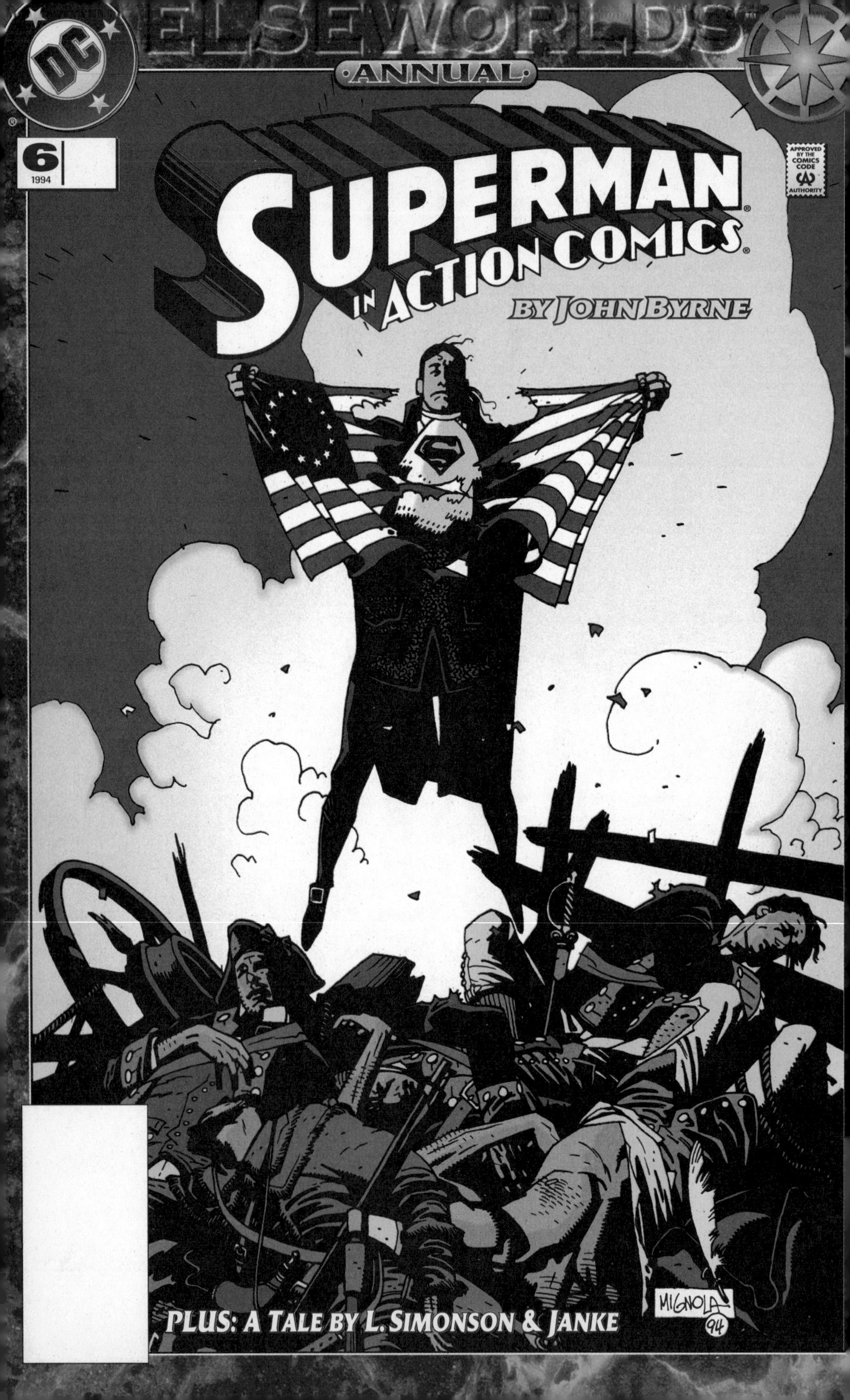
ELSEWORLDS
ANNUAL
DC
6
1994
APPROVED BY THE COMICS CODE AUTHORITY
SUPERMAN IN ACTION COMICS
BY JOHN BYRNE
MIGNOLA 94
PLUS: A TALE BY L. SIMONSON & JANKE

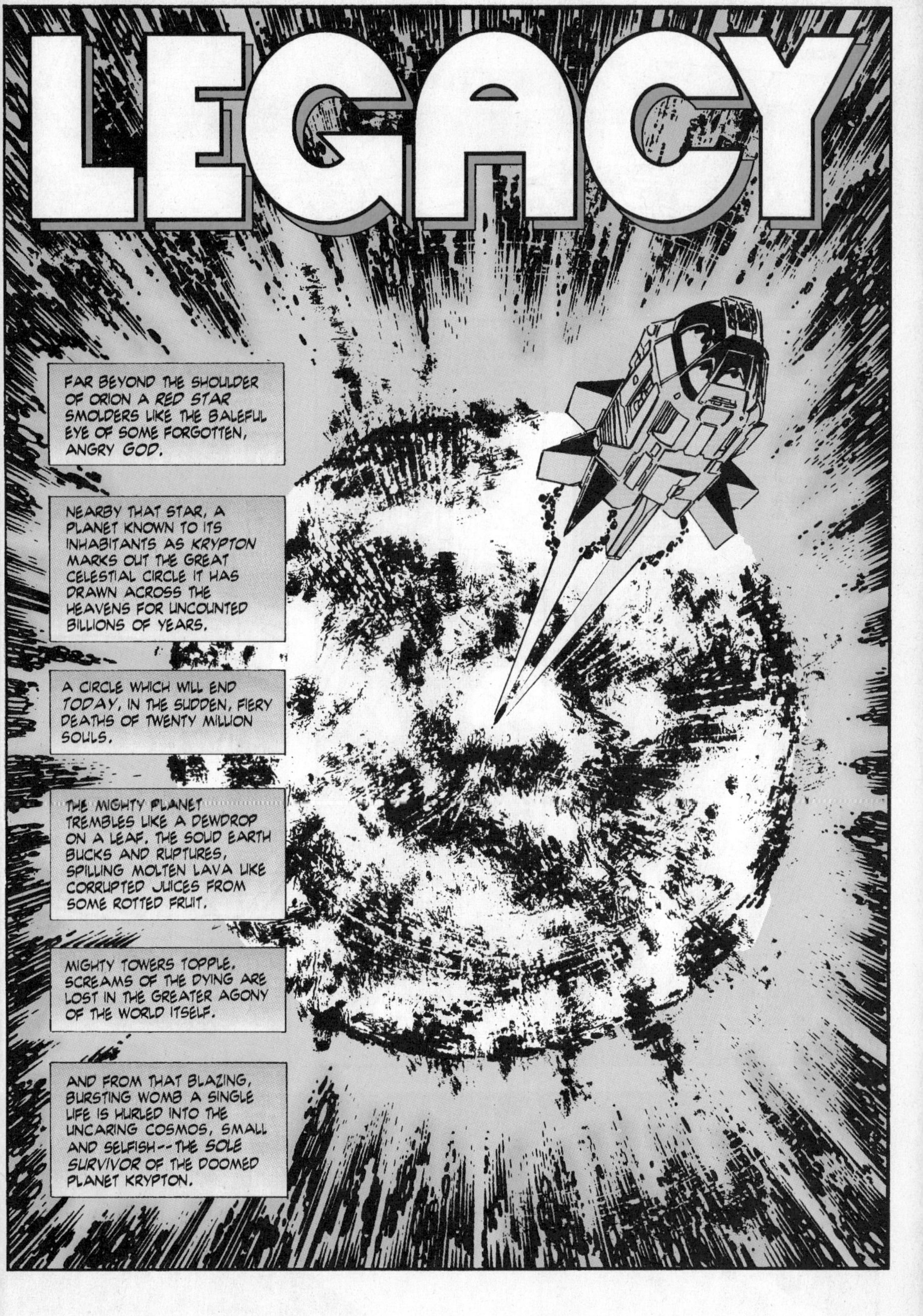
LEGACY
FAR BEYOND THE SHOULDER OF ORION A RED STAR SMOLDERS LIKE THE BALEFUL EYE OF SOME FORGOTTEN, ANGRY GOD.
NEARBY THAT STAR, A PLANET KNOWN TO ITS INHABITANTS AS KRYPTON MARKS OUT THE GREAT CELESTIAL CIRCLE IT HAS DRAWN ACROSS THE HEAVENS FOR UNCOUNTED BILLIONS OF YEARS.
A CIRCLE WHICH WILL END TODAY, IN THE SUDDEN, FIERY DEATHS OF TWENTY MILLION SOULS.
THE MIGHTY PLANET TREMBLES LIKE A DEWDROP ON A LEAF. THE SOLID EARTH BUCKS AND RUPTURES, SPILLING MOLTEN LAVA LIKE CORRUPTED JUICES FROM SOME ROTTED FRUIT.
MIGHTY TOWERS TOPPLE. SCREAMS OF THE DYING ARE LOST IN THE GREATER AGONY OF THE WORLD ITSELF.
AND FROM THAT BLAZING, BURSTING WOMB A SINGLE LIFE IS HURLED INTO THE UNCARING COSMOS, SMALL AND SELFISH--THE SOLE SURVIVOR OF THE DOOMED PLANET KRYPTON.

HIS NAME IS GAR-EL. HE IS SCION OF A PROUD AND FAMOUS FAMILY, ONE WHOSE NOBLE DEEDS STRETCH BACK TO THE VERY BEGINNINGS OF THE WORLD.

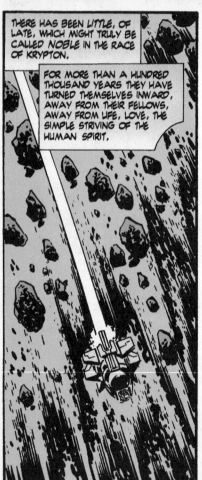

THERE HAS BEEN LITTLE, OF LATE, WHICH MIGHT TRULY BE CALLED *NOBLE* IN THE RACE OF KRYPTON.

FOR MORE THAN A HUNDRED THOUSAND YEARS THEY HAVE TURNED THEMSELVES INWARD, AWAY FROM THEIR FELLOWS, AWAY FROM LIFE, LOVE, THE SIMPLE STRIVING OF THE HUMAN SPIRIT.

NESTLED IN HIS STEEL AND PLASTIC POD, GAR-EL IS A PRIME EXAMPLE OF ALL THAT KRYPTON HAS BECOME, ALL THAT HAS BEEN LOST.

HE STUDIES THE INSTRUMENTS ARRAYED BEFORE HIM AND CHOKES BACK THE FEAR THAT BOILS IN HIS THROAT.

TRADITION HOLDS THAT FOR A KRYPTONIAN, LEAVING THE EMBRACE OF THE PLANET IS A CERTAIN *DEATH* SENTENCE.

ONLY ONE THING COULD HAVE COAXED GAR-EL INTO THE VOID, ONE THING TO HIM AN INCENTIVE GREATER EVEN THAN THE THREAT OF AGONIZING DEATH.

THE PROMISE OF SUPREME *POWER*.

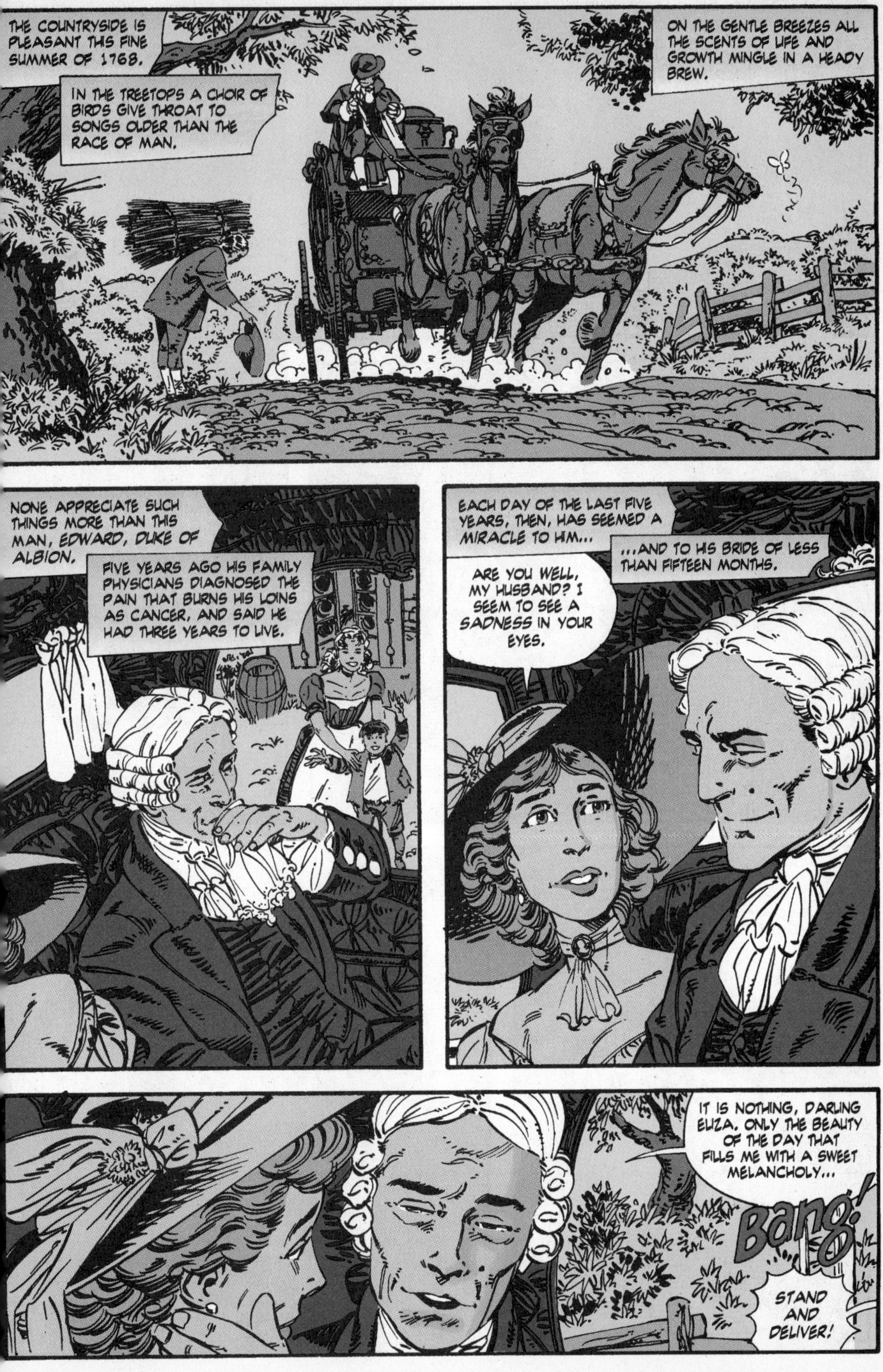
THE COUNTRYSIDE IS PLEASANT THIS FINE SUMMER OF 1768.
IN THE TREETOPS A CHOIR OF BIRDS GIVE THROAT TO SONGS OLDER THAN THE RACE OF MAN.
ON THE GENTLE BREEZES ALL THE SCENTS OF LIFE AND GROWTH MINGLE IN A HEADY BREW.
NONE APPRECIATE SUCH THINGS MORE THAN THIS MAN, EDWARD, DUKE OF ALBION.
FIVE YEARS AGO HIS FAMILY PHYSICIANS DIAGNOSED THE PAIN THAT BURNS HIS LOINS AS CANCER, AND SAID HE HAD THREE YEARS TO LIVE.
EACH DAY OF THE LAST FIVE YEARS, THEN, HAS SEEMED A MIRACLE TO HIM...
...AND TO HIS BRIDE OF LESS THAN FIFTEEN MONTHS.
ARE YOU WELL, MY HUSBAND? I SEEM TO SEE A SADNESS IN YOUR EYES.
IT IS NOTHING, DARLING ELIZA. ONLY THE BEAUTY OF THE DAY THAT FILLS ME WITH A SWEET MELANCHOLY...
BANG!
STAND AND DELIVER!

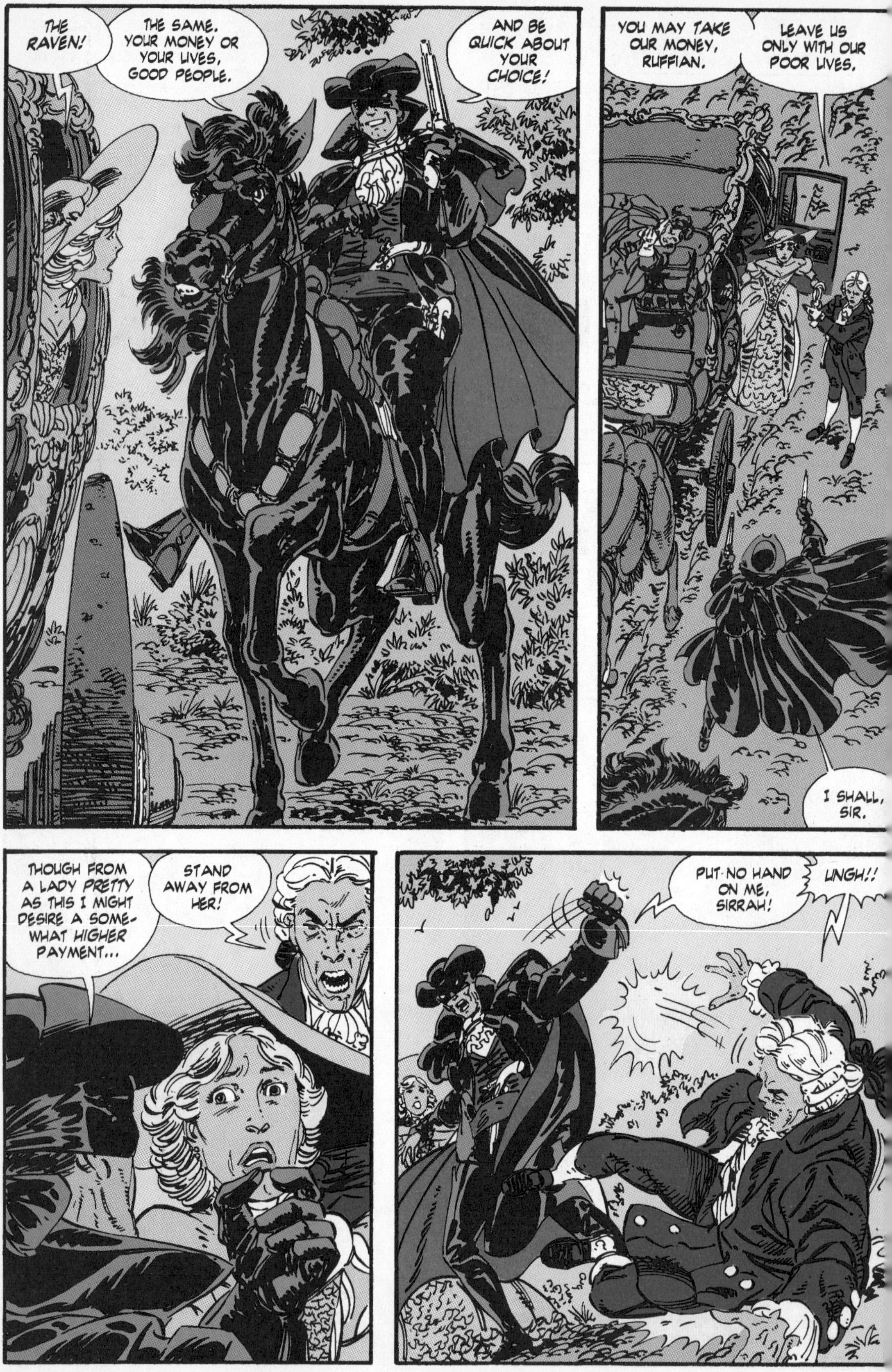
THE RAVEN!
THE SAME. YOUR MONEY OR YOUR LIVES, GOOD PEOPLE.
AND BE QUICK ABOUT YOUR CHOICE!
YOU MAY TAKE OUR MONEY, RUFFIAN.
LEAVE US ONLY WITH OUR POOR LIVES.
I SHALL, SIR.
THOUGH FROM A LADY PRETTY AS THIS I MIGHT DESIRE A SOME-WHAT HIGHER PAYMENT...
STAND AWAY FROM HER!
PUT NO HAND ON ME, SIRRAH!
UNGH!!

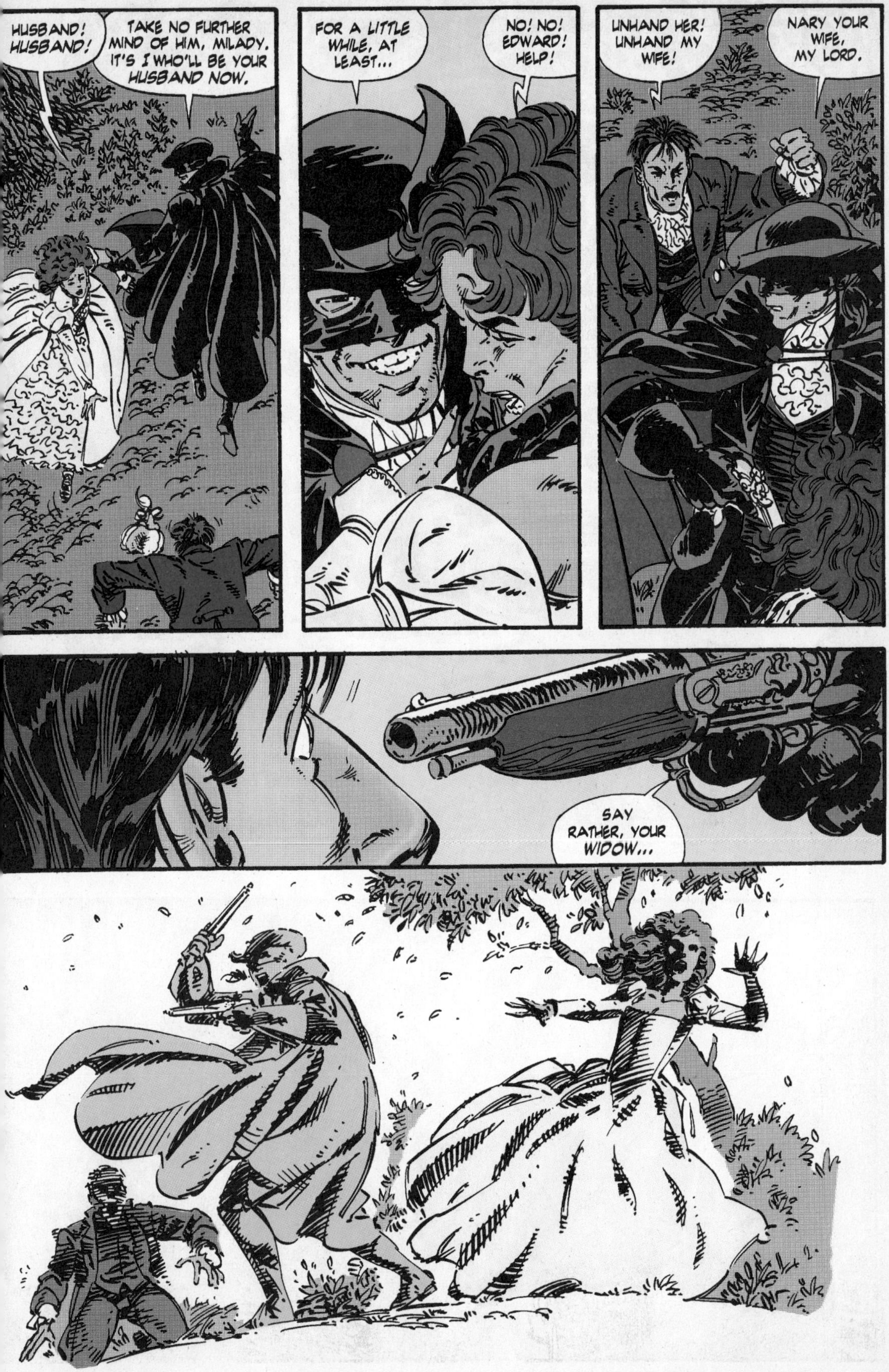
HUSBAND! HUSBAND!
TAKE NO FURTHER MIND OF HIM, MILADY. IT'S I WHO'LL BE YOUR HUSBAND NOW.
FOR A LITTLE WHILE, AT LEAST...
NO! NO! EDWARD! HELP!
UNHAND HER! UNHAND MY WIFE!
NARY YOUR WIFE, MY LORD.
SAY RATHER, YOUR WIDOW...

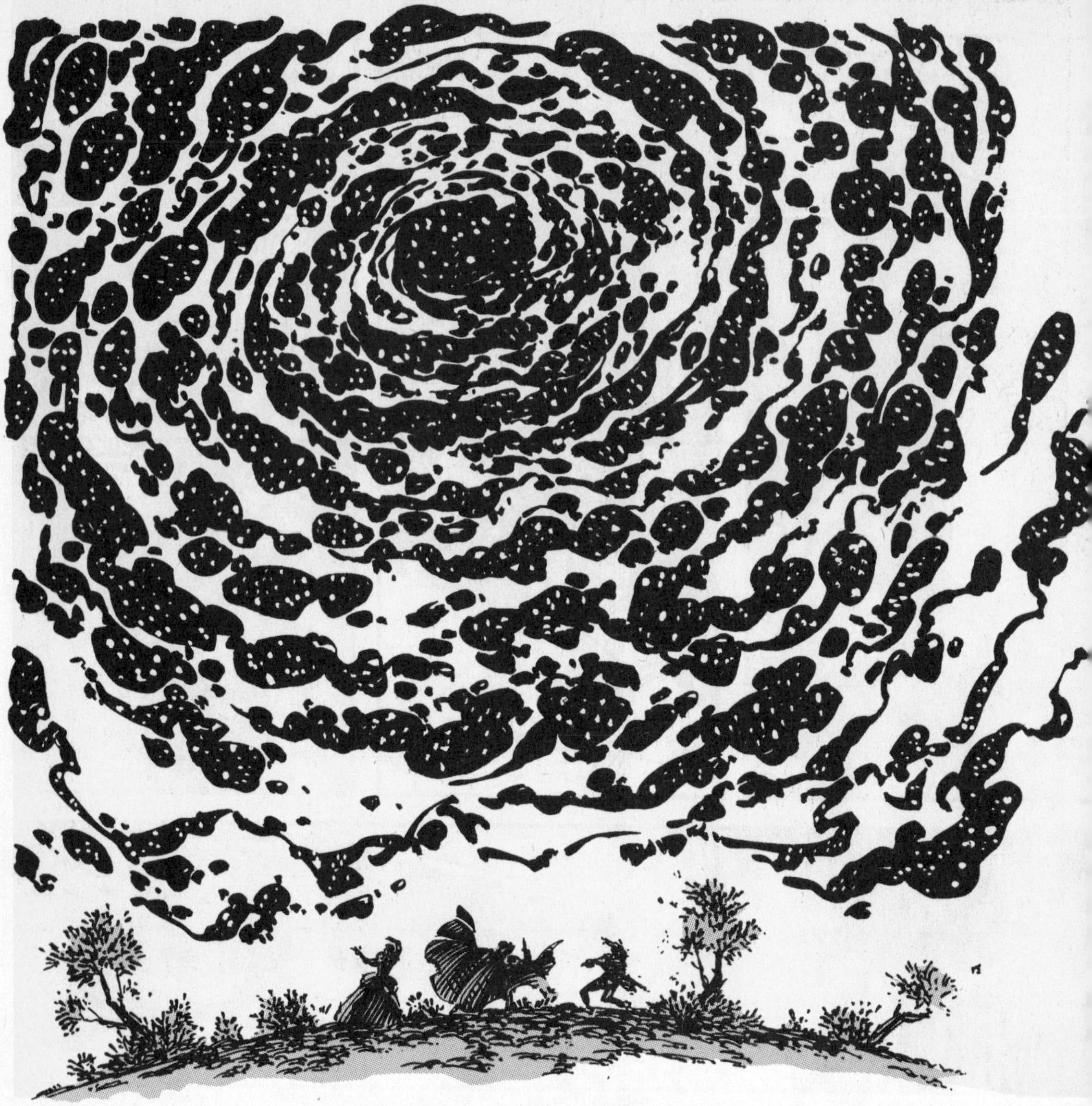

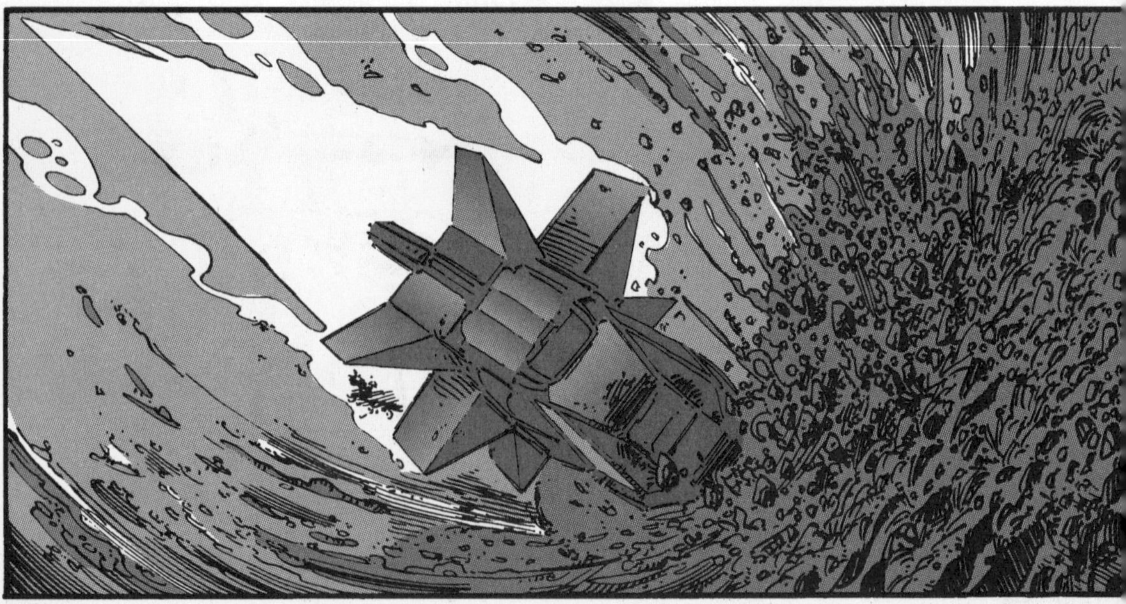

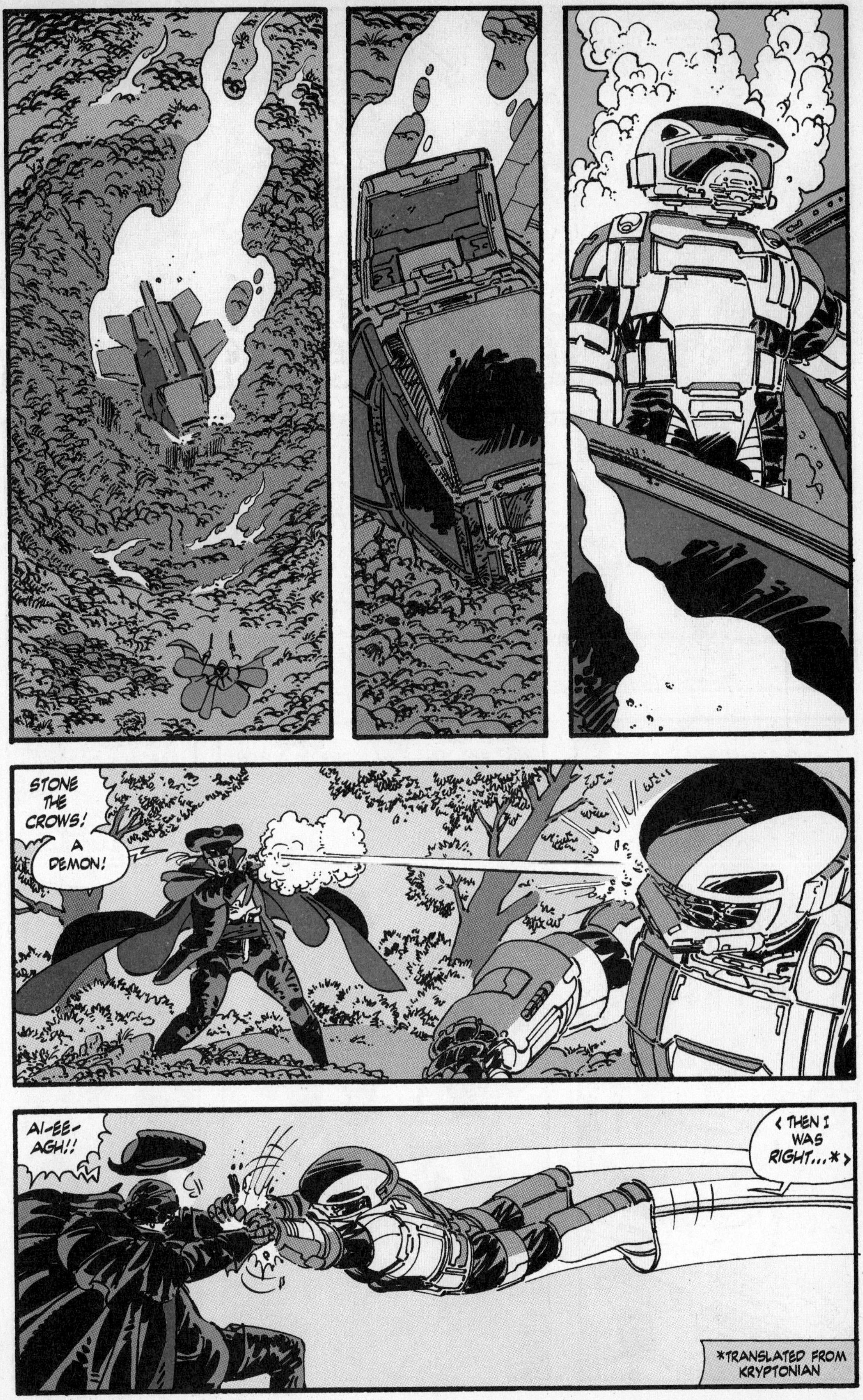

STONE THE CROWS! A DEMON!
AI-EE-AGH!!
< THEN I WAS RIGHT...* >
*TRANSLATED FROM KRYPTONIAN

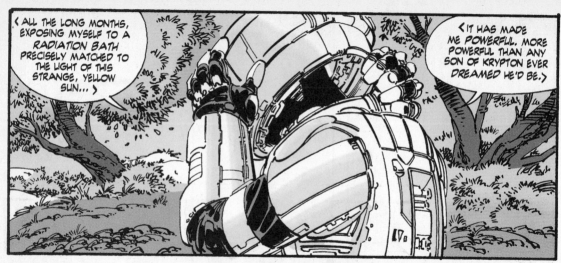

< ALL THE LONG MONTHS, EXPOSING MYSELF TO A RADIATION BATH PRECISELY MATCHED TO THE LIGHT OF THIS STRANGE, YELLOW SUN... >

< IT HAS MADE ME *POWERFUL*. MORE POWERFUL THAN ANY SON OF KRYPTON EVER DREAMED HE'D BE. >

< AND EVERY DAY I'M ON THIS PUNY PLANET I SHALL GROW EVER *STRONGER*, EVER *GREATER!* >

WHO... WHAT ARE YOU..?

< ENGLISH. YES, I THOUGHT I RECOGNIZED THE WORDS THAT FOOL SPOKE. >

WHO YOU ARE? SAY YOU NAME!

EDWARD, DUKE OF ALBION. AND... YOU..?

AM GAR-EL, LAST SON OF KRYPTON.

BUT I HAVE ALREADY DECIDED YOU OF EARTH SHALL CALL ME...

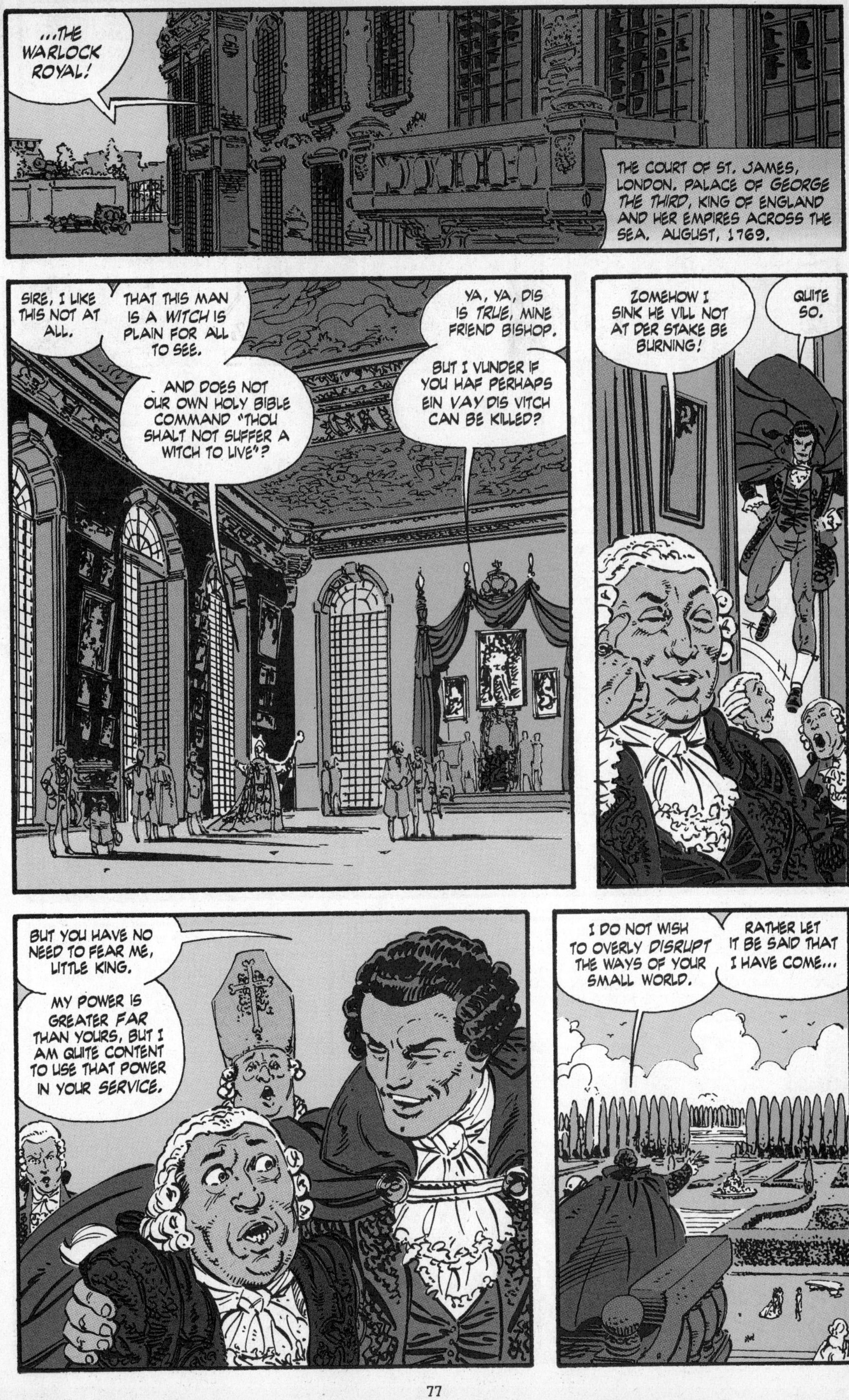
...THE WARLOCK ROYAL!
THE COURT OF ST. JAMES, LONDON. PALACE OF GEORGE THE THIRD, KING OF ENGLAND AND HER EMPIRES ACROSS THE SEA. AUGUST, 1769.
SIRE, I LIKE THIS NOT AT ALL.
THAT THIS MAN IS A WITCH IS PLAIN FOR ALL TO SEE.
AND DOES NOT OUR OWN HOLY BIBLE COMMAND "THOU SHALT NOT SUFFER A WITCH TO LIVE"?
YA, YA, DIS IS TRUE, MINE FRIEND BISHOP.
BUT I VUNDER IF YOU HAF PERHAPS EIN VAY DIS VITCH CAN BE KILLED?
ZOMEHOW I SINK HE VILL NOT AT DER STAKE BE BURNING!
QUITE SO.
BUT YOU HAVE NO NEED TO FEAR ME, LITTLE KING.
MY POWER IS GREATER FAR THAN YOURS, BUT I AM QUITE CONTENT TO USE THAT POWER IN YOUR SERVICE.
I DO NOT WISH TO OVERLY DISRUPT THE WAYS OF YOUR SMALL WORLD.
RATHER LET IT BE SAID THAT I HAVE COME...

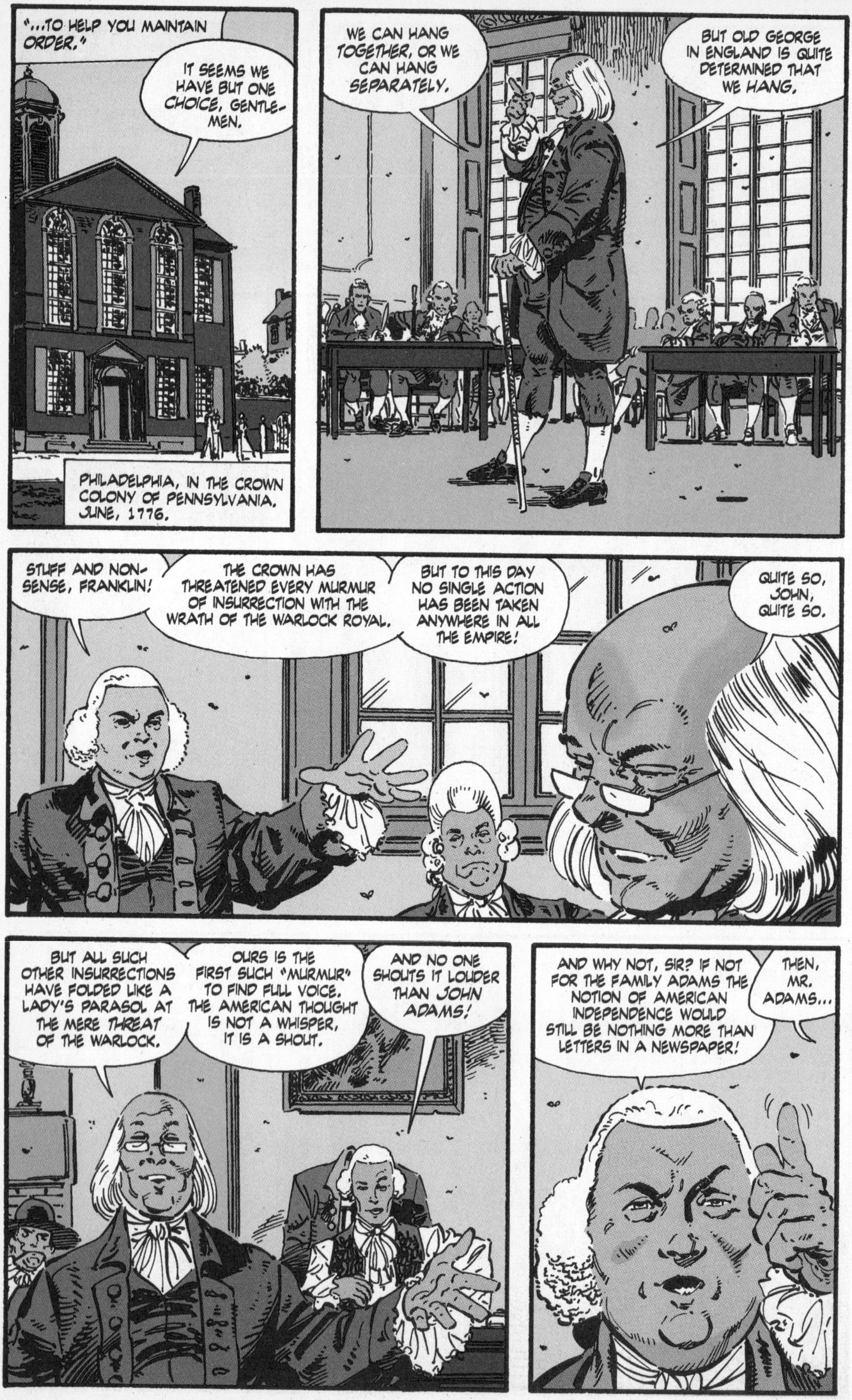
"...TO HELP YOU MAINTAIN ORDER."
IT SEEMS WE HAVE BUT ONE CHOICE, GENTLE-MEN.
PHILADELPHIA, IN THE CROWN COLONY OF PENNSYLVANIA. JUNE, 1776.
WE CAN HANG TOGETHER, OR WE CAN HANG SEPARATELY.
BUT OLD GEORGE IN ENGLAND IS QUITE DETERMINED THAT WE HANG.
STUFF AND NON-SENSE, FRANKLIN!
THE CROWN HAS THREATENED EVERY MURMUR OF INSURRECTION WITH THE WRATH OF THE WARLOCK ROYAL.
BUT TO THIS DAY NO SINGLE ACTION HAS BEEN TAKEN ANYWHERE IN ALL THE EMPIRE!
QUITE SO, JOHN, QUITE SO.
BUT ALL SUCH OTHER INSURRECTIONS HAVE FOLDED LIKE A LADY'S PARASOL AT THE MERE THREAT OF THE WARLOCK.
OURS IS THE FIRST SUCH "MURMUR" TO FIND FULL VOICE. THE AMERICAN THOUGHT IS NOT A WHISPER, IT IS A SHOUT.
AND NO ONE SHOUTS IT LOUDER THAN JOHN ADAMS!
AND WHY NOT, SIR? IF NOT FOR THE FAMILY ADAMS THE NOTION OF AMERICAN INDEPENDENCE WOULD STILL BE NOTHING MORE THAN LETTERS IN A NEWSPAPER!
THEN, MR. ADAMS...

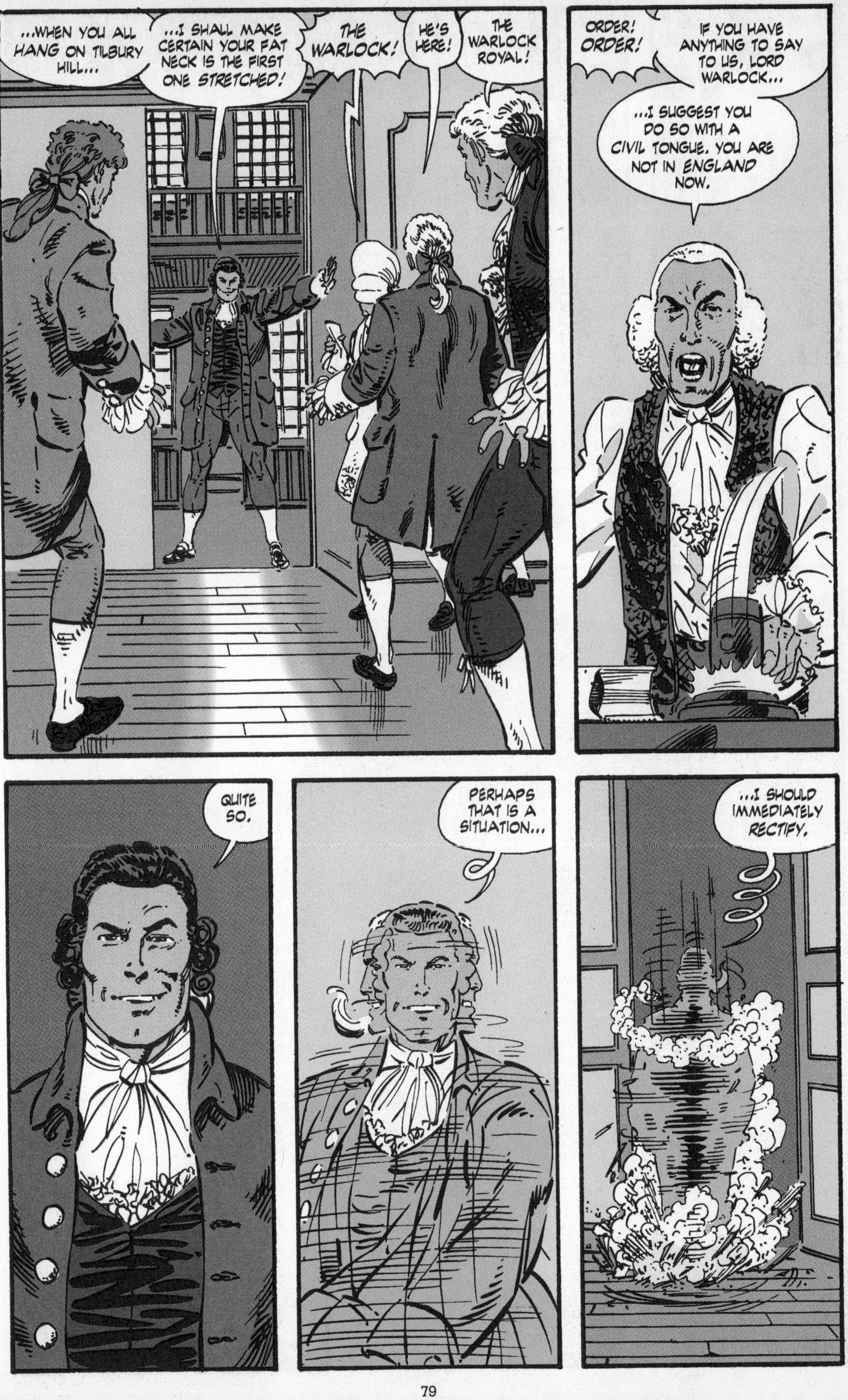
...WHEN YOU ALL HANG ON TILBURY HILL...
...I SHALL MAKE CERTAIN YOUR FAT NECK IS THE FIRST ONE STRETCHED!
THE WARLOCK!
HE'S HERE!
THE WARLOCK ROYAL!
ORDER! ORDER!
IF YOU HAVE ANYTHING TO SAY TO US, LORD WARLOCK...
...I SUGGEST YOU DO SO WITH A CIVIL TONGUE. YOU ARE NOT IN ENGLAND NOW.
QUITE SO.
PERHAPS THAT IS A SITUATION...
...I SHOULD IMMEDIATELY RECTIFY.

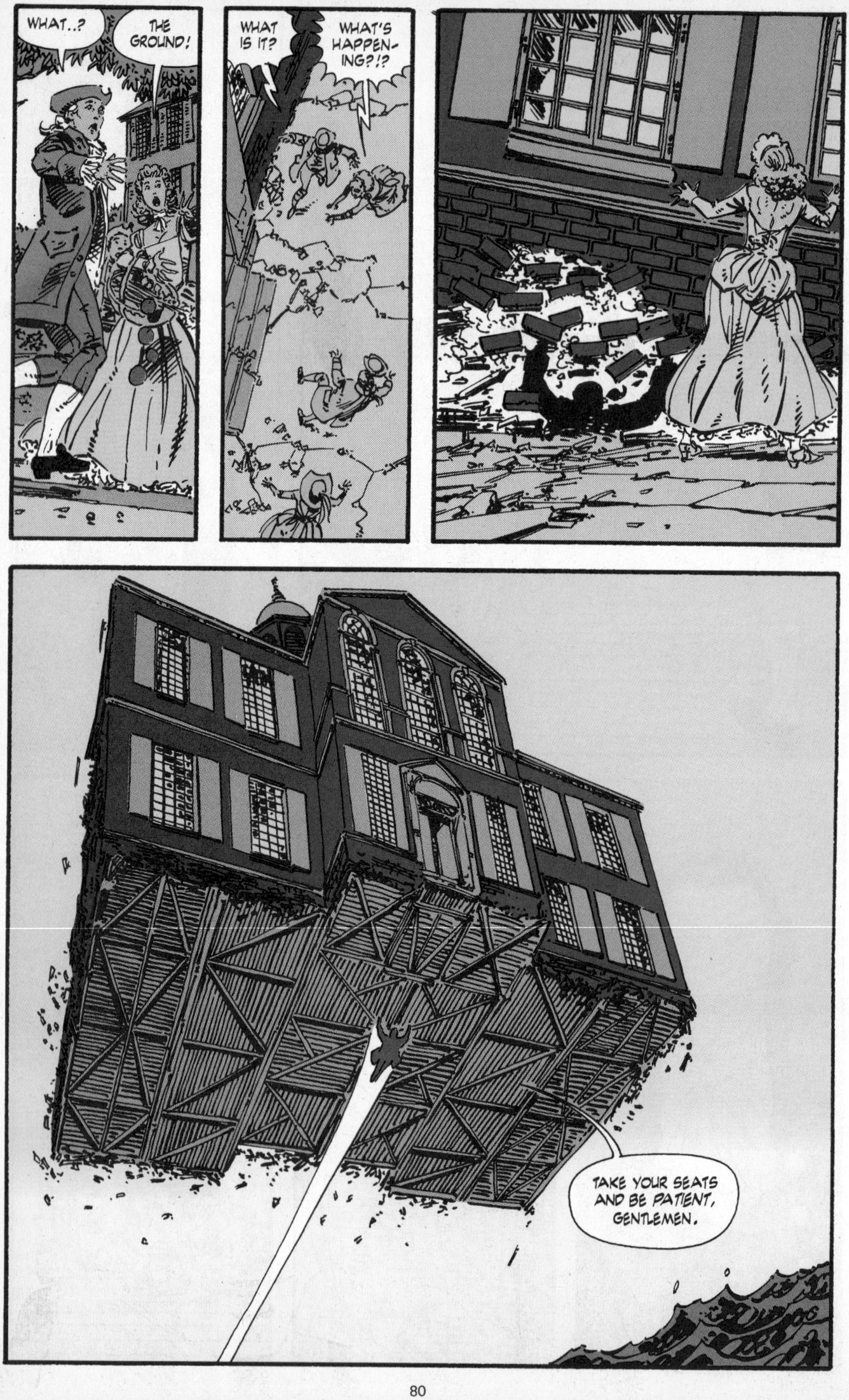
WHAT..?
THE GROUND!
WHAT IS IT?
WHAT'S HAPPEN-ING?!?
TAKE YOUR SEATS AND BE PATIENT, GENTLEMEN.

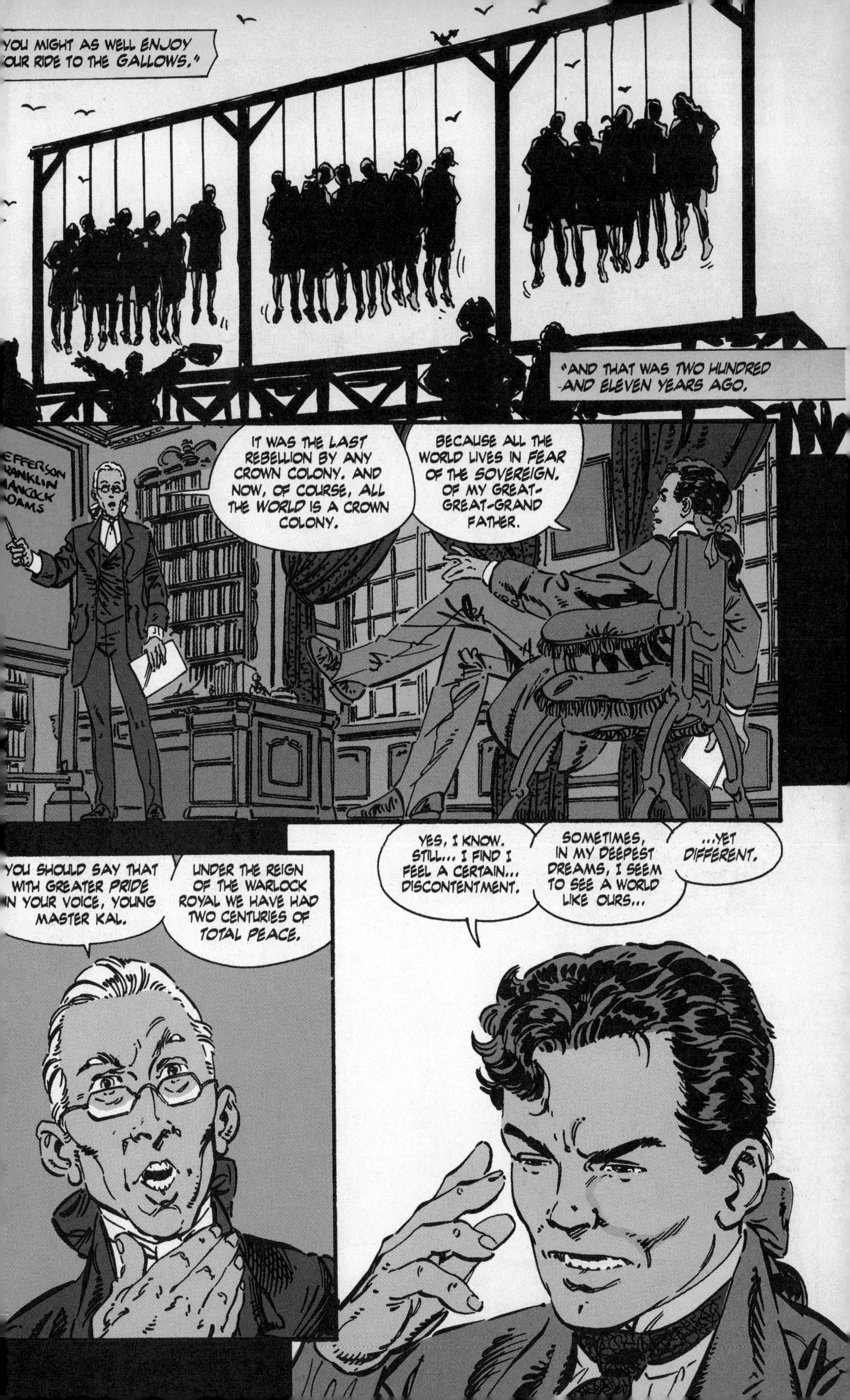

YOU MIGHT AS WELL ENJOY OUR RIDE TO THE GALLOWS."
"AND THAT WAS TWO HUNDRED AND ELEVEN YEARS AGO.
EFFERSON FRANKLIN HANCOCK ADAMS
IT WAS THE LAST REBELLION BY ANY CROWN COLONY. AND NOW, OF COURSE, ALL THE WORLD IS A CROWN COLONY.
BECAUSE ALL THE WORLD LIVES IN FEAR OF THE SOVEREIGN, OF MY GREAT-GREAT-GRAND FATHER.
YOU SHOULD SAY THAT WITH GREATER PRIDE IN YOUR VOICE, YOUNG MASTER KAL.
UNDER THE REIGN OF THE WARLOCK ROYAL WE HAVE HAD TWO CENTURIES OF TOTAL PEACE.
YES, I KNOW. STILL... I FIND I FEEL A CERTAIN... DISCONTENTMENT.
SOMETIMES, IN MY DEEPEST DREAMS, I SEEM TO SEE A WORLD LIKE OURS...
...YET DIFFERENT.

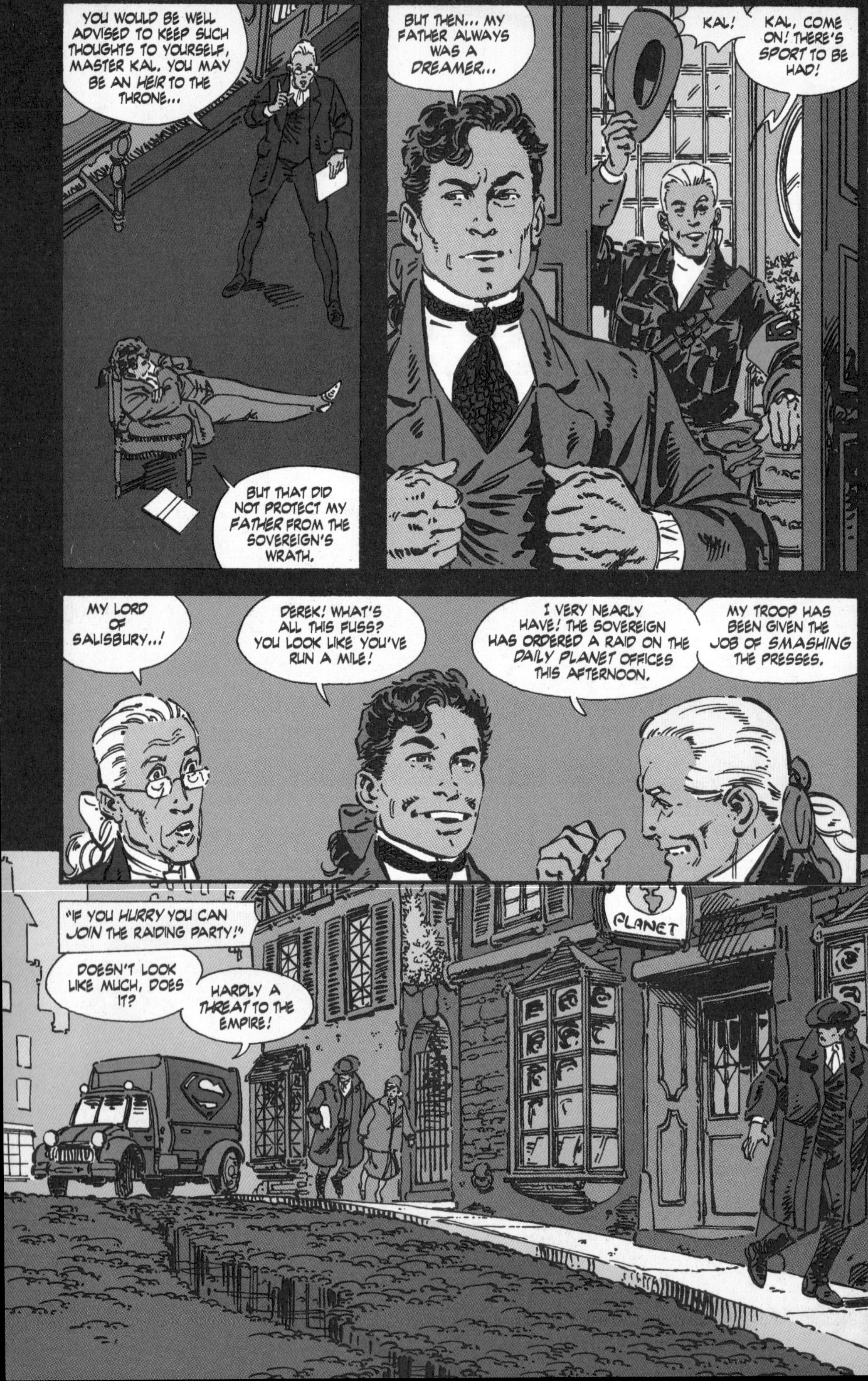
YOU WOULD BE WELL ADVISED TO KEEP SUCH THOUGHTS TO YOURSELF, MASTER KAL. YOU MAY BE AN HEIR TO THE THRONE...
BUT THAT DID NOT PROTECT MY FATHER FROM THE SOVEREIGN'S WRATH.
BUT THEN... MY FATHER ALWAYS WAS A DREAMER...
KAL!
KAL, COME ON! THERE'S SPORT TO BE HAD!
MY LORD OF SALISBURY...!
DEREK! WHAT'S ALL THIS FUSS? YOU LOOK LIKE YOU'VE RUN A MILE!
I VERY NEARLY HAVE! THE SOVEREIGN HAS ORDERED A RAID ON THE DAILY PLANET OFFICES THIS AFTERNOON.
MY TROOP HAS BEEN GIVEN THE JOB OF SMASHING THE PRESSES.
"IF YOU HURRY YOU CAN JOIN THE RAIDING PARTY!"
PLANET
DOESN'T LOOK LIKE MUCH, DOES IT?
HARDLY A THREAT TO THE EMPIRE!

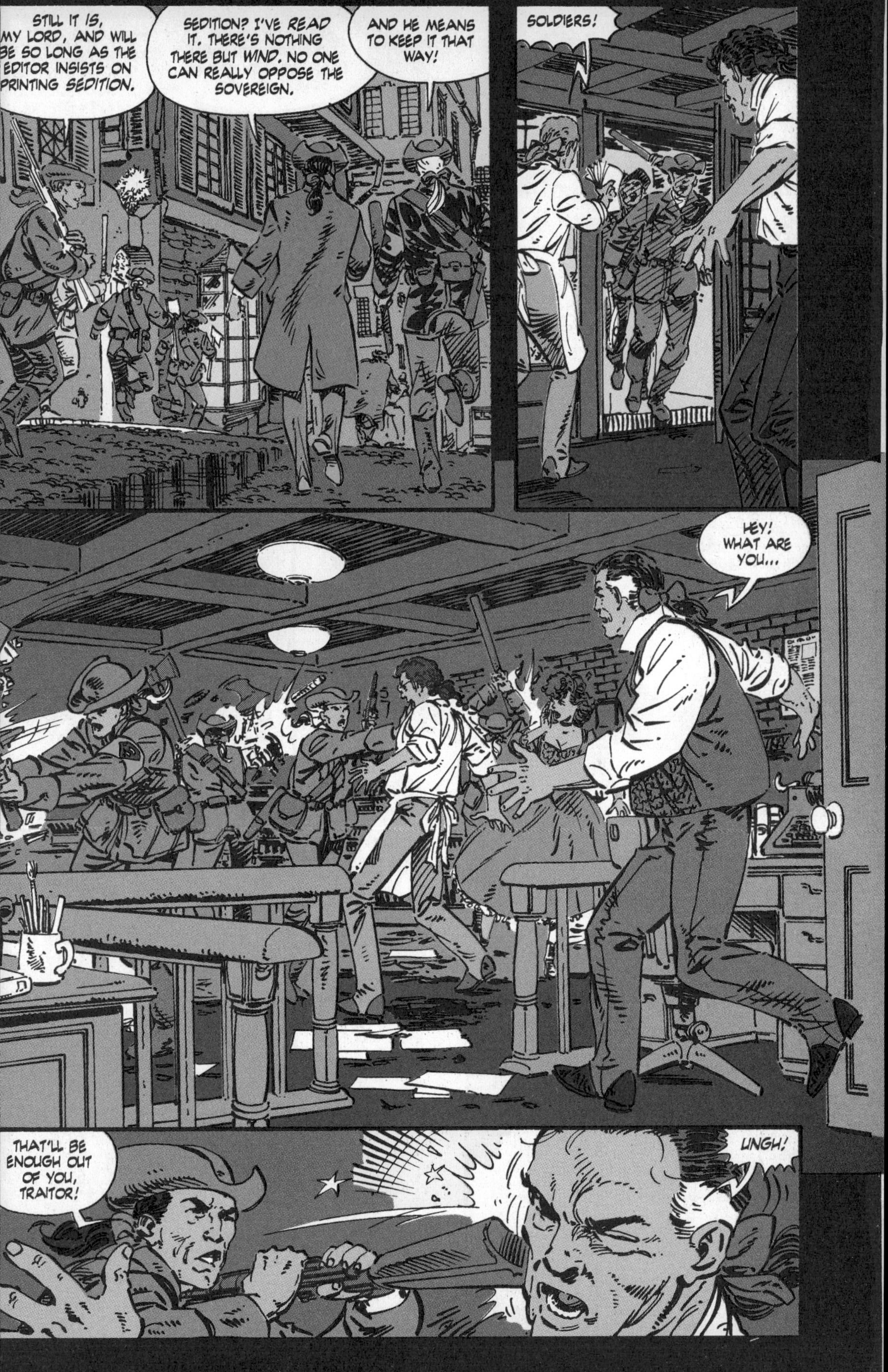
STILL IT IS, MY LORD, AND WILL BE SO LONG AS THE EDITOR INSISTS ON PRINTING SEDITION.
SEDITION? I'VE READ IT. THERE'S NOTHING THERE BUT WIND. NO ONE CAN REALLY OPPOSE THE SOVEREIGN.
AND HE MEANS TO KEEP IT THAT WAY!
SOLDIERS!
HEY! WHAT ARE YOU...
THAT'LL BE ENOUGH OUT OF YOU, TRAITOR!
UNGH!

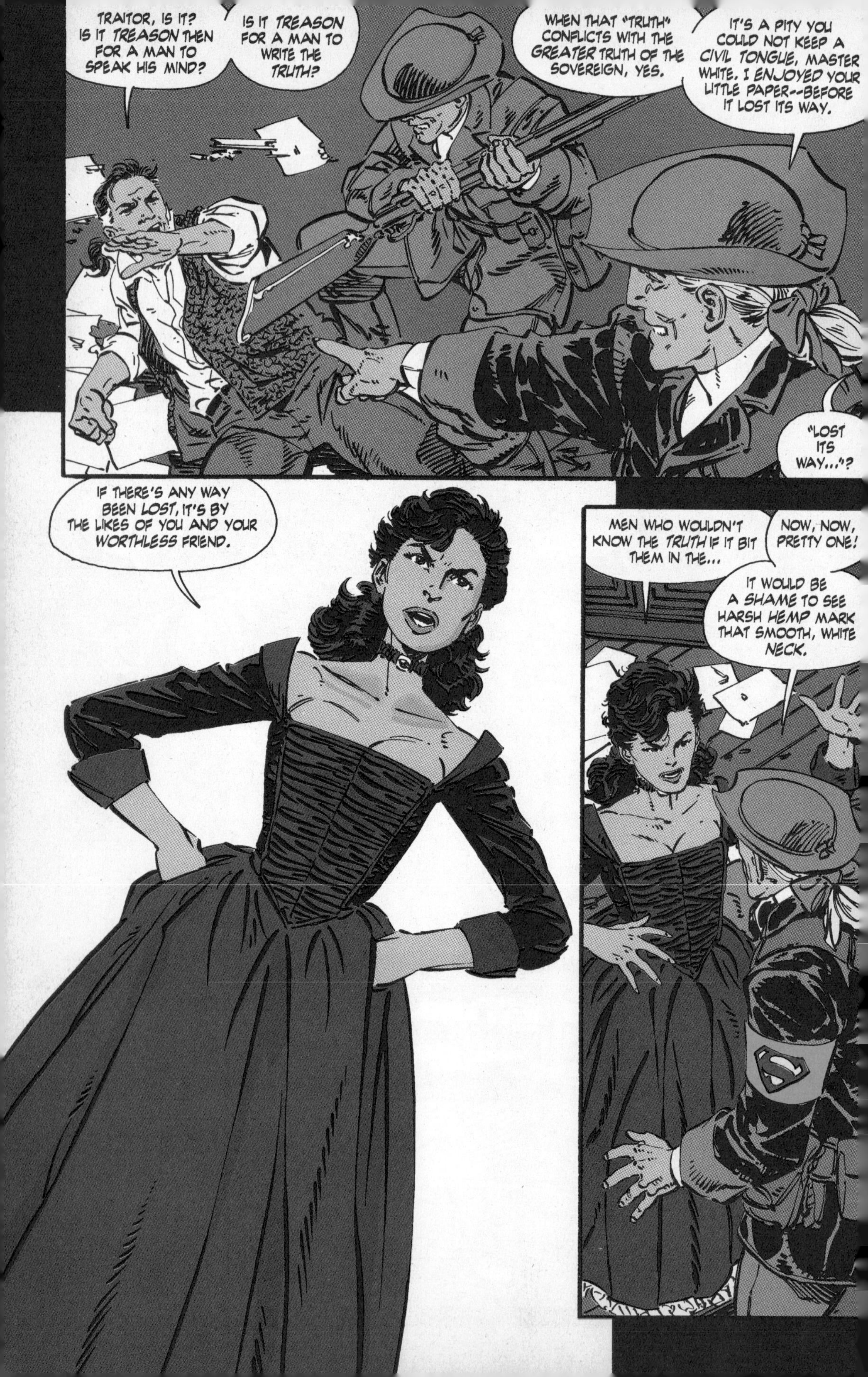
TRAITOR, IS IT? IS IT TREASON THEN FOR A MAN TO SPEAK HIS MIND?
IS IT TREASON FOR A MAN TO WRITE THE TRUTH?
WHEN THAT "TRUTH" CONFLICTS WITH THE GREATER TRUTH OF THE SOVEREIGN, YES.
IT'S A PITY YOU COULD NOT KEEP A CIVIL TONGUE, MASTER WHITE. I ENJOYED YOUR LITTLE PAPER--BEFORE IT LOST ITS WAY.
"LOST ITS WAY..."?
IF THERE'S ANY WAY BEEN LOST, IT'S BY THE LIKES OF YOU AND YOUR WORTHLESS FRIEND.
MEN WHO WOULDN'T KNOW THE TRUTH IF IT BIT THEM IN THE...
NOW, NOW, PRETTY ONE!
IT WOULD BE A SHAME TO SEE HARSH HEMP MARK THAT SMOOTH, WHITE NECK.

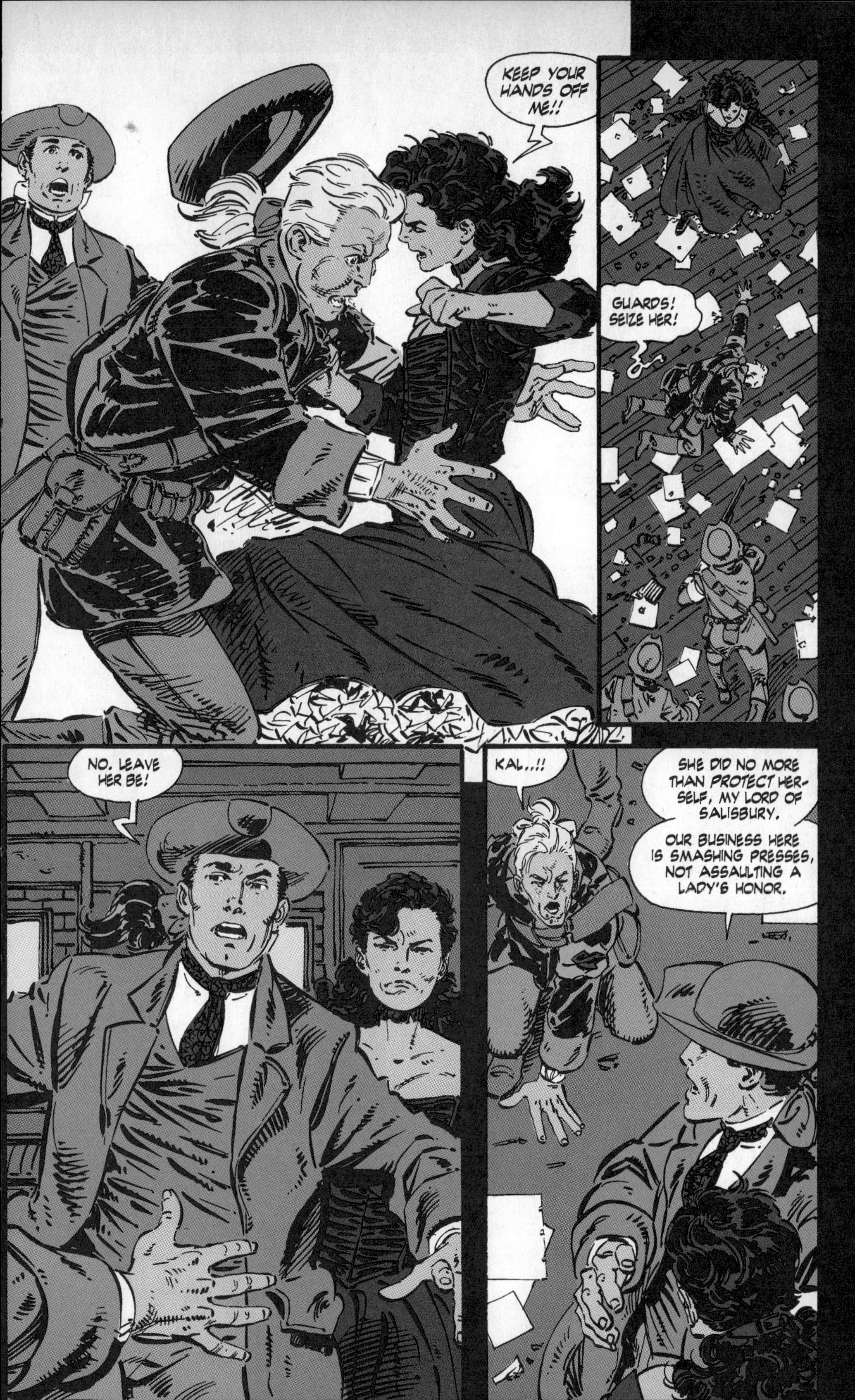
KEEP YOUR HANDS OFF ME!!
GUARDS! SEIZE HER!
NO. LEAVE HER BE!
KAL..!!
SHE DID NO MORE THAN PROTECT HER-SELF, MY LORD OF SALISBURY.
OUR BUSINESS HERE IS SMASHING PRESSES, NOT ASSAULTING A LADY'S HONOR.

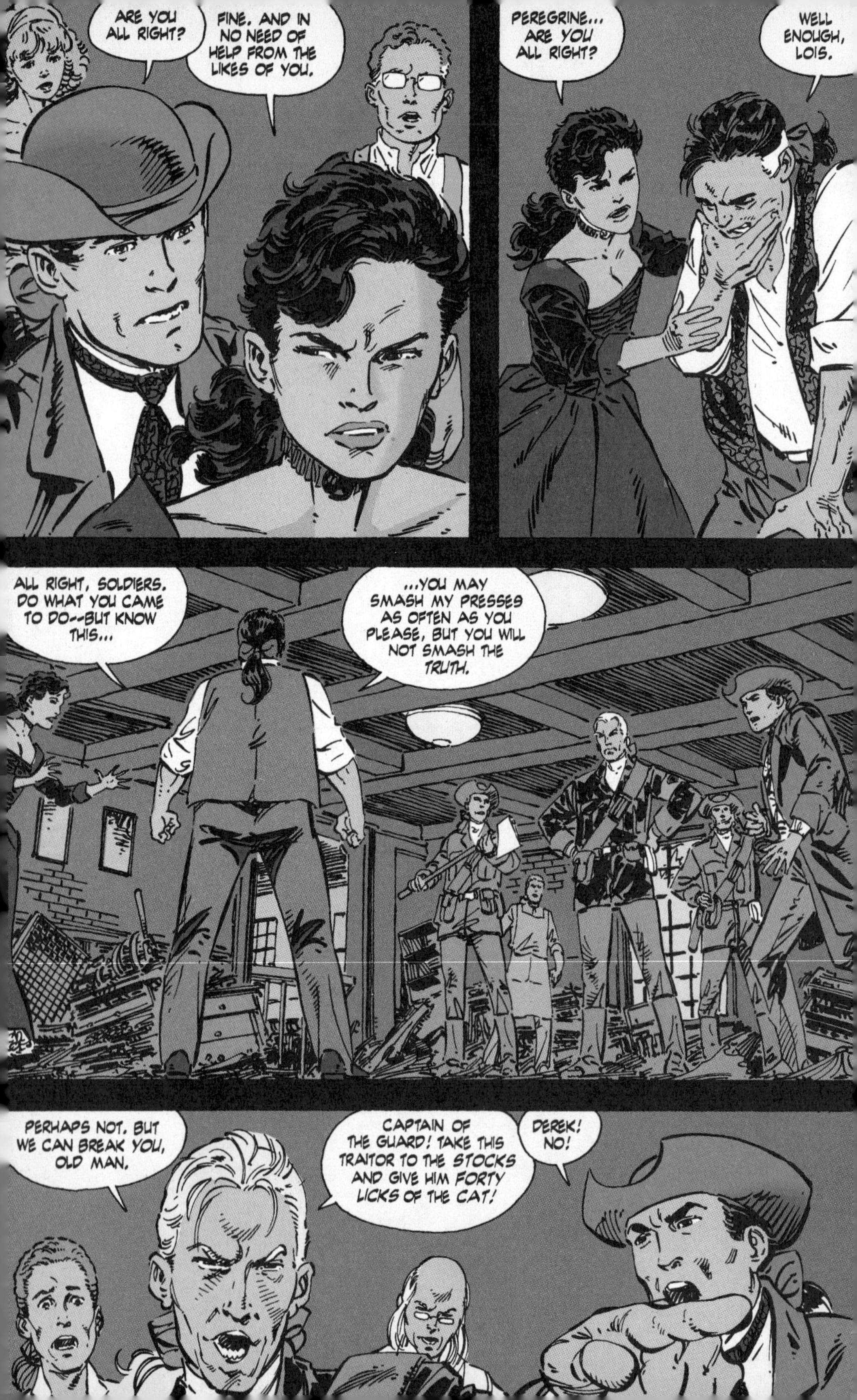
ARE YOU ALL RIGHT?
FINE. AND IN NO NEED OF HELP FROM THE LIKES OF YOU.
PEREGRINE... ARE YOU ALL RIGHT?
WELL ENOUGH, LOIS.
ALL RIGHT, SOLDIERS. DO WHAT YOU CAME TO DO--BUT KNOW THIS...
...YOU MAY SMASH MY PRESSES AS OFTEN AS YOU PLEASE, BUT YOU WILL NOT SMASH THE TRUTH.
PERHAPS NOT. BUT WE CAN BREAK YOU, OLD MAN.
CAPTAIN OF THE GUARD! TAKE THIS TRAITOR TO THE STOCKS AND GIVE HIM FORTY LICKS OF THE CAT!
DEREK! NO!

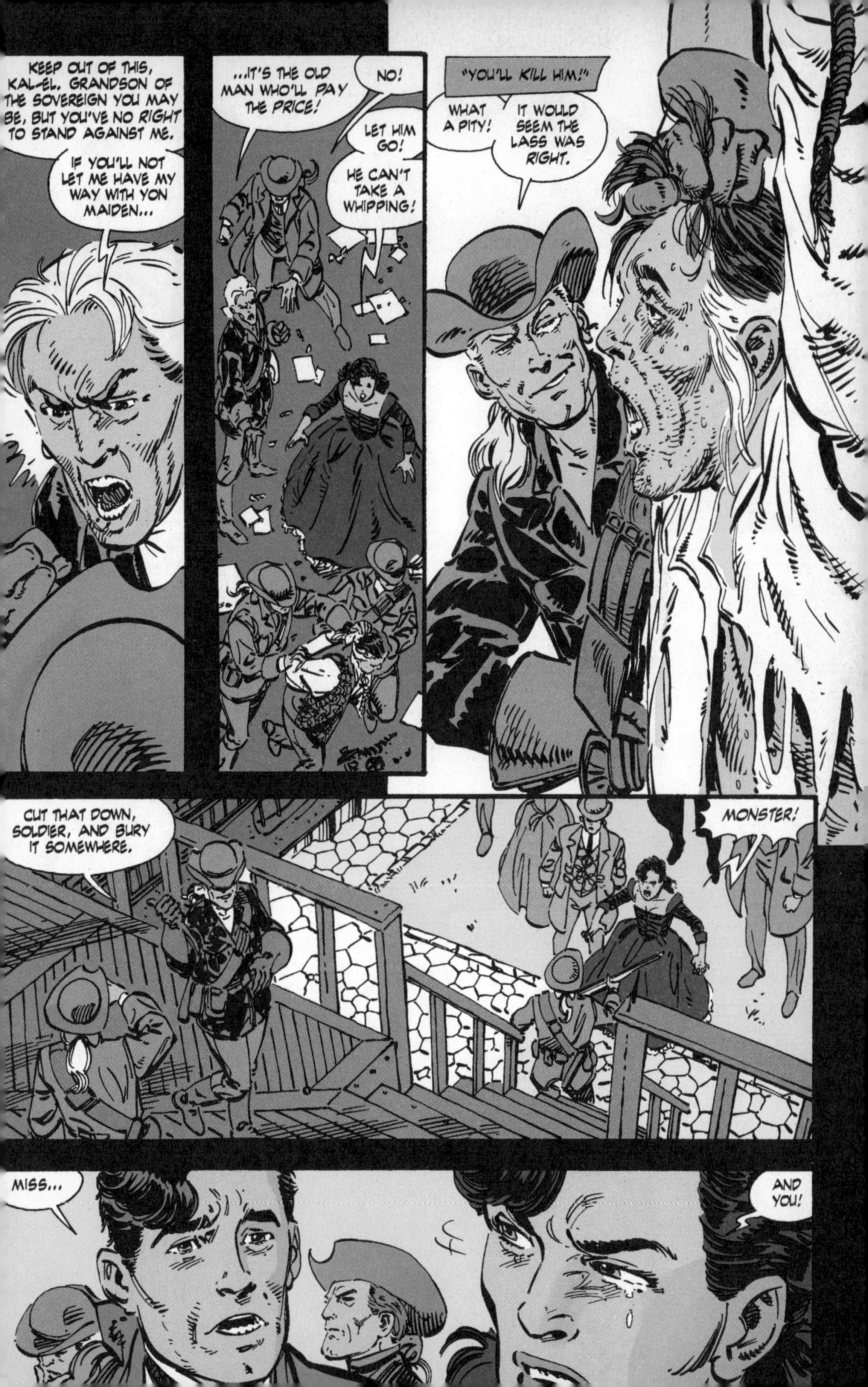
KEEP OUT OF THIS, KAL-EL. GRANDSON OF THE SOVEREIGN YOU MAY BE, BUT YOU'VE NO RIGHT TO STAND AGAINST ME.
IF YOU'LL NOT LET ME HAVE MY WAY WITH YON MAIDEN...
...IT'S THE OLD MAN WHO'LL PAY THE PRICE!
NO!
LET HIM GO!
HE CAN'T TAKE A WHIPPING!
"YOU'LL KILL HIM!"
WHAT A PITY!
IT WOULD SEEM THE LASS WAS RIGHT.
CUT THAT DOWN, SOLDIER, AND BURY IT SOMEWHERE.
MONSTER!
MISS...
AND YOU!

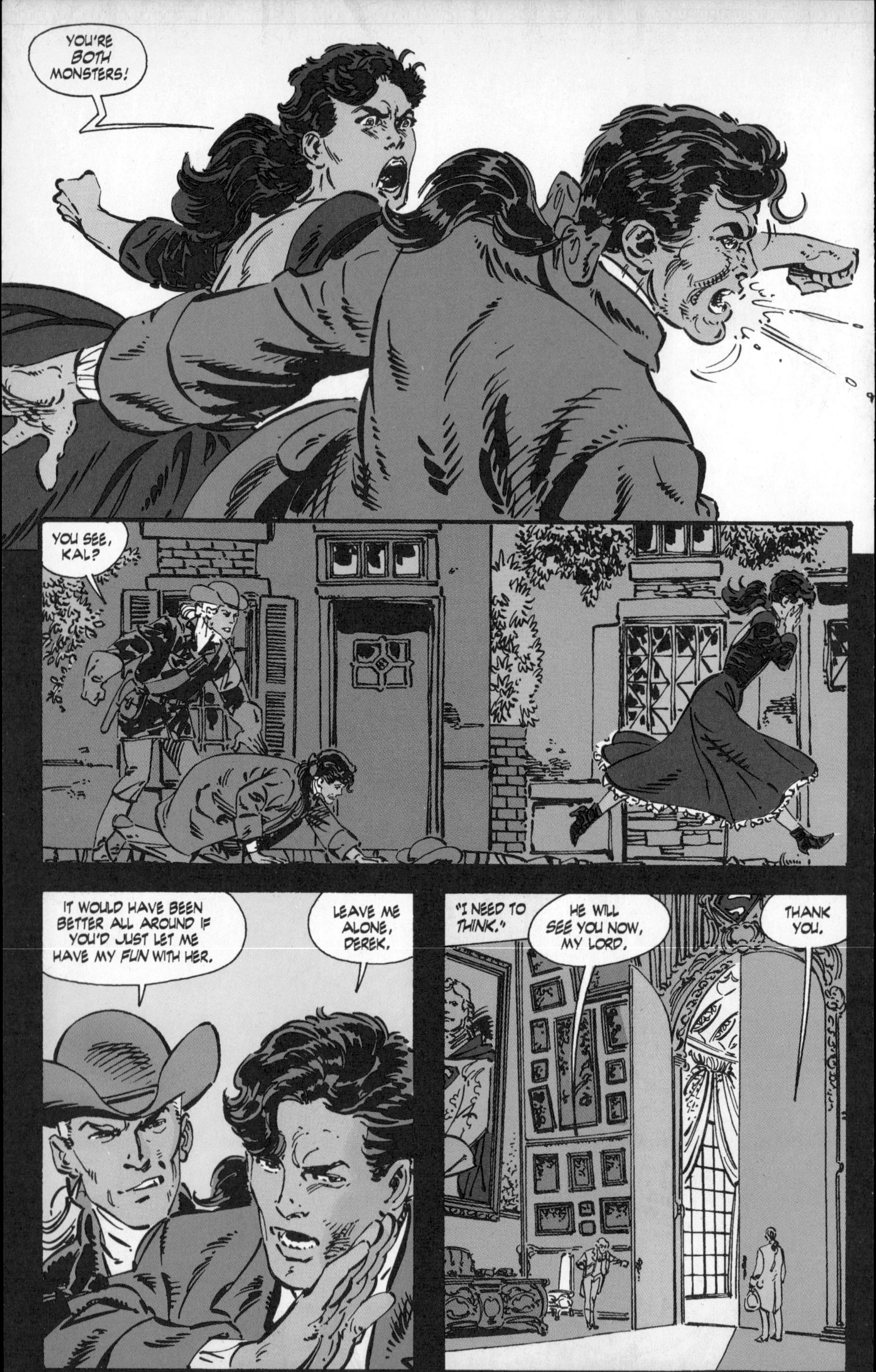
YOU'RE BOTH MONSTERS!
YOU SEE, KAL?
IT WOULD HAVE BEEN BETTER ALL AROUND IF YOU'D JUST LET ME HAVE MY FUN WITH HER.
LEAVE ME ALONE, DEREK.
"I NEED TO THINK."
HE WILL SEE YOU NOW, MY LORD.
THANK YOU.

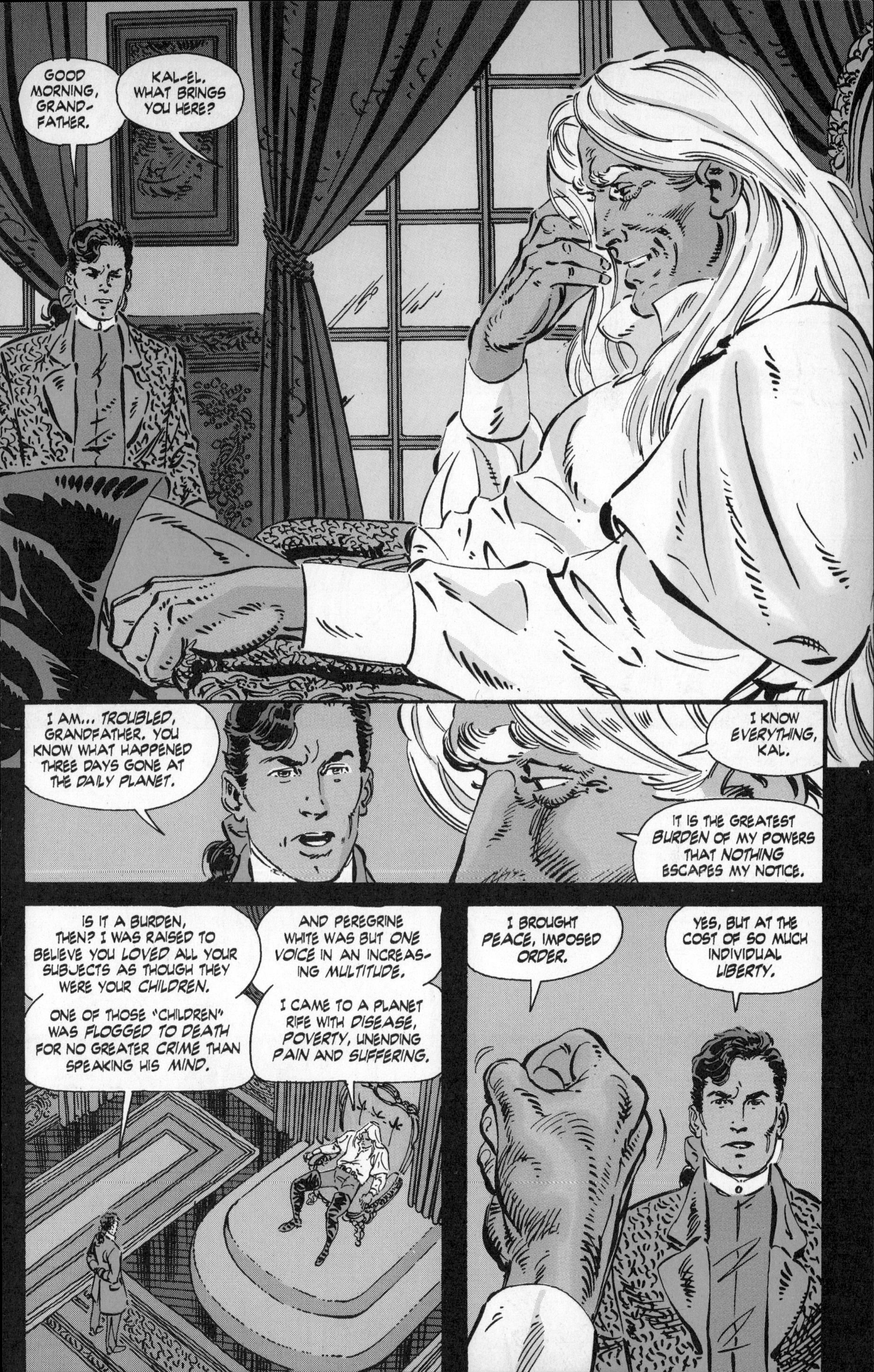
GOOD MORNING, GRAND-FATHER.
KAL-EL. WHAT BRINGS YOU HERE?
I AM... TROUBLED, GRANDFATHER. YOU KNOW WHAT HAPPENED THREE DAYS GONE AT THE DAILY PLANET.
I KNOW EVERYTHING, KAL.
IT IS THE GREATEST BURDEN OF MY POWERS THAT NOTHING ESCAPES MY NOTICE.
IS IT A BURDEN, THEN? I WAS RAISED TO BELIEVE YOU LOVED ALL YOUR SUBJECTS AS THOUGH THEY WERE YOUR CHILDREN.
ONE OF THOSE "CHILDREN" WAS FLOGGED TO DEATH FOR NO GREATER CRIME THAN SPEAKING HIS MIND.
AND PEREGRINE WHITE WAS BUT ONE VOICE IN AN INCREAS-ING MULTITUDE.
I CAME TO A PLANET RIFE WITH DISEASE, POVERTY, UNENDING PAIN AND SUFFERING.
I BROUGHT PEACE, IMPOSED ORDER.
YES, BUT AT THE COST OF SO MUCH INDIVIDUAL LIBERTY.

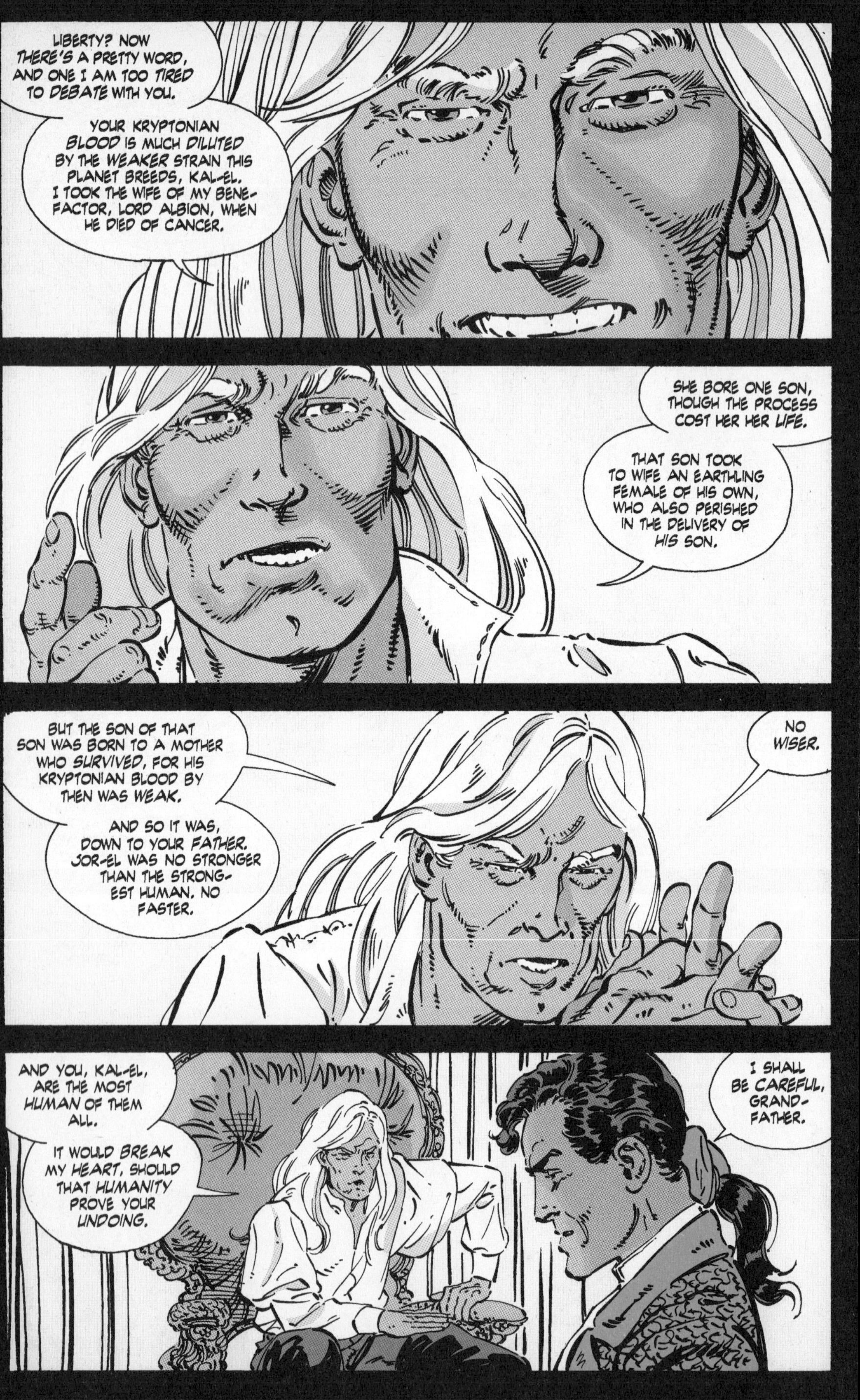
LIBERTY? NOW THERE'S A PRETTY WORD, AND ONE I AM TOO TIRED TO DEBATE WITH YOU.
YOUR KRYPTONIAN BLOOD IS MUCH DILUTED BY THE WEAKER STRAIN THIS PLANET BREEDS, KAL-EL. I TOOK THE WIFE OF MY BENEFACTOR, LORD ALBION, WHEN HE DIED OF CANCER.
SHE BORE ONE SON, THOUGH THE PROCESS COST HER HER LIFE.
THAT SON TOOK TO WIFE AN EARTHLING FEMALE OF HIS OWN, WHO ALSO PERISHED IN THE DELIVERY OF HIS SON.
BUT THE SON OF THAT SON WAS BORN TO A MOTHER WHO SURVIVED, FOR HIS KRYPTONIAN BLOOD BY THEN WAS WEAK.
AND SO IT WAS, DOWN TO YOUR FATHER. JOR-EL WAS NO STRONGER THAN THE STRONGEST HUMAN. NO FASTER.
NO WISER.
AND YOU, KAL-EL, ARE THE MOST HUMAN OF THEM ALL.
IT WOULD BREAK MY HEART, SHOULD THAT HUMANITY PROVE YOUR UNDOING.
I SHALL BE CAREFUL, GRANDFATHER.

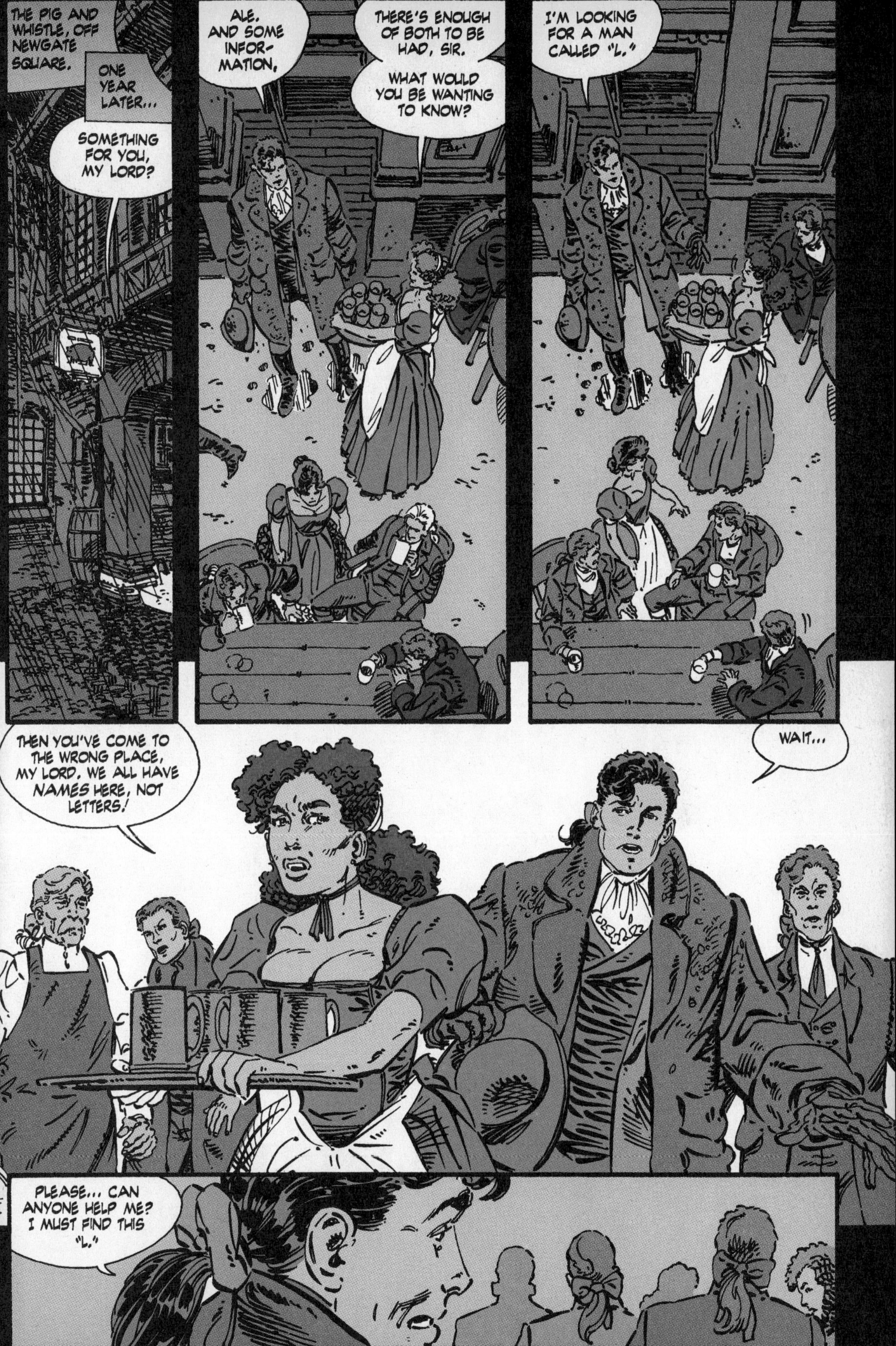

THE PIG AND WHISTLE, OFF NEWGATE SQUARE.
ONE YEAR LATER...
SOMETHING FOR YOU, MY LORD?
ALE. AND SOME INFORMATION.
THERE'S ENOUGH OF BOTH TO BE HAD, SIR.
WHAT WOULD YOU BE WANTING TO KNOW?
I'M LOOKING FOR A MAN CALLED "L."
THEN YOU'VE COME TO THE WRONG PLACE, MY LORD. WE ALL HAVE NAMES HERE, NOT LETTERS!
WAIT...
PLEASE... CAN ANYONE HELP ME? I MUST FIND THIS "L."

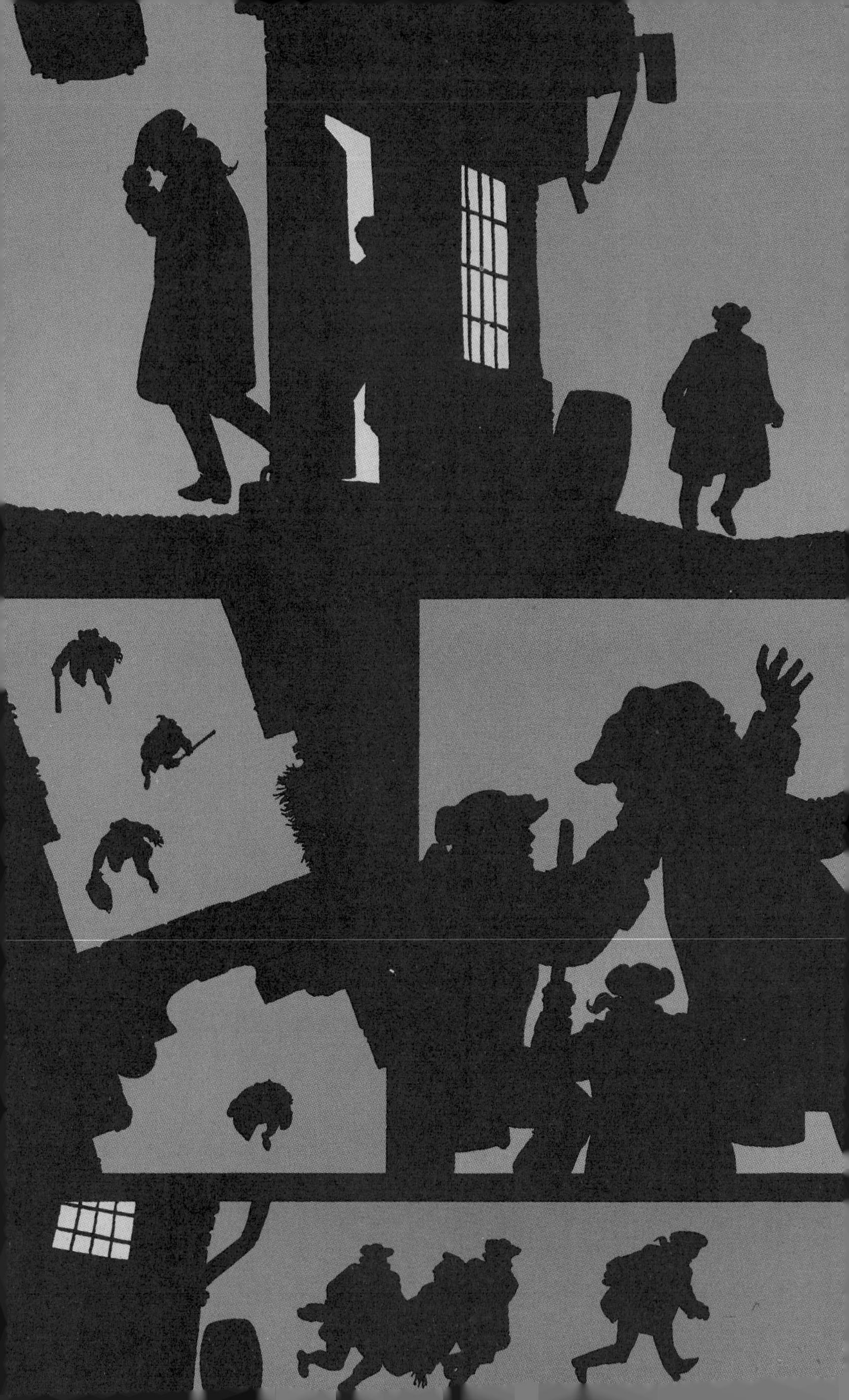

WAKE HIM UP.
AWAKE, ARE YOU, MY LORD? AWAKE ENOUGH TO FEEL IT WHEN WE SLIT YOUR THROAT.
WAIT;
ARE YOU... PLEASE; I MEAN NO HARM! I ONLY NEED TO MEET THIS MAN "L."
IT'S VITAL THAT I SPEAK WITH HIM.
AND WHAT DO YOU KNOW ABOUT "L"?

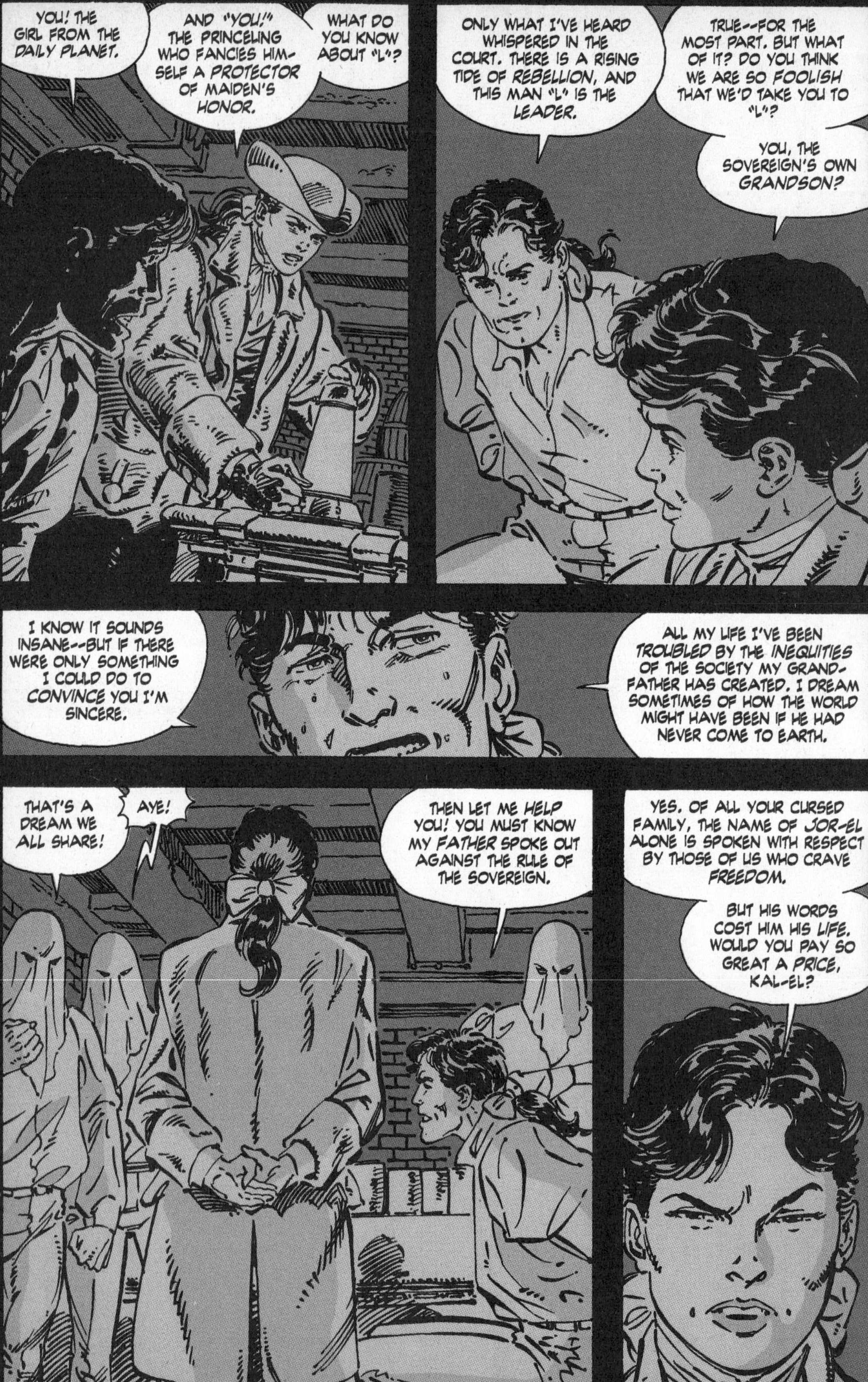
YOU! THE GIRL FROM THE DAILY PLANET.
AND "YOU!" THE PRINCELING WHO FANCIES HIMSELF A PROTECTOR OF MAIDEN'S HONOR.
WHAT DO YOU KNOW ABOUT "L"?
ONLY WHAT I'VE HEARD WHISPERED IN THE COURT. THERE IS A RISING TIDE OF REBELLION, AND THIS MAN "L" IS THE LEADER.
TRUE--FOR THE MOST PART. BUT WHAT OF IT? DO YOU THINK WE ARE SO FOOLISH THAT WE'D TAKE YOU TO "L"?
YOU, THE SOVEREIGN'S OWN GRANDSON?
I KNOW IT SOUNDS INSANE--BUT IF THERE WERE ONLY SOMETHING I COULD DO TO CONVINCE YOU I'M SINCERE.
ALL MY LIFE I'VE BEEN TROUBLED BY THE INEQUITIES OF THE SOCIETY MY GRANDFATHER HAS CREATED. I DREAM SOMETIMES OF HOW THE WORLD MIGHT HAVE BEEN IF HE HAD NEVER COME TO EARTH.
THAT'S A DREAM WE ALL SHARE!
AYE!
THEN LET ME HELP YOU! YOU MUST KNOW MY FATHER SPOKE OUT AGAINST THE RULE OF THE SOVEREIGN.
YES. OF ALL YOUR CURSED FAMILY, THE NAME OF JOR-EL ALONE IS SPOKEN WITH RESPECT BY THOSE OF US WHO CRAVE FREEDOM.
BUT HIS WORDS COST HIM HIS LIFE. WOULD YOU PAY SO GREAT A PRICE, KAL-EL?

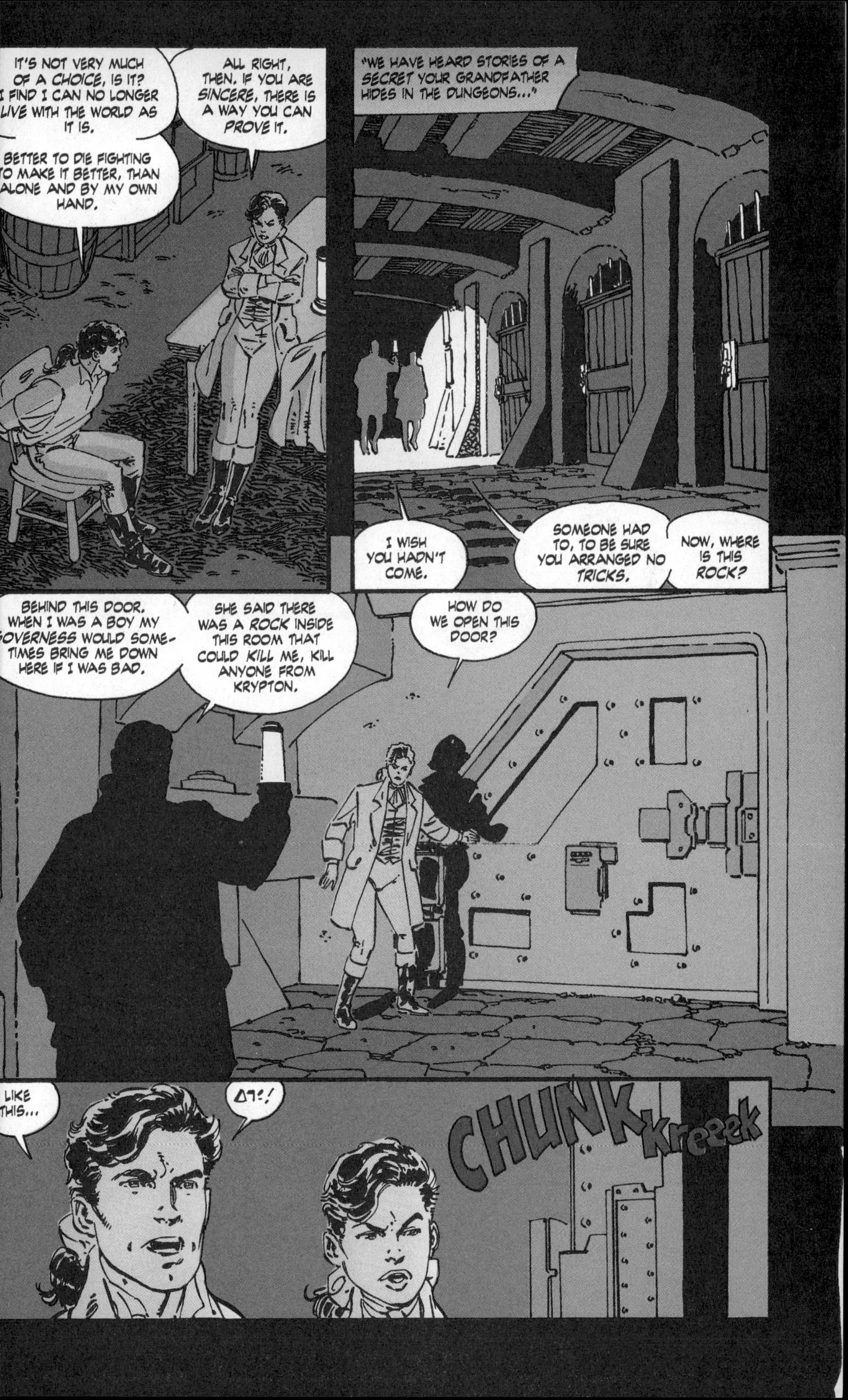

IT'S NOT VERY MUCH OF A CHOICE, IS IT? I FIND I CAN NO LONGER LIVE WITH THE WORLD AS IT IS.
BETTER TO DIE FIGHTING TO MAKE IT BETTER, THAN ALONE AND BY MY OWN HAND.
ALL RIGHT, THEN. IF YOU ARE SINCERE, THERE IS A WAY YOU CAN PROVE IT.
"WE HAVE HEARD STORIES OF A SECRET YOUR GRANDFATHER HIDES IN THE DUNGEONS..."
I WISH YOU HADN'T COME.
SOMEONE HAD TO, TO BE SURE YOU ARRANGED NO TRICKS.
NOW, WHERE IS THIS ROCK?
BEHIND THIS DOOR. WHEN I WAS A BOY MY GOVERNESS WOULD SOMETIMES BRING ME DOWN HERE IF I WAS BAD.
SHE SAID THERE WAS A ROCK INSIDE THIS ROOM THAT COULD KILL ME, KILL ANYONE FROM KRYPTON.
HOW DO WE OPEN THIS DOOR?
LIKE THIS...
CHUNK
Kreeek

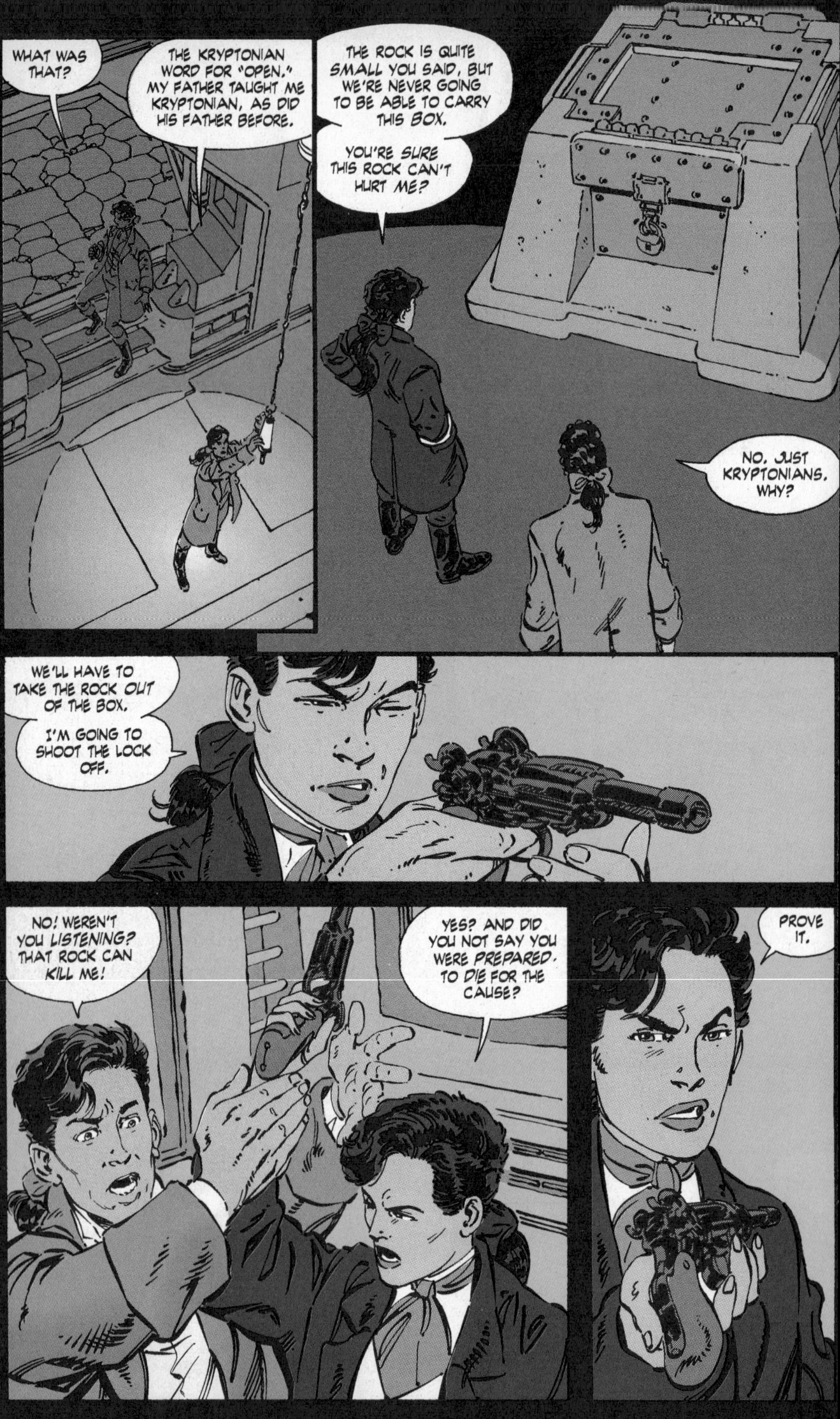
WHAT WAS THAT?
THE KRYPTONIAN WORD FOR "OPEN." MY FATHER TAUGHT ME KRYPTONIAN, AS DID HIS FATHER BEFORE.
THE ROCK IS QUITE SMALL YOU SAID, BUT WE'RE NEVER GOING TO BE ABLE TO CARRY THIS BOX.
YOU'RE SURE THIS ROCK CAN'T HURT ME?
NO. JUST KRYPTONIANS. WHY?
WE'LL HAVE TO TAKE THE ROCK OUT OF THE BOX.
I'M GOING TO SHOOT THE LOCK OFF.
NO! WEREN'T YOU LISTENING? THAT ROCK CAN KILL ME!
YES? AND DID YOU NOT SAY YOU WERE PREPARED TO DIE FOR THE CAUSE?
PROVE IT.

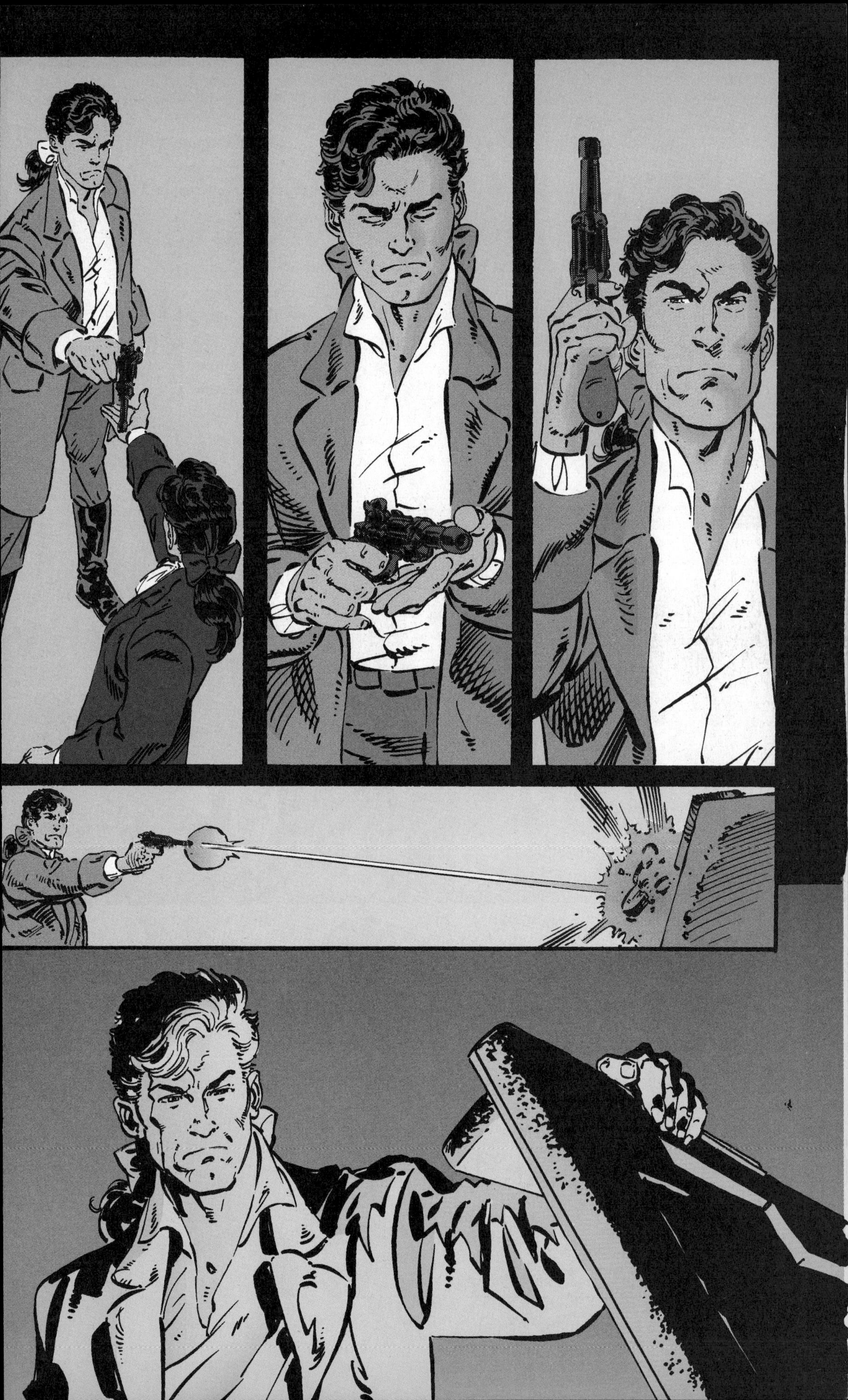

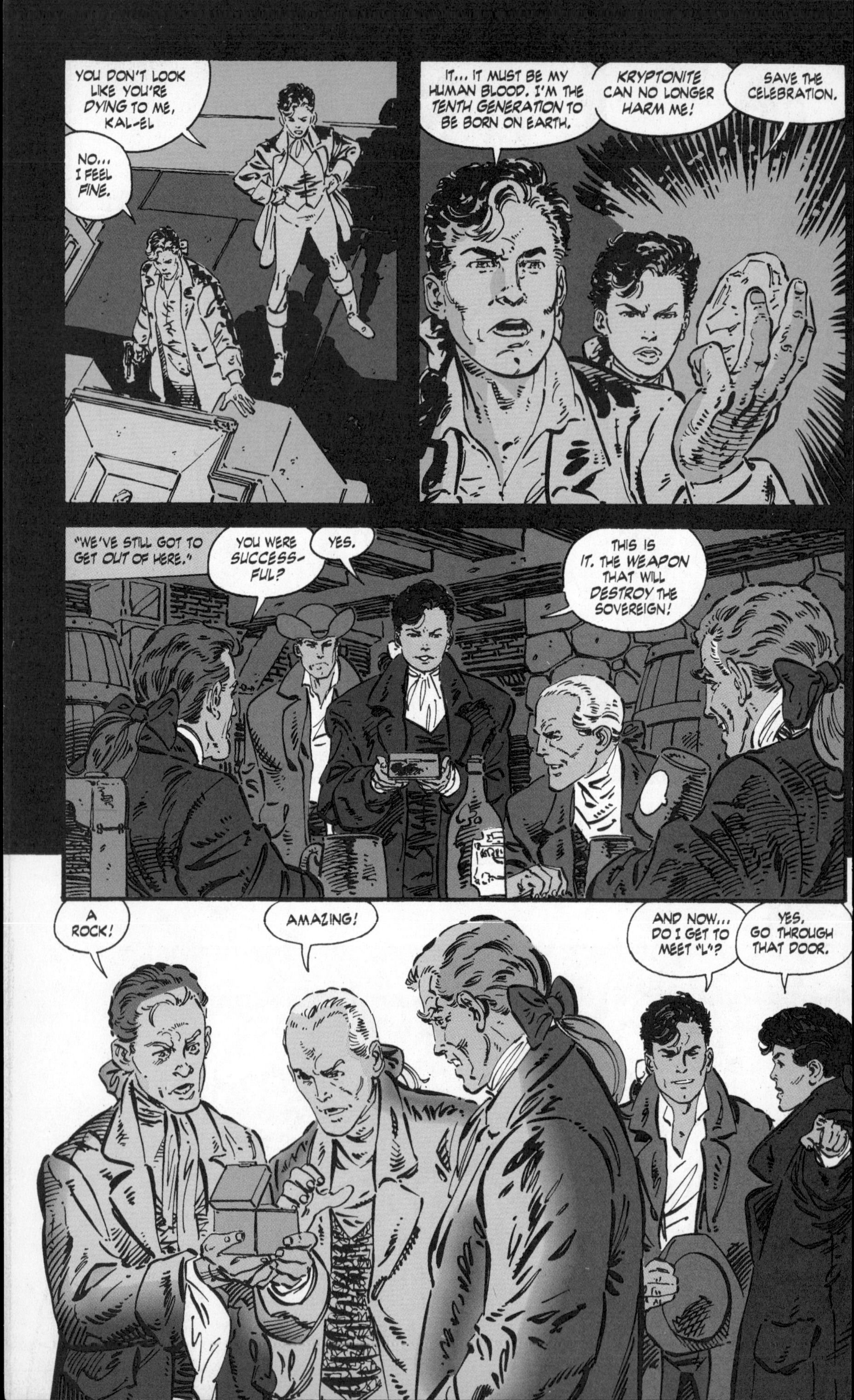
YOU DON'T LOOK LIKE YOU'RE DYING TO ME, KAL-EL
NO... I FEEL FINE.
IT... IT MUST BE MY HUMAN BLOOD. I'M THE TENTH GENERATION TO BE BORN ON EARTH.
KRYPTONITE CAN NO LONGER HARM ME!
SAVE THE CELEBRATION.
"WE'VE STILL GOT TO GET OUT OF HERE."
YOU WERE SUCCESS-FUL?
YES.
THIS IS IT. THE WEAPON THAT WILL DESTROY THE SOVEREIGN!
A ROCK!
AMAZING!
AND NOW... DO I GET TO MEET "L"?
YES. GO THROUGH THAT DOOR.

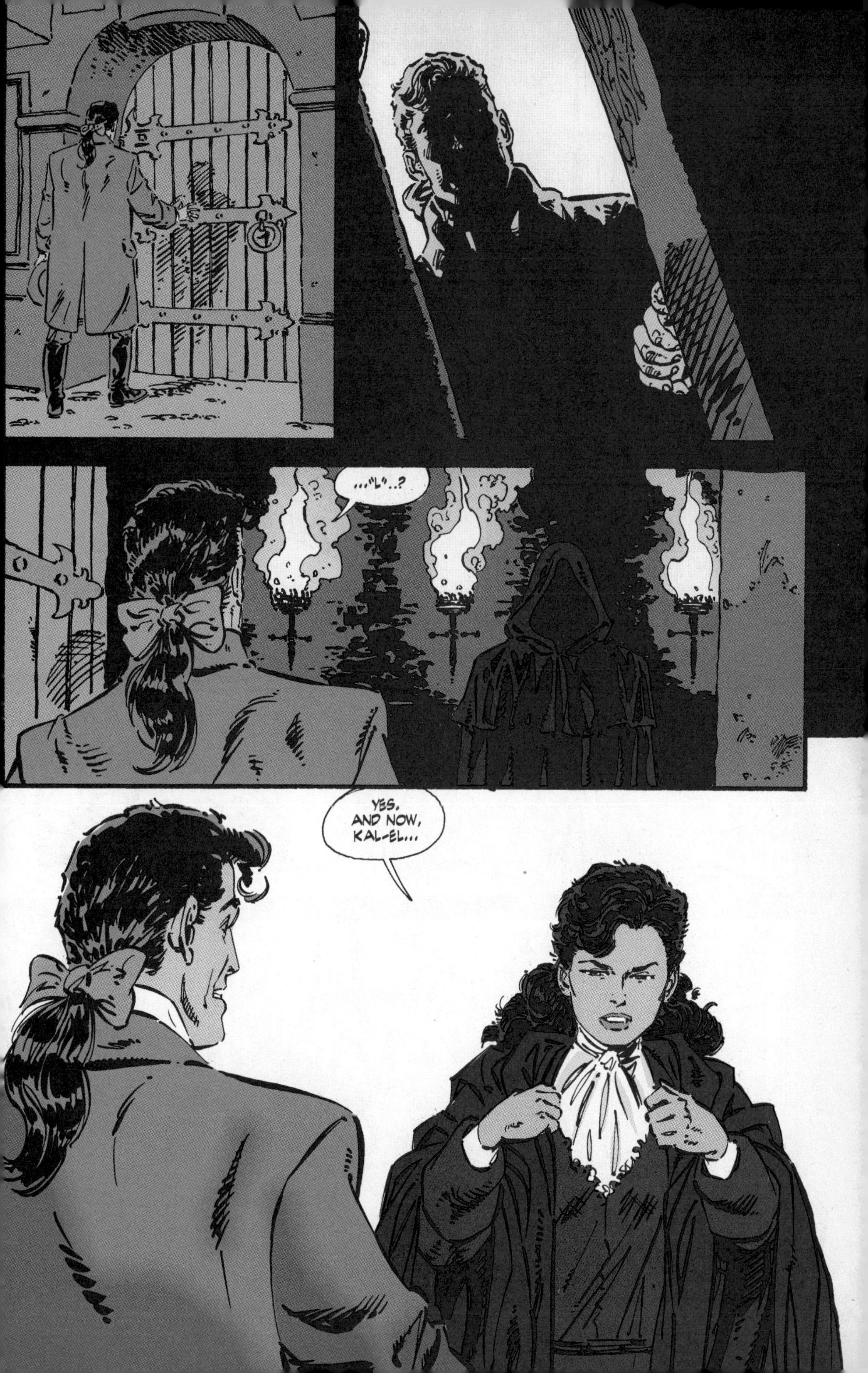
..."L"..?
YES. AND NOW, KAL-EL...

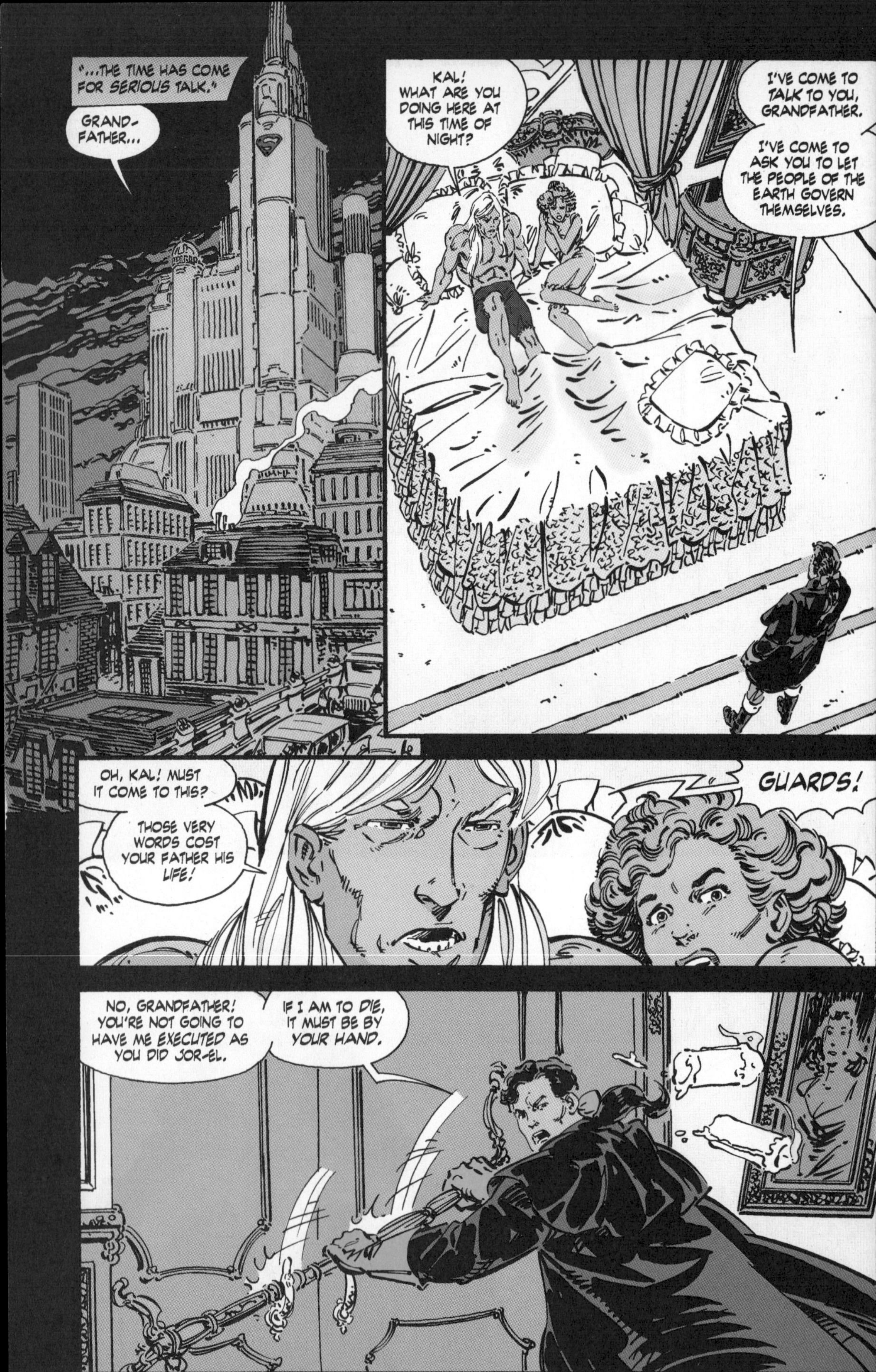
"...THE TIME HAS COME FOR SERIOUS TALK."
GRAND-FATHER...
KAL! WHAT ARE YOU DOING HERE AT THIS TIME OF NIGHT?
I'VE COME TO TALK TO YOU, GRANDFATHER.
I'VE COME TO ASK YOU TO LET THE PEOPLE OF THE EARTH GOVERN THEMSELVES.
OH, KAL! MUST IT COME TO THIS?
THOSE VERY WORDS COST YOUR FATHER HIS LIFE!
GUARDS!
NO, GRANDFATHER! YOU'RE NOT GOING TO HAVE ME EXECUTED AS YOU DID JOR-EL.
IF I AM TO DIE, IT MUST BE BY YOUR HAND.

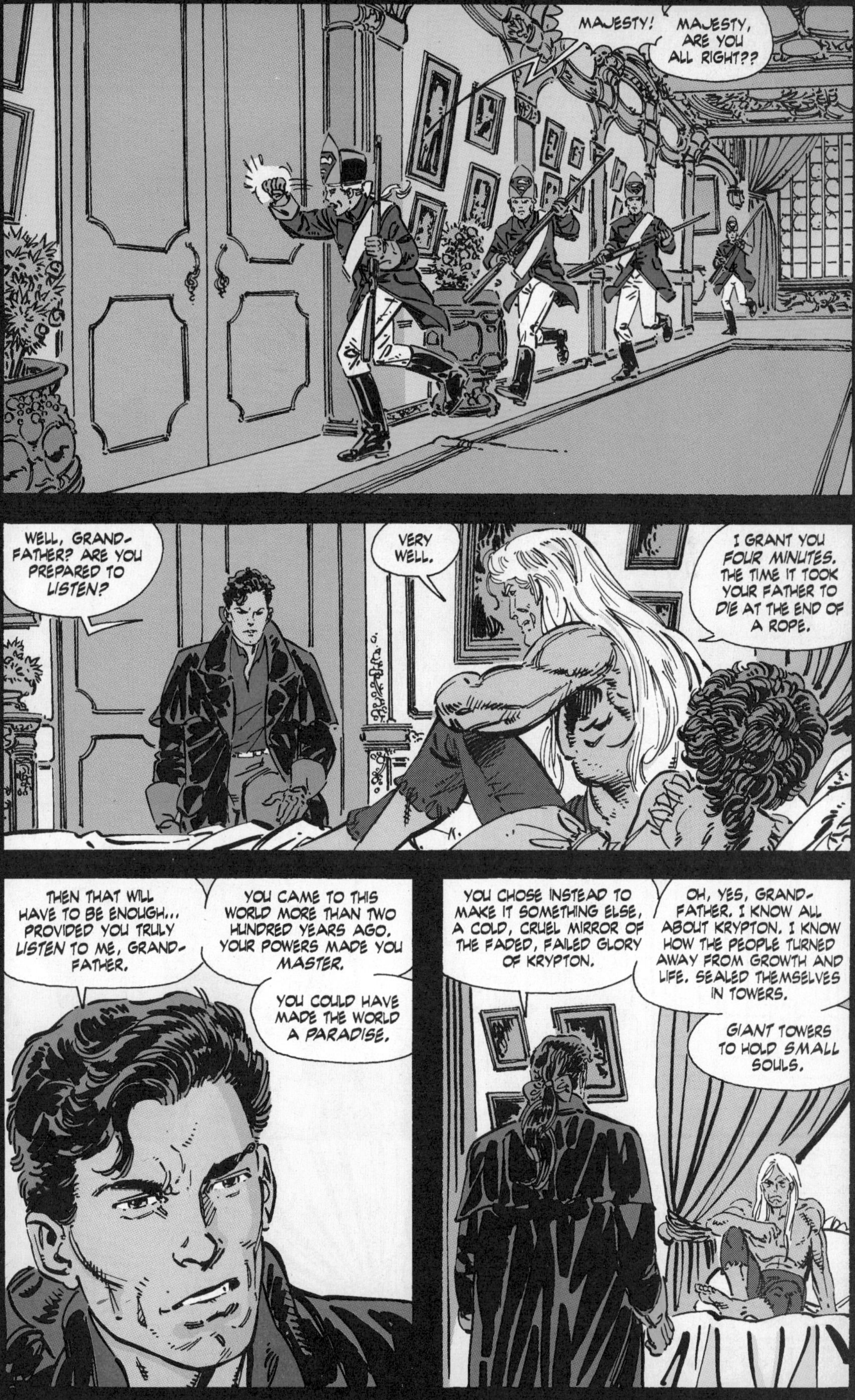
MAJESTY!
MAJESTY, ARE YOU ALL RIGHT??
WELL, GRAND-FATHER? ARE YOU PREPARED TO LISTEN?
VERY WELL.
I GRANT YOU FOUR MINUTES. THE TIME IT TOOK YOUR FATHER TO DIE AT THE END OF A ROPE.
THEN THAT WILL HAVE TO BE ENOUGH... PROVIDED YOU TRULY LISTEN TO ME, GRAND-FATHER.
YOU CAME TO THIS WORLD MORE THAN TWO HUNDRED YEARS AGO. YOUR POWERS MADE YOU MASTER.
YOU COULD HAVE MADE THE WORLD A PARADISE.
YOU CHOSE INSTEAD TO MAKE IT SOMETHING ELSE, A COLD, CRUEL MIRROR OF THE FADED, FAILED GLORY OF KRYPTON.
OH, YES, GRAND-FATHER. I KNOW ALL ABOUT KRYPTON. I KNOW HOW THE PEOPLE TURNED AWAY FROM GROWTH AND LIFE. SEALED THEMSELVES IN TOWERS.
GIANT TOWERS TO HOLD SMALL SOULS.

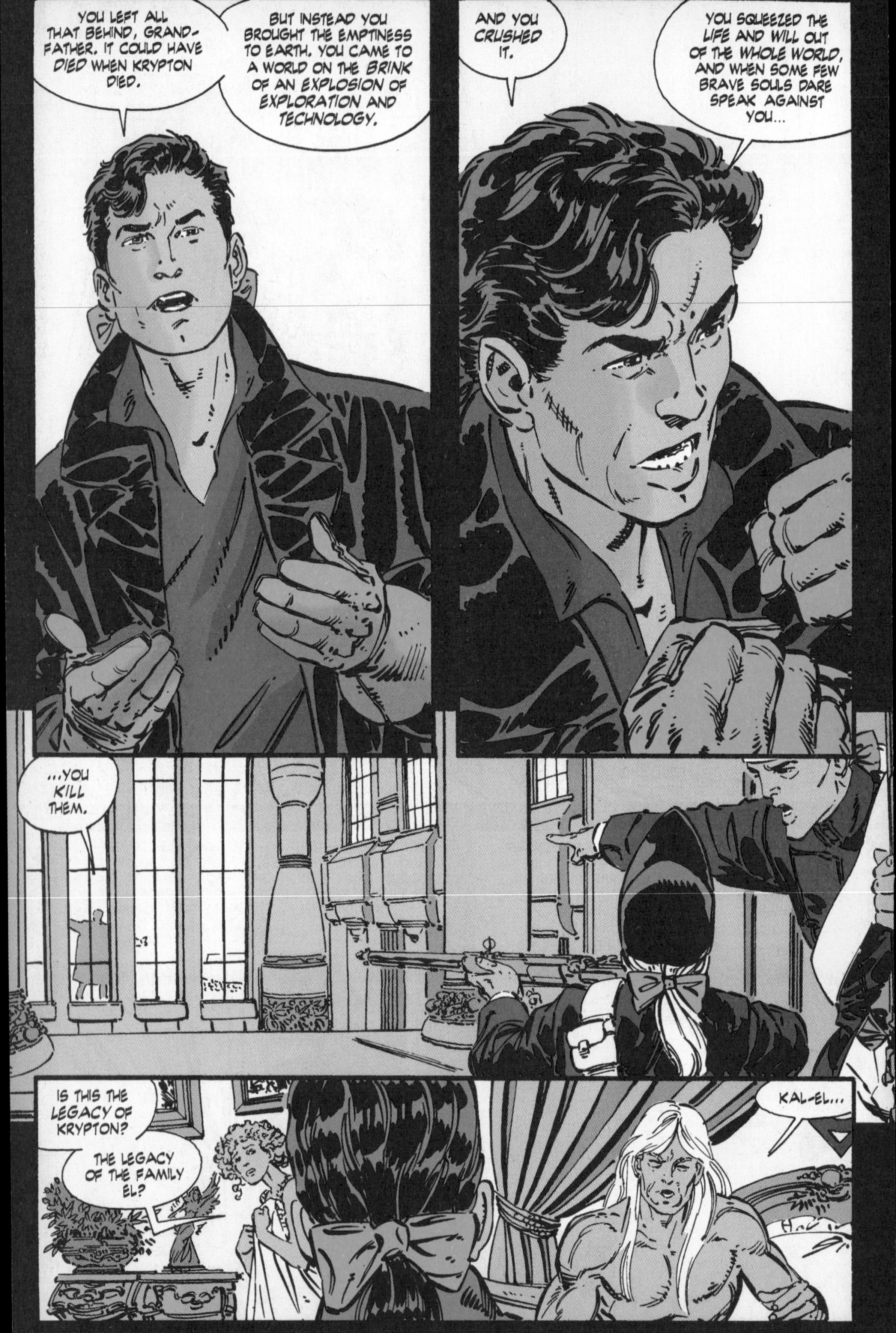
YOU LEFT ALL THAT BEHIND, GRAND-FATHER. IT COULD HAVE DIED WHEN KRYPTON DIED.
BUT INSTEAD YOU BROUGHT THE EMPTINESS TO EARTH. YOU CAME TO A WORLD ON THE BRINK OF AN EXPLOSION OF EXPLORATION AND TECHNOLOGY.
AND YOU CRUSHED IT.
YOU SQUEEZED THE LIFE AND WILL OUT OF THE WHOLE WORLD, AND WHEN SOME FEW BRAVE SOULS DARE SPEAK AGAINST YOU...
...YOU KILL THEM.
IS THIS THE LEGACY OF KRYPTON?
THE LEGACY OF THE FAMILY EL?
KAL-EL...

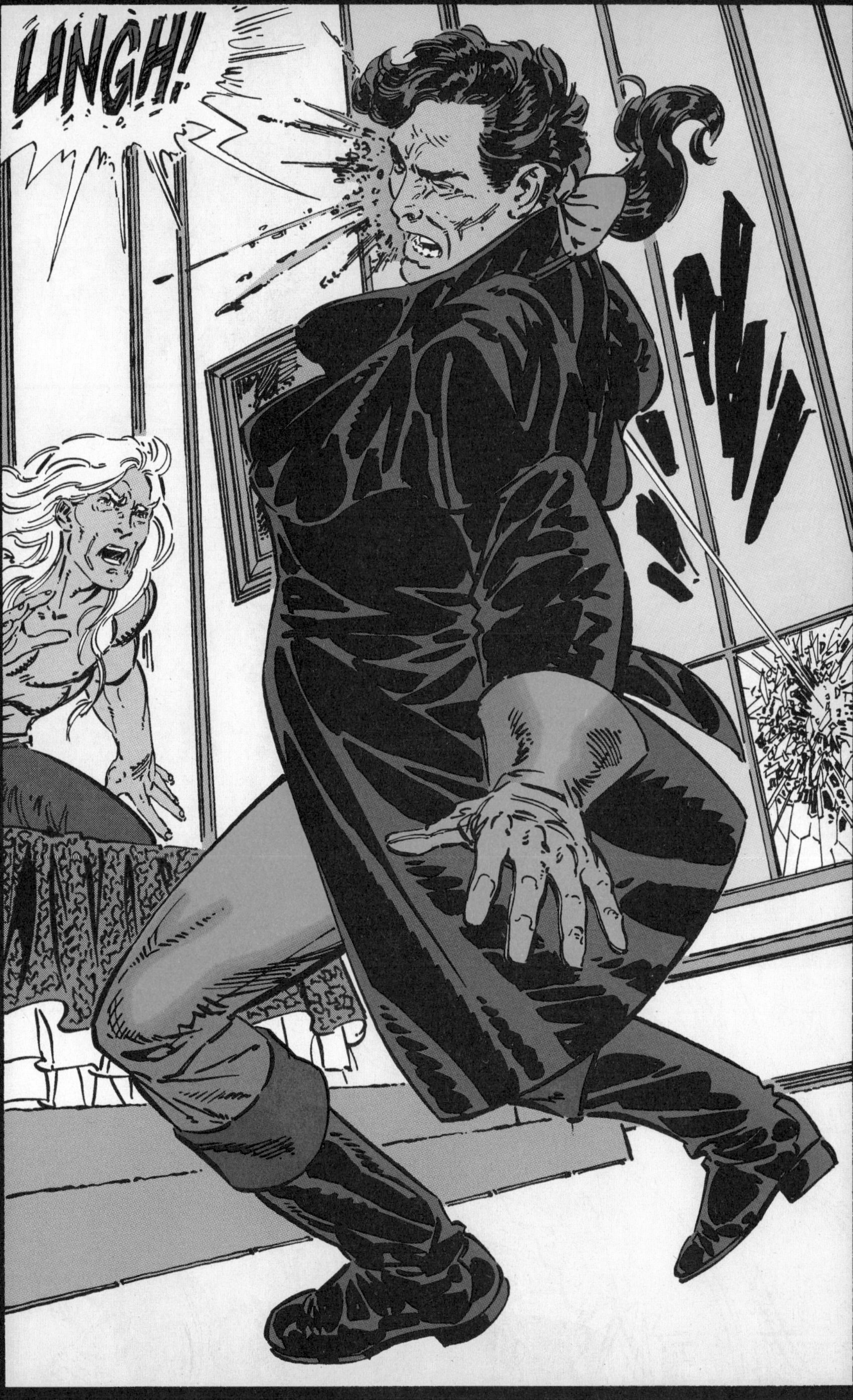
UNGH!

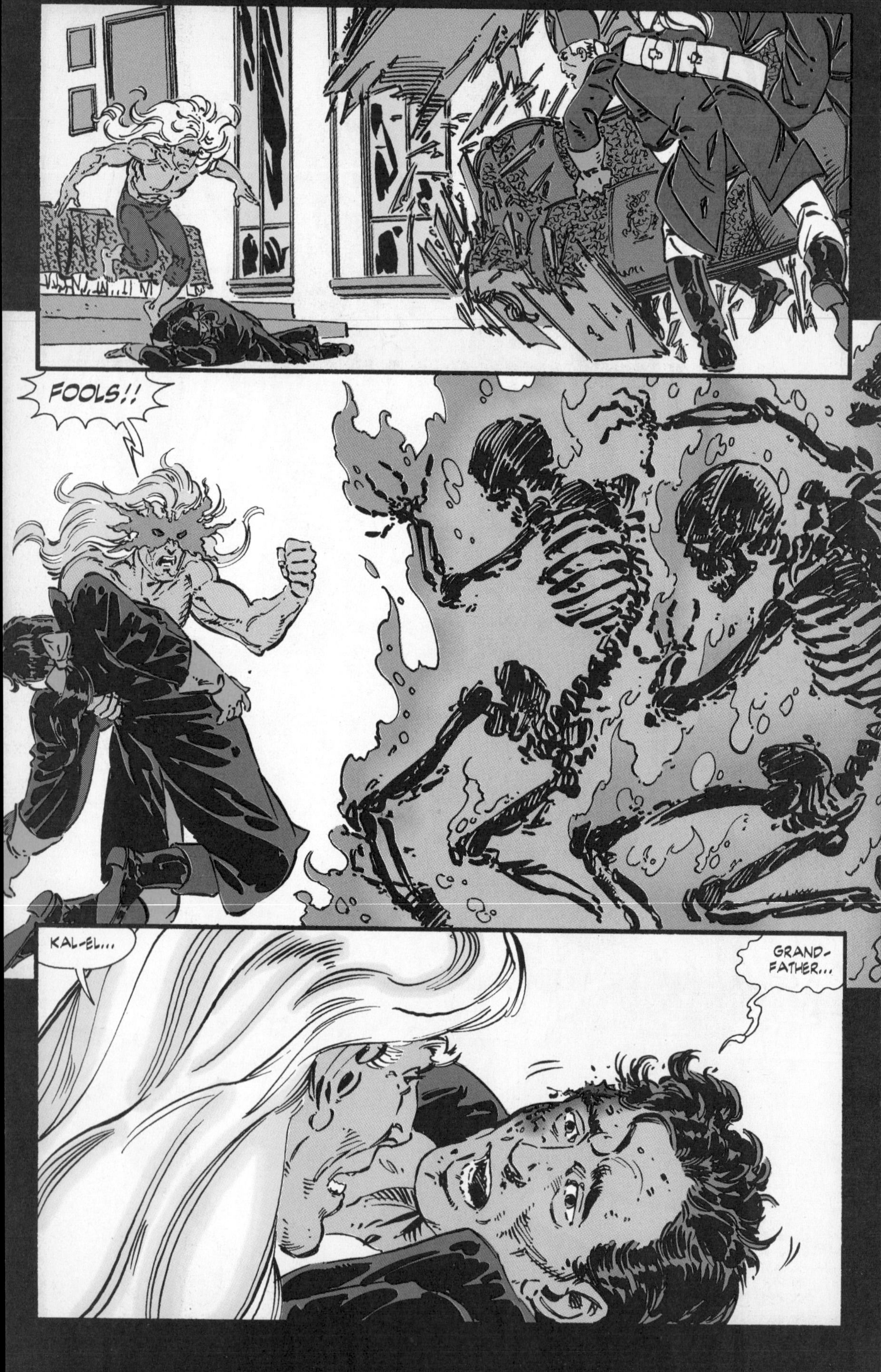
FOOLS!!
KAL-EL...
GRAND-
FATHER...

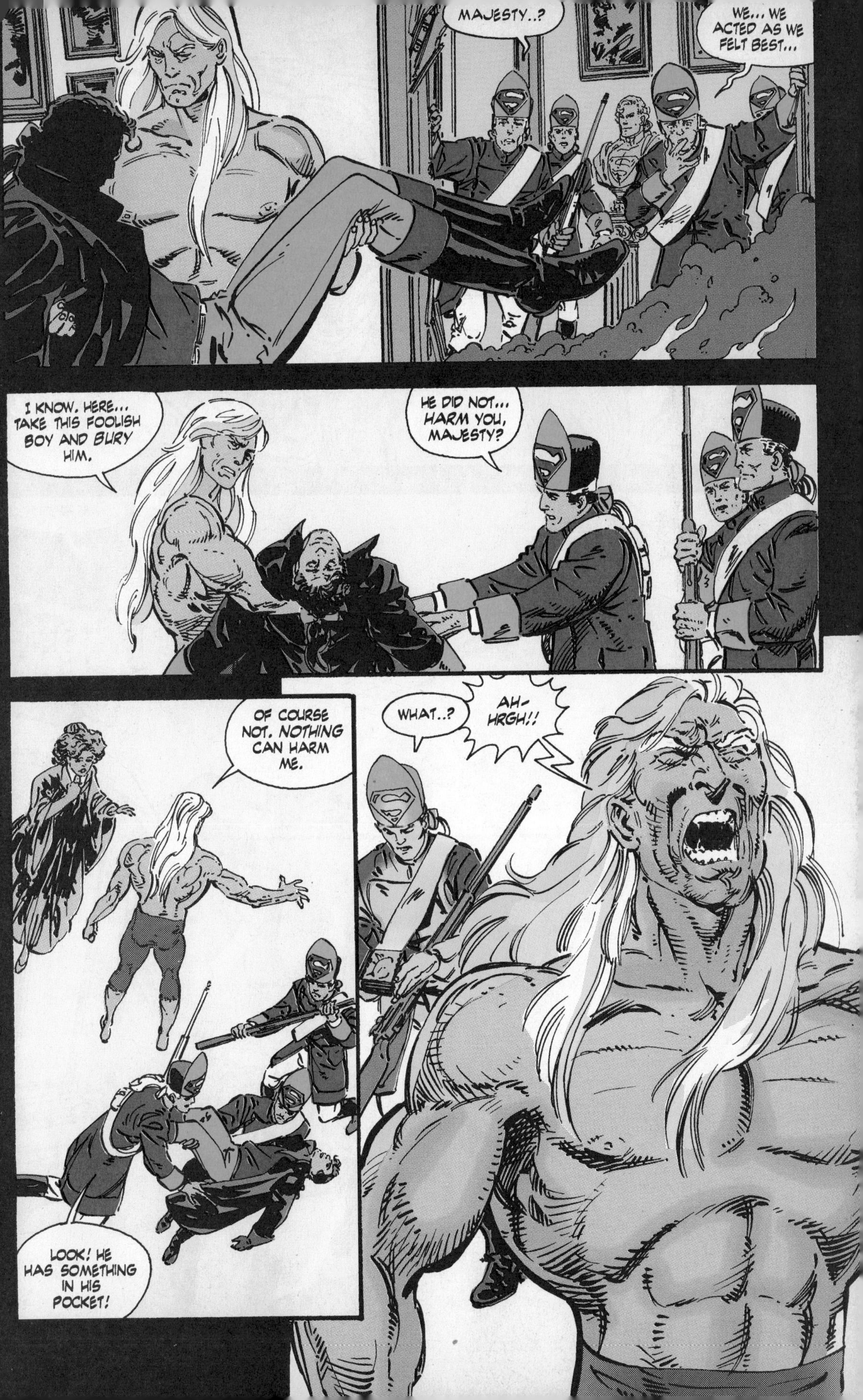
MAJESTY..?
WE... WE ACTED AS WE FELT BEST...
I KNOW. HERE... TAKE THIS FOOLISH BOY AND BURY HIM.
HE DID NOT... HARM YOU, MAJESTY?
OF COURSE NOT. NOTHING CAN HARM ME.
LOOK! HE HAS SOMETHING IN HIS POCKET!
WHAT..?
AH-HRGH!!

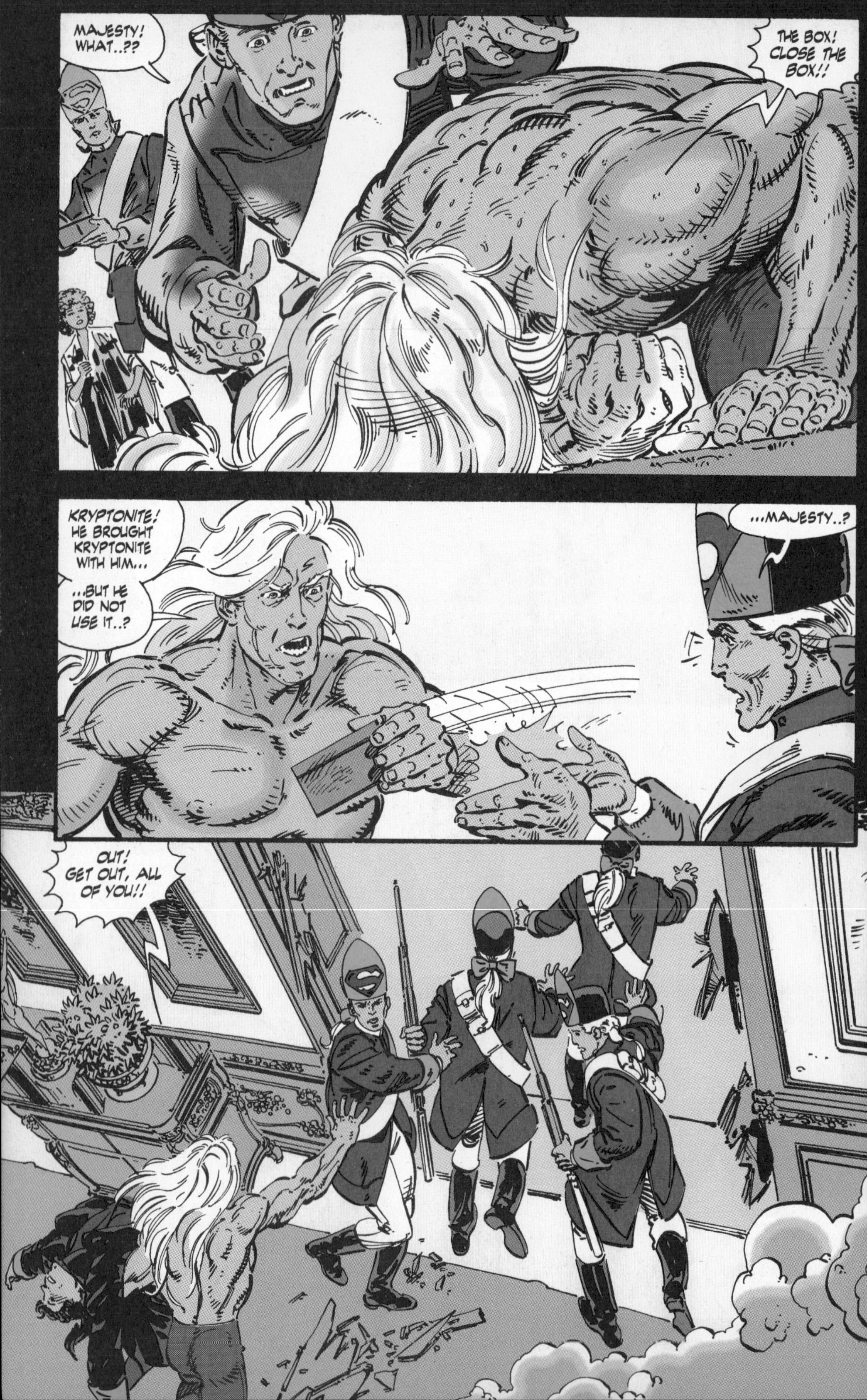
MAJESTY!
WHAT..??
THE BOX!
CLOSE THE
BOX!!
KRYPTONITE!
HE BROUGHT
KRYPTONITE
WITH HIM...
...BUT HE
DID NOT
USE IT..?
...MAJESTY..?
OUT!
GET OUT, ALL
OF YOU!!
...

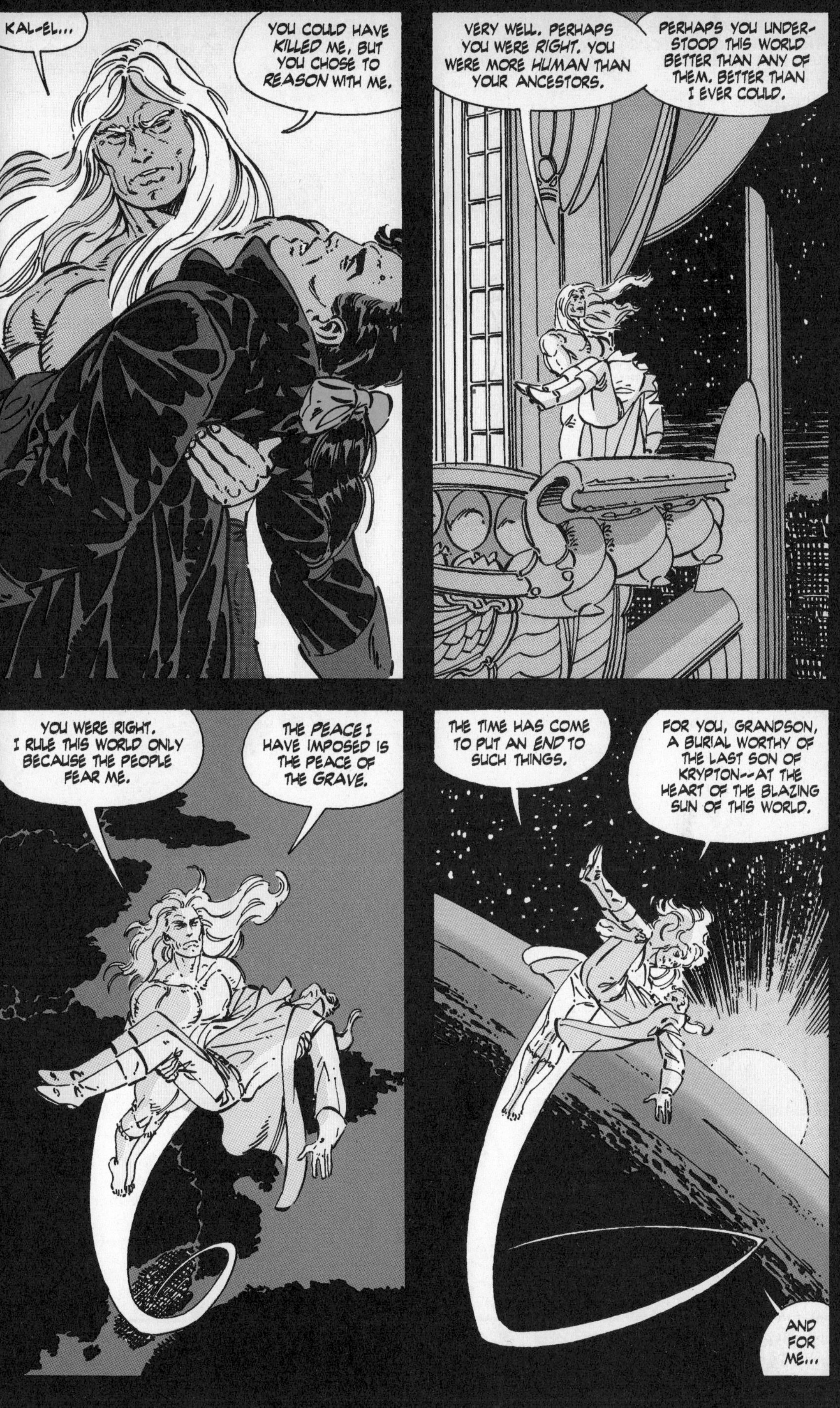
KAL-EL...
YOU COULD HAVE KILLED ME, BUT YOU CHOSE TO REASON WITH ME.
VERY WELL. PERHAPS YOU WERE RIGHT. YOU WERE MORE HUMAN THAN YOUR ANCESTORS.
PERHAPS YOU UNDERSTOOD THIS WORLD BETTER THAN ANY OF THEM. BETTER THAN I EVER COULD.
YOU WERE RIGHT. I RULE THIS WORLD ONLY BECAUSE THE PEOPLE FEAR ME.
THE PEACE I HAVE IMPOSED IS THE PEACE OF THE GRAVE.
THE TIME HAS COME TO PUT AN END TO SUCH THINGS.
FOR YOU, GRANDSON, A BURIAL WORTHY OF THE LAST SON OF KRYPTON--AT THE HEART OF THE BLAZING SUN OF THIS WORLD.
AND FOR ME...

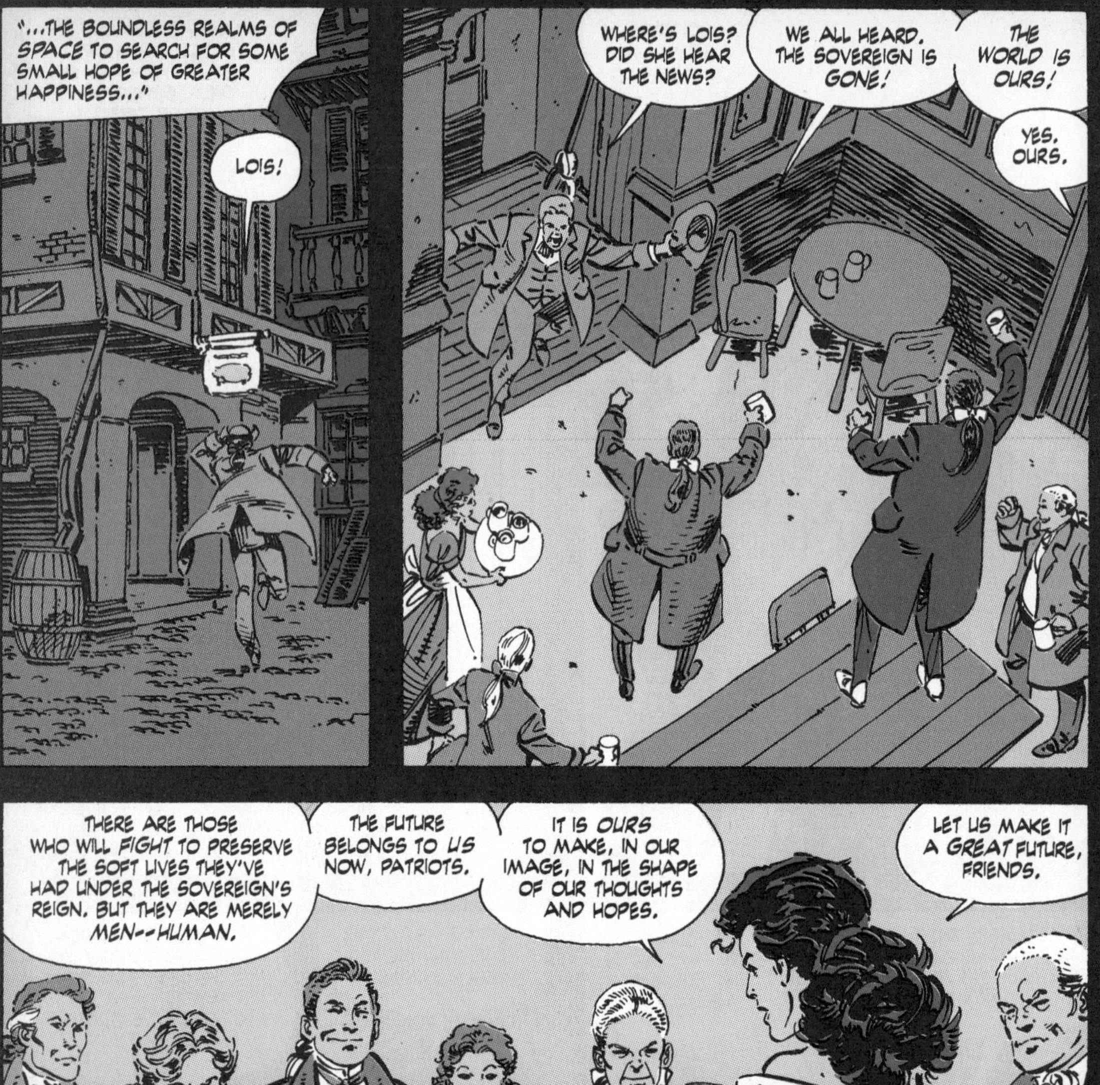
"...THE BOUNDLESS REALMS OF SPACE TO SEARCH FOR SOME SMALL HOPE OF GREATER HAPPINESS..."
LOIS!
WHERE'S LOIS? DID SHE HEAR THE NEWS?
WE ALL HEARD. THE SOVEREIGN IS GONE!
THE WORLD IS OURS!
YES. OURS.
THERE ARE THOSE WHO WILL FIGHT TO PRESERVE THE SOFT LIVES THEY'VE HAD UNDER THE SOVEREIGN'S REIGN. BUT THEY ARE MERELY MEN--HUMAN.
THE FUTURE BELONGS TO US NOW, PATRIOTS.
IT IS OURS TO MAKE, IN OUR IMAGE, IN THE SHAPE OF OUR THOUGHTS AND HOPES.
LET US MAKE IT A GREAT FUTURE, FRIENDS.
A FUTURE WORTHY OF THE BRAVE YOUNG MAN WHO BOUGHT IT FOR US--WITH HIS LIFE!
Freedom is nothing else but a chance to be better... enslavement is a certainty of the worse.
Albert Camus
Resistance, Rebellion, and Death
(1960)

JOHN BYRNE AUTHOR / GLENN WHITMORE COLORIST / CHRIS DUFFY ASST. EDITOR / FRANK PITTARESE ASSOC. EDITOR / MIKE CARLIN EDITOR

crucible of freedom

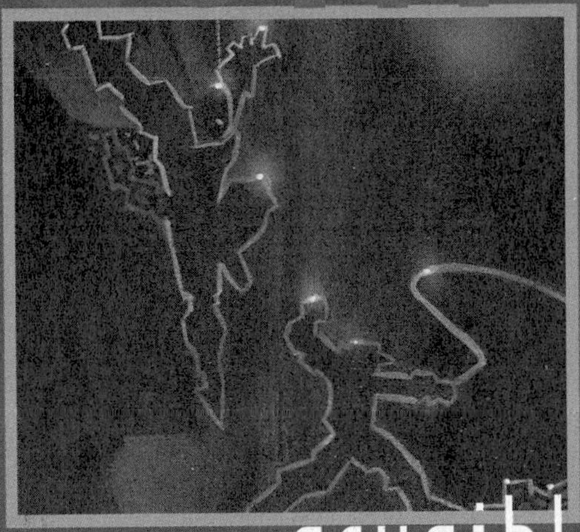

crucible of FREEDOM

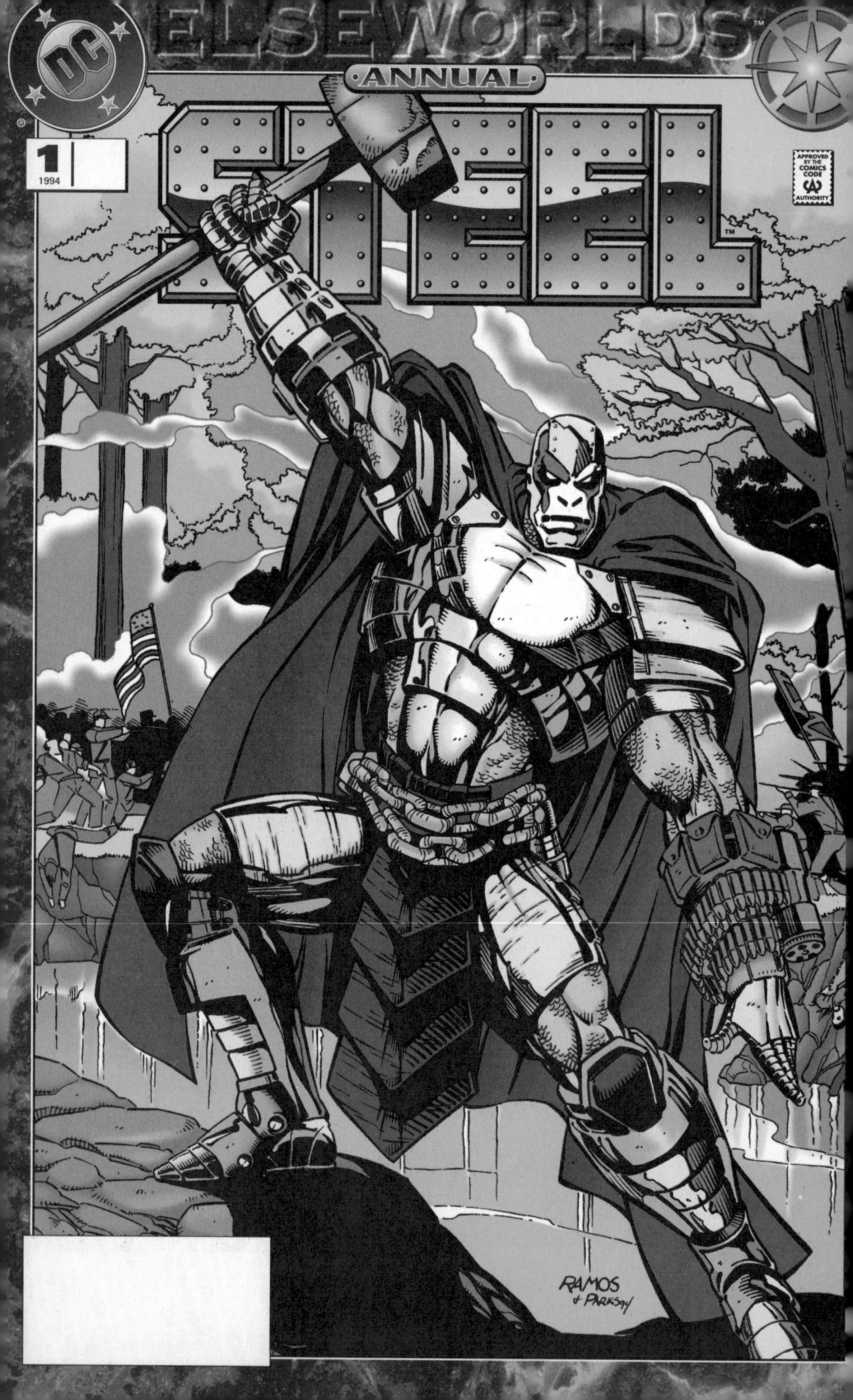
ELSEWORLDS
DC
ANNUAL
STEEL
1
1994
APPROVED BY THE COMICS CODE AUTHORITY
RAMOS & PARKSAY

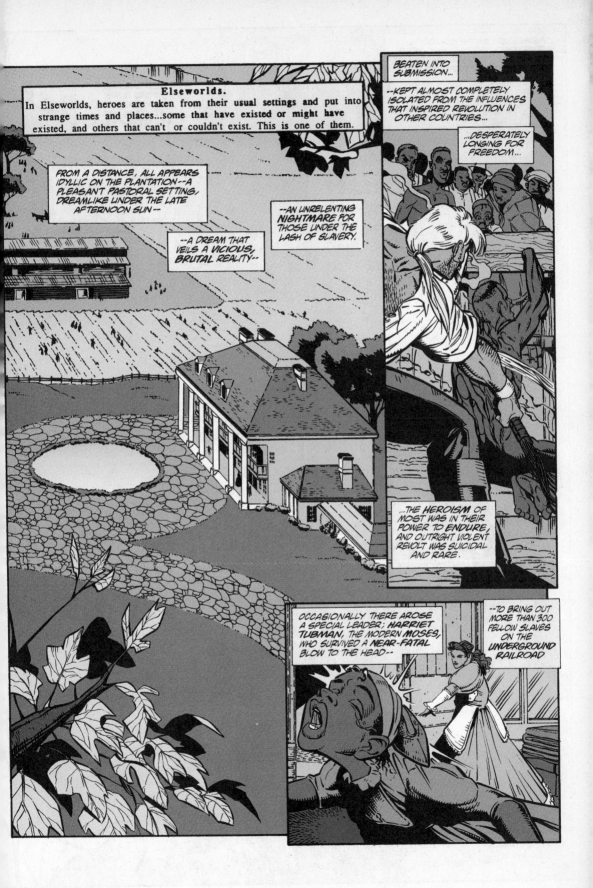

Elseworlds.

In Elseworlds, heroes are taken from their usual settings and put into strange times and places...some that have existed or might have existed, and others that can't or couldn't exist. This is one of them.

FROM A DISTANCE, ALL APPEARS IDYLLIC ON THE PLANTATION--A PLEASANT PASTORAL SETTING, DREAMLIKE UNDER THE LATE AFTERNOON SUN--

--A DREAM THAT VEILS A VICIOUS, BRUTAL REALITY--

--AN UNRELENTING NIGHTMARE FOR THOSE UNDER THE LASH OF SLAVERY.

BEATEN INTO SUBMISSION...

--KEPT ALMOST COMPLETELY ISOLATED FROM THE INFLUENCES THAT INSPIRED REVOLUTION IN OTHER COUNTRIES...

...DESPERATELY LONGING FOR FREEDOM...

...THE HEROISM OF MOST WAS IN THEIR POWER TO ENDURE, AND OUTRIGHT VIOLENT REVOLT WAS SUICIDAL AND RARE.

OCCASIONALLY THERE AROSE A SPECIAL LEADER; HARRIET TUBMAN, THE MODERN MOSES, WHO SURVIVED A NEAR-FATAL BLOW TO THE HEAD--

--TO BRING OUT MORE THAN 300 FELLOW SLAVES ON THE UNDERGROUND RAILROAD

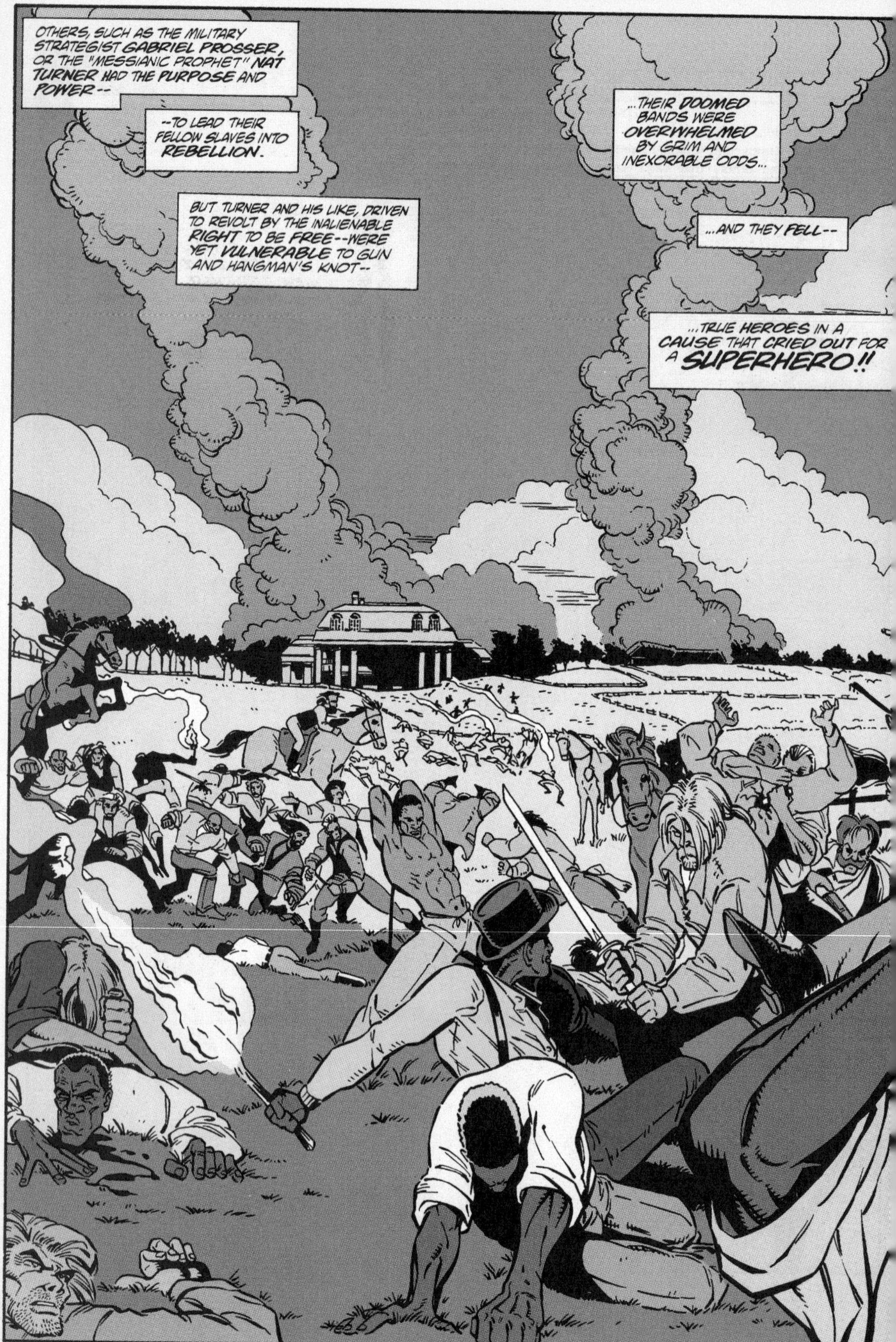
OTHERS, SUCH AS THE MILITARY STRATEGIST GABRIEL PROSSER, OR THE "MESSIANIC PROPHET" NAT TURNER HAD THE PURPOSE AND POWER--
--TO LEAD THEIR FELLOW SLAVES INTO REBELLION.
BUT TURNER AND HIS LIKE, DRIVEN TO REVOLT BY THE INALIENABLE RIGHT TO BE FREE--WERE YET VULNERABLE TO GUN AND HANGMAN'S KNOT--
...THEIR DOOMED BANDS WERE OVERWHELMED BY GRIM AND INEXORABLE ODDS...
...AND THEY FELL--
...TRUE HEROES IN A CAUSE THAT CRIED OUT FOR A SUPERHERO!!

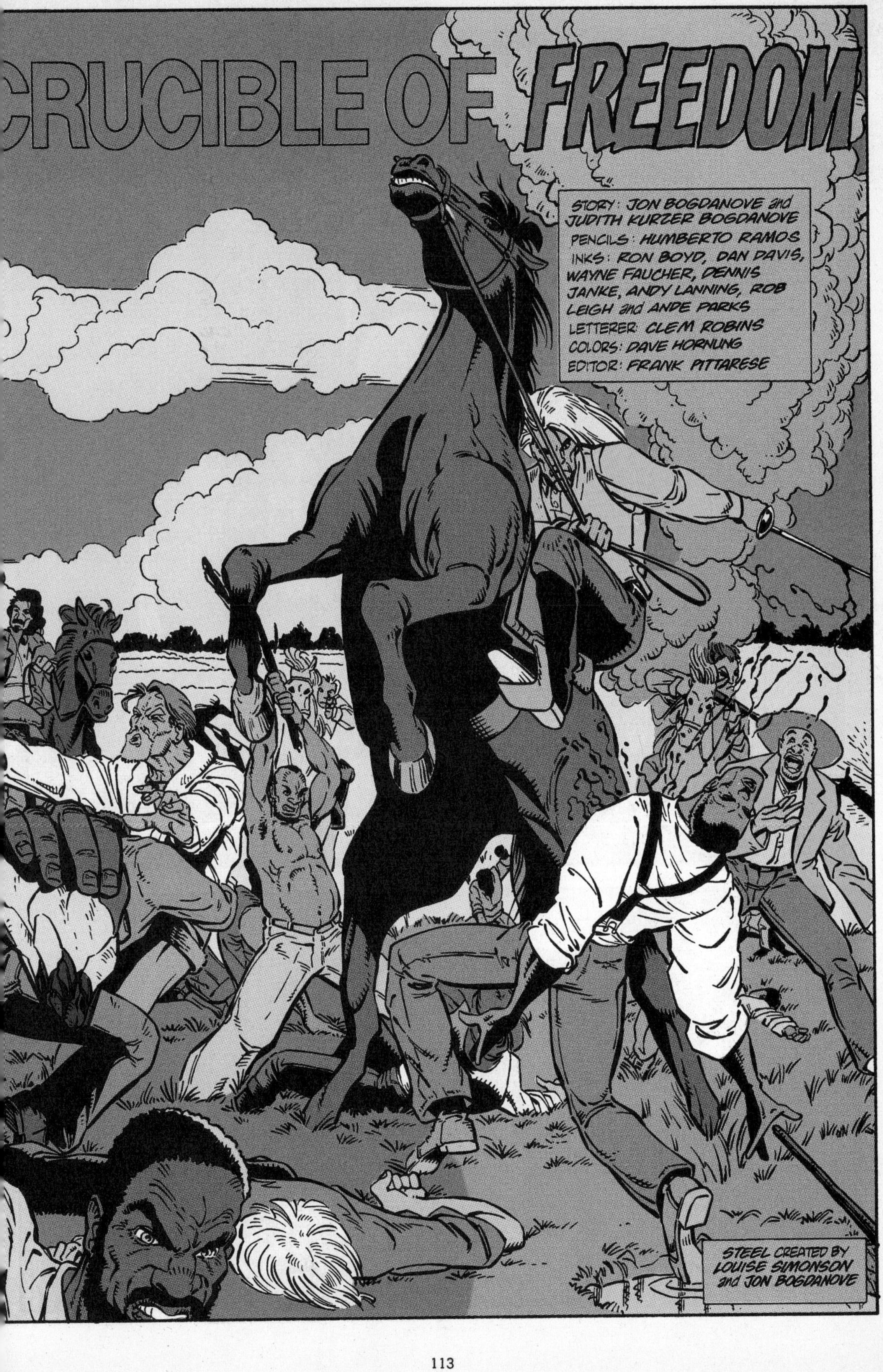
CRUCIBLE OF FREEDOM
STORY: JON BOGDANOVE and JUDITH KURZER BOGDANOVE
PENCILS: HUMBERTO RAMOS
INKS: RON BOYD, DAN DAVIS, WAYNE FAUCHER, DENNIS JANKE, ANDY LANNING, ROB LEIGH and ANDE PARKS
LETTERER: CLEM ROBINS
COLORS: DAVE HORNUNG
EDITOR: FRANK PITTARESE
STEEL CREATED BY LOUISE SIMONSON and JON BOGDANOVE

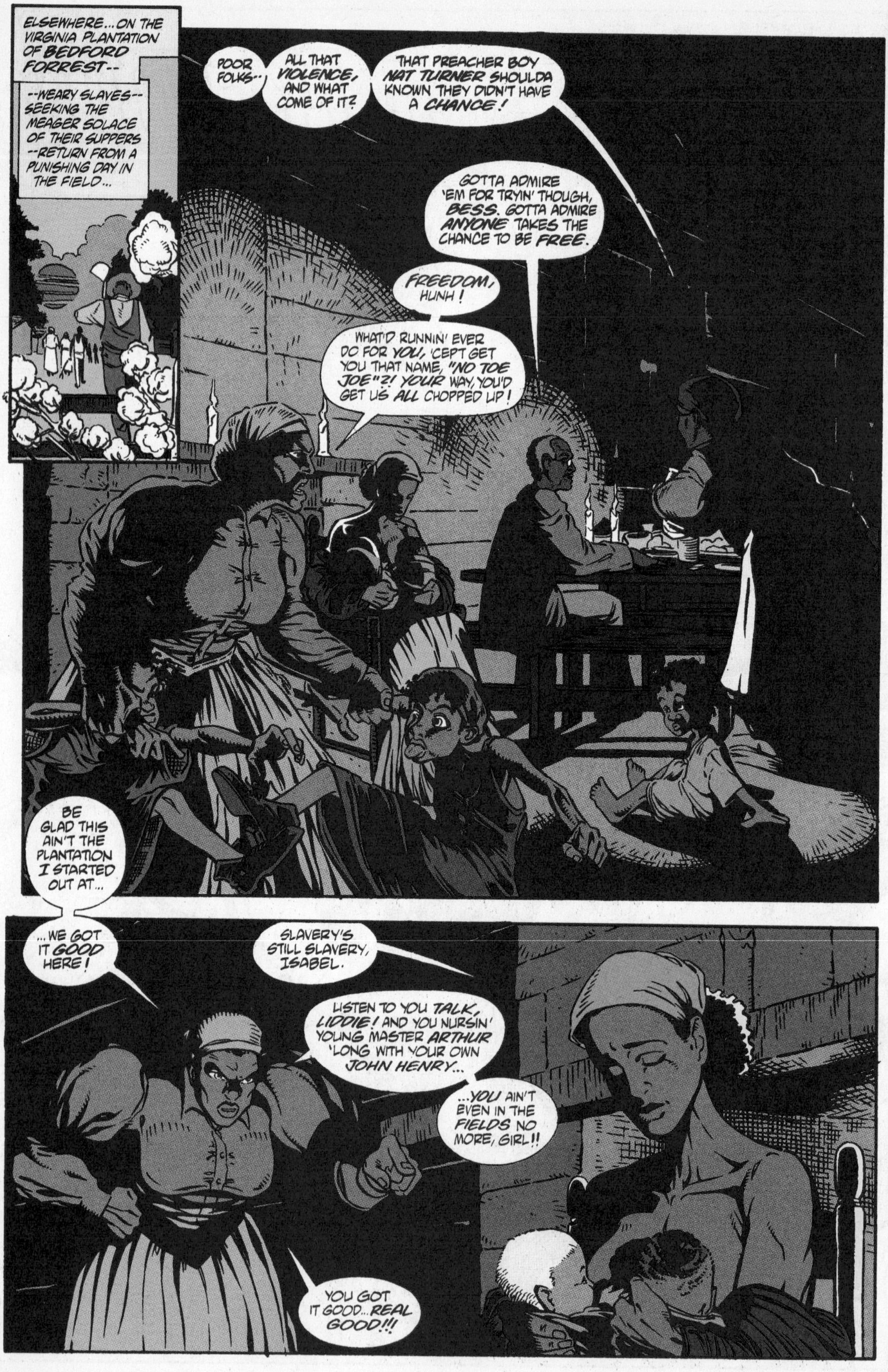
ELSEWHERE... ON THE VIRGINIA PLANTATION OF BEDFORD FORREST--
--WEARY SLAVES-- SEEKING THE MEAGER SOLACE OF THEIR SUPPERS --RETURN FROM A PUNISHING DAY IN THE FIELD...
POOR FOLKS--
ALL THAT VIOLENCE, AND WHAT COME OF IT?
THAT PREACHER BOY NAT TURNER SHOULDA KNOWN THEY DIDN'T HAVE A CHANCE!
GOTTA ADMIRE 'EM FOR TRYIN' THOUGH, BESS. GOTTA ADMIRE ANYONE TAKES THE CHANCE TO BE FREE.
FREEDOM, HUNH!
WHAT'D RUNNIN' EVER DO FOR YOU, 'CEPT GET YOU THAT NAME, "NO TOE JOE"?! YOUR WAY, YOU'D GET US ALL CHOPPED UP!
BE GLAD THIS AIN'T THE PLANTATION I STARTED OUT AT...
...WE GOT IT GOOD HERE!
SLAVERY'S STILL SLAVERY, ISABEL.
LISTEN TO YOU TALK, LIDDIE! AND YOU NURSIN' YOUNG MASTER ARTHUR 'LONG WITH YOUR OWN JOHN HENRY...
...YOU AIN'T EVEN IN THE FIELDS NO MORE, GIRL!!
YOU GOT IT GOOD... REAL GOOD!!!

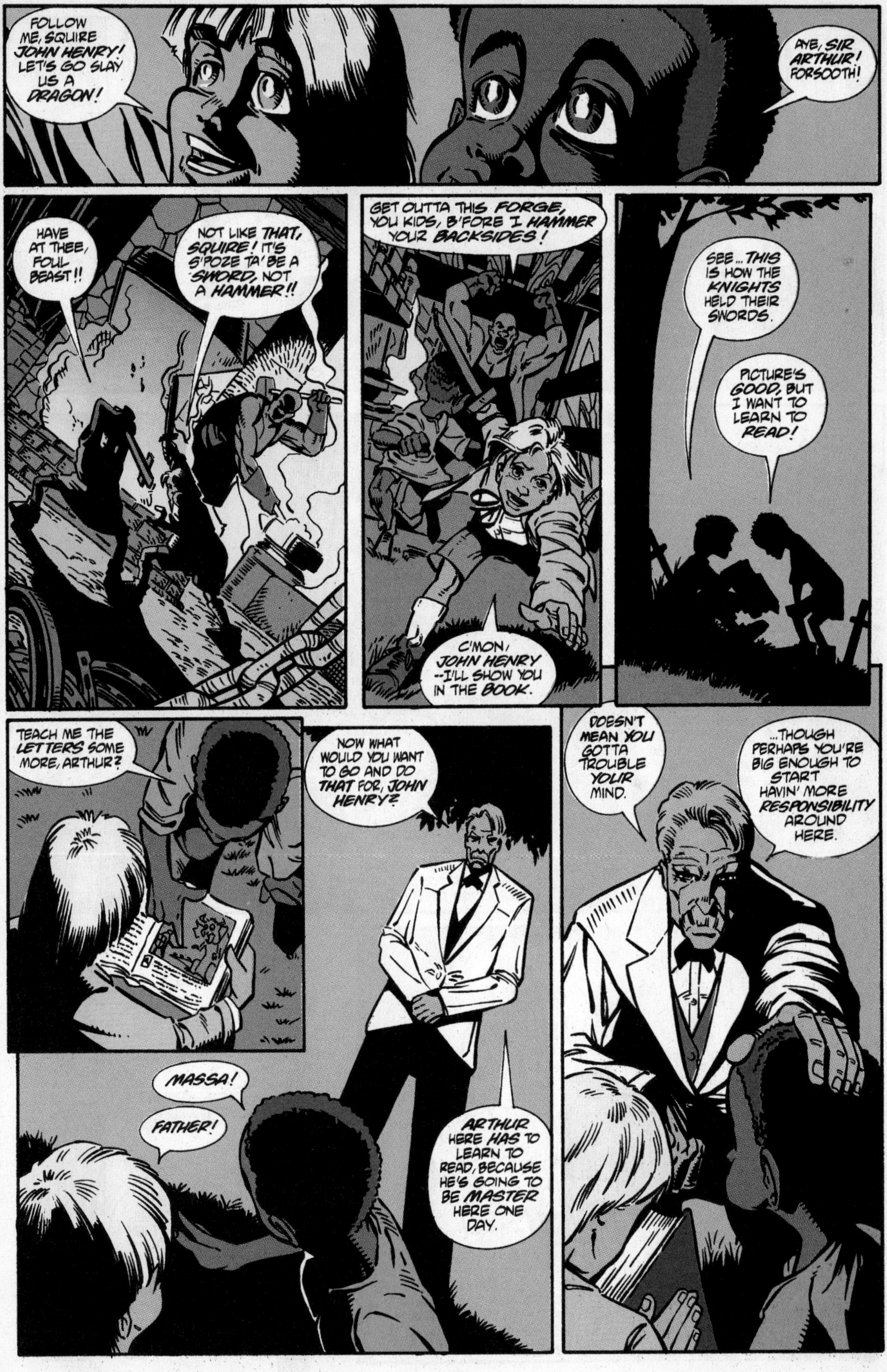
FOLLOW ME, SQUIRE JOHN HENRY! LET'S GO SLAY US A DRAGON!
AYE, SIR ARTHUR! FORSOOTH!
HAVE AT THEE, FOUL BEAST!!
NOT LIKE THAT, SQUIRE! IT'S S'POZE TA' BE A SWORD, NOT A HAMMER!!
GET OUTTA THIS FORGE, YOU KIDS, B'FORE I HAMMER YOUR BACKSIDES!
C'MON, JOHN HENRY --I'LL SHOW YOU IN THE BOOK.
SEE... THIS IS HOW THE KNIGHTS HELD THEIR SWORDS.
PICTURE'S GOOD, BUT I WANT TO LEARN TO READ!
TEACH ME THE LETTERS SOME MORE, ARTHUR?
NOW WHAT WOULD YOU WANT TO GO AND DO THAT FOR, JOHN HENRY?
MASSA!
FATHER!
ARTHUR HERE HAS TO LEARN TO READ, BECAUSE HE'S GOING TO BE MASTER HERE ONE DAY.
DOESN'T MEAN YOU GOTTA TROUBLE YOUR MIND.
...THOUGH PERHAPS YOU'RE BIG ENOUGH TO START HAVIN' MORE RESPONSIBILITY AROUND HERE.

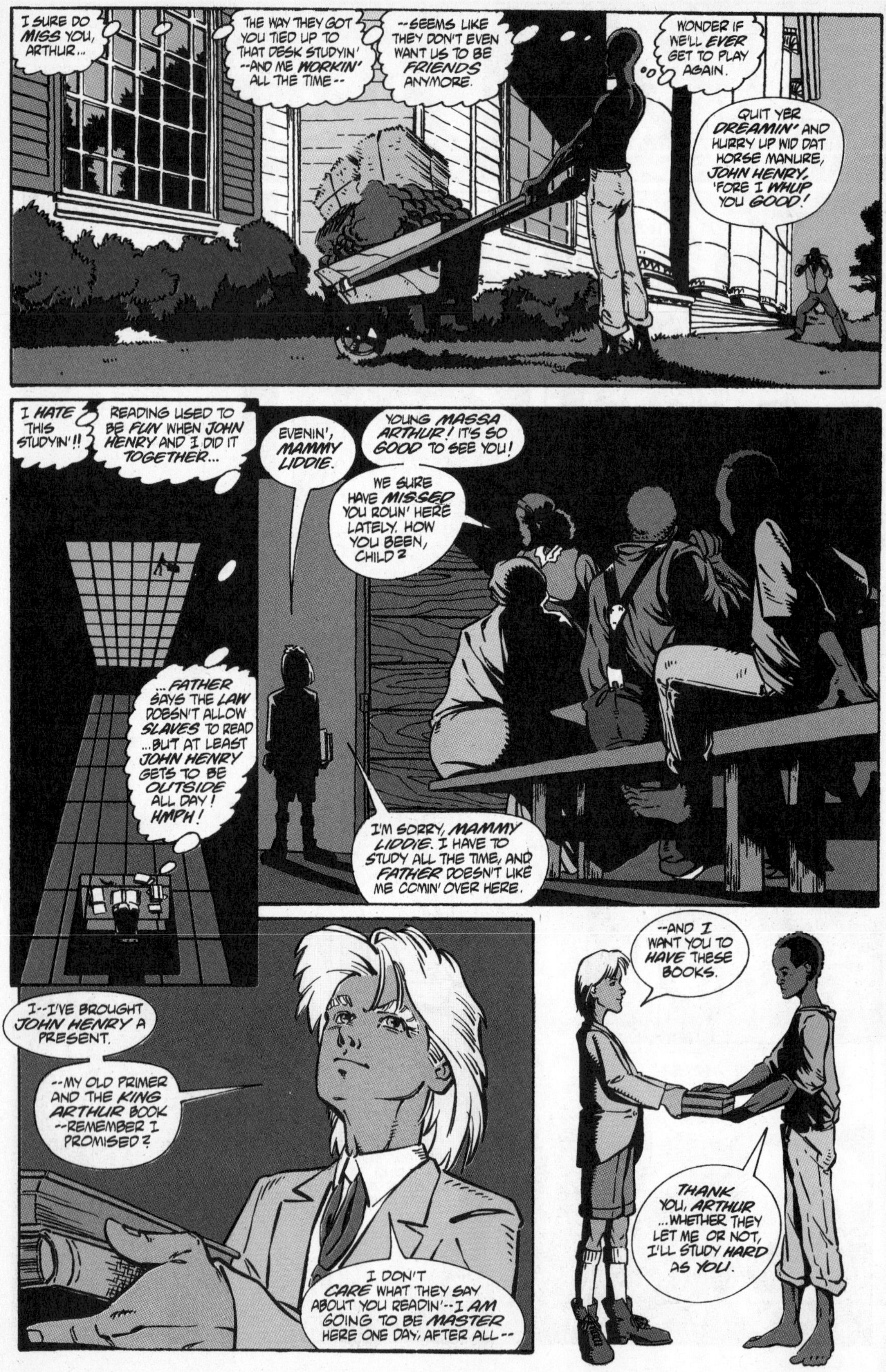

I SURE DO MISS YOU, ARTHUR...
THE WAY THEY GOT YOU TIED UP TO THAT DESK STUDYIN' --AND ME WORKIN' ALL THE TIME--
--SEEMS LIKE THEY DON'T EVEN WANT US TO BE FRIENDS ANYMORE.
WONDER IF WE'LL EVER GET TO PLAY AGAIN.
QUIT YER DREAMIN' AND HURRY UP WID DAT HORSE MANURE, JOHN HENRY, 'FORE I WHUP YOU GOOD!
I HATE THIS STUDYIN'!!
READING USED TO BE FUN WHEN JOHN HENRY AND I DID IT TOGETHER...
...FATHER SAYS THE LAW DOESN'T ALLOW SLAVES TO READ ...BUT AT LEAST JOHN HENRY GETS TO BE OUTSIDE ALL DAY! HMPH!
EVENIN', MAMMY LIDDIE.
YOUNG MASSA ARTHUR! IT'S SO GOOD TO SEE YOU!
WE SURE HAVE MISSED YOU ROUN' HERE LATELY. HOW YOU BEEN, CHILD?
I'M SORRY, MAMMY LIDDIE. I HAVE TO STUDY ALL THE TIME, AND FATHER DOESN'T LIKE ME COMIN' OVER HERE.
I--I'VE BROUGHT JOHN HENRY A PRESENT.
--MY OLD PRIMER AND THE KING ARTHUR BOOK --REMEMBER I PROMISED?
I DON'T CARE WHAT THEY SAY ABOUT YOU READIN'--I AM GOING TO BE MASTER HERE ONE DAY, AFTER ALL--
--AND I WANT YOU TO HAVE THESE BOOKS.
THANK YOU, ARTHUR ...WHETHER THEY LET ME OR NOT, I'LL STUDY HARD AS YOU.

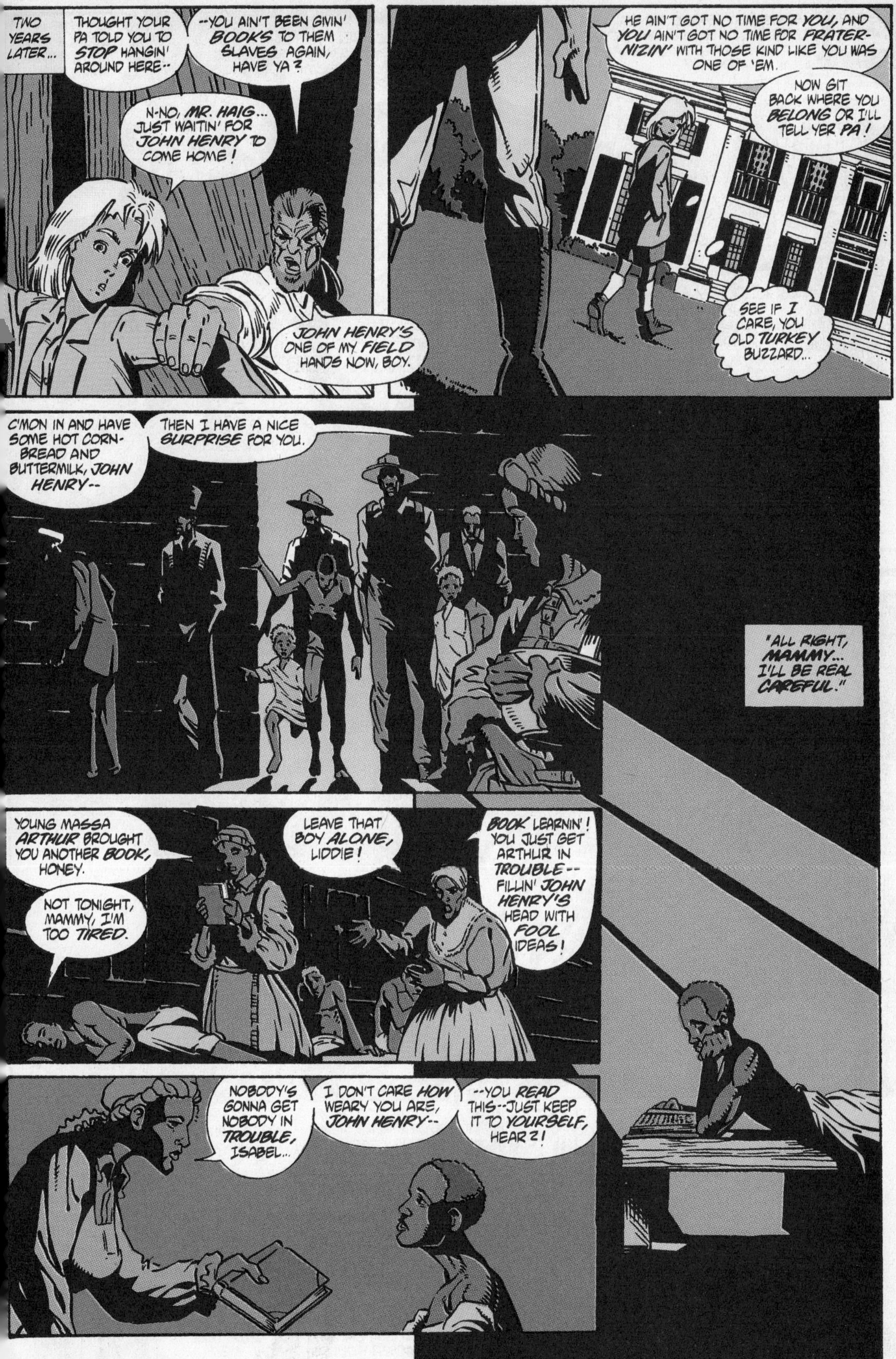

TWO YEARS LATER...
THOUGHT YOUR PA TOLD YOU TO STOP HANGIN' AROUND HERE--
--YOU AIN'T BEEN GIVIN' BOOKS TO THEM SLAVES AGAIN, HAVE YA?
N-NO, MR. HAIG... JUST WAITIN' FOR JOHN HENRY TO COME HOME!
JOHN HENRY'S ONE OF MY FIELD HANDS NOW, BOY.
HE AIN'T GOT NO TIME FOR YOU, AND YOU AIN'T GOT NO TIME FOR FRATER-NIZIN' WITH THOSE KIND LIKE YOU WAS ONE OF 'EM.
NOW GIT BACK WHERE YOU BELONG OR I'LL TELL YER PA!
SEE IF I CARE, YOU OLD TURKEY BUZZARD...
C'MON IN AND HAVE SOME HOT CORN-BREAD AND BUTTERMILK, JOHN HENRY--
THEN I HAVE A NICE SURPRISE FOR YOU.
YOUNG MASSA ARTHUR BROUGHT YOU ANOTHER BOOK, HONEY.
NOT TONIGHT, MAMMY, I'M TOO TIRED.
LEAVE THAT BOY ALONE, LIDDIE!
BOOK LEARNIN'! YOU JUST GET ARTHUR IN TROUBLE-- FILLIN' JOHN HENRY'S HEAD WITH FOOL IDEAS!
NOBODY'S GONNA GET NOBODY IN TROUBLE, ISABEL...
I DON'T CARE HOW WEARY YOU ARE, JOHN HENRY--
--YOU READ THIS--JUST KEEP IT TO YOURSELF, HEAR?!
"ALL RIGHT, MAMMY... I'LL BE REAL CAREFUL."

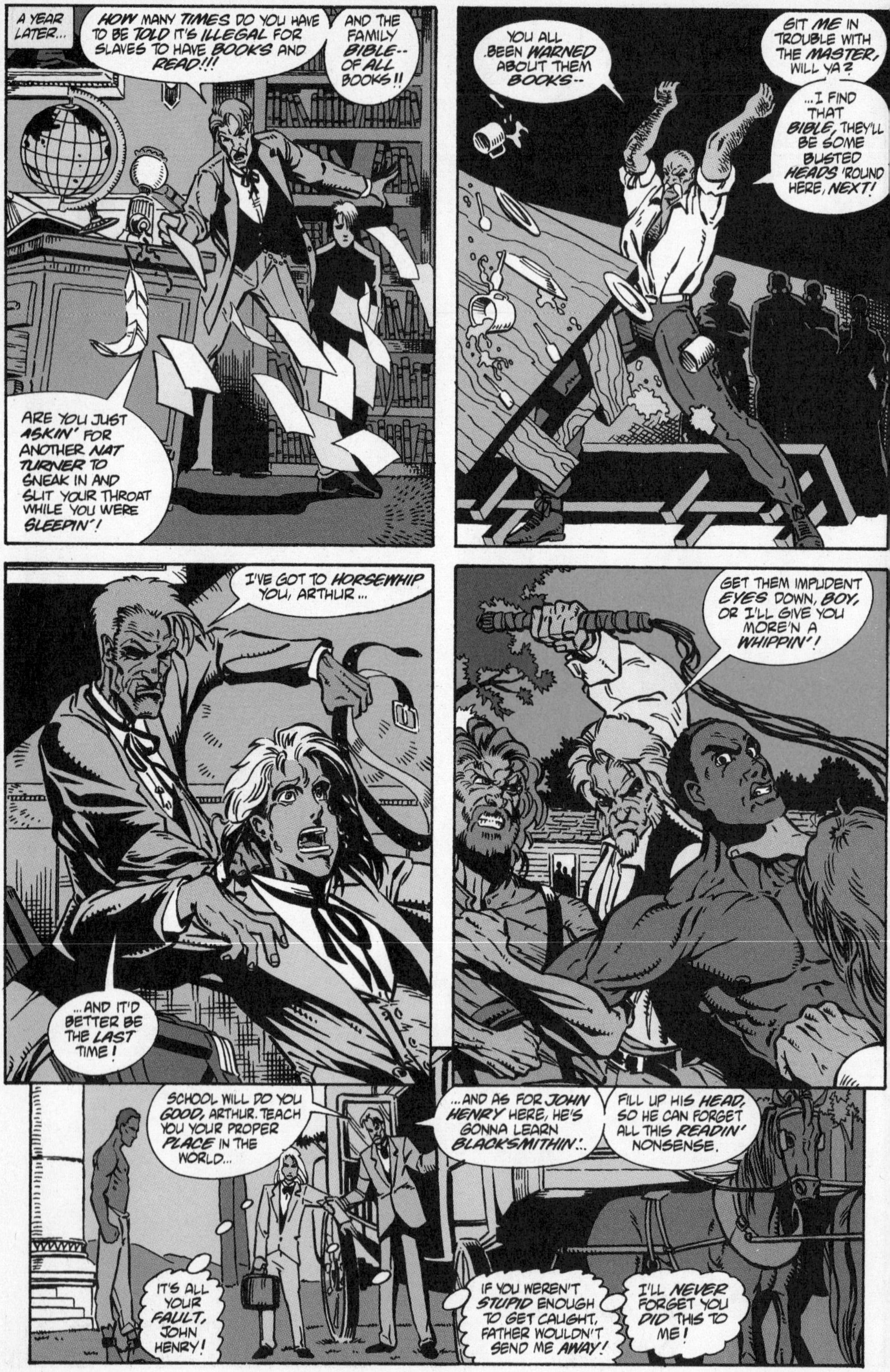
A YEAR LATER...
HOW MANY TIMES DO YOU HAVE TO BE TOLD IT'S ILLEGAL FOR SLAVES TO HAVE BOOKS AND READ!!!
AND THE FAMILY BIBLE-- OF ALL BOOKS!!
ARE YOU JUST ASKIN' FOR ANOTHER NAT TURNER TO SNEAK IN AND SLIT YOUR THROAT WHILE YOU WERE SLEEPIN'!
YOU ALL BEEN WARNED ABOUT THEM BOOKS--
GIT ME IN TROUBLE WITH THE MASTER, WILL YA?
...I FIND THAT BIBLE, THEY'LL BE SOME BUSTED HEADS 'ROUND HERE, NEXT!
I'VE GOT TO HORSEWHIP YOU, ARTHUR...
...AND IT'D BETTER BE THE LAST TIME!
GET THEM IMPUDENT EYES DOWN, BOY, OR I'LL GIVE YOU MORE'N A WHIPPIN'!
SCHOOL WILL DO YOU GOOD, ARTHUR. TEACH YOU YOUR PROPER PLACE IN THE WORLD...
...AND AS FOR JOHN HENRY HERE, HE'S GONNA LEARN BLACKSMITHIN'...
FILL UP HIS HEAD, SO HE CAN FORGET ALL THIS READIN' NONSENSE.
IT'S ALL YOUR FAULT, JOHN HENRY!
IF YOU WEREN'T STUPID ENOUGH TO GET CAUGHT, FATHER WOULDN'T SEND ME AWAY!
I'LL NEVER FORGET YOU DID THIS TO ME!

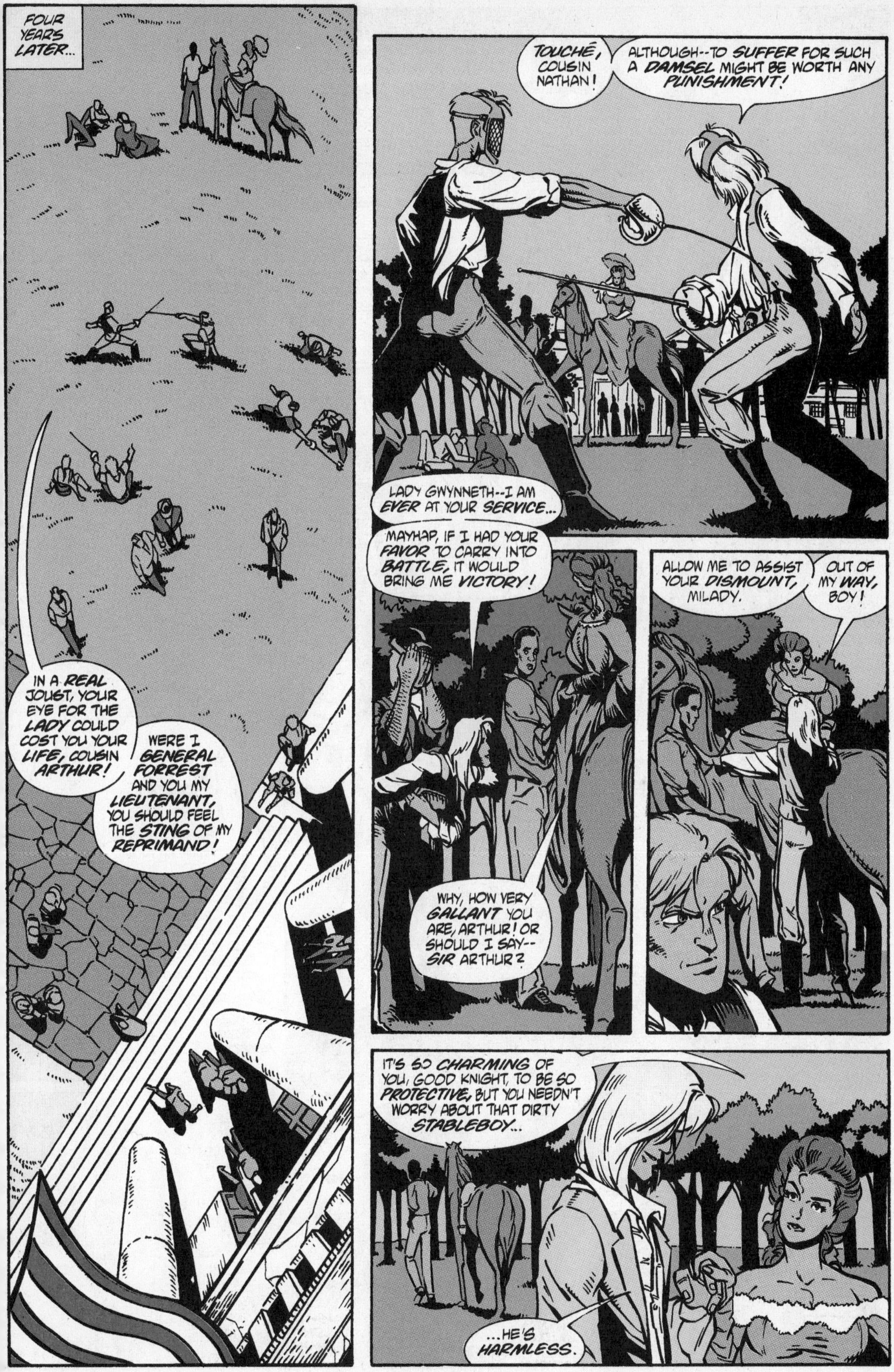
FOUR YEARS LATER...
IN A REAL JOUST, YOUR EYE FOR THE LADY COULD COST YOU YOUR LIFE, COUSIN ARTHUR!
WERE I GENERAL FORREST AND YOU MY LIEUTENANT, YOU SHOULD FEEL THE STING OF MY REPRIMAND!
TOUCHÉ, COUSIN NATHAN!
ALTHOUGH--TO SUFFER FOR SUCH A DAMSEL MIGHT BE WORTH ANY PUNISHMENT!
LADY GWYNNETH--I AM EVER AT YOUR SERVICE...
MAYHAP, IF I HAD YOUR FAVOR TO CARRY INTO BATTLE, IT WOULD BRING ME VICTORY!
WHY, HOW VERY GALLANT YOU ARE, ARTHUR! OR SHOULD I SAY-- SIR ARTHUR?
ALLOW ME TO ASSIST YOUR DISMOUNT, MILADY.
OUT OF MY WAY, BOY!
IT'S SO CHARMING OF YOU, GOOD KNIGHT, TO BE SO PROTECTIVE, BUT YOU NEEDN'T WORRY ABOUT THAT DIRTY STABLEBOY...
...HE'S HARMLESS.

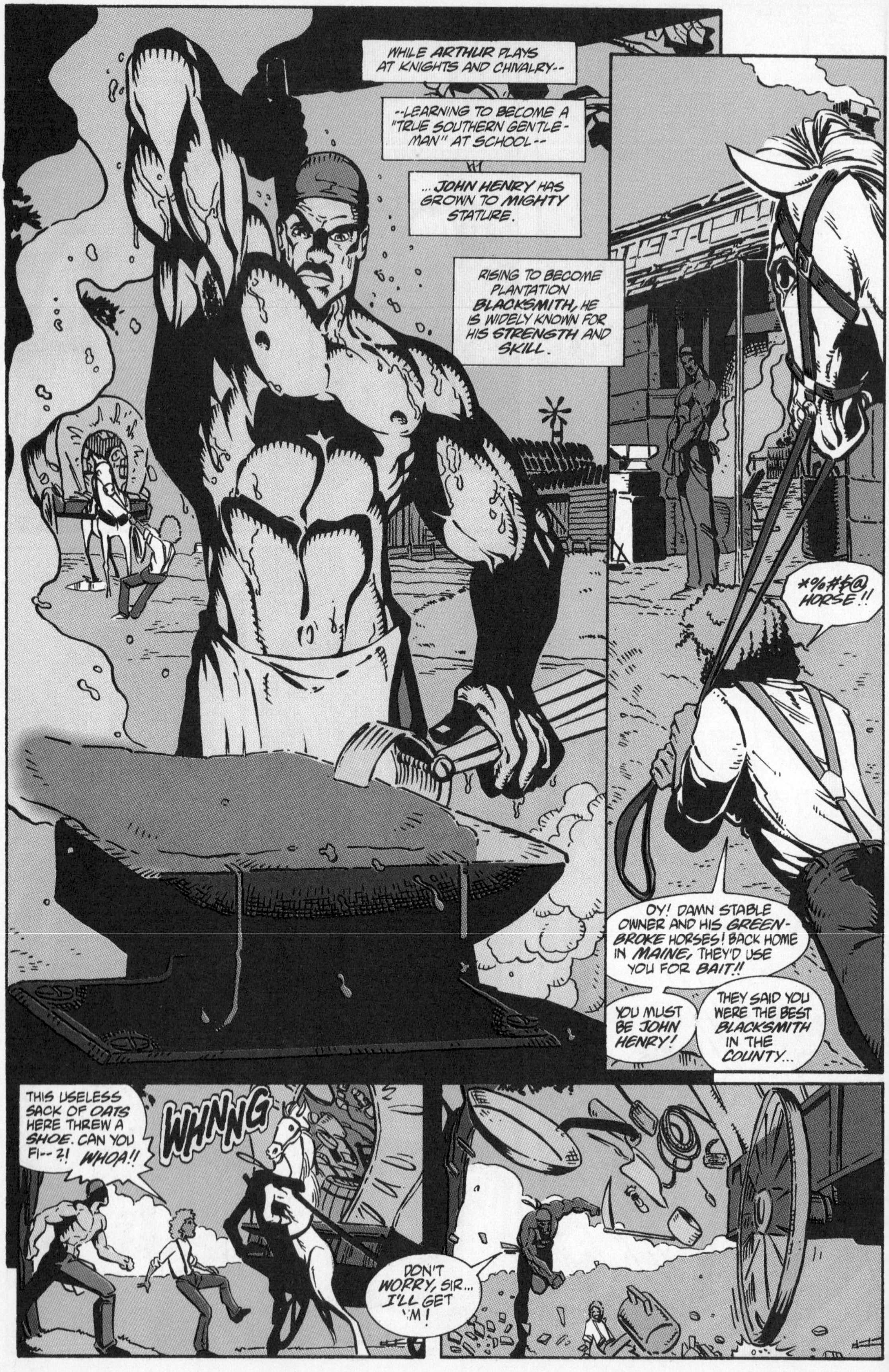
WHILE ARTHUR PLAYS AT KNIGHTS AND CHIVALRY--
--LEARNING TO BECOME A "TRUE SOUTHERN GENTLE-MAN" AT SCHOOL--
...JOHN HENRY HAS GROWN TO MIGHTY STATURE.
RISING TO BECOME PLANTATION BLACKSMITH, HE IS WIDELY KNOWN FOR HIS STRENGTH AND SKILL.
*%#$@ HORSE!!
OY! DAMN STABLE OWNER AND HIS GREEN-BROKE HORSES! BACK HOME IN MAINE, THEY'D USE YOU FOR BAIT!!
YOU MUST BE JOHN HENRY!
THEY SAID YOU WERE THE BEST BLACKSMITH IN THE COUNTY...
THIS USELESS SACK OF OATS HERE THREW A SHOE. CAN YOU FI-- ?! WHOA!!
WHNNG
DON'T WORRY, SIR... I'LL GET 'M!

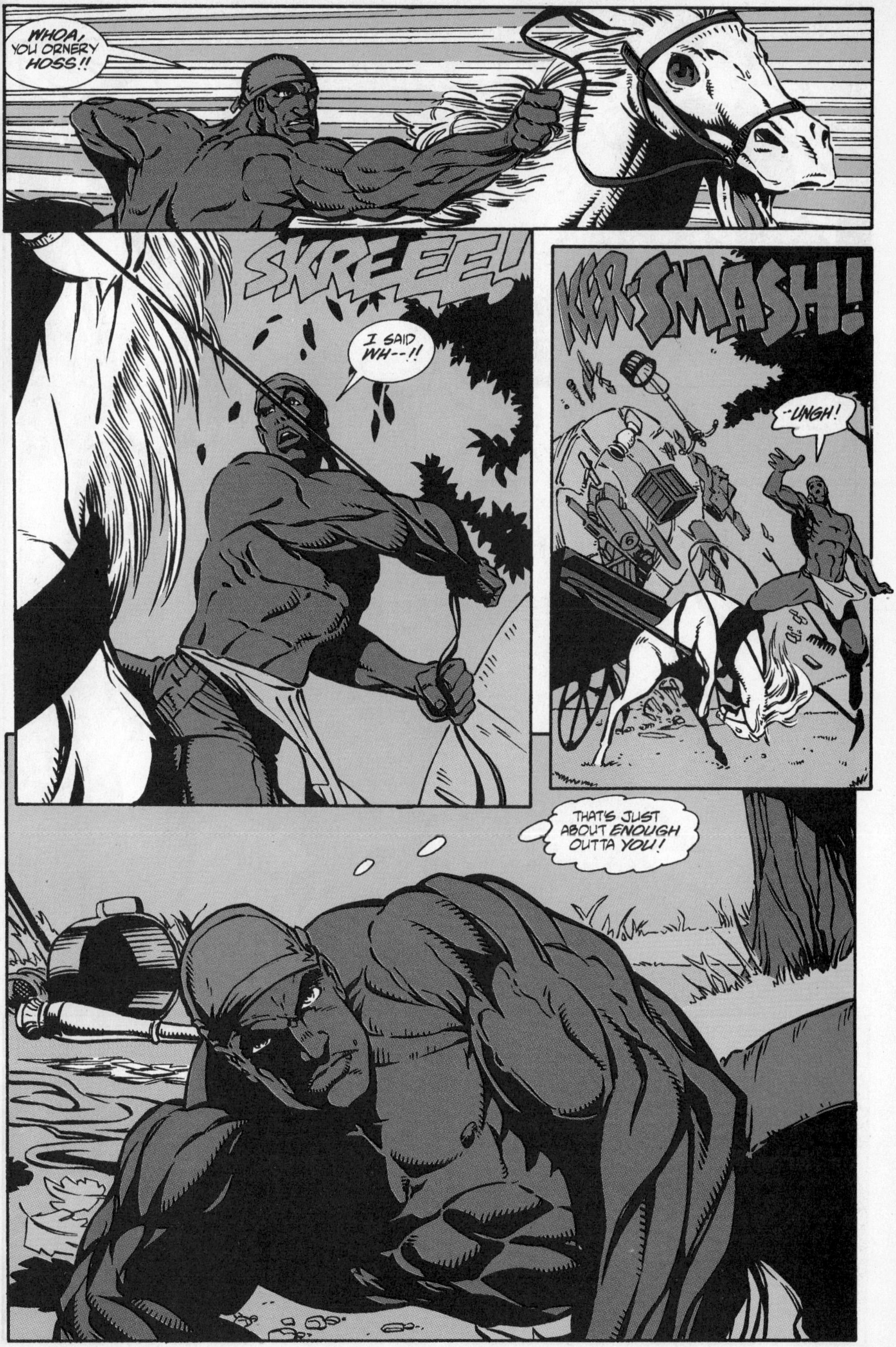
WHOA, YOU ORNERY HOSS!!
SKREEEE!
I SAID WH--!!
KER-SMASH!
--UNGH!
THAT'S JUST ABOUT ENOUGH OUTTA YOU!

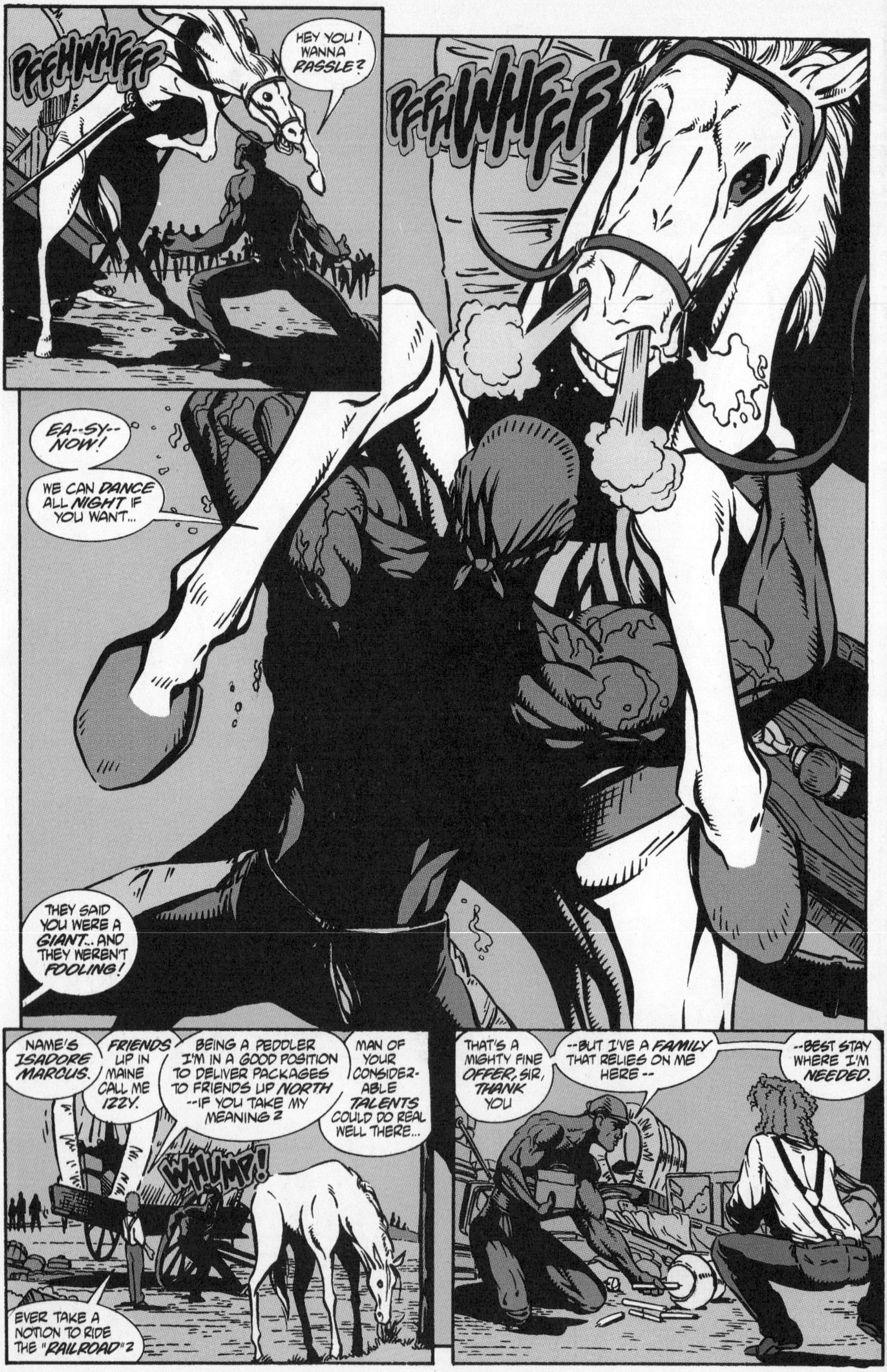
PFFHWHFFF
HEY YOU! WANNA RASSLE?
PFFHWHFFF
EA--SY-- NOW!
WE CAN DANCE ALL NIGHT IF YOU WANT...
THEY SAID YOU WERE A GIANT... AND THEY WEREN'T FOOLING!
NAME'S ISADORE MARCUS.
FRIENDS UP IN MAINE CALL ME IZZY.
BEING A PEDDLER I'M IN A GOOD POSITION TO DELIVER PACKAGES TO FRIENDS UP NORTH --IF YOU TAKE MY MEANING?
MAN OF YOUR CONSIDERABLE TALENTS COULD DO REAL WELL THERE...
WHUMP!
EVER TAKE A NOTION TO RIDE THE "RAILROAD"?
THAT'S A MIGHTY FINE OFFER, SIR, THANK YOU
--BUT I'VE A FAMILY THAT RELIES ON ME HERE --
--BEST STAY WHERE I'M NEEDED.

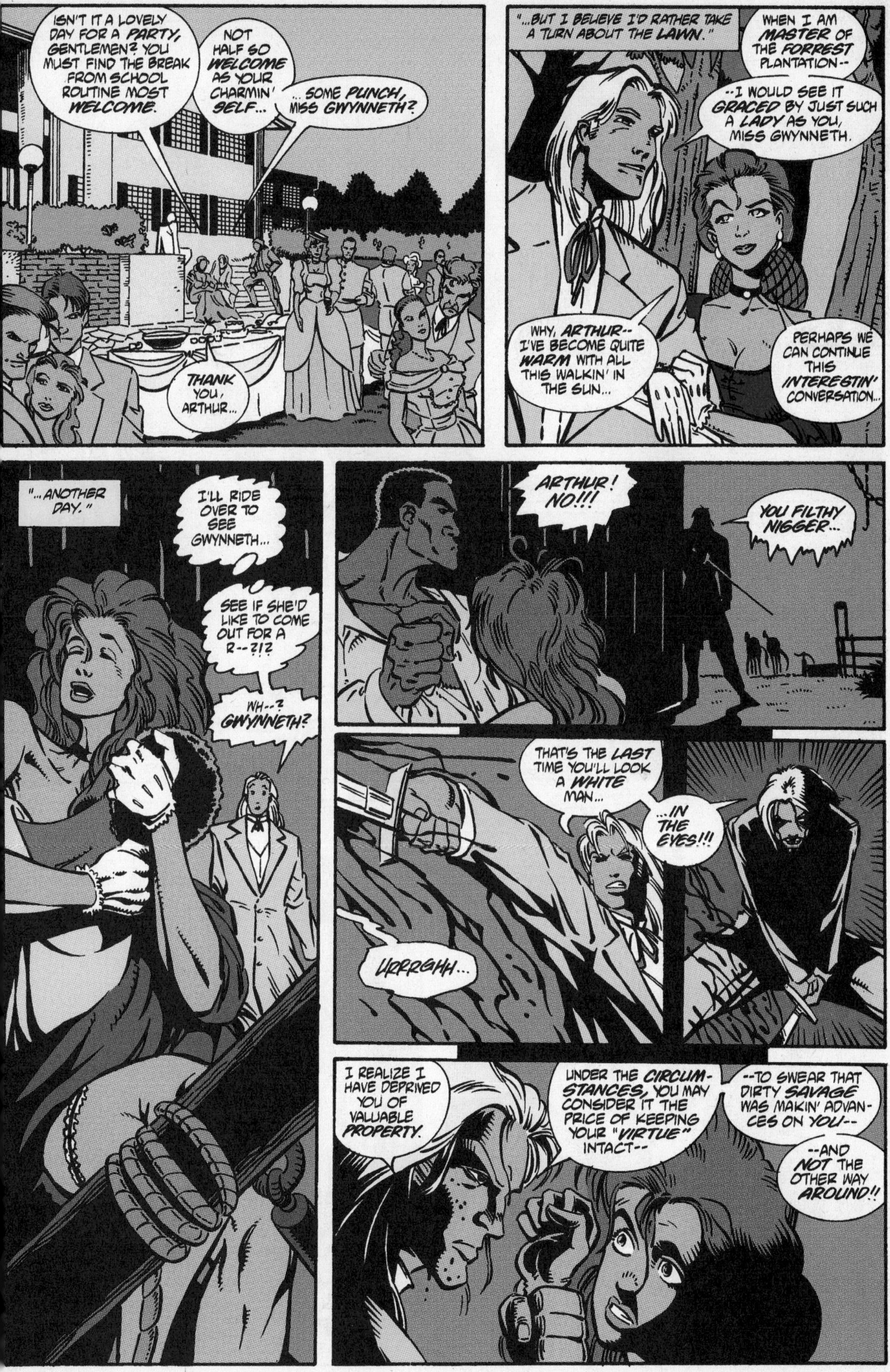
ISN'T IT A LOVELY DAY FOR A PARTY, GENTLEMEN? YOU MUST FIND THE BREAK FROM SCHOOL ROUTINE MOST WELCOME.
NOT HALF SO WELCOME AS YOUR CHARMIN' SELF...
...SOME PUNCH, MISS GWYNNETH?
THANK YOU, ARTHUR...
"...BUT I BELIEVE I'D RATHER TAKE A TURN ABOUT THE LAWN."
WHEN I AM MASTER OF THE FORREST PLANTATION--
--I WOULD SEE IT GRACED BY JUST SUCH A LADY AS YOU, MISS GWYNNETH.
WHY, ARTHUR-- I'VE BECOME QUITE WARM WITH ALL THIS WALKIN' IN THE SUN...
PERHAPS WE CAN CONTINUE THIS INTERESTIN' CONVERSATION...
"...ANOTHER DAY."
I'LL RIDE OVER TO SEE GWYNNETH...
SEE IF SHE'D LIKE TO COME OUT FOR A R--?!?
WH--? GWYNNETH?
ARTHUR! NO!!!
YOU FILTHY NIGGER...
THAT'S THE LAST TIME YOU'LL LOOK A WHITE MAN...
...IN THE EYES!!!
URRRGHH...
I REALIZE I HAVE DEPRIVED YOU OF VALUABLE PROPERTY.
UNDER THE CIRCUMSTANCES, YOU MAY CONSIDER IT THE PRICE OF KEEPING YOUR "VIRTUE" INTACT--
--TO SWEAR THAT DIRTY SAVAGE WAS MAKIN' ADVANCES ON YOU--
--AND NOT THE OTHER WAY AROUND!!

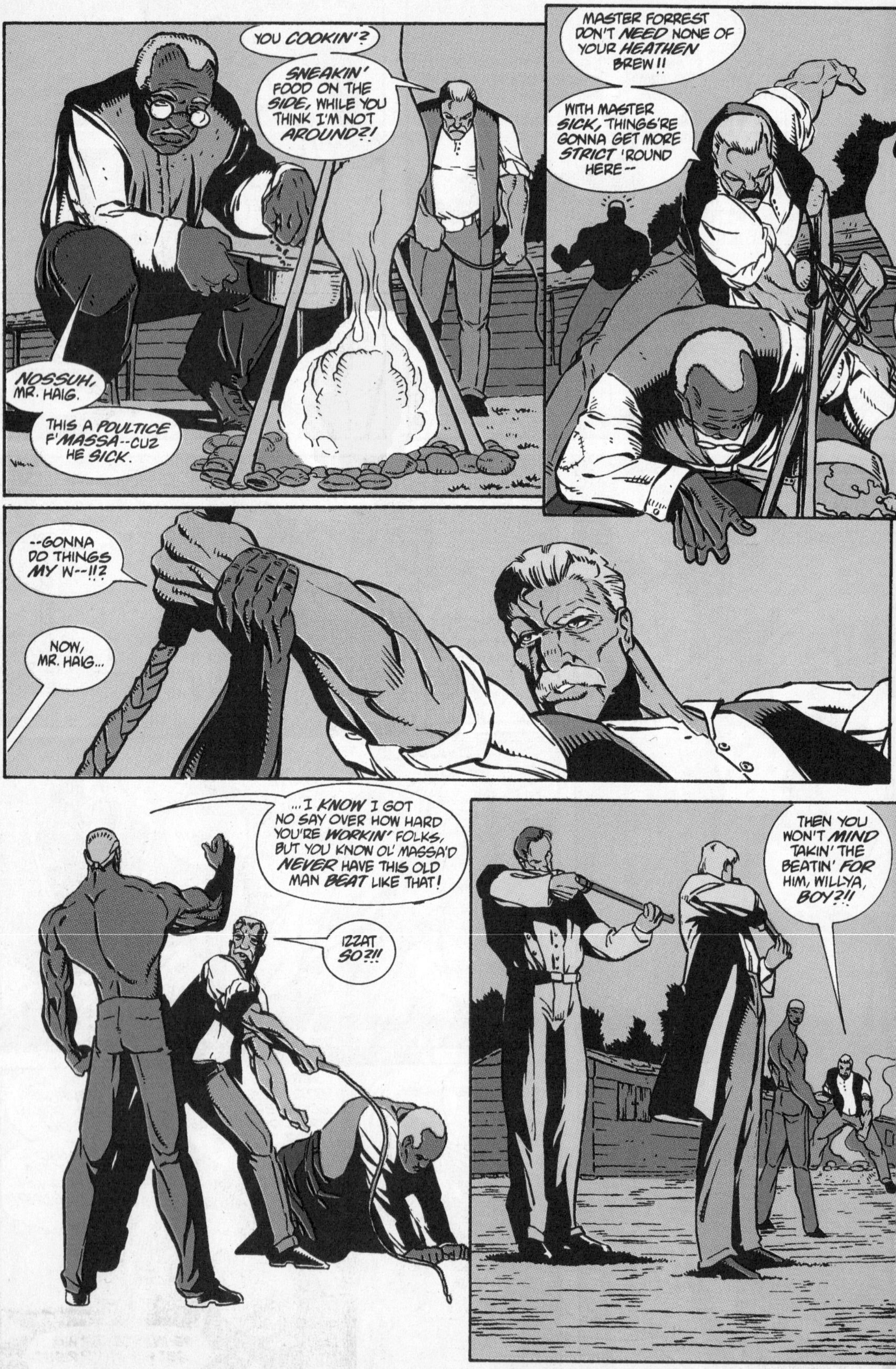
YOU COOKIN'?
SNEAKIN' FOOD ON THE SIDE, WHILE YOU THINK I'M NOT AROUND?!
NOSSUH, MR. HAIG.
THIS A POULTICE F'MASSA--CUZ HE SICK.
MASTER FORREST DON'T NEED NONE OF YOUR HEATHEN BREW!!
WITH MASTER SICK, THINGS'RE GONNA GET MORE STRICT 'ROUND HERE--
--GONNA DO THINGS MY W--!!?
NOW, MR. HAIG...
...I KNOW I GOT NO SAY OVER HOW HARD YOU'RE WORKIN' FOLKS, BUT YOU KNOW OL' MASSA'D NEVER HAVE THIS OLD MAN BEAT LIKE THAT!
IZZAT SO?!!
THEN YOU WON'T MIND TAKIN' THE BEATIN' FOR HIM, WILLYA, BOY?!!

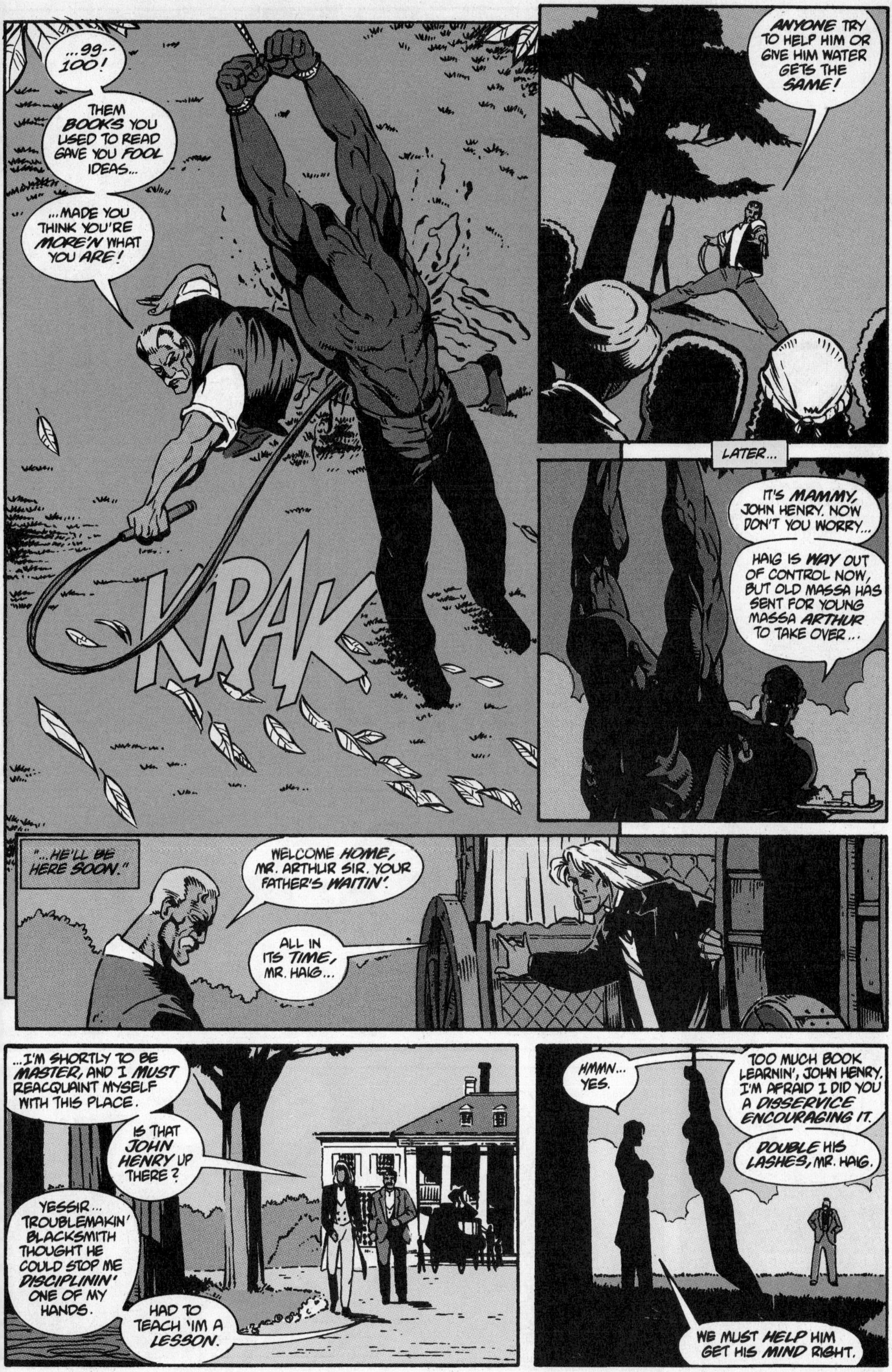
...99--100!
THEM BOOKS YOU USED TO READ GAVE YOU FOOL IDEAS...
...MADE YOU THINK YOU'RE MORE'N WHAT YOU ARE!
KRAK
ANYONE TRY TO HELP HIM OR GIVE HIM WATER GETS THE SAME!
LATER...
IT'S MAMMY, JOHN HENRY. NOW DON'T YOU WORRY...
HAIG IS WAY OUT OF CONTROL NOW, BUT OLD MASSA HAS SENT FOR YOUNG MASSA ARTHUR TO TAKE OVER...
"...HE'LL BE HERE SOON."
WELCOME HOME, MR. ARTHUR SIR. YOUR FATHER'S WAITIN'.
ALL IN ITS TIME, MR. HAIG...
...I'M SHORTLY TO BE MASTER, AND I MUST REACQUAINT MYSELF WITH THIS PLACE.
IS THAT JOHN HENRY UP THERE?
YESSIR... TROUBLEMAKIN' BLACKSMITH THOUGHT HE COULD STOP ME DISCIPLININ' ONE OF MY HANDS.
HAD TO TEACH 'IM A LESSON.
HMMN... YES.
TOO MUCH BOOK LEARNIN', JOHN HENRY. I'M AFRAID I DID YOU A DISSERVICE ENCOURAGING IT.
DOUBLE HIS LASHES, MR. HAIG.
WE MUST HELP HIM GET HIS MIND RIGHT.

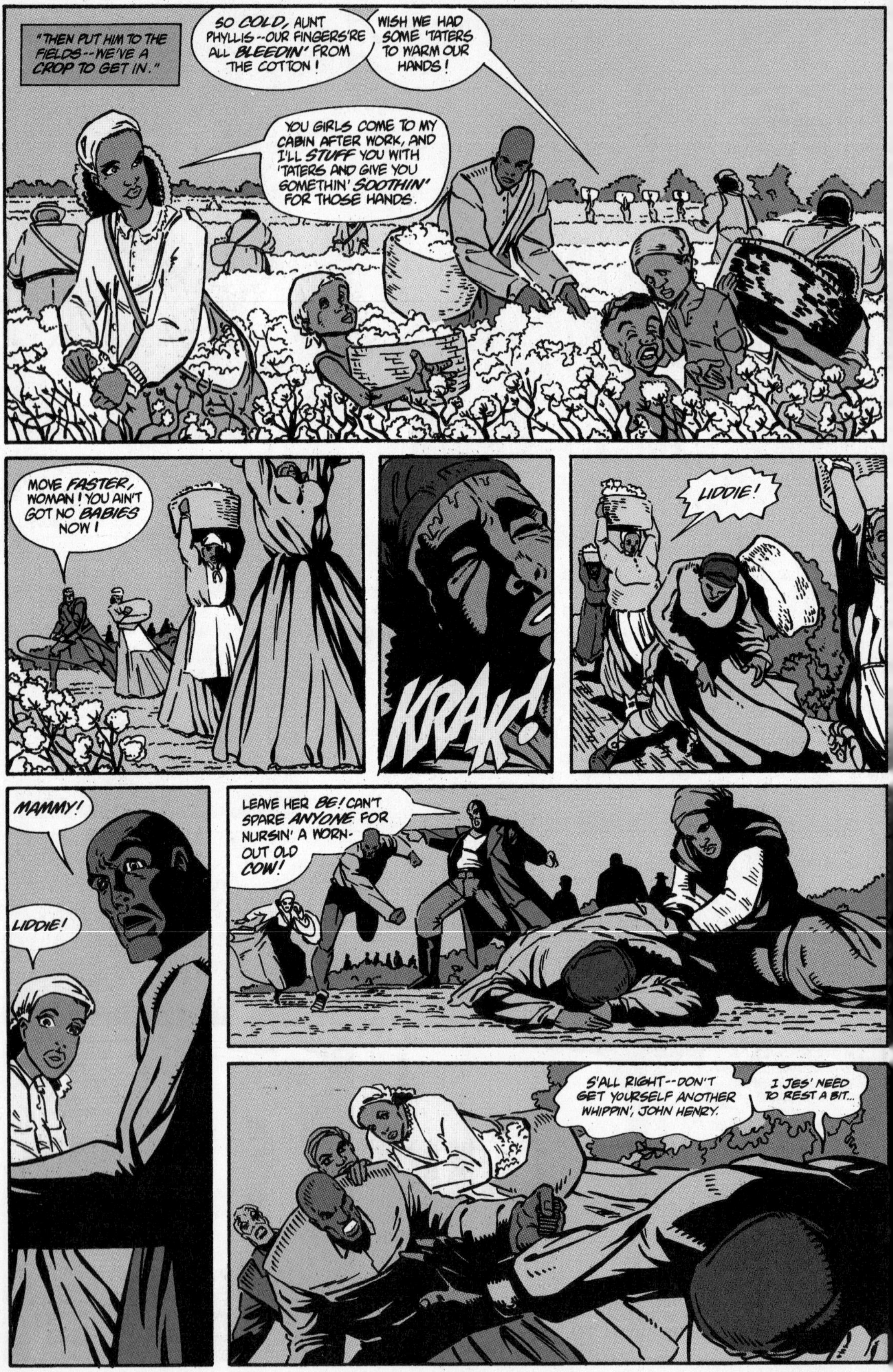
"THEN PUT HIM TO THE FIELDS--WE'VE A CROP TO GET IN."
SO COLD, AUNT PHYLLIS--OUR FINGERS'RE ALL BLEEDIN' FROM THE COTTON!
WISH WE HAD SOME 'TATERS TO WARM OUR HANDS!
YOU GIRLS COME TO MY CABIN AFTER WORK, AND I'LL STUFF YOU WITH 'TATERS AND GIVE YOU SOMETHIN' SOOTHIN' FOR THOSE HANDS.
MOVE FASTER, WOMAN! YOU AIN'T GOT NO BABIES NOW!
KRAK!
LIDDIE!
MAMMY!
LIDDIE!
LEAVE HER BE! CAN'T SPARE ANYONE FOR NURSIN' A WORN-OUT OLD COW!
S'ALL RIGHT--DON'T GET YOURSELF ANOTHER WHIPPIN', JOHN HENRY.
I JES' NEED TO REST A BIT...

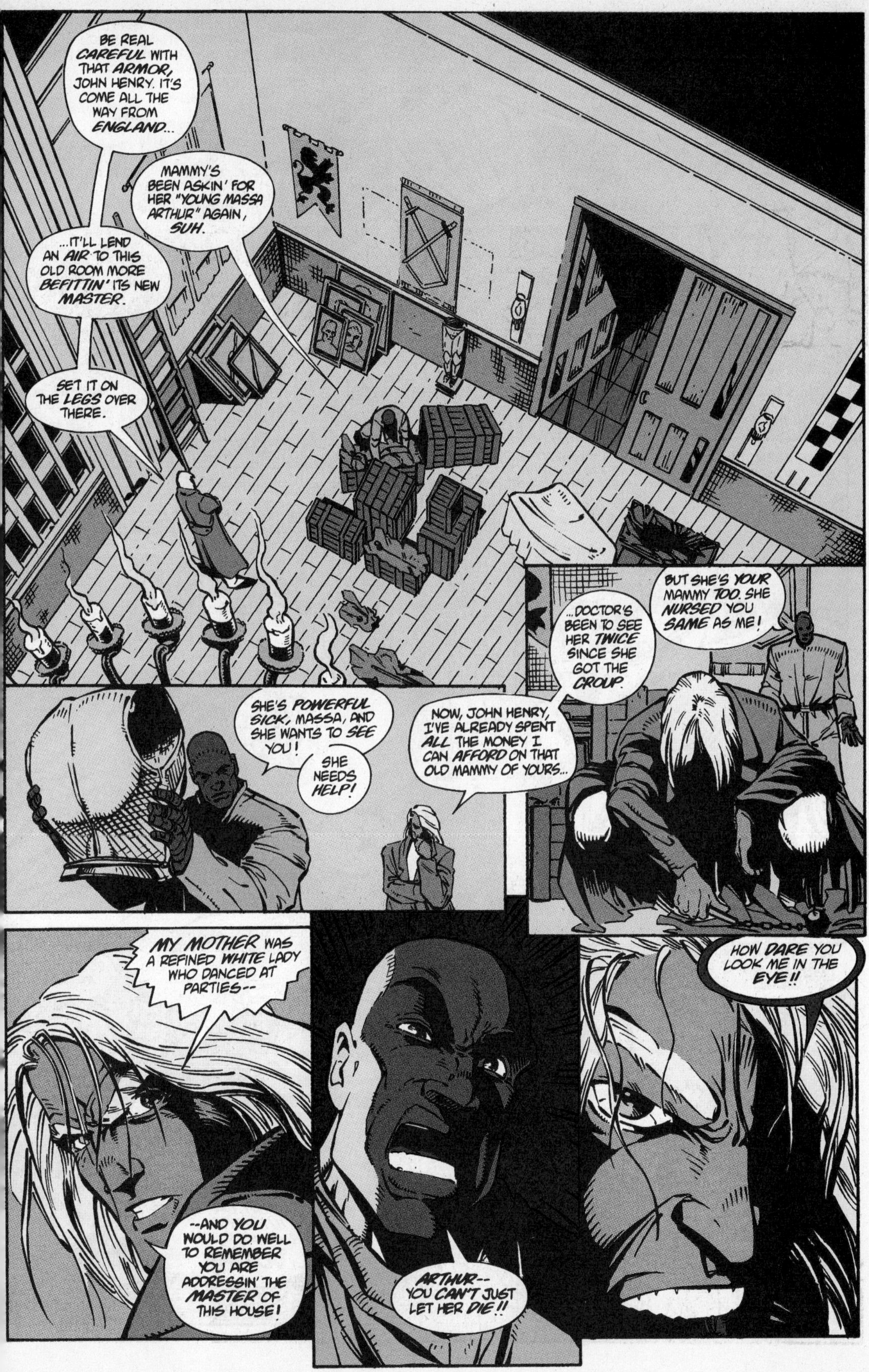

BE REAL CAREFUL WITH THAT ARMOR, JOHN HENRY. IT'S COME ALL THE WAY FROM ENGLAND...
...IT'LL LEND AN AIR TO THIS OLD ROOM MORE BEFITTIN' ITS NEW MASTER.
MAMMY'S BEEN ASKIN' FOR HER "YOUNG MASSA ARTHUR" AGAIN, SUH.
SET IT ON THE LEGS OVER THERE.
SHE'S POWERFUL SICK, MASSA, AND SHE WANTS TO SEE YOU!
SHE NEEDS HELP!
NOW, JOHN HENRY, I'VE ALREADY SPENT ALL THE MONEY I CAN AFFORD ON THAT OLD MAMMY OF YOURS...
...DOCTOR'S BEEN TO SEE HER TWICE SINCE SHE GOT THE CROUP.
BUT SHE'S YOUR MAMMY TOO. SHE NURSED YOU SAME AS ME!
MY MOTHER WAS A REFINED WHITE LADY WHO DANCED AT PARTIES--
--AND YOU WOULD DO WELL TO REMEMBER YOU ARE ADDRESSIN' THE MASTER OF THIS HOUSE!
ARTHUR-- YOU CAN'T JUST LET HER DIE!!
HOW DARE YOU LOOK ME IN THE EYE!!

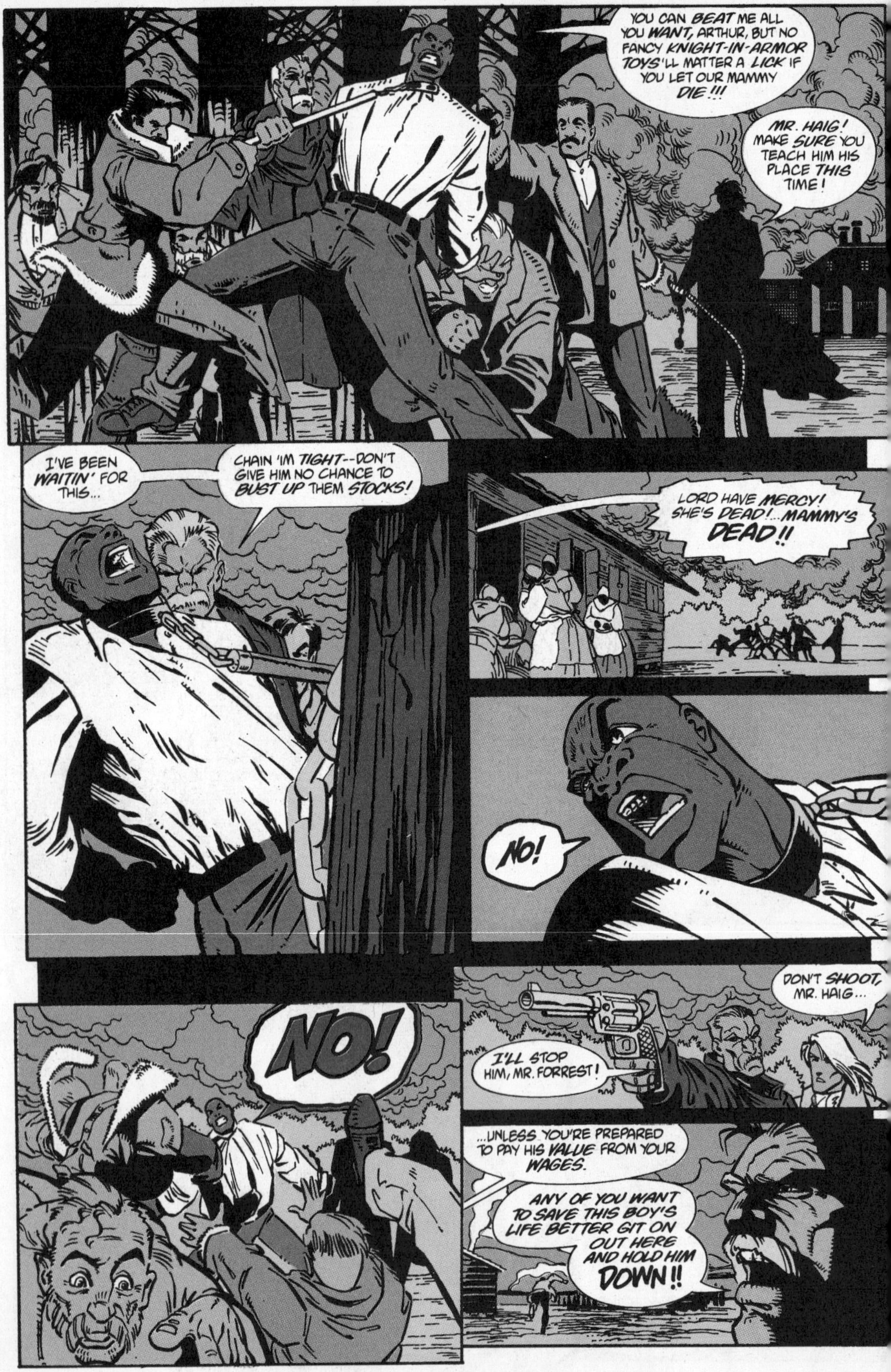
YOU CAN BEAT ME ALL YOU WANT, ARTHUR, BUT NO FANCY KNIGHT-IN-ARMOR TOYS'LL MATTER A LICK IF YOU LET OUR MAMMY DIE!!!
MR. HAIG! MAKE SURE YOU TEACH HIM HIS PLACE THIS TIME!
I'VE BEEN WAITIN' FOR THIS...
CHAIN 'IM TIGHT--DON'T GIVE HIM NO CHANCE TO BUST UP THEM STOCKS!
LORD HAVE MERCY! SHE'S DEAD!...MAMMY'S DEAD!!
NO!
NO!
DON'T SHOOT, MR. HAIG...
I'LL STOP HIM, MR. FORREST!
...UNLESS YOU'RE PREPARED TO PAY HIS VALUE FROM YOUR WAGES.
ANY OF YOU WANT TO SAVE THIS BOY'S LIFE BETTER GIT ON OUT HERE AND HOLD HIM DOWN!!

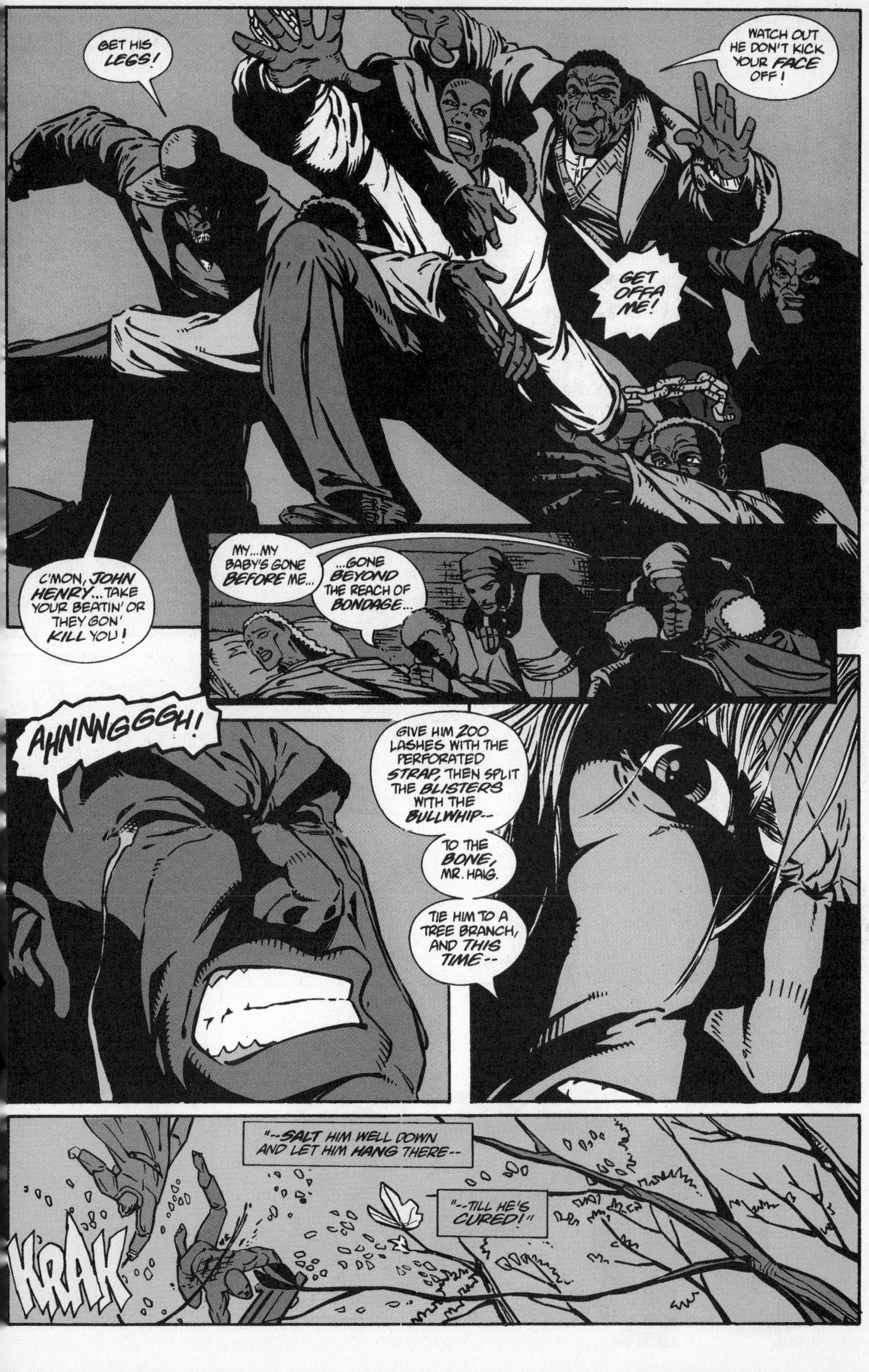
GET HIS LEGS!
WATCH OUT HE DON'T KICK YOUR FACE OFF!
GET OFFA ME!
C'MON, JOHN HENRY... TAKE YOUR BEATIN' OR THEY GON' KILL YOU!
MY... MY BABY'S GONE BEFORE ME...
...GONE BEYOND THE REACH OF BONDAGE...
AHNNNGGGH!
GIVE HIM 200 LASHES WITH THE PERFORATED STRAP, THEN SPLIT THE BLISTERS WITH THE BULLWHIP--
TO THE BONE, MR. HAIG.
TIE HIM TO A TREE BRANCH, AND THIS TIME--
"--SALT HIM WELL DOWN AND LET HIM HANG THERE--
"--TILL HE'S CURED!"
KRAK

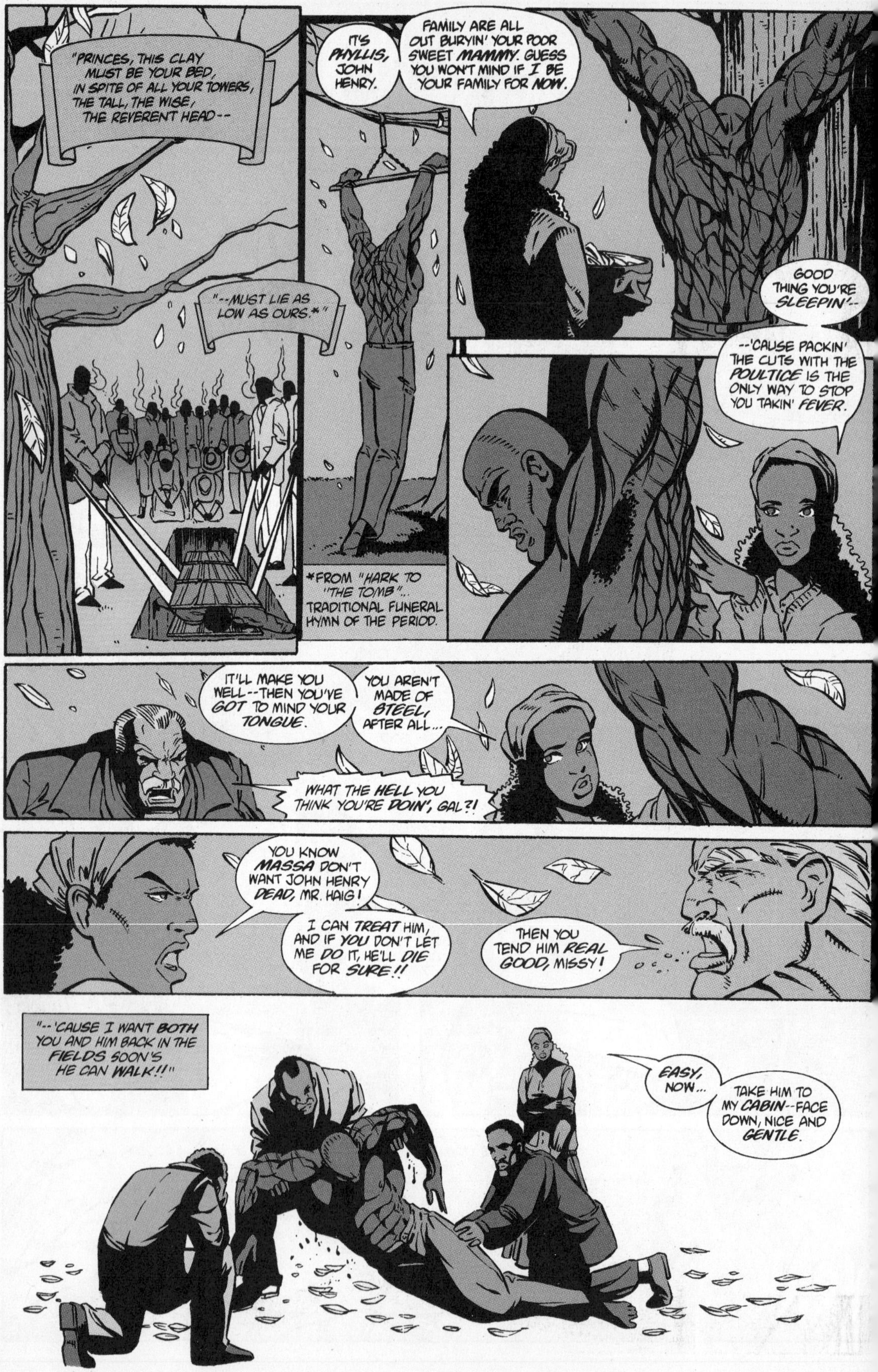
"PRINCES, THIS CLAY MUST BE YOUR BED, IN SPITE OF ALL YOUR TOWERS, THE TALL, THE WISE, THE REVERENT HEAD--
"--MUST LIE AS LOW AS OURS.*"
IT'S PHYLLIS, JOHN HENRY.
FAMILY ARE ALL OUT BURYIN' YOUR POOR SWEET MAMMY. GUESS YOU WON'T MIND IF I BE YOUR FAMILY FOR NOW.
*FROM "HARK TO THE TOMB"... TRADITIONAL FUNERAL HYMN OF THE PERIOD.
GOOD THING YOU'RE SLEEPIN'--
--'CAUSE PACKIN' THE CUTS WITH THE POULTICE IS THE ONLY WAY TO STOP YOU TAKIN' FEVER.
IT'LL MAKE YOU WELL--THEN YOU'VE GOT TO MIND YOUR TONGUE.
YOU AREN'T MADE OF STEEL, AFTER ALL...
WHAT THE HELL YOU THINK YOU'RE DOIN', GAL?!
YOU KNOW MASSA DON'T WANT JOHN HENRY DEAD, MR. HAIG!
I CAN TREAT HIM, AND IF YOU DON'T LET ME DO IT, HE'LL DIE FOR SURE!!
THEN YOU TEND HIM REAL GOOD, MISSY!
"--'CAUSE I WANT BOTH YOU AND HIM BACK IN THE FIELDS SOON'S HE CAN WALK!!"
EASY, NOW...
TAKE HIM TO MY CABIN--FACE DOWN, NICE AND GENTLE.

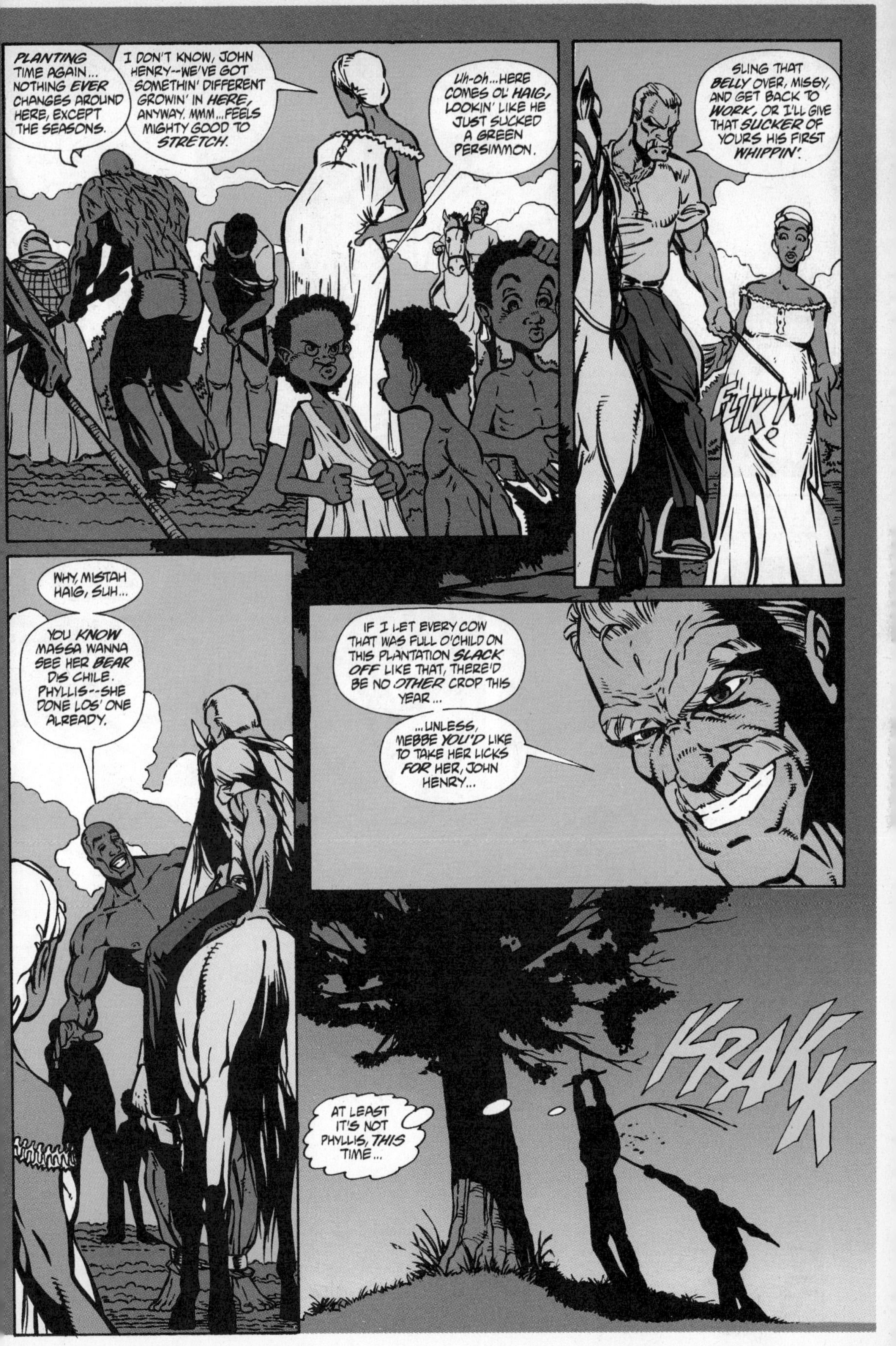
PLANTING TIME AGAIN... NOTHING EVER CHANGES AROUND HERE, EXCEPT THE SEASONS.
I DON'T KNOW, JOHN HENRY--WE'VE GOT SOMETHIN' DIFFERENT GROWIN' IN HERE, ANYWAY. MMM...FEELS MIGHTY GOOD TO STRETCH.
Uh-oh...HERE COMES OL' HAIG, LOOKIN' LIKE HE JUST SUCKED A GREEN PERSIMMON.
SLING THAT BELLY OVER, MISSY, AND GET BACK TO WORK, OR I'LL GIVE THAT SUCKER OF YOURS HIS FIRST WHIPPIN'.
FLIK!
WHY, MISTAH HAIG, SUH...
YOU KNOW MASSA WANNA SEE HER BEAR DIS CHILE. PHYLLIS--SHE DONE LOS' ONE ALREADY.
IF I LET EVERY COW THAT WAS FULL O'CHILD ON THIS PLANTATION SLACK OFF LIKE THAT, THERE'D BE NO OTHER CROP THIS YEAR...
...UNLESS, MEBBE YOU'D LIKE TO TAKE HER LICKS FOR HER, JOHN HENRY...
KRAKK
AT LEAST IT'S NOT PHYLLIS, THIS TIME...

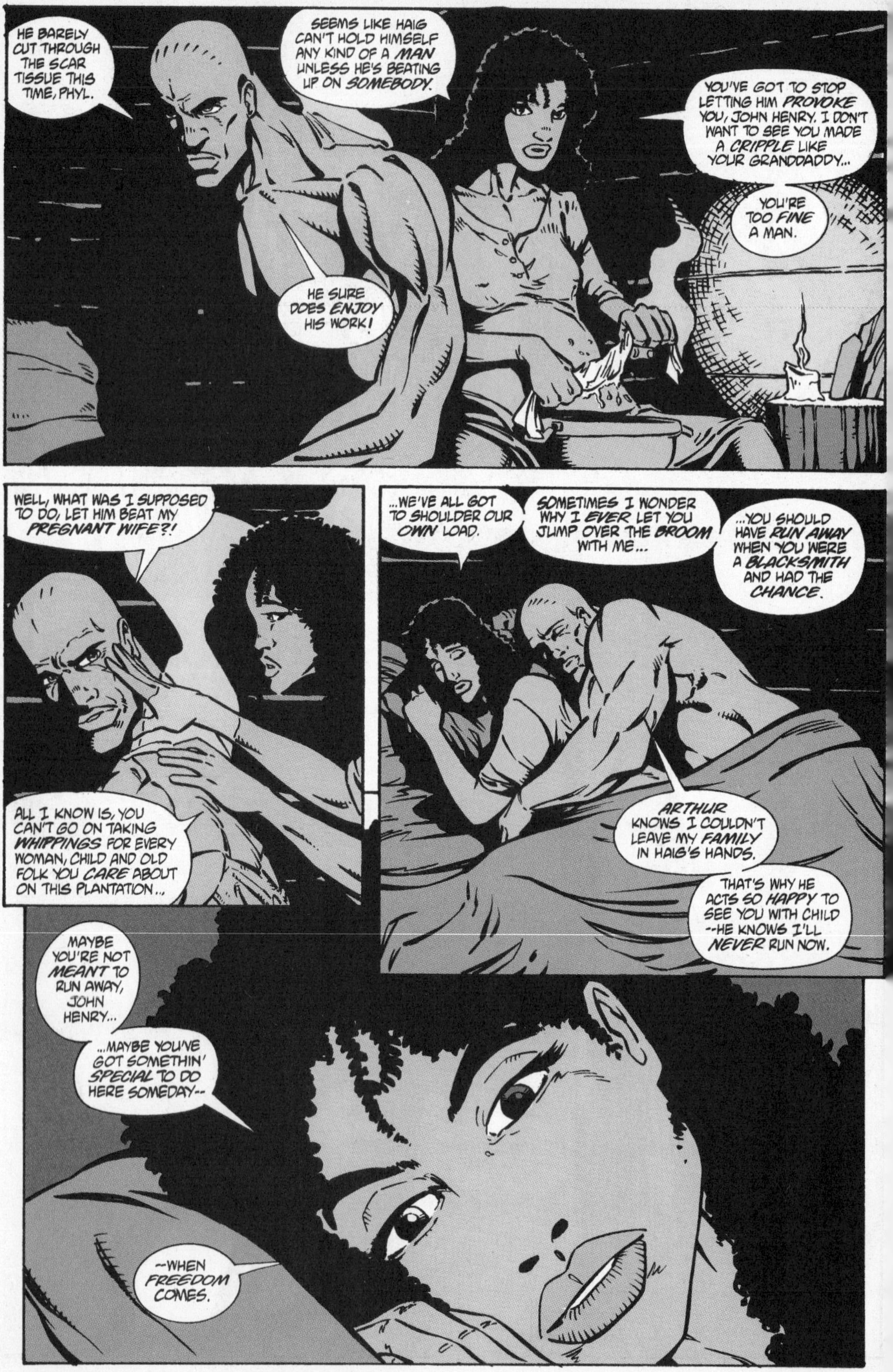
HE BARELY CUT THROUGH THE SCAR TISSUE THIS TIME, PHYL.
SEEMS LIKE HAIG CAN'T HOLD HIMSELF ANY KIND OF A MAN UNLESS HE'S BEATING UP ON SOMEBODY.
HE SURE DOES ENJOY HIS WORK!
YOU'VE GOT TO STOP LETTING HIM PROVOKE YOU, JOHN HENRY. I DON'T WANT TO SEE YOU MADE A CRIPPLE LIKE YOUR GRANDDADDY...
YOU'RE TOO FINE A MAN.
WELL, WHAT WAS I SUPPOSED TO DO, LET HIM BEAT MY PREGNANT WIFE?!
ALL I KNOW IS, YOU CAN'T GO ON TAKING WHIPPINGS FOR EVERY WOMAN, CHILD AND OLD FOLK YOU CARE ABOUT ON THIS PLANTATION...
...WE'VE ALL GOT TO SHOULDER OUR OWN LOAD.
SOMETIMES I WONDER WHY I EVER LET YOU JUMP OVER THE BROOM WITH ME...
...YOU SHOULD HAVE RUN AWAY WHEN YOU WERE A BLACKSMITH AND HAD THE CHANCE.
ARTHUR KNOWS I COULDN'T LEAVE MY FAMILY IN HAIG'S HANDS.
THAT'S WHY HE ACTS SO HAPPY TO SEE YOU WITH CHILD --HE KNOWS I'LL NEVER RUN NOW.
MAYBE YOU'RE NOT MEANT TO RUN AWAY, JOHN HENRY...
...MAYBE YOU'VE GOT SOMETHIN' SPECIAL TO DO HERE SOMEDAY--
--WHEN FREEDOM COMES.

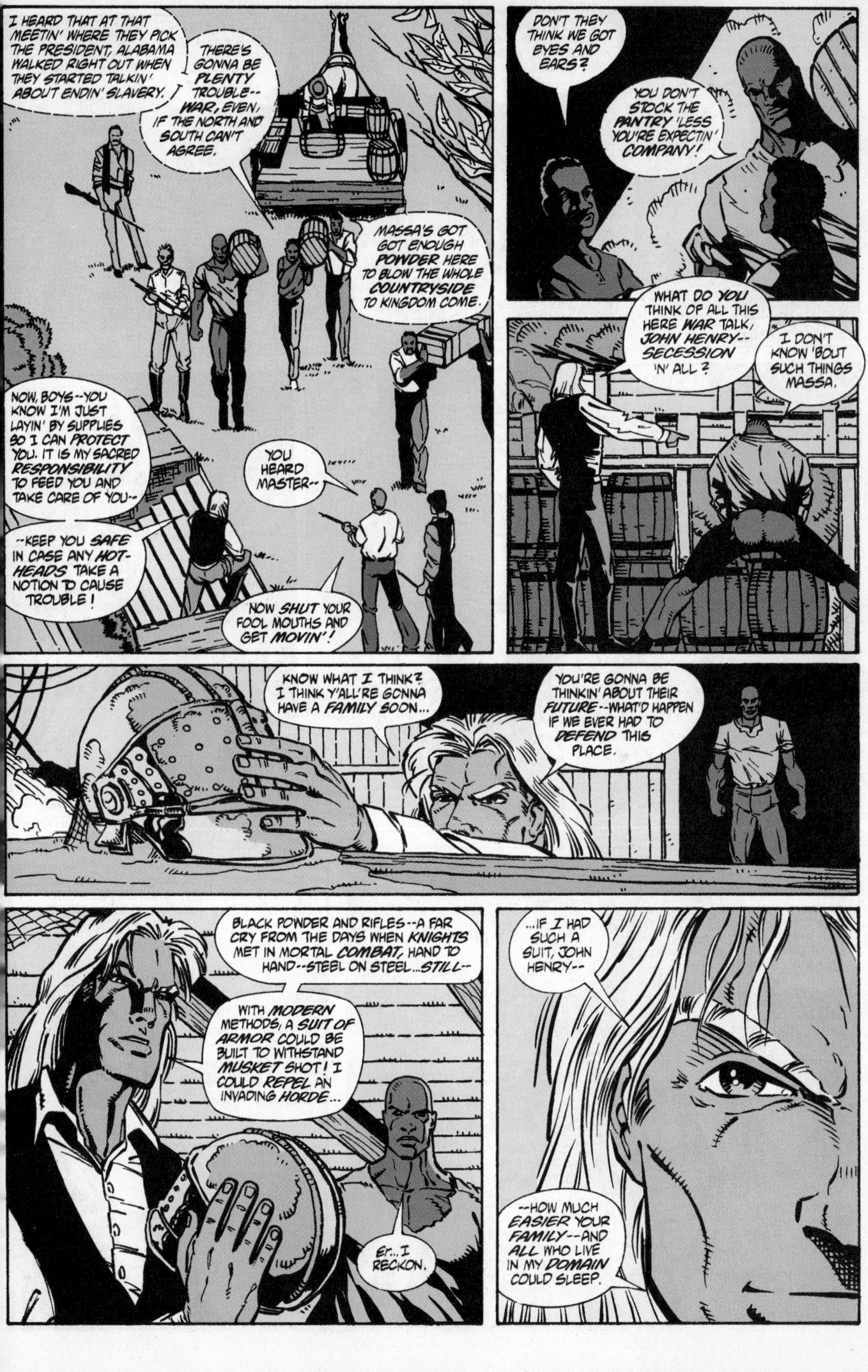
I HEARD THAT AT THAT MEETIN' WHERE THEY PICK THE PRESIDENT, ALABAMA WALKED RIGHT OUT WHEN THEY STARTED TALKIN' ABOUT ENDIN' SLAVERY.
THERE'S GONNA BE PLENTY TROUBLE-- WAR, EVEN, IF THE NORTH AND SOUTH CAN'T AGREE.
MASSA'S GOT GOT ENOUGH POWDER HERE TO BLOW THE WHOLE COUNTRYSIDE TO KINGDOM COME.
NOW, BOYS--YOU KNOW I'M JUST LAYIN' BY SUPPLIES SO I CAN PROTECT YOU. IT IS MY SACRED RESPONSIBILITY TO FEED YOU AND TAKE CARE OF YOU--
--KEEP YOU SAFE IN CASE ANY HOT-HEADS TAKE A NOTION TO CAUSE TROUBLE!
YOU HEARD MASTER--
NOW SHUT YOUR FOOL MOUTHS AND GET MOVIN'!
DON'T THEY THINK WE GOT EYES AND EARS?
YOU DON'T STOCK THE PANTRY 'LESS YOU'RE EXPECTIN' COMPANY!
WHAT DO YOU THINK OF ALL THIS HERE WAR TALK, JOHN HENRY-- SECESSION 'N' ALL?
I DON'T KNOW 'BOUT SUCH THINGS MASSA.
KNOW WHAT I THINK? I THINK Y'ALL'RE GONNA HAVE A FAMILY SOON...
YOU'RE GONNA BE THINKIN' ABOUT THEIR FUTURE--WHAT'D HAPPEN IF WE EVER HAD TO DEFEND THIS PLACE.
BLACK POWDER AND RIFLES--A FAR CRY FROM THE DAYS WHEN KNIGHTS MET IN MORTAL COMBAT, HAND TO HAND--STEEL ON STEEL...STILL--
WITH MODERN METHODS, A SUIT OF ARMOR COULD BE BUILT TO WITHSTAND MUSKET SHOT! I COULD REPEL AN INVADING HORDE...
Er... I RECKON.
...IF I HAD SUCH A SUIT, JOHN HENRY--
--HOW MUCH EASIER YOUR FAMILY--AND ALL WHO LIVE IN MY DOMAIN COULD SLEEP.

"YOU BUILD SUCH A SUIT FOR ME, JOHN HENRY, AND I'LL LET YOU BE *BLACKSMITH* AGAIN..."

I *TOLD* HIM, "AH'S *FORGOT* ALL 'BOUT 'SMITHIN' BY NOW, *MASSA*." HE WAS MIGHTY *ANGRY*, BUT HE COULDN'T DO ANYTHING ABOUT IT.

NOW *WHAT'D* YOU GO 'N SAY SUCH A THING FOR, *FOOL*?! SMITHS GET *PRIVILEGES*!

YOU COULD BETTER YOUR *FAMILY*-- MAYBE GET PHYLLIS A JOB UP TO THE *BIG HOUSE*!!

HUSH YOURSELF, ISABEL... AFTER ALL-- YOU'S THE *BEST* BLACKSMITH WHO *EVER* LIVED!

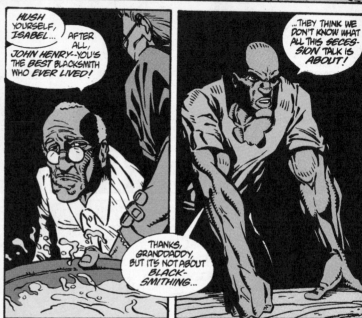

...THEY THINK WE DON'T KNOW WHAT ALL THIS *SECES-SION* TALK IS *ABOUT*!

THANKS, GRANDDADDY, BUT IT'S NOT ABOUT *BLACK-SMITHING*...

BUT *ARTHUR* WANTS *ME* TO INVENT A WEAPON THAT'LL HELP KEEP US SLAVES...

...AND KEEP HIS *BUTT* FROM GETTING SHOT UP AT THE SAME TIME!

I SAY *TAKE* THE JOB, JOHN HENRY...

...MAYBE IT'LL LEAD TO SOMETHIN' *BETTER* AND PUT *YOU* IN A BETTER POSITION TO KNOW WHAT'S *COMIN'*.

SORRY, FOLKS ...I TOLD HIM *NO*, AND IT'S *STILL NO*.

WE MAY BE SLAVES *NOW*... BUT I'M NOT ABOUT TO HELP *PERPETUATE* THAT CONDITION!!!

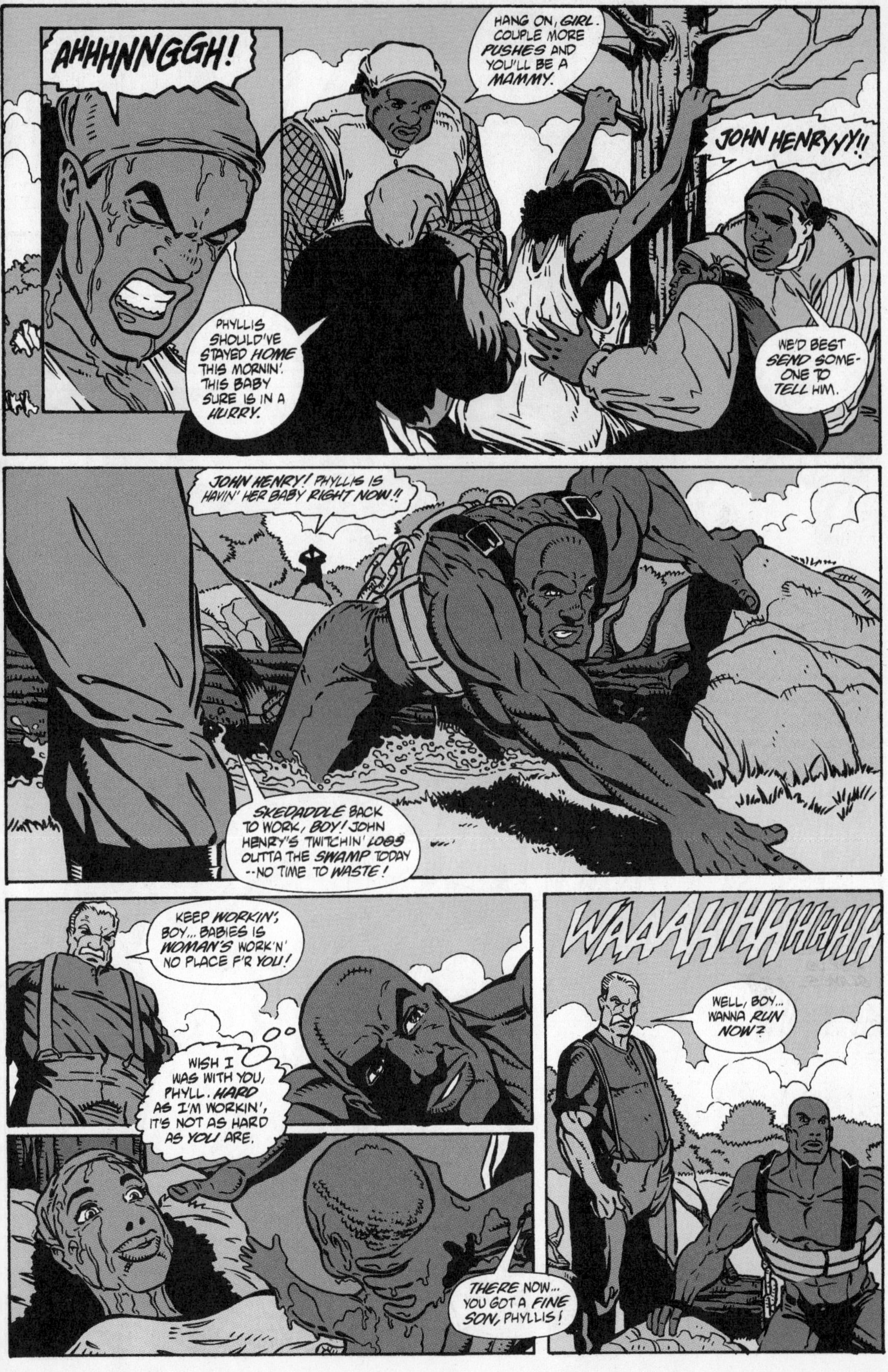
AHHHNNGGH!
HANG ON, GIRL. COUPLE MORE PUSHES AND YOU'LL BE A MAMMY.
JOHN HENRYYY!!
PHYLLIS SHOULD'VE STAYED HOME THIS MORNIN'. THIS BABY SURE IS IN A HURRY.
WE'D BEST SEND SOME-ONE TO TELL HIM.
JOHN HENRY! PHYLLIS IS HAVIN' HER BABY RIGHT NOW!!
SKEDADDLE BACK TO WORK, BOY! JOHN HENRY'S TWITCHIN' LOGS OUTTA THE SWAMP TODAY --NO TIME TO WASTE!
KEEP WORKIN', BOY... BABIES IS WOMAN'S WORK'N' NO PLACE F'R YOU!
WISH I WAS WITH YOU, PHYLL. HARD AS I'M WORKIN', IT'S NOT AS HARD AS YOU ARE.
THERE NOW... YOU GOT A FINE SON, PHYLLIS!
WAAAHHHHHHH
WELL, BOY... WANNA RUN NOW?

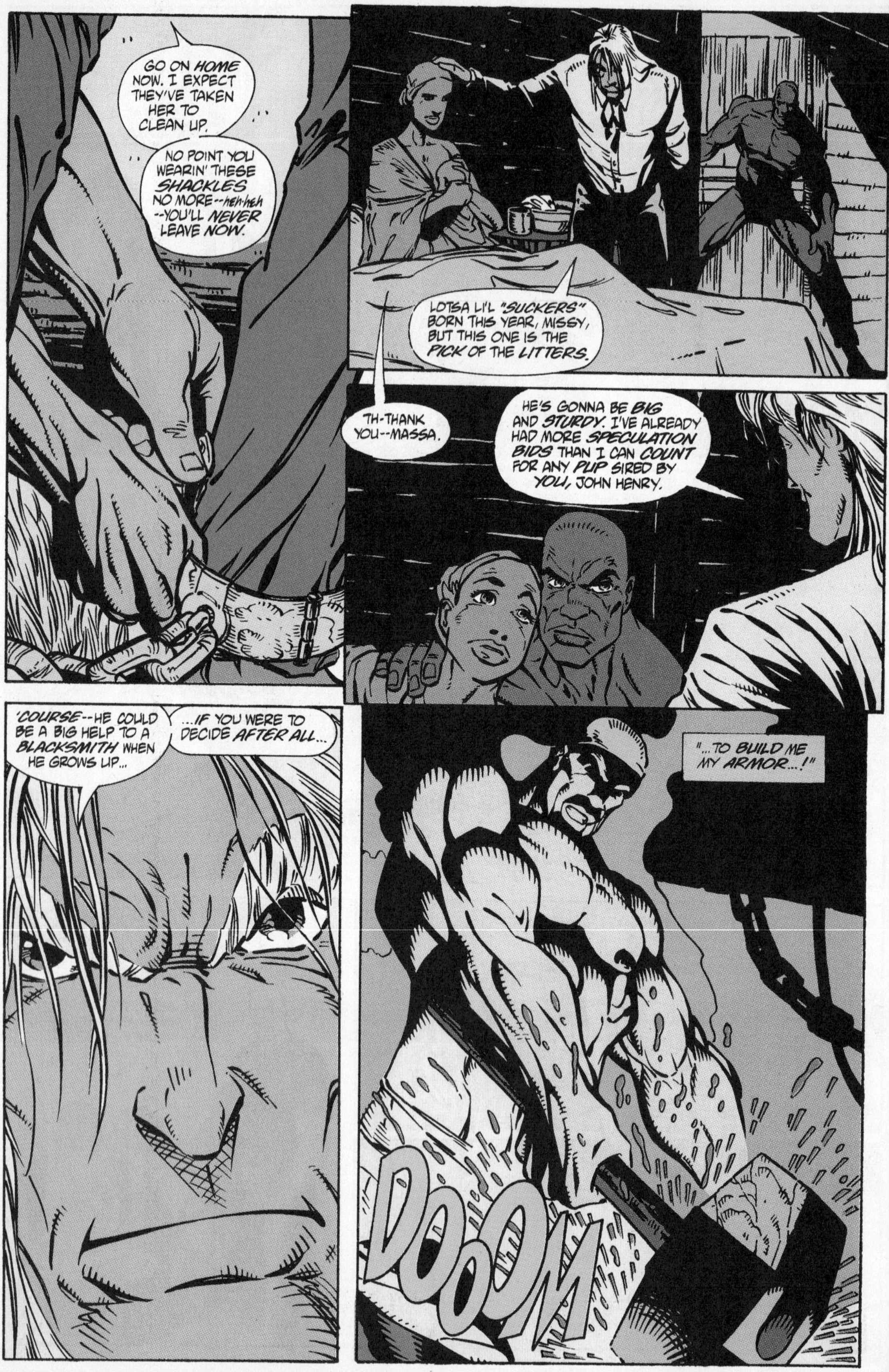
GO ON HOME NOW. I EXPECT THEY'VE TAKEN HER TO CLEAN UP.
NO POINT YOU WEARIN' THESE SHACKLES NO MORE--heh-heh --YOU'LL NEVER LEAVE NOW.
LOTSA LI'L "SUCKERS" BORN THIS YEAR, MISSY, BUT THIS ONE IS THE PICK OF THE LITTERS.
TH-THANK YOU--MASSA.
HE'S GONNA BE BIG AND STURDY. I'VE ALREADY HAD MORE SPECULATION BIDS THAN I CAN COUNT FOR ANY PUP SIRED BY YOU, JOHN HENRY.
'COURSE--HE COULD BE A BIG HELP TO A BLACKSMITH WHEN HE GROWS UP...
...IF YOU WERE TO DECIDE AFTER ALL...
"...TO BUILD ME MY ARMOR...!"
DOOOM

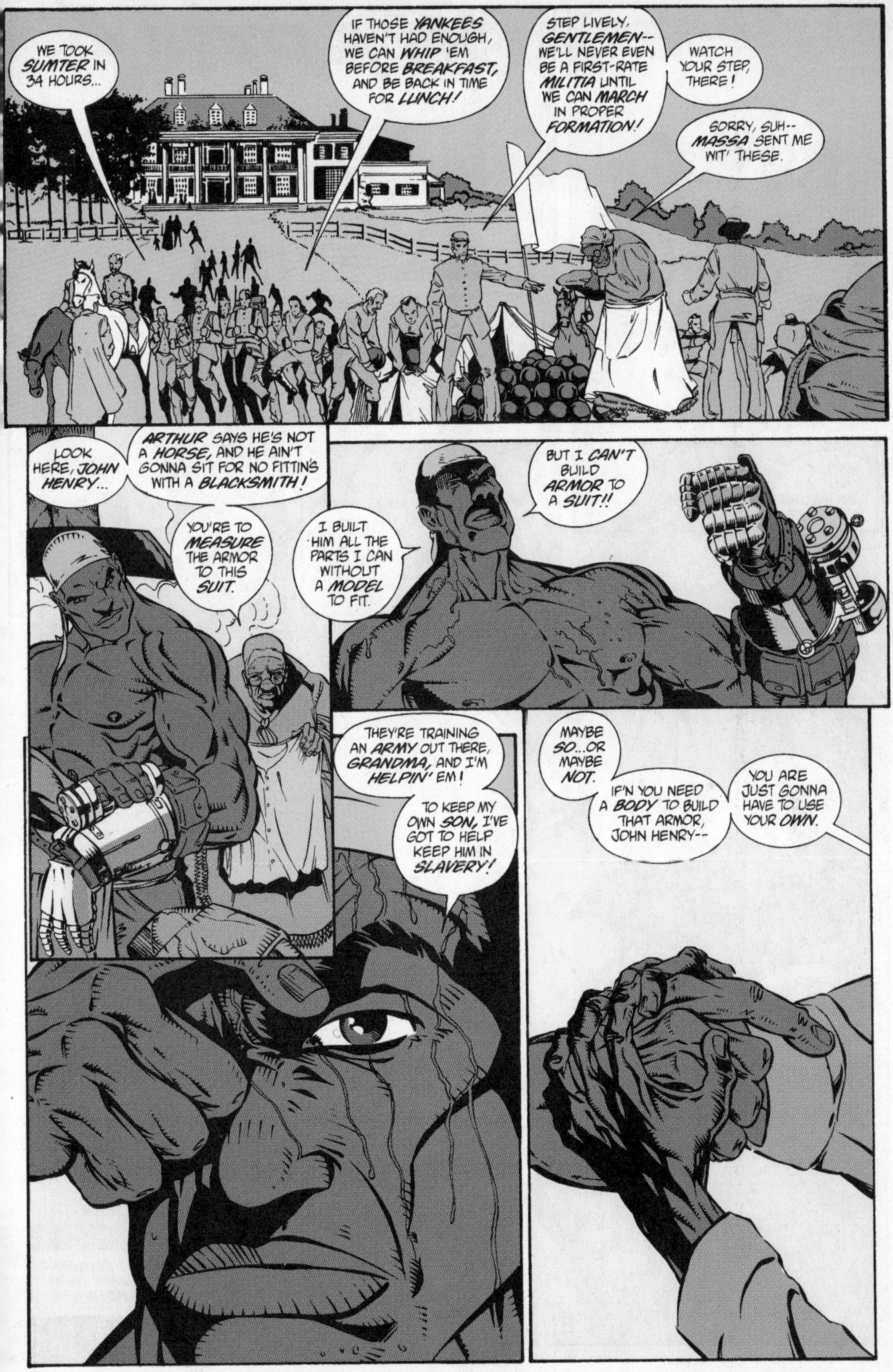

WE TOOK SUMTER IN 34 HOURS...
IF THOSE YANKEES HAVEN'T HAD ENOUGH, WE CAN WHIP 'EM BEFORE BREAKFAST, AND BE BACK IN TIME FOR LUNCH!
STEP LIVELY, GENTLEMEN-- WE'LL NEVER EVEN BE A FIRST-RATE MILITIA UNTIL WE CAN MARCH IN PROPER FORMATION!
WATCH YOUR STEP, THERE!
SORRY, SUH-- MASSA SENT ME WIT' THESE.
LOOK HERE, JOHN HENRY...
ARTHUR SAYS HE'S NOT A HORSE, AND HE AIN'T GONNA SIT FOR NO FITTIN'S WITH A BLACKSMITH!
YOU'RE TO MEASURE THE ARMOR TO THIS SUIT.
I BUILT HIM ALL THE PARTS I CAN WITHOUT A MODEL TO FIT.
BUT I CAN'T BUILD ARMOR TO A SUIT!!
THEY'RE TRAINING AN ARMY OUT THERE, GRANDMA, AND I'M HELPIN' 'EM!
TO KEEP MY OWN SON, I'VE GOT TO HELP KEEP HIM IN SLAVERY!
MAYBE SO...OR MAYBE NOT.
IF'N YOU NEED A BODY TO BUILD THAT ARMOR, JOHN HENRY--
YOU ARE JUST GONNA HAVE TO USE YOUR OWN.

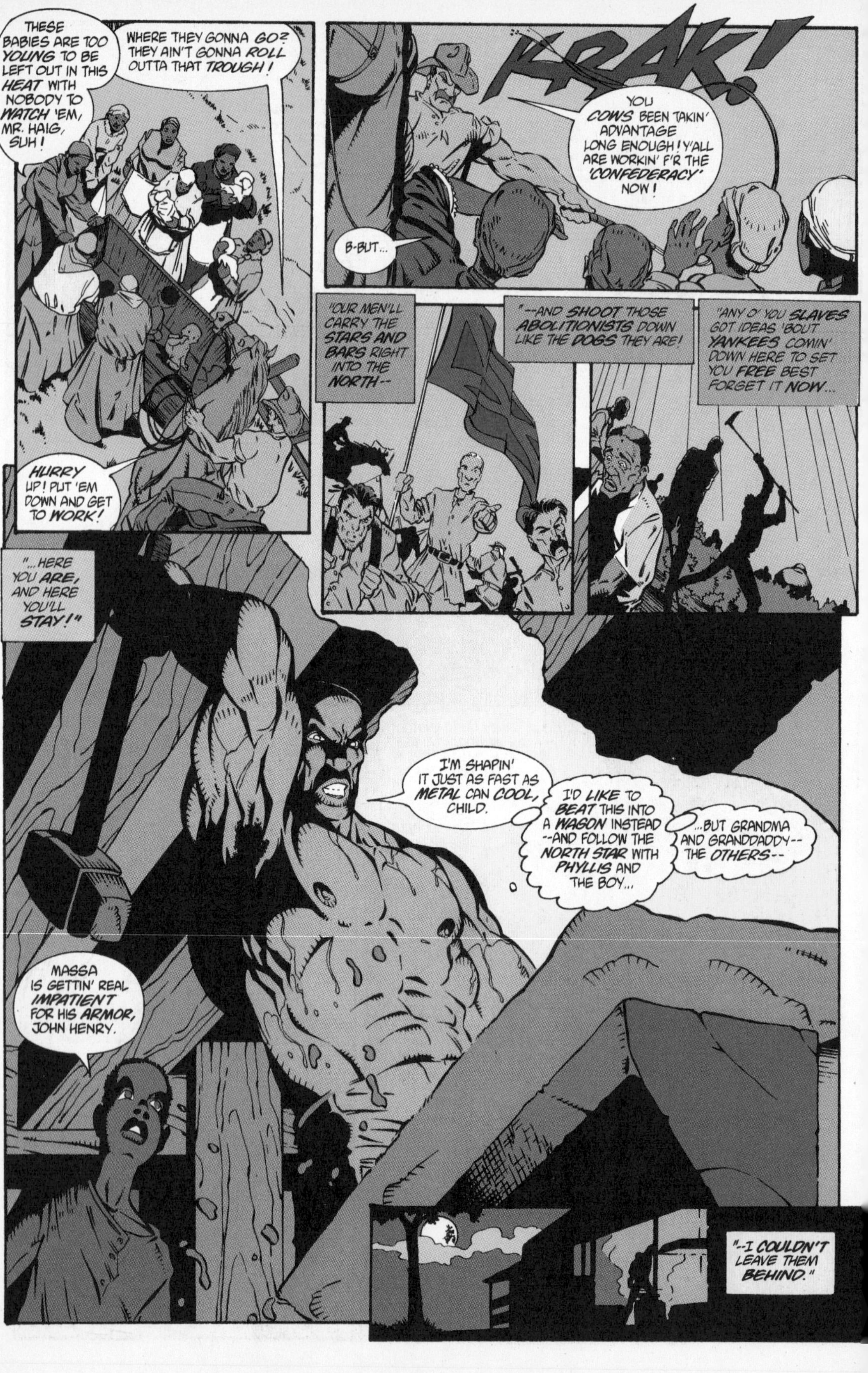
THESE BABIES ARE TOO YOUNG TO BE LEFT OUT IN THIS HEAT WITH NOBODY TO WATCH 'EM, MR. HAIG, SUH!
WHERE THEY GONNA GO? THEY AIN'T GONNA ROLL OUTTA THAT TROUGH!
HURRY UP! PUT 'EM DOWN AND GET TO WORK!
KRAK!
YOU COWS BEEN TAKIN' ADVANTAGE LONG ENOUGH! Y'ALL ARE WORKIN' F'R THE 'CONFEDERACY' NOW!
B-BUT...
"OUR MEN'LL CARRY THE STARS AND BARS RIGHT INTO THE NORTH--
"--AND SHOOT THOSE ABOLITIONISTS DOWN LIKE THE DOGS THEY ARE!
"ANY O' YOU SLAVES GOT IDEAS 'BOUT YANKEES COMIN' DOWN HERE TO SET YOU FREE BEST FORGET IT NOW...
"...HERE YOU ARE, AND HERE YOU'LL STAY!"
MASSA IS GETTIN' REAL IMPATIENT FOR HIS ARMOR, JOHN HENRY.
I'M SHAPIN' IT JUST AS FAST AS METAL CAN COOL, CHILD.
I'D LIKE TO BEAT THIS INTO A WAGON INSTEAD --AND FOLLOW THE NORTH STAR WITH PHYLLIS AND THE BOY...
...BUT GRANDMA AND GRANDDADDY-- THE OTHERS--
"--I COULDN'T LEAVE THEM BEHIND."

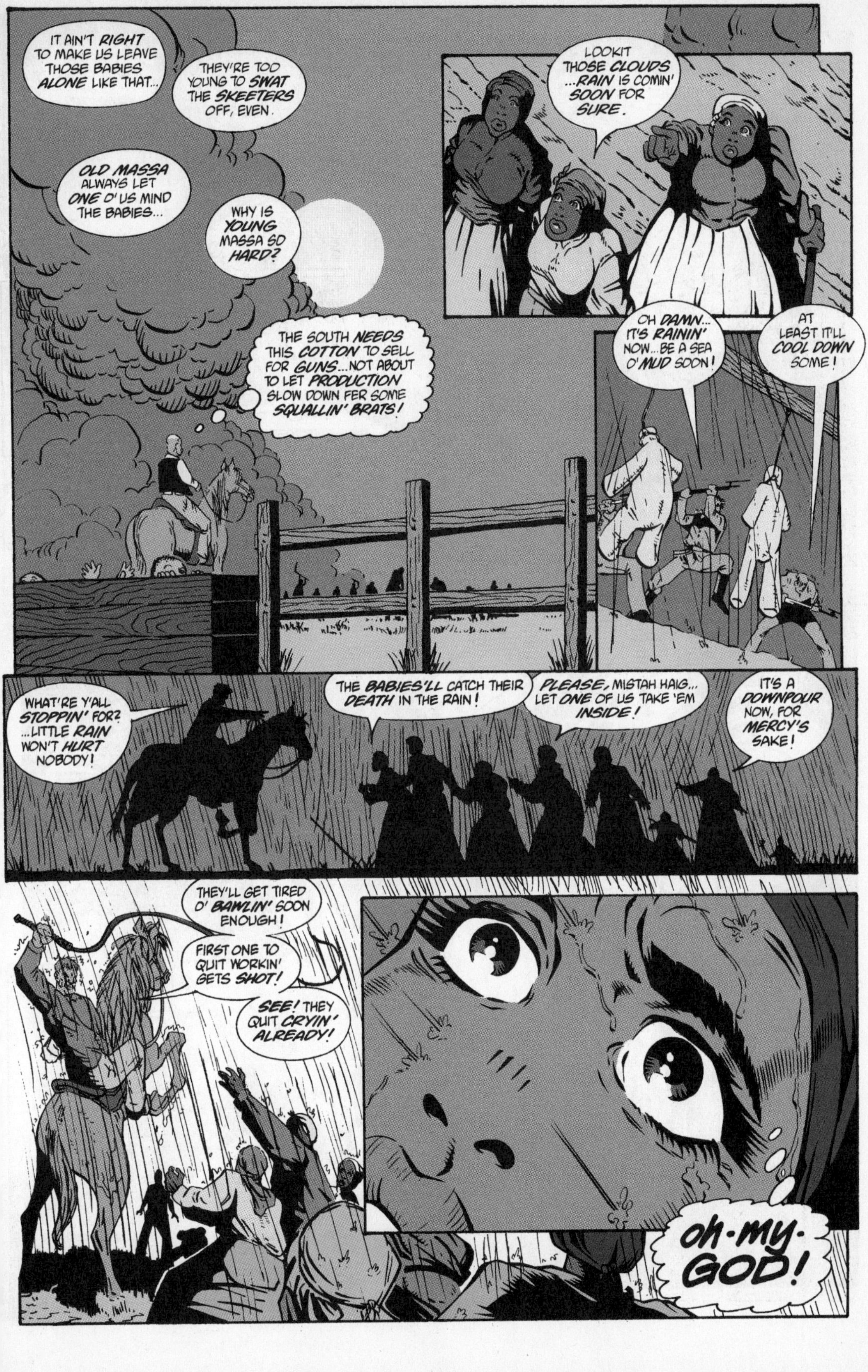
IT AIN'T RIGHT TO MAKE US LEAVE THOSE BABIES ALONE LIKE THAT...
THEY'RE TOO YOUNG TO SWAT THE SKEETERS OFF, EVEN.
OLD MASSA ALWAYS LET ONE O' US MIND THE BABIES...
WHY IS YOUNG MASSA SO HARD?
THE SOUTH NEEDS THIS COTTON TO SELL FOR GUNS...NOT ABOUT TO LET PRODUCTION SLOW DOWN FER SOME SQUALLIN' BRATS!
LOOKIT THOSE CLOUDS ...RAIN IS COMIN' SOON FOR SURE.
OH DAMN... IT'S RAININ' NOW...BE A SEA O' MUD SOON!
AT LEAST IT'LL COOL DOWN SOME!
WHAT'RE Y'ALL STOPPIN' FOR? ...LITTLE RAIN WON'T HURT NOBODY!
THE BABIES'LL CATCH THEIR DEATH IN THE RAIN!
PLEASE, MISTAH HAIG... LET ONE OF US TAKE 'EM INSIDE!
IT'S A DOWNPOUR NOW, FOR MERCY'S SAKE!
THEY'LL GET TIRED O' BAWLIN' SOON ENOUGH!
FIRST ONE TO QUIT WORKIN' GETS SHOT!
SEE! THEY QUIT CRYIN' ALREADY!
oh-my-GOD!

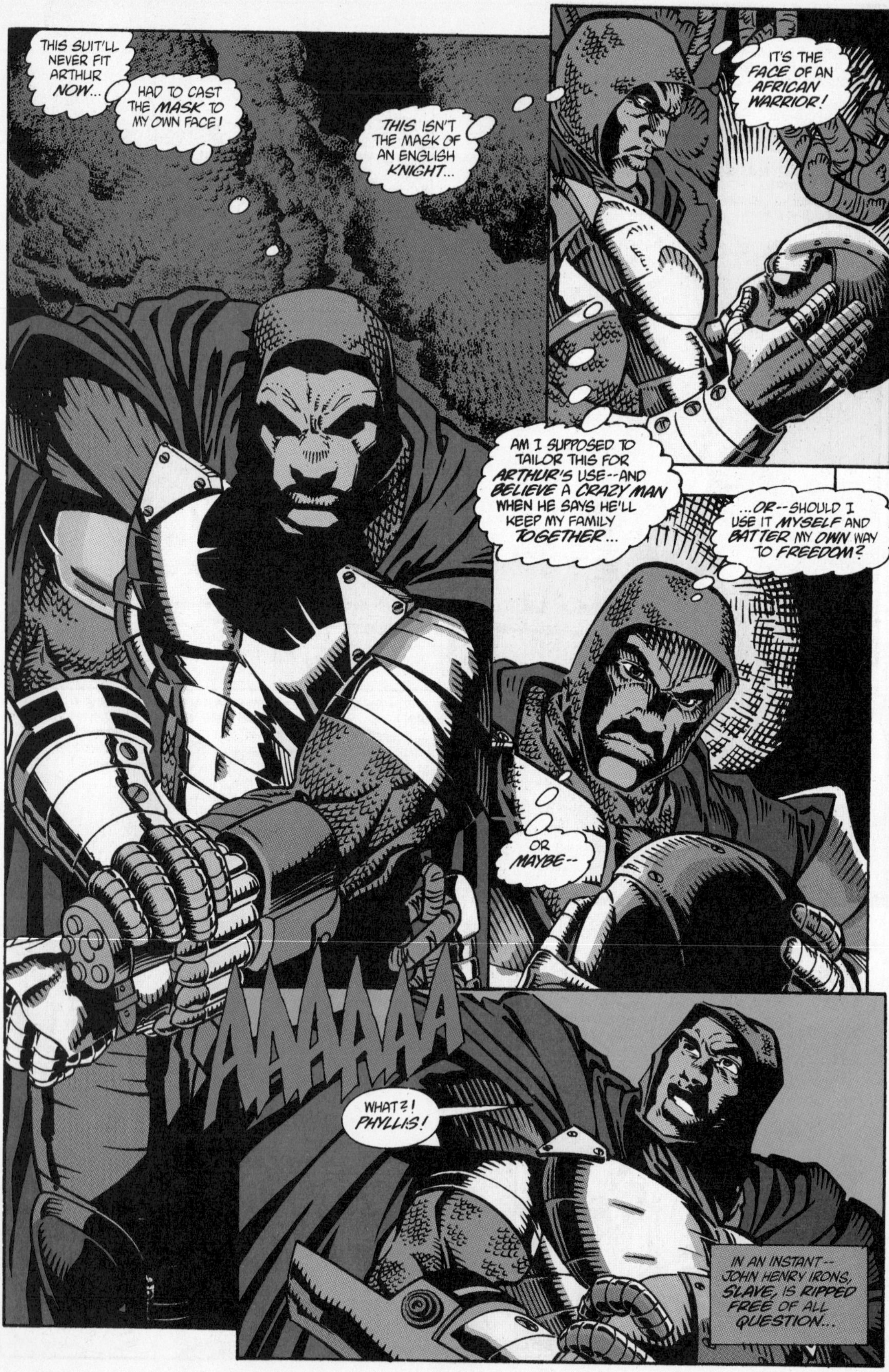
THIS SUIT'LL NEVER FIT ARTHUR NOW...
HAD TO CAST THE MASK TO MY OWN FACE!
THIS ISN'T THE MASK OF AN ENGLISH KNIGHT...
IT'S THE FACE OF AN AFRICAN WARRIOR!
AM I SUPPOSED TO TAILOR THIS FOR ARTHUR'S USE--AND BELIEVE A CRAZY MAN WHEN HE SAYS HE'LL KEEP MY FAMILY TOGETHER...
...OR--SHOULD I USE IT MYSELF AND BATTER MY OWN WAY TO FREEDOM?
OR MAYBE--
AAAAAA
WHAT?! PHYLLIS!
IN AN INSTANT--JOHN HENRY IRONS, SLAVE, IS RIPPED FREE OF ALL QUESTION...

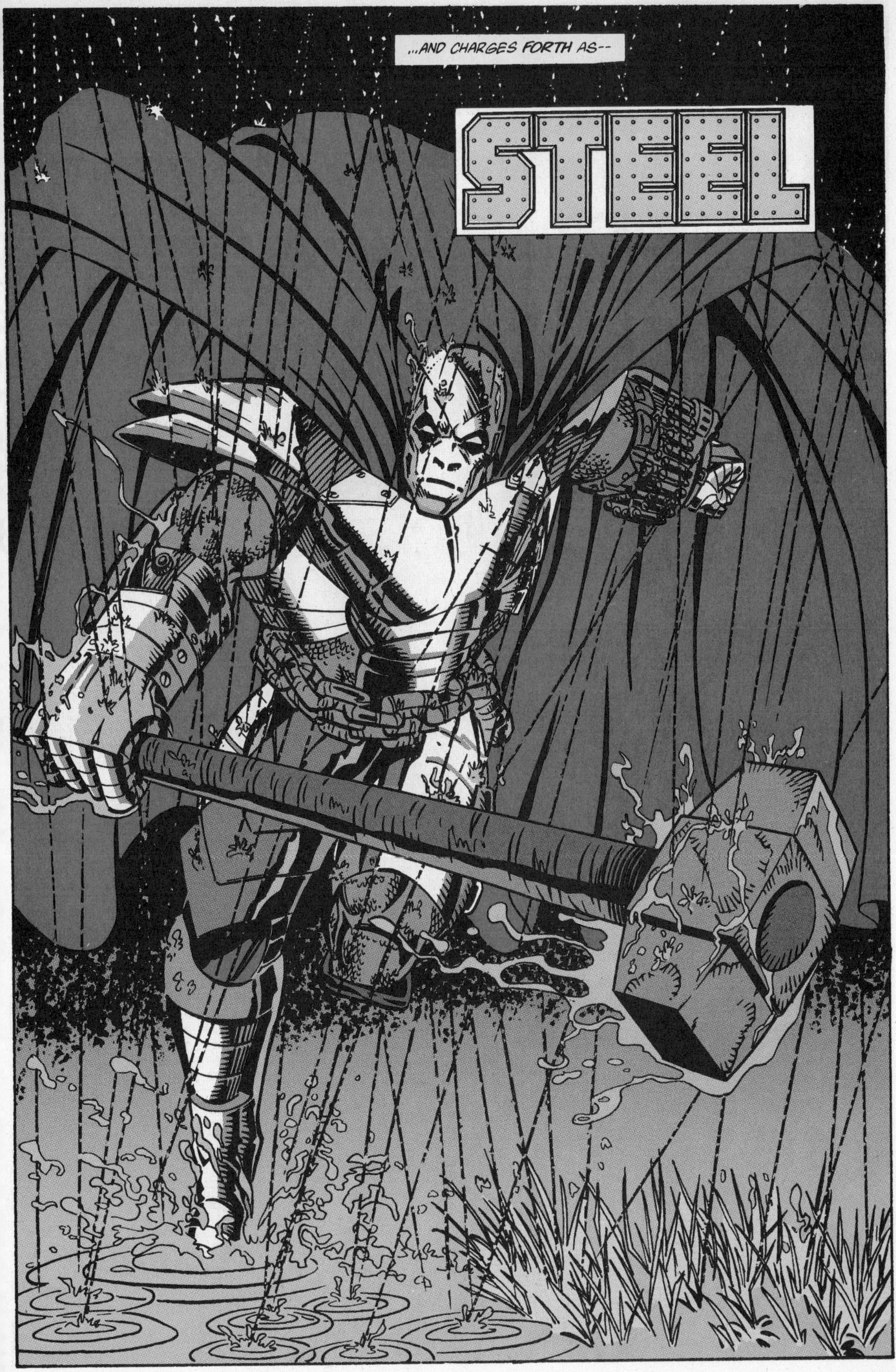
...AND CHARGES FORTH AS--
STEEL

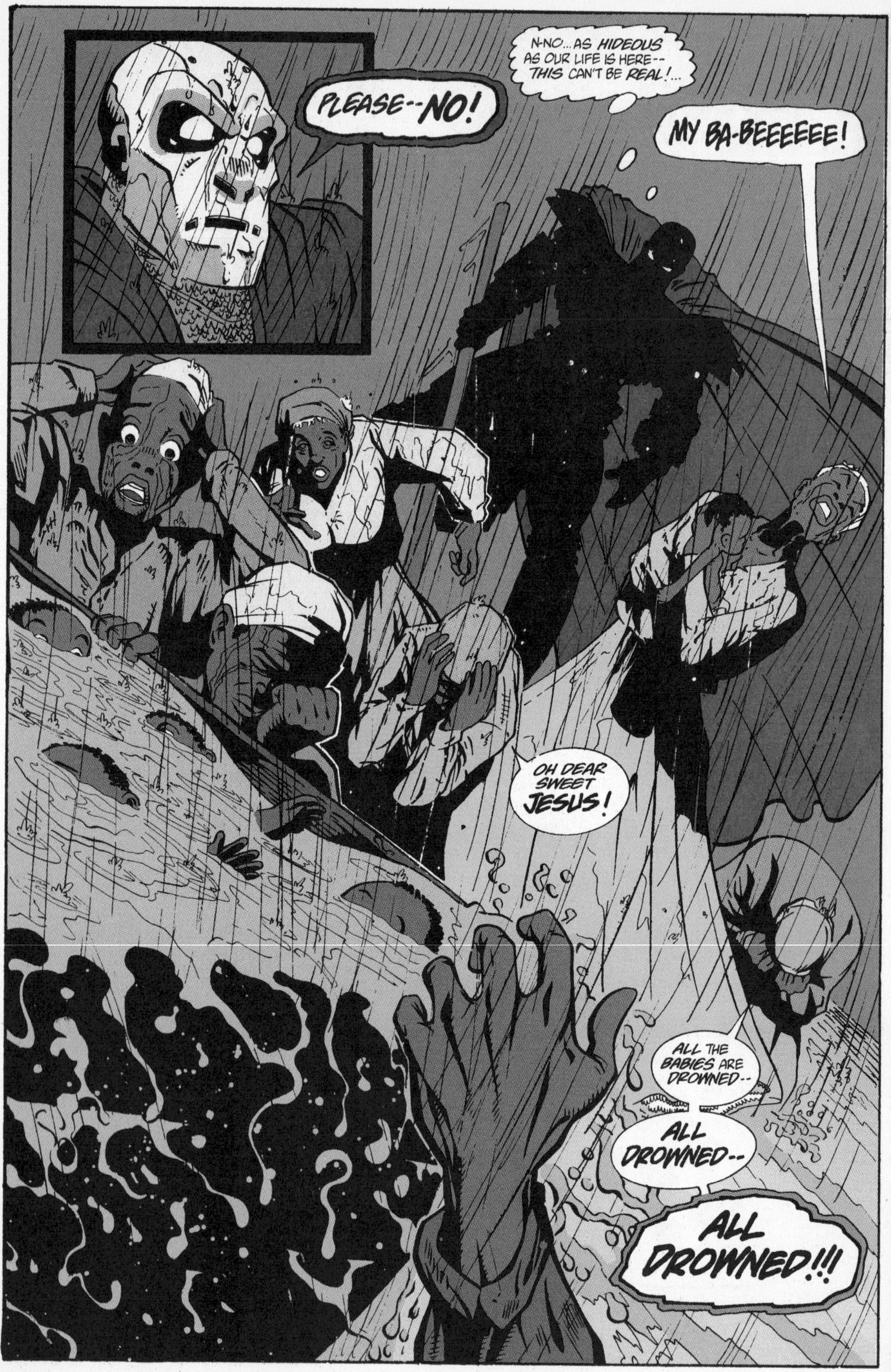
PLEASE--NO!
N-NO...AS HIDEOUS AS OUR LIFE IS HERE-- THIS CAN'T BE REAL!...
MY BA-BEEEEEE!
OH DEAR SWEET JESUS!
ALL THE BABIES ARE DROWNED--
ALL DROWNED--
ALL DROWNED!!!

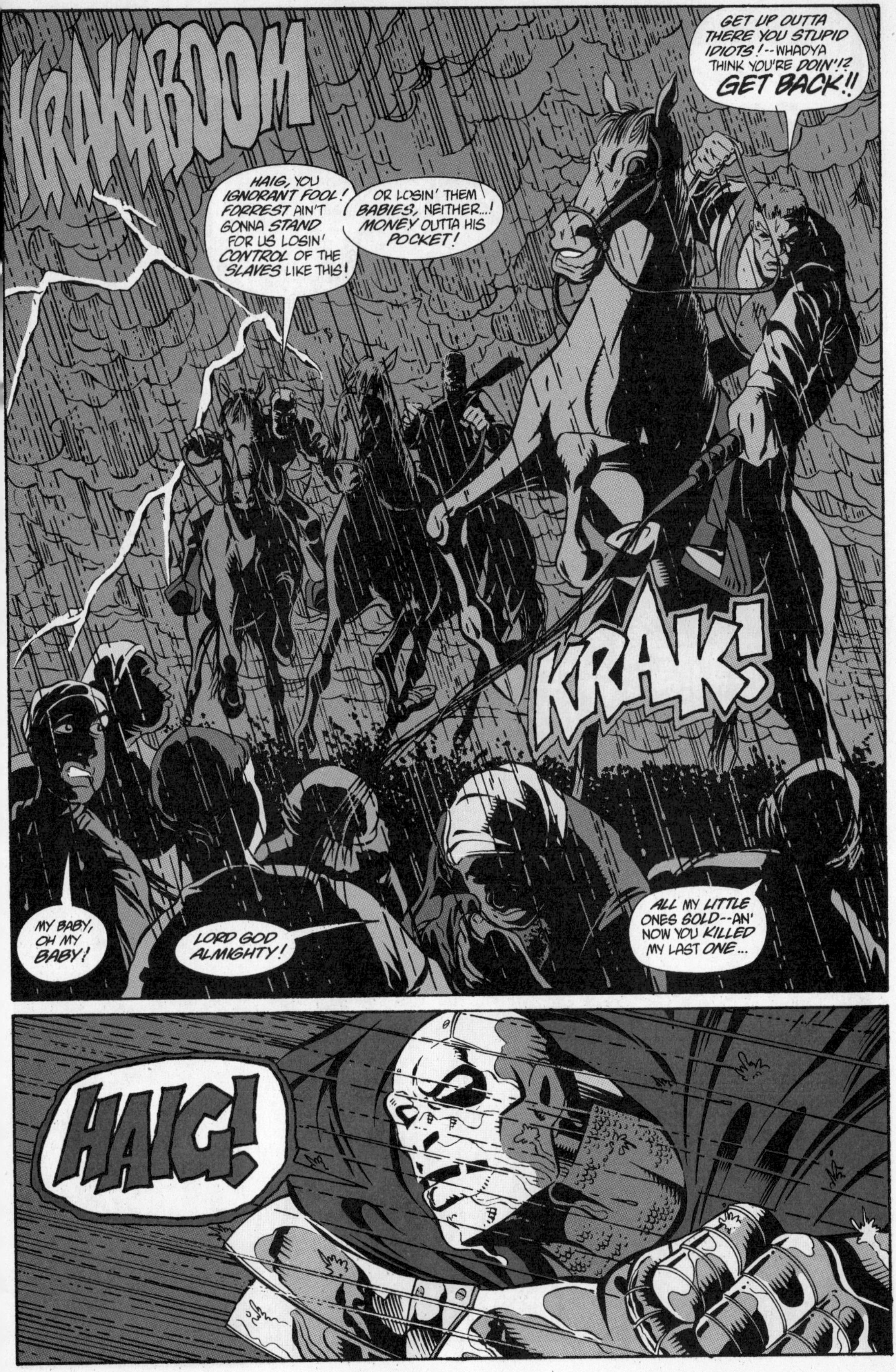
KRAKABOOM
GET UP OUTTA THERE YOU STUPID IDIOTS!--WHADYA THINK YOU'RE DOIN'!? GET BACK!!
HAIG, YOU IGNORANT FOOL! FORREST AIN'T GONNA STAND FOR US LOSIN' CONTROL OF THE SLAVES LIKE THIS!
OR LOSIN' THEM BABIES, NEITHER...! MONEY OUTTA HIS POCKET!
KRAK!
MY BABY, OH MY BABY!
LORD GOD ALMIGHTY!
ALL MY LITTLE ONES SOLD--AN' NOW YOU KILLED MY LAST ONE...
HAIG!

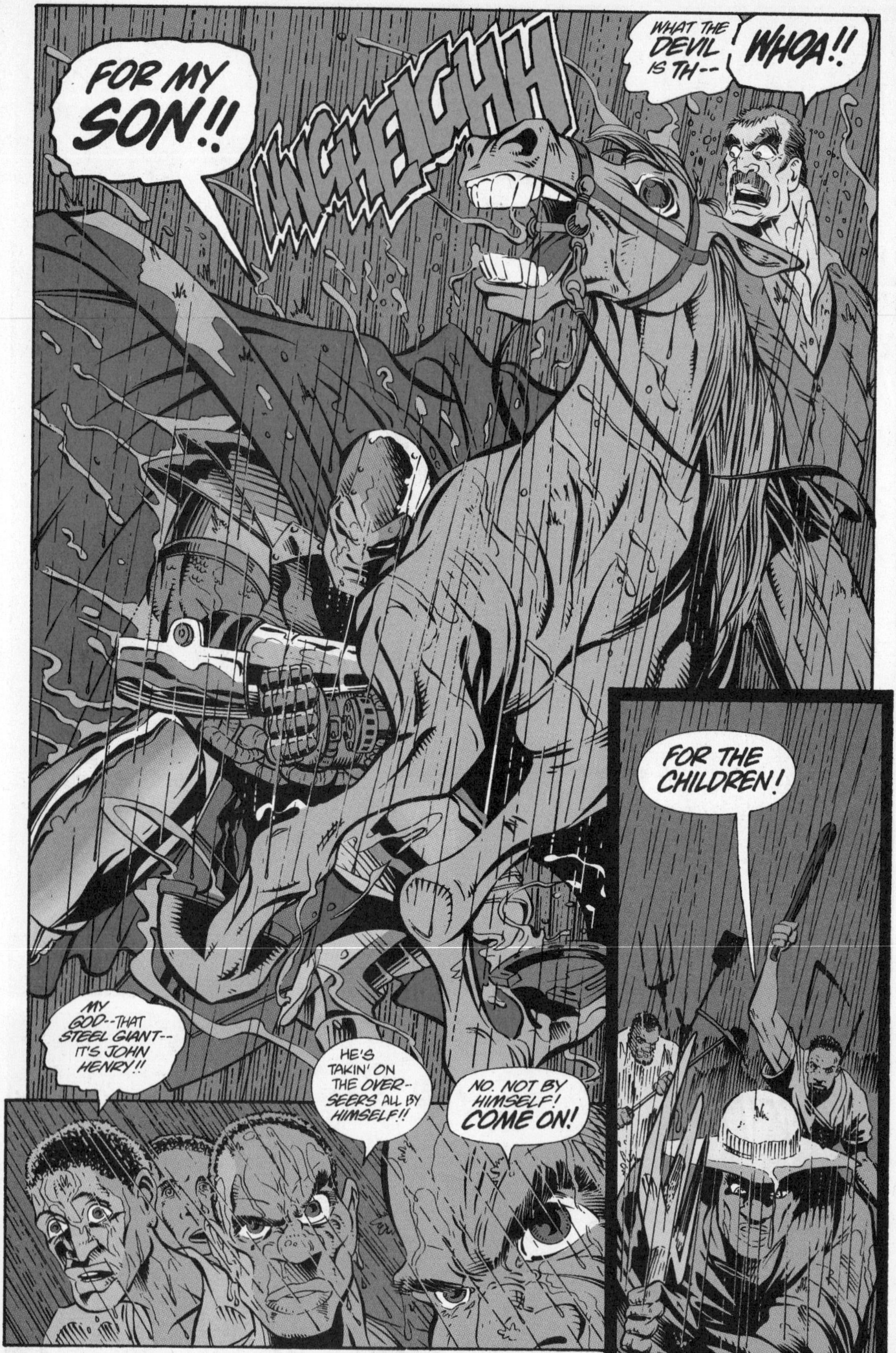
FOR MY SON!!
NNGHEIGHH
WHAT THE DEVIL IS TH--
WHOA!!
FOR THE CHILDREN!
MY GOD--THAT STEEL GIANT--IT'S JOHN HENRY!!
HE'S TAKIN' ON THE OVER-SEERS ALL BY HIMSELF!!
NO. NOT BY HIMSELF! COME ON!

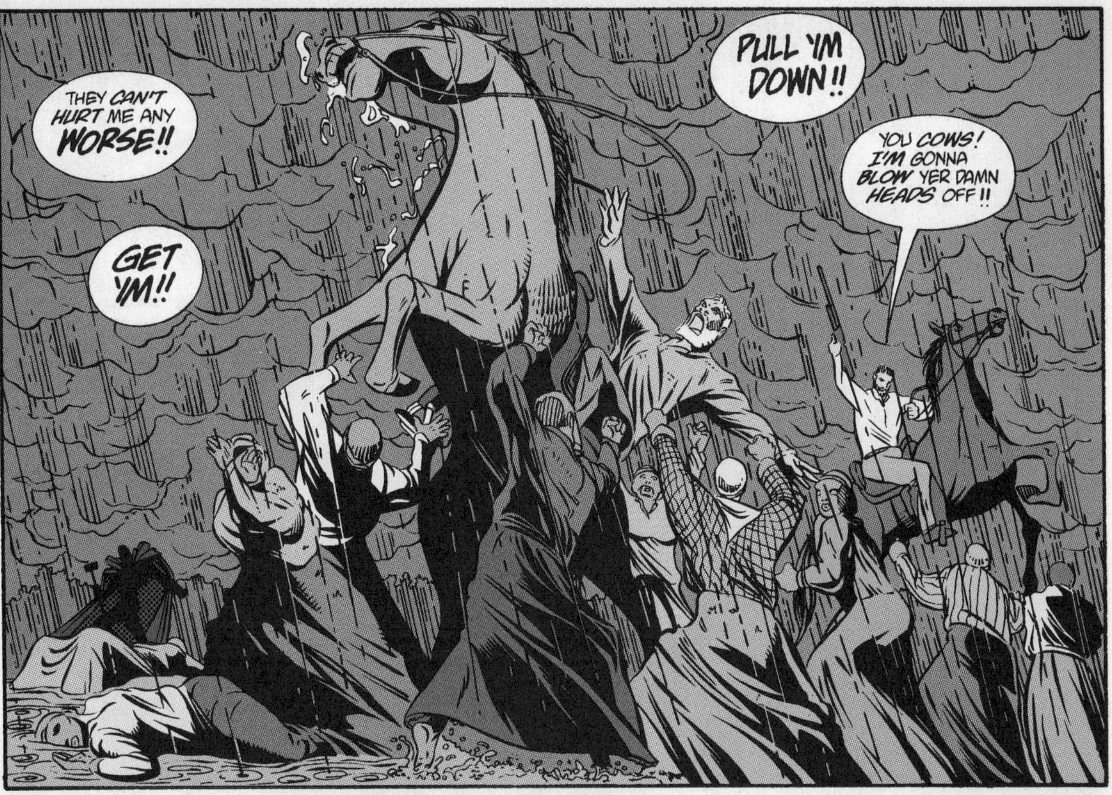

THEY CAN'T HURT ME ANY WORSE!!
PULL 'YM DOWN!!
YOU COWS! I'M GONNA BLOW YER DAMN HEADS OFF!!
GET 'YM!!

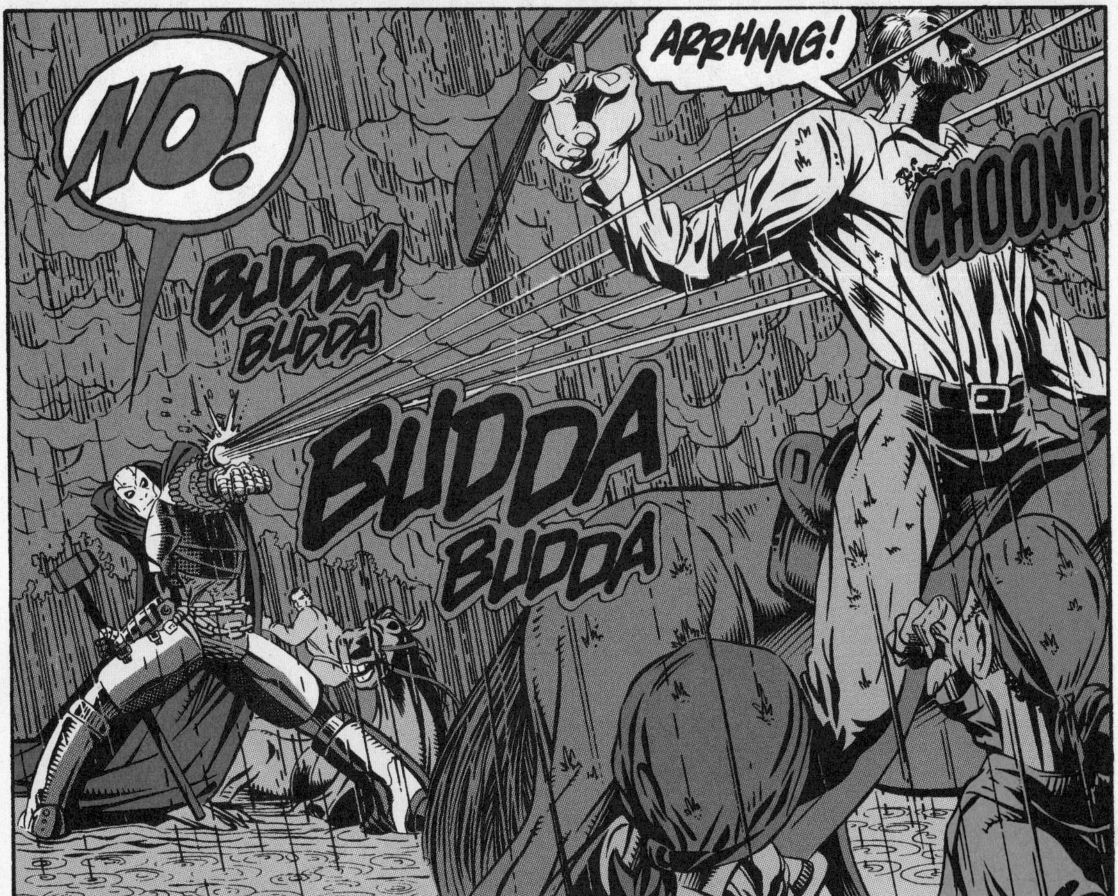

ARRHNNG!
NO!
CHOOM!
BUDDA BUDDA
BUDDA BUDDA

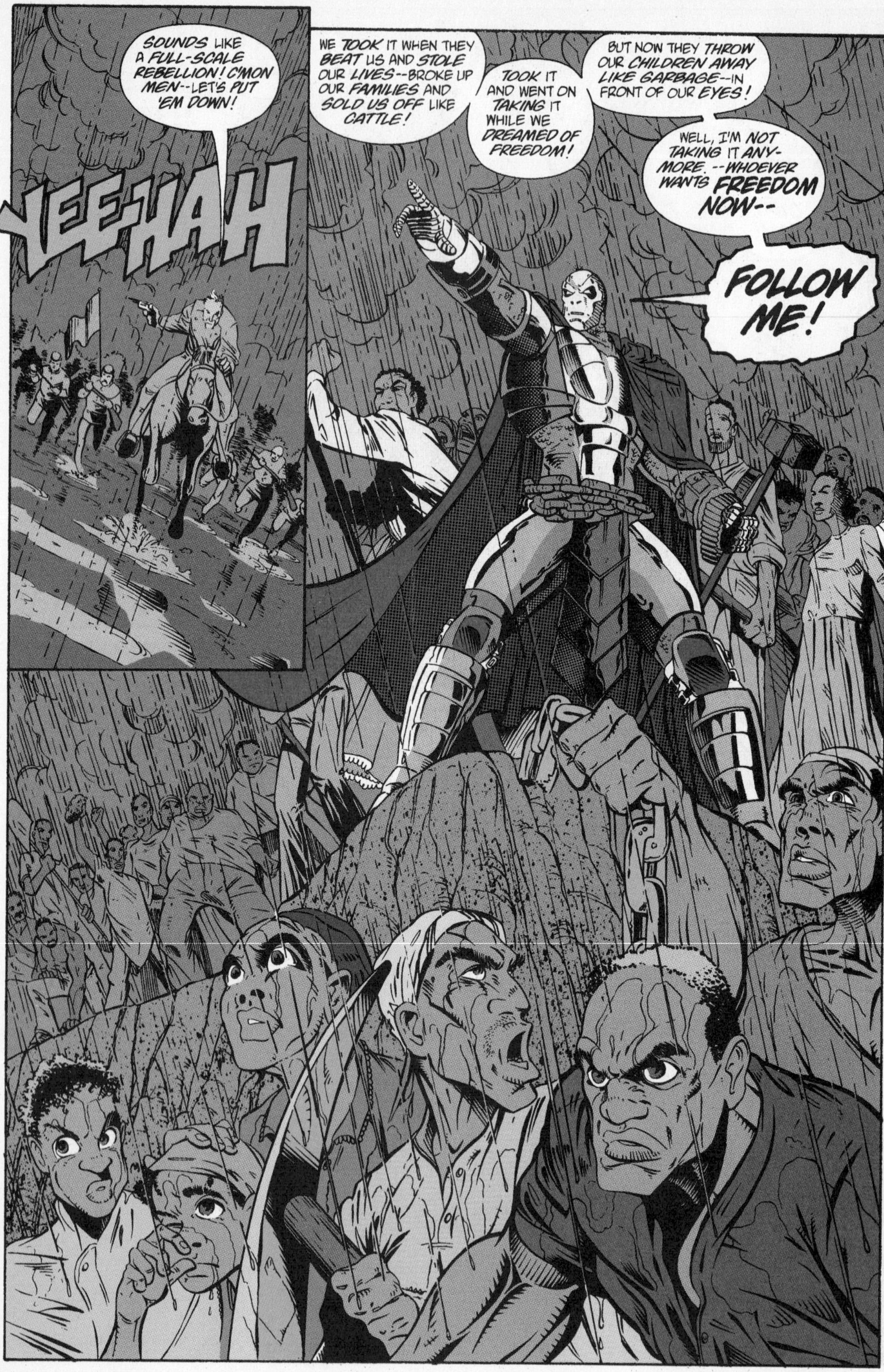
SOUNDS LIKE A FULL-SCALE REBELLION! C'MON MEN--LET'S PUT 'EM DOWN!
YEE-HAH
WE TOOK IT WHEN THEY BEAT US AND STOLE OUR LIVES--BROKE UP OUR FAMILIES AND SOLD US OFF LIKE CATTLE!
TOOK IT AND WENT ON TAKING IT WHILE WE DREAMED OF FREEDOM!
BUT NOW THEY THROW OUR CHILDREN AWAY LIKE GARBAGE--IN FRONT OF OUR EYES!
WELL, I'M NOT TAKING IT ANY-MORE. --WHOEVER WANTS FREEDOM NOW--
FOLLOW ME!

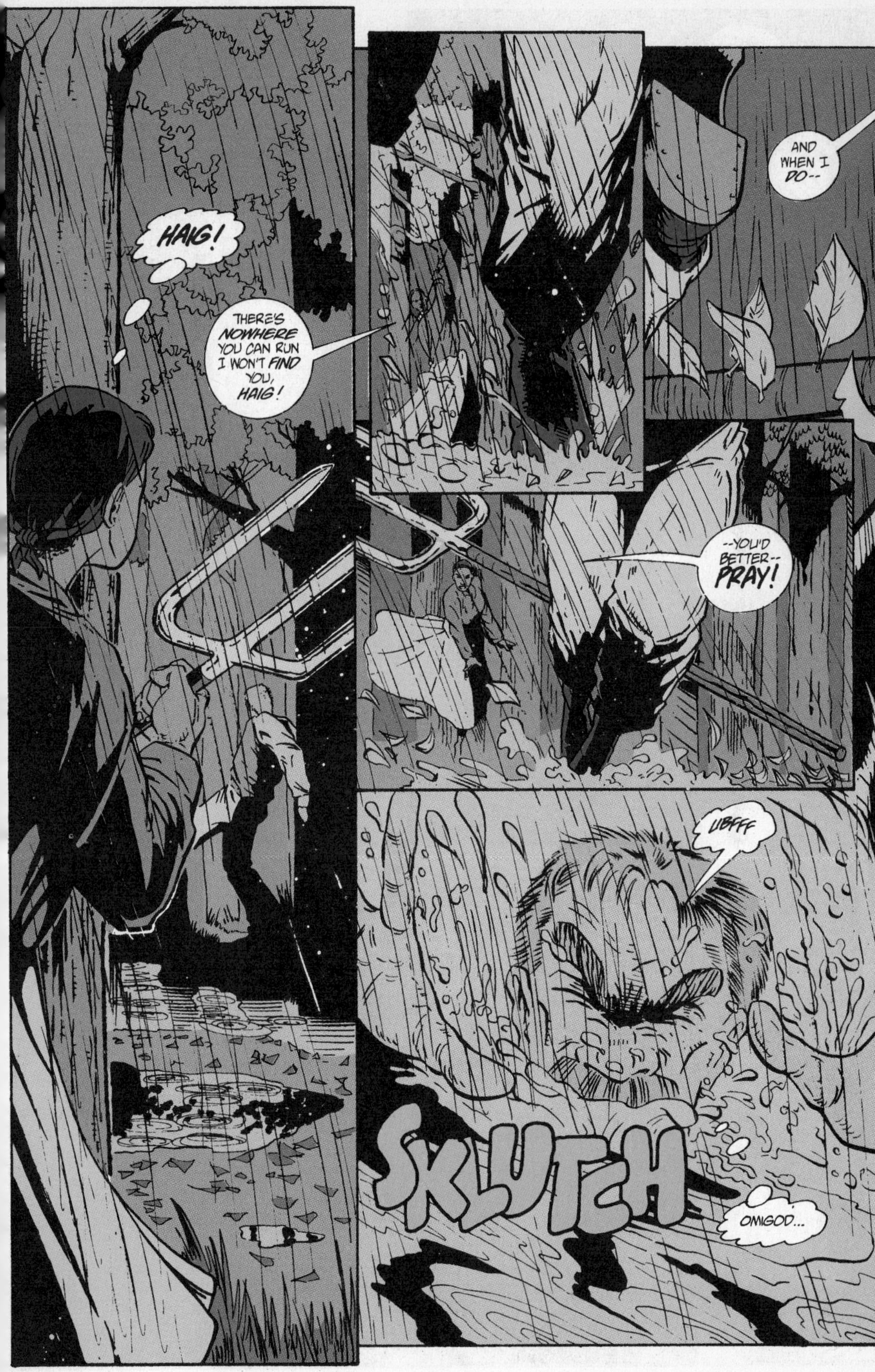
HAIG!
THERE'S NOWHERE YOU CAN RUN I WON'T FIND YOU, HAIG!
AND WHEN I DO--
--YOU'D BETTER--PRAY!
UBFFF
SKLUTCH
OMIGOD...

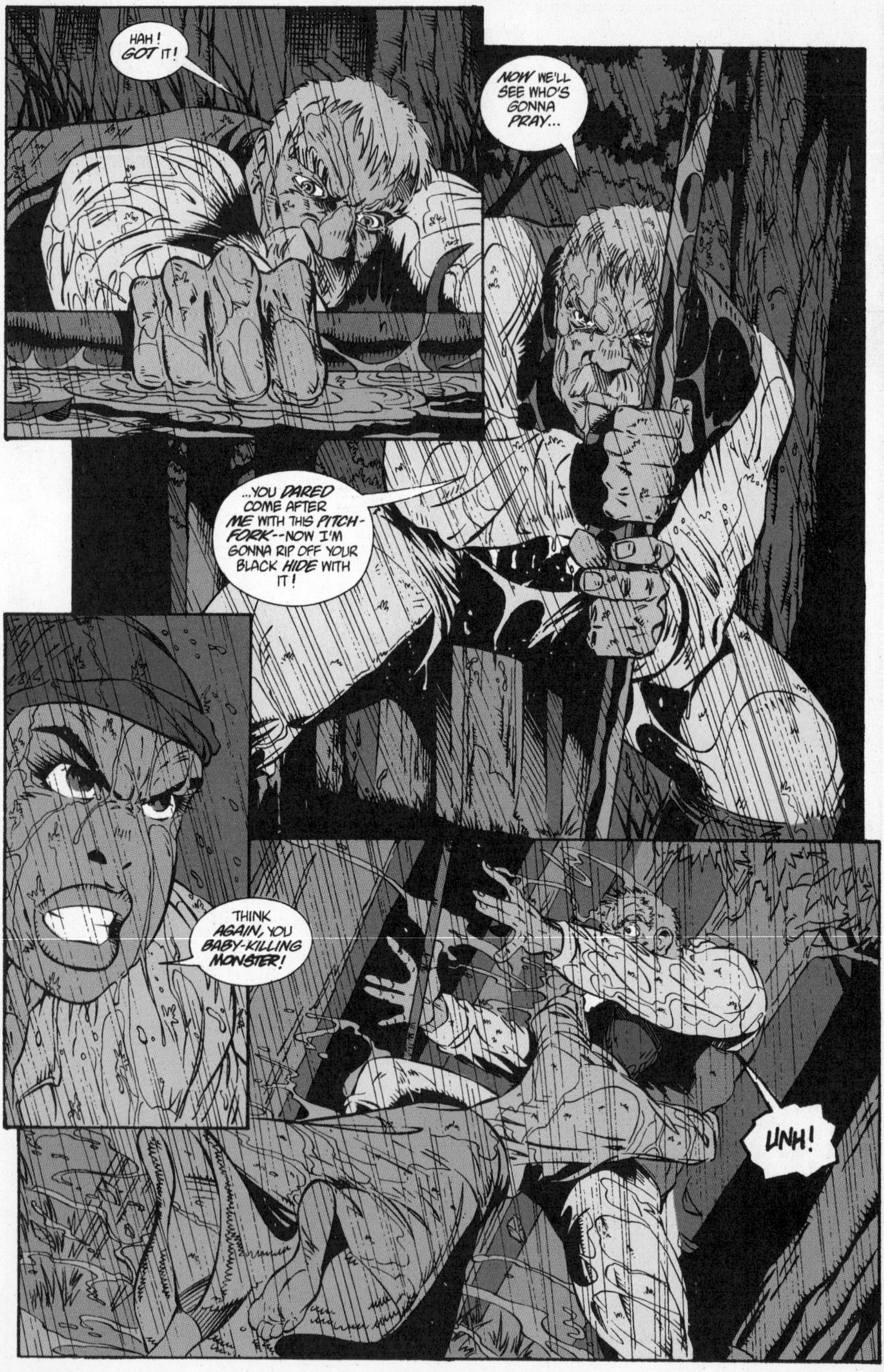
HAH! GOT IT!
NOW WE'LL SEE WHO'S GONNA PRAY...
...YOU DARED COME AFTER ME WITH THIS PITCH-FORK--NOW I'M GONNA RIP OFF YOUR BLACK HIDE WITH IT!
THINK AGAIN, YOU BABY-KILLING MONSTER!
UNH!

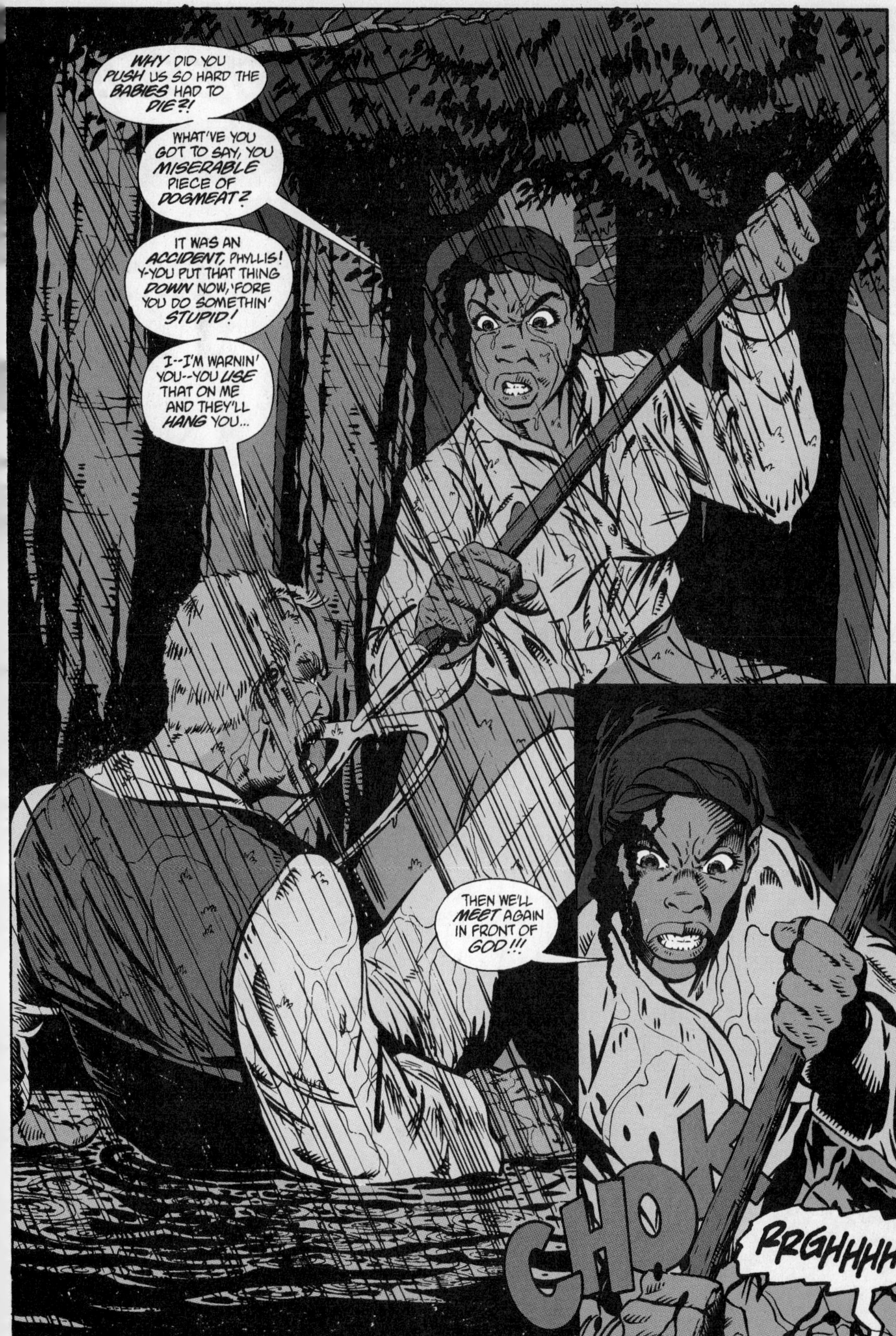

WHY DID YOU PUSH US SO HARD THE BABIES HAD TO DIE?!
WHAT'VE YOU GOT TO SAY, YOU MISERABLE PIECE OF DOGMEAT?
IT WAS AN ACCIDENT, PHYLLIS! Y-YOU PUT THAT THING DOWN NOW, 'FORE YOU DO SOMETHIN' STUPID!
I--I'M WARNIN' YOU--YOU USE THAT ON ME AND THEY'LL HANG YOU...
THEN WE'LL MEET AGAIN IN FRONT OF GOD!!!
CHOK
RRGHHHH...

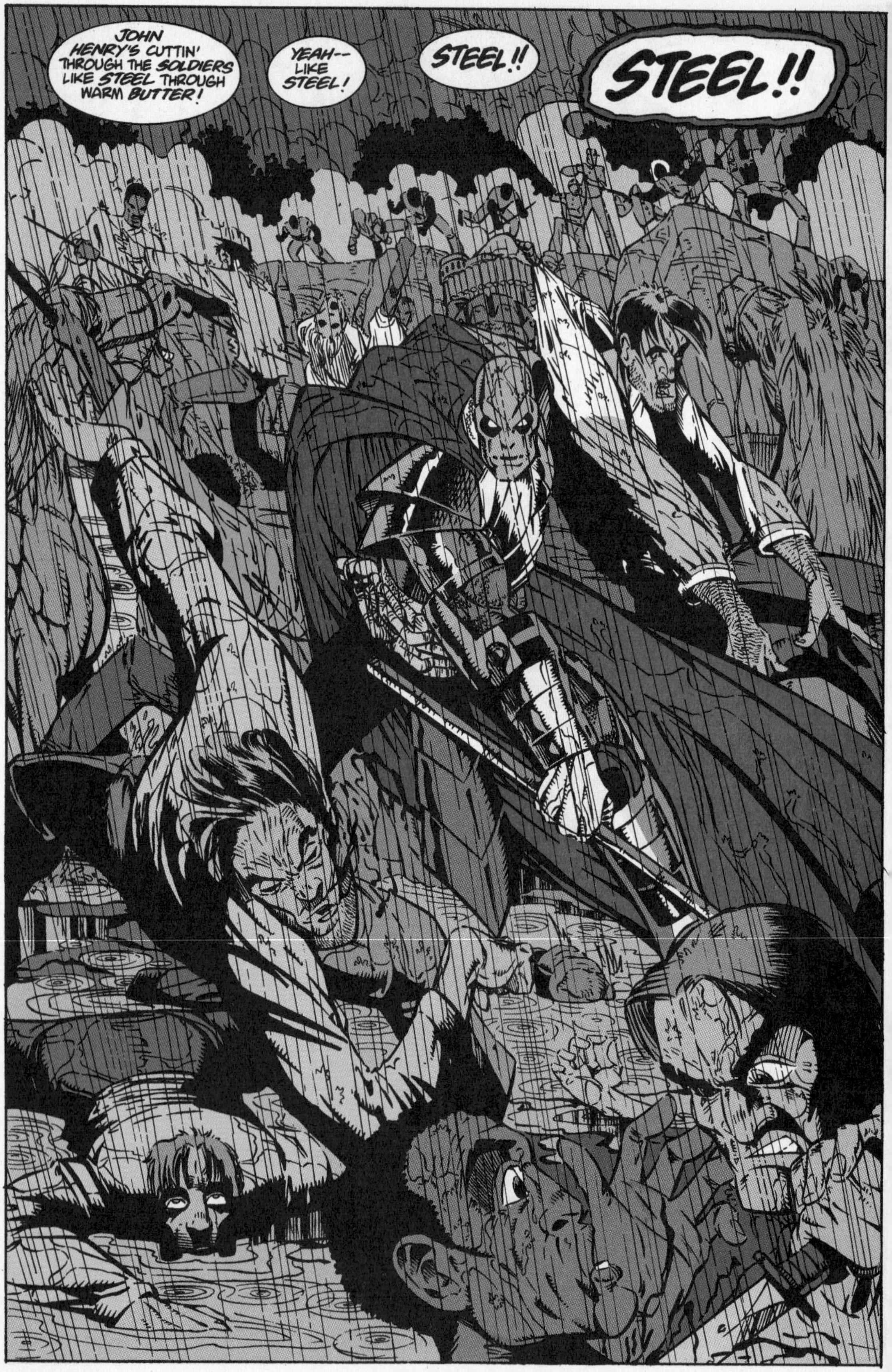
JOHN HENRY'S CUTTIN' THROUGH THE SOLDIERS LIKE STEEL THROUGH WARM BUTTER!
YEAH-- LIKE STEEL!
STEEL!!
STEEL!!

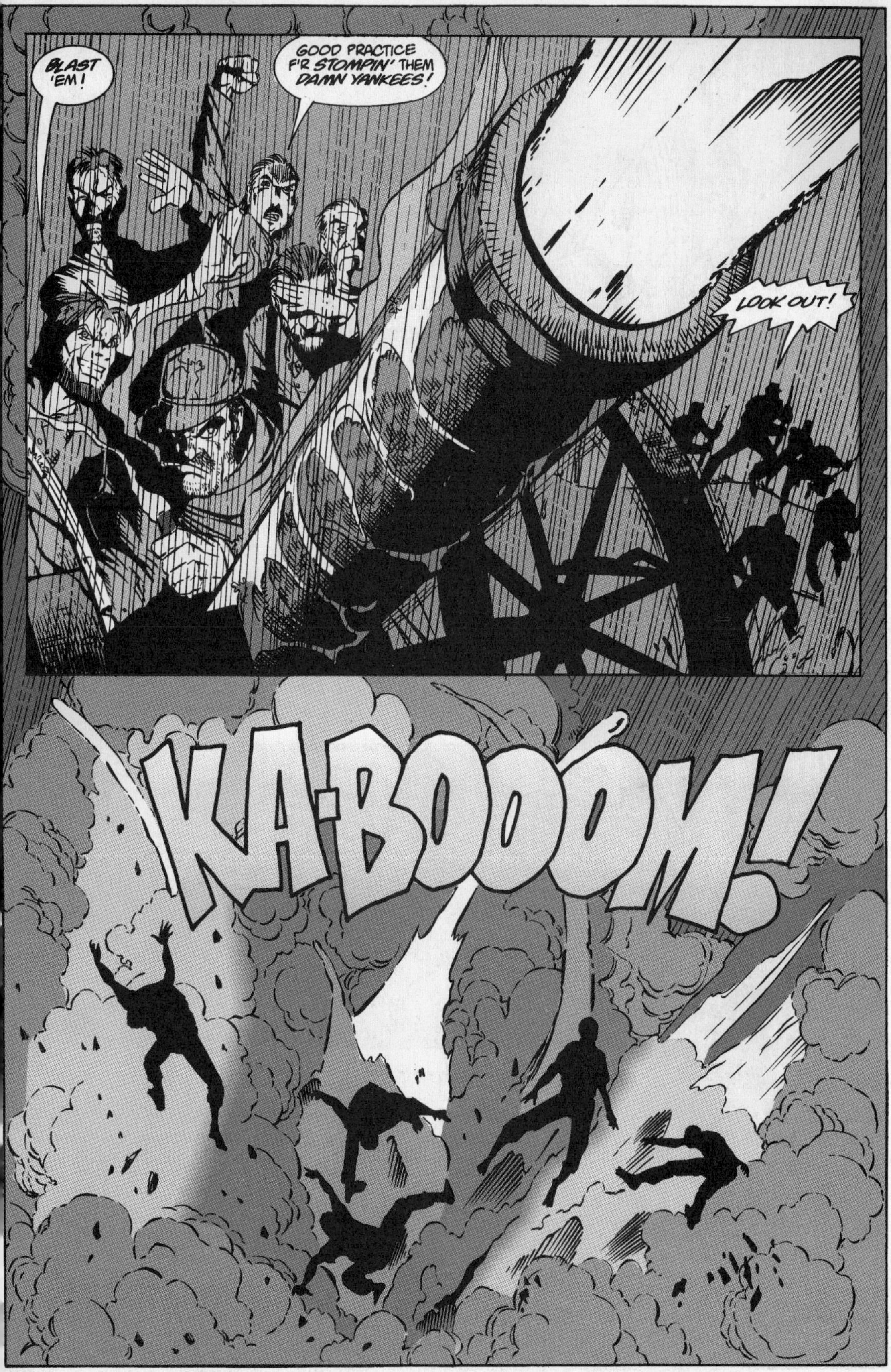
BLAST 'EM!
GOOD PRACTICE F'R STOMPIN' THEM DAMN YANKEES!
LOOK OUT!
KA-BOOOM!

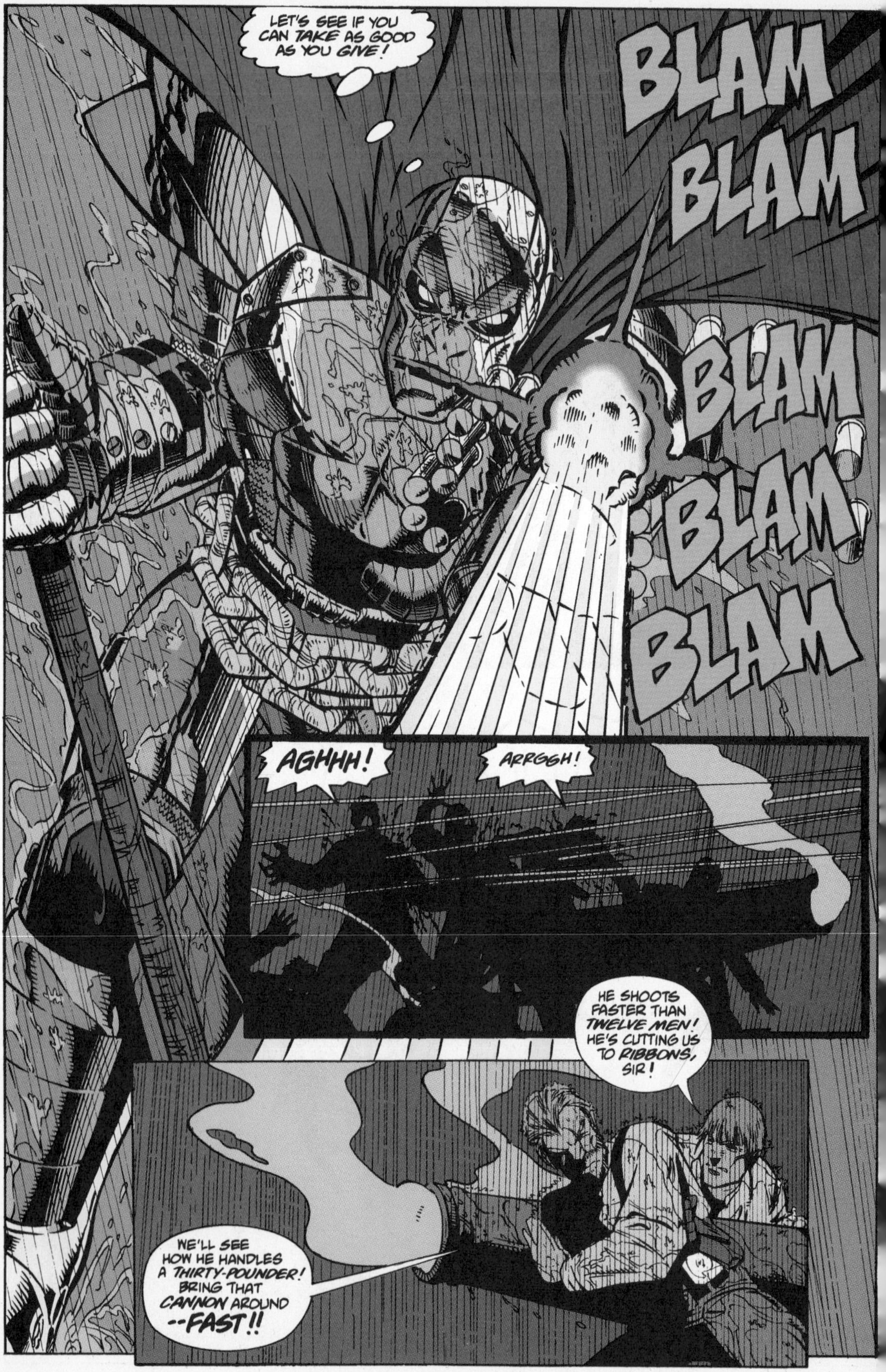
LET'S SEE IF YOU CAN TAKE AS GOOD AS YOU GIVE!
BLAM
BLAM
BLAM
BLAM
BLAM
AGHHH!
ARRGGH!
HE SHOOTS FASTER THAN TWELVE MEN! HE'S CUTTING US TO RIBBONS, SIR!
WE'LL SEE HOW HE HANDLES A THIRTY-POUNDER! BRING THAT CANNON AROUND --FAST!!

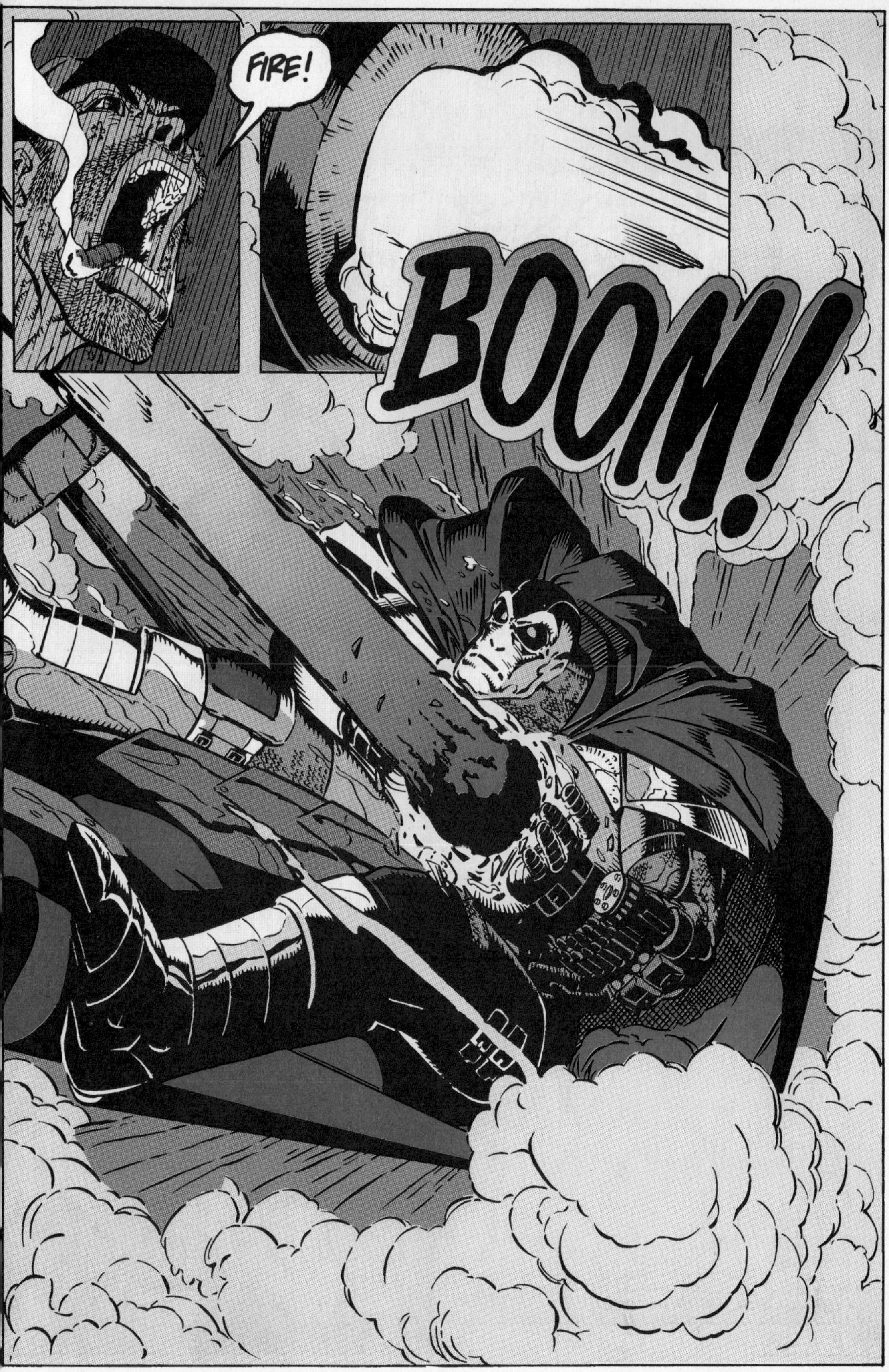
FIRE!
BOOM!

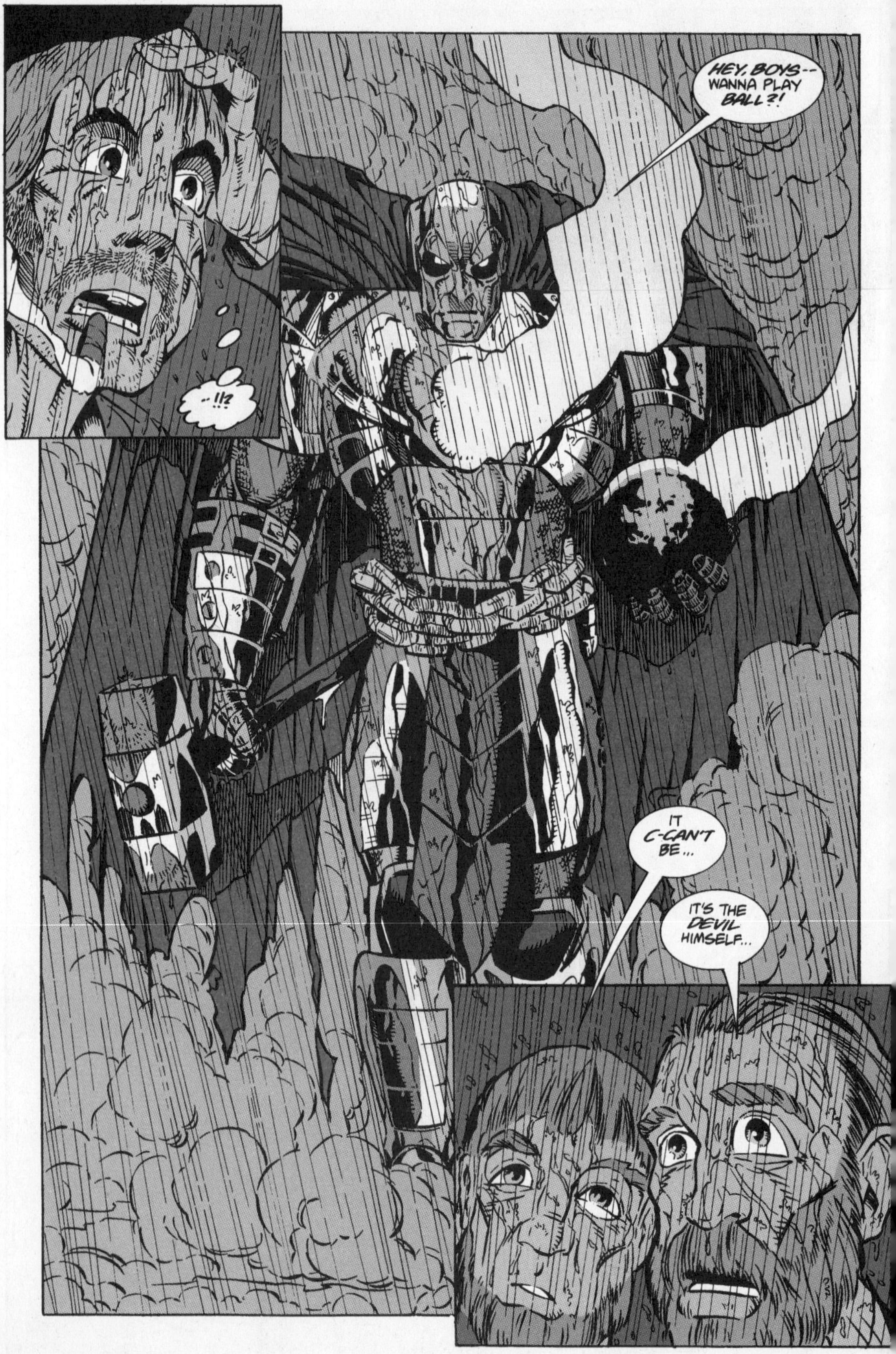
--!!?
HEY, BOYS-- WANNA PLAY BALL?!
IT C-CAN'T BE...
IT'S THE DEVIL HIMSELF...

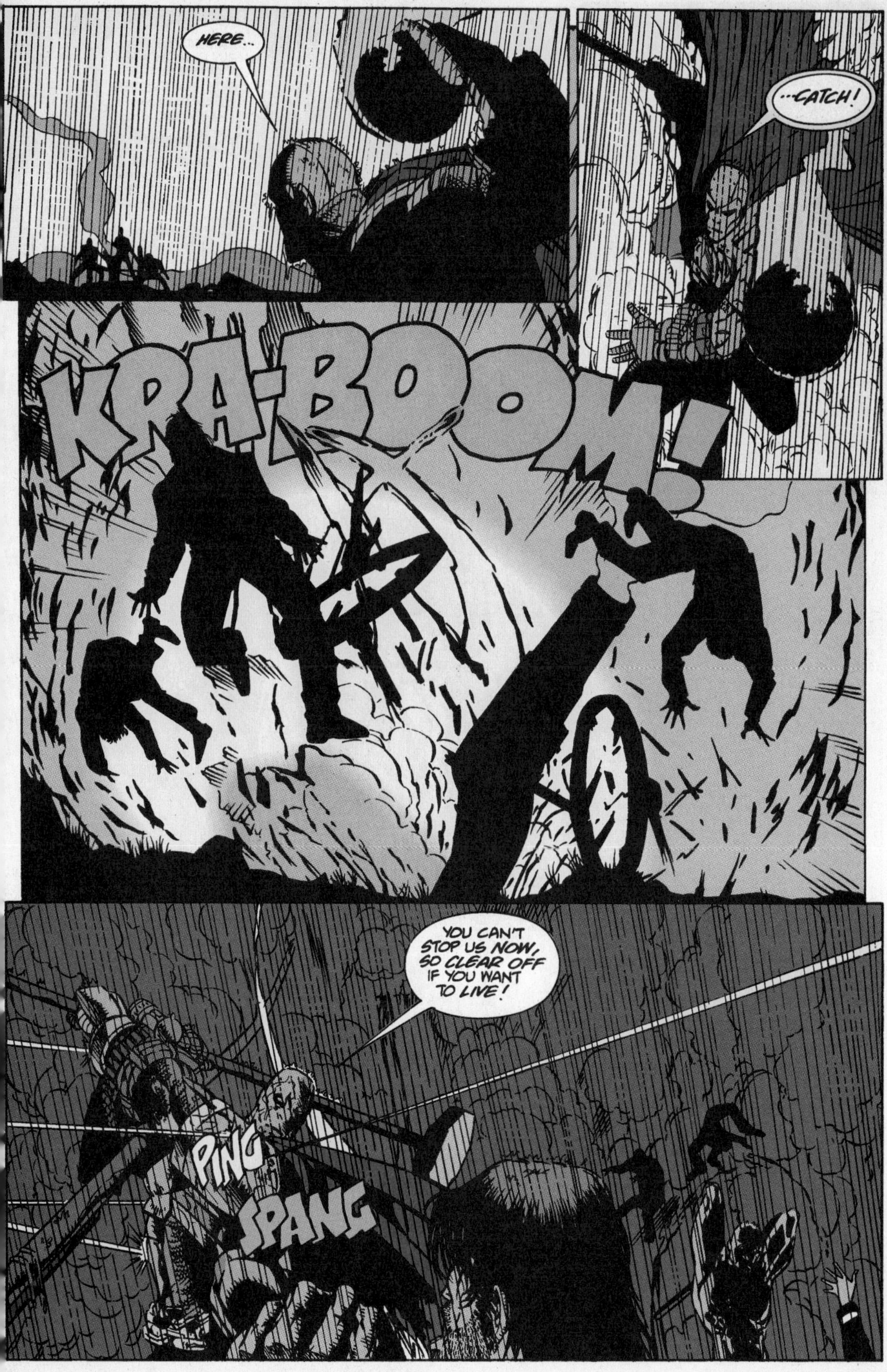
HERE...
...CATCH!
KRA-BOOM!
YOU CAN'T STOP US NOW, SO CLEAR OFF IF YOU WANT TO LIVE!
PING
SPANG

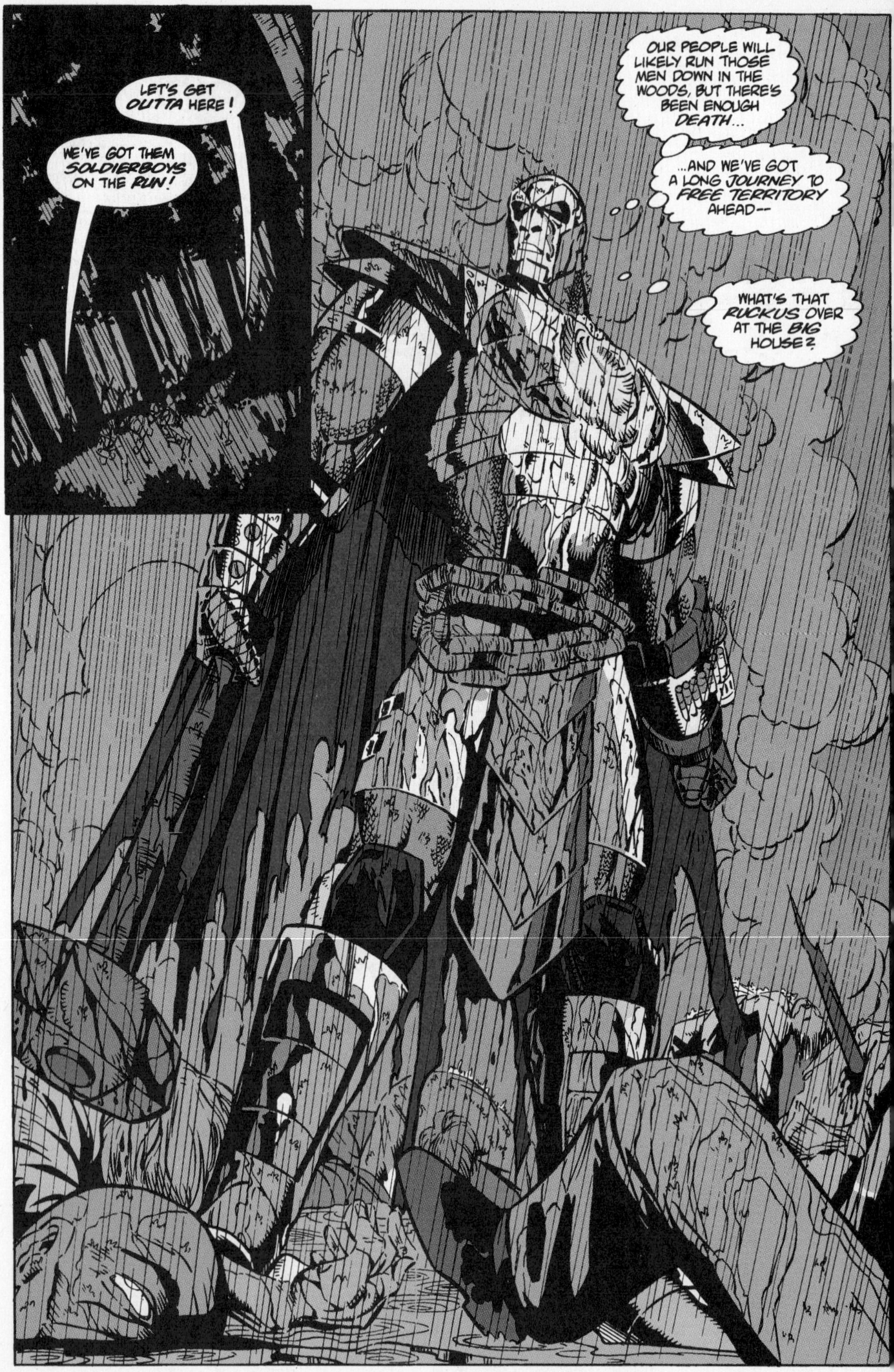
LET'S GET OUTTA HERE!
WE'VE GOT THEM SOLDIERBOYS ON THE RUN!
OUR PEOPLE WILL LIKELY RUN THOSE MEN DOWN IN THE WOODS, BUT THERE'S BEEN ENOUGH DEATH...
...AND WE'VE GOT A LONG JOURNEY TO FREE TERRITORY AHEAD--
WHAT'S THAT RUCKUS OVER AT THE BIG HOUSE?

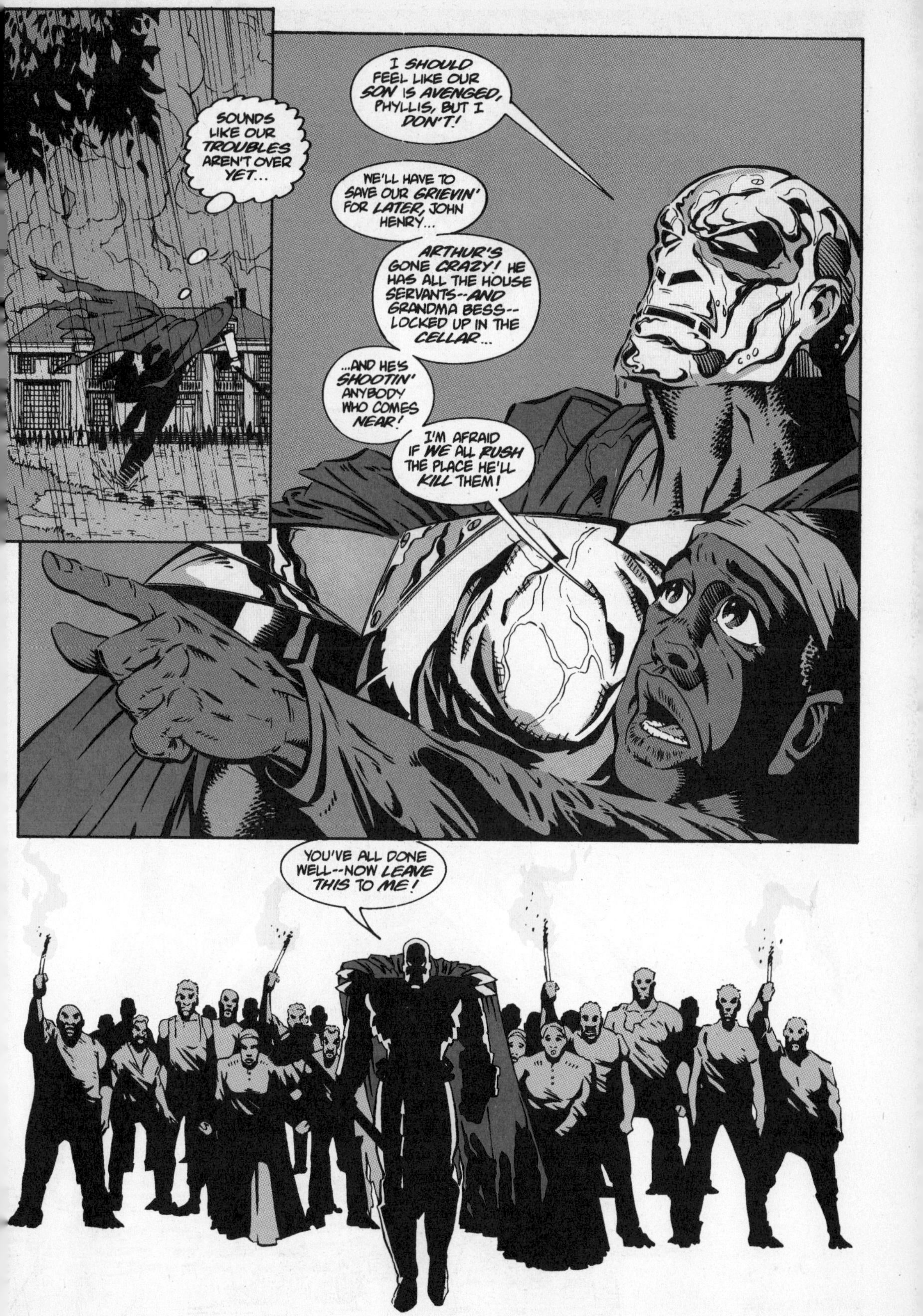
SOUNDS LIKE OUR TROUBLES AREN'T OVER YET...
I SHOULD FEEL LIKE OUR SON IS AVENGED, PHYLLIS, BUT I DON'T!
WE'LL HAVE TO SAVE OUR GRIEVIN' FOR LATER, JOHN HENRY...
ARTHUR'S GONE CRAZY! HE HAS ALL THE HOUSE SERVANTS--AND GRANDMA BESS--LOCKED UP IN THE CELLAR...
...AND HE'S SHOOTIN' ANYBODY WHO COMES NEAR!
I'M AFRAID IF WE ALL RUSH THE PLACE HE'LL KILL THEM!
YOU'VE ALL DONE WELL--NOW LEAVE THIS TO ME!

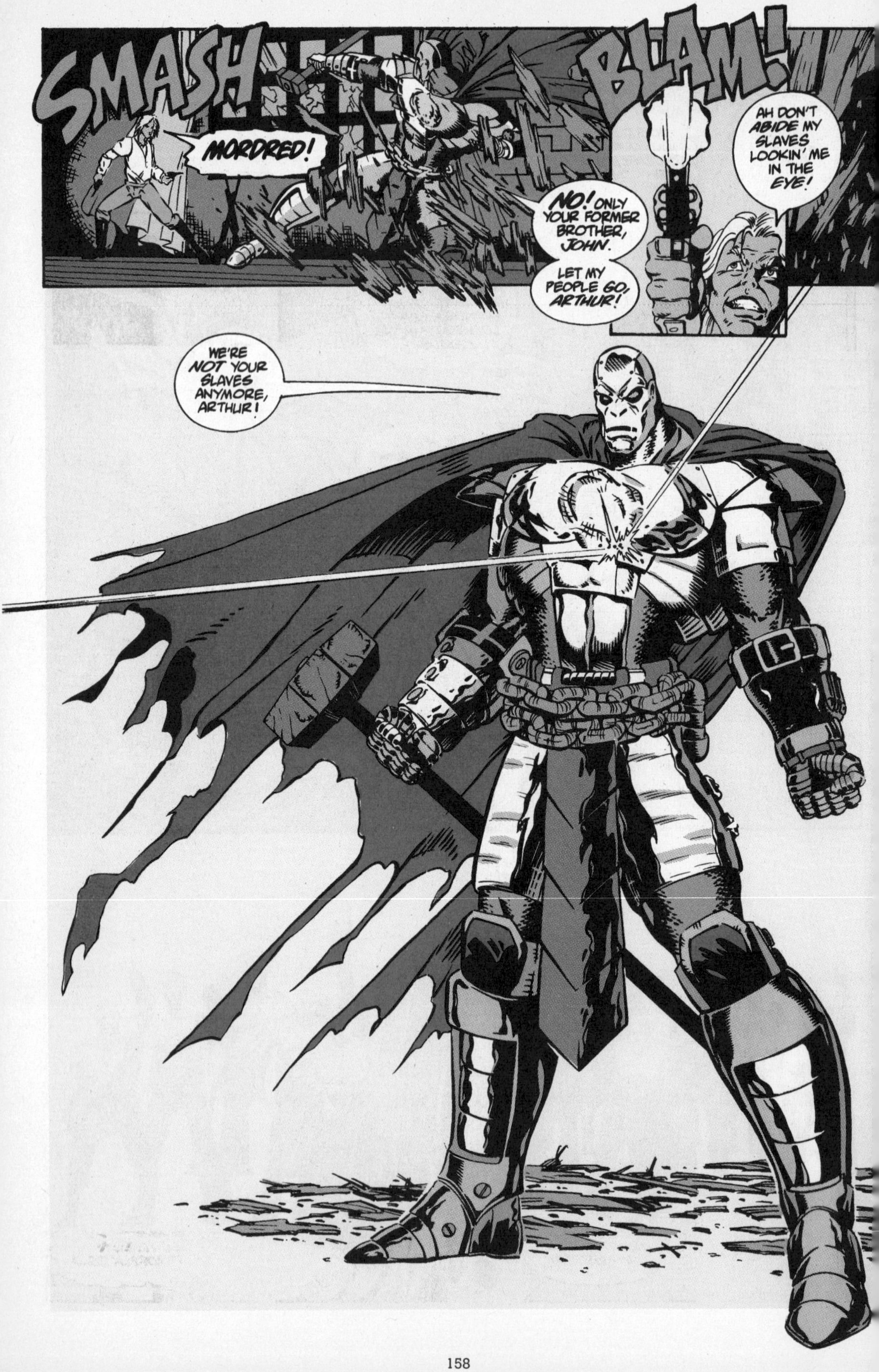
SMASH
MORDRED!
BLAM!
AH DON'T ABIDE MY SLAVES LOOKIN' ME IN THE EYE!
NO! ONLY YOUR FORMER BROTHER, JOHN.
LET MY PEOPLE GO, ARTHUR!
WE'RE NOT YOUR SLAVES ANYMORE, ARTHUR!

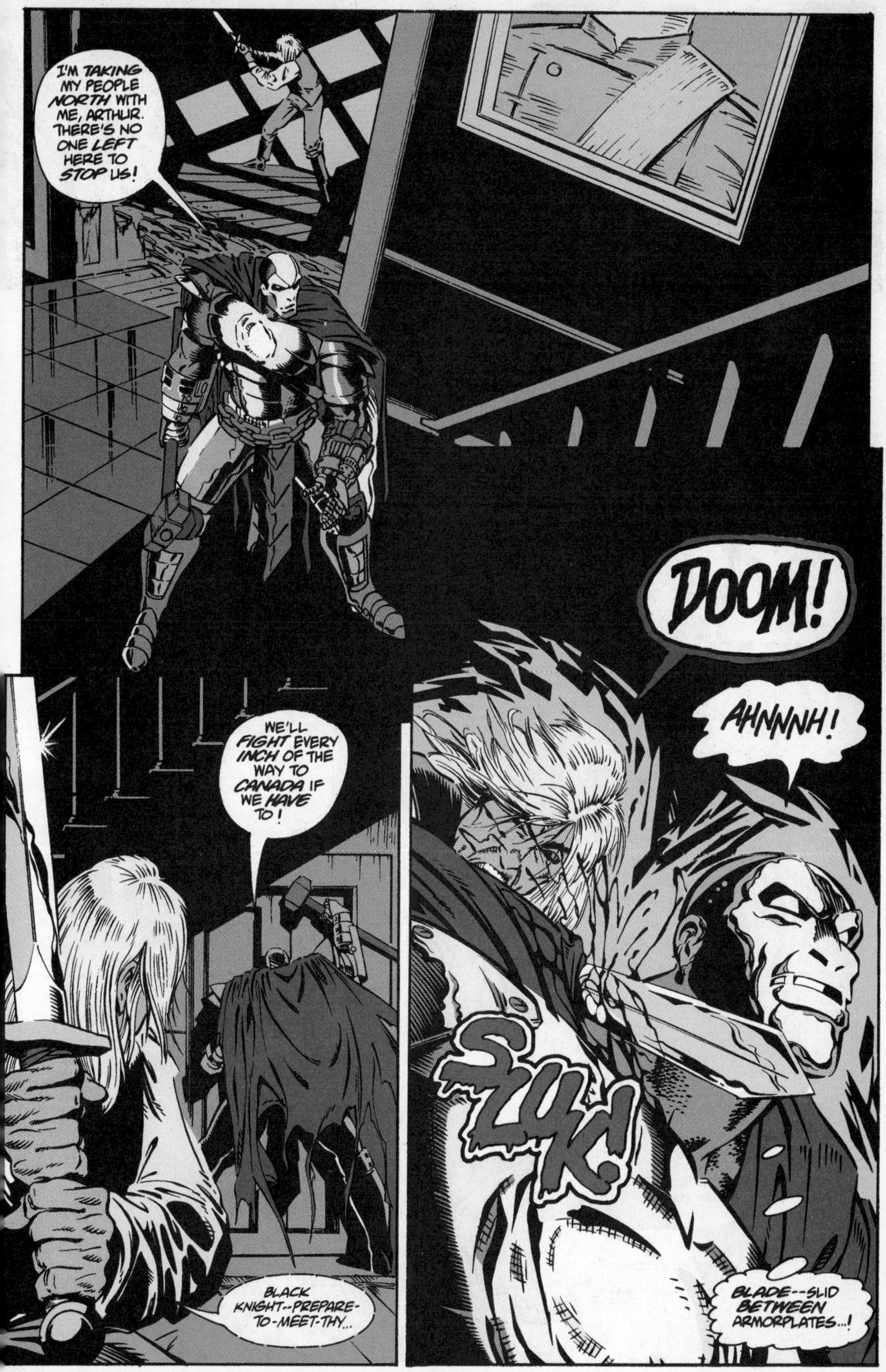
I'M TAKING MY PEOPLE NORTH WITH ME, ARTHUR. THERE'S NO ONE LEFT HERE TO STOP US!
WE'LL FIGHT EVERY INCH OF THE WAY TO CANADA IF WE HAVE TO!
BLACK KNIGHT--PREPARE-TO-MEET-THY...
DOOM!
AHNNNH!
SZUK!
BLADE--SLID BETWEEN ARMORPLATES...!

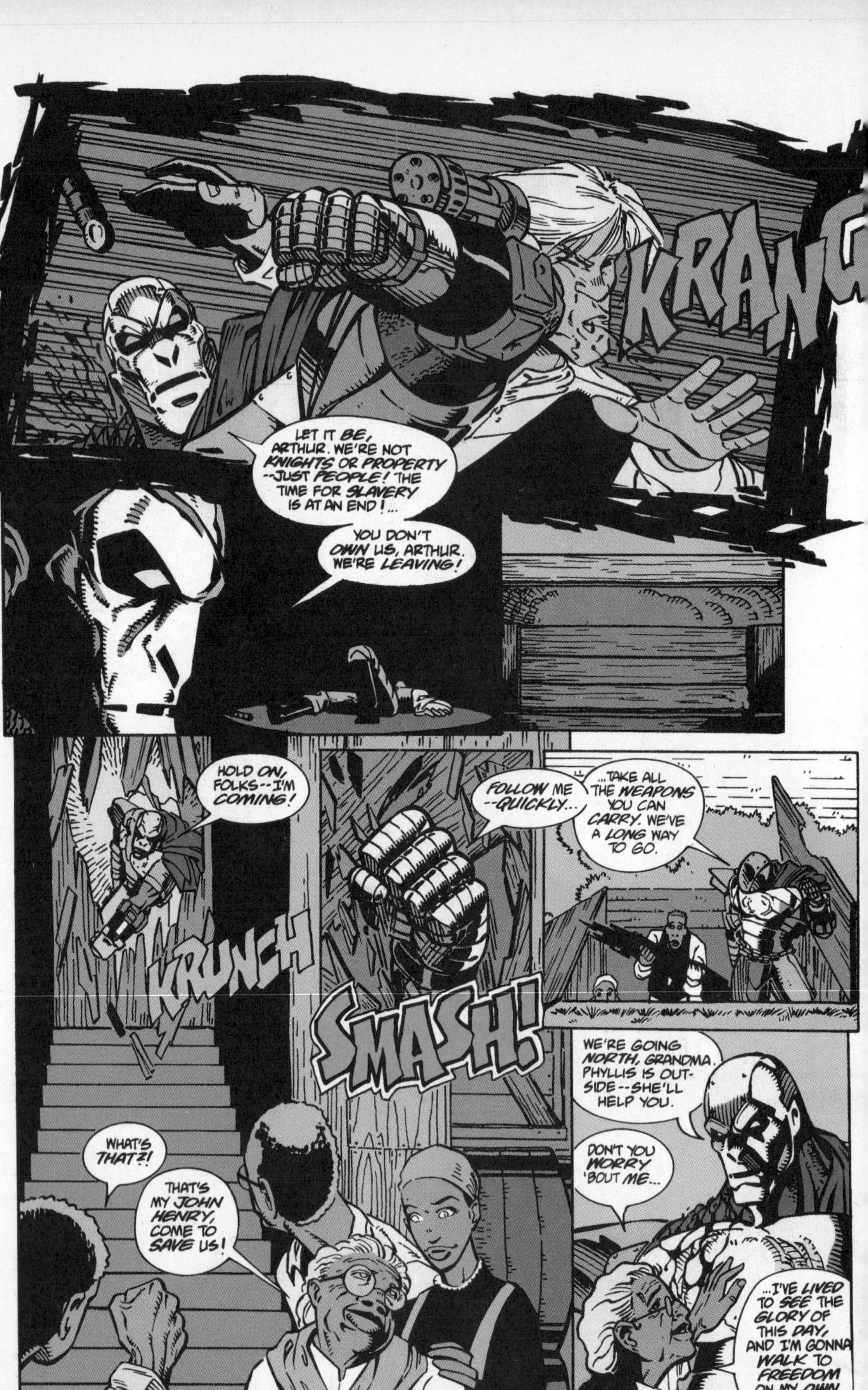
KRANG
LET IT BE, ARTHUR. WE'RE NOT KNIGHTS OR PROPERTY --JUST PEOPLE! THE TIME FOR SLAVERY IS AT AN END!...
YOU DON'T OWN US, ARTHUR. WE'RE LEAVING!
HOLD ON, FOLKS--I'M COMING!
KRUNCH
FOLLOW ME --QUICKLY...
...TAKE ALL THE WEAPONS YOU CAN CARRY. WE'VE A LONG WAY TO GO.
SMASH!
WHAT'S THAT?!
THAT'S MY JOHN HENRY, COME TO SAVE US!
WE'RE GOING NORTH, GRANDMA. PHYLLIS IS OUT-SIDE--SHE'LL HELP YOU.
DON'T YOU WORRY 'BOUT ME...
...I'VE LIVED TO SEE THE GLORY OF THIS DAY, AND I'M GONNA WALK TO FREEDOM ON MY OWN.

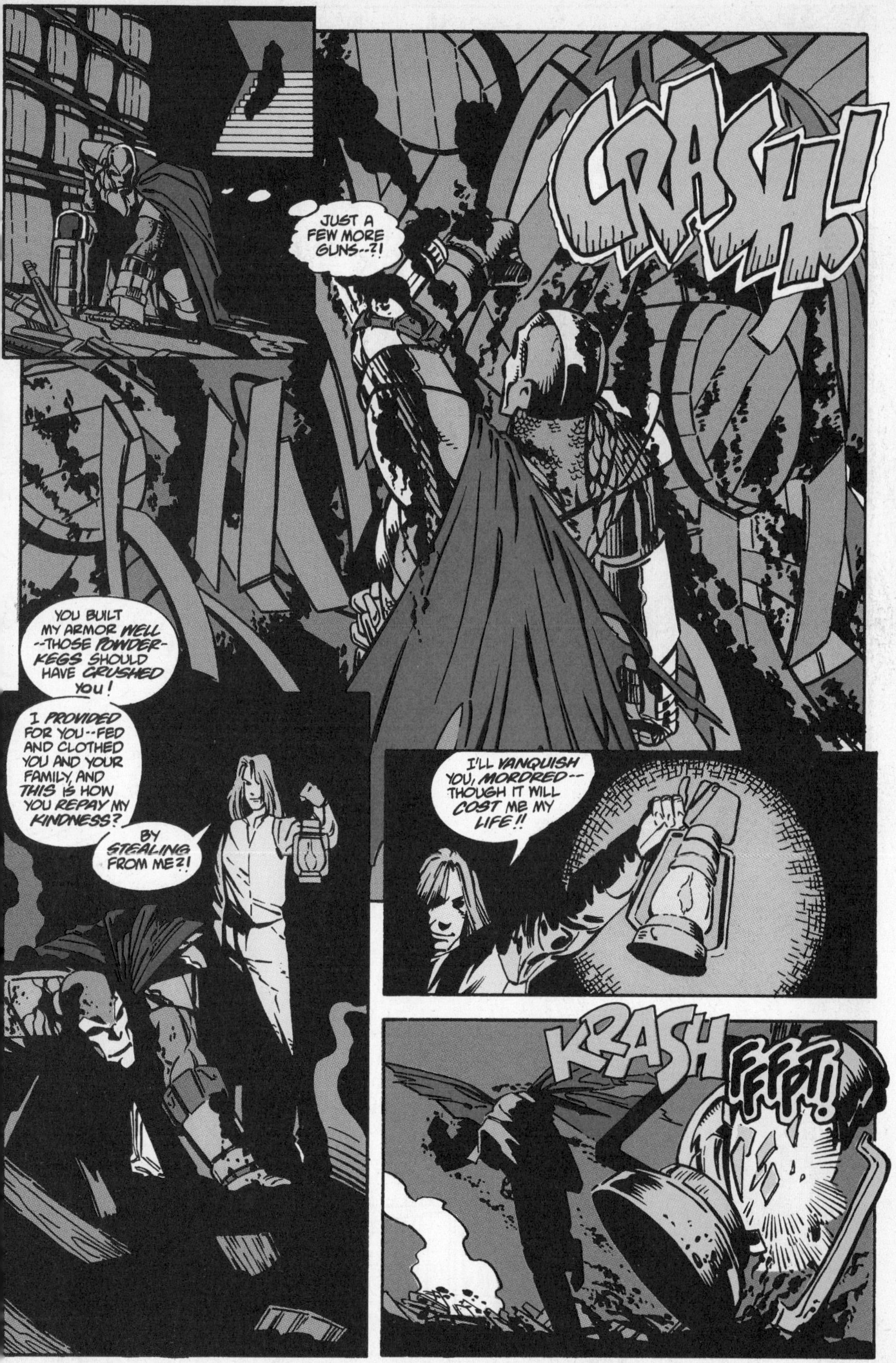
JUST A FEW MORE GUNS--?!
CRASH!
YOU BUILT MY ARMOR WELL --THOSE POWDER-KEGS SHOULD HAVE CRUSHED YOU!
I PROVIDED FOR YOU--FED AND CLOTHED YOU AND YOUR FAMILY, AND THIS IS HOW YOU REPAY MY KINDNESS?
BY STEALING FROM ME?!
I'LL VANQUISH YOU, MORDRED--THOUGH IT WILL COST ME MY LIFE!!
KRASH
FFFPT!

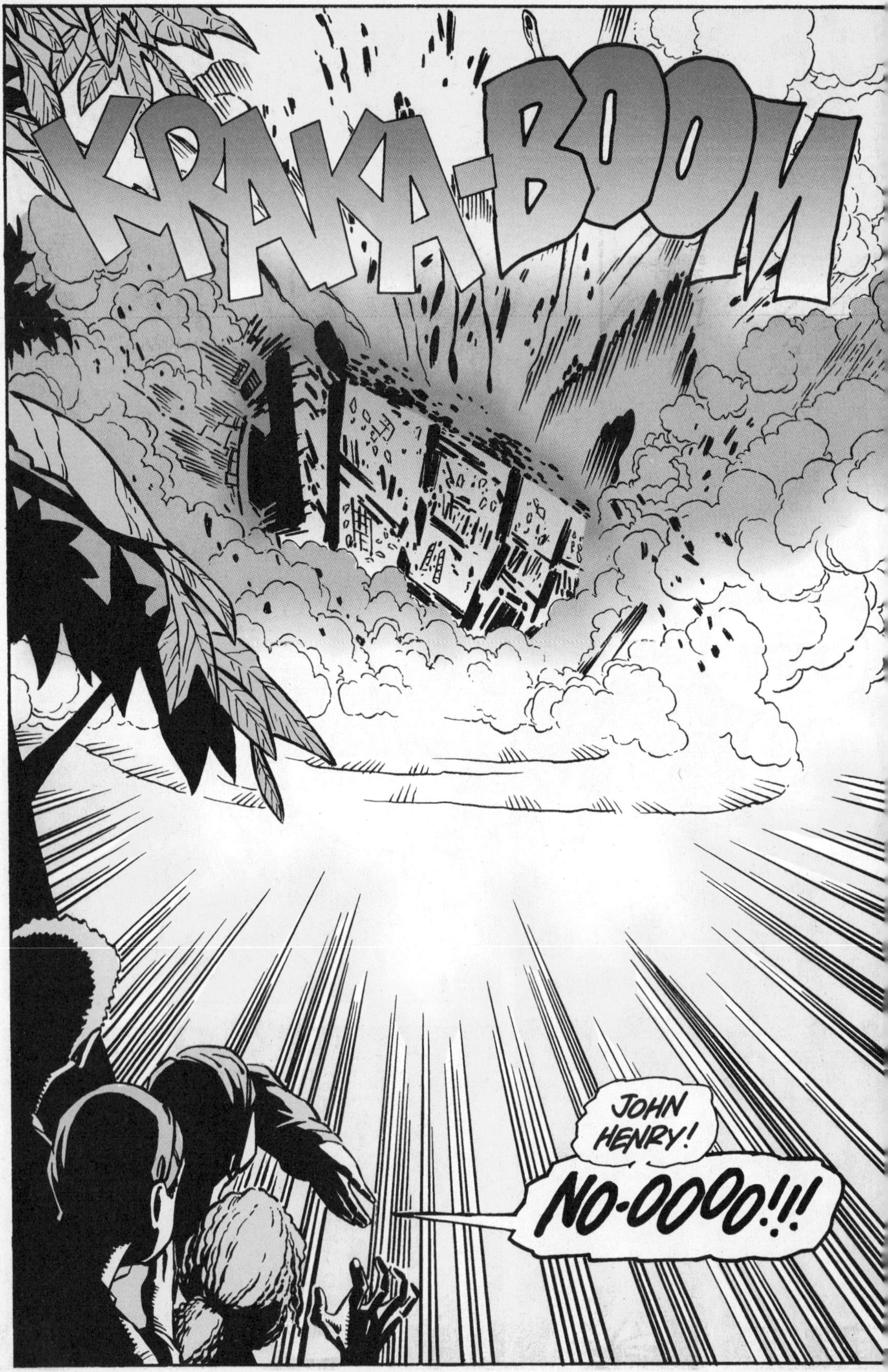
KRAKA-BOOM
JOHN HENRY!
NO-OOOO!!!

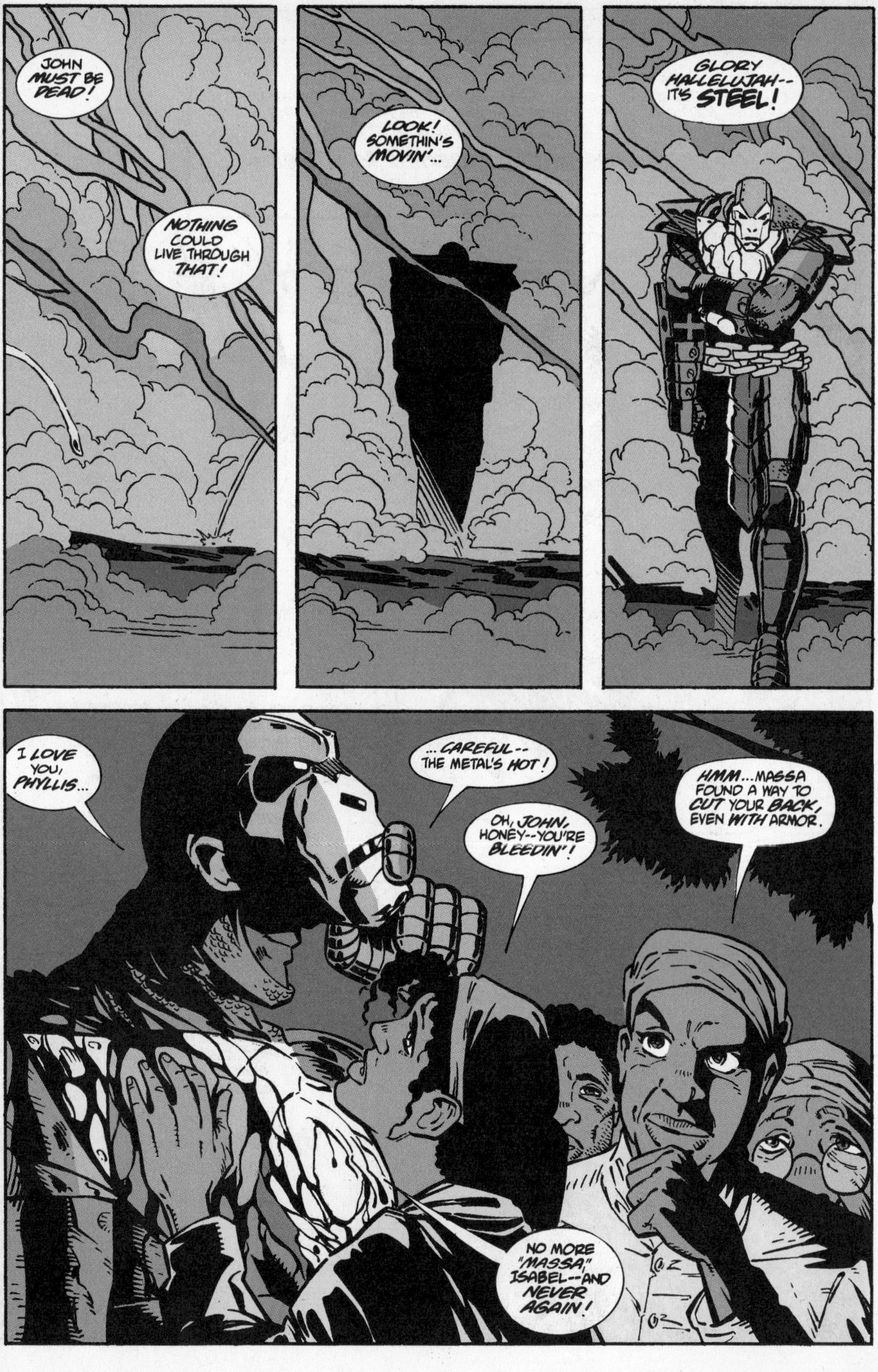
JOHN MUST BE DEAD!
NOTHING COULD LIVE THROUGH THAT!
LOOK! SOMETHIN'S MOVIN'...
GLORY HALLELUJAH-- IT'S STEEL!
I LOVE YOU, PHYLLIS...
...CAREFUL-- THE METAL'S HOT!
OH, JOHN, HONEY--YOU'RE BLEEDIN'!
HMM...MASSA FOUND A WAY TO CUT YOUR BACK, EVEN WITH ARMOR.
NO MORE "MASSA," ISABEL--AND NEVER AGAIN!

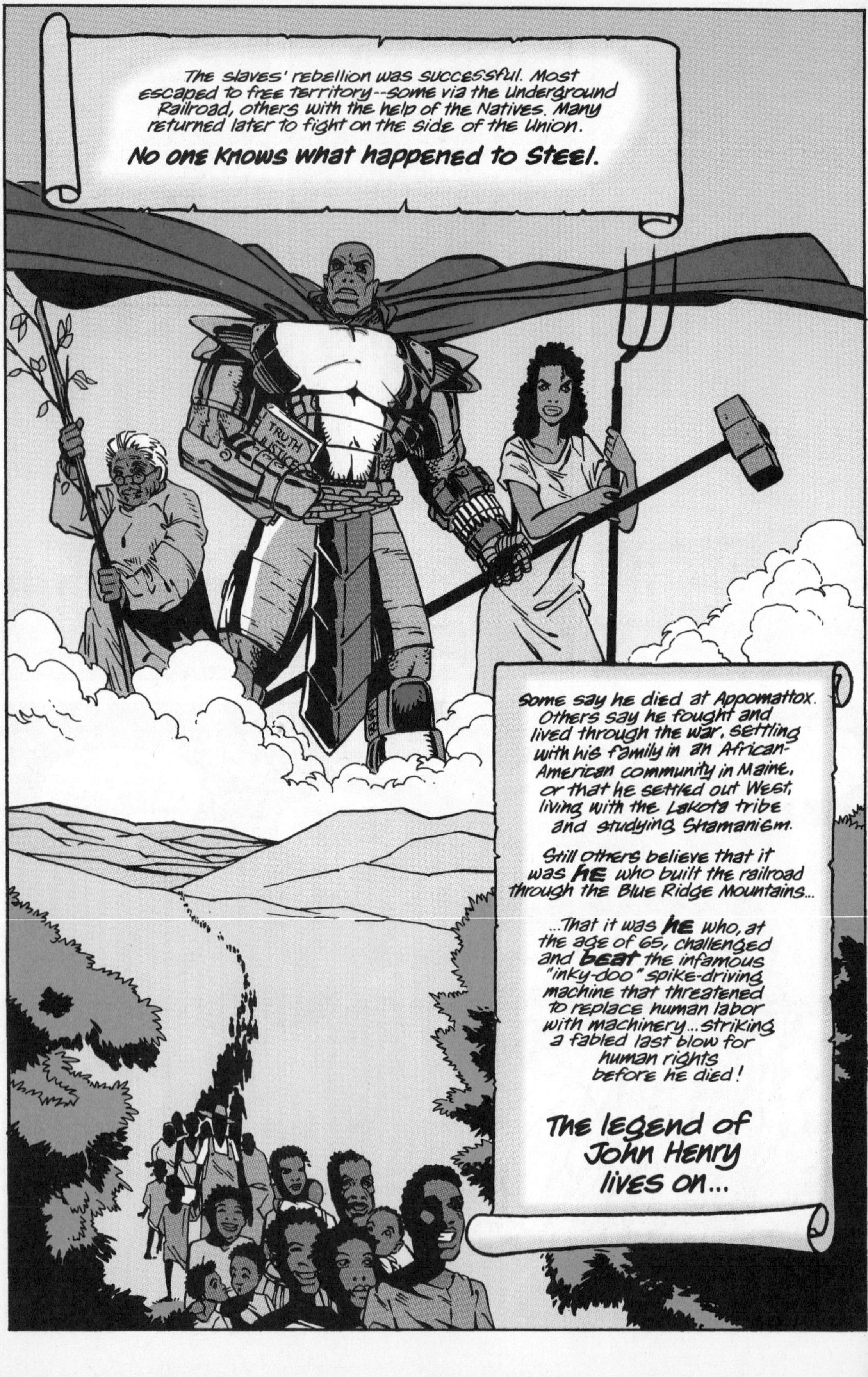
The slaves' rebellion was successful. Most escaped to free territory--some via the Underground Railroad, others with the help of the Natives. Many returned later to fight on the side of the Union.
No one knows what happened to Steel.
TRUTH JUSTICE
Some say he died at Appomattox. Others say he fought and lived through the war, settling with his family in an African-American community in Maine, or that he settled out West, living with the Lakota tribe and studying Shamanism.
Still others believe that it was HE who built the railroad through the Blue Ridge Mountains...
...That it was HE who, at the age of 65, challenged and beat the infamous "inky-doo" spike-driving machine that threatened to replace human labor with machinery...striking a fabled last blow for human rights before he died!
The legend of John Henry lives on...

citizen
WAYNE

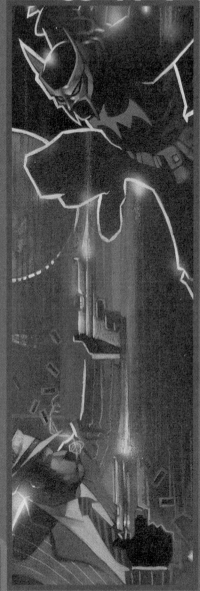

citizen
WAYNE.

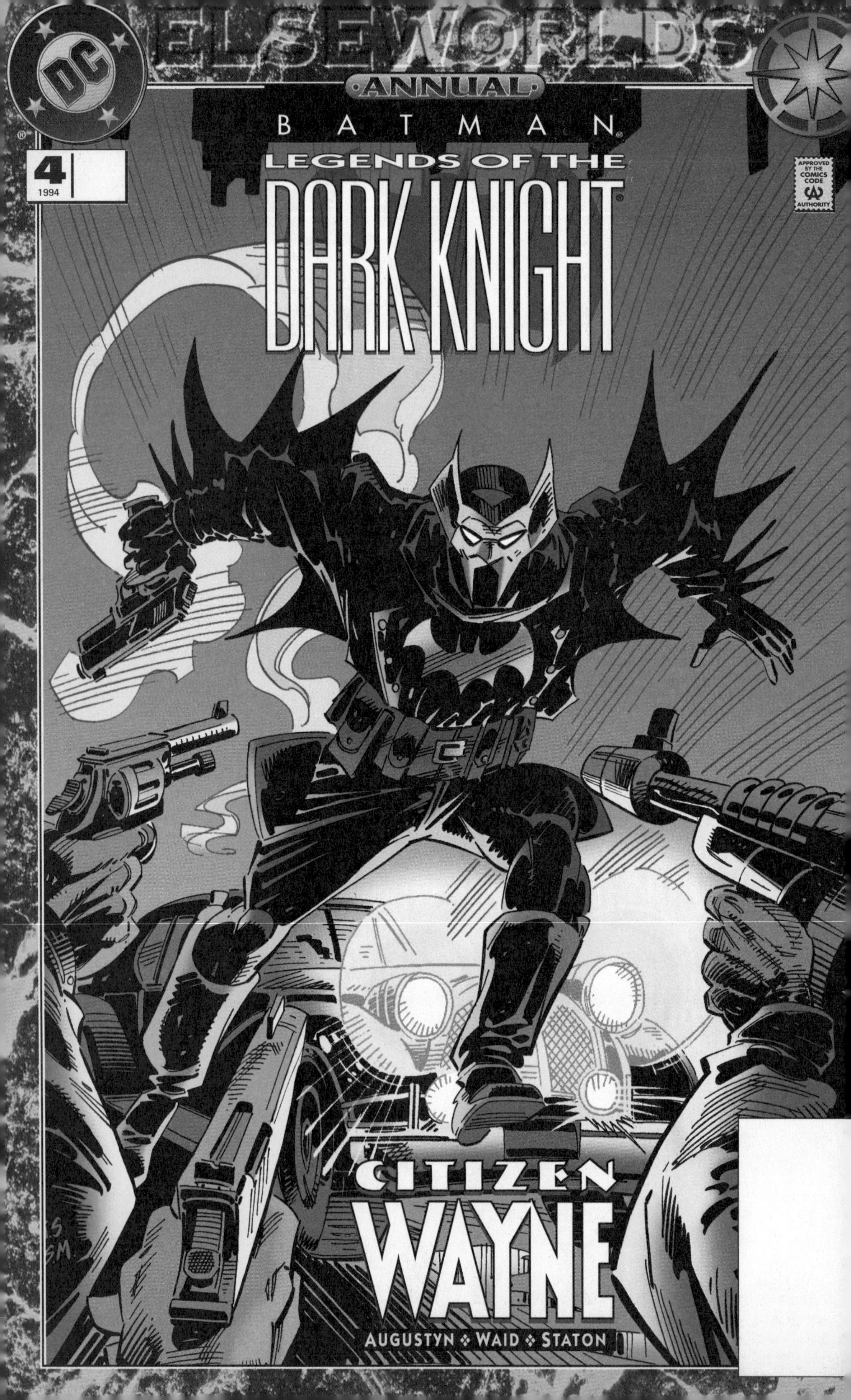

DC
ELSEWORLDS
ANNUAL
BATMAN
LEGENDS OF THE
DARK KNIGHT
4
1994
APPROVED BY THE COMICS CODE AUTHORITY
CITIZEN
WAYNE
AUGUSTYN ❖ WAID ❖ STATON

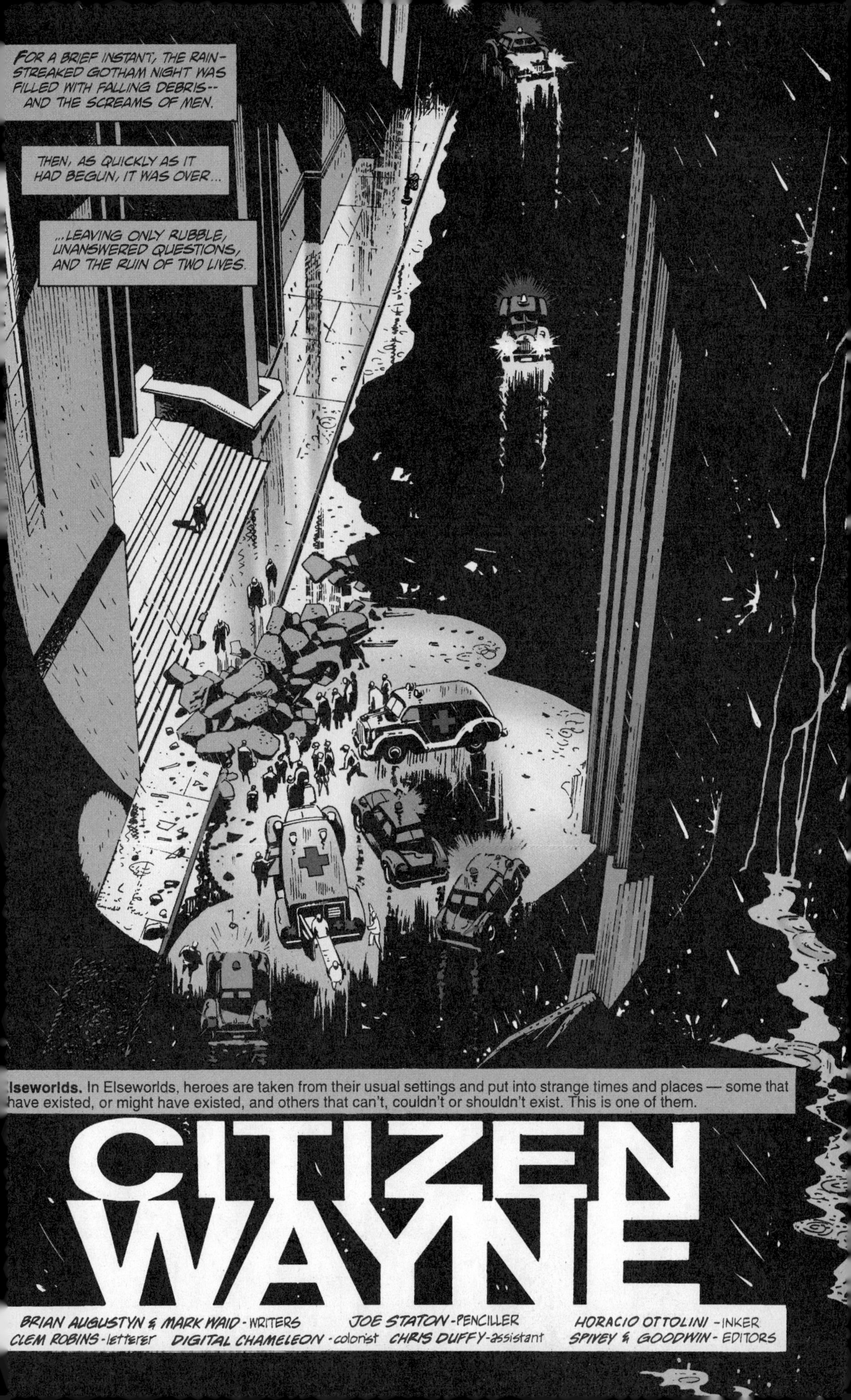
FOR A BRIEF INSTANT, THE RAIN-STREAKED GOTHAM NIGHT WAS FILLED WITH FALLING DEBRIS-- AND THE SCREAMS OF MEN.
THEN, AS QUICKLY AS IT HAD BEGUN, IT WAS OVER...
...LEAVING ONLY RUBBLE, UNANSWERED QUESTIONS, AND THE RUIN OF TWO LIVES.
lseworlds. In Elseworlds, heroes are taken from their usual settings and put into strange times and places — some that have existed, or might have existed, and others that can't, couldn't or shouldn't exist. This is one of them.
CITIZEN WAYNE
BRIAN AUGUSTYN & MARK WAID - WRITERS
JOE STATON - PENCILLER
HORACIO OTTOLINI - INKER
CLEM ROBINS - letterer
DIGITAL CHAMELEON - colorist
CHRIS DUFFY - assistant
SPIVEY & GOODWIN - EDITORS

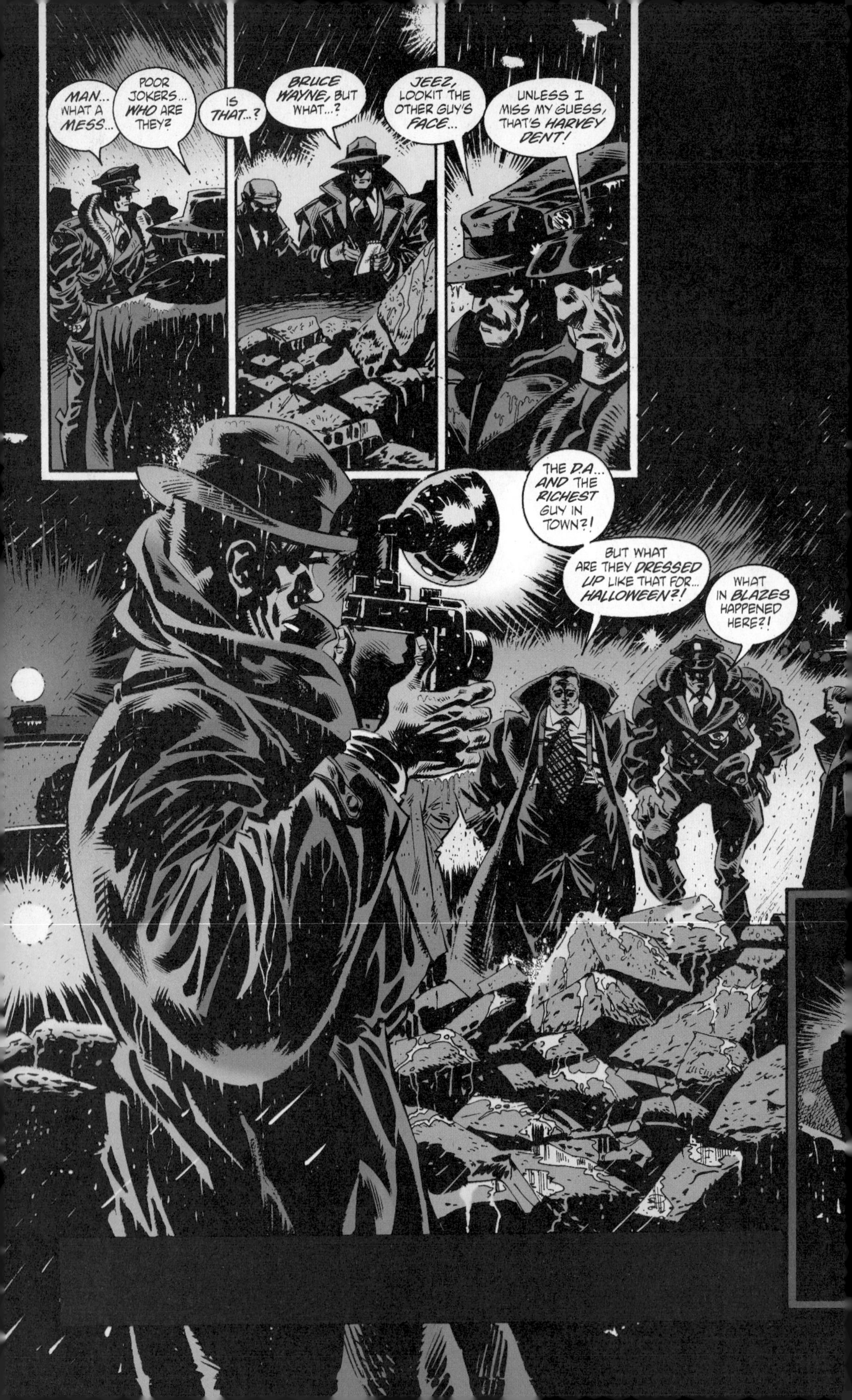

MAN... WHAT A MESS...
POOR JOKERS... WHO ARE THEY?
IS THAT...?
BRUCE WAYNE, BUT WHAT...?
JEEZ, LOOKIT THE OTHER GUY'S FACE...
UNLESS I MISS MY GUESS, THAT'S HARVEY DENT!
THE D.A... AND THE RICHEST GUY IN TOWN?!
BUT WHAT ARE THEY DRESSED UP LIKE THAT FOR... HALLOWEEN?!
WHAT IN BLAZES HAPPENED HERE?!

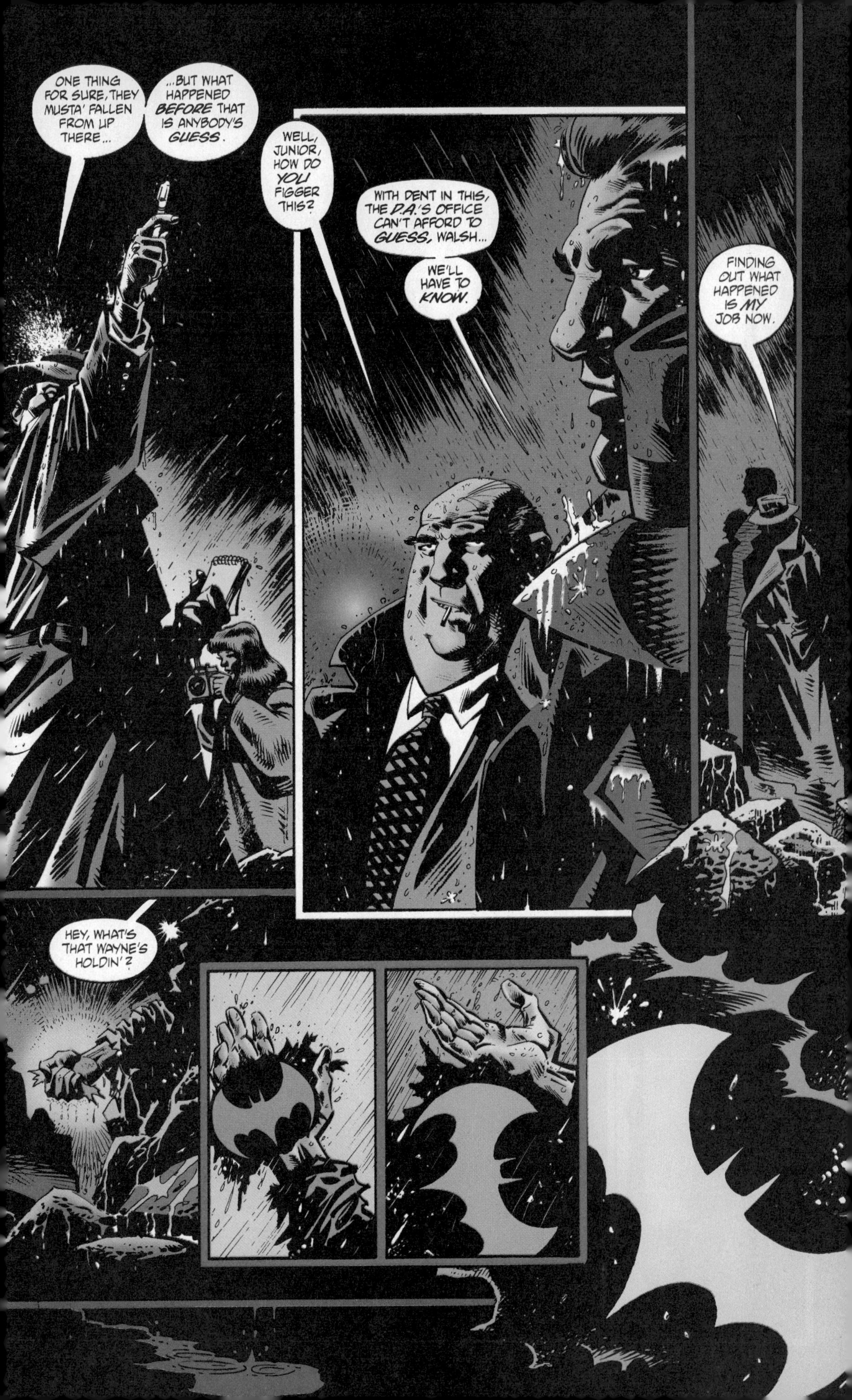

ONE THING FOR SURE, THEY MUSTA' FALLEN FROM UP THERE...
...BUT WHAT HAPPENED BEFORE THAT IS ANYBODY'S GUESS.
WELL, JUNIOR, HOW DO YOU FIGGER THIS?
WITH DENT IN THIS, THE D.A.'S OFFICE CAN'T AFFORD TO GUESS, WALSH...
WE'LL HAVE TO KNOW.
FINDING OUT WHAT HAPPENED IS MY JOB NOW.
HEY, WHAT'S THAT WAYNE'S HOLDIN'?

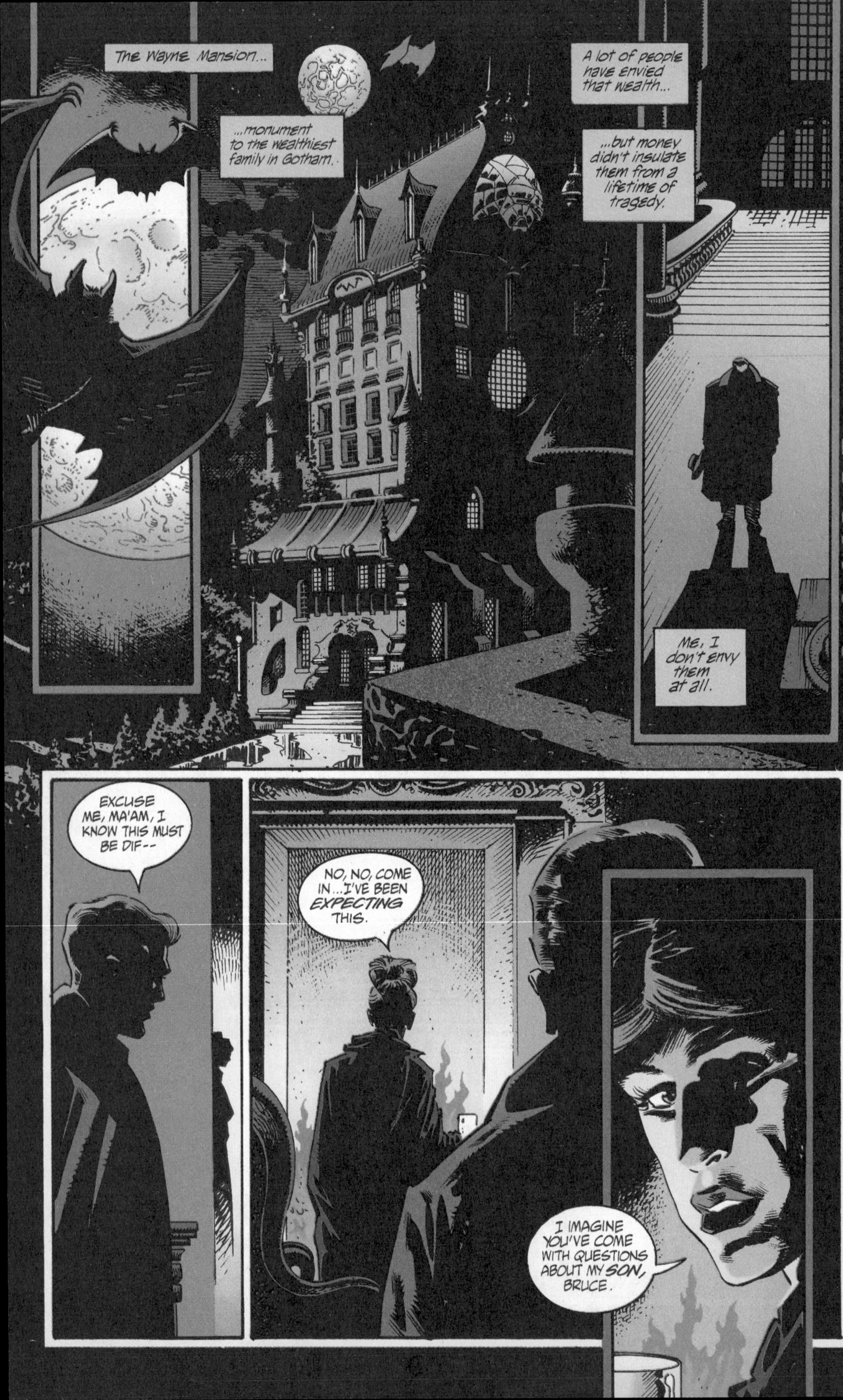

The Wayne Mansion...
...monument to the wealthiest family in Gotham.
A lot of people have envied that wealth...
...but money didn't insulate them from a lifetime of tragedy.
Me, I don't envy them at all.
EXCUSE ME, MA'AM, I KNOW THIS MUST BE DIF--
NO, NO, COME IN... I'VE BEEN EXPECTING THIS.
I IMAGINE YOU'VE COME WITH QUESTIONS ABOUT MY SON, BRUCE.

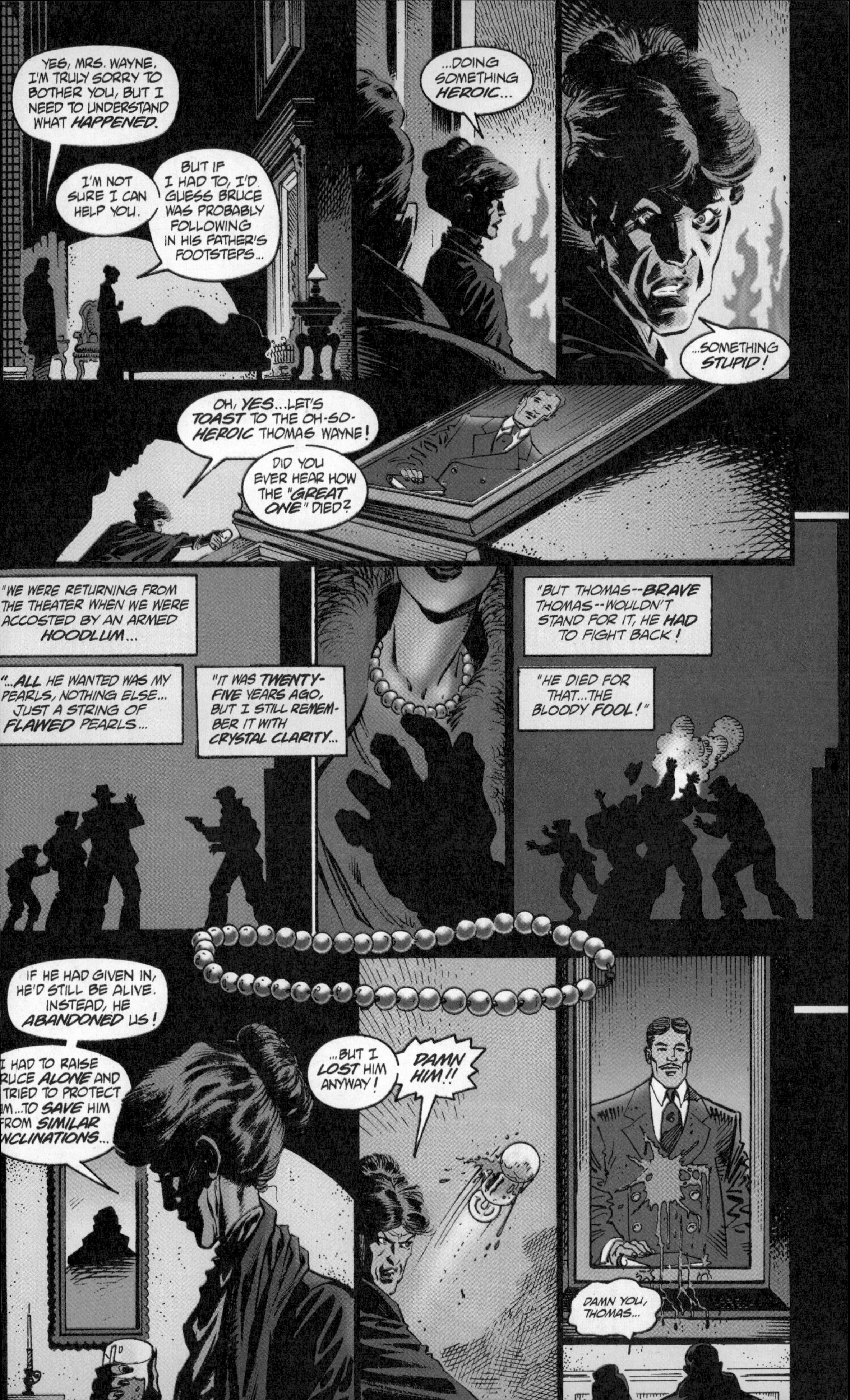
YES, MRS. WAYNE, I'M TRULY SORRY TO BOTHER YOU, BUT I NEED TO UNDERSTAND WHAT HAPPENED.
I'M NOT SURE I CAN HELP YOU.
BUT IF I HAD TO, I'D GUESS BRUCE WAS PROBABLY FOLLOWING IN HIS FATHER'S FOOTSTEPS...
...DOING SOMETHING HEROIC...
...SOMETHING STUPID!
OH, YES...LET'S TOAST TO THE OH-SO-HEROIC THOMAS WAYNE!
DID YOU EVER HEAR HOW THE "GREAT ONE" DIED?
"WE WERE RETURNING FROM THE THEATER WHEN WE WERE ACCOSTED BY AN ARMED HOODLUM...
"...ALL HE WANTED WAS MY PEARLS, NOTHING ELSE... JUST A STRING OF FLAWED PEARLS...
"IT WAS TWENTY-FIVE YEARS AGO, BUT I STILL REMEMBER IT WITH CRYSTAL CLARITY...
"BUT THOMAS--BRAVE THOMAS--WOULDN'T STAND FOR IT, HE HAD TO FIGHT BACK!
"HE DIED FOR THAT...THE BLOODY FOOL!"
IF HE HAD GIVEN IN, HE'D STILL BE ALIVE. INSTEAD, HE ABANDONED US!
I HAD TO RAISE RUCE ALONE AND TRIED TO PROTECT IM...TO SAVE HIM FROM SIMILAR NCLINATIONS...
...BUT I LOST HIM ANYWAY!
DAMN HIM!!
DAMN YOU, THOMAS...

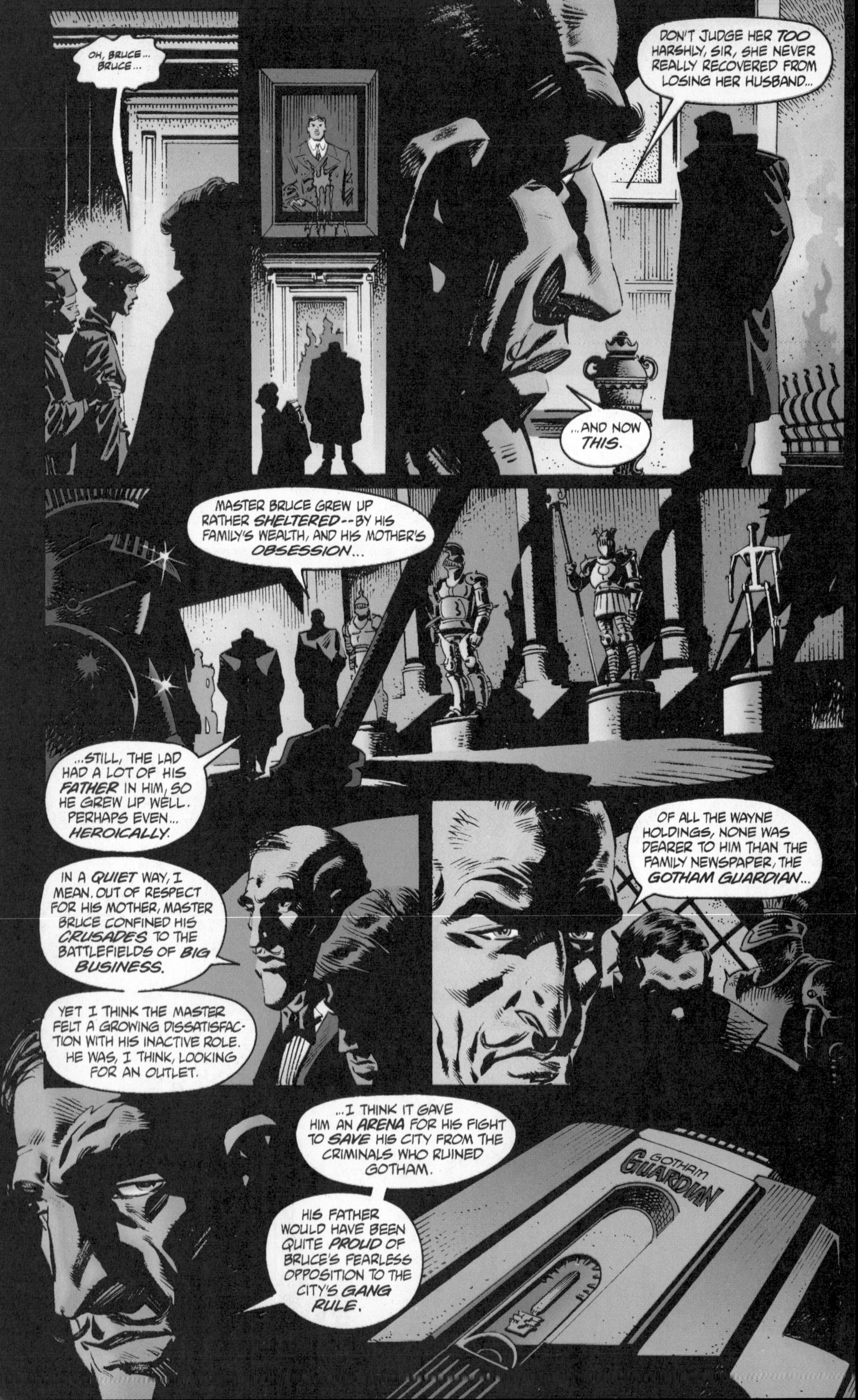
OH, BRUCE... BRUCE...
DON'T JUDGE HER TOO HARSHLY, SIR, SHE NEVER REALLY RECOVERED FROM LOSING HER HUSBAND...
...AND NOW THIS.
MASTER BRUCE GREW UP RATHER SHELTERED--BY HIS FAMILY'S WEALTH, AND HIS MOTHER'S OBSESSION...
...STILL, THE LAD HAD A LOT OF HIS FATHER IN HIM, SO HE GREW UP WELL. PERHAPS EVEN... HEROICALLY.
IN A QUIET WAY, I MEAN. OUT OF RESPECT FOR HIS MOTHER, MASTER BRUCE CONFINED HIS CRUSADES TO THE BATTLEFIELDS OF BIG BUSINESS.
YET I THINK THE MASTER FELT A GROWING DISSATISFACTION WITH HIS INACTIVE ROLE. HE WAS, I THINK, LOOKING FOR AN OUTLET.
OF ALL THE WAYNE HOLDINGS, NONE WAS DEARER TO HIM THAN THE FAMILY NEWSPAPER, THE GOTHAM GUARDIAN...
...I THINK IT GAVE HIM AN ARENA FOR HIS FIGHT TO SAVE HIS CITY FROM THE CRIMINALS WHO RUINED GOTHAM.
HIS FATHER WOULD HAVE BEEN QUITE PROUD OF BRUCE'S FEARLESS OPPOSITION TO THE CITY'S GANG RULE.
GOTHAM GUARDIAN

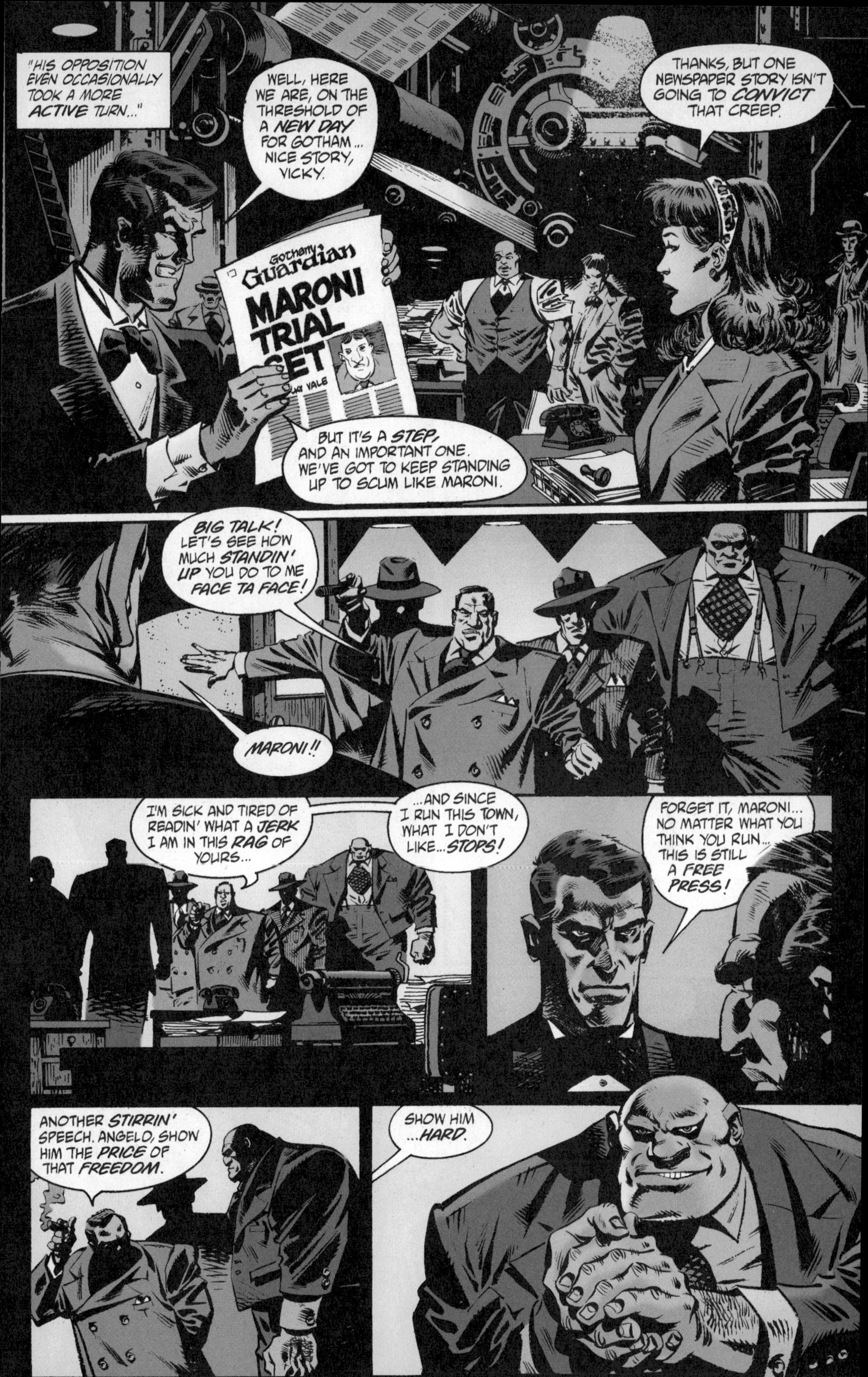
"HIS OPPOSITION EVEN OCCASIONALLY TOOK A MORE ACTIVE TURN..."
WELL, HERE WE ARE, ON THE THRESHOLD OF A NEW DAY FOR GOTHAM ... NICE STORY, VICKY.
THANKS, BUT ONE NEWSPAPER STORY ISN'T GOING TO CONVICT THAT CREEP.
Gotham Guardian
MARONI TRIAL SET
VALE
BUT IT'S A STEP, AND AN IMPORTANT ONE. WE'VE GOT TO KEEP STANDING UP TO SCUM LIKE MARONI.
BIG TALK! LET'S SEE HOW MUCH STANDIN' UP YOU DO TO ME FACE TA FACE!
MARONI!!
I'M SICK AND TIRED OF READIN' WHAT A JERK I AM IN THIS RAG OF YOURS...
...AND SINCE I RUN THIS TOWN, WHAT I DON'T LIKE... STOPS!
FORGET IT, MARONI... NO MATTER WHAT YOU THINK YOU RUN... THIS IS STILL A FREE PRESS!
ANOTHER STIRRIN' SPEECH. ANGELO, SHOW HIM THE PRICE OF THAT FREEDOM.
SHOW HIM ...HARD.

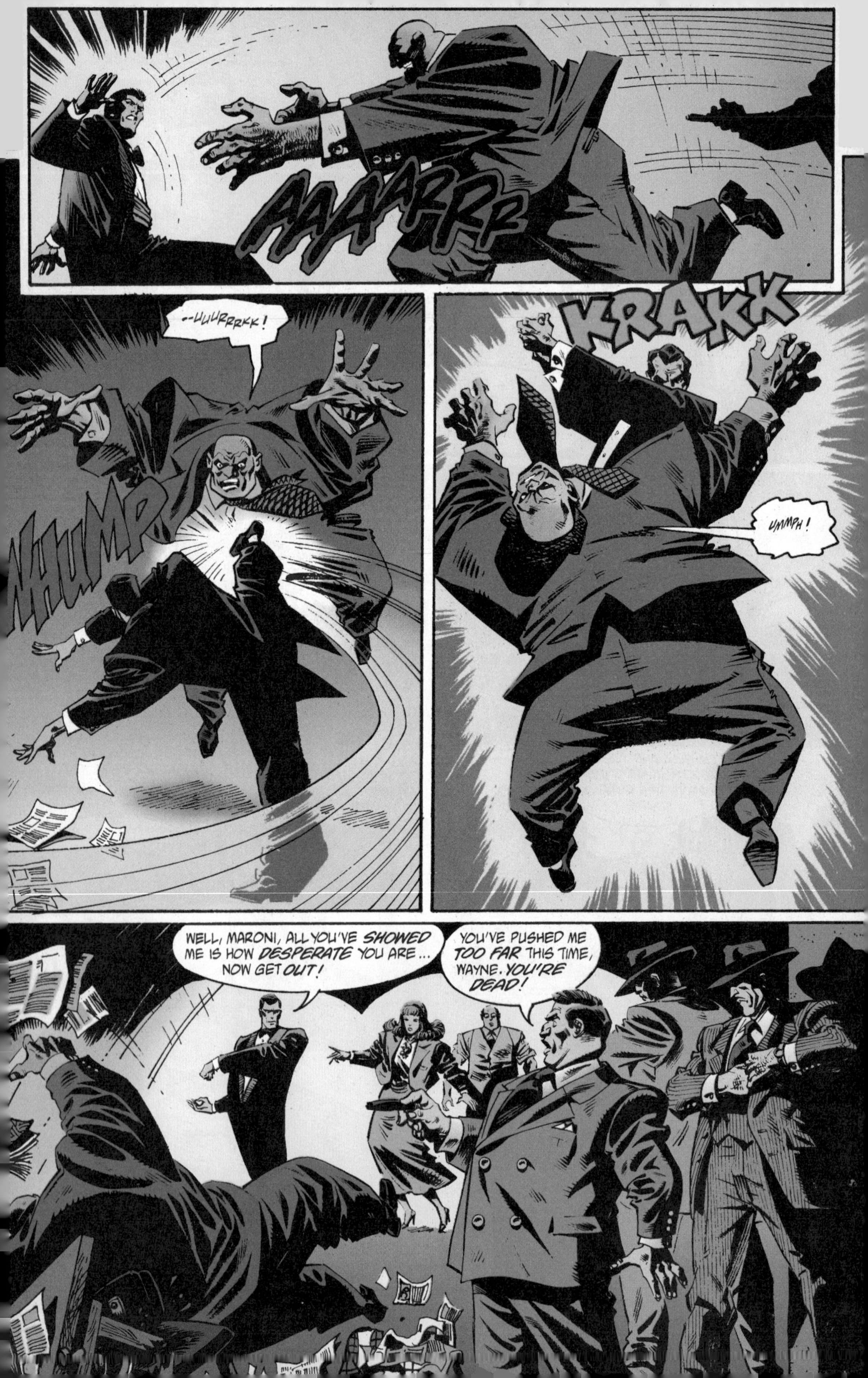
AAAARRR
--UUURRRKK!
NHUMP
KRAKK
UMMPH!
WELL, MARONI, ALL YOU'VE SHOWED ME IS HOW DESPERATE YOU ARE... NOW GET OUT!
YOU'VE PUSHED ME TOO FAR THIS TIME, WAYNE. YOU'RE DEAD!

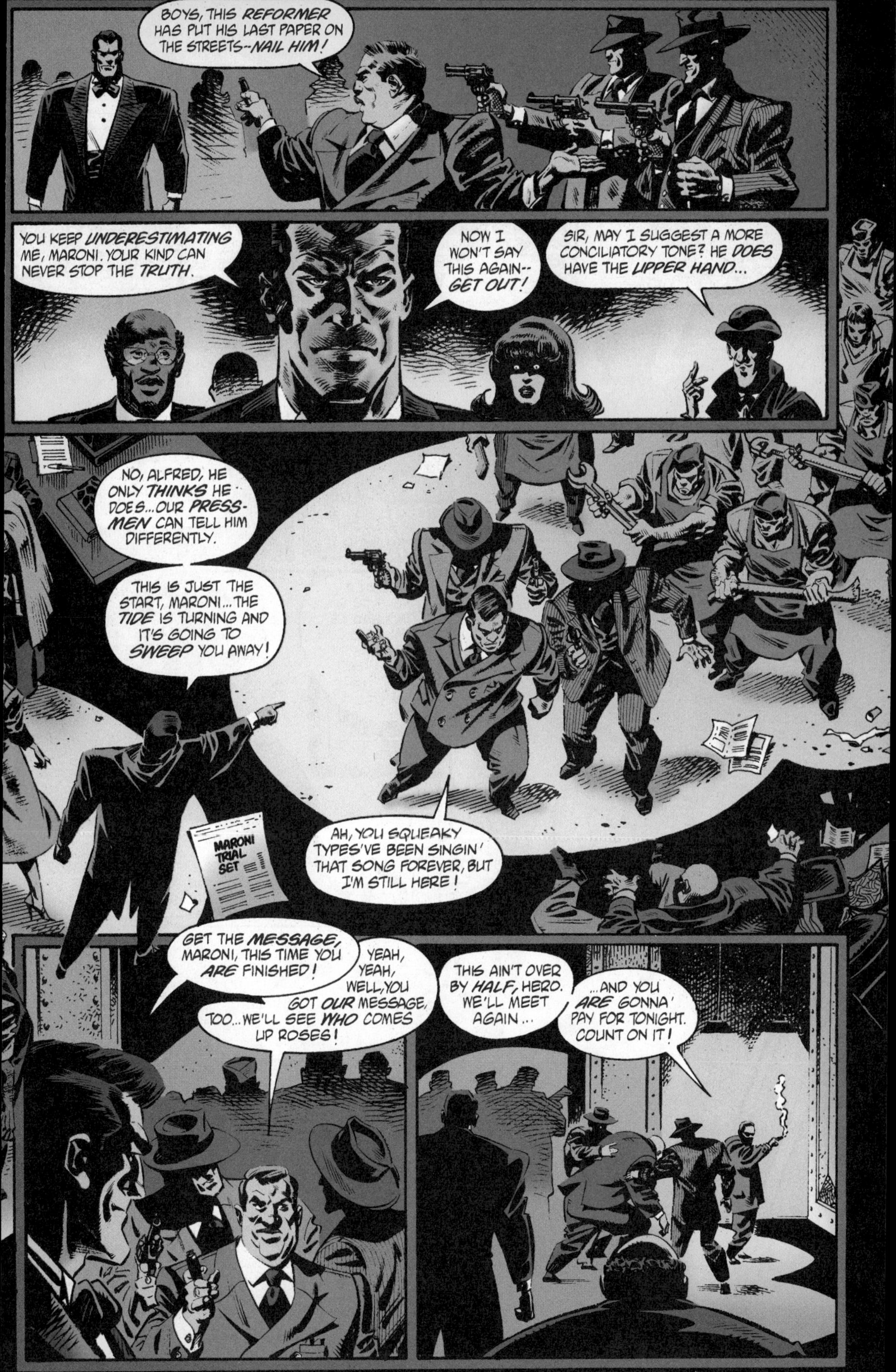
BOYS, THIS REFORMER HAS PUT HIS LAST PAPER ON THE STREETS--NAIL HIM!
YOU KEEP UNDERESTIMATING ME, MARONI. YOUR KIND CAN NEVER STOP THE TRUTH.
NOW I WON'T SAY THIS AGAIN-- GET OUT!
SIR, MAY I SUGGEST A MORE CONCILIATORY TONE? HE DOES HAVE THE UPPER HAND...
NO, ALFRED, HE ONLY THINKS HE DOES...OUR PRESS-MEN CAN TELL HIM DIFFERENTLY.
THIS IS JUST THE START, MARONI...THE TIDE IS TURNING AND IT'S GOING TO SWEEP YOU AWAY!
AH, YOU SQUEAKY TYPES'VE BEEN SINGIN' THAT SONG FOREVER, BUT I'M STILL HERE!
MARONI TRIAL SET
GET THE MESSAGE, MARONI, THIS TIME YOU ARE FINISHED!
YEAH, YEAH, WELL, YOU GOT OUR MESSAGE, TOO...WE'LL SEE WHO COMES UP ROSES!
THIS AIN'T OVER BY HALF, HERO. WE'LL MEET AGAIN...
...AND YOU ARE GONNA' PAY FOR TONIGHT. COUNT ON IT!

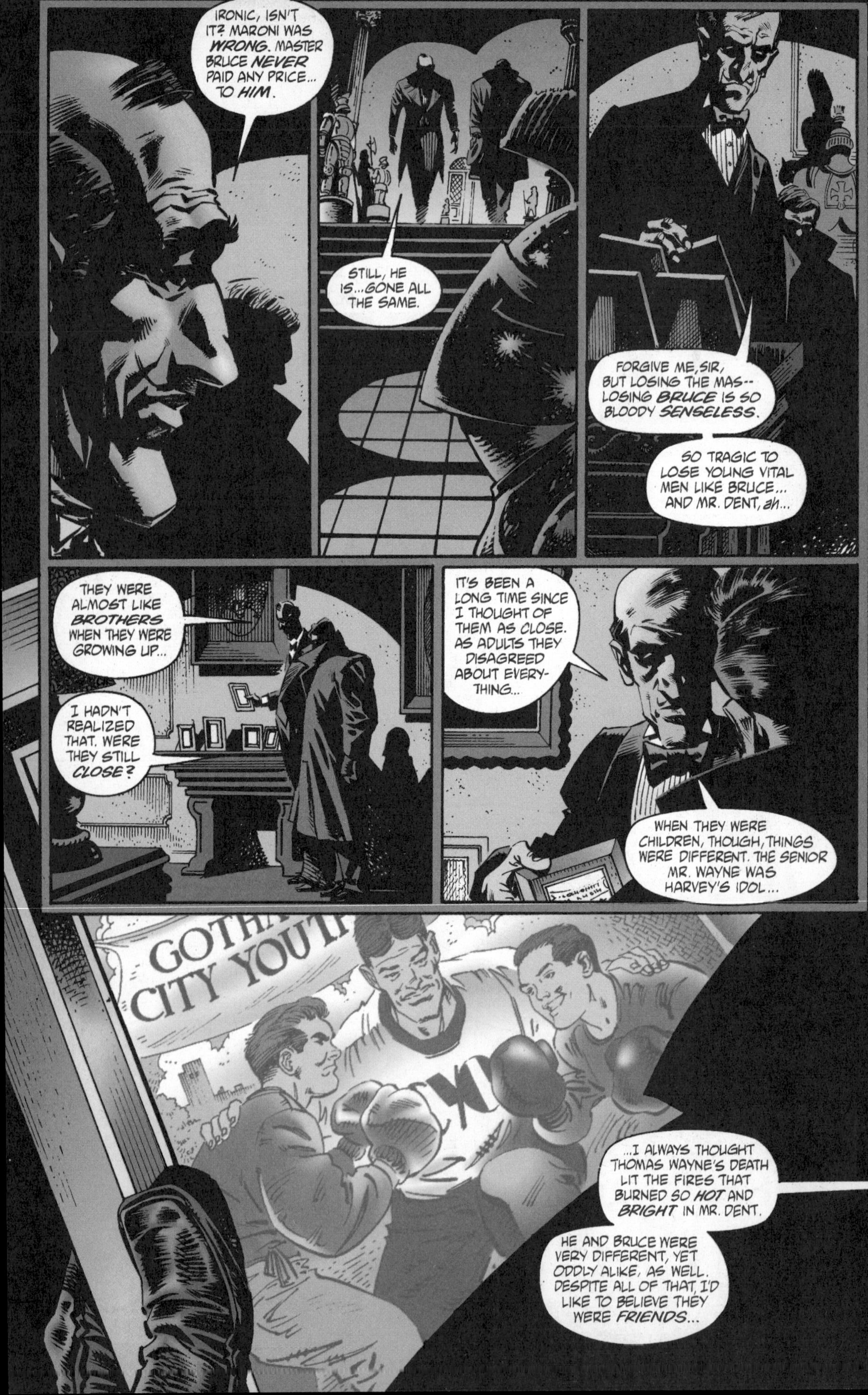

IRONIC, ISN'T IT? MARONI WAS WRONG. MASTER BRUCE NEVER PAID ANY PRICE... TO HIM.
STILL, HE IS...GONE ALL THE SAME.
FORGIVE ME, SIR, BUT LOSING THE MAS-- LOSING BRUCE IS SO BLOODY SENSELESS.
SO TRAGIC TO LOSE YOUNG VITAL MEN LIKE BRUCE... AND MR. DENT, ah...
THEY WERE ALMOST LIKE BROTHERS WHEN THEY WERE GROWING UP...
I HADN'T REALIZED THAT. WERE THEY STILL CLOSE?
IT'S BEEN A LONG TIME SINCE I THOUGHT OF THEM AS CLOSE. AS ADULTS THEY DISAGREED ABOUT EVERY-THING...
WHEN THEY WERE CHILDREN, THOUGH, THINGS WERE DIFFERENT. THE SENIOR MR. WAYNE WAS HARVEY'S IDOL...
GOTH
CITY YOUT
...I ALWAYS THOUGHT THOMAS WAYNE'S DEATH LIT THE FIRES THAT BURNED SO HOT AND BRIGHT IN MR. DENT.
HE AND BRUCE WERE VERY DIFFERENT, YET ODDLY ALIKE, AS WELL. DESPITE ALL OF THAT, I'D LIKE TO BELIEVE THEY WERE FRIENDS...

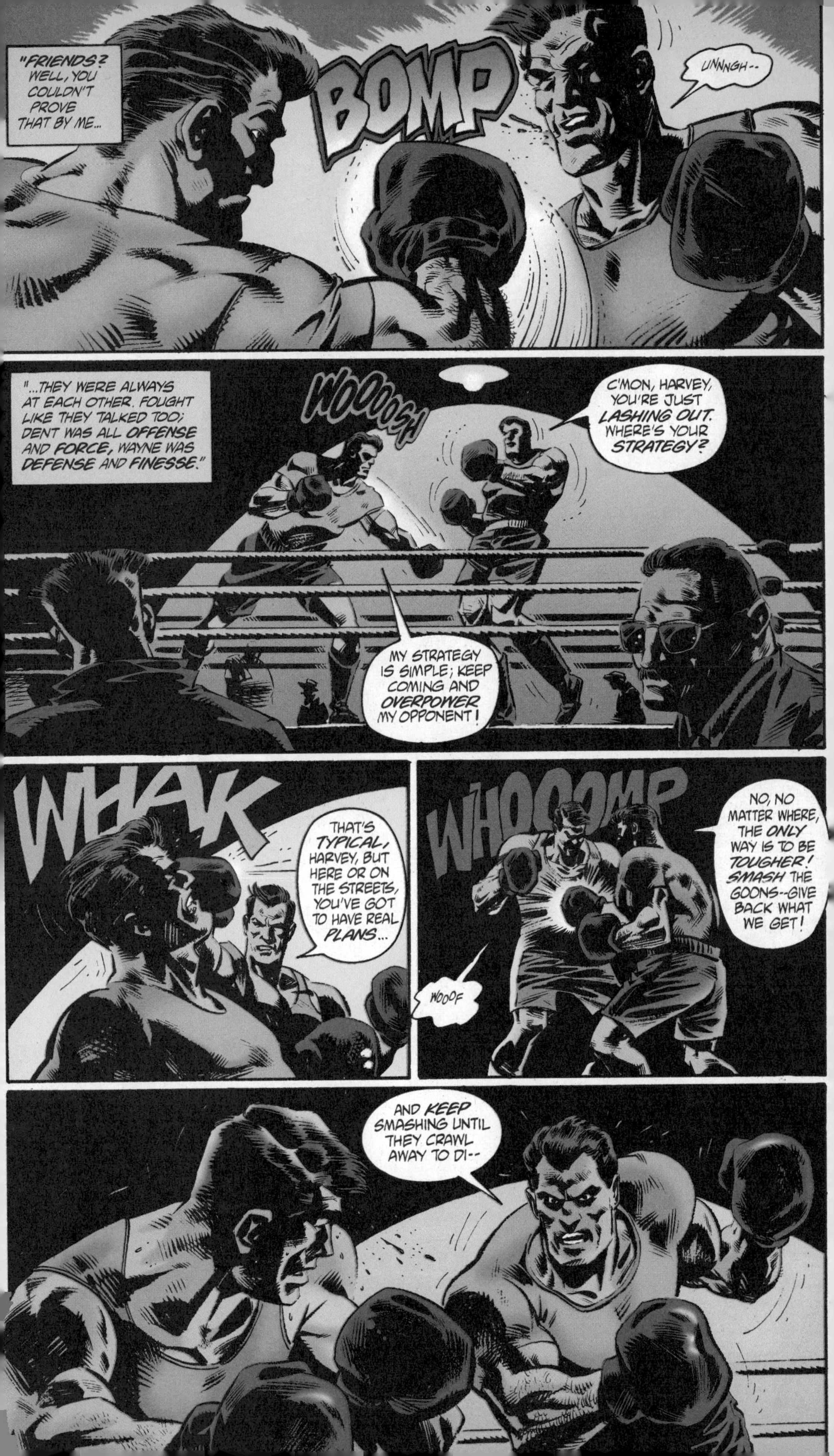
"FRIENDS? WELL, YOU COULDN'T PROVE THAT BY ME...
BOMP
UNNNGH--
"...THEY WERE ALWAYS AT EACH OTHER. FOUGHT LIKE THEY TALKED TOO; DENT WAS ALL OFFENSE AND FORCE, WAYNE WAS DEFENSE AND FINESSE."
WOOOOSH
C'MON, HARVEY, YOU'RE JUST LASHING OUT. WHERE'S YOUR STRATEGY?
MY STRATEGY IS SIMPLE; KEEP COMING AND OVERPOWER MY OPPONENT!
WHAK
THAT'S TYPICAL, HARVEY, BUT HERE OR ON THE STREETS, YOU'VE GOT TO HAVE REAL PLANS...
WHOOOMP
WOOOF
NO, NO MATTER WHERE, THE ONLY WAY IS TO BE TOUGHER! SMASH THE GOONS--GIVE BACK WHAT WE GET!
AND KEEP SMASHING UNTIL THEY CRAWL AWAY TO DI--

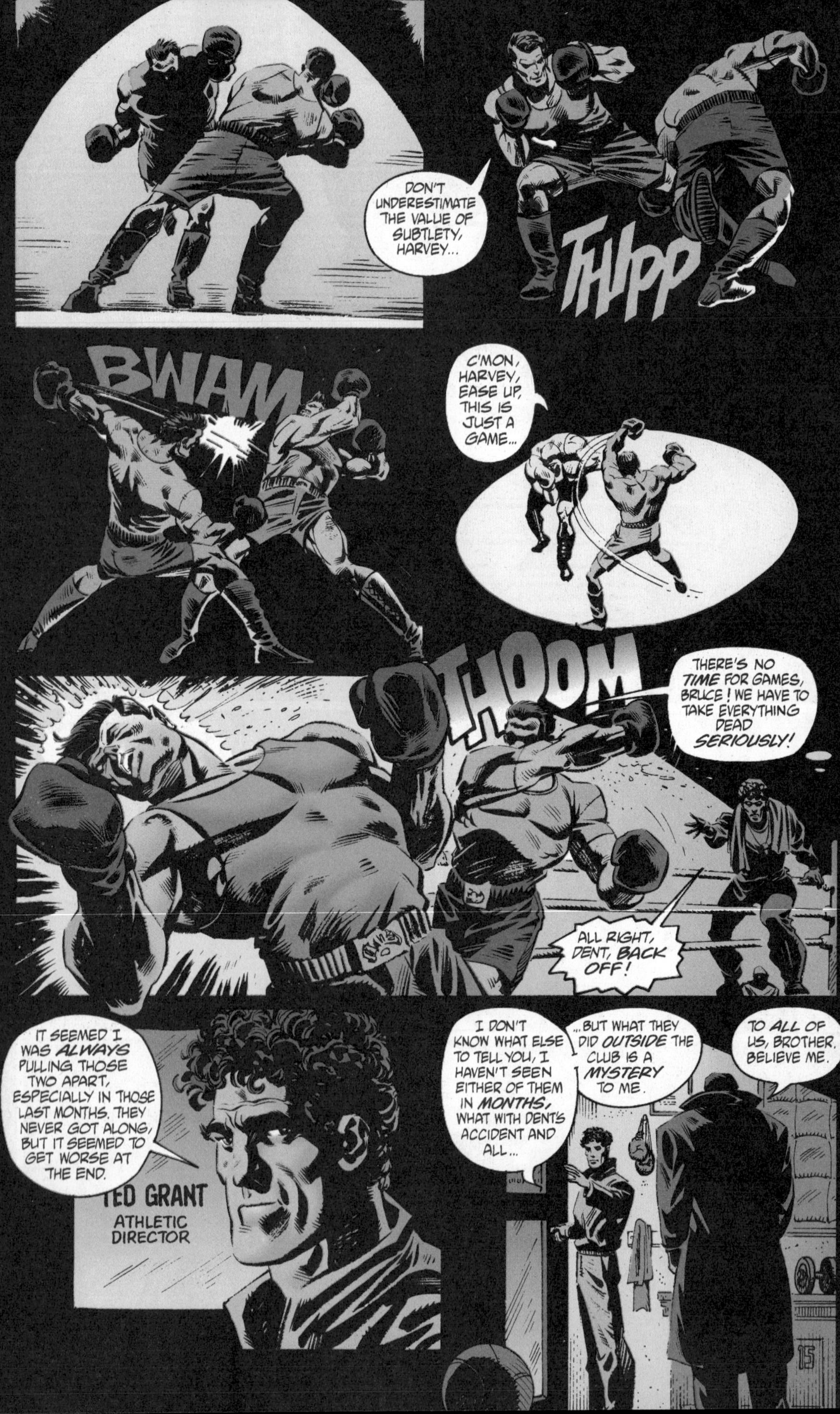
DON'T UNDERESTIMATE THE VALUE OF SUBTLETY, HARVEY...
THUPP
BWAM
C'MON, HARVEY, EASE UP, THIS IS JUST A GAME...
THOOM
THERE'S NO TIME FOR GAMES, BRUCE! WE HAVE TO TAKE EVERYTHING DEAD SERIOUSLY!
ALL RIGHT, DENT, BACK OFF!
IT SEEMED I WAS ALWAYS PULLING THOSE TWO APART, ESPECIALLY IN THOSE LAST MONTHS. THEY NEVER GOT ALONG, BUT IT SEEMED TO GET WORSE AT THE END.
TED GRANT
ATHLETIC DIRECTOR
I DON'T KNOW WHAT ELSE TO TELL YOU, I HAVEN'T SEEN EITHER OF THEM IN MONTHS, WHAT WITH DENT'S ACCIDENT AND ALL...
...BUT WHAT THEY DID OUTSIDE THE CLUB IS A MYSTERY TO ME.
TO ALL OF US, BROTHER, BELIEVE ME.
15

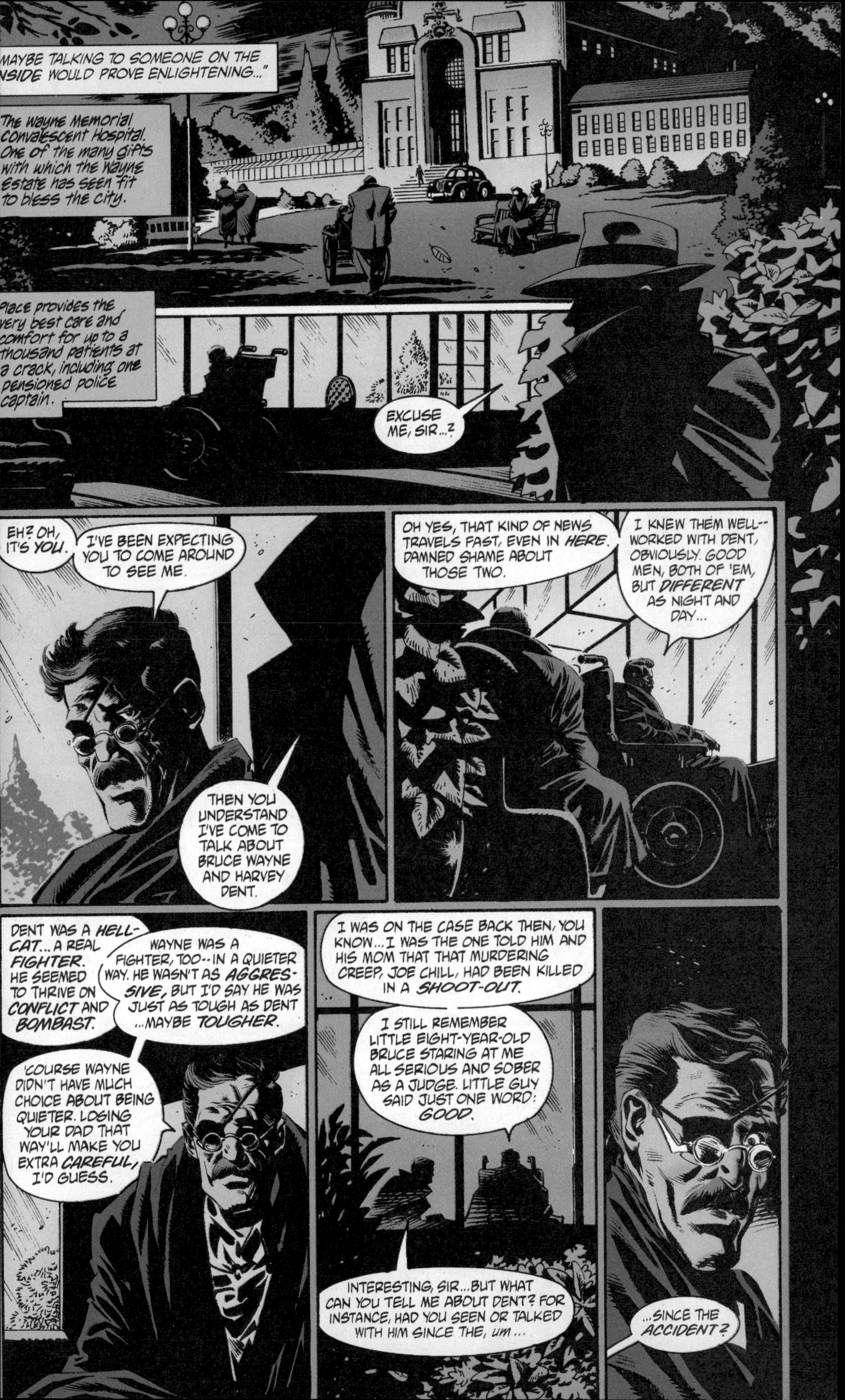

MAYBE TALKING TO SOMEONE ON THE INSIDE WOULD PROVE ENLIGHTENING..."
The Wayne Memorial Convalescent Hospital. One of the many gifts with which the Wayne Estate has seen fit to bless the city.
Place provides the very best care and comfort for up to a thousand patients at a crack, including one pensioned police captain.
EXCUSE ME, SIR...?
EH? OH, IT'S YOU.
I'VE BEEN EXPECTING YOU TO COME AROUND TO SEE ME.
THEN YOU UNDERSTAND I'VE COME TO TALK ABOUT BRUCE WAYNE AND HARVEY DENT.
OH YES, THAT KIND OF NEWS TRAVELS FAST, EVEN IN HERE. DAMNED SHAME ABOUT THOSE TWO.
I KNEW THEM WELL-- WORKED WITH DENT, OBVIOUSLY. GOOD MEN, BOTH OF 'EM, BUT DIFFERENT AS NIGHT AND DAY...
DENT WAS A HELL-CAT... A REAL FIGHTER. HE SEEMED TO THRIVE ON CONFLICT AND BOMBAST.
WAYNE WAS A FIGHTER, TOO-- IN A QUIETER WAY. HE WASN'T AS AGGRES-SIVE, BUT I'D SAY HE WAS JUST AS TOUGH AS DENT ...MAYBE TOUGHER.
'COURSE WAYNE DIDN'T HAVE MUCH CHOICE ABOUT BEING QUIETER. LOSING YOUR DAD THAT WAY'LL MAKE YOU EXTRA CAREFUL, I'D GUESS.
I WAS ON THE CASE BACK THEN, YOU KNOW... I WAS THE ONE TOLD HIM AND HIS MOM THAT THAT MURDERING CREEP, JOE CHILL, HAD BEEN KILLED IN A SHOOT-OUT.
I STILL REMEMBER LITTLE EIGHT-YEAR-OLD BRUCE STARING AT ME ALL SERIOUS AND SOBER AS A JUDGE. LITTLE GUY SAID JUST ONE WORD: GOOD.
INTERESTING, SIR... BUT WHAT CAN YOU TELL ME ABOUT DENT? FOR INSTANCE, HAD YOU SEEN OR TALKED WITH HIM SINCE THE, UM ...
...SINCE THE ACCIDENT?

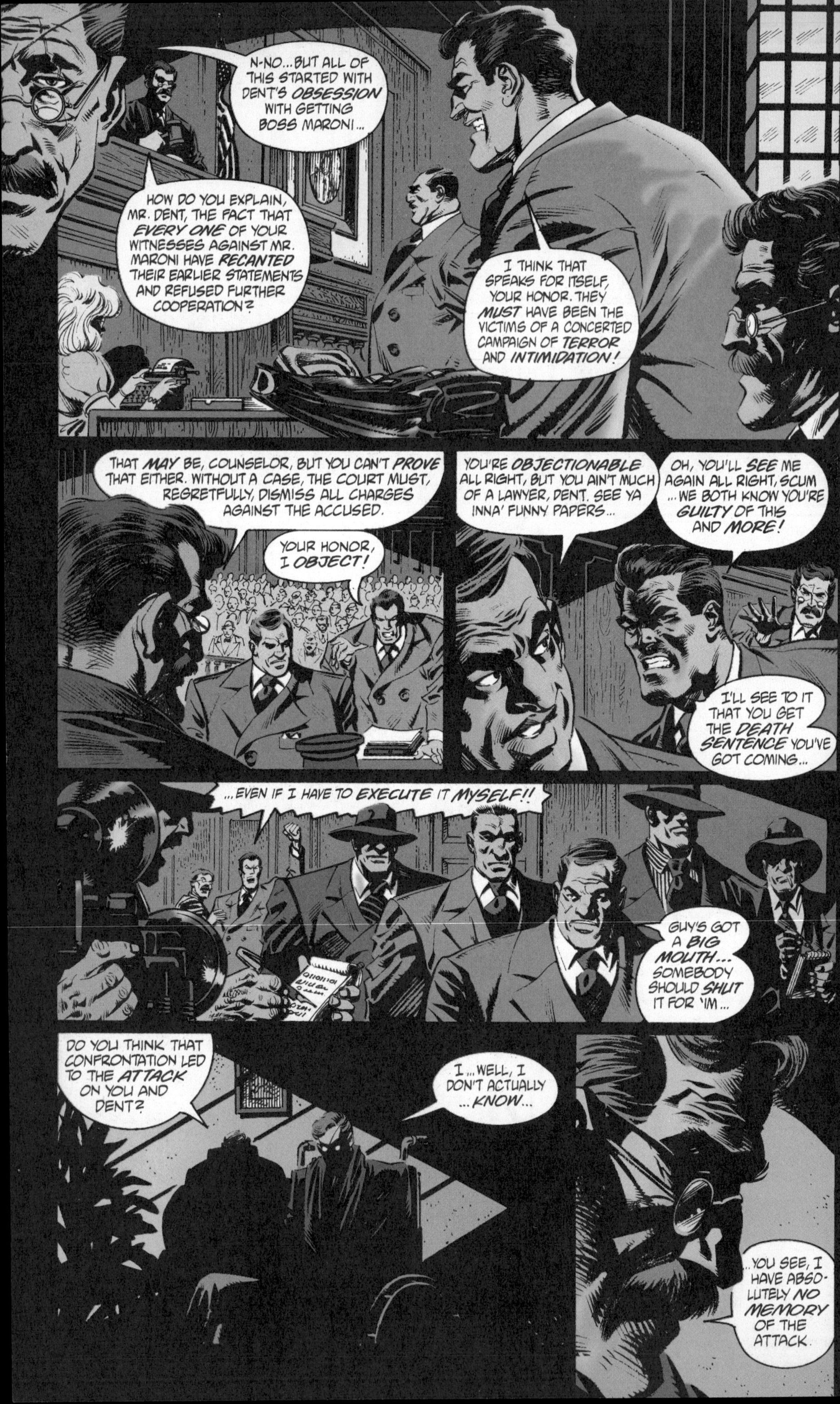
N-NO... BUT ALL OF THIS STARTED WITH DENT'S OBSESSION WITH GETTING BOSS MARONI...
HOW DO YOU EXPLAIN, MR. DENT, THE FACT THAT EVERY ONE OF YOUR WITNESSES AGAINST MR. MARONI HAVE RECANTED THEIR EARLIER STATEMENTS AND REFUSED FURTHER COOPERATION?
I THINK THAT SPEAKS FOR ITSELF, YOUR HONOR. THEY MUST HAVE BEEN THE VICTIMS OF A CONCERTED CAMPAIGN OF TERROR AND INTIMIDATION!
THAT MAY BE, COUNSELOR, BUT YOU CAN'T PROVE THAT EITHER. WITHOUT A CASE, THE COURT MUST, REGRETFULLY, DISMISS ALL CHARGES AGAINST THE ACCUSED.
YOUR HONOR, I OBJECT!
YOU'RE OBJECTIONABLE ALL RIGHT, BUT YOU AIN'T MUCH OF A LAWYER, DENT. SEE YA INNA' FUNNY PAPERS...
OH, YOU'LL SEE ME AGAIN ALL RIGHT, SCUM ...WE BOTH KNOW YOU'RE GUILTY OF THIS AND MORE!
I'LL SEE TO IT THAT YOU GET THE DEATH SENTENCE YOU'VE GOT COMING...
...EVEN IF I HAVE TO EXECUTE IT MYSELF!!
GUY'S GOT A BIG MOUTH... SOMEBODY SHOULD SHUT IT FOR 'IM...
DO YOU THINK THAT CONFRONTATION LED TO THE ATTACK ON YOU AND DENT?
I...WELL, I DON'T ACTUALLY ...KNOW...
...YOU SEE, I HAVE ABSOLUTELY NO MEMORY OF THE ATTACK.

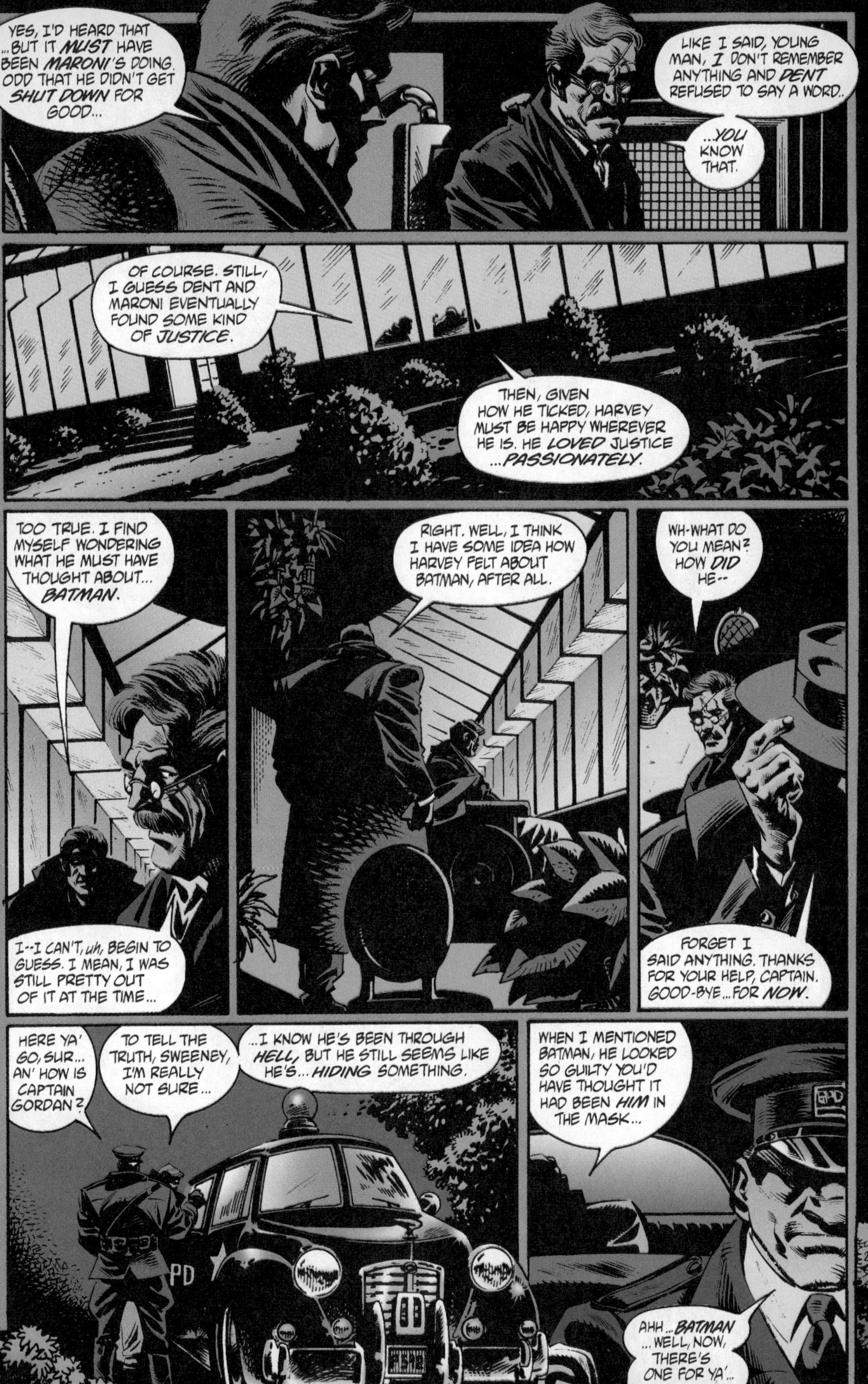

YES, I'D HEARD THAT ...BUT IT MUST HAVE BEEN MARONI'S DOING. ODD THAT HE DIDN'T GET SHUT DOWN FOR GOOD...
LIKE I SAID, YOUNG MAN, I DON'T REMEMBER ANYTHING AND DENT REFUSED TO SAY A WORD..
...YOU KNOW THAT.
OF COURSE. STILL, I GUESS DENT AND MARONI EVENTUALLY FOUND SOME KIND OF JUSTICE.
THEN, GIVEN HOW HE TICKED, HARVEY MUST BE HAPPY WHEREVER HE IS. HE LOVED JUSTICE ...PASSIONATELY.
TOO TRUE. I FIND MYSELF WONDERING WHAT HE MUST HAVE THOUGHT ABOUT... BATMAN.
I--I CAN'T, uh, BEGIN TO GUESS. I MEAN, I WAS STILL PRETTY OUT OF IT AT THE TIME...
RIGHT. WELL, I THINK I HAVE SOME IDEA HOW HARVEY FELT ABOUT BATMAN, AFTER ALL.
WH-WHAT DO YOU MEAN? HOW DID HE--
FORGET I SAID ANYTHING. THANKS FOR YOUR HELP, CAPTAIN. GOOD-BYE...FOR NOW.
HERE YA' GO, SUR... AN' HOW IS CAPTAIN GORDAN?
TO TELL THE TRUTH, SWEENEY, I'M REALLY NOT SURE...
...I KNOW HE'S BEEN THROUGH HELL, BUT HE STILL SEEMS LIKE HE'S... HIDING SOMETHING.
PD
WHEN I MENTIONED BATMAN, HE LOOKED SO GUILTY YOU'D HAVE THOUGHT IT HAD BEEN HIM IN THE MASK...
GPD
AHH... BATMAN ...WELL, NOW, THERE'S ONE FOR YA'...

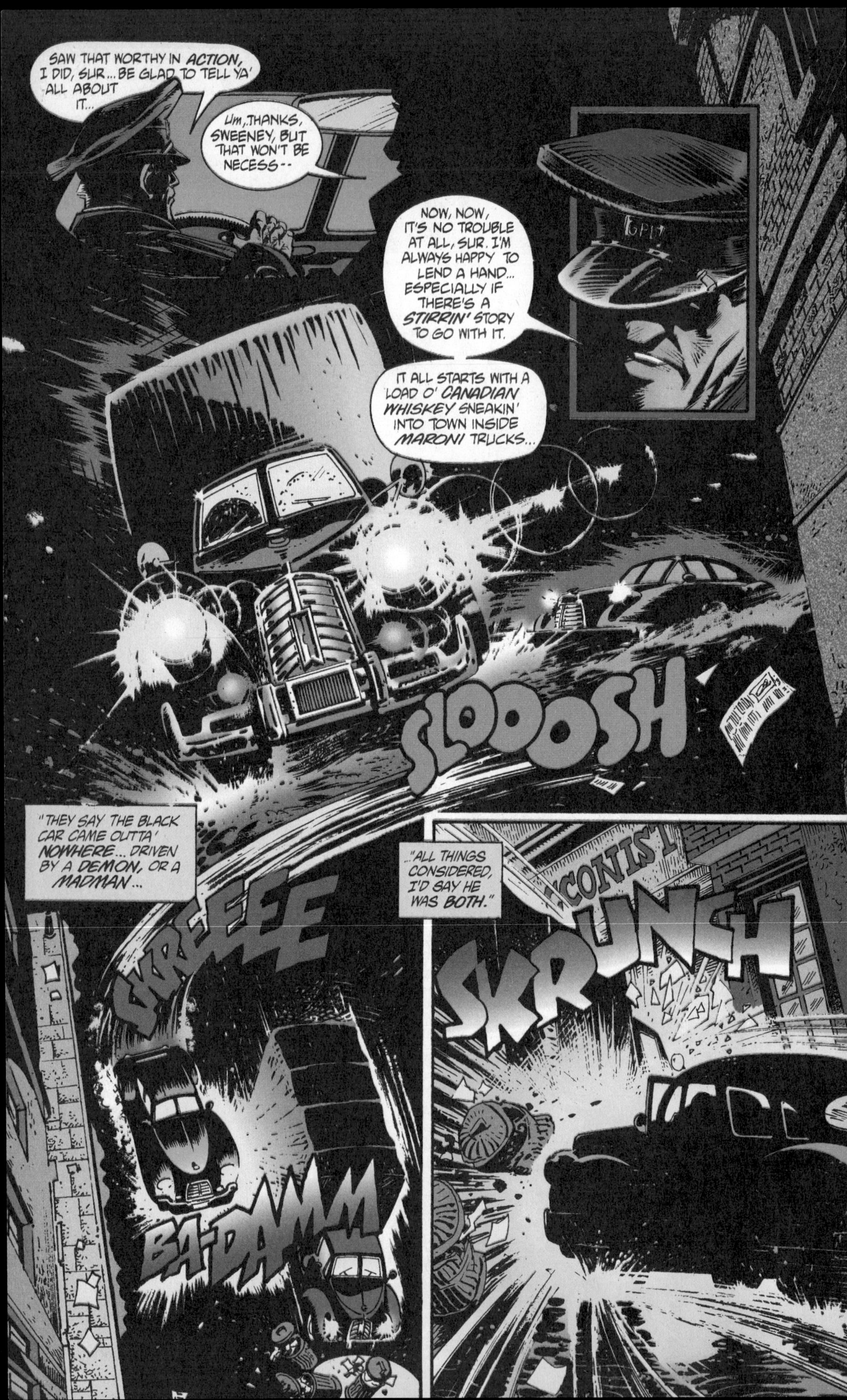
SAW THAT WORTHY IN ACTION, I DID, SUR... BE GLAD TO TELL YA' ALL ABOUT IT...
Um, THANKS, SWEENEY, BUT THAT WON'T BE NECESS--
NOW, NOW, IT'S NO TROUBLE AT ALL, SUR. I'M ALWAYS HAPPY TO LEND A HAND... ESPECIALLY IF THERE'S A STIRRIN' STORY TO GO WITH IT.
IT ALL STARTS WITH A LOAD O' CANADIAN WHISKEY SNEAKIN' INTO TOWN INSIDE MARONI TRUCKS...
SLOOOSH
"THEY SAY THE BLACK CAR CAME OUTTA' NOWHERE... DRIVEN BY A DEMON, OR A MADMAN...
SKREEEE
BA-DAMM
..."ALL THINGS CONSIDERED, I'D SAY HE WAS BOTH."
SKRUNCH

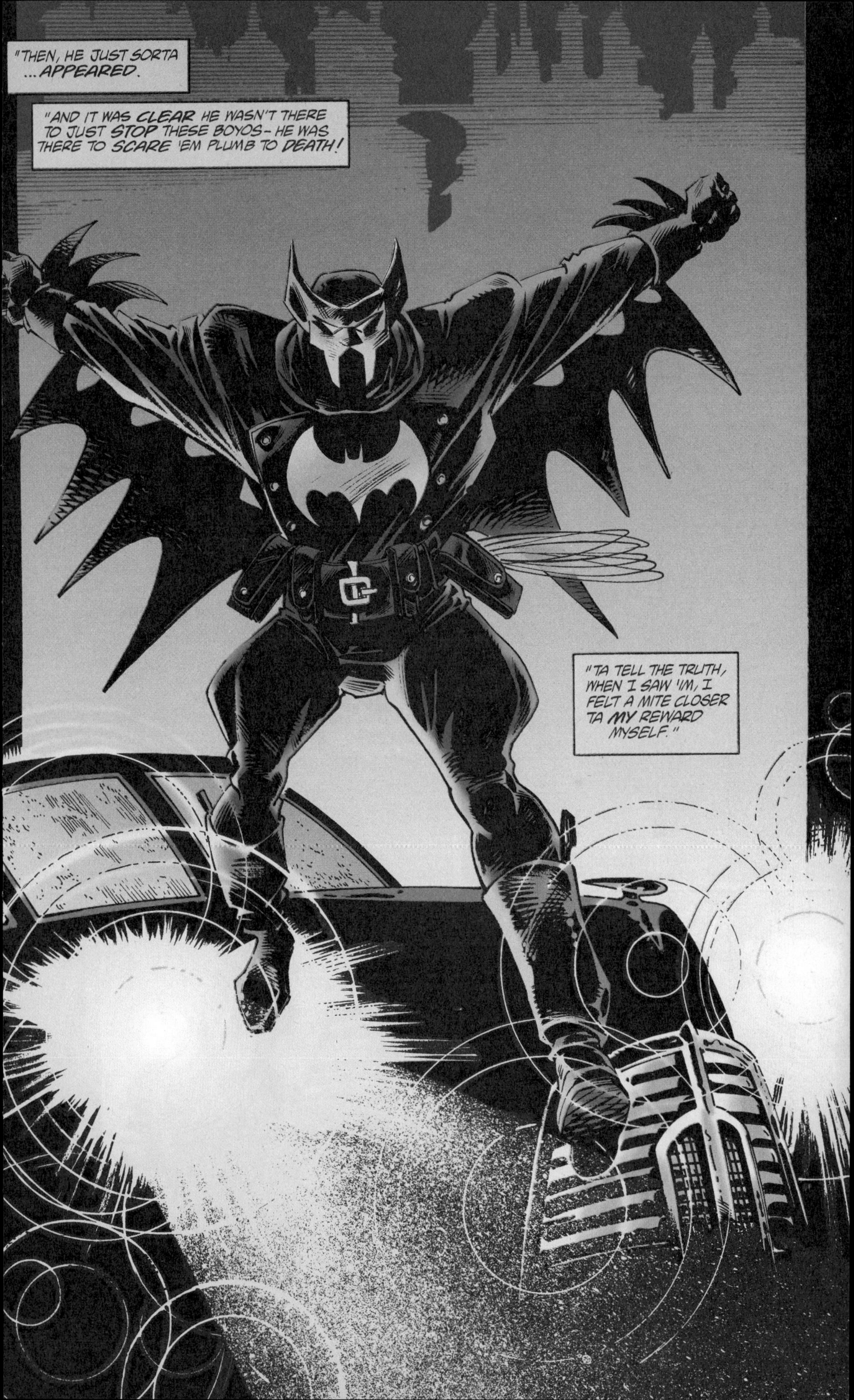
"THEN, HE JUST SORTA ...APPEARED.
"AND IT WAS CLEAR HE WASN'T THERE TO JUST STOP THESE BOYOS- HE WAS THERE TO SCARE 'EM PLUMB TO DEATH!
"TA TELL THE TRUTH, WHEN I SAW 'IM, I FELT A MITE CLOSER TA MY REWARD MYSELF."

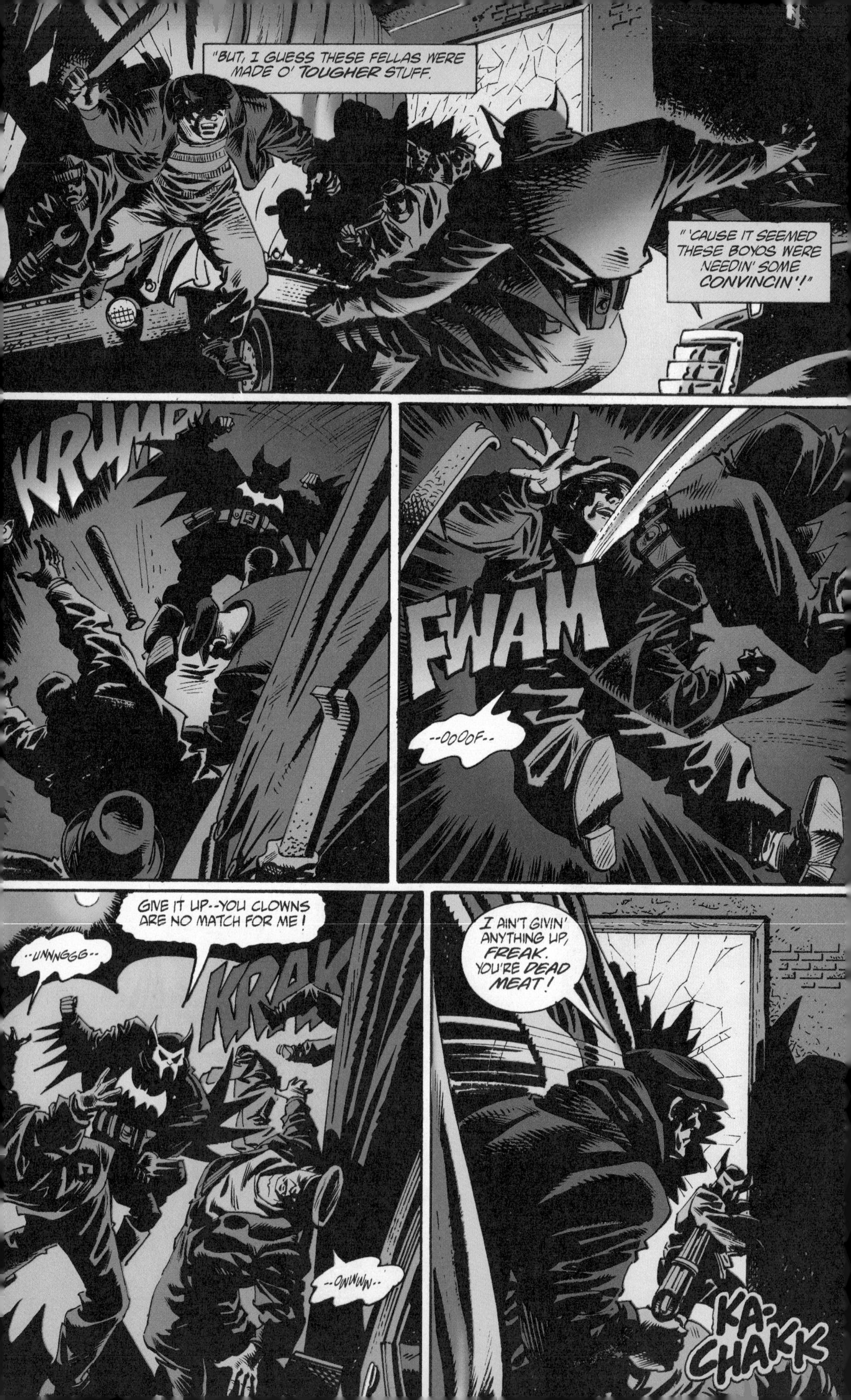
"BUT, I GUESS THESE FELLAS WERE MADE O' TOUGHER STUFF.
"'CAUSE IT SEEMED THESE BOYOS WERE NEEDIN' SOME CONVINCIN'!"
KRUMP
FWAM
--OOOOF--
GIVE IT UP--YOU CLOWNS ARE NO MATCH FOR ME!
--UNNNGGG--
KRAK
--OWWWW--
I AIN'T GIVIN' ANYTHING UP, FREAK. YOU'RE DEAD MEAT!
KA-CHAKK

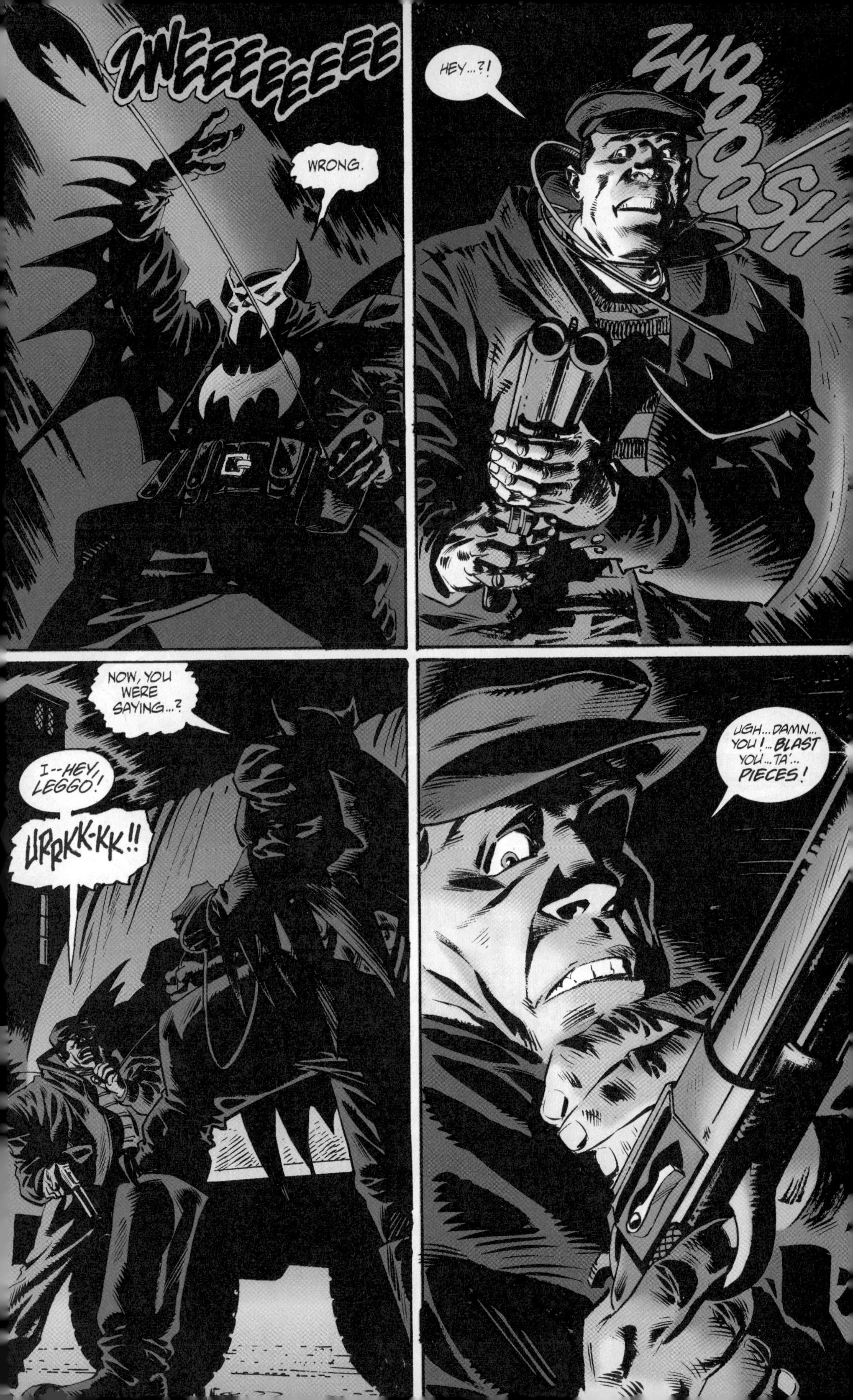
ZWEEEEEEEEE
WRONG.
HEY...?!
ZWOOOSH
NOW, YOU WERE SAYING...?
I--HEY, LEGGO!
URRKK-KK!!
UGH...DAMN... YOU!...BLAST YOU...TA'... PIECES!

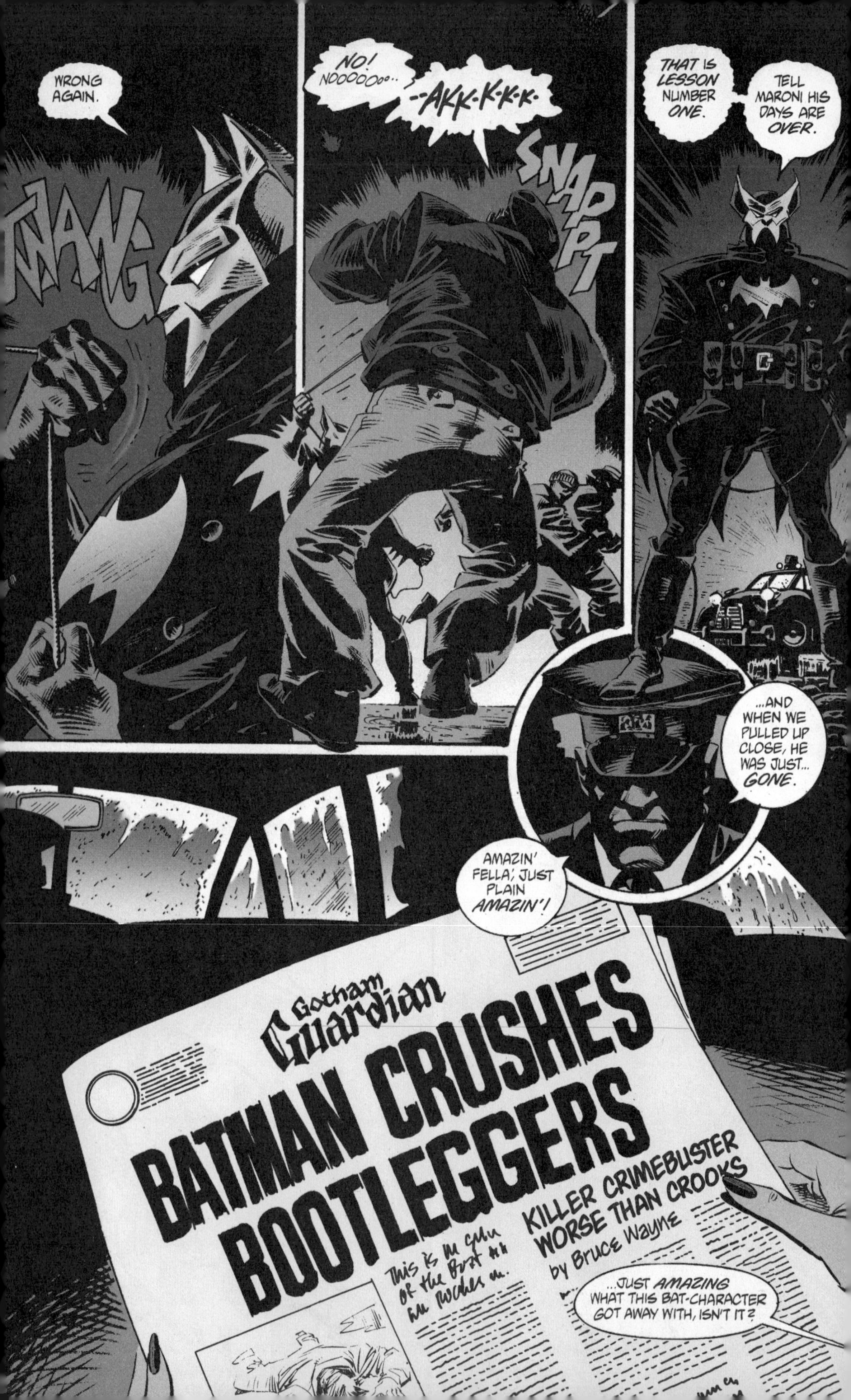
WRONG AGAIN.
THWANG
NO! NOOOOOOoo...
-AKK-K-K-K-
SNAPPT
THAT IS LESSON NUMBER ONE.
TELL MARONI HIS DAYS ARE OVER.
...AND WHEN WE PULLED UP CLOSE, HE WAS JUST... GONE.
AMAZIN' FELLA; JUST PLAIN AMAZIN'!
Gotham Guardian
BATMAN CRUSHES BOOTLEGGERS
KILLER CRIMEBUSTER WORSE THAN CROOKS
by Bruce Wayne
...JUST AMAZING WHAT THIS BAT-CHARACTER GOT AWAY WITH, ISN'T IT?

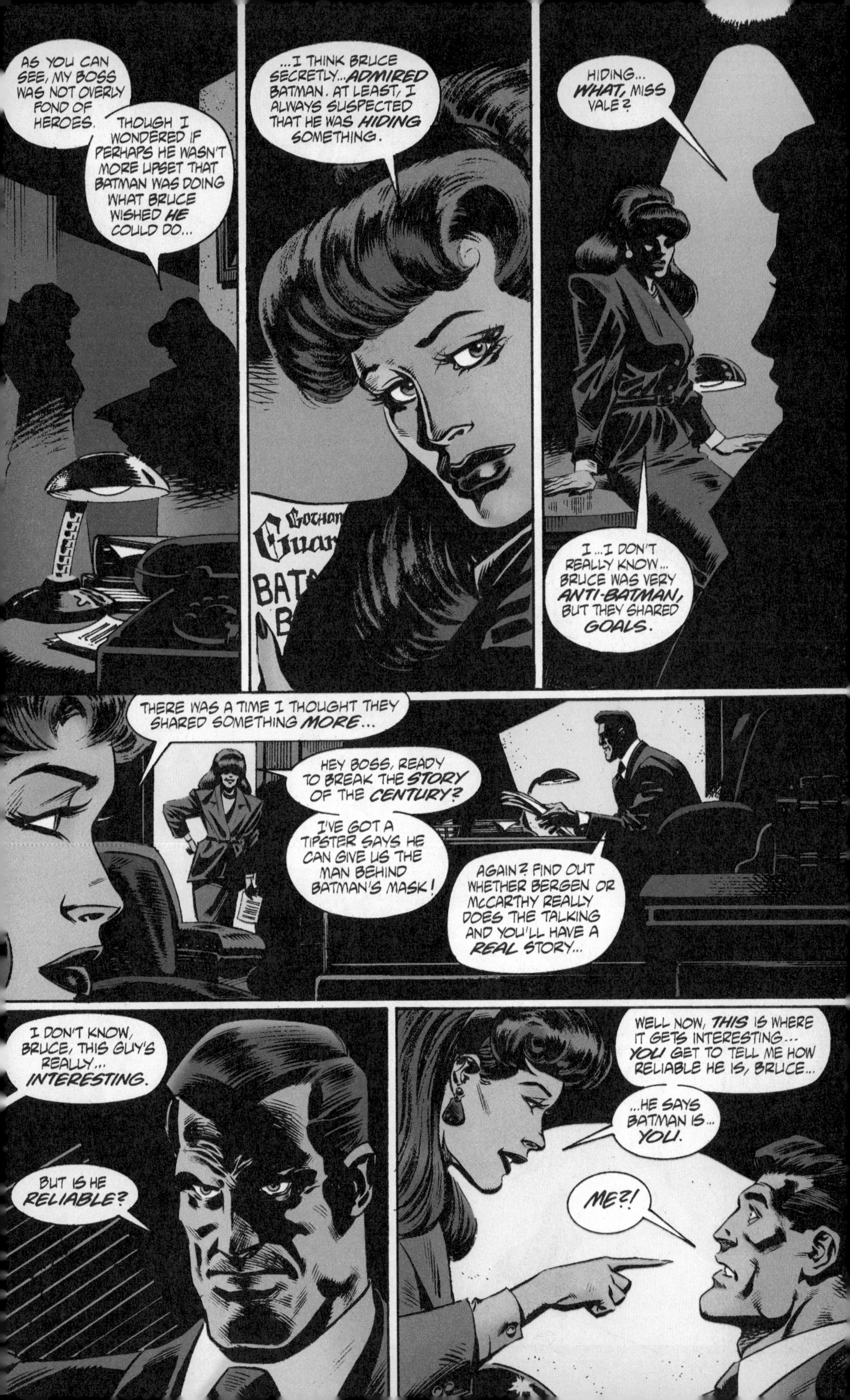

AS YOU CAN SEE, MY BOSS WAS NOT OVERLY FOND OF HEROES.
THOUGH I WONDERED IF PERHAPS HE WASN'T MORE UPSET THAT BATMAN WAS DOING WHAT BRUCE WISHED HE COULD DO...
...I THINK BRUCE SECRETLY...ADMIRED BATMAN. AT LEAST, I ALWAYS SUSPECTED THAT HE WAS HIDING SOMETHING.
HIDING... WHAT, MISS VALE?
I...I DON'T REALLY KNOW... BRUCE WAS VERY ANTI-BATMAN, BUT THEY SHARED GOALS.
THERE WAS A TIME I THOUGHT THEY SHARED SOMETHING MORE...
HEY BOSS, READY TO BREAK THE STORY OF THE CENTURY?
I'VE GOT A TIPSTER SAYS HE CAN GIVE US THE MAN BEHIND BATMAN'S MASK!
AGAIN? FIND OUT WHETHER BERGEN OR McCARTHY REALLY DOES THE TALKING AND YOU'LL HAVE A REAL STORY...
I DON'T KNOW, BRUCE, THIS GUY'S REALLY... INTERESTING.
BUT IS HE RELIABLE?
WELL NOW, THIS IS WHERE IT GETS INTERESTING... YOU GET TO TELL ME HOW RELIABLE HE IS, BRUCE...
...HE SAYS BATMAN IS... YOU.
ME?!

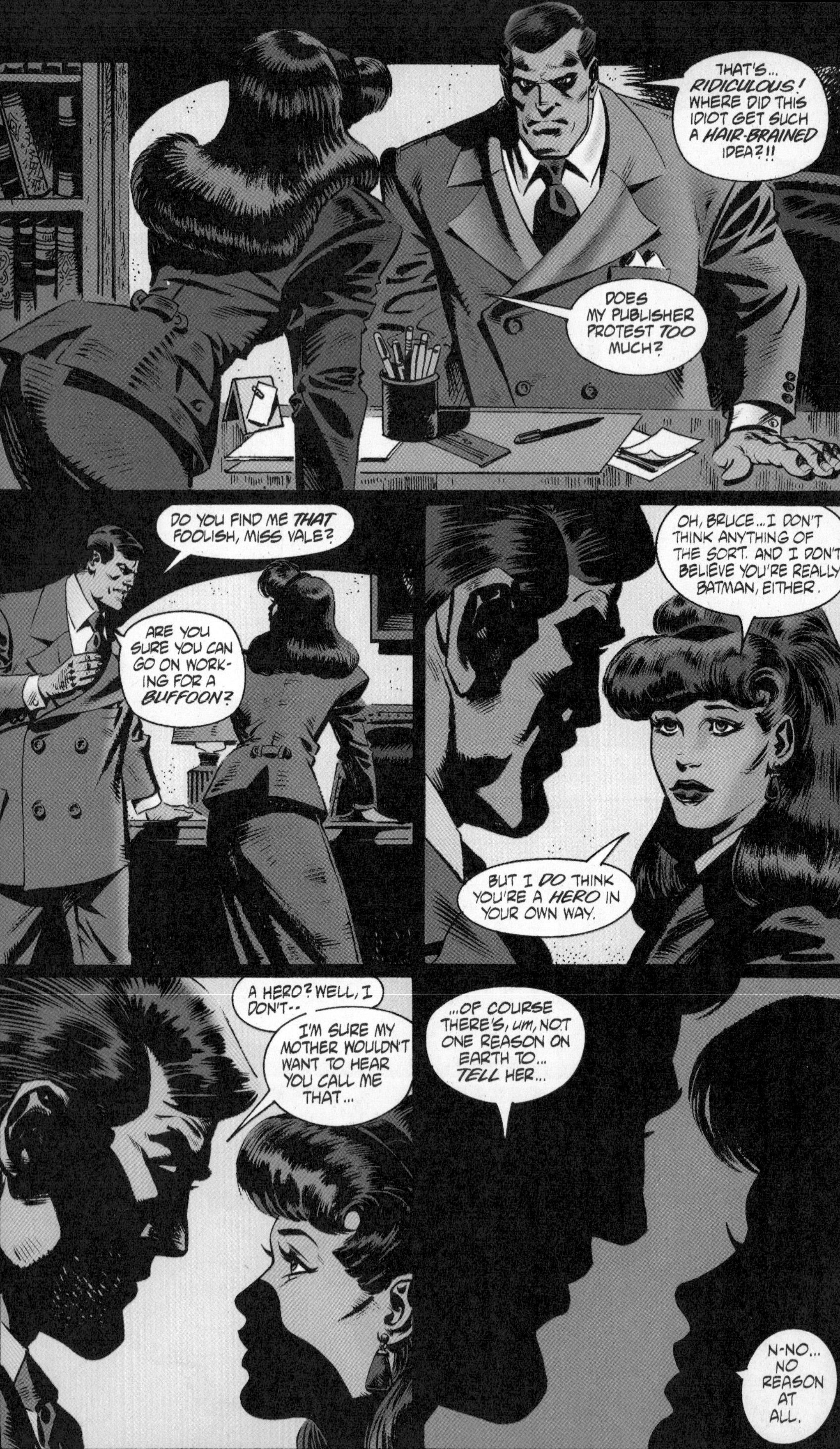
THAT'S... RIDICULOUS! WHERE DID THIS IDIOT GET SUCH A HAIR-BRAINED IDEA?!!
DOES MY PUBLISHER PROTEST TOO MUCH?
DO YOU FIND ME THAT FOOLISH, MISS VALE?
ARE YOU SURE YOU CAN GO ON WORKING FOR A BUFFOON?
OH, BRUCE... I DON'T THINK ANYTHING OF THE SORT. AND I DON'T BELIEVE YOU'RE REALLY BATMAN, EITHER.
BUT I DO THINK YOU'RE A HERO IN YOUR OWN WAY.
A HERO? WELL, I DON'T--
I'M SURE MY MOTHER WOULDN'T WANT TO HEAR YOU CALL ME THAT...
...OF COURSE THERE'S, um, NOT ONE REASON ON EARTH TO... TELL HER...
N-NO... NO REASON AT ALL.

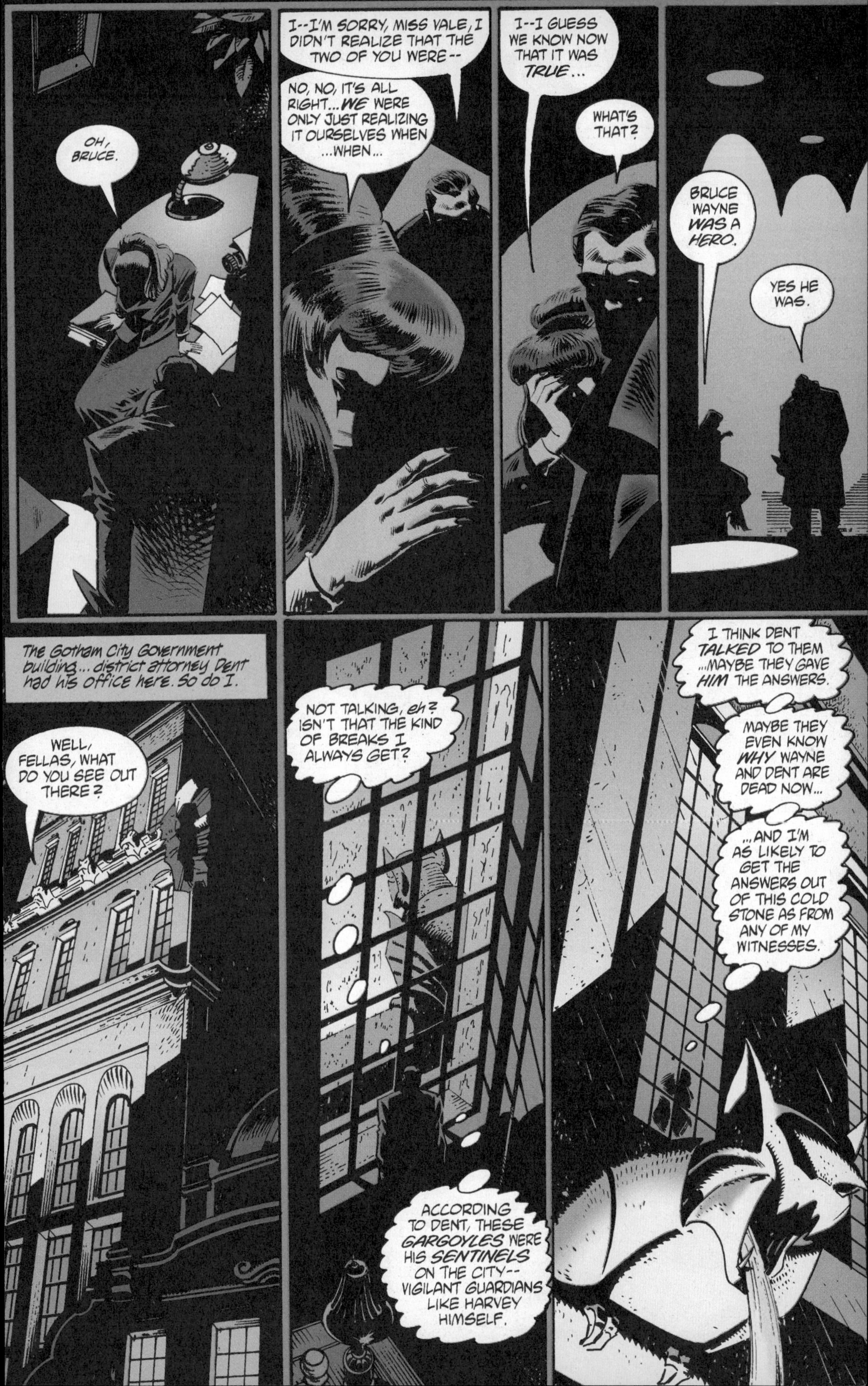
OH, BRUCE.
I--I'M SORRY, MISS VALE, I DIDN'T REALIZE THAT THE TWO OF YOU WERE--
NO, NO, IT'S ALL RIGHT... WE WERE ONLY JUST REALIZING IT OURSELVES WHEN ...WHEN...
I--I GUESS WE KNOW NOW THAT IT WAS TRUE...
WHAT'S THAT?
BRUCE WAYNE WAS A HERO.
YES HE WAS.
The Gotham City Government building... district attorney Dent had his office here. So do I.
WELL, FELLAS, WHAT DO YOU SEE OUT THERE?
NOT TALKING, eh? ISN'T THAT THE KIND OF BREAKS I ALWAYS GET?
ACCORDING TO DENT, THESE GARGOYLES WERE HIS SENTINELS ON THE CITY-- VIGILANT GUARDIANS LIKE HARVEY HIMSELF.
I THINK DENT TALKED TO THEM ...MAYBE THEY GAVE HIM THE ANSWERS.
MAYBE THEY EVEN KNOW WHY WAYNE AND DENT ARE DEAD NOW...
...AND I'M AS LIKELY TO GET THE ANSWERS OUT OF THIS COLD STONE AS FROM ANY OF MY WITNESSES.

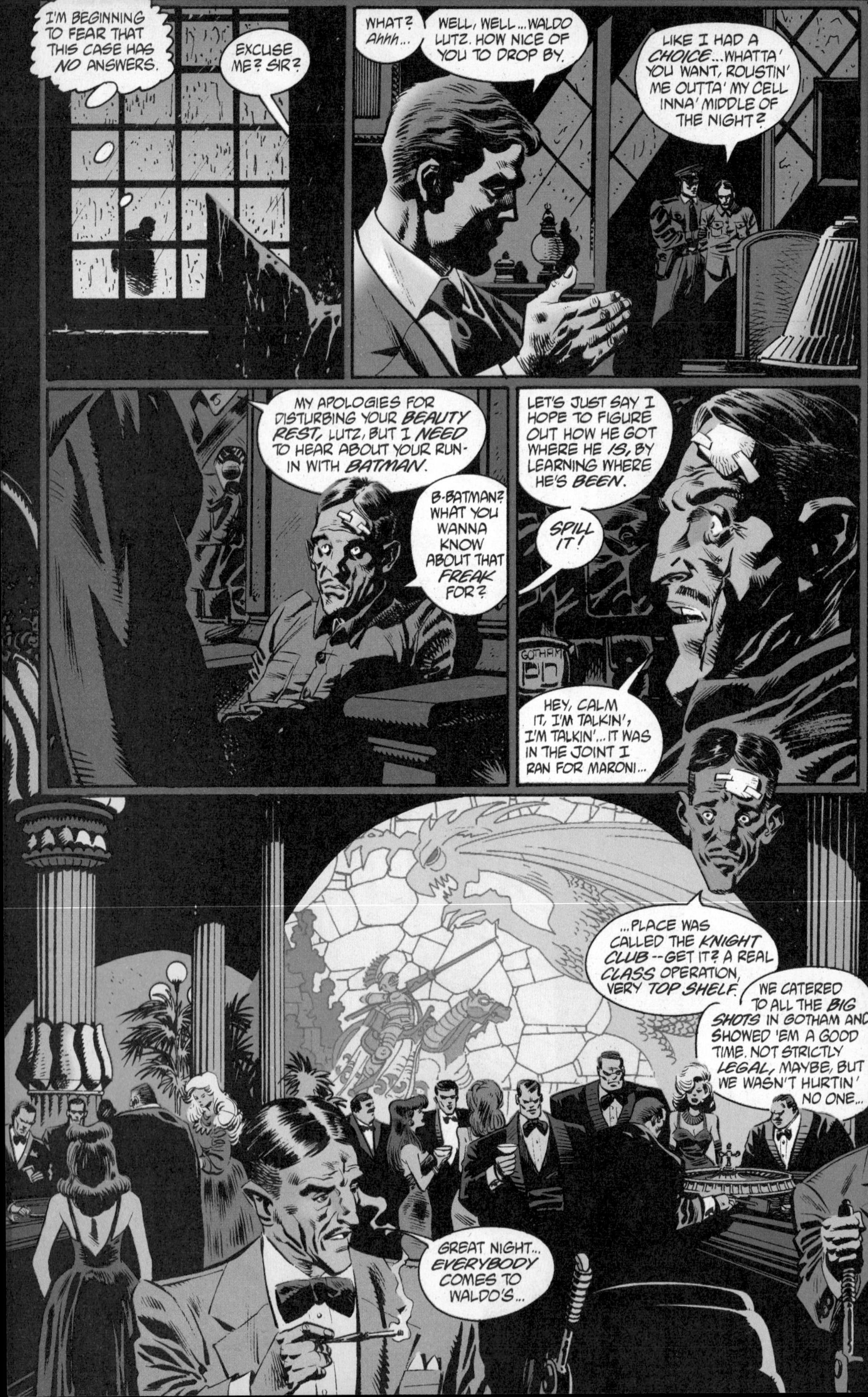
I'M BEGINNING TO FEAR THAT THIS CASE HAS *NO* ANSWERS.
EXCUSE ME? SIR?
WHAT? *Ahhh...*
WELL, WELL... WALDO LUTZ. HOW NICE OF YOU TO DROP BY.
LIKE I HAD A *CHOICE*... WHATTA' YOU WANT, ROUSTIN' ME OUTTA' MY CELL INNA' MIDDLE OF THE NIGHT?
MY APOLOGIES FOR DISTURBING YOUR *BEAUTY REST*, LUTZ, BUT I *NEED* TO HEAR ABOUT YOUR RUN-IN WITH *BATMAN*.
B-BATMAN? WHAT YOU WANNA KNOW ABOUT THAT *FREAK* FOR?
LET'S JUST SAY I HOPE TO FIGURE OUT HOW HE GOT WHERE HE *IS*, BY LEARNING WHERE HE'S *BEEN*.
SPILL IT!
GOTHAM
HEY, CALM IT, I'M TALKIN', I'M TALKIN'... IT WAS IN THE JOINT I RAN FOR MARONI...
...PLACE WAS CALLED THE *KNIGHT CLUB* -- GET IT? A REAL *CLASS* OPERATION, VERY *TOP SHELF*.
WE CATERED TO ALL THE *BIG SHOTS* IN GOTHAM AND SHOWED 'EM A GOOD TIME. NOT STRICTLY *LEGAL*, MAYBE, BUT WE WASN'T HURTIN' NO ONE...
GREAT NIGHT... *EVERYBODY* COMES TO WALDO'S...

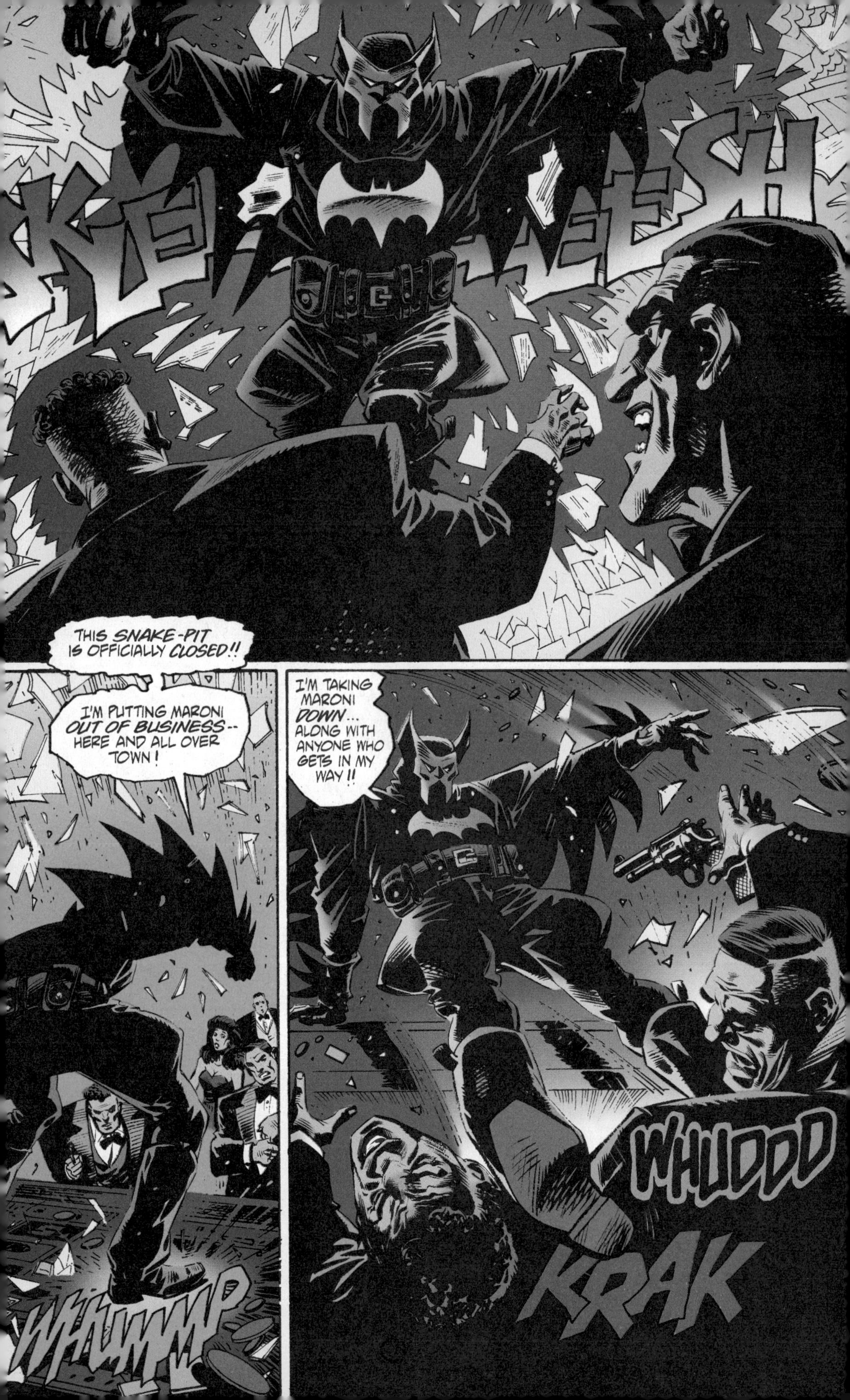
KERASH
THIS SNAKE-PIT IS OFFICIALLY CLOSED!!
I'M PUTTING MARONI OUT OF BUSINESS -- HERE AND ALL OVER TOWN!
WHUMMP
I'M TAKING MARONI DOWN... ALONG WITH ANYONE WHO GETS IN MY WAY!!
WHUDDD
KRAK

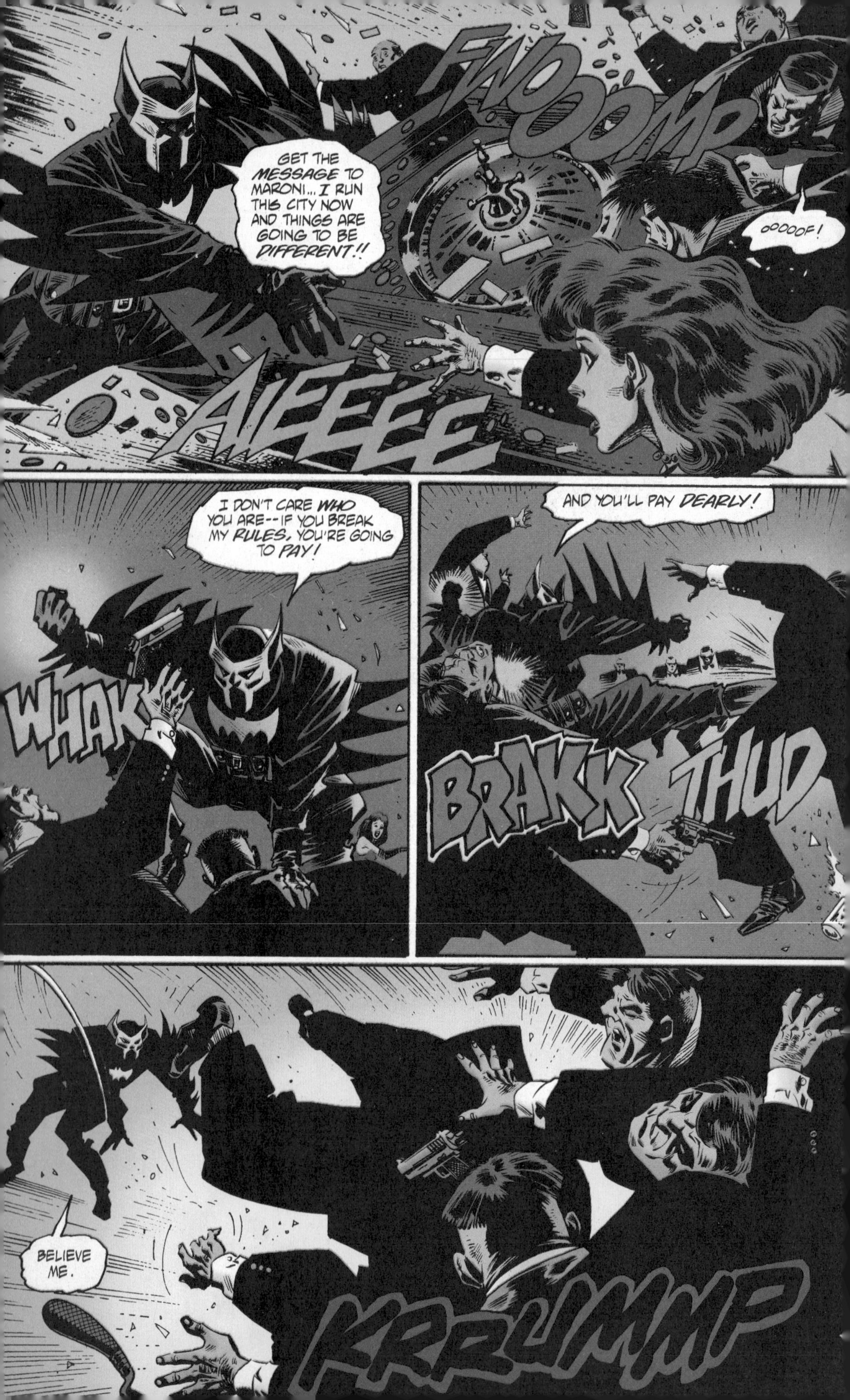
FWOOOOMP
GET THE MESSAGE TO MARONI... I RUN THIS CITY NOW AND THINGS ARE GOING TO BE DIFFERENT!!
OOOOOF!
AIEEEE
I DON'T CARE WHO YOU ARE--IF YOU BREAK MY RULES, YOU'RE GOING TO PAY!
WHAK
AND YOU'LL PAY DEARLY!
BRAKK
THUD
BELIEVE ME.
KRRUMMP

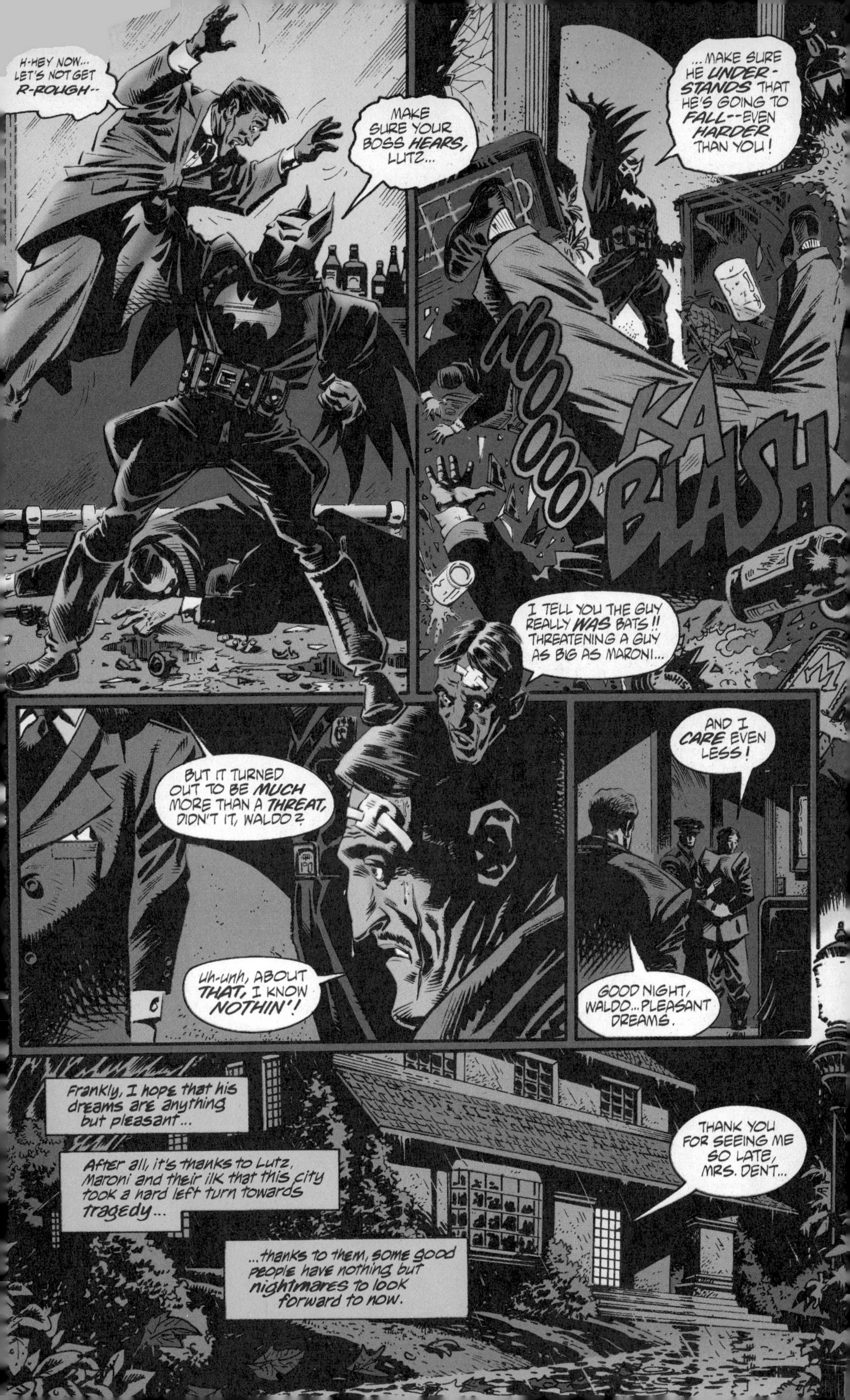

H-HEY NOW... LET'S NOT GET R-ROUGH--
MAKE SURE YOUR BOSS HEARS, LUTZ...
...MAKE SURE HE UNDERSTANDS THAT HE'S GOING TO FALL--EVEN HARDER THAN YOU!
NOOOOOO
KA BLASH
I TELL YOU THE GUY REALLY WAS BATS!! THREATENING A GUY AS BIG AS MARONI...
BUT IT TURNED OUT TO BE MUCH MORE THAN A THREAT, DIDN'T IT, WALDO?
Uh-unh, ABOUT THAT, I KNOW NOTHIN'!
AND I CARE EVEN LESS!
GOOD NIGHT, WALDO... PLEASANT DREAMS.
Frankly, I hope that his dreams are anything but pleasant...
After all, it's thanks to Lutz, Maroni and their ilk that this city took a hard left turn towards tragedy...
THANK YOU FOR SEEING ME SO LATE, MRS. DENT...
...thanks to them, some good people have nothing but nightmares to look forward to now.

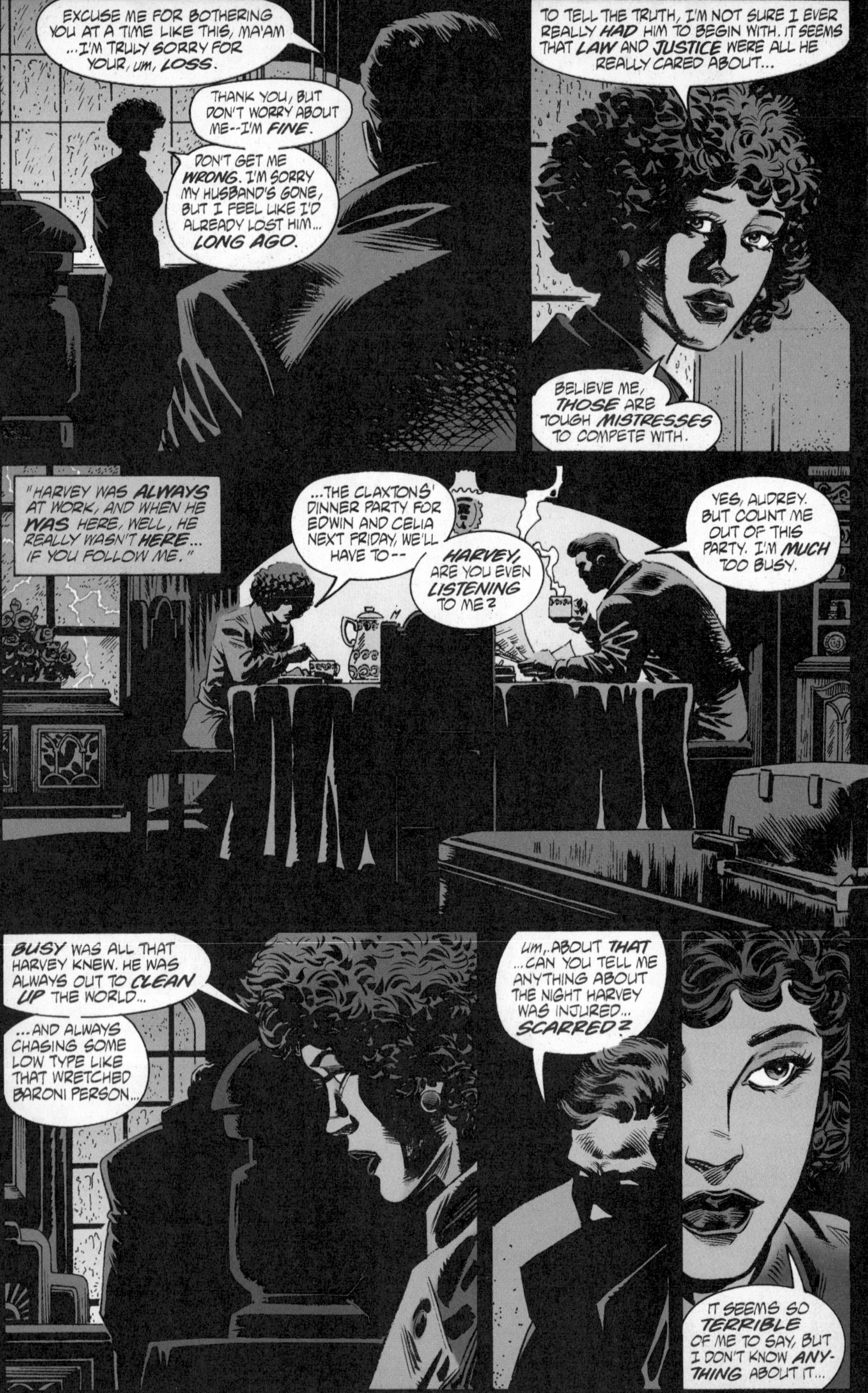

EXCUSE ME FOR BOTHERING YOU AT A TIME LIKE THIS, MA'AM ...I'M TRULY SORRY FOR YOUR, UM, LOSS.
THANK YOU, BUT DON'T WORRY ABOUT ME--I'M FINE.
DON'T GET ME WRONG. I'M SORRY MY HUSBAND'S GONE, BUT I FEEL LIKE I'D ALREADY LOST HIM... LONG AGO.
TO TELL THE TRUTH, I'M NOT SURE I EVER REALLY HAD HIM TO BEGIN WITH. IT SEEMS THAT LAW AND JUSTICE WERE ALL HE REALLY CARED ABOUT...
BELIEVE ME, THOSE ARE TOUGH MISTRESSES TO COMPETE WITH.
"HARVEY WAS ALWAYS AT WORK, AND WHEN HE WAS HERE, WELL, HE REALLY WASN'T HERE... IF YOU FOLLOW ME."
...THE CLAXTONS' DINNER PARTY FOR EDWIN AND CELIA NEXT FRIDAY, WE'LL HAVE TO--
HARVEY, ARE YOU EVEN LISTENING TO ME?
YES, AUDREY. BUT COUNT ME OUT OF THIS PARTY. I'M MUCH TOO BUSY.
BUSY WAS ALL THAT HARVEY KNEW. HE WAS ALWAYS OUT TO CLEAN UP THE WORLD...
...AND ALWAYS CHASING SOME LOW TYPE LIKE THAT WRETCHED BARONI PERSON...
UM,.ABOUT THAT ...CAN YOU TELL ME ANYTHING ABOUT THE NIGHT HARVEY WAS INJURED... SCARRED?
IT SEEMS SO TERRIBLE OF ME TO SAY, BUT I DON'T KNOW ANYTHING ABOUT IT...

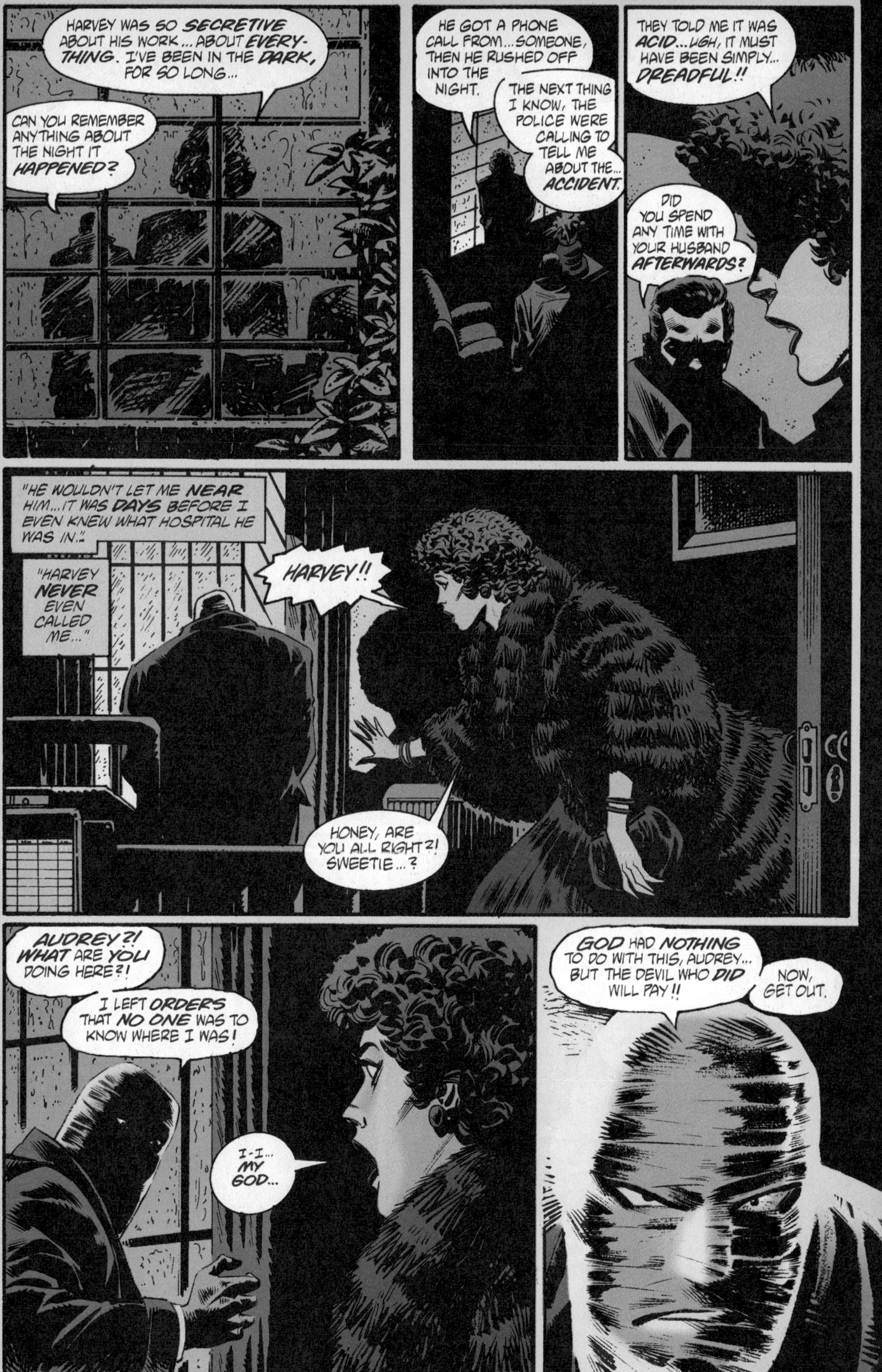
HARVEY WAS SO SECRETIVE ABOUT HIS WORK... ABOUT EVERYTHING. I'VE BEEN IN THE DARK, FOR SO LONG...
CAN YOU REMEMBER ANYTHING ABOUT THE NIGHT IT HAPPENED?
HE GOT A PHONE CALL FROM... SOMEONE, THEN HE RUSHED OFF INTO THE NIGHT.
THE NEXT THING I KNOW, THE POLICE WERE CALLING TO TELL ME ABOUT THE... ACCIDENT.
THEY TOLD ME IT WAS ACID... UGH, IT MUST HAVE BEEN SIMPLY... DREADFUL!!
DID YOU SPEND ANY TIME WITH YOUR HUSBAND AFTERWARDS?
"HE WOULDN'T LET ME NEAR HIM... IT WAS DAYS BEFORE I EVEN KNEW WHAT HOSPITAL HE WAS IN..."
"HARVEY NEVER EVEN CALLED ME..."
HARVEY!!
HONEY, ARE YOU ALL RIGHT?! SWEETIE...?
AUDREY?! WHAT ARE YOU DOING HERE?!
I LEFT ORDERS THAT NO ONE WAS TO KNOW WHERE I WAS!
I-I... MY GOD...
GOD HAD NOTHING TO DO WITH THIS, AUDREY... BUT THE DEVIL WHO DID WILL PAY!!
NOW, GET OUT.

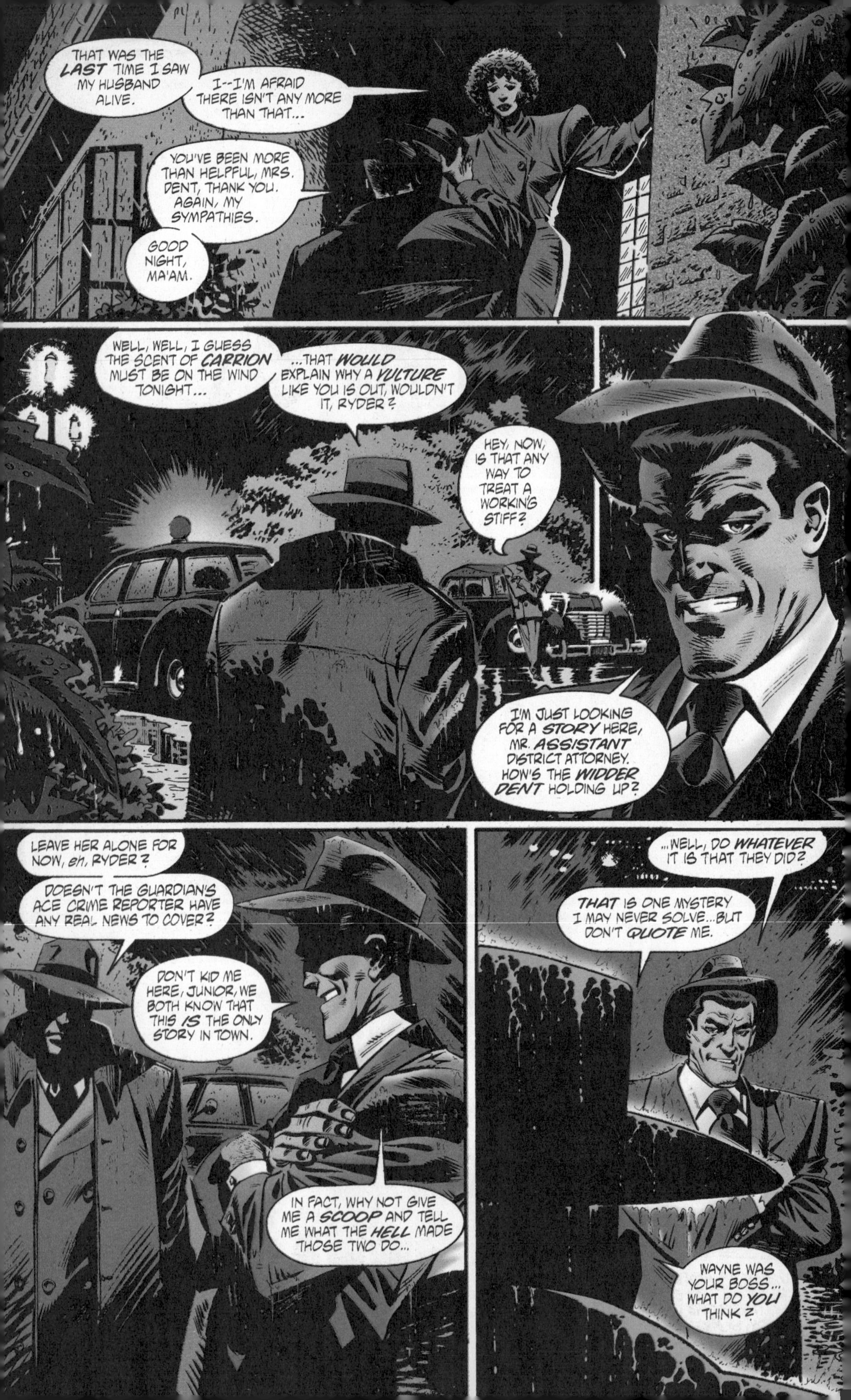
THAT WAS THE LAST TIME I SAW MY HUSBAND ALIVE.
I--I'M AFRAID THERE ISN'T ANY MORE THAN THAT...
YOU'VE BEEN MORE THAN HELPFUL, MRS. DENT, THANK YOU. AGAIN, MY SYMPATHIES.
GOOD NIGHT, MA'AM.
WELL, WELL, I GUESS THE SCENT OF CARRION MUST BE ON THE WIND TONIGHT...
...THAT WOULD EXPLAIN WHY A VULTURE LIKE YOU IS OUT, WOULDN'T IT, RYDER?
HEY, NOW, IS THAT ANY WAY TO TREAT A WORKING STIFF?
I'M JUST LOOKING FOR A STORY HERE, MR. ASSISTANT DISTRICT ATTORNEY. HOW'S THE WIDDER DENT HOLDING UP?
LEAVE HER ALONE FOR NOW, eh, RYDER?
DOESN'T THE GUARDIAN'S ACE CRIME REPORTER HAVE ANY REAL NEWS TO COVER?
DON'T KID ME HERE, JUNIOR, WE BOTH KNOW THAT THIS IS THE ONLY STORY IN TOWN.
IN FACT, WHY NOT GIVE ME A SCOOP AND TELL ME WHAT THE HELL MADE THOSE TWO DO...
...WELL, DO WHATEVER IT IS THAT THEY DID?
THAT IS ONE MYSTERY I MAY NEVER SOLVE...BUT DON'T QUOTE ME.
WAYNE WAS YOUR BOSS... WHAT DO YOU THINK?

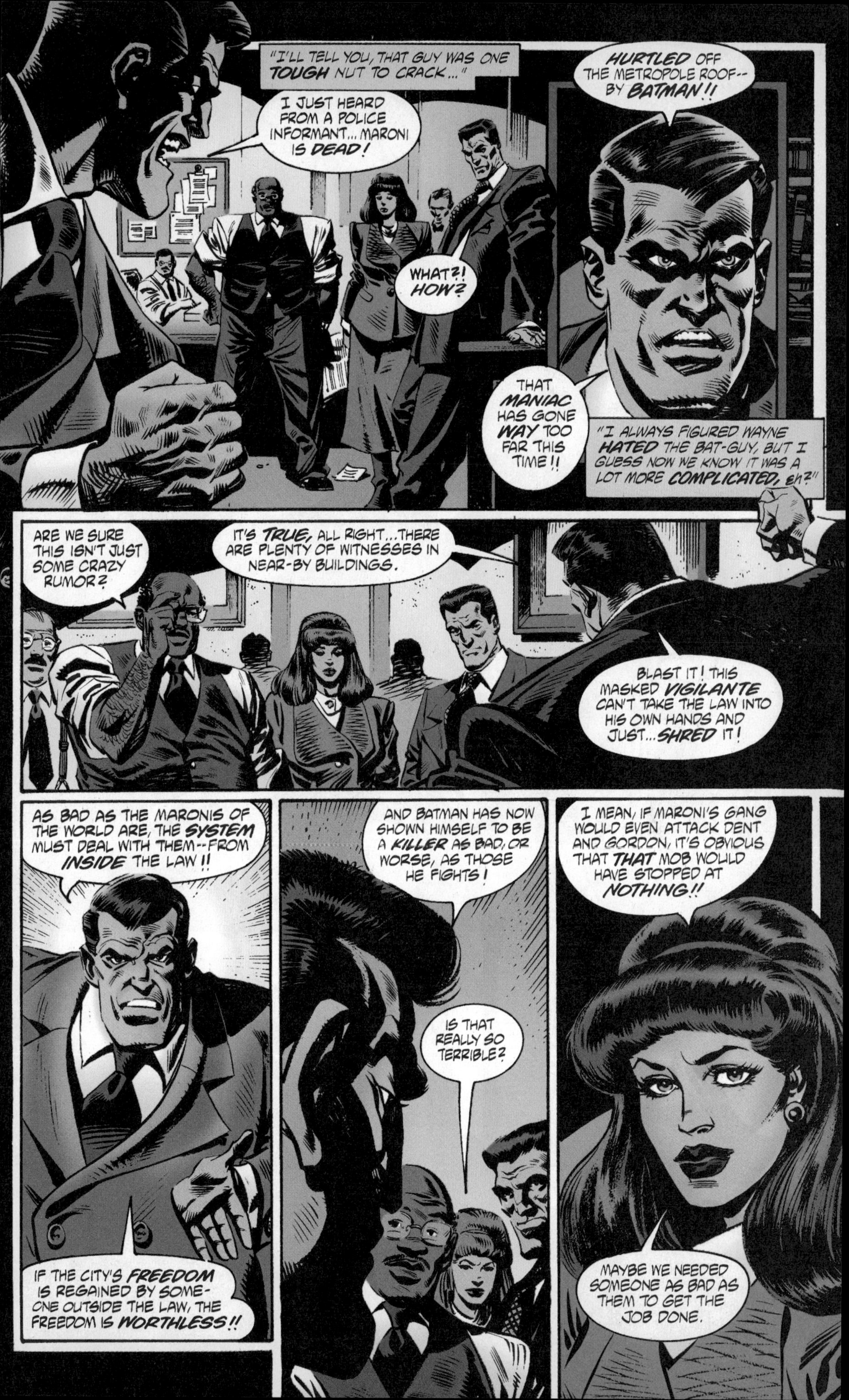
"I'LL TELL YOU, THAT GUY WAS ONE TOUGH NUT TO CRACK..."
I JUST HEARD FROM A POLICE INFORMANT... MARONI IS DEAD!
WHAT?! HOW?
HURTLED OFF THE METROPOLE ROOF-- BY BATMAN!!
THAT MANIAC HAS GONE WAY TOO FAR THIS TIME!!
"I ALWAYS FIGURED WAYNE HATED THE BAT-GUY, BUT I GUESS NOW WE KNOW IT WAS A LOT MORE COMPLICATED, eh?"
ARE WE SURE THIS ISN'T JUST SOME CRAZY RUMOR?
IT'S TRUE, ALL RIGHT... THERE ARE PLENTY OF WITNESSES IN NEAR-BY BUILDINGS.
BLAST IT! THIS MASKED VIGILANTE CAN'T TAKE THE LAW INTO HIS OWN HANDS AND JUST... SHRED IT!
AS BAD AS THE MARONIS OF THE WORLD ARE, THE SYSTEM MUST DEAL WITH THEM--FROM INSIDE THE LAW!!
IF THE CITY'S FREEDOM IS REGAINED BY SOME-ONE OUTSIDE THE LAW, THE FREEDOM IS WORTHLESS!!
AND BATMAN HAS NOW SHOWN HIMSELF TO BE A KILLER AS BAD, OR WORSE, AS THOSE HE FIGHTS!
IS THAT REALLY SO TERRIBLE?
I MEAN, IF MARONI'S GANG WOULD EVEN ATTACK DENT AND GORDON, IT'S OBVIOUS THAT THAT MOB WOULD HAVE STOPPED AT NOTHING!!
MAYBE WE NEEDED SOMEONE AS BAD AS THEM TO GET THE JOB DONE.

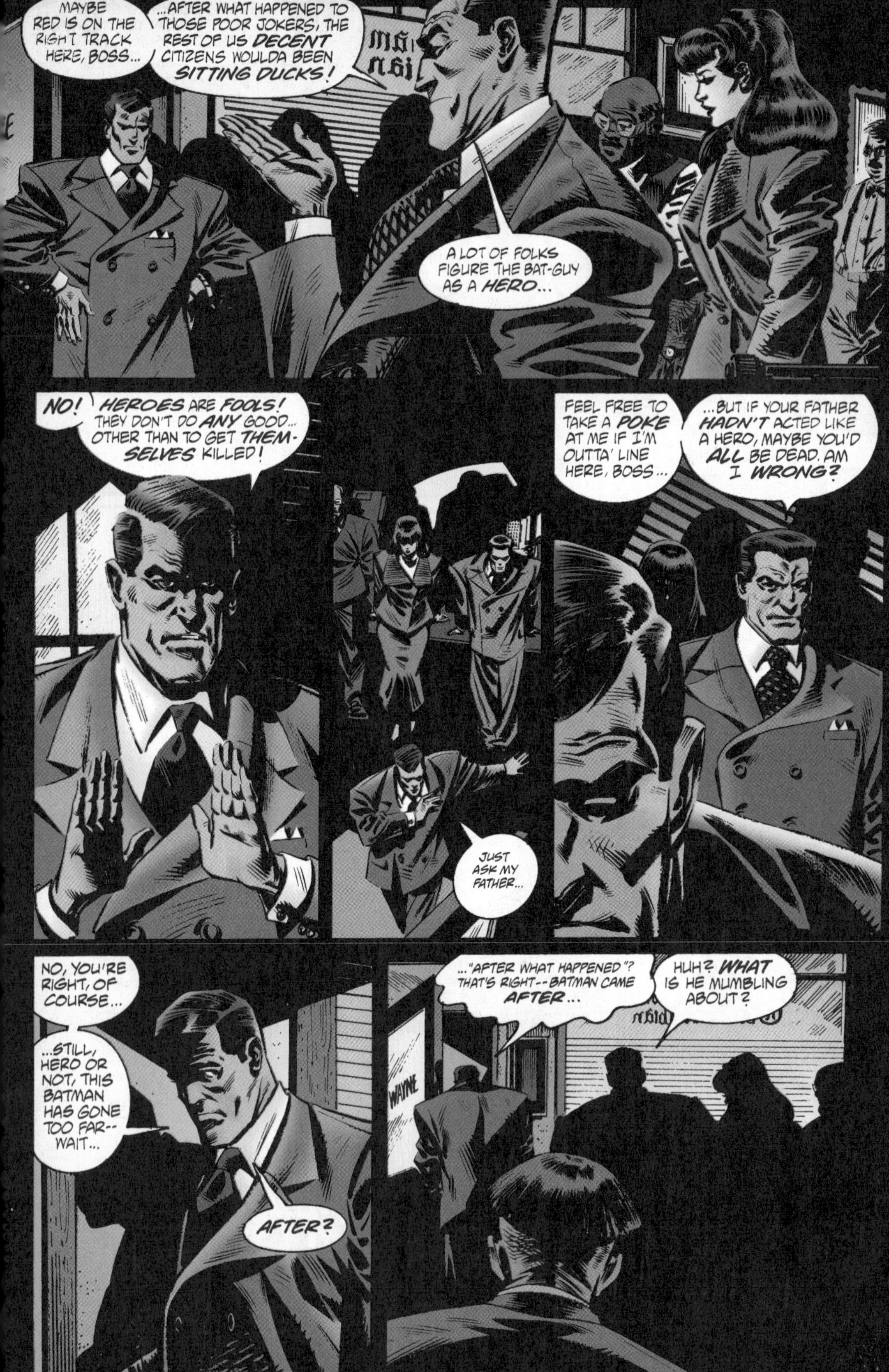
MAYBE RED IS ON THE RIGHT TRACK HERE, BOSS...
...AFTER WHAT HAPPENED TO THOSE POOR JOKERS, THE REST OF US DECENT CITIZENS WOULDA BEEN SITTING DUCKS!
A LOT OF FOLKS FIGURE THE BAT-GUY AS A HERO...
NO!
HEROES ARE FOOLS! THEY DON'T DO ANY GOOD... OTHER THAN TO GET THEMSELVES KILLED!
JUST ASK MY FATHER...
FEEL FREE TO TAKE A POKE AT ME IF I'M OUTTA' LINE HERE, BOSS...
...BUT IF YOUR FATHER HADN'T ACTED LIKE A HERO, MAYBE YOU'D ALL BE DEAD. AM I WRONG?
NO, YOU'RE RIGHT, OF COURSE...
...STILL, HERO OR NOT, THIS BATMAN HAS GONE TOO FAR-- WAIT...
AFTER?
..."AFTER WHAT HAPPENED"? THAT'S RIGHT--BATMAN CAME AFTER...
HUH? WHAT IS HE MUMBLING ABOUT?
WAYNE

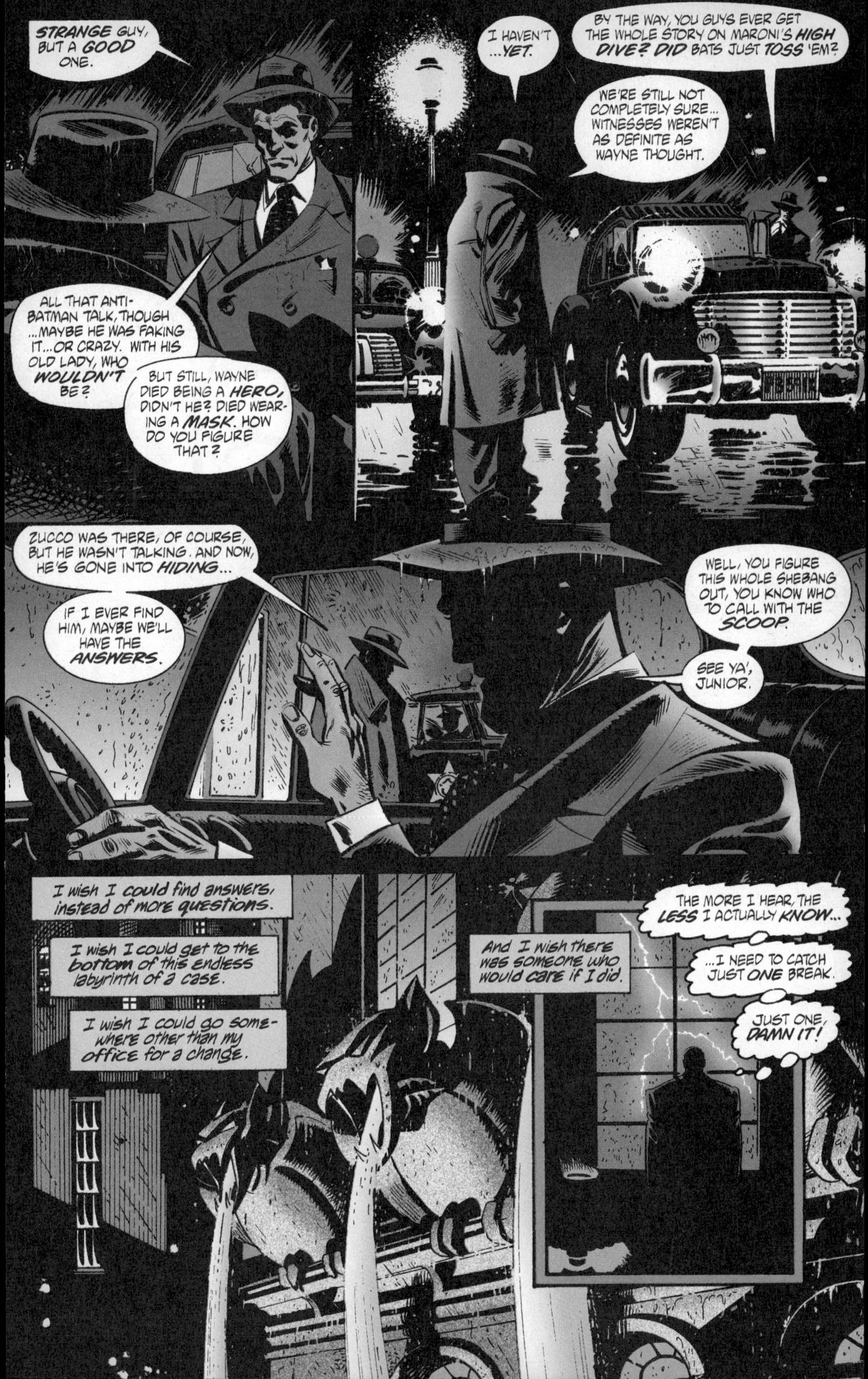

STRANGE GUY, BUT A GOOD ONE.
I HAVEN'T ...YET.
BY THE WAY, YOU GUYS EVER GET THE WHOLE STORY ON MARONI'S HIGH DIVE? DID BATS JUST TOSS 'EM?
WE'RE STILL NOT COMPLETELY SURE... WITNESSES WEREN'T AS DEFINITE AS WAYNE THOUGHT.
ALL THAT ANTI-BATMAN TALK, THOUGH ...MAYBE HE WAS FAKING IT...OR CRAZY. WITH HIS OLD LADY, WHO WOULDN'T BE?
BUT STILL, WAYNE DIED BEING A HERO, DIDN'T HE? DIED WEARING A MASK. HOW DO YOU FIGURE THAT?
ZUCCO WAS THERE, OF COURSE, BUT HE WASN'T TALKING. AND NOW, HE'S GONE INTO HIDING...
IF I EVER FIND HIM, MAYBE WE'LL HAVE THE ANSWERS.
WELL, YOU FIGURE THIS WHOLE SHEBANG OUT, YOU KNOW WHO TO CALL WITH THE SCOOP.
SEE YA', JUNIOR.
I wish I could find answers, instead of more questions.
I wish I could get to the bottom of this endless labyrinth of a case.
I wish I could go somewhere other than my office for a change.
And I wish there was someone who would care if I did.
THE MORE I HEAR, THE LESS I ACTUALLY KNOW...
...I NEED TO CATCH JUST ONE BREAK.
JUST ONE, DAMN IT!

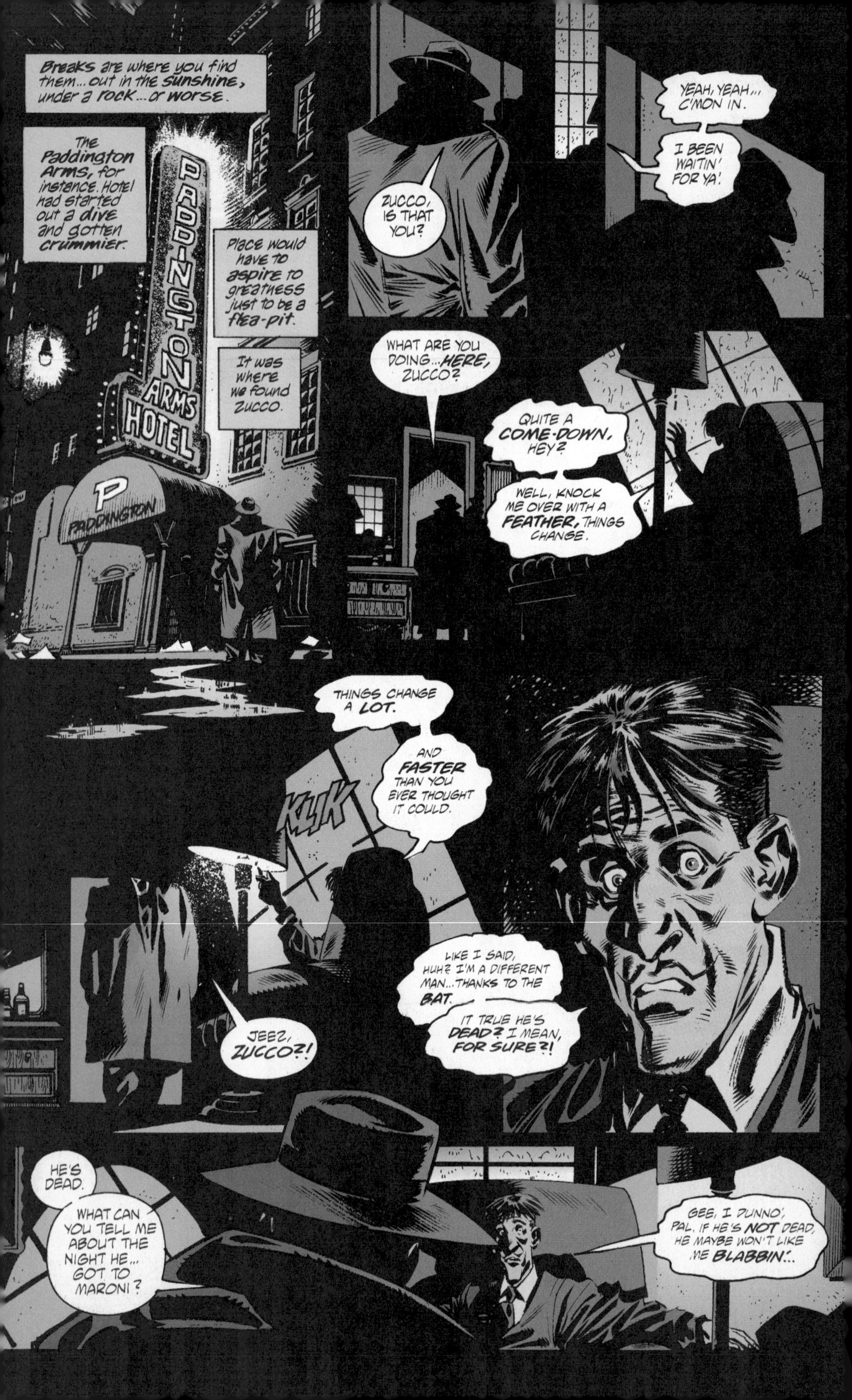

Breaks are where you find them... out in the sunshine, under a rock... or worse.
The Paddington Arms, for instance. Hotel had started out a dive and gotten crummier.
PADDINGTON ARMS HOTEL
Place would have to aspire to greatness just to be a flea-pit.
It was where we found Zucco.
P PADDINGTON
ZUCCO, IS THAT YOU?
YEAH, YEAH... C'MON IN.
I BEEN WAITIN' FOR YA'.
WHAT ARE YOU DOING... HERE, ZUCCO?
QUITE A COME-DOWN, HEY?
WELL, KNOCK ME OVER WITH A FEATHER, THINGS CHANGE.
THINGS CHANGE A LOT.
AND FASTER THAN YOU EVER THOUGHT IT COULD.
KLIK
JEEZ, ZUCCO?!
LIKE I SAID, HUH? I'M A DIFFERENT MAN... THANKS TO THE BAT.
IT TRUE HE'S DEAD? I MEAN, FOR SURE?!
HE'S DEAD.
WHAT CAN YOU TELL ME ABOUT THE NIGHT HE... GOT TO MARONI?
GEE, I DUNNO', PAL. IF HE'S NOT DEAD, HE MAYBE WON'T LIKE ME BLABBIN'...

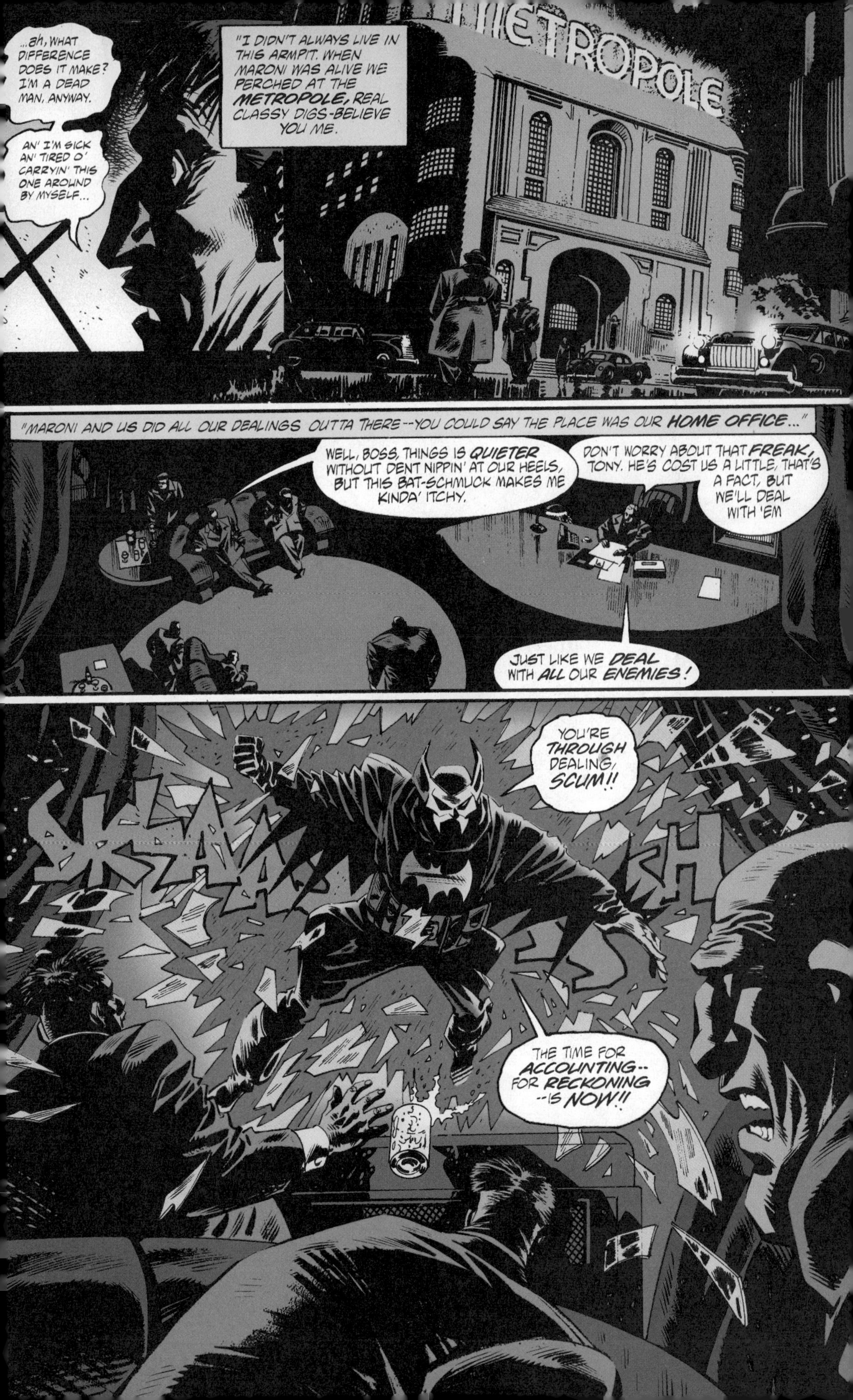
...ah, WHAT DIFFERENCE DOES IT MAKE? I'M A DEAD MAN, ANYWAY.
AN' I'M SICK AN' TIRED O' CARRYIN' THIS ONE AROUND BY MYSELF...
"I DIDN'T ALWAYS LIVE IN THIS ARMPIT. WHEN MARONI WAS ALIVE WE PERCHED AT THE METROPOLE, REAL CLASSY DIGS-BELIEVE YOU ME.
METROPOLE
"MARONI AND US DID ALL OUR DEALINGS OUTTA THERE--YOU COULD SAY THE PLACE WAS OUR HOME OFFICE..."
WELL, BOSS, THINGS IS QUIETER WITHOUT DENT NIPPIN' AT OUR HEELS, BUT THIS BAT-SCHMUCK MAKES ME KINDA' ITCHY.
DON'T WORRY ABOUT THAT FREAK, TONY. HE'S COST US A LITTLE, THAT'S A FACT, BUT WE'LL DEAL WITH 'EM
JUST LIKE WE DEAL WITH ALL OUR ENEMIES!
SKRAAASH
YOU'RE THROUGH DEALING, SCUM!!
THE TIME FOR ACCOUNTING-- FOR RECKONING --IS NOW!!

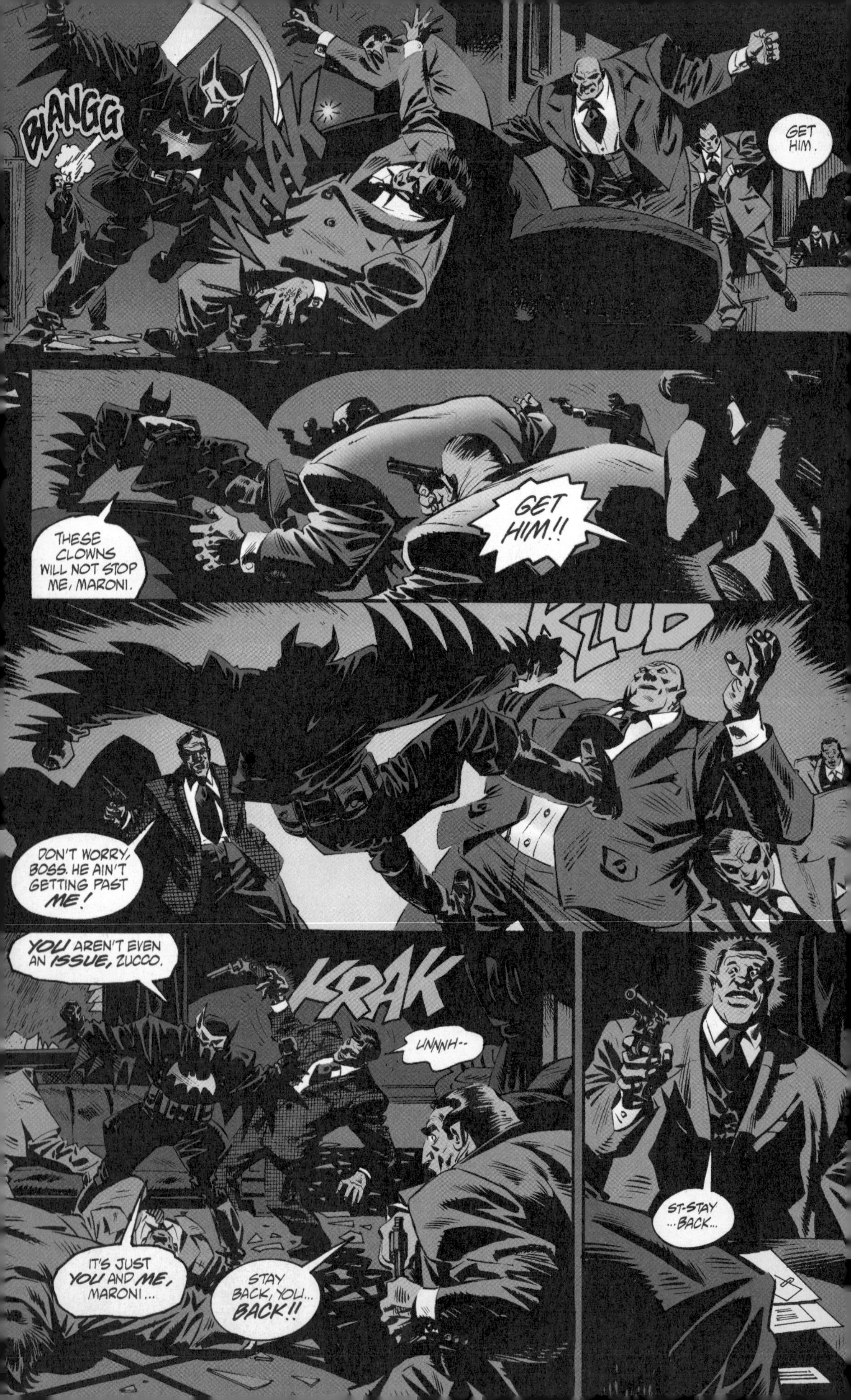
BLANGG
WHAK
GET HIM.
THESE CLOWNS WILL NOT STOP ME, MARONI.
GET HIM!!
KLUD
DON'T WORRY, BOSS. HE AIN'T GETTING PAST ME!
YOU AREN'T EVEN AN ISSUE, ZUCCO.
KRAK
UNNNH--
IT'S JUST YOU AND ME, MARONI...
STAY BACK, YOU... BACK!!
ST-STAY ...BACK...

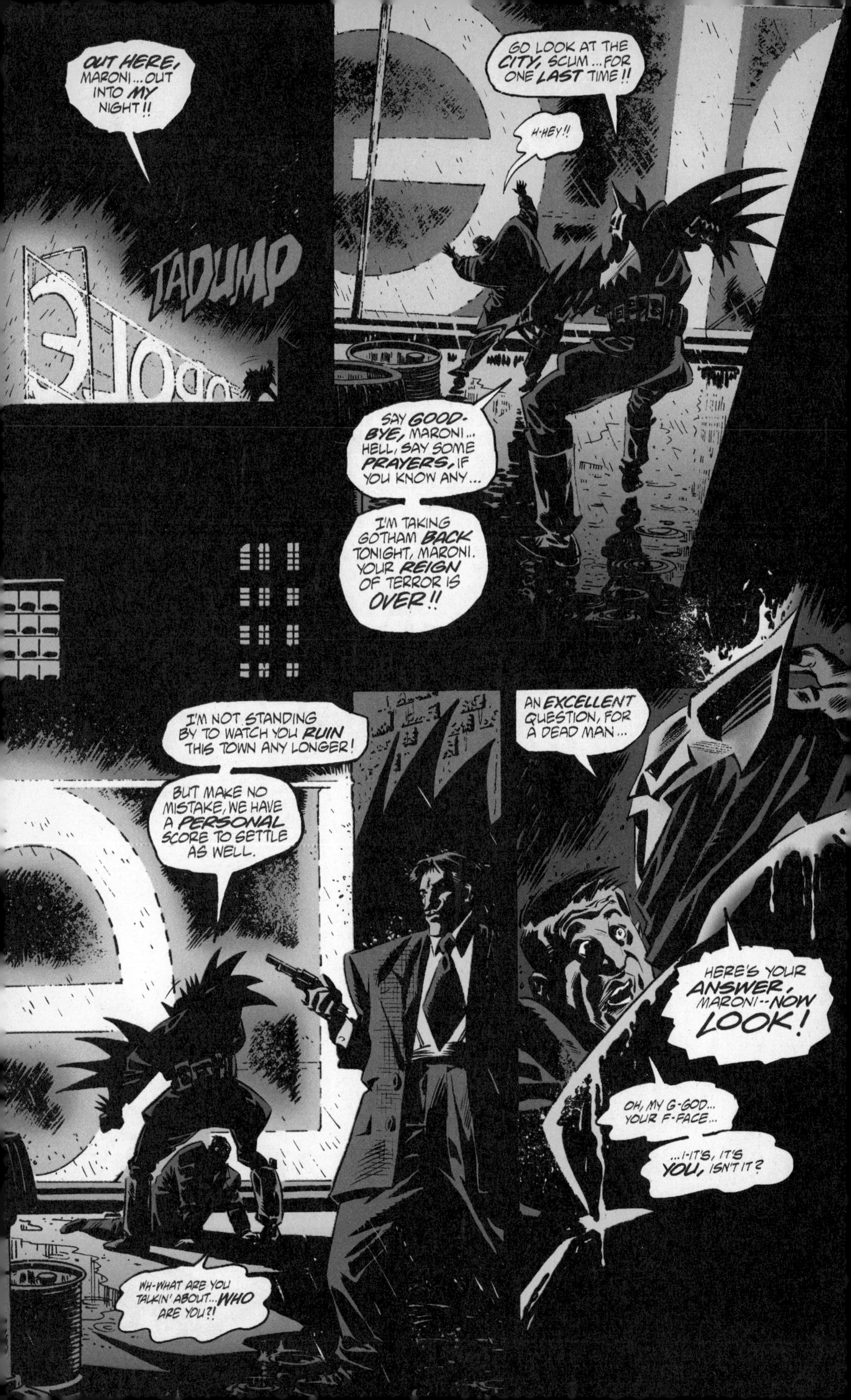
OUT HERE, MARONI ... OUT INTO MY NIGHT!!
TADUMP
GO LOOK AT THE CITY, SCUM ... FOR ONE LAST TIME!!
H-HEY!!
SAY GOOD-BYE, MARONI... HELL, SAY SOME PRAYERS, IF YOU KNOW ANY...
I'M TAKING GOTHAM BACK TONIGHT, MARONI. YOUR REIGN OF TERROR IS OVER!!
I'M NOT STANDING BY TO WATCH YOU RUIN THIS TOWN ANY LONGER!
BUT MAKE NO MISTAKE, WE HAVE A PERSONAL SCORE TO SETTLE AS WELL.
WH-WHAT ARE YOU TALKIN' ABOUT... WHO ARE YOU?!
AN EXCELLENT QUESTION, FOR A DEAD MAN...
HERE'S YOUR ANSWER, MARONI--NOW LOOK!
OH, MY G-GOD... YOUR F-FACE...
...I-IT'S, IT'S YOU, ISN'T IT?

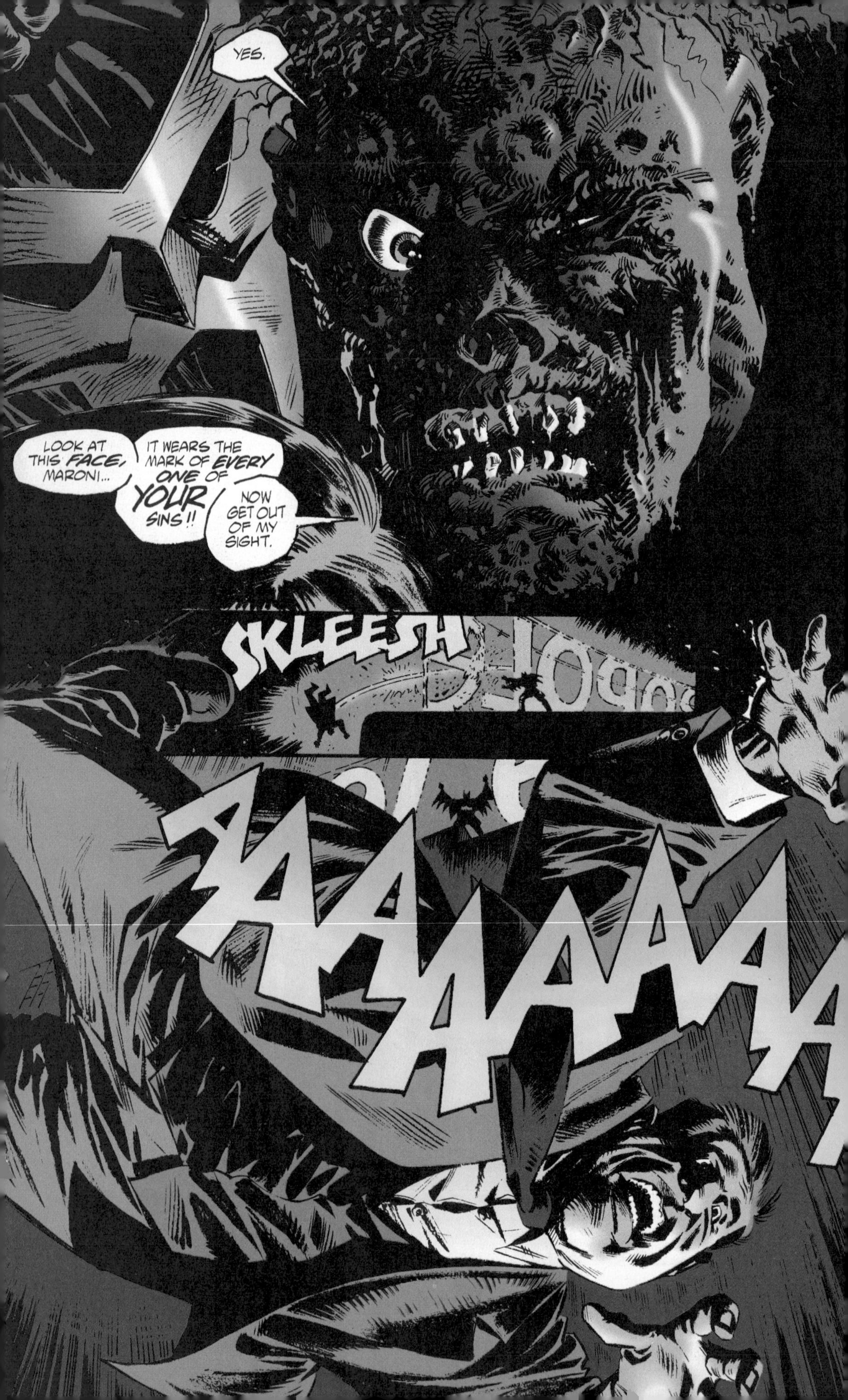
YES.
LOOK AT THIS FACE, MARONI...
IT WEARS THE MARK OF EVERY ONE OF YOUR SINS!!
NOW GET OUT OF MY SIGHT.
SKLEESH
AAAAAAA

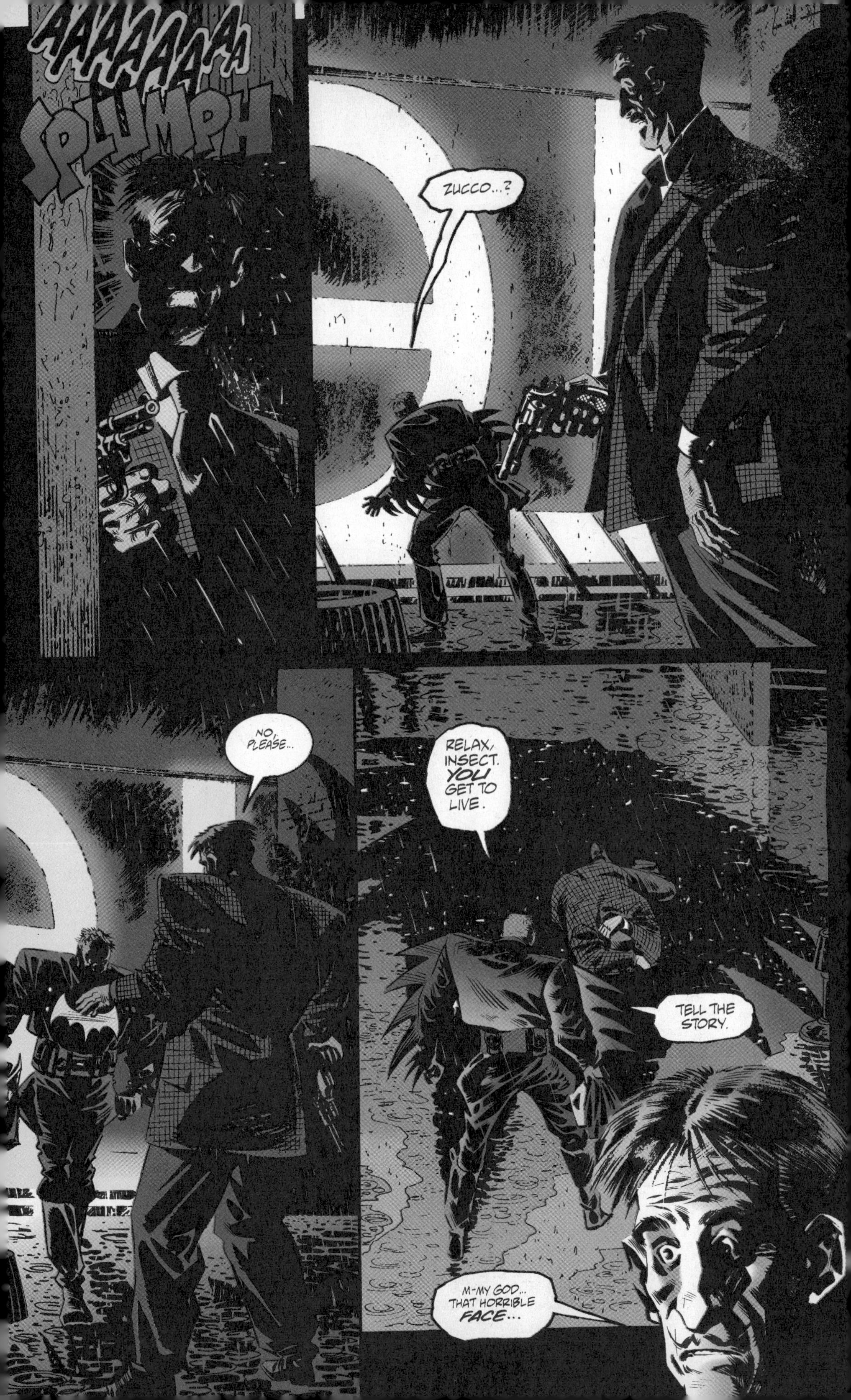
AAAAAAAA
SPLUMPH
ZUCCO...?
NO, PLEASE...
RELAX, INSECT. YOU GET TO LIVE.
TELL THE STORY.
M-MY GOD... THAT HORRIBLE FACE...

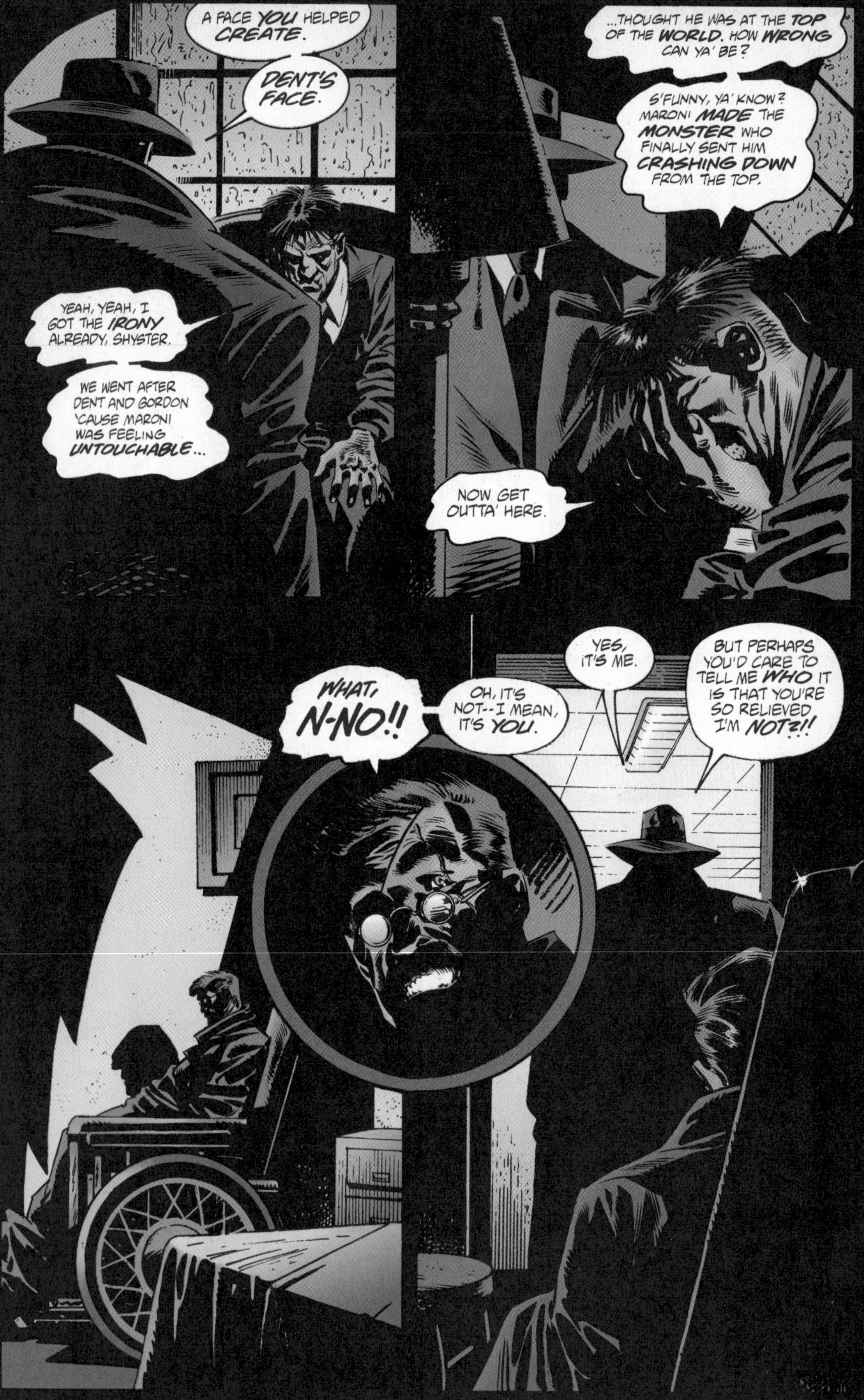

A FACE YOU HELPED CREATE.
DENT'S FACE.
YEAH, YEAH, I GOT THE IRONY ALREADY, SHYSTER.
WE WENT AFTER DENT AND GORDON 'CAUSE MARONI WAS FEELING UNTOUCHABLE...
...THOUGHT HE WAS AT THE TOP OF THE WORLD. HOW WRONG CAN YA' BE?
S'FUNNY, YA' KNOW? MARONI MADE THE MONSTER WHO FINALLY SENT HIM CRASHING DOWN FROM THE TOP.
NOW GET OUTTA' HERE.
WHAT, N-NO!!
OH, IT'S NOT--I MEAN, IT'S YOU.
YES, IT'S ME.
BUT PERHAPS YOU'D CARE TO TELL ME WHO IT IS THAT YOU'RE SO RELIEVED I'M NOT?!!

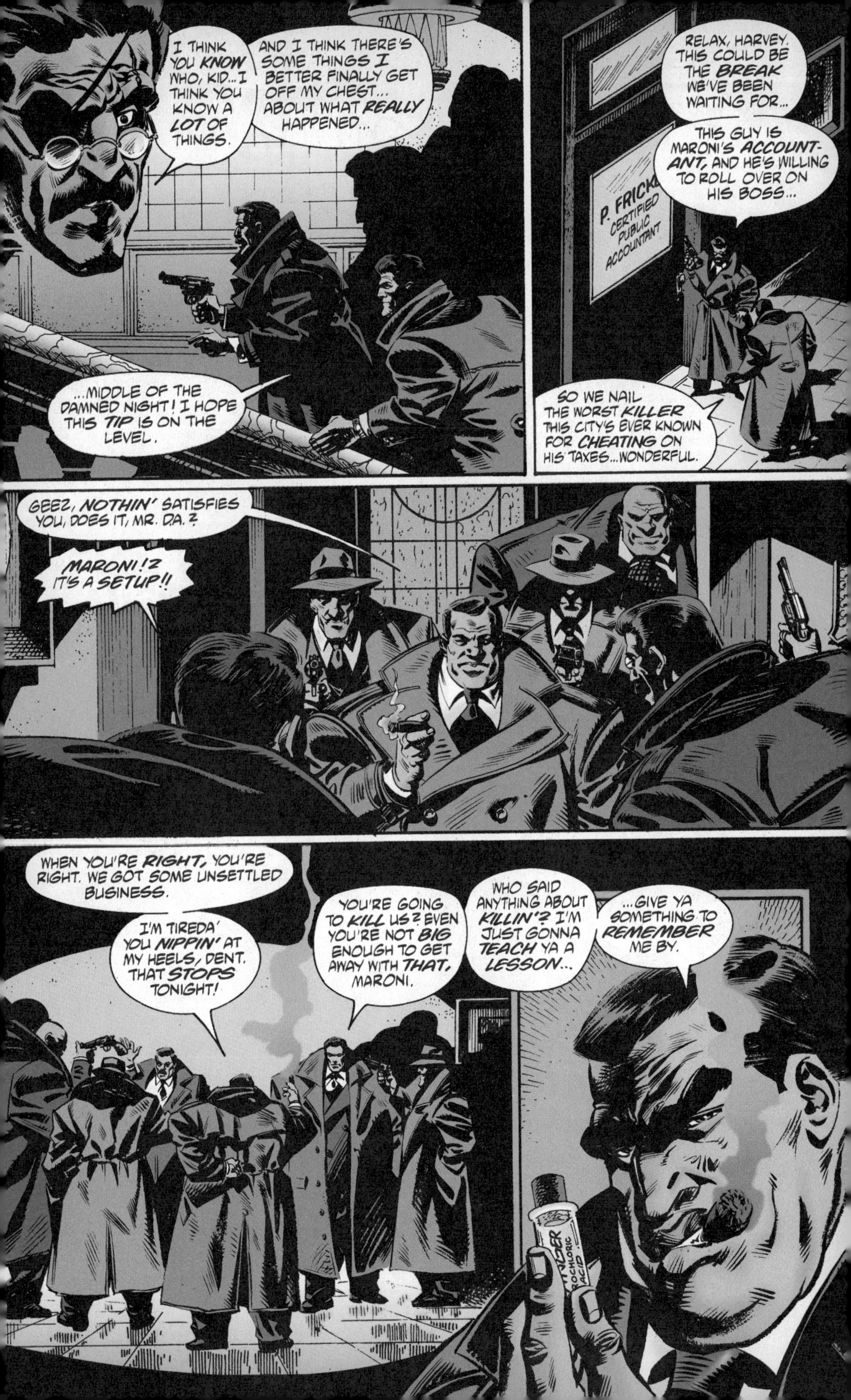
I THINK YOU KNOW WHO, KID... I THINK YOU KNOW A LOT OF THINGS.
AND I THINK THERE'S SOME THINGS I BETTER FINALLY GET OFF MY CHEST... ABOUT WHAT REALLY HAPPENED...
...MIDDLE OF THE DAMNED NIGHT! I HOPE THIS TIP IS ON THE LEVEL.
RELAX, HARVEY. THIS COULD BE THE BREAK WE'VE BEEN WAITING FOR...
THIS GUY IS MARONI'S ACCOUNT-ANT, AND HE'S WILLING TO ROLL OVER ON HIS BOSS...
P. FRICK
CERTIFIED PUBLIC ACCOUNTANT
SO WE NAIL THE WORST KILLER THIS CITY'S EVER KNOWN FOR CHEATING ON HIS TAXES... WONDERFUL.
GEEZ, NOTHIN' SATISFIES YOU, DOES IT, MR. D.A.?
MARONI!? IT'S A SETUP!!
WHEN YOU'RE RIGHT, YOU'RE RIGHT. WE GOT SOME UNSETTLED BUSINESS.
I'M TIREDA' YOU NIPPIN' AT MY HEELS, DENT. THAT STOPS TONIGHT!
YOU'RE GOING TO KILL US? EVEN YOU'RE NOT BIG ENOUGH TO GET AWAY WITH THAT, MARONI.
WHO SAID ANYTHING ABOUT KILLIN'? I'M JUST GONNA TEACH YA A LESSON...
...GIVE YA SOMETHING TO REMEMBER ME BY.

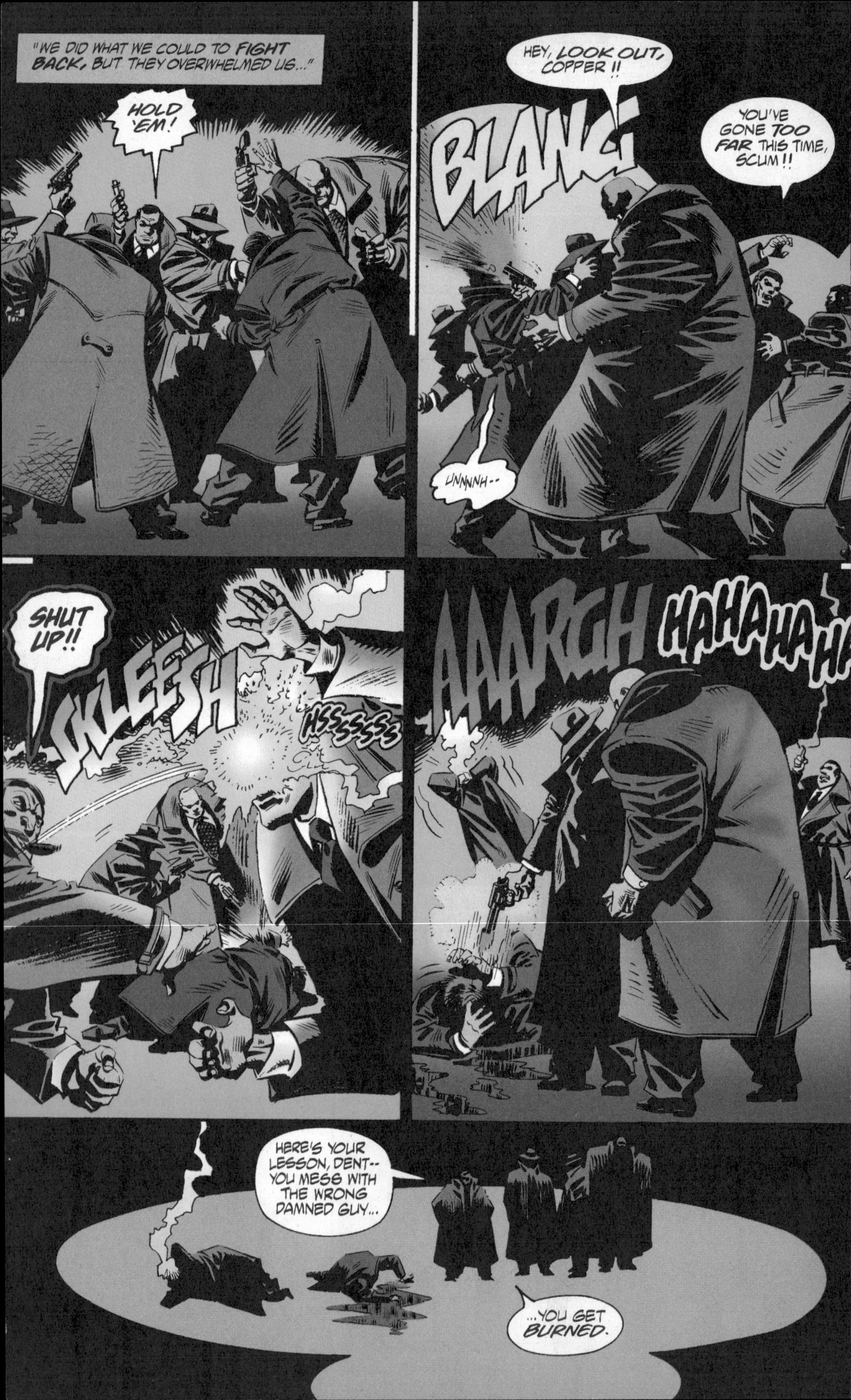
"WE DID WHAT WE COULD TO FIGHT BACK, BUT THEY OVERWHELMED US..."
HOLD 'EM!
HEY, LOOK OUT, COPPER !!
BLANG
YOU'VE GONE TOO FAR THIS TIME, SCUM !!
UNNNNH--
SHUT UP!!
SKLEESH
HSSSSSSS
AAARGH
HAHAHAHA
HERE'S YOUR LESSON, DENT-- YOU MESS WITH THE WRONG DAMNED GUY...
...YOU GET BURNED.

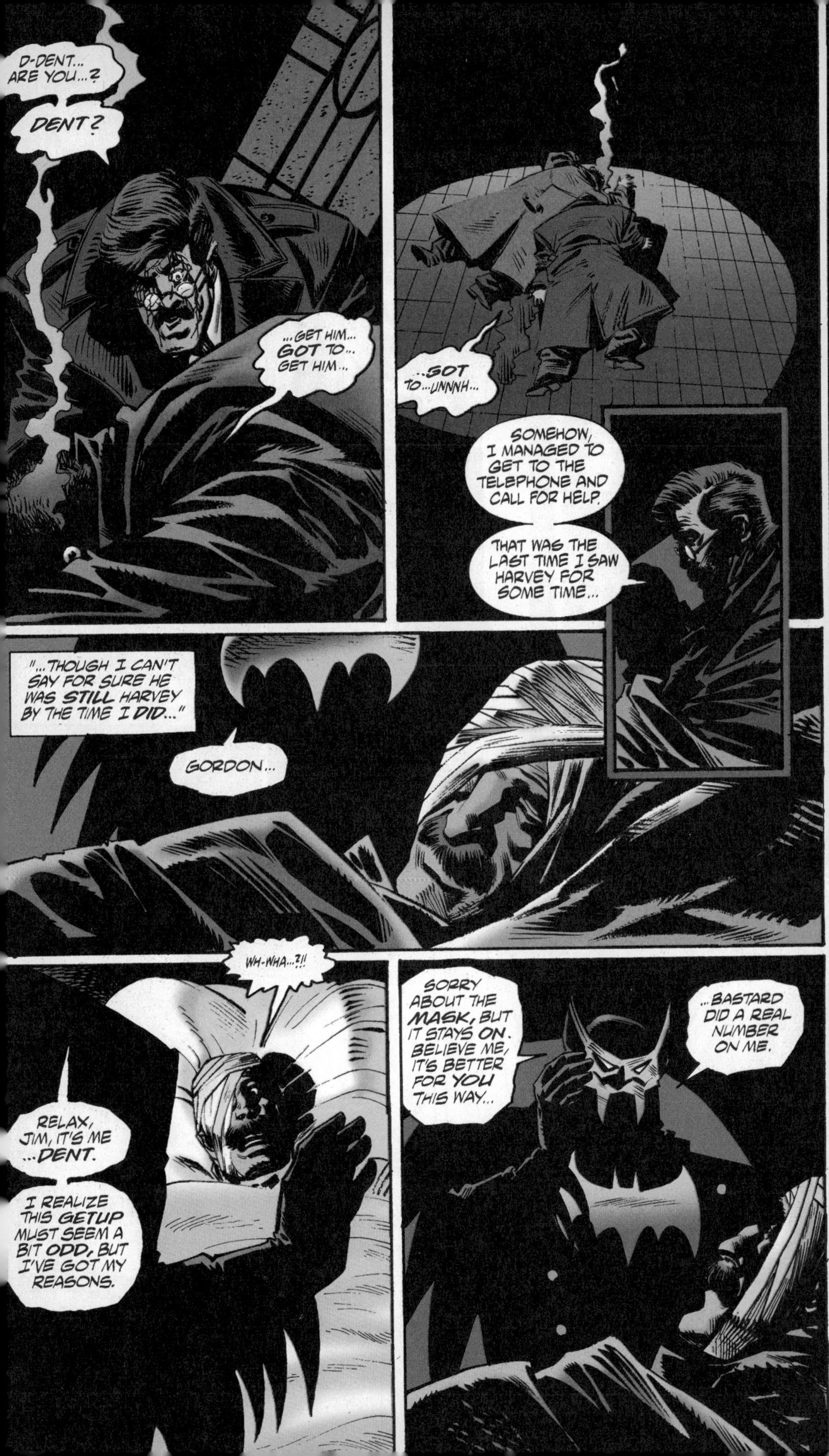
D-DENT... ARE YOU...?
DENT?
...GET HIM... GOT TO... GET HIM...
...GOT TO...UNNNH...
SOMEHOW, I MANAGED TO GET TO THE TELEPHONE AND CALL FOR HELP.
THAT WAS THE LAST TIME I SAW HARVEY FOR SOME TIME...
"...THOUGH I CAN'T SAY FOR SURE HE WAS STILL HARVEY BY THE TIME I DID..."
GORDON...
WH-WHA...?!!
RELAX, JIM, IT'S ME ...DENT.
I REALIZE THIS GETUP MUST SEEM A BIT ODD, BUT I'VE GOT MY REASONS.
SORRY ABOUT THE MASK, BUT IT STAYS ON. BELIEVE ME, IT'S BETTER FOR YOU THIS WAY...
...BASTARD DID A REAL NUMBER ON ME.

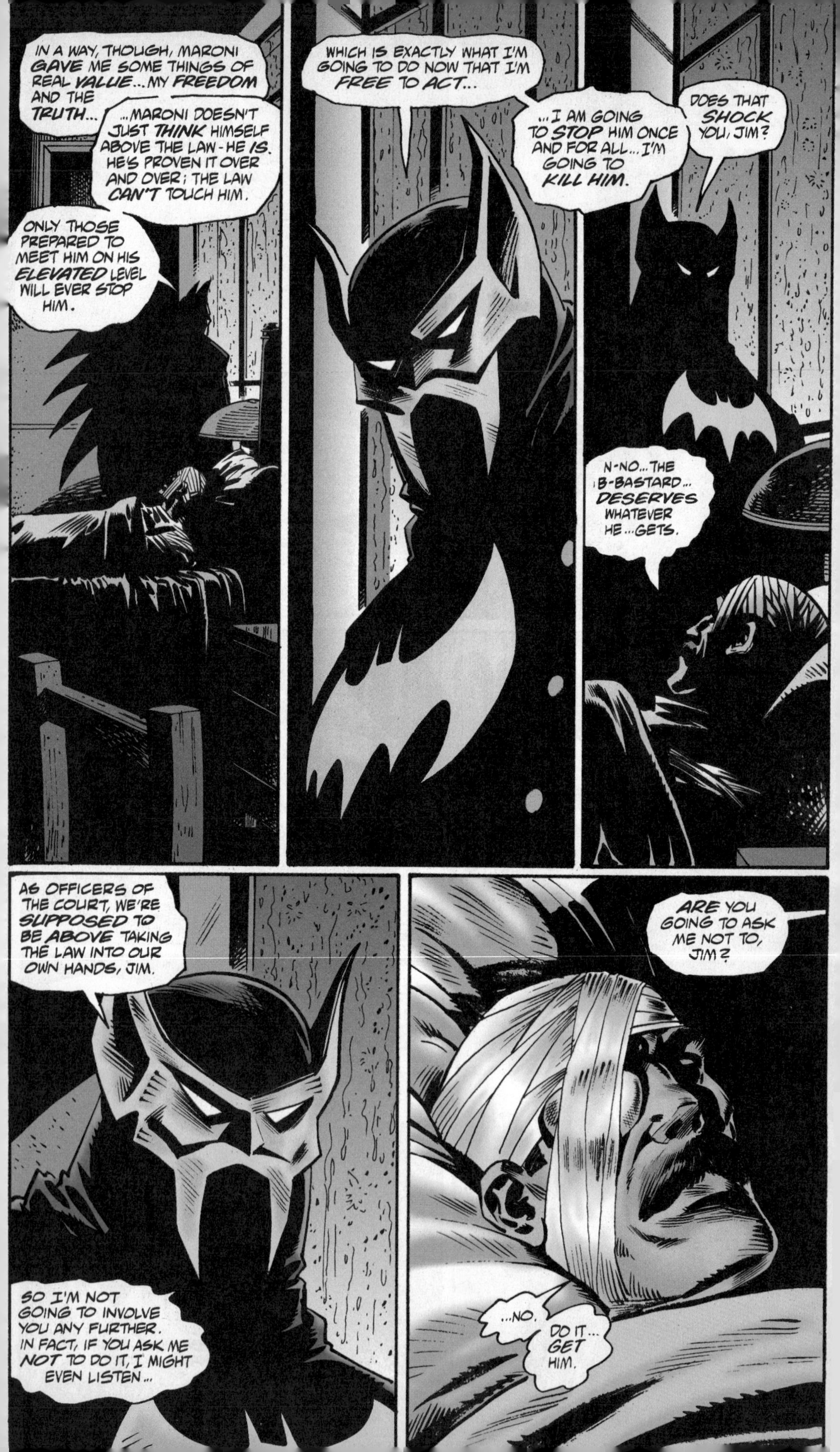
IN A WAY, THOUGH, MARONI GAVE ME SOME THINGS OF REAL VALUE... MY FREEDOM AND THE TRUTH...
...MARONI DOESN'T JUST THINK HIMSELF ABOVE THE LAW - HE IS. HE'S PROVEN IT OVER AND OVER; THE LAW CAN'T TOUCH HIM.
ONLY THOSE PREPARED TO MEET HIM ON HIS ELEVATED LEVEL WILL EVER STOP HIM.
WHICH IS EXACTLY WHAT I'M GOING TO DO NOW THAT I'M FREE TO ACT...
...I AM GOING TO STOP HIM ONCE AND FOR ALL... I'M GOING TO KILL HIM.
DOES THAT SHOCK YOU, JIM?
N-NO... THE B-BASTARD... DESERVES WHATEVER HE ...GETS.
AS OFFICERS OF THE COURT, WE'RE SUPPOSED TO BE ABOVE TAKING THE LAW INTO OUR OWN HANDS, JIM.
SO I'M NOT GOING TO INVOLVE YOU ANY FURTHER. IN FACT, IF YOU ASK ME NOT TO DO IT, I MIGHT EVEN LISTEN...
ARE YOU GOING TO ASK ME NOT TO, JIM?
...NO.
DO IT... GET HIM.

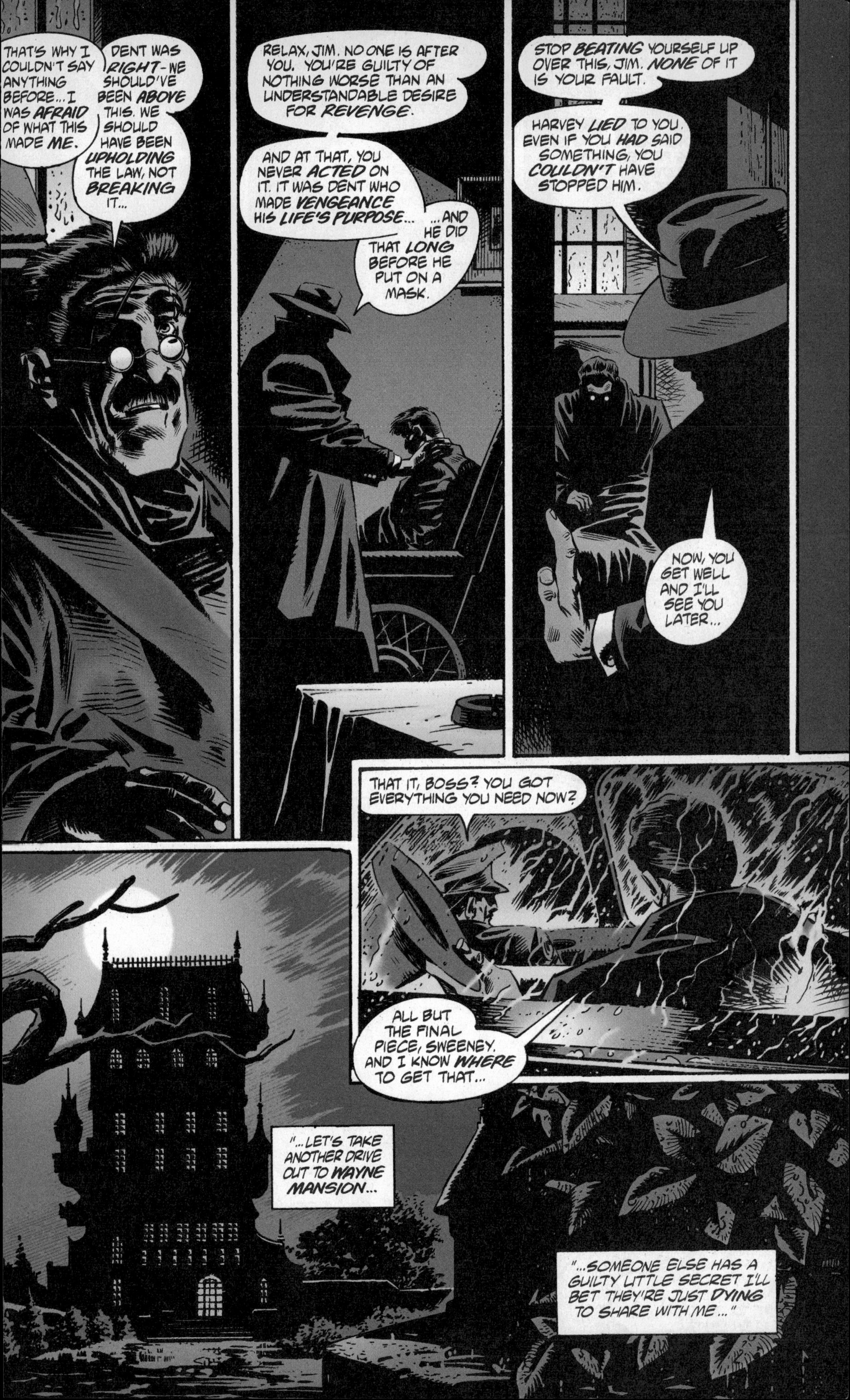
THAT'S WHY I COULDN'T SAY ANYTHING BEFORE... I WAS AFRAID OF WHAT THIS MADE ME.
DENT WAS RIGHT - WE SHOULD'VE BEEN ABOVE THIS. WE SHOULD HAVE BEEN UPHOLDING THE LAW, NOT BREAKING IT...
RELAX, JIM. NO ONE IS AFTER YOU. YOU'RE GUILTY OF NOTHING WORSE THAN AN UNDERSTANDABLE DESIRE FOR REVENGE.
AND AT THAT, YOU NEVER ACTED ON IT. IT WAS DENT WHO MADE VENGEANCE HIS LIFE'S PURPOSE...
...AND HE DID THAT LONG BEFORE HE PUT ON A MASK.
STOP BEATING YOURSELF UP OVER THIS, JIM. NONE OF IT IS YOUR FAULT.
HARVEY LIED TO YOU. EVEN IF YOU HAD SAID SOMETHING, YOU COULDN'T HAVE STOPPED HIM.
NOW, YOU GET WELL AND I'LL SEE YOU LATER...
THAT IT, BOSS? YOU GOT EVERYTHING YOU NEED NOW?
ALL BUT THE FINAL PIECE, SWEENEY. AND I KNOW WHERE TO GET THAT...
"...LET'S TAKE ANOTHER DRIVE OUT TO WAYNE MANSION...
"...SOMEONE ELSE HAS A GUILTY LITTLE SECRET I'LL BET THEY'RE JUST DYING TO SHARE WITH ME..."

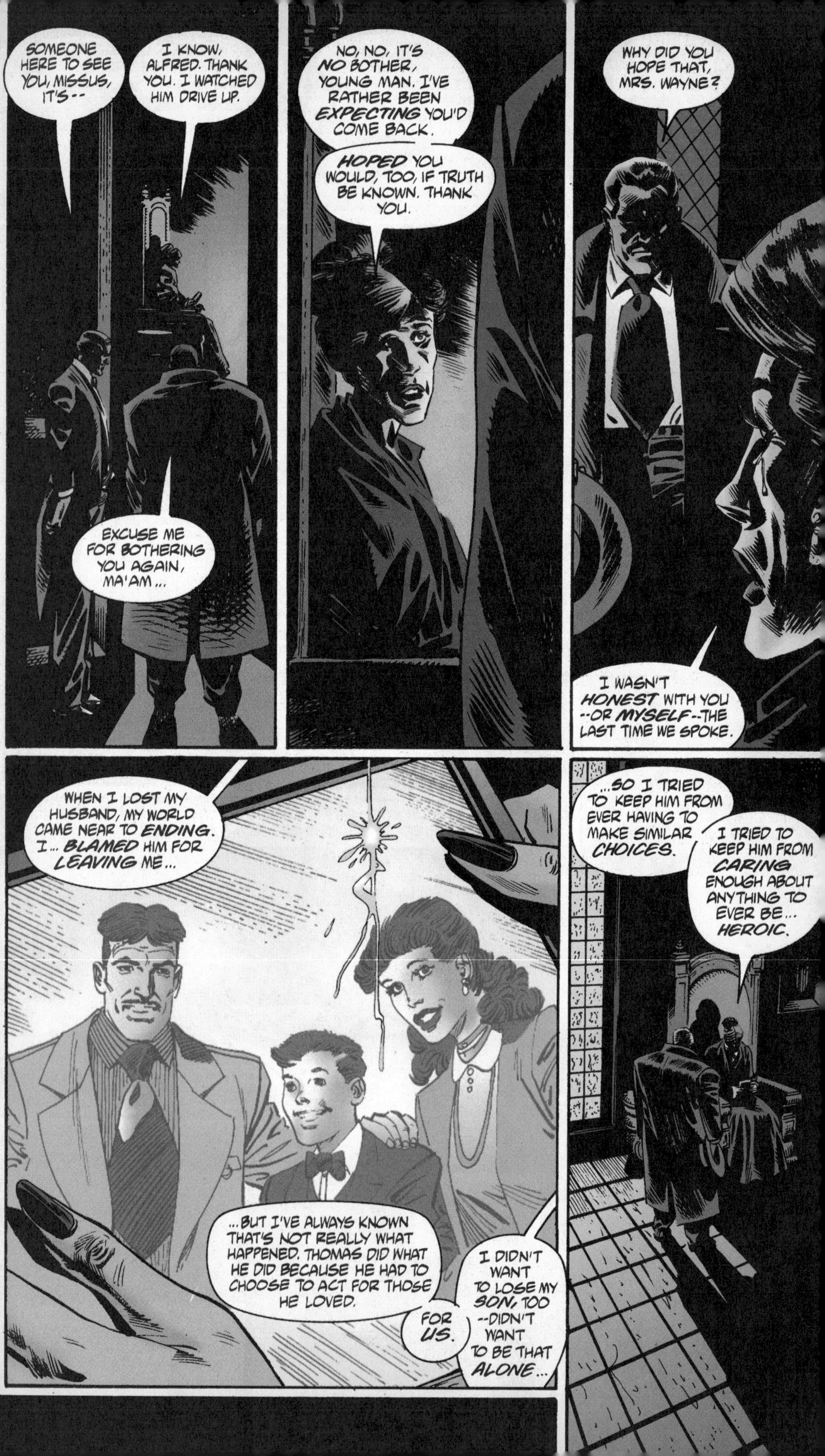
SOMEONE HERE TO SEE YOU, MISSUS, IT'S --
I KNOW, ALFRED. THANK YOU. I WATCHED HIM DRIVE UP.
EXCUSE ME FOR BOTHERING YOU AGAIN, MA'AM...
NO, NO, IT'S NO BOTHER, YOUNG MAN. I'VE RATHER BEEN EXPECTING YOU'D COME BACK.
HOPED YOU WOULD, TOO, IF TRUTH BE KNOWN. THANK YOU.
WHY DID YOU HOPE THAT, MRS. WAYNE?
I WASN'T HONEST WITH YOU --OR MYSELF--THE LAST TIME WE SPOKE.
WHEN I LOST MY HUSBAND, MY WORLD CAME NEAR TO ENDING. I... BLAMED HIM FOR LEAVING ME...
...BUT I'VE ALWAYS KNOWN THAT'S NOT REALLY WHAT HAPPENED. THOMAS DID WHAT HE DID BECAUSE HE HAD TO CHOOSE TO ACT FOR THOSE HE LOVED.
FOR US.
I DIDN'T WANT TO LOSE MY SON, TOO --DIDN'T WANT TO BE THAT ALONE...
...SO I TRIED TO KEEP HIM FROM EVER HAVING TO MAKE SIMILAR CHOICES.
I TRIED TO KEEP HIM FROM CARING ENOUGH ABOUT ANYTHING TO EVER BE... HEROIC.

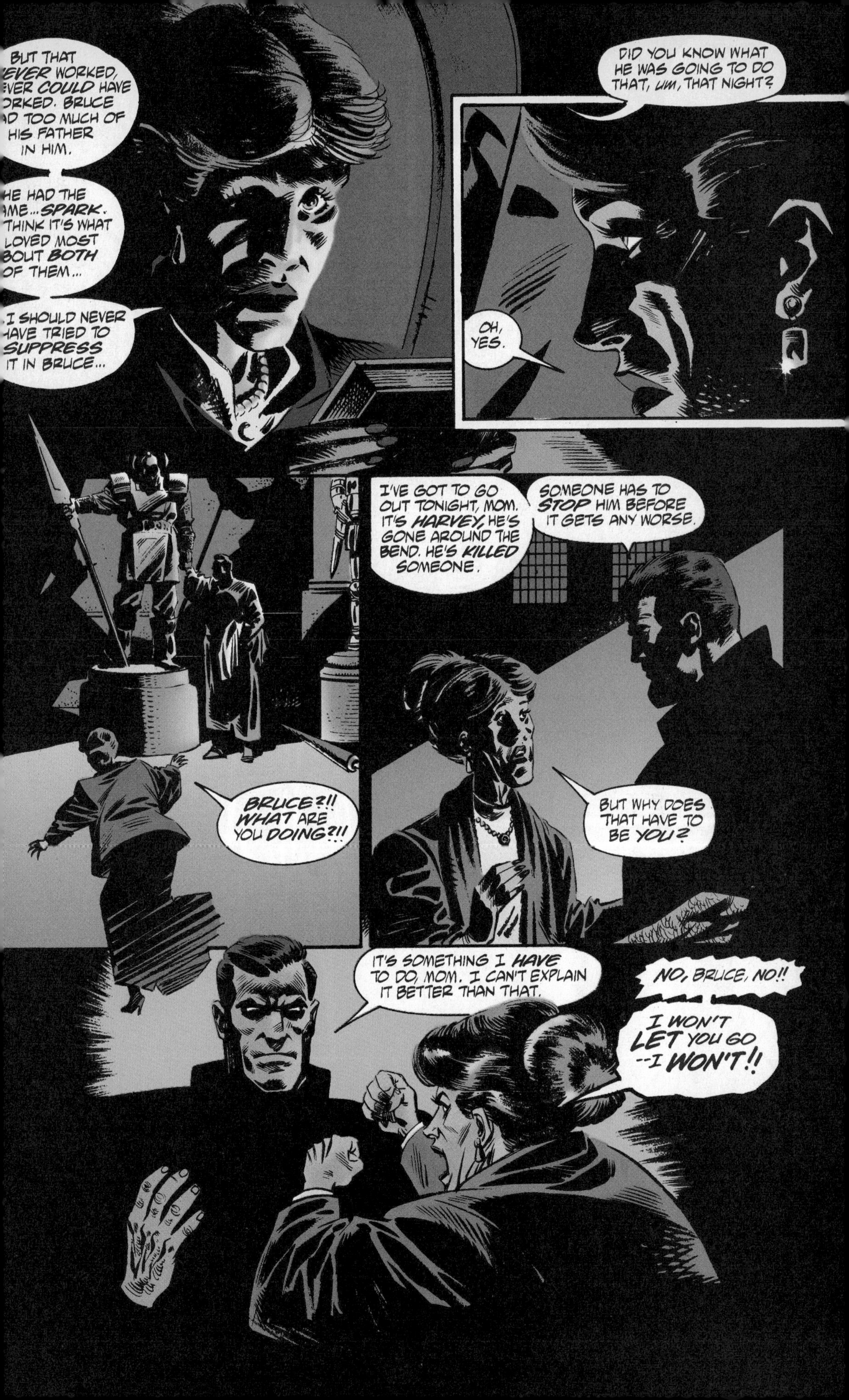
BUT THAT NEVER WORKED, NEVER COULD HAVE WORKED. BRUCE HAD TOO MUCH OF HIS FATHER IN HIM.
HE HAD THE SAME...SPARK. I THINK IT'S WHAT I LOVED MOST ABOUT BOTH OF THEM...
...I SHOULD NEVER HAVE TRIED TO SUPPRESS IT IN BRUCE...
DID YOU KNOW WHAT HE WAS GOING TO DO THAT, UM, THAT NIGHT?
OH, YES.
BRUCE?!! WHAT ARE YOU DOING?!!
I'VE GOT TO GO OUT TONIGHT, MOM. IT'S HARVEY, HE'S GONE AROUND THE BEND. HE'S KILLED SOMEONE.
SOMEONE HAS TO STOP HIM BEFORE IT GETS ANY WORSE.
BUT WHY DOES THAT HAVE TO BE YOU?
IT'S SOMETHING I HAVE TO DO, MOM. I CAN'T EXPLAIN IT BETTER THAN THAT.
NO, BRUCE, NO!!
I WON'T LET YOU GO --I WON'T!!

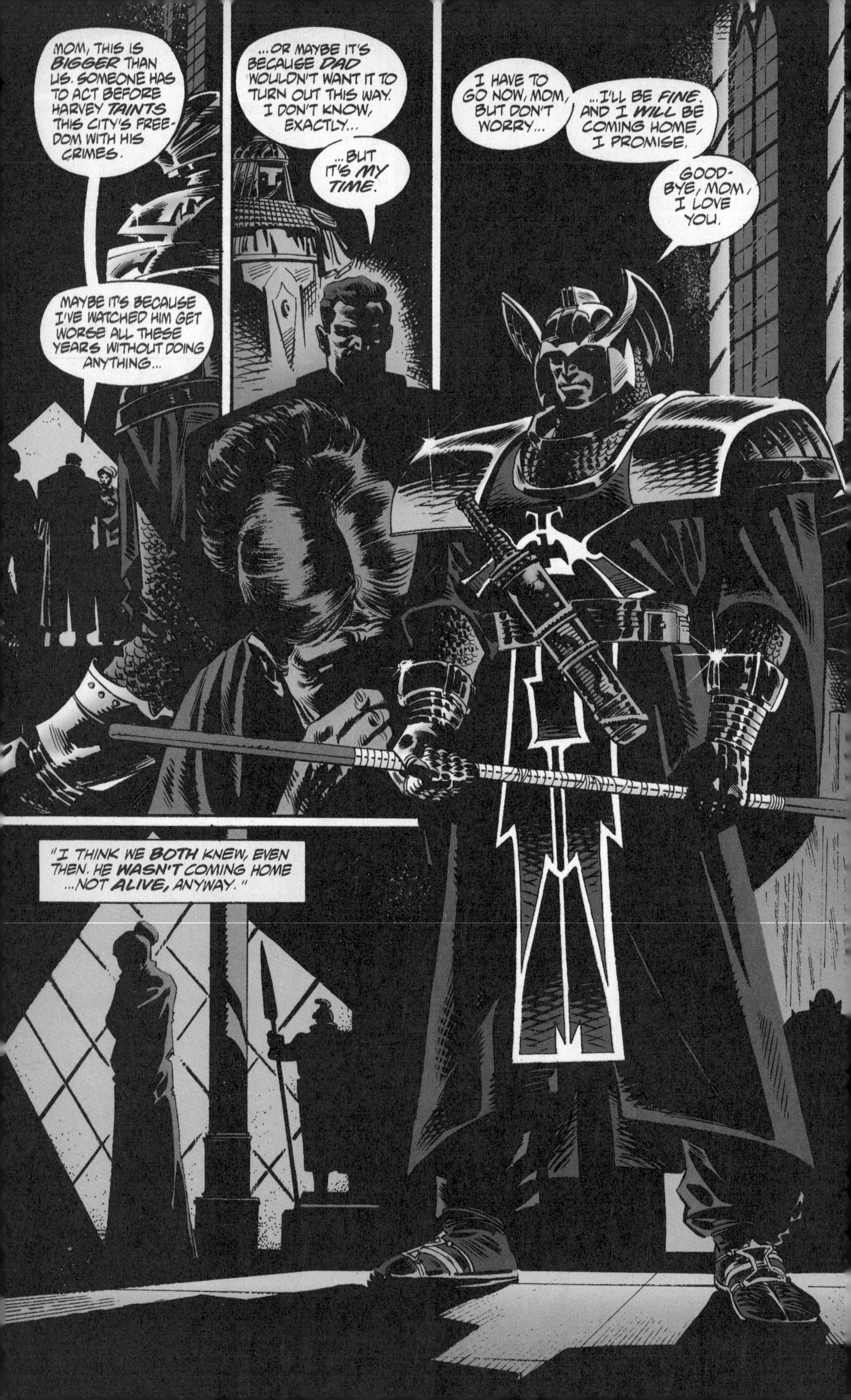
MOM, THIS IS BIGGER THAN US. SOMEONE HAS TO ACT BEFORE HARVEY TAINTS THIS CITY'S FREEDOM WITH HIS CRIMES.
MAYBE IT'S BECAUSE I'VE WATCHED HIM GET WORSE ALL THESE YEARS WITHOUT DOING ANYTHING...
...OR MAYBE IT'S BECAUSE DAD WOULDN'T WANT IT TO TURN OUT THIS WAY. I DON'T KNOW, EXACTLY...
...BUT IT'S MY TIME.
I HAVE TO GO NOW, MOM, BUT DON'T WORRY...
...I'LL BE FINE. AND I WILL BE COMING HOME, I PROMISE.
GOOD-BYE, MOM, I LOVE YOU.
"I THINK WE BOTH KNEW, EVEN THEN. HE WASN'T COMING HOME ...NOT ALIVE, ANYWAY."

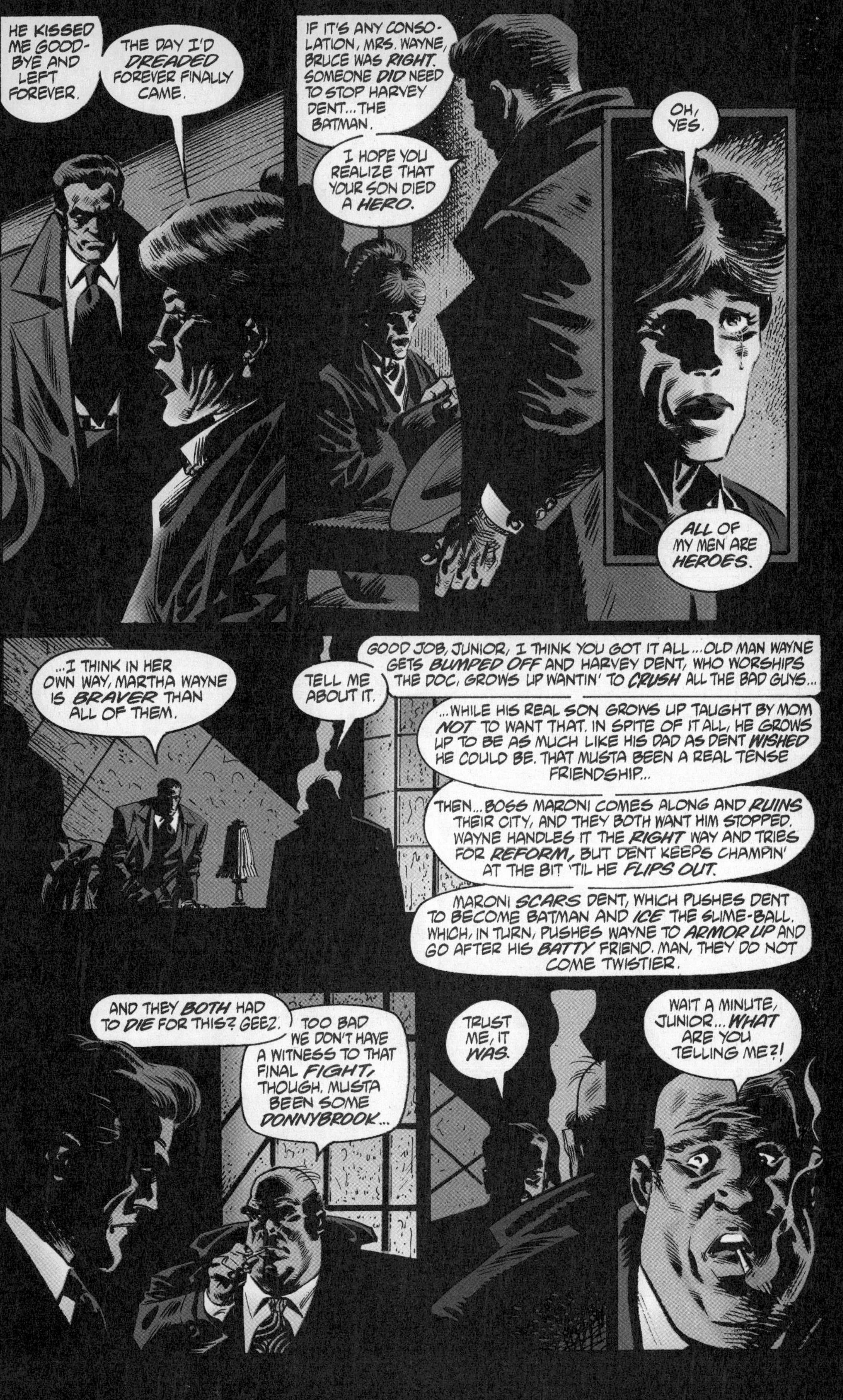
HE KISSED ME GOOD-BYE AND LEFT FOREVER.
THE DAY I'D DREADED FOREVER FINALLY CAME.
IF IT'S ANY CONSOLATION, MRS. WAYNE, BRUCE WAS RIGHT. SOMEONE DID NEED TO STOP HARVEY DENT... THE BATMAN.
I HOPE YOU REALIZE THAT YOUR SON DIED A HERO.
OH, YES.
ALL OF MY MEN ARE HEROES.
...I THINK IN HER OWN WAY, MARTHA WAYNE IS BRAVER THAN ALL OF THEM.
TELL ME ABOUT IT.
GOOD JOB, JUNIOR, I THINK YOU GOT IT ALL... OLD MAN WAYNE GETS BUMPED OFF AND HARVEY DENT, WHO WORSHIPS THE DOC, GROWS UP WANTIN' TO CRUSH ALL THE BAD GUYS...
...WHILE HIS REAL SON GROWS UP TAUGHT BY MOM NOT TO WANT THAT. IN SPITE OF IT ALL, HE GROWS UP TO BE AS MUCH LIKE HIS DAD AS DENT WISHED HE COULD BE. THAT MUSTA BEEN A REAL TENSE FRIENDSHIP...
THEN... BOSS MARONI COMES ALONG AND RUINS THEIR CITY, AND THEY BOTH WANT HIM STOPPED. WAYNE HANDLES IT THE RIGHT WAY AND TRIES FOR REFORM, BUT DENT KEEPS CHAMPIN' AT THE BIT 'TIL HE FLIPS OUT.
MARONI SCARS DENT, WHICH PUSHES DENT TO BECOME BATMAN AND ICE THE SLIME-BALL. WHICH, IN TURN, PUSHES WAYNE TO ARMOR UP AND GO AFTER HIS BATTY FRIEND. MAN, THEY DO NOT COME TWISTIER.
AND THEY BOTH HAD TO DIE FOR THIS? GEEZ.
TOO BAD WE DON'T HAVE A WITNESS TO THAT FINAL FIGHT, THOUGH. MUSTA BEEN SOME DONNYBROOK...
TRUST ME, IT WAS.
WAIT A MINUTE, JUNIOR... WHAT ARE YOU TELLING ME?!

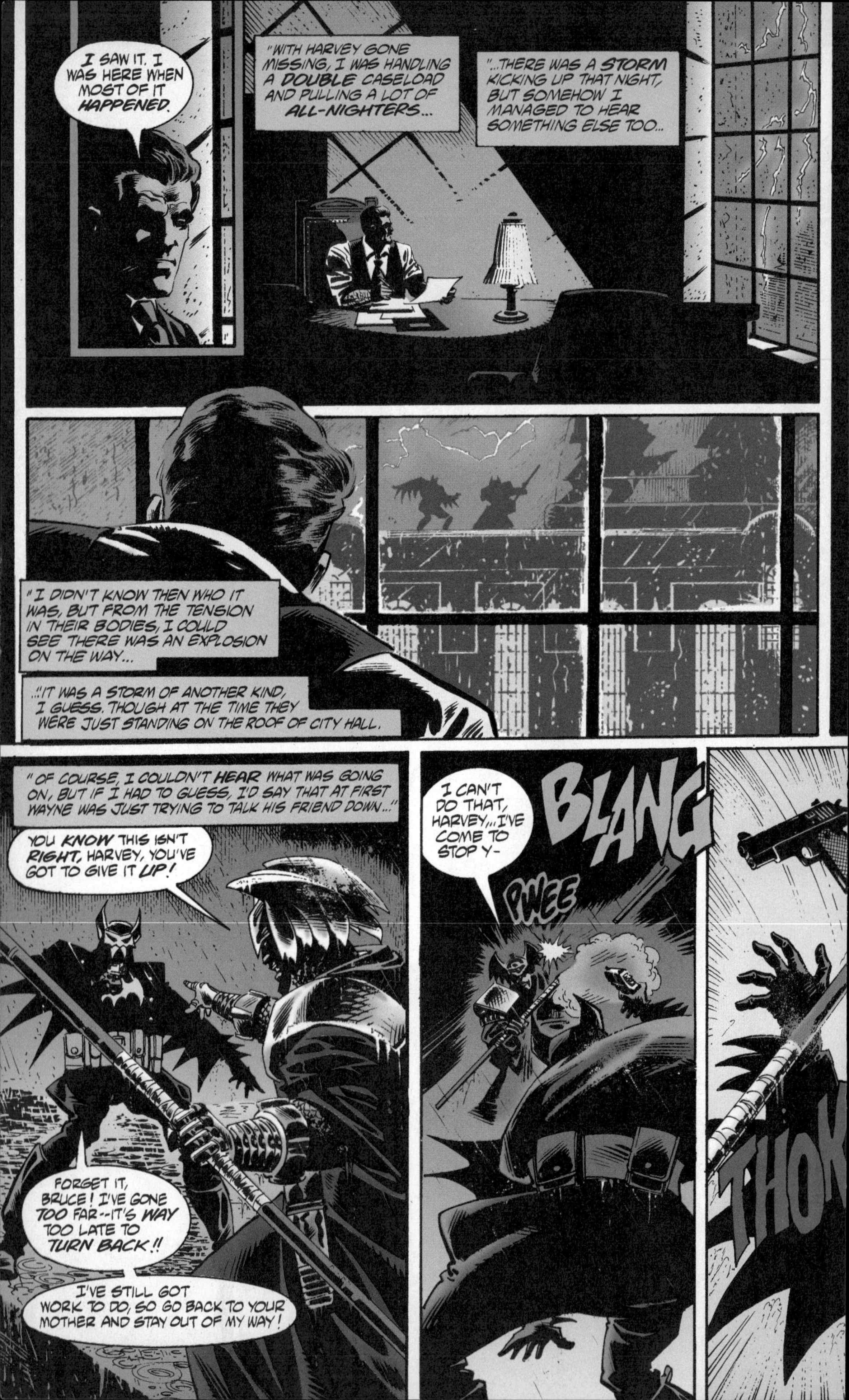
I SAW IT. I WAS HERE WHEN MOST OF IT HAPPENED.
"WITH HARVEY GONE MISSING, I WAS HANDLING A DOUBLE CASELOAD AND PULLING A LOT OF ALL-NIGHTERS...
"...THERE WAS A STORM KICKING UP THAT NIGHT, BUT SOMEHOW I MANAGED TO HEAR SOMETHING ELSE TOO...
"I DIDN'T KNOW THEN WHO IT WAS, BUT FROM THE TENSION IN THEIR BODIES, I COULD SEE THERE WAS AN EXPLOSION ON THE WAY...
...IT WAS A STORM OF ANOTHER KIND, I GUESS. THOUGH AT THE TIME THEY WERE JUST STANDING ON THE ROOF OF CITY HALL.
"OF COURSE, I COULDN'T HEAR WHAT WAS GOING ON, BUT IF I HAD TO GUESS, I'D SAY THAT AT FIRST WAYNE WAS JUST TRYING TO TALK HIS FRIEND DOWN..."
YOU KNOW THIS ISN'T RIGHT, HARVEY, YOU'VE GOT TO GIVE IT UP!
FORGET IT, BRUCE! I'VE GONE TOO FAR--IT'S WAY TOO LATE TO TURN BACK!!
I'VE STILL GOT WORK TO DO, SO GO BACK TO YOUR MOTHER AND STAY OUT OF MY WAY!
I CAN'T DO THAT, HARVEY... I'VE COME TO STOP Y-
BLANG
PWEE
THOK

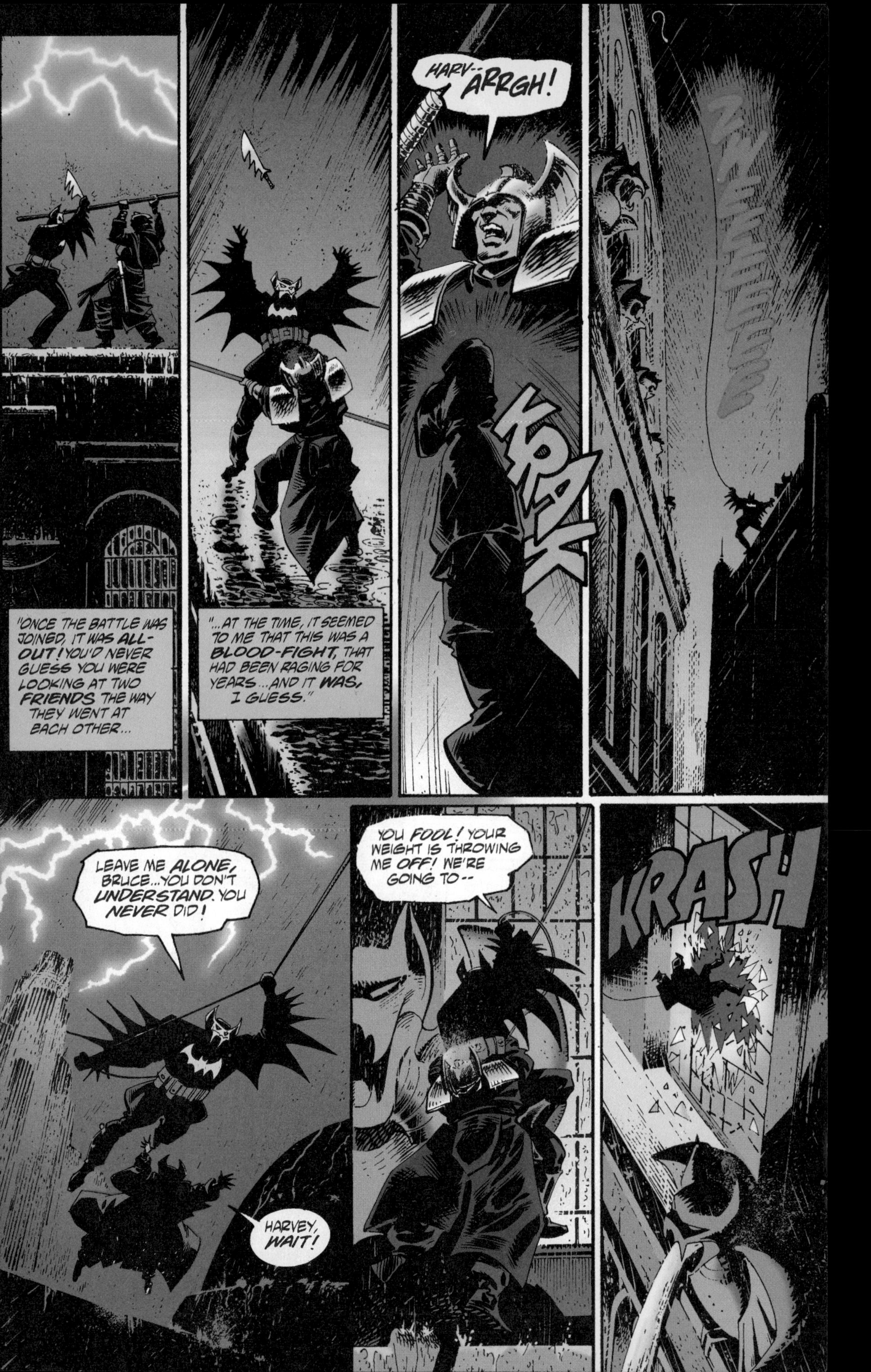

"ONCE THE BATTLE WAS JOINED, IT WAS ALL-OUT! YOU'D NEVER GUESS YOU WERE LOOKING AT TWO FRIENDS THE WAY THEY WENT AT EACH OTHER...
"...AT THE TIME, IT SEEMED TO ME THAT THIS WAS A BLOOD-FIGHT, THAT HAD BEEN RAGING FOR YEARS... AND IT WAS, I GUESS."
HARV-- ARRGH!
KRAK
LEAVE ME ALONE, BRUCE...YOU DON'T UNDERSTAND. YOU NEVER DID!
HARVEY, WAIT!
YOU FOOL! YOUR WEIGHT IS THROWING ME OFF! WE'RE GOING TO --
KRASH

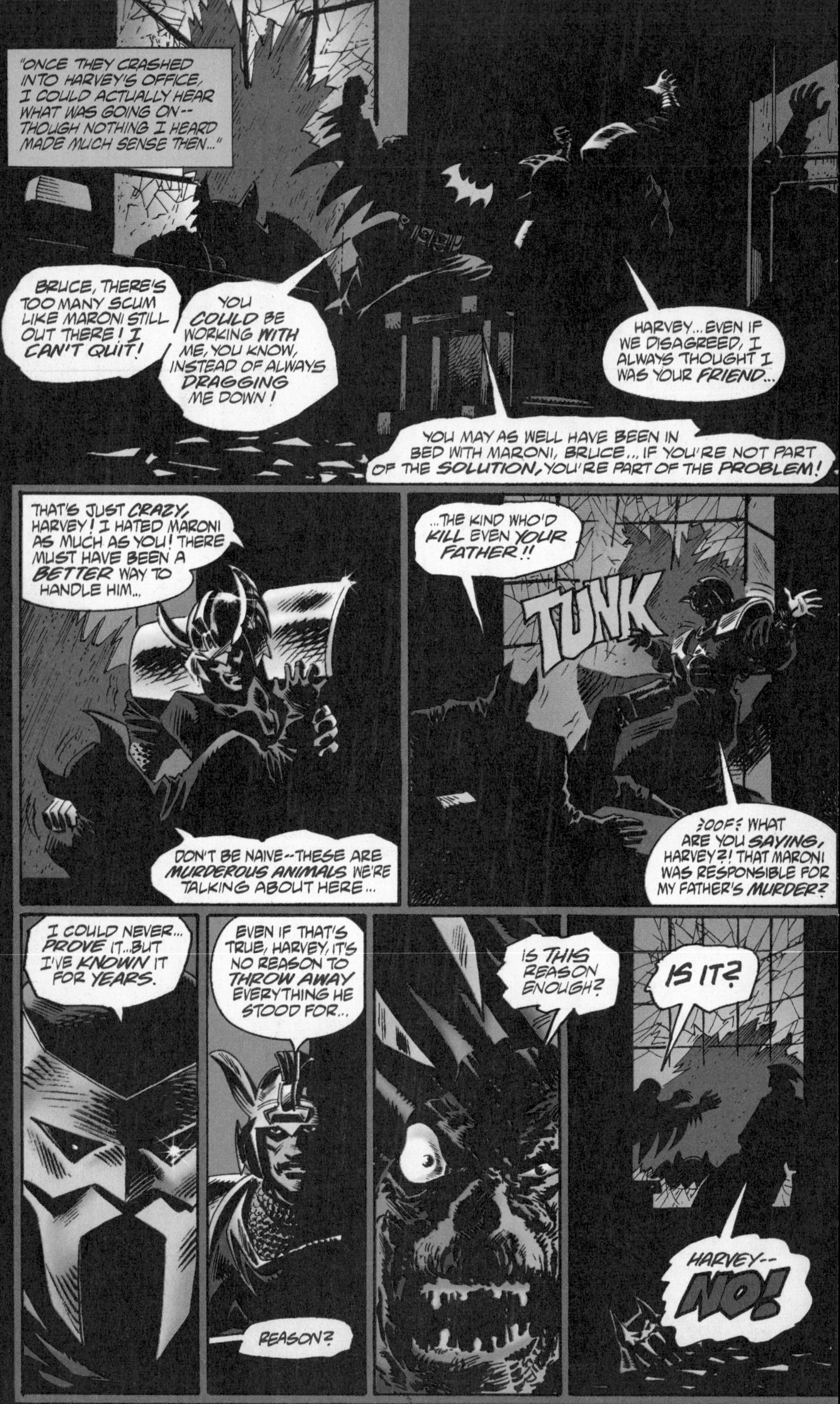
"ONCE THEY CRASHED INTO HARVEY'S OFFICE, I COULD ACTUALLY HEAR WHAT WAS GOING ON-- THOUGH NOTHING I HEARD MADE MUCH SENSE THEN..."
BRUCE, THERE'S TOO MANY SCUM LIKE MARONI STILL OUT THERE! I CAN'T QUIT!
YOU COULD BE WORKING WITH ME, YOU KNOW, INSTEAD OF ALWAYS DRAGGING ME DOWN!
HARVEY... EVEN IF WE DISAGREED, I ALWAYS THOUGHT I WAS YOUR FRIEND...
YOU MAY AS WELL HAVE BEEN IN BED WITH MARONI, BRUCE... IF YOU'RE NOT PART OF THE SOLUTION, YOU'RE PART OF THE PROBLEM!
THAT'S JUST CRAZY, HARVEY! I HATED MARONI AS MUCH AS YOU! THERE MUST HAVE BEEN A BETTER WAY TO HANDLE HIM...
DON'T BE NAIVE--THESE ARE MURDEROUS ANIMALS WE'RE TALKING ABOUT HERE...
...THE KIND WHO'D KILL EVEN YOUR FATHER!!
TUNK
OOF! WHAT ARE YOU SAYING, HARVEY?! THAT MARONI WAS RESPONSIBLE FOR MY FATHER'S MURDER?
I COULD NEVER... PROVE IT... BUT I'VE KNOWN IT FOR YEARS.
EVEN IF THAT'S TRUE, HARVEY, IT'S NO REASON TO THROW AWAY EVERYTHING HE STOOD FOR...
REASON?
IS THIS REASON ENOUGH?
IS IT?
HARVEY-- NO!

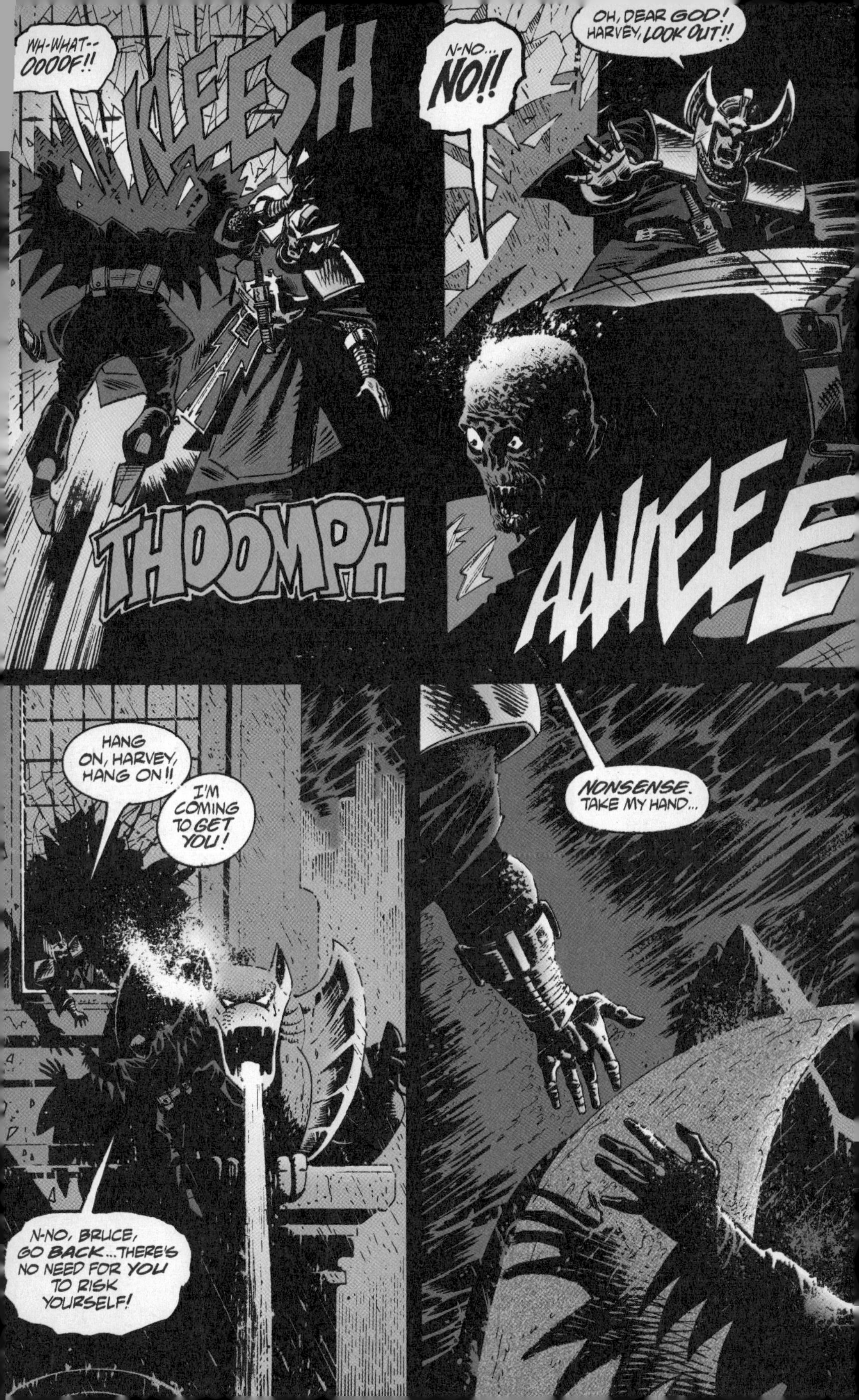
WH-WHAT--
OOOOF!!
KLEESH
THOOMPH
N-NO...
NO!!
OH, DEAR GOD! HARVEY, LOOK OUT!!
AAIEEE
HANG ON, HARVEY, HANG ON!!
I'M COMING TO GET YOU!
N-NO, BRUCE, GO BACK...THERE'S NO NEED FOR YOU TO RISK YOURSELF!
NONSENSE. TAKE MY HAND...

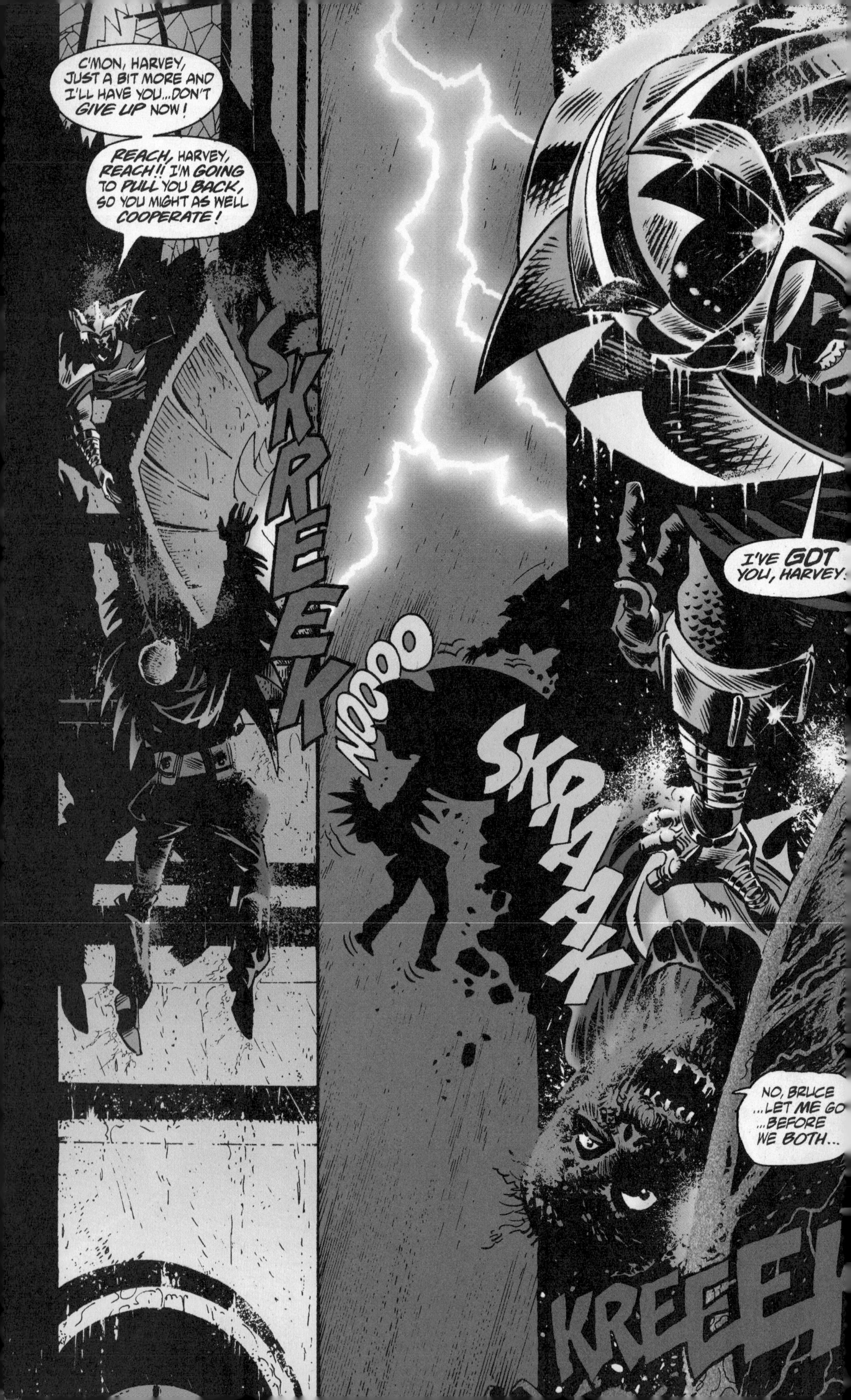
C'MON, HARVEY, JUST A BIT MORE AND I'LL HAVE YOU...DON'T GIVE UP NOW!
REACH, HARVEY, REACH!! I'M GOING TO PULL YOU BACK, SO YOU MIGHT AS WELL COOPERATE!
SKREEEK
NOOOOO
SKRAAAK
I'VE GOT YOU, HARVEY.
NO, BRUCE ...LET ME GO ...BEFORE WE BOTH...
KREEE

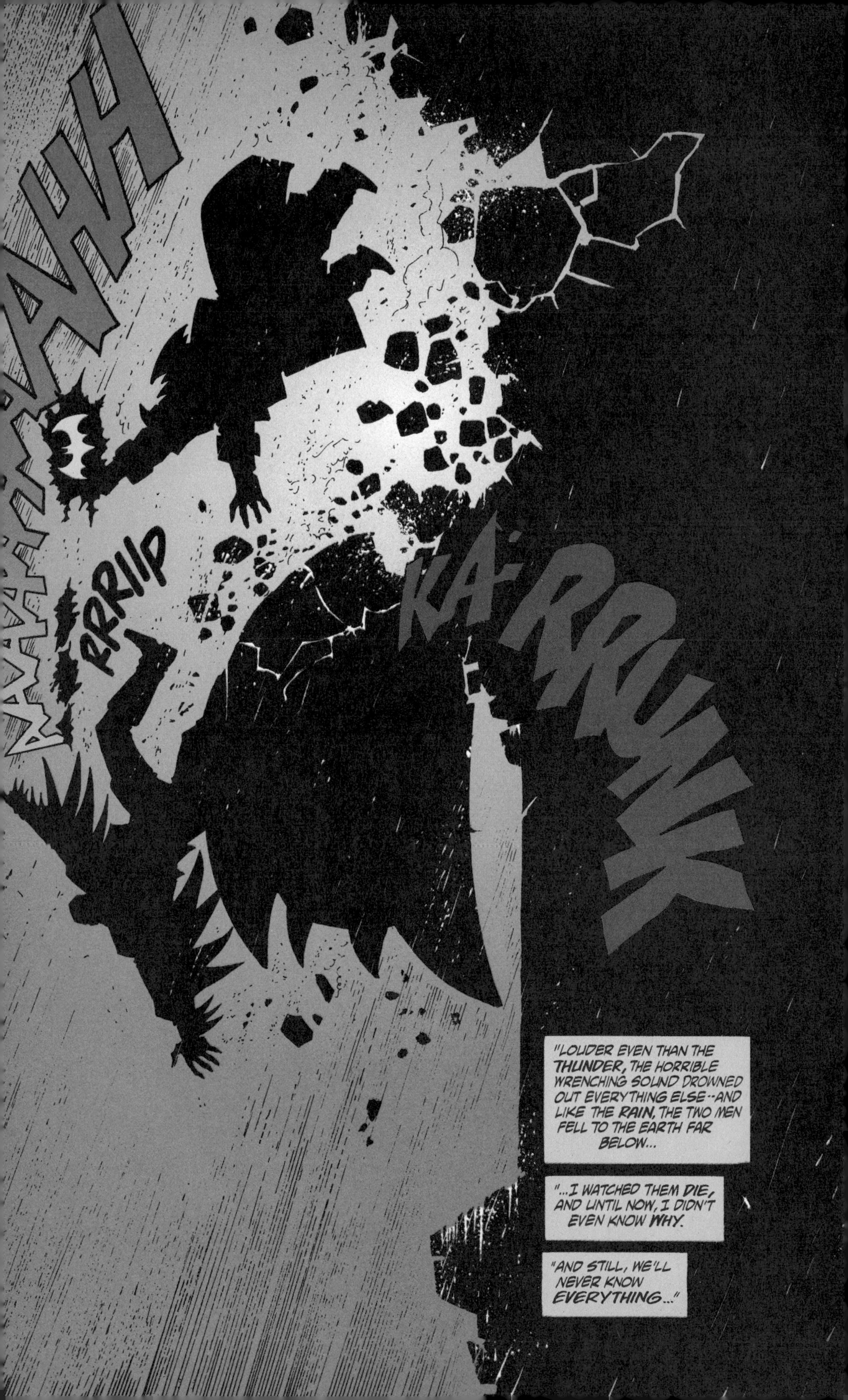
RRRIIP
KA-RRUNK
"LOUDER EVEN THAN THE THUNDER, THE HORRIBLE WRENCHING SOUND DROWNED OUT EVERYTHING ELSE--AND LIKE THE RAIN, THE TWO MEN FELL TO THE EARTH FAR BELOW...
"...I WATCHED THEM DIE, AND UNTIL NOW, I DIDN'T EVEN KNOW WHY.
"AND STILL, WE'LL NEVER KNOW EVERYTHING..."

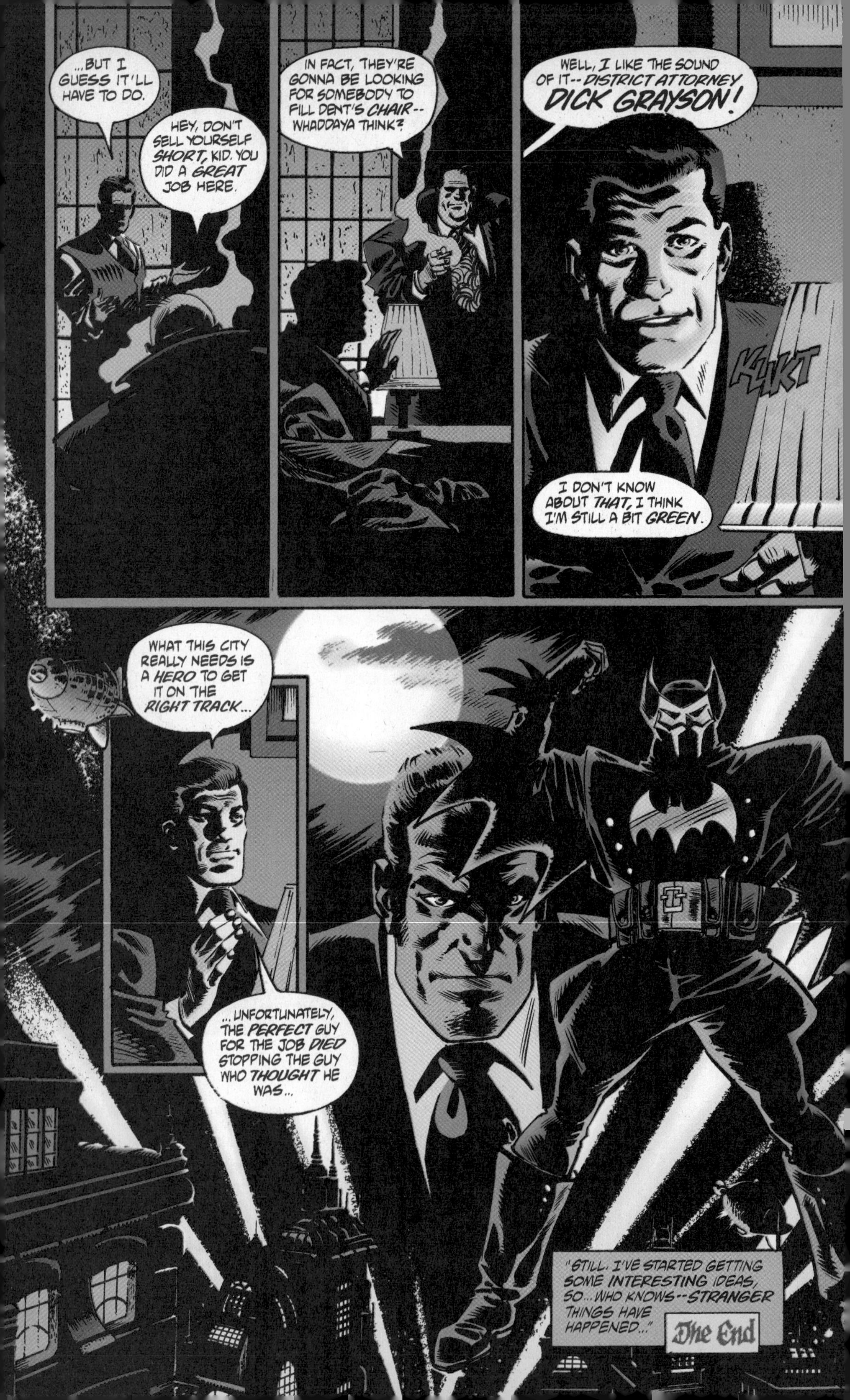
...BUT I GUESS IT'LL HAVE TO DO.
HEY, DON'T SELL YOURSELF SHORT, KID. YOU DID A GREAT JOB HERE.
IN FACT, THEY'RE GONNA BE LOOKING FOR SOMEBODY TO FILL DENT'S CHAIR-- WHADDAYA THINK?
WELL, I LIKE THE SOUND OF IT-- DISTRICT ATTORNEY DICK GRAYSON!
KLIKT
I DON'T KNOW ABOUT THAT, I THINK I'M STILL A BIT GREEN.
WHAT THIS CITY REALLY NEEDS IS A HERO TO GET IT ON THE RIGHT TRACK...
...UNFORTUNATELY, THE PERFECT GUY FOR THE JOB DIED STOPPING THE GUY WHO THOUGHT HE WAS...
"STILL, I'VE STARTED GETTING SOME INTERESTING IDEAS, SO... WHO KNOWS--STRANGER THINGS HAVE HAPPENED..."
The End

ELSEWORLDS TITLES AVAILABLE FROM DC

ELSEWORLDS.
CONSIDER THE POSSIBILITIES.